MUSIC IN SOCIETY:
A Guide to the
Sociology of Music

MUSIC IN SOCIETY:
A Guide to the
Sociology of Music

by
Ivo Supičić

SOCIOLOGY OF MUSIC NO. 4

PENDRAGON PRESS
STUYVESANT, NY

THE SOCIOLOGY OF MUSIC SERIES

No. 1   *The Social Status of the Professional Musician from the Middle Ages to the 19th Century,* Walter Salmen, General Editor (1983) ISBN 0-918728-16-9

No. 2   *Big Sounds from Small Peoples: The music industry in small countries* by Roger Wallis and Krister Malm (1984) ISBN 0-918728-39-8

No. 3   *A Music for the Millions: antibellum democratic attitudes and the birth of American popular music* by Nicholas Tewa (1984) ISBN 0-918720-38-Y

Library of Congress Cataloging-in-Publication Data

Supičić, Ivo.
    Music in society.

    (Sociology of music; no. 4)
    Translation of: Elementi sociologije muzike.
    Bibliography: p.
    Includes index.
    1. Music and society.   I. Title.   II. Series.
ML3795.S8813 1987   780'.07   85-28414
ISBN 0-918728-35-5

TABLE OF CONTENTS

Introduction   xi

PART ONE — THE SOCIOLOGY OF MUSIC

Chapter 1. The Sociology of Music and Related Disciplines   3
I.   Approaches to the Sociology of Music   6
II.   The Sociology of Music and Music History   9
III.   A Social History of Music   16
IV.   A Note on the Sociology of Music and   25
       Ethnomusicology
V.   Aesthetic Studies and Sociological Research   28
VI.   Musicology, Sociology, Philosophy   38

Chapter 2. Subject and Methods   45
I.   Sociohistorical and Socioartistic Conditionings   47
II.   Questions and Problems   56
III.   Methods and Approaches   68
IV.   Sociological Explications   72

v

CONTENTS

PART TWO — MUSIC IN SOCIETY

Introduction   79

Chapter 1. Music and the Public   83
I.   Social Groups in Musical Life   85
II.   Music as a Social Phenomenon   88
III.   Types of Relationships between Music and Public   90
IV.   Types of Musical Publics   97

Chapter 2. Social Roles of Various Audiences   103
I.   The Musical Public as a Social Factor   105
II.   Presence and Absence of a Musical Public   107
III.   Attitudes of the Public   110
IV.   Social Demand   114
V.   Motivations for Music   116
VI.   Evolution of Musical Taste   119

Chapter 3. Music and Social Stratifications   123
I.   Social Differentiation and Musical Practice   125
II.   Musical Style and Social Groups   129
III.   A Sociohistorical Aspect: Aristocracy and Middle   133
       Class

Chapter 4. Music in Social Life   141
I.   Social Distinction Through Music   143
II.   Amateur Performances and Public Concerts   149
III.   Early Forms of Musical "Mass" Culture   155
IV.   Musical Subcultures and Acculturation   165

Chapter 5. The Expansion of Musical "Consumption"   169
I.   Democratization of Musical Life   171
II.   The Disfunctionalization of Music   174
III.   The Mass Media and Mass Musical Culture   180

Chapter 6. The Social Status and Role of the Musician   193
I.   Collective Attitudes Toward Musicians   195
II.   The Musical Profession   202

CONTENTS

III. Musicians in Other Professions   211
IV. Professional Organizations of Musicians   215

Chapter 7. Music and Economics   221
I. Types of Societies and Musical Functions   224
II. Labor and Musical Reception   228
III. Music for Work   231
IV. Influence of Economic Sources on Music   238
V. Copying, Printing, and Publishing   245
VI. Earnings and Royalties   248

Chapter 8. Music and Technique   253
I. Production of Instruments   255
II. Music and Architecture   267

Chapter 9. Sociopsychological Conditions   271
I. Music and Social Symbolization   273
II. Music, Political Life, and Ideologies   281
III. Music, Ceremony, and Ritual   293
IV. A Note on Court Music   304
V. Sacred and Secular Music   309

Chapter 10. Socioartistic Aspects of Music   319
I. Tradition, Invention, and Innovation   323
II. Originality and Historical Relativity   328
III. Change, Evolution, and Progress in Music   333
IV. Sociological Perspectives and Human Horizons   342

Conclusion   357

Bibliography   363

Index   477

Acknowledgments

I would like to express my sincere thanks and profound indebtedness to Professor Barry S. Brook for all his help and support in preparing this book for the American edition. I also extend my deep gratitude to him and to Mrs. Sarah Reichard for the enormous amount of work they undertook in the difficult task of translation from French into English.

I.S.

Introduction

This study has two distinct but not unrelated aspects. First, it is an investigation into the sociology of music as an autonomous and specialized discipline; and second, it is an examination of certain fundamental facts that may be considered within the purview of the sociology of music itself.

If such an analysis and study—even a preliminary one—is to be properly focused and fruitful, we must first try to determine the subject and methods of the sociology of music, its position and boundaries in respect to musicology, and most especially, its relationship to the aesthetics of music and to music history. It is equally indispensable to ascertain what the sociology of music as a separate scholarly discipline embraces, where its investigation leads, and finally, what its position is vis-à-vis sociology in general.

The conjunction of these two basic aspects of our investigation of the sociology of music—that of a study *on* the sociology of music as an autonomous and specialized discipline, and that of research with*in* the sociology of music itself—seems fruitful, however, from still another point of view: the very solutions of the problems raised by the sociological approach and the appearance of new problems in the course of sociological research will certainly contribute to the cumulative definition of its subject and structure, its purpose and methods, and naturally, its limits.

The sociology of music is only now beginning to establish itself as a specialized scholarly discipline. It is not yet entirely delimited and defined, and the existing literature, though relatively abundant, is inconclusive and fragmentary. In view of the lack of basic research, a more or less complete definition of its subject and methods probably will not be forthcoming for some time. To be sure, it is virtually impossible to create a new discipline through an exhaustive determination of its subject, methods, structure, and perspectives. Only in the course of its application can a science be gradually defined, its structure perfected, and its perspectives developed and enlarged. Nevertheless, studies in the sociology of music are now so numerous, and the interest in its development so clear, that it seems entirely justified to devote to it a separate work bestowing upon the subject all the attention it deserves.

Still, many questions will undoubtedly remain unanswered, left for further specialized research, because of the considerable complexity and scope of material dealt with in the sociology of music. The treatment of the material demands from the researcher a thorough knowledge not only of music history but also of the allied disciplines of history and sociology. The scope of the task embraces the vast horizons of the entire history of music and delves into its most diverse social aspects.

The first part of the present work, then, deals with a critical philosophy of the sociology of music, and includes observations on this new scholarly discipline. The methodological problems raised in the course of sociological research will also be examined.

In part two, some fundamental problems within the sociology of music will be analyzed in light of the results obtained in the first part. By an examination of certain positive facts, we will venture some preliminary conclusions, open up some new perspectives, and set some guidelines. The principal goal will be to illustrate the relationships between music and social life, taken in its largest sense. As this work is a *guide* to the sociology of music, we have used only a part of the literature and corresponding sources. Fuller documentation should be envisioned within a more specialized elaboration of available material.

Furthermore, we are not attempting here a complete social history of music—not only because the present state of socio-historical research would make such an attempt premature, but also because that is not our goal. The social history of music and the sociology of music should not be confused, although they are closely aligned. It is essential, on the other hand, that the study of the sociology of music be founded on the well-defined, specific facts that the social history of music can provide. Thus, while it is necessary to differentiate between historical and sociological analyses of music, they must not be considered unrelated.

Finally, it must be obvious that a definitive study of the subjects dealt with in the present work cannot come to pass until there is more research done in specialized areas. Today the sociology of music remains the concern of a rather small number of scholars, although interest in it is certainly growing. In fact, the sociology of music is attracting an increasingly large share of the attention of contemporary musicologists, ethno-musicologists and sociologists. It is also beginning to find a place in university programs, and already a number of institutions are engaged in studies of the sociology of music in various ways through their research programs. A specialized journal, the *International Review of the Aesthetics and Sociology of Music* (IRASM) has been in existence (in English, French, and German) since 1970. The second symposium of the International Musicological Society (Zagreb, 1974) was devoted exclusively to the sociology of music. The subject also figured at the twelfth and thirteenth congresses of the IMS (Berkeley, California, 1977; and Strasbourg, 1982). But it will remain for future generations of scholars to carry out and complete the necessary work in depth. To make this possible, we must lay down the foundations on which their work may evolve. However, it is important to remember that the sociology of music as a discipline will not develop and move forward without strong and systematic collaboration between musicologists and sociologists of many diverse specializations and orientations.

PART ONE

Sociology of Music

CHAPTER ONE

SOCIOLOGY OF MUSIC
AND RELATED DISCIPLINES

The sociology of music may be defined as the study of music insofar as it is a social phenomenon, or as the study of the social aspects of music. Its concern should be with the study of specific social facts, and not with all of the extramusical elements surrounding music—an area of investigation that, by an abusive extension, has sometimes been given the name of sociology.[1]

Scholarly inquiry into the objectives, problems, and methods of the sociology of music depends to a considerable extent on the investigator's position with regard to purely sociological matters, and the findings he considers valuable and consonant with general sociology.[2] Here the sociology of music finds itself in a sort of "formal" dependency, since it has not yet fully established its own methods of research. However, the sociology of music (though it may evolve toward greater autonomy) will always remain somewhat dependent on sociology, on its spirit and orientation. And although that dependency can never completely disappear, it may possibly be reduced in a certain

---

[1] See François Lesure, "Musicologie et sociologie," *La revue musicale* CCXXI (1953): 4.

[2] In the present state of sociological research on music, an initial methodological acceptance of several points of view already existing in sociology could (under certain circumstances and without leading to a sort of eclecticism) be useful to or enriching for sociological studies in music.

sense, because with time the sociology of music will probably develop its own methods, and will deal with more and more specialized problems, bring to them original solutions.

If, however, the sociology of music is to broaden its perspectives, exploring specific material more deeply and discovering those problems unique to it, and if new procedures and methods of investigation are to be developed, it will require support from the results acquired by musicology (taken in the largest sense of the term). Here is thus another equally important dependency to which the sociology of music is inevitably subject: that is, "material" dependency upon musicological scholarship (notably the history of music and ethnomusicology), which endows it with specificity with respect to the other domains of sociology. In addition to the previously mentioned liaison (seen on a grander scale) of those two essential aspects of study (study *in* the sociology of music and study *on* the sociology of music) which, while being clearly distinct, are not to be separated, and which develop along parallel lines while giving each other mutual assistance, we now confront the fact that the position of the sociology of music is unique. It is situated at the crossroads of sociology and musicology, and requires an elaboration of its own.[3]

I • APPROACHES TO THE SOCIOLOGY OF MUSIC

The problems addressed by the sociology of music were

---

[3]On this subject see, for example, Hans Mersmann, "Soziologie als Hilfswissenschaft der Musikgeschichte," *Archiv für Musikwissenschaft* X/1 (1953): 1–15; François Lesure, op. cit.; Alphons Silbermann, "Die Stellung der Musiksoziologie innerhalb der Soziologie und der Musikwissenschaft," *Kölner Zeitschrift für Soziologie und Sozialpsychologie* I (1958): 102–105; Tibor Kneif, "Der Gegenstand musiksoziologischer Erkenntnis," *Archiv für Musikwissenschaft* XXIII (1966): 213–36; Gerhard Albersheim, "Reflexionen über Musikwissenschaft und Soziologie," *The International Review of Music Aesthetics and Sociology* I/2 (1970): 200–8; and Helmut Reinold, "Zur Bedeutung musiksoziologischen Denkens für die Musikgeschichte," *Texte zur Musiksoziologie*, ed. Tibor Kneif (Cologne: Arno Volk, 1975), 21–5.

formulated for the first time toward the end of the nineteenth and at the beginning of the twentieth century, in a few works by Georg Simmel, Karl Bücher, Jules Combarieu, Charles Lalo and Max Weber.[4] From its inception, by a process characteristic of contemporary science, the sociology of music has been involved in the specialized differentiation of its research from that of related fields of study. And to questions concerning its domain and its autonomy were later added those of its unification and systematization. The studies done so far, of course, are less works of synthesis (even of limited scope) than they are analyses of particular (and already fairly numerous) problems. With respect to some of those problems, we might mention as early examples the essays of Max Kaplan and Constantin Brailoïu concerning, respectively, the musical life of a town and that of a village;[5] those of Theodore Caplow, Jacques Chailley, Roger Girod, René König and Alphons Silbermann concerning music and the radio; or a study such as that of Jacques Descotes on music for work environments.[6] Other studies, such as those

---

[4]See Georg Simmel, "Psychologische und ethnologische Studien über Musik," *Zeitschrift für Völkerpsychologie und Sprachwissenschaft* XIII (1882): 261–305; *Georg Simmel: The Conflict in Modern Culture,* tr. K. Peter Etzkorn (New York: Teachers College, 1968), 98–140; Karl Bücher, *Arbeit und Rhythmus* (Leipzig: Teubner, 1892); Jules Combarieu, *La musique, ses lois, son évolution* (Paris: Flammarion, 1907); Charles Lalo, *L'art et la vie sociale* (Paris: Doin, 1921); Max Weber, *Die rationalen und soziologischen Grundlagen der Musik* (Munich: Drei Masken, 1921). Eng. tr., *The Rational and Social Foundations of Music,* (New York: Southern Illinois U. Press, 1958). On the beginnings of the sociology of music see Walter Serauky, "Wesen und Aufgaben der Musiksoziologie," *Zeitschrift für Musikwissenschaft* XVI/4 (1934): 232–44, and K. Peter Etzkorn, "Sociologists and Music," *Music and society. The later writings of Paul Honigsheim* (New York-London-Sydney-Toronto: John Wiley & Sons, 1973), 3–40.

[5]Max Kaplan, *Music in the City, a Sociological Survey of Musical Facilities and Activities in Pueblo, Colorado* (Pueblo, Colorado: M. Kaplan, 1944); Constantin Brailoïu, "Vie musicale d'un village," *Recherches sur le répertoire de Dragus— Roumanie, 1929–1932* (Paris: Institut Universitaire Roumain, 1960).

[6]See Theodore Caplow, "The Influence of Radio on Music as a Social Institution"; Jacques Chailley, "La Radio et le développement de l'instinct harmonique chez les auditeurs"; Roger Girod, "Recherches sociologiques et

of Marcel Belvianes and Alphons Silbermann, do not live up to the promise of their titles, which lead one to suppose that they are concerned with essentially sociological synthesis.[7] Nevertheless, we occasionally do find studies that come close to an introductory sociological synthesis or to a broader grasp of material, such as those of Kurt Blaukopf, Hans Engel, Theodor W. Adorno and Tibor Kneif, but such studies are rare.[8] We could also refer to a few essays that define the principles of the sociology of music or try to justify its elaboration as a separate

développement de la culture musicale"; René König, "Sur quelques problèmes sociologiques de l'émission radiophonique musicale," *Cahiers d'études de radiotélévision* III–IV (1955): 279–91, 401–12, 338–43, 348–65; Alphons Silbermann, *La musique, la radio et l'auditeur* (Paris: P.U.F., 1954); Jacques Descotes, "La musique fonctionnelle," *Polyphonie* VII–VIII (1951): 71–92.

[7] See Marcel Belvianes, *Sociologie de la musique* (Paris: Payot, 1951); and Alphons Silbermann, *Introduction à une sociologie de la musique* (Paris: P.U.F., 1955).

[8] See Elie Siegmeister, *Music and Society* (New York: Critics Group, 1938). *Musik und Gesellschaft,* Ger. tr. (Berlin: Dietz, 1948); Kurt Blaukopf, *Musiksoziologie. Eine Einführung in die Grundbegriffe mit besonderer Berücksichtigung der Soziologie der Tonsysteme* (Cologne-Berlin: Gustav Kiepenheuer, 1951); 2nd ed. (Niederteufen: Arthur Niggli, 1972); Alphons Silbermann, *Wovon lebt die Musik, Die Prinzipien der Musiksoziologie* (Regensburg: Gustav Bosse, 1957). Eng. tr., The Sociology of Music (London: Routledge and Kegan Paul, 1963). *Les principes de la sociologie de la musique,* Fr. tr. (Geneva-Paris: Droz, 1968); Hans Engel, *Musik und Gesellschaft, Bausteine zu einer Musiksoziologie* (Berlin-Halensee-Wunsiedel: Max Hesse, 1960); Theodor W. Adorno, *Einleitung in die Musiksoziologie, Zwölf theoretische Vorlesungen* (Frankfurt am Main: Suhrkamp, 1962); Karl Gustav Fellerer, *Soziologie der Kirchenmusik* (Cologne-Opladen: Westdeutscher Verlag, 1963); Ivo Supičić, *Elementi sociologije muzike* (Zagreb: Jugoslavenska akademija znanosti i umjetnosti, 1964). Pol. tr., *Wstęp do socjologii muzyki* (Warsaw: Państwowe Wydawnictwo Naukowe, 1969). Fr. tr., *Musique et société, Perspectives pour une sociologie de la musique* (Zagreb: Institut de Musicologie, Académie de musique, 1971); Tibor Kneif, *Musiksoziologie* (Cologne: H. Gerig, 1971), and "Musiksoziologie," *Einführung in die systematische Musikwissenschaft,* ed. Carl Dahlhaus (Cologne: H. Gerig, 1975, 2nd ed.), 171–202; Peter Rummenhöller, *Einführung in die Musiksoziologie* (Wilhelmshaven: Heinrichshofen, 1978); Elisabeth Haselauer, *Handbuch der Musiksoziologie* (Vienna-Cologne-Graz: Böhlaus, 1980); Kurt Blaukopf, *Musik im Wandel der Gesellschaft* (Munich-Zurich: Piper, 1982); Christian Kaden, *Musiksoziologie* (Berlin: Verlag Neue Musik, 1984).

discipline.[9] More recently some other specialized works have been added to those already existing, concerning respectively among other things the professional musician, the amateurs of music and the mass media, and written by Jacqueline De Clercq, Nicole Berthier, Pierre-Michel Menger, Michel de Coster, and Kurt Blaukopf.[10] Anthologies of texts about the sociology of music have also appeared.[11] This relative immaturity and slow development have also characterized branches of the sociology of arts other than music—the sociology of literature, for instance.[12]

II • SOCIOLOGY OF MUSIC AND MUSIC HISTORY

Although investigation of the subject began more than half a

---

[9]Walter Serauky, "Wesen und Aufgaben der Musiksoziologie," *Zeitschrift für Musikwissenschaft* XVI/4 (1934): 232–44; Paul Honigsheim, "Musiksoziologie," *Handwörterbuch der Sozialwissenschaften* (Stuttgart-Tübingen-Göttingen, 1960) XXXIV: 485–94; François Lesure, "Pour une sociologie historique des faits musicaux," *Report of the Eighth Congress of the IMS—New York, 1961* (Kassel: Bärenreiter, 1961) I: 333–46; Alphons Silbermann, "Die Ziele der Musiksoziologie," *Kölner Zeitschrift für Soziologie und Sozialpsychologie* II (1962): 322–35, and "Die Pole der Musiksoziologie," ibid. III (1963): 425–48; Ivo Supičić, "Problèmes de la sociologie musicale," *Cahiers internationuax de sociologie* XXXVII (1964): 119–29, and "Pour une sociologie de la musique," *Revue d'esthétique* XIX/1 (1966): 66–76; Tibor Kneif, "Gegenwartsfragen der Musiksoziologie," *Acta musicologica* XXXVIII/2–4 (1966): 72–118; Alfred Willener, "Music and Sociology," *Cultures* I/1 (1973): 233–49; W.V. Blomster, "Sociology of Music: Adorno and Beyond," *Thelos* 9/2 (1976): 81–112.

[10]Jacqueline De Clercq, *La profession de musicien—une enquête* (Brussels: Editions de l'Institut de Sociologie, 1970); Nicole Berthier, *Mélomanes et cultures musicales. Etude d'un statut socio-culturel* (Grenoble: Université des Sciences Sociales de Grenoble, 1975); Pierre-Michel Menger, *Le paradoxe du musicien. Le compositeur, le mélomane et l'Etat dans la société contemporaine* (Paris: Flammarion, 1983); Michel De Coster, *Le disque, art ou affaires? Analyse sociologique d'une industrie culturelle* (Grenoble: Presses Universitaires de Grenoble, 1976); Kurt Blaukopf, *Musik im Wandel der Gesellschaft* (Munich-Zurich: Piper, 1982).

[11]See Tibor Kneif, ed., *Texte zur Musiksoziologie* (Cologne: Arno Volk Verlag, 1975); Antonio Serravezza, ed., *La sociologia della musica* (Turin: E.D.T., 1980).

[12]See Albert Memmi, "Cinq propositions pour une sociologie de la

century ago, the sociology of music is still developing and many of its questions remain unexplored. It has been fostered largely by the discipline of music history, within which field, more than any other, sociological questions have been raised. In their formulation, these questions have gradually been differentiated from those relevant to music history itself. The development of music history as a scholarly discipline in the nineteenth and twentieth centuries[13] and the ever-increasing study of other related aspects of music have contributed to a more precise description of specifically sociological phenomena, in which music from the entire span of music history may be studied from the point of view of its integration into society. On the other hand, developments in biographical research have contributed to the discovery of the social and historical conditioning of musical creativity, and of the opportunities and limitations placed on the composer and his artistic output in various eras and societies. The history of music has also raised the important question of the relationship of the public to music, another sociological problem that cannot be clarified sufficiently by a purely music-historical approach.[14] Ethnomusicological research has, in its turn, produced a number of sociological problems: for example, that posed by the increasingly numerous discoveries

---

littérature," *Cahiers internationaux de sociologie* XXVI (1959): 149–59; Robert Escarpit, et al., *Le littéraire et le social, Eléments pour une sociologie de la littérature* (Paris: Flammarion, 1970) and Lucien Goldman, et al., *Sociologie de la littérature, Recherches récentes et discussions* (Brussels: Editions de l'Institut de Sociologie, 1970). See also Jean Ducrocq, Suzy Halimi, and Maurice Lévy, *Roman et société en Angleterre au XVIIIᵉ siècle* (Paris: P.U.F., 1978); and André Corvisier, *Arts et sociétés dans l'Europe du XVIIIᵉ siècle* (Paris: P.U.F., 1978).

[13]The history of music has developed considerably since the eighteenth century, but it has been its evolution in the following centuries, above all, that has determined the maturation of sociological questions concerning music.

[14]For information regarding the relatively recent public, see, for example, the papers read at the congress of the International Music Council (Rome, September 27–30, 1962) on "Music and Its Public," *The World of Music* V/1–2 (1963), and those of the Second symposium of the IMS (Zagreb, 1974), published in *IRASM* V/1 (1974) and VI/1 (1975).

concerning the practical functions and precise social purposes of ethnic music.[15]

That all of these questions have not been sufficiently examined until now is fairly explainable; they have been formulated, for the most part, by music historians, ethnomusicologists, or aestheticians, not by sociologists. However, by their very nature they are sociological questions, and call for a specifically sociological elucidation. Therefore, we can easily understand that those who have raised such questions have been uncomfortable with them and, except for a few tentative answers and some general observations, they have left them, for the most part, without solution.

At the same time, there exist other obstacles to the development of the sociology of music. First, there are still some traces of a certain "romantic" point of view—more prevalent, perhaps, among practicing musicians and the general public than among musicologists—that rejects the sociological approach to music and the sociological explication of some of its aspects. There is a certain fear of seeing the musical fact and its intrinsic worth devalued, a fear of seeing the autonomy of the musician limited or of submitting music to an analytic approach that might reduce a cherished art to a mere collection of facts. Sometimes such an attitude originates from an asociological (and thus purely aestheticist) conception of music as a completely autonomous and closed universe, which in essence concerns nothing "extra-artistic," and which cannot be clarified, at least partly, by sociological research. This attitude is no longer valid.

Of course, we can well understand the grounds for an aversion to the sociological explication of musical facts—especially, for example, when it reflects opposition to those

---

[15]See Jaap Kunst, *Ethnomusicology* (The Hague: Martinus Nijhoff, 1955); Alan P. Merriam, *The Anthropology of Music* (Evanston, Ill.: Northwestern U. Press, 1964); Bruno Nettl, *Theory and Method in Ethnomusicology* (New York: Free Press, 1964); Mantle Hood, *The Ethnomusicologist* (New York: McGraw Hill, 1971); 2nd ed. (Kent, Ohio: The Kent State U. Press, 1982); Charles Hamm, Bruno Nettl, and Ronald Byrnside, *Contemporary Music and Music Cultures* (Englewood Cliffs, N.J.: Prentice-Hall, 1975).

sociologistic trends toward more or less *reducing* artistic facts to social phenomena, thereby eliminating to some extent the relative autonomy and unquestionable specificity of music; or when it represents a confusion of these reductionist trends with an authentic conception of the sociology of music. Indeed, almost the entire history of musical scholarship gives evidence of its struggle to achieve emancipation and autonomy—the very struggle, in fact, that had been necessary for the emancipation and relative autonomy of the art of music itself. Occasionally, the theorists in the seventeenth, eighteenth and even into part of the nineteenth century still denied these qualities, instead submitting musical scholarship to other disciplines such as grammar or mathematics, or even relegating music to the status of an incomplete or inferior art. On the other hand, in one respect the majority of "19th-century musical scholars did their work almost too well in claiming a place for themselves in the academic hierarchy. This led to a premature specialization and forstered the kind of isolationism all too common in highly specialized fields. Musicology, or any humanistic discipline for that matter, thrives on interdisciplinary stimulation.... Sometimes the effort to gain a foothold as a 'scientific' study led to a narrowness of viewpoint that no reputable scientist would endorse ... There has been a tendency to emphasize the *historical* at the expense of the *systematic* aspects of our study.... "[16] Yet the sociological approach to music is essentially a "systematic" one. Without displacing the historical approach, it is complementary to it. And as for musicology in general, its maturity can be measured nowadays "in part by the ease with which it absorbs concepts and techniques from other fields in order to help attain its own humanistic objectives."[17]

An authentic conception of the sociology of music excludes

---

[16]Vincent Duckles, "Patterns in the Historiography of 19th-Century Music," *Acta musicologica* XLII/1–2 (1970) 82.

[17]Barry S. Brook, "Music, Musicology, and Related Disciplines: On Perspective and Interconnectedness," in *A Musical Offering: Essays in Honor of Martin Bernstein*, ed. Edward H. Clinkscale and Claire Brook (New York: Pendragon Press, 1977) 72.

all interference that might distort valid conceptions of music and its true nature, or diminish its aesthetic and artistic values. On the contrary, it should be stressed that the sociology of music is both bearer and messenger of true *musical* values. It transmits them indirectly, it is true, but it transmits them nonetheless by means of its very course of study, which in itself leads to the discovery of the *social* values and functions of music. According to Alphons Silbermann, the sociology of music has five functions: "(1) General characterization of the structure and function of the socio-musical organization as a phenomenon which, for the satisfaction of its needs, stems from the interaction of the individual with the group. (2) The determination of the relationship of socio-musical organization to socio-cultural changes. (3) Structural analysis of socio-musical groups, from the view points of: the functional interdependence of their members, the behavior of the groups, the constitution and the effects of roles and norms established within the groups, and the exercise of controls. (4) A typology of groups, based upon their functions. (5) Practical foresight and planning of necessary alterations in the life of music."[18]

Still, it is worthwhile to point out that in its investigations into social functions and values of music, the sociology of music throws into relief the capacity of that art to *outlive*, through its own artistic and human values, the socio-historical conditionings and circumstances that influence its creation.[19] The more clearly the sociology of music brings out the social functions and values of music as well as its goals and its purely artistic and human values, the more clearly can one demonstrate that music—despite its deep social roots—has always been and continues to

---

[18]Alphons Silbermann, *The Sociology of Music*, tr. Corbet Stewart (London: Routledge and Kegan Paul, 1963) 62.

[19]See Ingmar Bengtsson, "Some comments and another discussion," *IRASM* I/2 (1970): 195–9, where the author, however, remarks that such values or aspects either are contended to exist *a priori*, or (somewhat more empirically) are shown to exist through the alleged ability of music to supersede (how far?) its historical and social conditions, and asks where did the link between "social conditions" and "permanent" or "absolute" values disappear to?

be capable of surpassing the limitations of place and milieu of its origins and later performances, precisely because of these artistic and human values; and these limitations can be surpassed just to the extent that these values are revealed as deeper, more elevated, or universal.[20] Therein lies the cultural value of the sociology of music, which, far from destroying values, helps in its own way to support them.

Another obstacle to the integration of the sociology of music into musicology derives from the fact that a conception of the sociology of music that would contribute to a more complete and profound knowledge of music has not yet been sufficiently developed. Sociological research into musical matters has until now produced rather limited results. Furthermore, certain sociological approaches toward music have been criticized, with reason, for their surrender to verbosity, for their gratuitously abstract or pseudophilosophical (and pseudosociological) efforts, which are far removed from the scholarly work of positive analysis of concrete material. On the other hand, it is difficult for such positive analyses to carry us far enough toward a synthesis if they are not oriented, at least by a basic theoretical and methodological introduction, to the subject, goals, and methods of the discipline in question. Without such an approach, the integration of the sociology of music into musicology remains problematic.

One last difficulty arises in part from the preceding problem. The sociology of music is excluded by some musicologists from the framework of musicology either because its importance has been minimized,[21] or because it is considered a part of sociology.

---

[20] See the interesting discussion about an aspect of this question between Paul Henry Lang, Georg Knepler and Frits Noske, in particular Noske's pertinent formulation: "Social conditions cannot prevent a composer from creating good music, but they may prevent him from writing different music," in "Musical Style Changes and General History," *IMS Report of the Tenth Congress—Ljubljana, 1967* (Kassel-Ljubljana: Bärenreiter-U. of Ljubljana, 1970) 251–70.

[21] See Carl Dahlhaus, "Das musikalische Kunstwerk als Gegenstand der Soziologie," *IRASM* V/1 (1974) 11–26.

But if the sociology of music can have only a peripheral importance for general sociology, such is not the case for musicology. Belonging to sociology only in its aims and methods, the sociology of music belongs in its subject matter to musicology. Capable of analyses of fundamental relevance to musicology, the sociology of music makes use of some musicological disciplines or subdisciplines as auxiliary sciences.

Despite this, certain musicologists do not grant a place to the sociology of music within musicology, even theoretically. Lloyd Hibberd, for example, who outlined a table of all the principal musicological disciplines in his "Musicology Reconsidered," did not mention the sociology of music.[22] Likewise, Jacques Chailley in his *Précis de musicologie* included the aesthetics and the philosophy of music, but did not devote the slightest attention to our discipline.[23] Suzanne Clercx tackled briefly, in her definition of musicology, the "social role" of music (which should have been designated "social function," because in sociology performance of a "role" is attributed only to persons or groups of persons) as one of the subjects to be studied by musicology, but not as a separate discipline.[24] Other systematizations of musicology, so far as they concern (or rather, more or less neglect) the sociology of music, will not be mentioned here, as they belong to a more general field of research. However, this matter should not be forgotten or ignored, especially since it has been treated by outstanding musicologists in the past and is still present in contemporary musical scholarship.[25]

---

[22]See Lloyd Hibberd, "Musicology reconsidered," *Acta musicologica* XXI/1 (1959) 25–31.

[23]See Jacques Chailley, et al., *Précis de musicologie* (Paris: P.U.F., 1958); in its second edition (Paris: P.U.F., 1984) this work no longer includes the aesthetics and philosophy of music.

[24]See Suzanne Clercx, "Définition de la musicologie et sa position à l'égard des disciplines qui lui sont connexes," *Revue belge de musicologie* I (1946–47) 113–16.

[25]See, for example, Hugo Riemann, *Grundriss der Musikwissenschaft* (Leipzig: 1908); Glen Haydon, *Introduction to Musicology* (New York: 1941); reprint (Chapel Hill, N.C.: 1959); Frank L. Harrison, Mantle Hood, and Claude V.

The foregoing examples testify to some of the difficulties previously noted, which are obstacles to the development of the sociology of music and to its integration into musicology. Yet only if an interaction can be established and maintained between sociologists of music, ethnomusicologists and music historians will the sociology of music play anything more than an occasional and peripheral role within the general field of musicology. That there is not enough "literature in the sociology of music is not due to any particular difficulty within the field, but rather to the fact that music is generally considered a less socially important occupation than many others, at least in our industrial societies."[26]

III • A SOCIAL HISTORY OF MUSIC

A new area of exploration and research that has already proved fruitful has appeared within musicology—more particularly within music history. The first elements or guidelines for a *social history* of music have been formulated. We may point to the studies undertaken by Paul H. Lang and Roman I. Gruber, whose works have gone beyond the limits of a pure and strict music history. The former deals with social facts relating to

---

Palisca, *Musicology* (Englewood Cliffs, N.J.: Prentice-Hall, 1965, 2nd ed.); Walter Wiora, *Historische und systematische Musikwissenschaft* (Tutzing: Hans Schneider, 1972); *Ideen zur Geschichte der Musik* (Darmstadt: Wissenschaftliche Buchgesellschaft, 1980); Oskár Elschek, "Gegenwartsprobleme der musikwissenschaftlichen Systematik," *Acta musicologica* XLV/1 (1973) 1–23. See also a selected bibliography in *Perspectives in Musicology*, ed. Barry S. Brook, Edward O.D. Downes, and Sherman Van Solkema (New York: Norton, 1972) 335–46; Jack Westrup, *An Introduction to Musical History* (London: Hutchinson U. Library, 1955; 2nd ed. 1973); Carl Dahlhaus, ed. *Einführung in die systematische Musikwissenschaft* (Cologne: Hans Gerig, 1971; 2nd ed. 1975); Carl Dahlhaus, *Grundlagen der Musikgeschichte* (Cologne: Hans Gerig, 1977); Eng. tr., *Foundations of Music History* (Cambridge-London-New York: Cambridge U. Press, 1983); and Charles Seeger, *Studies in Musicology 1935–1975* (Berkeley-Los Angeles-London: U. of California Press, 1977).

[26]Alfred Willener, "Music and Sociology," *Cultures* I/1 (1973) 234.

music on a rather general level; the latter envisions the interrelation of musical culture with general culture, and with political and economic life as well.[27] We may also add to these the more recent works of Arnold Hauser, Walter Wiora and others.[28] More specialized contributions have also been forthcoming: for example, those for specific periods such as the Middle Ages and the baroque or the Romantic eras, by André Pirro, Jacques Chailley, Manfred F. Bukofzer and Alfred Einstein.[29] Other studies refer to particular countries within a given era, such as those by Wilfrid Mellers, Nanie Bridgman, and Robert Wangermée.[30] Leo Balet, Marcel Beaufils and Eberhard Preussner have studied German bourgeois music, the structure of the musical public, and musical life in eighteenth-century Germany.[31]

---

[27]See Paul H. Lang, *Music in Western Civilization* (New York: Norton, 1941) and Roman I. Gruber, *Istoria muzykal'noj kul'tury* (Moscow-Leningrad: Gosizd, 1941–59), 2 vols.

[28]See Arnold Hauser, *The Social History of Art* (London: Routledge and Kegan Paul, 1951) 2 vols.; Walter Wiora, *Die vier Weltalter der Musik* (Stuttgart: Kohlhammer, 1961); Eng. tr., *The Four Ages of Music* (New York: Norton, 1965); George Dyson, *The Progress of Music* (London: Oxford U. Press, 1932).

[29]See André Pirro, *Histoire de la musique de la fin du XIVe siècle à la fin du XVIe* (Paris: H. Laurens, 1940); Jacques Chailley, *Histoire musicale du Moyen Age* (Paris: P.U.F., 1950); Manfred F. Bukofzer, *Music in the Baroque Era* (New York: Norton, 1947); Alfred Einstein, *Music in the Romantic Era* (New York: Norton, 1947).

[30]See Wilfrid Mellers, *Music and Society, England and the European Tradition* (London: Dennis Dobson, 1950); Nanie Bridgman, *La vie musicale au Quattrocento et jusqu'à la naissance du madrigal (1400–1530)* (Paris: Gallimard, 1964); Robert Wangermée, *La musique flamande dans la société des XVe et XVIe siècles*, 2nd ed. (Brussels: Arcade, 1966); Eng. tr., *Flemish Music and Society in the Fifteenth and Sixteenth Centuries* (New York: Praeger, 1968), and especially Barry S. Brook, *La Symphonie française dans la seconde moité du XVIIe siècle* (Paris: Institut de Musicologie de l'Université de Paris-Sorbonne, 1962) 3 vols; Karl Gustav Fellerer, *Musik und Leben im 19. Jahrhundert* (Regensburg: G. Bosse, 1984).

[31]See Leo Balet, *Die Verbürgerlichung der deutschen Kunst, Literatur und Musik im 18. Jahrhundert,* (Leipzig-Strassburg-Zürich: Heitz, 1936) Marcel Beaufils, *Par la musique vers l'obscur, Essai sur la musique bourgeoise et l'éveil d'une conscience allemande au XVIIIe siècle* (Marseille: F. Robert, 1942); 2nd ed., *Comment l'Allemagne est devenue musicienne* (Paris: Laffont, 1983); Eberhard

Walter Wiora made an interesting study of the relationships of the composer to his environment.[32] Other questions in the social history of music have been treated by Ernst H. Meyer, Paul Loubet de Sceaury, Stefania Lobaczewska, Walter L. Woodfill, Georg Knepler, François Lesure, Barry S. Brook and Jean Mongrédien.[33] On a strictly socio-historical level, some other more or less important editions concerning a social history of music have appeared more recently, among which should be specially stressed those of Albert Dunning, Walter Salmen, Henry Raynor, William Weber, Sabine Žak, Gianfranco Zàccaro, Bruno Brévan and Christopher Ballantine.[34] All these works, in the

---

Preussner, *Die bürgerliche Musikkultur, Ein Beitrag zur deutschen Musikgeschichte des 18. Jahrhunderts,* 2nd ed. (Kassel-Basel: Bärenreiter, 1950).

[32]See Walter Wiora, *Komponist und Mitwelt* (Kassel-Basel: Bärenreiter, 1964).

[33]See Ernst H. Meyer, *English Chamber Music* (London: Laurence and Wishart, 1946); Paul Loubet de Sceaury, *Musiciens et facteurs d'instruments de musique sous l'Ancien Régime, Statuts corporatifs* (Paris: A. Pedone, 1949); Stefania Lobaczewska, *Zarys historii form muzycznych, Próba ujęcia socjologicznego* (Kraków: 1950); Walter L. Woodfill, *Musicians in English Society, from Elizabeth to Charles I* (Princeton: Princeton U. Press, 1953); Georg Knepler, *Musikgeschichte des 19. Jahrhunderts* (Berlin: Henschelverlag, 1961) 2 vols.; François Lesure, *Musica e Società* (Milan: Istituto editoriale italiano, 1966); Ger. tr., *Musik und Gesellschaft im Bild* (Kassel-Basel: Bärenreiter, 1966); Eng. tr., *Music and Art in Society* (Pittsburgh: Pennsylvania State U. Press, 1968); Barry S. Brook, "La symphonie concertante: Its Musical and Sociological Bases," *IRASM* VI/1 (1975) 9–28; Jean Mongrédien, *La musique en France des Lumières au Romantisme (1789-1830)* (Paris: Flammarion, 1986).

[34]See Henry Raynor, *The social history of music from the Middle Ages to Beethoven* (London: Barrie & Jenkins, 1972), and *Music and Society since 1815* (New York, Schocken Books, 1976); Albert Dunning, *Die Staatsmotette (1480-1555)* (Utrecht: Oosthoek, 1970); William Weber, *Music and the Middle Class* (London: Croom Helm, 1975); Sabine Žak, *Musik als "Ehr und Zier" im mittelalterlichen Reich. Studien zur Musik im höfischen Leben, Recht und Zeremoniell* (Neuss: Päffgen Verlag, 1979); Gianfranco Zàccaro, *Storia sociale della musica* (Rome: Newton Compton Editori, 1979); Bruno Brévan, *Les changements de la vie musicale parisienne de 1744 à 1799* (Paris: P.U.F., 1980); Walter Salmen, ed., *Der Sozialstatus des Berufmusikers vom 17. bis 19. Jahrhundert* (Kassel-Basel, Bärenreiter, 1971), and the enlarged American translation *The Social Status of the Professional Musician from the Middle Ages to the 19th century* (New York: Pendragon Press, 1983); Christopher Ballantine, *Music and its Social Meanings*

variety of their approaches, their methods and their matter, have permitted, with some others, to constitute a field of investigation the frameworks of which are being concretized with ever more precision in the elaboration of its own object and perspectives. These essays, along with others, are witness to the maturation and formulation of specifically sociological problems concerning music and its history. In the meantime, however, new problems have arisen, which now require definition and research.

Actually, one has occasionally been led, implicitly or explicitly, to identify the sociology of music not only with a "sociological" aesthetics of music[35] but also with a social history of music, as Kurt Blaukopf did.[36] However, the sociology of music should not be identified with any sort of history at all, whether social (and "world-wide"!) or not. Its value should not be deemed provisional, as Blaukopf first proposed in affirming that the sociology of music, as a separate discipline, will become superfluous and will disappear when musicology adopts the sociological point of view in its investigations.[37] Such a position, which would eliminate the autonomy of the sociology of music, is methodologically incorrect even though it might seem to enrich musicological research. The widening and deepening of exploration in any scholarly field leads inevitably to specialization and to ever more ramified subdivisions. There is no reason for sociology and musicology to be exempt. On the other hand,

---

(New York: Gordon and Breach, 1984); Michel Faure, *Musique et société du Second Empire aux années vingt* (Paris: Flammarion, 1985).

[35]See below, p. 28–9.

[36]See Kurt Blaukopf, *Musiksoziologie* (Cologne-Berlin: Kiepenheuer, 1951), 5, where the author distinguished a *general* sociology of music from a *special* sociology of music. He assigned to the first the study of tonal systems from a sociological point of view, and identified the second with a "world-wide history of music." Although it may be acceptable to hold that the sociology of music in general (but not a special sociology of music, as the author would have it) would have for study all the sociological facts concerning music, within the spatial and temporal limits determined by the culture, one could hardly ignore all that would be gratuitous in such a distinction and attribution of areas of jurisdiction concerning a "general" or "special" sociology of music.

[37]*Ibid.*, 8.

to adopt the sociological point of view in musicology—a vague exigency—is not sufficient. Similarly, as long as it cannot be reduced to the application of that point of view to the *history of music*, the sociology of music will never become synonymous with the *social history of music*, which is only one of its points of departure. As for Blaukopf, he revoked his theory of the "transitional" character of the sociology of music in the second edition of his book,[38] considering that it is also possible today "to adduce practical arguments that rule out the ascription of a merely provisional importance to the sociology of music. This discipline has developed its own specific methods—for example in the analysis of the way music is received, of musical behavior and so forth—and these methods are at least as closely related to sociology, psychology and psycho-acoustics as they are to musicology. Apart from this, the sociology of music now includes fields that certainly do not fall within the purview of musicology, such as the study of the transformation of musical information in the technical media, and audience research."[39] Clearly, the (social) history of music and musicology in general have failed to pose certain questions raised by the sociology of music. These questions exist; the sociology of music is required to answer them.

The fact that the social history of music does not have the range of the sociology of music does not lessen its importance. On the contrary, it conserves all of its own values and is also an integral part of that artistic history of man (or that human history of art) considered by many to be fundamental: "A history of the human imagination in cooperation with intelligence, sensibility or activity; an extensive research into the aspirations, desires, and inventions that create and modify, from one era to the next, the reality experienced by all; in short, a history describing not only the life of art in relation to man but also the life of man in

---

[38]See Kurt Blaukopf, *Musiksoziologie*, 2nd ed. (Niederteufen: Arthur Niggli, 1972), 5–6.

[39]Kurt Blaukopf, "Ivo Supičić, Musique et société, Perspectives pour une sociologie de la musique—Zagreb 1971," *The World of Music* XIV/2 (1972), 64.

relation to art; and ... the action of art upon man. Science, customs, philosophy, war, revolutions, economic conditions, industry, *and art* must be studied in their living inter-relation-ships—changing, perpetual and *mutual.*"[40] Such a conception of a social history of art would have definite methodological and substantive importance, because it would require problems to be examined in a richer and more productive manner. In the light of this human complexity, we could rightly ask: To what extent can music be isolated from it?[41] Still, the task of a social history of music, although highly significant, will always remain in a certain sense more humble and limited than that of the sociology of music. The social history of music involves comprehension of the *concrete.* Its aim is to delineate the history of music in connection with the history of societies, to establish in chronological order the ties that may unite them; in sum, to study them comparatively. And the comparative method is one of the essential components of this discipline. It is through the use of this method, and through the scrutiny of the materials provided by music history and by social and cultural history that a social history of music can reveal the concrete and singular relationships existing between music and society.

The sociology of music, on the other hand, does not limit itself to comprehension of the concrete. While presuming the fundamental importance of this comprehension, the sociology of music goes beyond it, aiming at another level of understanding of the material, namely at a *typology.* "Typology is a kind of generalization used in the social sciences for the purpose of classifying, comparing, and deducing relationships among various classes of cultural phenomena ... We would try to formulate the 'typology' of each group in terms of characteristic traits, socio–cultural—economic backgrounds, esthetic and intellectual influences, formal and stylistic patterns, and so forth. Each typology could also be considered as a theoretical

---

[40]Etienne Souriau, "Autorité humaine de la musique," *Polyphonie* VII–VIII (1951), 24.

[41]See *Ibid.,* 25.

'model' for purposes of comparison or deduction."[42] But to make sense, typology must correspond to reality.[43] The social facts and functions of music that are *common* to a social group, global society, certain period in history or particular civilization. can be considered as *typical* of that group, society, etc. The social facts and functions of music that show, on the contrary, a greater stability or duration within history, thus manifesting certain fundamental relationships that go beyond the given social group, society, period of history or civilization have to be considered as transcending the typical, as being *supertypological*. Thus the social *role* of musicians seems to be much more constant through history and consequently obeys supertypological laws, while their social *status* seems more variable, conforming consequently to different types. But concrete musical and social facts, which are not either "typical" or "supertypological" do not fall within the scope of the *specific* subject of the sociology of music. Music history (social or not) and ethnomusicology both study concrete musical facts in depth on factual grounds, taking them in their singularity. The sociology of music, on the contrary, grasps these facts at a more profound level, considering whatever is common to all of them from the sociological point of view. In this sense, the sociology of music goes further in the exploration and explication of musical facts. Actually neither the social history of music nor music history can achieve their goals without considerable recourse to abstraction, or, of course, selecting from singular facts their particularly important aspects. But this would be done solely to link particulars to particulars, never to bring about an essentially sociological typification, which is the task of the sociology of music.

---

[42]Gilbert Chase, "American Musicology and the Social Sciences," *Perspectives in Musicology*, ed. B.S. Brook, E.O.D. Downes, and S. Van Solkema (New York: Norton, 1972), 225.

[43]About Max Weber's concept of "idealtypisch," see Henri-Irénée Marrou, *De la connaissance historique*, 3rd ed. (Paris: Seuil, 1958), 159–168, and about Weber's sociology of music in general Kurt Blaukopf, "Tonsysteme und ihre gesellschaftliche Geltung in Max Webers Musiksoziologie," *IRASM* I/2 (1970) 159–67.

In order to succeed, however, the sociology of music does need the social history of music and music history itself as auxiliary disciplines; indeed, it cannot do without them, nor can the social history of music do without music history. These disciplines, together with ethnomusicology, provide the indispensable basis on which the sociology of music must be built. Therefore, we can conclude that the inductive method is one of the fundamental techniques of the sociology of music.[44] This method retains a universal value in the sociology of music, especially concerning the typology of the relationships established by the social history of music between musical facts as *artistic* facts and extramusical social facts as *social* facts. The goal of the social history of music is to establish the relationships between these facts, considered in their singularity and in chronological order. To establish what is *typical* in these relationships, be it at the core of a given historical period or of a particular society, or more extensively; in very rare cases, perhaps, to be able to endow those facts with an almost universal or supertypological significance and, finally, to draw sociological conclusions from it all—such is the goal of the sociology of music. This discipline is, then, by the nature of the knowledge it seeks, aimed toward more general views, which must be based upon precise and determinable facts. According to Georg Knepler, "music history concentrates on genetic and music sociology on structural matters. Music sociology has the task of presenting a cross section of musical culture at a given historical moment, never forgetting that all the facts, relationships, and artifacts it reveals are the result of historical change and are subject to change again as soon as one's momentary picture is mapped and even while it is being mapped . . . Music history and music sociology complement one another—only the stress is different. The use of empirical methods is not a necessary criterion of sociology; sociological methods can be used in the analysis of musical cultures of the

---

[44]See below, p. 70.

past to whatever extent available material allows."[45] Still, everything that has been said on the subject of music history is equally valid, from the methodological point of view, when applied to ethnomusicology. This discipline, as a "study of primitive and traditional musics of the whole world" (C. Marcel-Dubois), or as a study "of learned non-European musics" (C. Braïloïu) is closely connected with or even belongs to music history, considered in its most general sense.

Therefore, the sociology of music is not, and cannot be, practiced in a vacuum. It must be pursued as a distinct and unique field of study, but its close links with other related disciplines must also be respected. Those related disciplines furnish indispensable services, which the sociology of music can then render in kind. An example would be the musical language of the Middle Ages: "before attempting to discover the secrets of its technique, it is important to understand the *sense*, the meaning of this language. Music then had a very precise social and spiritual role to play: much more than ours does today. Without having defined this role, without knowing its limits, without having considered all the conditions that regulated the initimate correspondance between the purpose and the expression of this language and between its motives and its means—it would be useless to attempt to recount its history."[46] In contrast, it is of secondary methodological importance to determine whether or not the sociology of music should incorporate a social history of music into its own structure. What is more important to establish is that, even when they deal with a common *subject matter*, the sociology of music and the social history of music do not focus on identical *objects* for study.

As Georges Gurvitch explained, while nineteenth-century sociology was one-dimensional, twentieth-century sociology is clearly multidimensional. It is a sociology in depth: social reality

---

[45]Georg Knepler, "Music Historiography in Eastern Europe," *Perspectives in Musicology* (New York: Norton, 1972), 231. Compare this view with that held by Barry S. Brook, p. 82 below.

[46]Vladimir Fédorov, "Notes sur la musicologie médiévale: son objet de demain," *Polyphonie III* (1949) 32.

is presented as existing in levels, steps and layers, one below another. These interact with and interpenetrate each other, but they also come into conflict in relationships of tension. To these "vertical" polarizations and antagonisms are added, at each level, horizontal tensions or dynamics. The degrees in depth or the diverse levels of social facts, however, are independent of degrees of value and reality. On the contrary, they concern, for the most part, that which is more or less directly accessible to external observation.[47]

Now, the social history of music grasps its subject matter at the first level of horizontal dialectic, one that is concrete and more accessible, concerning the relationships between a musical fact and an extramusical social fact, one that is principally at the factual and historically verifiable level. It is certainly true that this grasp does not constitute a complete sociological analysis. But that it constitutes an indispensable point of departure seems equally incontestable. We can ask nevertheless whether in research it is always possible to delimit the scope of sociology and that of history, and to distinguish what belongs, on the analytical level, to the sociology of music, from what belongs to music history or to the social history of music.[48] The serious work that could promote the sociology of music resides today, and will for quite some time, in research at the factual level: in dealing with concrete musical and social facts, when united and classified will lead to valid sociological conclusions.

IV • A NOTE ON THE SOCIOLOGY OF MUSIC AND ETHNOMUSICOLOGY

As it was stressed by Alan P. Merriam, "the uses and functions of

---

[47] See Georges Gurvitch, *La vocation actuelle de la sociologie* (Paris: P.U.F., 1957) I, 63–6.

[48] See in this connection the position of Christoph-Hellmut Mahling, "Soziologie der Musik und musikalische Sozialgeschichte," *IRASM* I/1 (1970) 92–4, and Elisabeth Haselauer, *Handbuch der Musiksoziologie* (Vienna-Cologne-Graz: Böhlaus, 1980) 143–4.

music represent one of the most important problems in ethno-musicology, for in the study of human behavior we search constantly . . . not only for the descriptive facts about music, but, more important, for the meaning of music . . . We wish to know not only what a thing is, but, more significantly, what it does for people and how it does it."[49] It happens that the sociology of music aims at the same target looking for functions and uses of music in society in order to understand what it was created for and in service of whom it is performed. In this aspect we should view a profound similarity of method and goal between the two disciplines. What Merriam says about ethnomusicology can be perfectly well applied to the sociology of music: "When we speak of the uses of music, we are referring to the ways in which music is employed in human society, to the habitual practice or customary exercise of music either as a thing in itself or in conjunction with other activities . . . Music is *used* in certain situations and becomes a part of them, but it may or may not also have a deeper *function* . . . 'Use' then, refers to the situation in which music is employed in human action; 'function' concerns the reasons for its employment and particularly the broader purpose which it serves."[50]

In fact, ethnomusicology has already developed the study of uses and functions of ethnic music in its own field of investigation to a considerable degree; the sociology of music has to contribute to this study in art music in order to help music history and musicology in general to better understand and grasp their object from this point of view. At the present state of research, ethnomusicology and the sociology of music can help each other in this field, ethnomusicology bringing first of all a richer articulation of numerous functions it discovers in ethnic music on the factual level and the sociology of music a deeper insight into various uses and functions of both art and ethnic music as they can be viewed from the sociological standpoint.

---

[49]Alan P. Merriam, *The Anthropology of Music* (Evanston, Illinois: Northwestern University Press, 1964) 209.
[50]*Ibid.,* 210.

Merriam briefly describes a few kinds of functions which ethnic music assumes, among others the functions of stimulating, expressing, and sharing emotions; the function of aesthetic enjoyment; the function of entertainment; the function of communication; the function of symbolic representation; the function of physical response; the function of validation of social institutions and religious rituals; the function of contribution to the continuity and stability of culture; and the function of contribution to the integration of society.[51] According to him, "it is quite possible that this list of the functions of music may require condensation or expansion, but in general it summarizes the role of music in human culture."[52]

To which extent ethnomusicological and sociological studies of music can be close to one another is also demonstrated in considerations made by Mantle Hood in the introductory pages of his book *The Ethnomusicologist*, where he states that "a truly significant study of music or dance or theater cannot be isolated from its socio-cultural context and the scale of values it implies."[53] And he gives for the sake of comparative illustration two contrasting examples: the United States and the island of Bali in Indonesia. "Viewed as a total society, the United States regards the arts as nonessential, low on its scale of values . . . Possession of a first and second automobile has high priority over direct support of the arts . . . It can also be pointed out that dollar support of the arts, in one form or another, by private foundations, some institutions of higher learning, and benevolent individuals is probably greater in the United States than any other country in the world. However, dollar support is not necessarily an index of consumer valuation in determining the attitude of a society toward the arts."[54]

Now, to envisage things more broadly, we shall quote Charles Seeger: "In his article "Ethnomusicology" in the *Harvard Diction-*

---

[51]See *Ibid.,* 219-226.

[52]*Ibid.,* 227.

[53]Mantle Hood, *The Ethnomusicologist* (Kent, Ohio: Kent State University Press, 1982 2nd ed.) 10.

[54]*Ibid.,* 12-13.

ary of Music (1969), Mantle Hood states categorically, 'Ethno-musicology is an approach to the study of *any* music, not only in terms of itself but also in relation to its cultural context.' He continues, 'Currently the term has two broad applications: (1) the study of all music outside the European art tradition, including survivals of earlier forms of that tradition in Europe and alsewhere; (2) the study of all varieties of music found in one locale or region, e.g., the 'ethnomusicology' of Tokyo or Los Angeles or Santiago would comprise the study in that locality of all types of European art music, the music of ethnic enclaves, folk, popular and commercial music, musical hybrids, etc.; in other words, all music being used by the people of a given area.' . . . Ultimately, there would be no roles for separate studies, musicology and ethnomusicology; but there would still be a distinction between the musicological and ethnomusicologi-cal *approaches*, the first to the thing in itself, the second, to the thing in its cultural context as one of quite a number of other contexts. . . "[55] As it is well known, these views are not shared by all musicologists and ethnomusicologists.

V • AESTHETIC STUDIES AND SOCIOLOGICAL RESEARCH

The relationships between music history and the sociology of music do not lead to the mutual isolation of the two disciplines, but rather to their complementing one another. Let us now examine whether the same is true for the aesthetics of music and the sociology of music.

An identification of the sociology of art with aesthetics, or more specifically of the sociology of music with the aesthetics of music—an identification which at times was equated with an elimination of aesthetics from the domain of science—has undoubtedly been generally discarded today.[56] It is true that the

---

[55]Charles Seeger, "Foreword" to Mantle Hood. *The Ethnomusicologist* (Kent, Ohio: Kent State University Press, 1982, 2nd ed.) v-vi.

[56]However, see Alphons Silbermann, *Introduction à une sociologie de la*

concept of *sociological aesthetics* seemed to resolve the question of the relationship between aesthetics and the sociology of art by synthesizing the two;[57] its deficiency stemmed from the fact that it was in truth neither aesthetics nor sociology, but rather a strange mixture of philosophy of art and various sciences, often associated parasitically with one of the most serious errors of modern scientism: sociologism.[58] However, the sociology of art has gradually won its place among the family of sciences exploring the artistic universe; by its very existence as a separate discipline, it inevitably poses the problem of its relationship to aesthetics.

Without considering here the existing theories of specific authors, whether they be associated with sociologism or of an asociological bent, we must reflect on these two basic attitudes reduced to their logical essence and the purity of their philosophical roots, and thus freed of other elements often intermingled in the particular theories espoused by various authors.

In the overall cognitive approach to music within musicology itself, two fundamentally opposing errors are to be avoided at the very outset: the first assumes an attitude that is basically *asociological;* the second takes as its point of departure a

---

musique (Paris: P.U.F., 1955), where the author's manner of expression leads us to suppose that the sociology of music should replace the aesthetics of music. For his more recent point of view see "Soziologie der Musik," *Empirische Kunstsoziologie* (Stuttgart: F. Enke, 1973) 69-109.

[57] See H.H. Needham, *Le développement de l'esthétique sociologique en France et en Angleterre au XIXe siècle* (Paris: Librairie Ancienne Honoré Champion, 1926). For example, see Charles Lalo, *Notions d'esthétique* (Paris: P.U.F., 1948), 77ff., and "Méthodes et objets de l'esthétique sociologique," *Revue internationale de philosophie* VII (1949) 5-41; Raymond Bayer, *Histoire de l'esthétique* (Paris: Armand Colin, 1961) 229-242; and Roger Bastide, *Art et société* (Paris: Payot, 1977).

[58]These observations especially concern much of the work of earlier authors such as Taine and Guyau, as well as some of the works of Charles Lalo, who had later taken a position against "totalitarian sociologism." See Charles Lalo, "Méthodes et objets de l'esthétique sociologique," *Revue internationale de philosophie* VII (1949) 10. As to the position of Guyau, see F. J. W. Harding, *Jean-Marie Guyau (1854-1888): Aesthetician and Sociologist* (Geneva: Librairie Droz, 1973).

sociologistic stance. These two postures arise from preconceived and erroneous philosophical ideas, which disfigure the authentic nature of musicology; the resulting approaches suffer from a fundamental methodological fallacy. They not only pervade the basic principles that underly this discipline and its methods, but frequently, by denaturing these principles, they permeate the problems and even the very solutions as well with which musicology is concerned.

These remarks require some clarification. We can formulate two principal conceptions of musicology. According to the first, musicology is a meld of strictly scholarly disciplines, including primarily music history (and other associated disciplines), ethnomusicology and the sociology of music. Armand Machabey has defined it as a discipline that researches, formulates and resolves problems relating to the history of music, its aesthetics, and to music itself in its various manifestations.[59] For Jacques Handschin and François Lesure, however, musicology is "that historical discipline which has as its subject 'not music as a given fact by itself, but man insofar as he expresses himself in music,'[60] that discipline which in the last analysis reflects only a fraction of the history of civilization."[61] Such a conception is acceptable only if it also grants the aesthetics of music a place in the totality of knowledge about music—a place, by this definition outside of the scholarly discipline of musicology itself, considering the importance given to philosophic speculation in the aesthetic understanding of music. If, on the other hand, a conception of musicology were to deny the objective value of aesthetic knowledge, it should be rejected. It is needless to emphasize the impoverishment that such a denial would bring not only to the aesthetics of music, but also to the knowledge and understanding of music as a whole, and finally, to musicology itself. It is also superfluous to point out the discrepancy—

---

[59]Armand Machabey, *La musicologie* (Paris: P.U.F., 1962) 119.

[60]Reference is made to Jacques Handschin, "Musicologie et musique," *La revue internationale de musique* IX (winter 1950-51) 221.

[61]François Lesure, "Musicologie et sociologie," *La revue musicale* CCXXI (1953): 4.

which in this conception is inescapable—with the fact that the aesthetics of music is now also a scholarly discipline. But a conception of musicology as a historical discipline, having "as its subject . . . man insofar as he expresses himself in music," or music considered in its relationships with man, would expose musicology to two dangers: first, of being too restrictive in defining musicology solely as a historical discipline; second, of being somewhat too vague, although correct in its humanistic perspective. On the other hand, if we accept the view formulated by Jacques Handschin, "then anthropology becomes by definition the social science that has the most relevance to musicology."[62] Still, it should be emphasized, as Claude Palisca did, that we cannot call musicology simply the history of music, because "there is much in the discipline that is not properly history. There is criticism and analysis, lexicography, bibliography, paleography, philology, archaeology, and sociology. All of these activities of the musicologist contribute to the history of music, of course, but it is misleading to think of the musicologist only as a historian, because often his emphasis is not in the chronicle, but in some aspect of the thing being chronicled."[63]

Now we can also consider a second concept: that the aesthetics of music is an integral part of musicology, taken in a larger sense. This concept is also justifiable, as it seeks to demonstrate that aesthetic knowledge enters into the totality of scientific knowledge of music. Undoubtedly, it is essential to distinguish between two orders of knowledge that are clearly distinct in themselves: *scientific* and *philosophical* knowledge. But it would be a mistake to equate the aesthetics of music with purely philosophical knowledge, especially as valuable results

---

[62]Gilbert Chase, "American Musicology and the Social Sciences," *Perspectives in Musicology* 207. See also Alan P. Merriam, *The Anthropology of Music* (Evanston, Ill.: Northwestern University Press, 1964), and "Musical Instruments as Objects of Historical and Anthropological Research," Round Table II, *IMS Report of the Eleventh Congress—Copenhagen 1972* (Copenhagen: Edition Wilhelm Hansen, 1974) 131-65.

[63]Claude V. Palisca, "The Scope of American Musicology," *Musicology*, Frank L. Harrison, Mantle Hood, and Claude V. Palisca ed., 120-121.

THE SOCIOLOGY OF MUSIC

have been obtained from aestheticians and musicologists who have contributed, as did Walter Wiora, to the formulation of an aesthetics of music embracing both science *and* philosophy, as a complex and integral scientific-philosophical knowledge.[64] For instance, as Carl Dahlhaus put it, if sometimes "esthetic experience is apparently independent of historical knowledge, or at least may be so," it is also true sometimes that more exact analysis shows that historical knowledge is quite often founded on esthetic judgement, as well as vice versa . . . Many esthetic judgements are established by way of historical judgements . . . But to admit that originality or its absence is an esthetic criterion implies that there are esthetic experiences that include historical knowledge and would be impossible without it . . . "[65] On the other hand, "anyone who confined himself strictly within a historian's limits might of course establish that a piece of music repeated something said earlier, but such a historian could not speak about derivativeness as a shortcoming."[66] Although "the criterion of originality, however, . . . is itself historically limited; its validity does not extend back before the eighteenth century,"[67] "in the accusation of the derivativeness, historical and aesthetic aspects are inseparably interlocked."[68] This is obviously only one example, among many, of the mutual interpenetration of historical and aesthetic explanations,[69] and of scientific and philosophical aspects. . . .

The content of the aesthetics of music consists in objects of

---

[64]See for example Walter Wiora, "Das musikalische Kunstwerk und die systematische Musikwissenschaft," *Deuxième Congrès international d'Esthétique et de Science de l'art* (Paris: F. Alcan, 1937): 223-226; and "Historische und systematische Musikforschung," *Die Musikforschung* I (1948) 171-191. See also the collection of his writings, *Historische und systematische Musikwissenschaft* (Tutzing: H. Schneider, 1972); and *Das musikalische Kunstwerk* (Tutzing: H. Schneider, 1983).

[65]Carl Dahlhaus, *Esthetics of Music* (Cambridge: Cambridge University Press, 1982) 71.

[66]*Ibid.*

[67]*Ibid.*, p. 72.

[68]*Ibid.*, p. 71.

[69]On recent relationships between the aesthetics of music and musicology,

thought that are either typical features of a given historical period of music, musical style, form or work (the words "style" and "form" being used here in their broadest sense), or typical of some universal aspect of music or a musical culture. It is from specific musical data—facts collected by musicology that concern either a historical aspect of music or some of its general characteristics—that these objects of thought are abstracted inductively by the aesthetics of music. However, these facts ought to be compared to the previously acquired philosophical truths that concern them. Scientific induction and philosophical deduction must be combined so that the proper content of the aesthetics of music can emerge. Neither of these methods alone is sufficient for the elaboration of an authentic aesthetics of music. Each must, one the contrary, support the other in that undertaking. One should not justify an aesthetics of music founded exclusively on either philosophical analyses or the observation of concrete facts. Now that these preliminary remarks have been presented, we can better understand the significance and range of both the asociological and sociologistic concepts in the totality of artistic and musical knowledge.

In fact, these two concepts of art are at the same time concepts of the *knowledge* of art. They are also mutually exclusive, because the asociological concept repudiates sociological knowledge of art as an essential and integral part of that knowledge, capable of revealing its nature and clarifying its history; and the sociologistic concept repudiates the autonomous value of a specifically aesthetic and philosophical knowledge of art, and could be considered an "imperialist" conception of the understanding of the artistic universe. Sociologism encroaches on domains that are not authentically sociological, and it appropriates to itself areas of jurisdiction that do not pertain to an authentic sociology of art. Asociological concepts, however, are sometimes developed in an inverse sense, and at times go so far as to propose that there is no true science or, at least, sociology of art. The result is

see our study; "Contemporary Aesthetics of Music and Musicology," *Acta musicologica* XLVII/2 (1975) 193-207.

aestheticism, individualistic relativism, and sometimes inadequate subjectivism toward the work of art. In this sense, aestheticism and sociologism represent a misuse, respectively, of aesthetics and sociology.[70]

As for the terms "aesthetics" and "aestheticism," they are rightly questioned in Alan P. Merriam's *Anthropology of Music* as to their universal applicability, as are other fundamental aesthetic concepts about music formulated within European civilization. He tries to show that at least some of these concepts are quite alien to other musical cultures. The European musical aesthetics is "essentially verbal,"which—according to Merriam—is not a general, universal characterization. To this typically Western characteristic he added five others, stressing in particular the ascribing of beauty to art products and the treatment of form "for its own sake."[71] Merriam's effort to distinguish particular and universal values in different musical cultures is an important contribution to the comparative aesthetic-sociological study of music.

Furthermore, insofar as social facts have a relationship to music, the sociology of music should be distinguished from musical sociologism, which with regard to music, is only a pseudoscientific position on a philosophically erroneous base. But it is also necessary to distinguish the aesthetics of music, as a science *and* philosophy of musical facts and artistic values, from pure aestheticism, which is merely an extrapolation from aesthetics and does not admit the scientific competence of

---

[70]Similarly, historicism is "a misuse of history," being able to "present as a model to the present, a musical era reconstructed musically." Jacques Handschin, "Musicologie et musique," *La revue internationale de musique* IX (winter 1950-51) 226.

[71]Alan P. Merriam, *The Anthropology of Music*, 260-263. Cf. also W. Charlton, "Aestheticism," *The British Journal of Aesthetics* XII/2 (1972) 122. Aestheticism would contain the following ideas: "(i) To appreciate a thing aesthetically we must consider it apart from anything else, and apart from any purpose, use or significance it may have. (ii) Aesthetic appreciation is a matter of calm contemplation. . . (iii) The object must be contemplated and valued for its own sake."

sociology as an integral part of the study of music. The repudiation of the aesthetics of music by many music historians is partly due to a certain parasitic aestheticist literature that they may sometimes confuse with the authentic aesthetics of music. Whereas aestheticism has neither justification nor consistency, the authentic aesthetics of music should be respected. Likewise, the sociology of music as well as music history furnishes indispensable data to the aesthetics of music, whereas sociologism ought to be considered devoid of meaning. The aesthetics of music and the sociology of music should aim for a differentiation and, above all, a purification and *liberation* from aestheticism and sociologism. The sociology of music shares this same goal with sociology in general: "to put between parentheses, as much as possible, the evaluative coefficient . . . which is proper to sociological knowledge.[72]

We are thus provided with a glimpse of the essential methodological difference between the aesthetics of music and the sociology of music. While the aesthetics of music, which integrates philosophical analysis, cannot survive without this basic rational approach, the sociology of music, which remains exclusively a science, must proceed on the inductive route of factual analysis. It is true that the sociology of music is not a science in the positivist sense of the word, yet it maintains a close relationship with the implicit or explicit philosophy of the sociologist. But it does not proceed in its analyses and research via a speculative or deductive philosophical path in combination with an inductive scientific path: it is *limited* to the latter.

There is not only a difference of method and nature between the two disciplines: the subjects with which they are concerned are not identical either. While the subject matter of the sociology of music is delimited by the study of social facts concerning music, the subject of the aesthetics of music (and, even more, of general aesthetics)[73] has a considerably broader scope. The

---

[72]Georges Gurvitch, "Les cadres sociaux de la connaissance sociologique," *Cahiers internationaux de sociologie* XXVI (1959) 166.

[73]It was possible to define general aesthetics as "the study of works and

aesthetics of music ought to envision music globally, leading to an integrated view of music and musical art. It should also take into consideration all aspects of music—not only the social ones—in order to attempt to explain the subject as fully as possible. Moreover, by virtue of its strictly scientific nature, the sociology of music is obliged to refrain from value judgments concerning the artistic and aesthetic aspects of music, as well as the human values inherent in this art. And this observation is equally valid for music history. However, this does not mean that music history and the sociology of music should deal only with purely historical or sociological facts and values; both areas of study should reveal not only matters of historical and sociological value, but also historical and sociological facts that may be of specifically aesthetic, artistic, and human value, as well as aesthetic, artistic and human facts of historical and sociological value.

Both sociology and music history, though, should examine the aesthetic, artistic and human values of music only as sociological or historical *facts*, not as aesthetic, artistic and human *values*. It is not within their purview to judge the aesthetic, artistic and human *values* of the historical and socio-logical *facts* they discover and examine, although they can contribute to this evaluation in a somewhat extrinsic manner by furnishing factual data. These value judgements, which necessi-tate a philosophical intervention, belong rather to the province

---

procedures of art, as a typical human activity particularly evident in the fine arts." Etienne Souriau, "Les limites de l'esthétique," *Atti del III. Congresso Internazionale di Estetica* (Turin: Ed. della Rivista di estetica, 1957) 32. See also his "Objet et méthodes de l'esthétique," *Bulletin de psychologie* XIV (1959) 781-83. According to Olivier Revault d'Allonnes, on the contrary, "an attempt to define aesthetics 'in itself' is absurd from the very beginning. One could only lay claim to uncovering what the tasks of aestheticians are today. And to say that one can understand the facts of art, is to look for conditions of possibility of that understanding." See his interesting article "Peut-on connaître les faits d'art?" *Médiations* II (1961) 61-78. This point of view is more or less shared, for example, by Carl Dahlhaus, *Musikästhetik*, 7-10. Eng. tr. *Esthetics of Music*, vii-viii: 1-4; and Enrico Fubini, "Music Aesthetics and Philosophy," *IRASM* I/1 (1970) 94-7.

of aesthetics and, above all, the philosophy of music.[74] If the sociology of music is thus the transmitter of values, nonetheless it is not authorized to make value judgements.

Thus, aesthetics and an authentically conceived sociology of music, far from opposing each other, complement and fortify one another. The aesthetics of music ought never to succumb to one of its constant temptations, which is to adopt an *a priori* position, such as that represented by an asociological attitude of aesthetic subjectivism. It should always strive for consistency in the verification of facts examined inductively, so that these facts can provide it with confirmation and proof. The aesthetics of music is therefore obligated to delineate facts that are delivered to it by music history, the sociology of music, and the entire field of musicology. One of the tasks of the sociology of music is to show whether, how and in what measure musical substance itself is fashioned and influenced by social facts. Consequently, it is a necessary adjunct to the aesthetics of music. In this sense only can the idea of a "sociological" aesthetics of music, or better still, a sociologically oriented aesthetics, be accepted. The sociology of music ought to function as an auxiliary discipline without affecting the autonomy of the aesthetics of music. Traditional sociological aesthetics, on the contrary, preoccupied with empiricism or dominated by sociologism, has only made a degrading mockery of it.

The sociology of music is equally in need of musical aesthetics. In order to study musical facts in relation to extramusical social facts, it is imperative that these facts be well determined and defined within their own specific context, without forgetting, however, that the musical phenomenon implies social aspects and cannot be fully defined by a single method.[75]

---

[74]On the problem of values in aesthetics, one can consult for example Mikel Dufrenne, "Valeurs et valeurs esthétiques;" and Roman Ingarden, "La valeur esthétique et le problème de son fondement objectif," *Atti del III. Congresso Internazionale di Estetica* (Turin: Ed. della Rivista di estetica, 1957) 145-48, 167-73.

[75]See François Lesure, "Review," *IRASM* I/2 (1970) 220-21; and Friedrich Blume, "Historische Musikforschung in der Gegenwart," *Report of the IMS*

Now, musical facts ought to be discovered, described and verified by music history. And the aesthetics of music, being based on music history, must appreciate and define musical facts as well, in order to offer the sociology of music a part of its conceptual apparatus. For its part, the sociology of music must develop for its own needs an operational framework of sociological concepts relevant to the social facts that it examines (unless it borrows them, if only partially, from general sociology). But if it is a question of developing an operational framework that conforms strictly to music and to music alone, it is to the aesthetics of music, supported by music history and music theory, that the sociology of music must turn. Since the aesthetics of music is a scientific-philosophical discipline, it follows that the operational conceptual framework of the sociology of music will depend, in part, on an element foreign to the sociology of music as such. Moreover, the operational conceptual framework of general sociology is also dependent upon a philosophical element. This poses the problem of the relationships of the sociology of music with both general sociology and philosophy.

VI • MUSICOLOGY, SOCIOLOGY, PHILOSOPHY

Problems concerning the sociology of music are not unrelated to problems concerning general sociology; and the latter are not unrelated to the problems of philosophy. Consequently, although it is essentially a science, the sociology of music, as well as all sociology, cannot be entirely separated from philosophy but should be clearly differentiated from it. The distinction mentioned between scientific knowledge and philosophical knowledge does not signify opposition or mutual exclusion, for

---

Tenth Congress—Ljubljana, 1967 (Kassel-Ljubljana: Bärenreiter-U. of Ljubljana, 1970). See especially p. 20: "Surely we are only [transmitters,] and, whatever we are to aim at, it is not the dictatorship of *one* method, but the *synthesis of all possible methods.*"

purely scientific knowledge, like that proposed by classical positivism, does not exist in the domain of sociology any more than it does in aesthetics or in history.

The relationships between sociology and philosophy can be looked at from a point of view relative to philosophy or from one relative to sociology. It is also possible to present the historical point of view, in order to show how these relationships have varied from one era to another, going for example (at least in theory) from a state of separation, through a complementary relationship, to fusion or reciprocal implication. Here we will look at them in their essence and try to show what is the authentic condition of sociological knowledge with regard to philosophical knowledge, referring especially to questions which touch on the sociology of music.

Sociological knowledge has a certain dependence upon philosophical knowledge. The dangers which follow their separation have been justly denounced. Such a separation "hinders all development of sociological theory, because the theory of any science—most particularly a humanistic science— is impossible without a collaboration with philosophy. To repudiate the theory for fear of philosophy is to take no account of precisely that situation in which facts must be sought in order to be discovered, or of the fact that each science possesses its own conceptual and operational framework, which constructs the specific field of its study."[76]

But here the question arises whether a complete and total separation of sociological theory from philosophy is possible, and if it has ever existed in reality or in practice, no matter whether it might be, on the part of the sociologist, an unavowed and implicit philosophy or a frank and explicit one. We know not only how much knowledge in general (and sociological theory in particular) can be influenced by social—and thus existential—factors (a subject studied today as part of the sociology of knowledge), but how much it may be similarly

---

[76]Georges Gurvitch, "Réflexions sur les rapports entre philosophie et sociologie," *Cahiers internationaux de sociologie* XXII (1957) 6.

THE SOCIOLOGY OF MUSIC

influenced also by philosophical elements.[77] An adumbration of philosophy is indisputably present in sociological knowledge. It is present there in two ways: first, starting with the very use of concepts; then, by the placement or formulation of problems, which depends not only upon the exigencies of the subject under investigation, but also upon the personality of the scholar, upon his culture, and ultimately upon his implicit or explicit philosophy. What has been said with good reason about history and the historian is, *mutatis mutandis*, perfectly applicable to sociology and the sociologist: "there is no true history . . . which can be independent of a philosophy of man and of life, from which it borrows its fundamental concepts, its systems of explication, and, beforehand, the very questions it will pose to the past in the name of its conception of man. Truth in history is a function of truth in philosophy, put to work by the historian . . . The more intelligent he is, the more cultivated, rich in experience, and open to all human values he becomes—the more he will become able to reconstruct the past, and the more his knowledge will have a potential for richness and truth."[78] This point of view does not, however, imply any subjectivism. It only opposes radical positivistic objectivism. In the fact of sociological knowledge, as well as in the face of a knowledge of works of art, "the truth of our attitude resides neither, properly speaking, in subjectivism nor in an impossible objectivism."[79] This is a perspective that musicology should not fail to keep in view.

Without any doubt, therefore, truth exists in sociology, as in history. And sociology, like history, has its specific truth. This truth is factual, not rational. In order to arrive at its own truth,

---

[77]See the interesting study by Pitirim A. Sorokin, "Notes on the Interdependence of Philosophy and Sociology," *Revue internationale de philosophie* XIII (1950) 268-77, where the author puts into relief the presence of these factors and elements in sociological theory throughout its history.

[78]Henri Irénée Marrou, *De la connaissance historique* (Paris: Seuil, 1958, 3rd ed.) 237, 38.

[79]Ivo Supičić, *La musique expressive* (Paris: P.U.F., 1957) 85.

however, sociology requires that the sociologist have a full measure of rational equipment at his command. The diversity and multiplicity of sociological conceptualizations clearly testify that these conceptualizations depend at least as much—if not more—on a philosophical rationalization as on a purely scientific statement of facts, which, stated alone would preclude such conceptualizations. It is possible, certainly, for this rationalization to be realized and developed largely *a priori*—a process totally unacceptable, however, to an authentically conceived sociology. But the statement of sociological facts cannot be arrived at without the intellectual equipment of the sociologist, without a body of operational concepts whose elaboration depends partly on a philosophical application of the mind. This condition of sociological knowledge is understandable if we consider that it relates to the human being, and that it is essential for the sociologist to have authentic philosophical views on man and a proper evaluation of the respective importance and value of diverse human activities of an economic, political, artistic, moral, religious and spiritual or other order. Those views must be purged as much as possible of all the philosophical, psychological, and social coefficients which might obscure them and impair the authenticity of sociological knowledge. We could here also quote T.W. Adorno: "to the extent that the sociology of music is considered with the ideological content and effects of music, it contributes to a decisive doctrine for society. It is therefore impelled to examine the question of truth in music. Sociologically, this obligation comes back to music—socially— in the form of a true or false conscience. The sociology of music would be obliged to elucidate what is entailed by the examination of manifestations and criteria for such a conscience . . . Finally, it would also be necessary to inquire into the historical, social, and intra-musical conditions of a musical conscience. The problem inevitably arises: is a true social conscience free of ideology in music, or else—which is more plausible—do they interpenetrate each other, and for what reasons? The affirmative element in all art—and particularly that of music, is heir to ancient magic: the sound by which all music begins already possesses something

41

of it . . . It is only by the explication of the idea of truth that the sociology of music would acquire its theoretical dignity."[80]

If the presence of the philosophical element at the basis of sociological knowledge appears inevitable and legitimate, normal and fruitful, it should not justify, however, the use of philosophical *methods* and procedures in the treatment and the solutions of specifically sociological problems. To agree to the intervention of philosophy at this level would be to compromise the scientific character and methods belonging to sociological knowledge (notably the inductive method) and to make of sociology a social philosophy and of the sociology of music a sociological aesthetics. But if nothing "would be more dangerous for sociological theory—and therefore, for the whole of sociology—than a liaison with a particular philosophical doctrine,"[81] this is only true, to be precise, for the treatment and the solutions of sociological problems, not for their conceptualization and their formulation. Given the importance of a proper conceptualization and an authentic formulation of sociological questions for their very solution, it is not a matter of indifference to know which philosophical conceptions can provide motivational force and support. In this sense, sociological knowledge should only benefit from a well-founded, valid, and true philosophical contribution.

Historically, philosophy, and especially social philosophy, has often been a parasite of sociology, or has led it in false and aberrant directions; but in the end it has also fertilized and inspired it, awakened it to its own vitality, and helped it to find itself. At one time distinct and authentically conceived, the two disciplines should now only support each other.

It is not just general philosophy, but more particularly social philosophy, which can render basic data fruitful in the conceptualization of sociological problems as well as in their formulation. If it is correct "that whoever tries to define philosophy makes

---

[80]Theodor W. Adorno, "Sociologie de la musique," *Musique en jeu* II (1971) 11-12.

[81]Georges Gurvitch, "Réflexions sur les rapports entre philosophie et sociologie," *Cahiers internationaux de sociologie* XXII (1957) 7.

known, in truth, only his own philosophy,"[82] it is also correct that in defining sociology, one defines one's own sociology—or better still, one's philosophy of sociology. It is enough to open any work on sociology to confirm this.[83] Furthermore, it is accurate that "at present philosophy supplies to sociology, by its working hypotheses, by its guiding suggestions and its anticipated interpretations, even more than it receives in data for its own elaboration."[84]

Certain philosophical disciplines, however—moral philosophy, for example, and especially social philosophy—cannot be elaborated in a satisfying and complete manner without taking sociology and the facts established by sociology into account. Between social philosophy and the aesthetics of music there exists that basic methodological analogy wherein both participate in philosophy and, at the same time, must rely on inductively established facts for the solution to their problems. They are both placed between philosophy and the respective sciences that concern them.

The exclusion of unwarranted philosophical interventions in the treatment and the solution of sociological problems is, of course, required so that sociology may be guaranteed its own distinct subject and methods. However, a certain partial dependence by sociology on philosophy, in those aspects already mentioned, does not put into question the character of scientific objectivity in sociology, as an old positivistic error might let us suppose, claiming all scientific knowledge to be "objective" and all philosophical knowledge to be "subjective." For the very

---

[82]René Hubert, "Réflexions sur les rapports actuels de la sociologie et de la philosophie," *Revue internationale de philosophie* XIII (1950) 255.

[83]See for example the following works: Pierre Francastel, "Problèmes de la sociologie de l'art," *Traité de sociologie* (Paris: P.U.F., 1960) II, 278-96, and *Etudes de sociologie de l'art* (Paris: Denoël Gonthier, 1970); Herbert Read, *Art and Society* (London: Faber & Faber, 1967); Jean Duvignaud, *Sociologie de l'art* (Paris: P.U.F., 1972); Roger Bastide, *Art et société* (Paris: Payot, 1977), where the authors' conceptions of the sociology of art remain strictly dependent on their philosophical and aesthetic ideas.

[84]René Hubert, *op. cit.*, 266.

notion of objectivity has sense only with regard to a subject, and it is only through defining a subject that objectivity can be established. Knowledge, be it scientific or philosophical, can only become objective to the extent that it is based on reality and possesses truth. The fluctuating evolution of science itself, with its many instances of progress beyond achievements formerly considered scientifically and objectively acquired, does not allow us to consider scientific knowledge as always accompanied by absolute objectivity. We can find more objectivity, and therefore more truth, in a philosophical corollary as old as philosophy itself than in a scientific conclusion established by today's most exacting scientific methods, which will be made meaningless tomorrow by new discoveries or other even more exact methods. This is why, if it is valid and authentic, the initial philosophic intervention in the conceptualization and statement of sociological problems does not alter at all the scientific character of sociological knowledge and does not remove the possibility of attaining objective truths.

Now, what has been said of sociological knowledge in general is also of value for the sociological knowledge of music. On the other hand, if the sociology of music is to succeed in revealing itself, in time, as necessary and effective in the analysis of musical facts, it will also be able to eliminate gradually the *a priori* approaches of the aesthetics of music, while opening new perspectives on facts that, until now, were studied only as part of musical aesthetics.

In sum, the sociology of music depends in part not only on musicology and on general sociology, but also on the aesthetics of music and on philosophy. The importance of *ideas* should not be ignored in the sociology of music. It is only necessary to be wary of a danger that Theodore Caplow has rightly underlined, a risk the sociologist of art runs, perhaps unconsciously: that of letting his personal aesthetic ideas, dressed in the language of the social sciences, pass for sociology.[85]

---

[85]See Theodore Caplow, "The Influence of Radio on Music as a Social Institution," *Cahiers d'études de radio-télévision* III-IV (1955) 279.

CHAPTER TWO

SUBJECT AND METHODS

The preceding considerations establish that the sociology of music must partly renounce the notion of originality. This fact is reflected in the use it makes or can make of certain concepts, in its goals, and in its methods. We have seen this in its partial dependence on the *concepts* of general sociology (and through this, on philosophy) as well as on music history and the aesthetics of music. Concerning its *goals,* the sociology of music shares those of sociology in general, in studying sociological facts that relate specifically to music. And lastly, concerning its *methods,* it borrows largely from other sociological disciplines, especially when dealing with general procedures or applications more or less universal in sociology, such as methods of observation, historical description, comparison, classification, or definition. Within this domain, however, there remains a vast terrain that belongs solely to the sociology of music.

I • SOCIOHISTORICAL AND SOCIOARTISTIC CONDITIONINGS

The fundamental goal of the sociology of music may be divided into two parts: first, to examine the relationship of music to diverse global societies as well as to various social groups within those societies; second, to examine how music itself is a social phenomenon, or rather, to examine the social aspects within music. But in examining the social element in music, the sociology of music also examines the historical element. Although it is not to be confused with a *social history* of music, it is nevertheless *historical sociology* of music, because the social and artistic facts with which it deals are also historical facts. Here, once more, we find that fundamental difference between the sociology of music and a history of music (social or not). The history of music, by itself, is the study of musical facts in an *artistic* context, and the social history of music views these same musical facts both as *artistic* facts and, relating them to extra-musical social facts, as *social* facts; also with that, its scope of exploration is exhausted. On the other hand, the sociology of music concerns itself not only with the typical relationships between musical artistic facts, and extramusical social facts, but also with these same musical facts as *social* facts themselves. The musical and the social must not be opposed, since they mutually interpenetrate; many musical facts imply, in effect, some social aspects.

The questions that lend themselves to study in the sociology of music can be referred to in terms of *social conditioning* in music. The idea of social conditioning in the sociology of music appears to be essential from a substantive as well as a methodological point of view, implying as it does that musical activity depends on the artistic personality of the musician and that, at the same time, the specific social conditions of a given period are imposed on that personality. One task for the sociology of music would also be to "establish a new scale of values capable of serving the comparative study of musical art and social life. Or, if we wish, to search for the respective parts played by creator, techniques, and social milieu in the birth of the work of art."[1] It has been stated, for example, that "no doubt political, economic, and religious events had been a factor of prime importance in the creative process and in musical practice during the last centuries

---

[1]François Lesure, "Musicologie et sociologie," *La revue musicale* CCXXI (1953) 9.

of the Middle Ages."[2] But this is only one example, since social conditioning has affected the music of all ages. Karl Marx's generalization is that men make their own history; they do not, however, make it under self-chosen conditions, but under imposed conditions mandated by tradition. This assertion applies equally to the history of music. In the sociology of music, however, the idea of conditioning must be adequately determined, and its proposed effect verified by facts. It is true already that a preliminary analysis of the facts admits the possible validity of this idea, but these findings must be precisely tested in the history of music (as a living process), in order that the sociology of music may interpret them scientifically.

But first we must dissipate a misunderstanding and confront an objection to this approach. It has been said that to introduce the perspective of conditioning into the sociology of music is to falsify that study from its inception, given that music and musical life are not separated from society and from social life, but part of them.[3] This position amounts to nothing but a play on words. Since music and musical activities *are* a part of society and social life, it is possible for them to be conditioned by society and its life. If music were not incorporated into society, social conditionings would have no relevance—they would not even exist. But if we allow that music is incorporated into the social structure, it would be senseless to suggest that the different spheres of social, cultural and artistic activities would not influence each other. Thus, since musical activities are more or less integrated into extramusical social activities, they can be conditioned by the latter and, to a certain extent, affect them in return. To study the social conditionings of music, therefore, is to study music within social reality, not outside of it.

The idea of social conditioning presumes that, in his artistic activity, the musician is not absolutely free, but that his musical

---

[2]Charles Van Den Borren, "Musicologie et géographie," *La Renaissance dans les provinces du nord,* Collected works published under the direction of François Lesure (Paris: C.N.R.S., 1956) 19.

[3]See the account by Pavel Beylin in *Report of the IMS Tenth Congress—Ljubljana 1967* (Kassel-Ljubljana: Bärenreiter-U. of Ljubljana, 1970), 417.

activity is to some extent linked to objective conditions formed by the currents of history and society and transmitted through social means, which affect both the artist and the social and artistic-cultural ambiance in which he lives and works. Consequently, the specific effects of social conditioning will differ in various social and artistic-cultural contexts, as well as in diverse historical moments. "Whatever different kinds of innovations musicians of genius may have achieved, they themselves have only been able to adapt to given situations, each one making use of the instrumental material of his times; submitting himself to conditions which allow him to be heard (church concerts, chamber music, the orchestra, presentations of ballet or opera, etc.); expressing himself in the context of usual forms (motet, suite, concerto, etc.); occasionally fulfilling special functions (organist, *maître de chapelle*, director of music or of the theater, etc.) which oblige him to supply a special repertoire; and even more, having to account for the number and variety of performers, instrumentalists, and singers at his disposal."[4] Thus the social conditioning of musical activity has to do with the action of certain specific social conditions on the musical activity of the artist, by whom they are experienced as a substratum, opportunity, or starting point, which cannot be avoided. These social conditions are inevitable limitations, objectively imposed. They are both restrictive and enriching. The pressure they exert can be stronger or weaker; however—since it is a matter of conditioning—it never transforms itself into necessity, consciously felt as such. This would exclude the creative freedom of the artist, or preclude innovation, at least in more developed societies (primitive ones often impose heavy taboos).

Nevertheless, in a certain sense these limitations appear to be necessary. If they are valuable, it is precisely as social conditionings, not as social necessity. In other words, these unavoidable limitations influence the artistic activity of the musician, conditioning it and imposing restrictions or orientations on him, but

---

[4]André Schaeffner, "Musique populaire et art musical," *Journal de psychologie* I-II (1951) 253.

do not determine his activity in an absolute manner. They do not make a puppet of the artist, condemning him to follow passively a predetermined historical evolution; on the contrary, they allow considerable room for his creative freedom and reaction to the artistic, historical, and social realities he confronts. Thus, without being able to bend social or historical evolution arbitrarily to his will, the artist can create, in the historical, artistic, and social spheres where his activities are reflected, innovative trends that combine with preexisting ones. He can thus give, through his artistic activity, a specific orientation to the dynamic mass of history inherited from the past. Recalling Frits Noske's formulation quoted earlier,[5] we can amplify it by saying that social conditionings can prevent a composer from creating neither *good* music, nor *new* music. Noske himself gives an example of just such a case: "During the seventeenth century, a group of Dutch musicians was clearly restricted in its creative freedom, namely the Roman Catholic composers . . . Although there was no question of oppression or persecution, these Catholics were often chicaned. They were compelled to hold their services in private houses (so-called hidden churches) . . . The rather ridiculous rule was that their liturgical music should not be heard in the streets or by the neighbors. This not only excluded the use of house organs; it also prevented the Catholics from assembling a choir in their 'church.' The latter impediment was a serious one, for musical practice in seventeenth-century Holand was rather old-fashioned. People still used to sing *a capella*, either with or without melodic instruments which doubled the vocal parts . . . Now the Catholics were forced to practice another kind of liturgical music, less noisy than choral singing. This was the small concertato mass and motet, written for one to four voices with a basso continuo played on the harpsichord. Through their contacts with Rome and Venice, Dutch musicians became acquainted with the concertato style and started to write works appropriated to the conditions of the Catholic church in Holland . . . Thus the Catholic composers

---

[5]See above p. 14, footnote 20, F. Noske, *op. cit.*

introduced a completely novel style in Holland, in fact the most modern kind of music of their time. Here we have an example of limitation provoking a progressive attitude."[6]

If it is therefore indefensible to state that musical activity is entirely independent of society and history, it is equally illogical to hold that musical activity is totally determined by an absolute necessity somehow imposed by history or society. The study of sociology and of history does not confirm this. It is proper to conclude, consequently, that the social conditioning of musical activity necessarily exists, but not that it is *identical* to social or historical necessity. We must distinguish conditionality from necessity. In the history of music, at any given period, only certain general orientations appear necessary, within which creative freedom and the play of diverse conditions can determine particular directions. But to identify those general orientations of music history at any given moment which can be proven necessary to their times remains a task which the sociology of music will be able to deal with—especially by collaboration with music history—only in a much more advanced stage of its development; this is one of its most difficult problems.[7]

On the other hand, the social conditioning of music seems to present itself as a domain for fruitful explorations; though the idea of social conditioning has been sufficiently precisely

---

[6]Frits Noske, Discussion in "Musical Style Changes and General History," *Report of the IMS Tenth Congress*, 265-66.

[7]The following remarks are also pertinent: "To try to identify certain correlations between this differential division of practice (of behaviors) on the one hand, and different aspects of the historical, economic and political situation of the milieu under consideration on the other: This is indeed already a small advance in the understanding of the problem, but not yet enough to resolve it. . . we must push the study even deeper, inquiring into the processes by which the recorded facts are produced. In our sense, now, sociological facts of this sort are specifically produced by a series of human acts which are structured and organized in a particular fashion. This network of actions constitutes the principal subject matter of sociology." Roger Girod, "Recherches sociologiques et développement de la culture musicale," *Cahiers d'études de Radio-Télévision* III-IV (1955) 340.

determined, its subtleties need, nevertheless, to be discussed.[8] Thus a fundamental distinction can be made between *socio-historical* conditionings, which concern extramusical social conditions, and *socioartistic* conditionings, which concern essentially musical sociological conditions.[9] In the sociology of music we must study the place, impact, and importance of sociohistorical conditionings of music—extramusical social conditions that serve as a basis for artistic musical activities. We must also study the influence, range, and significance of socioartistic conditionings of music—sociological aspects that occur within the range of artistic musical activities. The study of the former is much more extensive and important. This distinction is not, however, sufficient: These conditionings can be divided into more specialized categories. The value of these classifications and further distinctions, however, is mostly of pragmatic value. They should be regarded only as flexible and changing points of reference aimed at facilitating sociological research, never as rigid categories.

Each of the two fundamental conditionings—sociohistorical and socioartistic—could be further diversified, according to its

---

[8]See for example Richard Wollheim, "Sociological Explanation of the Arts: Some Distinctions," *Atti del III. Congresso Internazionale di Estetica* (Turin: Ed. della Rivista di estetica, 1957) 404-10, where the author proposes to distinguish between the causal, expressive and anecdotal sociological explorations of art.

[9]In *L'art et la vie sociale* (Paris: Doin, 1921) 6, Charles Lalo made a distinction between "the study of non-aesthetic social conditions" of art and "the study of properly called aesthetic social conditions," but still attributed them both to sociological aesthetics. See the critique of his position in Roger Bastide, "Les problèmes de la sociologie de l'art," *Cahiers internationaux de sociologie* IV (1948) 160-71, and *Art et société* (Paris: Payot, 1977). See also Robert Hoebaer, "L'intérêt pour l'art musical, Essai d'analyse sociologique," *Bulletin de l'Institut de Recherches Economiques et Sociales* VIII (Louvain: 1956) 699, where in reply, the author assigns the mission of studying social milieus, or "the social non-aesthetic conditions" of art, to the history of art. See also Radhakamal Mukerjee, "Art as a Social Science," *The Sociological Review* XXXVI/1-4 (1944) 65. With reason, this author, sees the proper subject of the sociology of art in the study of the social conditions of art, as does Roger Bastide, who, however, does not differentiate it quite clearly from sociological aesthetics.

application to musical creation, performance, diffusion or consumption. Furthermore, the specificity of the sociology of music in comparison to other branches of the sociology of art rests in the social existence of musical work—a fact that does not pertain in the same way to the plastic arts. What is at issue, here, is to distinguish a work of music as an expression of a milieu from its performance, which brings it to life through interpreters (orchestra, choir, soloists) for a public physically present (at a concert) or virtually so (radio, recordings).[10] Paul Beaud considers that "the non-semantic aspect of musical communication is a sizable obstacle to the comprehension of surrounding phenomena. The diversity of problems which it raises makes the construction of an analytical system even more difficult than in the other arts. How, in fact, to synthesize the multiple approaches which music imposes: the sociology of its creation and the sociology of its reception, and also the sociology of its reproduction, of its means of diffusion, etc."[11]

A musical work is thus conditioned, from its creation to its concrete realization, by the social context in which that creation and those realizations have taken place. In regard to *sociohistorical* conditionings, the sociology of music must examine the influence of extramusical social conditions first on musical creation and musical works, then on musical performance and diffusion, and finally on musical consumption—that is, on the reception, reactions, and demands of the public in regard to the creation and performance of musical works. The sociology of music must also study the influence of socioartistic conditionings on the creation of musical works, as well as on their performance and interpretation. These latter conditionings, by their very nature, refer primarily to musical works and activities, and this is why these works and these activities themselves must be examined from this point of view. Socioartistic conditionings,

---

[10]See René Bonnot, "Sociologie de la musique," *Traitè de sociologie,* ed. Georges Gurvitch (Paris: P.U.F., 1960) II, 297.

[11]Paul Beaud, "L'électro-acoustique," in: Paul Beaud, and Alfred Willener, *Musique et vie quotidienne* (Paris: Mame, 1973) 24.

however, also concern the musical public—a public whose tastes, demands, and responses are conditioned by traditions and inherited or accepted tastes and preferences.

At this point another classification is imposed on the study of sociohistorical conditionings of music: a classification depending not on the specific subject matter of the sociology of music, which is dictated by the nature of musical art (creation-perform-ance-listening), but rather depending on the connection of this discipline to sociology in general—general sociology this time imposing the nature of the classification. This classification also should have no absolute value, but rather an exclusively instrumental one, serving only as a foothold for an easier analysis of the material. Above all, this classification takes into consideration the sociohistorical conditions of music vis-à-vis social groups and strata, social classes and global societies (or societies taken in their totality).[12]

As to *socioartistic* conditionings, they can be examined on various levels other than those just mentioned. They may be looked at "microhistorically"—those particular influences ex-erted, for example, by one musical work on another; or "historically"—more extensive influences, exerted, for example, by one style or one technique on a musical work or works; or "macrohistorically"—influences even more generalized and global in nature, for example, those exerted by the musical language characteristic of a widespread musical culture on the creation of entire generations of composers. It is here, especially, that induction and assessment of historical facts ought to have prime importance, and that a classification should not be made *a priori*. On the other hand, there should not be a discontinuous classification—one of closed categories—but rather a gradation of influences of greater or lesser importance and of longer or shorter duration. Thus it is historical analysis, especially, which must determine the classification to be accepted in each

---

[12]Compare this classification with that by Georges Gurvitch in *Déterminismes sociaux et liberté humaine* (Paris: P.U.F., 1955), 191-282; and in *La vocation actuelle de la sociologie* (Paris: P.U.F., 1957, 2nd ed.) I, 281-502.

particular case, as examined from the point of view of socio-artistic conditionings. And what has been said for musical creation and performance remains valid for musical diffusion and consumption. A special differentiation, however, must be made in respect to the public, in the sense that relevant socioartistic conditionings ought to be examined on the levels mentioned above for sociohistorical conditionings (social groups and strata, social classes, and global societies).

In addition to sociohistorical and socioartistic conditionings, the sociology of music still must examine those that we call "inverse": that is, those reflecting social pressure exerted by music on society, on various social groups, and on social life in general—in other words, the influence and action of music and musicians within different cultures and societies.[13]

II • QUESTIONS AND PROBLEMS

The social conditionings of music offer a wide range of particular items for study.[14] One element of the sociohistorical conditionings of music is that of the *social role* and *status* of musicians, both as individuals and as a group. The sociology of music is not only a sociology of musical art, but of musicians as well.[15] Not only the musician's social situation itself is important,

---

[13]"In fact, certain theorists of sociological aesthetics (who are already somewhat outdated) tend to believe, in the manner of Guyau, for example, that music... [would be] only a sort... of expression mirroring society but having no action upon it; something which would be a result and not a cause; determined but not determining. Now music has always had this power of acting on Society..." Etienne Souriau, "Allocution" to the International Congress on the sociological aspects of music on the radio, *Cahiers d'études de Radio-Télévision* III-IV (1955) 268-69.

[14]For James H. Barnett these facts are, in the sociology of art, the artist, the work of art and the public. See "Research Areas in the Sociology of Art," *Sociology and Social Research* XLII/6 (1958) 401-5.

[15]"When one researches the conditions which determine the birth of a work of art, a style, or a school, one can proceed in two different ways: first, in reference to the artist... second, in reference to the work of art itself." Robert

however; also of importance are the consequences of his station in society for musical creation and practice. It is above all in relation to musical works—their dissemination and consumption as well as their artistic qualities—that this social situation is of interest. Now the role and the social status of musicians, individually and as a group, must be examined principally in the following respects: as to their inclusion in various social groups, economic conditions, and professional situations. In particular, the sociology of music must study the relationships of groups of musicians with other professional groups, for example, publishers, printers, librarians, music sellers, critics and entrepreneurs; then, the relationships of these same groups of musicians with different organizations and institutions; and finally, their relationships with the social classes and the hierarchy of social strata and social groups to which they belong. This matter and others, such as music and social interaction, music and communication, the social acceptance of music, music and social control, etc., are treated in a more systematic way, also from the interactionist point of view, as examplified in the work of Alan S. Rumbelow.[16] According to Robert R. Hornyak, "he has provided some definite parameters to a field which had excellent potential for future study".[17]

One area worthy of examination concerns *professionalism* and *amateurism,* and the fluctuations from one to the other within musical activity. Some of the available facts are of equal interest to composers and performers; others concern one more than the other. Although composers are sometimes performers,

---

Hoebaer, "L'intérêt pour l'art musical, Essai d'analyse sociologique," *Bulletin de l'Institut de Recherches Economiques et Sociales* VII (1956) 700.

[16]Alan S. Rumbelow, *Music and Social Groups: An Interactionist Approach to the Sociology of Music* (Ph.D. dissertation: U. of Minnesota, 1969). Order number 70-15802. Two chapters of this thesis, "Music and Communication," and "The Social Acceptance of Music," have been published under the title "Sociology of Music and Musical Aesthetics," *Journal of the Indian Musicological Society* VII/2 (1976) 5-44.

[17]Review of *op. cit.* of A. S. Rumbelow by R. Robert Hornyak, *Council for Research in Music Education* XL (winter 1974) 17.

it is the latter, being far more numerous, who at times play the most diversified and complex social roles, and provide the greatest amount of facts for study. Among these facts are: structuring of performers into groups, the cohesion within these groups, the relationships among their members, their inclusion in a social class, the integration of performing ensembles into the profession, and the structuring of the latter into groups. We will not go so far as to say, however, that an ensemble of performers constitutes a real "society" of musicians (an opinion expressed by Maurice Halbwachs, and repeated by André Schaeffner) and that it ought to be studied as such, since in sociology the term "society" has a precise technical meaning that is not appropriate here.[18]

Another important area to explore is that of *social demand:* "if, in certain respects, the social demand for a particular art (painting, sculpture, music, etc.) is conditioned by an aesthetic orientation, certain other factors, among them those of an economic nature, are brutally nonaesthetic."[19] And it is social demand precisely as a demand motivated by extra-artistic factors that we can examine in two ways: first, in the most general and most profound sense—when it derives from the collective desires, emotions, beliefs, will and ways of feeling and thinking within the society, in which the musician participates, in a more or less conscious manner, and which influence, to a certain degree, his art. We could call this *indirect* demand. Second, we can examine social demand in a more immediate and specific sense, easier to identify and study, because this demand, although deriving from the first, is revealed on the much more concrete level of events—in history and in social life. This is the *direct* demand exerted by a group, a social class, an institution, an organization, or an individual, and is addressed directly to the musician.

Concerning the first aspect, Jacques Chailley remarks by way of illustration: "With Beethoven, Schumann, and especially

---

[18]See André Schaeffner, "Musique populaire et art musical," *Journal de psychologie* I-II (1951) 252.

[19]Etienne Souriau, "L'insertion temporelle de l'oeuvre d'art," *Journal de psychologie* I-II (1951) 49.

Chopin, music learned to express . . . the personal feeling of the musician . . . Romanticism, in the nineteenth century, had thus re-established the function of mediation of primitive music, but, paradoxically, in reverse. This time, it was not the audience who charged the musician with the task of expressing its collective feelings, but the musician who gathered the audience in order to impose on them his own way of feeling . . . But, in this revival of primitive contact, the musician himself was, unconsciously, the direct product of collective feeling, the typical man, one could say, of his era"[20] and of his social milieu. And from this participation (personalized or not) in collective representations, aspirations and feelings—participation by which musicians always prove to be members of a society by their very musical activities—a species of normativity, need or demand is derived, to which musicians accede to some degree, whether they are conscious of it or not.

The second, or direct, aspect of social demand, when addressed to the composer, often concerns musical works of circumstance, such as those of which Albert Schweitzer and André Schaeffner spoke in reference to Bach. For these are precisely the circumstances from which specific demands arise, while, on the other hand, these same demands may constitute the circumstances from which the musician cannot escape: "This idea of a work of circumstance was not yet common among our men of letters when Albert Schweitzer noted that 'all Bach's works are basically works of circumstance in the most profound sense of the word; he wrote them because circumstances demanded them from him.'[21] Some of these circumstances could have been the different posts he held, and the necessity of teaching his children or pupils, for whom so many works were especially composed such as: *Clavierübungen, Orgelbüchlein,* etc., up to *Wohltemperiertes Clavier.* For Bach as well as other musicians, circumstances comprise all that is imposed from without, and

---

[20]Jacques Chailley, *40,000 ans de musique,* 75.

[21]Albert Schweitzer, *J. S. Bach, le musicien poète* (Leipzig: Breitkopf, 1905), 171. See also 112, 158-60, 176-77.

which the composer would not perhaps have chosen 'of his own volition'[22]: the idea for a work, its length, its subject matter, its instrumentation or vocal distribution. Some very beautiful pages [of music] . . . (*The Venusberg* of Wagner, *Martyre de Saint-Sébastien* of Debussy, three or four scenes in *Petrouchka* . . .) were, in fact, brought about by circumstances."[23] Throughout history, moreover, the social demand addressed directly to the musican has assumed many forms—it may be an actual command, or possibly a contract between the musician and the person (or institution) who ordered the work.

Another aspect worthy of study is that of the *transposition* or transferal of problems that occupy or agitate society (at its various levels) into musical art, where those problems are dealth with in a specifically artistic manner.[24] This aspect is particularly accentuated in those forms and genres of music that are linked with the expression of words, although it may also be present in purely instrumental works. In the light of this transposition, music is regarded above all as a participant in social life, either by expressing it (that is, in perpetuating some of its aspects) or by opposing it. Here musical art appears as an integral part of collective experiences, whether as approbation, or as disapproval of some sort.[25]

As Charles Lalo wrote, a revolt against a certain milieu is, in its way, as social a fact as a manifestation of conformist approval of that milieu.[26] Music as a sign or symbol, and more especially

---

[22]Editor's note in the introduction to *Variété* by Paul Valéry.

[23]André Schaeffner, "Musique populaire et art musical," 254. Regarding Bach, see also for example Karl Geiringer, *Johann Sebastian Bach, The Culmination of an Era* (New York: Oxford U. Press, 1966) 15-106.

[24]See Georges Gurvitch, "Discussion," *Cahiers internationaux de sociologie* XXVI (1959) 161.

[25]Musical works can also be a tool for better understanding of the social group in which they are created or where they are performed, as well as toward a better grasp of the collective conscience of the group. See Etienne Souriau, "L'art et la vie sociale," *Cahiers internationaux de sociologie* V (1948) 92-94.

[26]See Charles Lalo, "Méthodes et objets de l'esthétique sociologique," *Revue internationale de philosophie* VII (1949) 37.

"subversive" music—such as that associated with evolutions and revolutions in society—is an appropriate example of music that rises out of a social event. However, the uniqueness of the sociology of music as compared to other branches of the sociology of art resides in the fact that it deals with an art whose means of expression are not conceptual. As a consequence, correlations between music and society, at least until now, have been more easily found by studying the destination and the social functions of the musical work rather than its social roots. According to Adorno, "the sociology of music . . . ought to show how, in music, social conditions are specifically expressed . . . To do this necessarily involves deciphering the social content of music . . . This is most likely to succeed in the domain of technology. Society involves itself in works of art at the corresponding technical level. Affinities between techniques of material production and of artistic production are much closer than the division of scientific work would admit."[27] Much prudence is nonetheless necessary in analyses which aim toward this type of discovery, especially vis-à-vis enterprises such as Adorno suggests, as has been among others clearly shown by Carl Dahlhaus,[28] and anticipated in a general way by Tibor Kneif: "While the sociology of knowledge in general, and related branches in the aesthetic objectivization of social life such as the sociology of literature and art in particular, can often bring convincing proof of such correlations, similar clarifying results in the sociology of music are made more difficult, if not impossible, as only the art form is available for investigation, and not the content as well."[29]

Thus, as it was stressed by Paul Beaud, it seems that the non-semantic aspect of musical communication is an important obstacle to the comprehension of phenomena which surroud it.

---

[27]Theodor W. Adorno, "Sociologie de la musique," *Musique en jeu* 2 (1971) 10-11.

[28]See Carl Dahlhaus, "Soziologische Dechiffrierung von Musik—zu Th. W. Adornos Wagnerkritik," *IRASM* I/2 (1970) 137-147.

[29]Tibor, Kneif, "Der Gegenstand musiksoziologischer Erkenntnis," *Archiv für Musikwissenschaft* XXIII (1966) 227.

The diversity of problems which it raises makes the construction of a system of analysis even more problematic than in other arts. How effectively can we synthesize the multiple approaches that music requires: the sociology of creation, of reception, but also of reproduction, of means of diffusion, etc.?[30] Jean-Jacques Nattiez, on the other hand thinks, that "it is not because music is a-semantic (or differently semantic, or less semantic than literature and the plastic arts) that the sociology of music is difficult,"[31] but he does not give any convincing argument for this view. However, he is right in stressing that sometimes in the sociological interpretation of musical significance the elision by which one passes from social structures to musical structures, and vice-versa is finally in question: "To pass from social structures (or from their destruction) to musical structures (or to their anarchy) wrote F. Müller, implies a questionable analogical and causal reasoning. This reasoning, though, is widely held."[32] Parenthetically, Olivier Revault d'Allonnes was also aware of the difficulty of analyzing such a genre which would suppose "that one possesses sure scholarly methods for passing from music, and only music itself, to the social position and function of that music, which is not at all the case."[33] Nevertheless, we should add three remarks: that a procedure described by Nattiez does not characterize either all the socio-logical approaches of music or all the scholars who adopt them; that it does not present an example of good or appropriate method, but on the contrary a counter-example of a well-founded approach; and that it is only with technical and formal analyses that a complementary historical analysis can clarify the

---

[30]See Paul Beaud, "L'électro-acoustique," in: *Musique et vie quotidienne*, by Paul Beaud and Alfred Willener (Paris: Mame, 1973) 24.

[31]Jean-Jacques Nattiez, *Fondements d'une sémiologie de la musique* (Paris: Union Générale d'Edition, 1975) 415.

[32]F. Müller, "Du maniérisme dans la musique contemporaine," *Music en jeu*, 1 (1970) 9, quoted in: Jean-Jacques Nattiez, "Sur les relations entre sociologie et sémiologie musicales," *IRASM*, V/1 (1974) 71.

[33]Olivier Revault d'Allonnes, "Musique et politique," *V. H. 101*, 4 (1970-71) 99.

social functions and the practical utilisations of a work of art, as well as those musical consequences proper to these functions and utilisations for the work in question.

A further problem which can be raised in the sociological approach of music is that of knowing whether or not the musical works have to be envisaged as individual products or simply as examples or representatives of the forms and genres to which they belong. Certain more recent analytical methods have tried to abandon or to relegate to the background the approaches of generalization and examplification. As Carl Dahlhaus put it, "in the analyses which deserve this name the individual product does not appear any more as the representative of a pattern, but on the contrary the pattern is a means and a point of departure to arrive to a description of the individuality of the work".[34] For an authentic sociological approach it is not a question of stating, in a monotonous manner, simplistic sociological theses such as those of the unavoidable existence of social functions of any musical work, or of the obligatory expression of social conditions through it. Nor is it a question of finding only those examples or models that confirm these general theses and illustrate, through those deliberately chosen cases, some preconceived sociological categories of musical works. Instead, it is a question of showing which individual work has or has not its own social identity and function in the milieu of its creation and performance. Only afterwards can the same question be formulated about entire groups, series or forms of works.

The study of social *functions* of music within different societies, as well as the study of variations and differentiations in musical functions, offer areas of fundamental interest to the sociologist. For the relationships between musical works—their language, technique, expression and character, as well as their style, form, and genre—on the one hand, and the given social contexts—most especially the social groups, classes, and global social structures, on the other—provide the sociology of music

---

[34]Carl Dahlhaus, "Das musikalische Kunstwerk als Gegenstand der Soziologie," 13.

with one of its most important questions.[35] These relationships can be studied from two points of view: in respect to the social contexts in which these works are *born,* and in respect to those in which they are later *performed.* But we must also distinguish between real social functions and those bestowed on musical works by the composer at the moment of their creation, for these do not always coincide. The study of these relationships leads, however, to another basic problem in connection with the presentation of works before the public: the problem of what is strictly transitory and what transcends the moment or the era of its appearance. As Georges Gurvitch rightly observed in his remarks about the theater, which, *mutatis mutandis,* have equal validity for music, this problem has its limits: "Without any doubt, interesting statements could thus be made about the relationship between the type of global society (for example, feudalism, enlightened absolutism, economic liberalism, organized capitalism, communism, etc.) and the content of theatrical production. But this statement of the problem has its limitations, some of which had already been foreseen by Marx: he pointed out that the ancient tragedies or the works of Shakespeare continue to exert a powerful effect on us, even though our global social structures are completely different from those in which these works were born, and even though these works bear incontestable marks of their own times."[36]

It is an essential concern of the sociology of music to consider also the *"respective roles which are played by those who find themselves in contact with musical material*: creators, interpreters, listeners—these latter, too often neglected, being neither numeri-

---

[35]See Robert Hoebaer, "L'intérêt pour l'art musical," *Bulletin de l'Institut de Recherches Economiques et Sociales* VII (1956) 701, where the author contests altogether the idea that one can connect the subject of the musical work "to the milieu where it was born." Here, as in the position held by Tibor Kneif and others, it would be necessary to establish first what the words "Inhalt," "sujet," etc. actually signify within their terminology, since we know that these terms can embrace widely differing meanings.

[36]Georges Gurvitch, "Sociologie du théâtre," *Les lettres nouvelles* XXXV (1956) 203.

cally nor qualitatively the least important."[37] This last aspect, the role of the public in the history of music, deserves special attention.[38] In sociology a considerable number of definitions of the public in general have already been formulated, and opinions on this subject still differ widely.[39] Yet the sociology of music ought to formulate a more exact idea of the social reality that is the musical public. Moreover, it is impossible to study the social conditionings affecting music—which imply social relationships and functions—without referring to specific social groups into which the musical public falls, and which are fundamental to these relationships and functions. It is especially important to see to what extent a public is representative of the society of which it is part, either globally or of one or more layers; to observe how it is diversified socially, and to determine with which attitudes and requirements it confronts music in different eras and milieus, and according to which various social diversifications. The study of the sociology of music includes not only the reactions of the public, but also its actions, although these so often join and mingle with each other so that reactions acquire the functions of actions. The sociology of music ought to direct its research in two ways: first, toward studying the behavior and typical actions of various groupings and categories of particular publics; and then, if possible, toward discovering what social action is characteristic of the musical public in general. The sociology of music also must investigate the different degrees of cohesiveness between those people within the public who are

---

[37]Jacques Chailley, "Problèmes de la musique contemporaine et de l'auditeur devant l'histoire du langage," *La revue internationale de musique* XIII (1952) 210.

[38]As has been correctly affirmed, "the initial temporal insertion of the work is not yet really complete, in spite of its physically-realized existence, in so far as this fact of *collective aperception* that completes its presence has not been realized." Etienne Souriau, "L'insertion temporelle de l'oeuvre d'art," *Journal de psychologie* I-II (1951) 56.

[39]See for example Gabriel Tarde, *L'opinion et la foule* (Paris: Alcan, 1901); Emile Dekany, "Une forme 'élémentaire' de la vie sociale: Le Public," *Revue internationale de sociologie* XLIV (1936) 263-77; Mikel Dufrenne, "Pour une sociologie du public," *Cahiers internationaux de sociologie* VI (1949) 101-12.

possessed of common interests, and their eventual transformations into proper groups—that is, into structured or organized
collective units; and consequently, the influence of these
transformations on the attitudes, reactions, and needs of this
same public with respect to the creation and the performance of
musical works.

Related to the question of the musical public, we find a further
aspect for study in the problem of the diffusion and performance
of music, aspects which are closely linked, although clearly
distinguished from each other. The question of *diffusion* concerns
the various ways of disseminating music; from the presentation
of music actually played before the public, to the use of
"intermediaries," such as scores, records and the radio. As
Irmgard Bontinck rightly stressed, until recently the sociology
of music was thought to be primarily concerned with the impact
of the social environment upon music, and that of social change
upon changes in musical life in general.[40] "But lately it has been
pointed out that this confrontation of 'society,' on the one hand,
and 'music,' on the other, will not lead to satisfactory results.[41]
The technological changes brought about by the mass media in
our century call for a revised methodological approach. Live
music is not longer entirely representative of musical culture . . .
Thanks to the possibilities offered by technology, music
communicated through the technical media attains the status of
a 'social fact' (*fait social*), as defined by Emile Durkheim.[42]"[43] The
economic aspects of musical diffusion are also particularly
important. As Adorno said, "the task approached today in
various places, or searching for and analyzing the *economic base*

---

[40]See Irmgard Bontinck, "Mass Media and New Types of Youth Music,"
IRASM VI/1 (1975) 47.

[41]The author of this quote, Kurt Blaukopf, is referring to "New Patterns of
Musical Behaviour of the Young Generation in Industrial Societies," *New
Patterns of Musical Behaviour of the Young Generation in Industrial Societies*, ed.
Irmgard Bontinck (Vienna: Universal Edition,1974), 13.

[42]Emile Durkheim's definition appeared in *Les règles de la méthode sociologique*
(Paris: 1963, 15th ed.).

[43]Irmgard Bontinck, "Mass Media and New Types of Youth Music," 48.

of music is essential for the sociology of music; [this is] the moment when the relation between society and music is actualized. Of prime concern are questions of musical life: not only to what extent and with what result is it determined by economical motivations, but also—most important and far-reaching—[how it is determined] by the laws and modifications of economic structures."[44] The question of *performance*, in contrast, primarily concerns the musical repertoire. This must be viewed by the sociology of music as unfolding within a given social framework. The aspects to examine here would mainly be the following: in what measure is the repertoire dependent on this framework? When and how has interpretation itself been dependent on it? Has there or has there not been conflict, correspondence, or interpenetration of the social framework with the music performed—in what manner and to what extent? Relative to the social framework, what has been the duration of certain works in the repertoire? Have their performance and their interpretation been varied in relation to different social structures and junctures?

Finally, with regard to those categories of facts that concern socioartistic conditionings: these, in the main, pose the broad problems of *tradition*, *invention*, and *originality*, as well as *change*, *evolution* and *progress* in music, which are at the very core of musical activity—especially creative activity, if we assume that "the musician cannot create without reference to the relativity of history" and to this "historical curve" into which he must "know how to insert his creative personality."[45] The continuity of this curve encompasses many problems of a sociological nature: The tendency of composers to classify themselves by national, philosophical, or purely artistic schools (and thus to play a role together in art, in music, and even in social life); the relationships of music with the other arts; their points of contact and parallel orientations showing social influences and pressures;[46] the

---

[44]Theodor W. Adorno, "Sociologie de la musique," *Musique en jeu* II (1971) 9-10.

[45]Gisèle Brelet, *Esthétique et création musicale* (Paris: P.U.F., 1947), 16, 15.

[46]On the aesthetic relationships of music with the other arts, see for example

preservation of traditions by different institutions, organizations or associations, as well as by establishments of musical education— these questions are also of great interest to the sociology of music. The problems they pose deserve a more precise and complete elucidation within the sociological perspective.

III • METHODS AND APPROACHES

A wide-ranging study of all aspects of music would not be complete without a systematic confrontation of these aspects, not only *within* each of the two broad fundamental categories of social conditionings of music (sociohistorical and socioartistic), but also in their *reciprocal* relationships. Although sociohistorical and socioartistic conditionings coexist and interpenetrate, they must be kept distinct in sociological study and then united later; in other words, they must be understood not only in isolation, but also in their interconnections. But here, as Tibor Kneif rightly pointed out, many methodological pitfalls must be guarded against, whatever their philosophical base—whether it be an *a priori* point of view that takes music to be, in the sense of organicist theory, a self-evident part of society as a whole; or one that considers music to be understood and explained by the recognition of its origins; or even one that holds music explicable in relationship to other arts.[47] The historical bases for a sociology of music should be, according to François Lesure, "the study of the milieu producing the work, and that of the recipients of the work; not one without the other, since the milieu is as much responsible for the art, as the art is creator of the milieu."[48] Hence this study is complex, but the subject matter offered to sociological research in music is intimately linked to its methods.

Etienne Souriau, *La correspondance des arts, Eléments d'esthétique comparée* (Paris: Flammarion, 1947) and Thomas Munro, *Les arts et leurs relations mutuelles* (Paris: P.U.F., 1954). Tr. from English.

[47]See Tibor Kneif, *Musiksoziologie,* 14-28.

[48]François Lesure, "Musicologie et sociologie," *La revue musicale* CCXXI (1953) 9.

Social conditionings make up that subject matter, but they are at the same time one of the essential methods of examining its problems.[49]

A musical work, which has inevitably come under certain influences of given sociohistorical and socioartistic conditionings, can exert pressure not only of a socioartistic but also of a sociohistorical nature on later musical works. In other words, there is a "vertical," or *indirect*, influence exerted by sociohistorical conditionings through existing musical works, which, to some extent, embody those conditions. There also exists a more important "horizontal," or *direct*, influence exerted by these same conditionings, which is immediate and contemporary with the creation of the works it affects. There is also an *indirect* influence of socioartistic conditionings on the musical art of each period, through the action exerted by musical art on society (and society, while subject to this action, is not without its own reaction to musical art). But this indirect influence is universally much weaker than that of sociohistorical conditionings (since the action that musical art exerts on diverse societies generally appears to be less than that which societies exert upon musical art). Finally, there is the *direct* influence of socioartistic conditionings, not necessarily manifested immediately; this is the influence exerted by previous musical activities or works on subsequent activities or works, and concerns only their artistic qualities. Thus, the first methodological requirement is to study the mutual relationships and connections of different social conditionings of music.

The extent and importance of the influence exerted by each of

---

[49]"It is the nature of the objects studied that determines which methods are best adapted to their study. In aesthetics, as elsewhere, the most fundamental methodological problem is not to know *if* induction is better than deduction, or observation better than experimentation for in this domain these procedures are closely combined (although in different proportions according to the domains envisaged and the evolutionary state of the science). It is much more important to find out *what* is better... to submit to induction, deduction, observation, experimentation, definition, conjecture, hypothesis, etc." Charles Lalo, "Méthodes et objets de l'esthétique sociologique," 5.

these specific social conditionings, directly or indirectly—by society on music, or vice-versa—should be examined first by *induction*, a method that will lead to more general conclusions in sociology of music. At this point it joins with music history and the social history of music, the two disciplines that must deal with specific facts and demonstrate their relatedness: the former, between single musical facts of earlier and later periods, in order to provide a foundation necessary for the study of socioartistic conditionings; the latter, between musical facts (as artistic facts) and extramusical social facts (as social facts) in order to acquire a base essential for the study of the sociohistorical conditionings of music. This first level of research belongs to music history and the social history of music. The sociology of music must dig deeper to find its true subject matter.[50] Ultimately, however, it is through a combined use of both inductive and deductive methods that significant research can be carried out in the sociology of music. This is its second methodological requirement.

A matter of further precision is now imposed in order to satisfy a third methodological requirement: the precise *definition* of particular terms that relate to given social conditionings. Be it a matter of the relationship of a musical or extramusical term with a musical term, or a matter of socioartistic or sociohistorical conditions, each term must be specified and determined exactly. In the study of the sociohistorical conditionings of a given musical work, for example, it is not sufficient to state *which* conditionings (i.e., economic, technical, political, etc.) are involved. We must also know to which specific element of the musical work (i.e., content, language, technique, expression, or form) they refer, and how. And when musical facts themselves are studied as social facts, they must be treated with no less precision.

A fourth methodological step, essential for the sociology of music as well as for sociology in general, consists of looking at problems, limited though they may be, by gradually *enlarging*

---

[50]See above, p. 23.

the social context of the facts studied: by moving from their particularity to the totality that encircles them (and sometimes vice-versa). In this way we come to understand these facts in greater depth and to explain them more completely, stressing either important and characteristic details or more general aspects. Moreover, it is correct that "in general, when we pose a problem in sociology . . . we always arrive, in the end, at total social phenomena . . . we always arrive at situations of totality."[51]

Assuming that the sociology of music need not introduce aesthetic criteria or value judgements into the delimitation of its subject matter, a fifth method necessarily results, which we could call the method of totality or *integrality*. This method allows us to demonstrate that the sociology of music must not only study living musical works—that is, those regularly found in the repertoire and appreciated for their artistic qualities—but must embrace the totality of music history: everything past and outdated from an aesthetic point of view, as well as everything current and valid. Still, living musical works represent a particularly interesting subject for study, since we can assume that there are sociological as well as purely aesthetic reasons for their survival. Nevertheless, the sociology of music cannot be confined to the study of living musical works alone, because this would overlook the totality of music history of which they are only a part and from which they derive. This totality can explain some of their aspects, but the method of integrality also embraces the purely sociological side. In other words, the sociology of music must look at *all* the social elements that relate to music.

A sixth method available to the sociology of music is one also essential for the social history of music: the *comparative* method, which is implied in the very idea of social conditioning.[52] As

---

[51]Georges Gurvitch, "Discussion," *Cahiers internationaux de sociologie* XXVI (1959) 161.

[52]It has been stated, with good reason, that "the comparative method. . . is the most fruitful process in sociology," although it may be exact only in a certain sense; whether it be "pre-eminently destined for sociological aesthetics" is another matter. See Charles Lalo, "Méthodes et objets de l'esthétique sociologique," 20.

71

applied to the sociology of music, this method has a double purpose: it can be used for either the systematic comparison of musical facts to social facts, or for comparison of musical facts to other musical facts, in order to discover their typical correlations. In its double application, this method derives directly from the very subject matter proposed for the sociological examination of music, and is imposed of necessity. Moreover, it can be applied doubly in yet another way: first, in the comparative study of terms occurring at *diverse* moments of history (we can include here very small segments of time, as well as entire historical periods); second, in the comparative study of terms that occur simultaneously within the *same* historical moment (and we can include here very small dimensions of space, as well as the very largest). With this approach, the sociology of music approaches in method the specialized discipline that— at one point in its evolution—was called comparative musicology, which we now call ethnomusicology. What differentiates the comparative method of ethnomusicology from that of the sociology of music, however, is that the first bears essentially on particular historical data of ethnic music, while the second is engaged in establishing general or typical relationships of sociological nature.

IV • SOCIOLOGICAL EXPLICATIONS

In regard to the sociological explications of music, an initial disclaimer is required on two counts: first, in terms of what the sociology of music can explicate in a general way, and second, in terms of what it can explicate in its present state of development. The sociology of music can not claim to furnish today broad syntheses or explications of great thrust, while we still await an exploration of matters in depth. "It is obvious, moreover, that such a tentative elaboration can provide some general views in the long run, but it poses delicate problems of method and requires one to arrive at an objective study of works considered as complex evidence of individual and social activities which are still poorly defined, and, in any case, not reducible to some abstract pseudo-historical scheme."[53] Furthermore, in the sociology of music, as in sociology in general, *to explicate* does not necessarily mean to explicate in a causal fashion. We can explicate, from a sociological perspective, by functional correlations, by integration within the whole, and finally even by the calculus of probability."[54] But even the statistical method, interesting as it may be, has no general or exclusive importance in the sociology of music. Certainly, the method will allow us to deal very well with the number of people in a society, class, or social group who devote their time and efforts to music as composers, performers, employees and collaborators, tradesmen, instrument makers, theorists, critics, professors or consumers. We can also use statistics to deal with the numbers "of printings of musical publications. Such elements are among the most valuable to the sociologist who desires to appraise the diffusion of a work."[55] The statistical method can also assist our study of patterns in the sale of scores, with a view to establishing the interest in a certain genre of music or in a certain composer, within one society.[56] But we see "only too many indications of weariness in face of the growing numbers of statistical studies, inventories, and inquiries, which lack the essential requirement of having been undertaken and conducted as a function of

[53]Pierre Francastel, "Compte-rendu," *L'Année sociologique,* Series 3 (1951) 519.

[54]Georges Gurvitch, "Les cadres sociaux de la connaissance sociologique," *Cahiers internationaux de sociologie* XXVI (1959) 167.

[55]François Lesure, "Histoire d'une édition posthume: Les 'Airs' de Sébastien le Camus (1678)," *Revue belge de musicologie* VIII/2,3,4 (1954) 126. The author cites seven documents covering the whole period of the ancien régime, and whose publication he has been able to establish.

[56]See Arthur Honegger, "Le musicien dans la société moderne," *L'artiste dans la société* contemporaine (Liège: UNESCO; Vaillant-Carmane, 1954) 64; where the author has shown the small catalogue established by the *Editions Durand* indicating the diminishing sale of certain modern works.

something else."[57] What the sociology of music needs especially is "a specific body of material rich in characteristic facts."[58] It is true, for example, that the use of a genre can give sociological evidence of a well-defined musical center at a certain musical period,[59] it is also true that this evidence can exist as a characteristic and significant fact established by the method of observation, and not as a precise quantitative fact established by the statistical method.

From the methodological point of view, it is thus necessary to reject as ill founded the sociologistic absolutism that would consider the sociology of music to be the unique and supreme tool for explicating all artistic musical facts. It is also in this sense that sociological explication has its limits. Alphons Silbermann stresses the viewpoint (which some other authors share) that "the study of the sociological ramifications of music is of no service in clarifying the nature and essence of music itself. But it is the ultimate goal of Adorno's approach to the sociology of music."[60] Carl Dahlhaus, for example, discusses whether or not the sociology of music is a "central" or only a "peripheral" discipline—a mere auxiliary to music history or to the aesthetics of music.[61] Thus perplexities and controversies concerning the discipline still exist. We must discard, however, the position that would limit, a priori, the explicative possibilities of the sociology of music. We can no longer accept the idea that this will always be the same scientific discipline, qualified to bring a further and more profound explication of all musical phenomena—be they the aesthetics, the sociology or the history of music. Otherwise, we would fall into a pseudoscientific and methodologically

---

[57]André Schaeffner, "Ethnologie musicale ou musicologie comparée," Les Colloques de Wégimont I (Brussels: Elsevier, 1956) 23.

[58]Ibid., 23.

[59]See Floris Van Der Mueren, "Ecole bourguignonne, école néerlandaise ou début de la Renaissance," Revue belge de musicologie XII/1-4 (1958) 54.

[60]Alphons Silbermann, Empirische Kunstsoziologie, 74.

[61]See Carl Dahlhaus, "Das musikalische Kunstwerk als Gegenstand der Soziologie," IRASM V/1 (1974) 11; and "Vorwort" to Texte zur Musiksoziologie, ed. Tibor Kneif (Cologne: Arno Volk, 1975) 1.

indefensible position, of which aestheticism and sociologism are sometimes both the results and/or the cause.

On the other hand, as was rightly stressed by Barry S. Brook, "to place hierarchical values on the different kinds of things musicologists may do in the practice of their profession, whether it be bibliography, historical synthesis or 'the higher criticism,' is a disservice to our discipline."[62] Arthur Mendel's distinction between two different stages of musicological work may, however, prove acceptable: the first stage should establish the facts of a lower order and the second stage those of a higher order (e.g., characteristics of style).[63] Perhaps more stages than these two could be foreseen. But the important thing to note is that a division into two or more levels of abstraction or generalization does not imply a hierarchical gradation of different disciplines within the field of musicology. According to Edward E. Lowinsky, each musicological discipline has its autonomous structure, and there are no steps that would lead from these structures to evaluation and critical judgement. Critical judgment, which includes evaluation also, is seen by Lowinsky as being much closer to its nature to criticism in literature and the fine arts than it is to musical science, even when it has music as its object. Critical judgment is neither the end result nor the peak achievement of the process of scientific research.[64]

The solution to this question of determining the disciplines most competent to deal with the possible explication of musical facts resides in a pluralistic conception. A certain pluralism of competencies determined by the subject examined, and a certain modifying coefficient—that facts discovered by one discipline can contribute to results acquired in another—must be recognized. The sociologistic attitude, opposed to such a

---

[62]Barry S. Brook, "Music, Musicology, and Related Disciplines: On Perspective and Interconnectedness," 71-72.

[63]Arthur Mendel, "Evidence and Explanation," *IMS Report of the Eighth Congress—New York, 1961* (Kassel-Basel: Bärenreiter, 1961), vol. I.

[64]Cf. Edward E. Lowinsky, "Character and Purposes of American Musicology," *JAMS* XVIII (1965) 2, 224.

pluralism, suffers from a profound futility of method. From the sociologistic point of view, one can never arrive at an objective study of the field one should like to explicate, because one examines only the domain of social facts, without investigating the specific domain to which they must be compared. And one ends in reducing this domain to those facts without ever having analyzed it by and for itself. It is absolutely necessary for the sociology of music to avoid running a risk that has rightly been denounced in a parallel discipline—the sociology of literature— a veritable *"risk of destruction: scientific explication has quite often resulted, in this domain, in destroying its own object."*[65] It is thus of primary methodological importance in sociological study to safe- guard, from the very beginning, the specificity of the artistic musi- cal fact—a fact of autonomous validity. Célestin Deliège has also stated that "if it is possible to make a structural analysis [of music] without appealing to sociology, the reverse is not true. It is presumptuous to claim that one can integrate the object of the sociological analysis into a reality which encompasses it and partially determines it, without having penetrated the secrets of that object other than intuitively, without having previously decoded it. Structural analysis is thus a necessary means of research in the sociology of art."[66]

In this perspective, sociologism must be rejected as a method- ologically outdated position, since from the very first, before undertaking an objective examination of the subject, it proclaims that art and musical works in given social contexts are *only* the result of socially determined pressure. Sociologism considers them neither for their "own sake," nor as part of an artistic and human universe that these works imply and presume, which conditions them—a universe that the sociology of music (and sociologism as well) cannot be capable of revealing without a complementary aesthetic, psychological and philosophical analysis. On the other hand, the contemporary "aesthetics of

---

[65] Albert Memmi, "Cinq propositions pour une sociologie de la littérature," 154.
[66] Célestin Deliège, "Une incidence d'Adorno," *L'Arc* XL (1970) 107.

sociological orientation refuses a rigid conception of relationships between art and society, aiming rather at the individualization from one case to another, of how such relationships
have been arranged in the framework of complex and multiform
problems which emerge from them."[67] "For to put a work of art
into a sociological perspective . . . does not mean to consider it
as a species of *epiphenomenon*—that is, only as the reflection of a
situation; it only means putting it into a situation of functional
correlation."[68] Thus, "reduction, if it is possible at all, can only be
a result—a long-range result—at the end of scientific research,
and cannot be posed at the beginning."[69] Otherwise, it would be
an *a priori* procedure characteristic of certain philosophical
attitudes, and not of rigorously scientific procedures, to which
the sociology of music, as a science, has to remain faithful. As we
have already pointed out, music is always, in a certain sense, a
"reflection." In what sense? Precisely in that it is always
historically situated and socially conditioned, associated with
different extramusical sources that occasion and underly it.[70]
But the sociology of music must demonstrate the truth of this
statement, if it can, and not accept it as if it had already been
proven in its own sphere. Thus, when Alphons Silbermann
erroneously interprets this point of view, writing "there is
nothing to object to in this conception, if one wishes to be
content with allowing the sociology of music to remain closed to
the simple causality of music history,"[71] he seems not only to
misunderstand the true concept of "conditioning" and to accept

---

[67]"L'estetica di orientamento sociologico rifiuta una concezione rigida dei
rapporti tra arte e società, mirando piuttosto a individuare di volta in volta
come si sono configurati tali rapporti nell'ambito dei complessi e multiformi
problemi che da essi sorgono," Enrico Fubini, *L'estetica contemporanea* (Turin:
Loeschner, 1976) 167.

[68]Georges Gurvitch, "Les cadres sociaux de la connaissance sociologique,"
167.

[69]Albert Memmi, "Cinq propositions pour une sociologie de la littérature,"
154.

[70]See Ivo Supičić *La musique expressive*, 19.

[71]Alphons Silbermann, "Ivo Supičić, *Musique et Société. Perspectives pour une
sociologie de la musique* (Zagreb: Institut de Musicologie-Académie de Musique,

it in the sense opposite to its real meaning, but also, ignoring the real bases of the whole concept of the sociology of music presented here, to oversimplify it one-sidedly, reducing these bases to influences to which they cannot be reduced. It is clear that if "conditioning" and "necessity" do not mean the same thing, then, similarly, "conditioning" cannot be reduced to "causality."[72]

In conclusion, the sociology of music must take into consideration, as much as possible and with a broad overview, all the levels of meaning and aspects of social facts concerning the music studied. In areas where the sociology of music has yet to venture, it must at least determine the basic elements to be dealt with therein, with an eye to further, more complete examination in the future. Generally, the various musicological disciplines study only various aspects of musical facts by detaching them from the whole, without even attempting to look at the totality of these facts. Music history and ethnomusicology, it is true, today seek more and more to understand on an elevated number of levels the facts they study, but for the most part they investigate special relationships and the continuity of structures. By means of its typological method, the sociology of music must search for discontinuous types in matters that concern sociohistorical conditionings, and must look for typical facts, in order to arrive rightly at an essentially sociological typification.

1971), 205" *Kölner Zeitschrift für Soziologie und Sozialpsychologie* XXV/3 (1973) 660.

[72] See above, p. 50-1.

PART TWO

Music in Society

INTRODUCTION

In this study of sociohistorical conditionings—the most important study in the sociology of music—we shall not present in introduction a chronological and systematic social history of music. Considering the present state of knowledge, it would be foolhardy to claim that this could be done in a complete and more or less detailed manner; the material for study is too vast and unexplored. Neither do we have any interest in addressing a general point of view that others have already adopted in order to follow, from century to century, the development of music in relation to historical and social developments.[1] Such is not the spirit of this work, which is, above all, a work of approach, oriented toward the exposition of certain fundamental or characteristic facts related to several periods in music history, and the identification of social aspects of music, in order to illustrate the subject matter and perspectives of the sociology of music. As K.P. Etzkorn stressed, "a sociological approach to music must start with what is the essential musical situation . . . trying to locate contained musical situations and to learn from

---

[1]Concerning this observation, see for example: Paul H. Lang, *Music in Western Civilization* (New York: Norton, 1941); Roman I. Gruber, *History of Musical Culture* (Moscow-Leningrad: Gosizd, 1941-1959) 2 vols (in Russian), and Arnold Hauser, *The Social History of Art* (London: Routledge and Kegan Paul, 1951) 2 vols.

them how they became conventionalized, how the participants in these social situations of music making have acquired the particular expressions that become obligatory."[2] This task is all the more justifiable in that some works that have up to now qualified as "sociologies of music" are lacking in determined facts, which could substantiate some theoretical considerations that have been extensively developed in the meantime. Walter Wiora rightly remarked that the number of those writings that contain worthwhile knowledge pertaining to the sociology of music is much greater than the number of writings that devote themselves explicitly to the sociology of music,[3] and that it should now be necessary, far more than before, to undertake or to encourage written works in which this knowledge, which was formerly rather implicit, be made deliberately explicit.[4] Many works, such as those by Walter Salmen, Arnold Schering, Paul H. Lang, Manfred Bukofzer, etc., present materials that require further study in a specifically sociological perspective and supplemented by information from all possible sources (newspapers, church records, etc). Certainly, we also "have studies on musical reception as a sociology of reception, we have studies of sociology of production, we have all these sociologies of—but they do not amount to the sociology of music because they do not start with music."[5] In addition, as Barry S. Brook emphasized, "it is necessary to explore the area of the past *at the same time* as that of today, in order to evaluate thoroughly the possibilities of the sociology of music."[6] The goal envisioned here is thus to clear the ground, to open several principal routes, and to determine a certain order of basic problems. Consequently, we have utilized only selected elements from music history and the social history of music as a basis for precisely the sociological perspectives we wanted to reach.

---

[2]K. Peter Etzkorn, "Discussion," *IRASM* VI/1 (1975) 82.
[3]Walter Wiora, "Discussion," *IRASM* VI/1 (1975) 182.
[4]See *Ibid.,* 183.
[5]K. Peter Etzkorn, "Discussion," *IRASM* VI/1 (1975) 87.
[6]Barry S. Brook, "Discussion," *IRASM* VI/1 (1975) 85.

CHAPTER ONE

MUSIC AND THE PUBLIC

I • SOCIAL GROUPS IN MUSICAL LIFE

It has been often observed in the course of history, starting with primitive societies, that a musical fact was related to a social fact. "Of all the objects which a Black African population uses, musical instruments are the most bound to the play of its institutions, to the rhythm of its activities. All divisions between musical instruments correspond to divisions in the society or among the rites it practices ... One type of instrument is far from having an identical function in all the societies which use it."[1] But divisions appear everywhere according to sex, profession, or rituals in which individuals or groups of individuals participate; these divisions are those of the society.

"In many societies, certain songs are for singing and certain instruments for playing by individuals of one or the other sex only. Throughout the Western world, children carry traditions on music which can be considered folk songs. These are not learned from the elders, who have usually either forgotten or pay no attention to them. Constantin Brailoĭu believed that traditions of children's songs were universal and exhibited

---

[1]André Schaeffner, *Les Kissis, une société noire et ses instruments de musique* (Paris: Hermann, 1951) 3.

music-technical traits in common."[2] André Schaeffner reported that, in the village of Katako, in Africa's Boga country, he found an instrument normally belonging to young girls in the hands of men: it was a question of men taking over the social functions of women for a certain length of time.[3]

In France, as another example, we could note an instrument, the toulouhou of the central Pyrenees, which is exclusively reserved to a given community, the boys;[4] and, more generally, the use of a musical instrument as the symbol of the chief of an organization or tribe.[5] In the Congo there were even trials that were pleaded musically, where defendant and prosecutor, assisted first by their groups (who alternately offered their chanted interventions) then by the wood drum (by its conclusion—the battery pronouncing judgement), composed a clearly structured musical "suite."[6] The further we look back into the history of humanity, the more we see music existing not in the form of entertainment or as a purely artistic manifestation, but as an element bound up in the most earthy details of daily social life.[7]

In the middle of the sixteenth century in Paris, in a highly civilized society, "musical participation was inseparable from the various stages of family life: betrothals, marriages, days of churching for birth, all sorts of anniversaries; it was inseparable from professional life: 'chef-d'oeuvres' of new masters, feast days of the guilds' patron saints, festivals of the corporations (some of these, such as that for the clerks of Châtelet, had a very

---

[2]Charles Seeger, "The Music Compositional Process as a Function in a Nest of Functions and in Itself a Nest of Functions," in *Studies in Musicology 1935-1975* (Berkeley-Los Angeles-London: U. of California Press, 1977) 151.

[3]See André Schaeffner *"Ethnologie musicale ou musicologie comparée,"* 30, and "Musique et structures sociales" (Sociétés d'Afrique Noire) *Revue française de sociologie* IV (1962) 389-390.

[4]See Claudie Marcel-Dubois, "Le toulouhou des Pyrénées centrales," *Les Colloques de Wegimont III-1956, Ethnomusicologie II* (Paris: Société d'Edition "Les Belles Lettres," 1960) 16.

[6]See Gilbert Rouget, "A propos de la forme dans les musiques de tradition orale," *Les Colloques de Wégimont* I (Brussels: Elsevier, 1956) 135.

[7]See Marius Schneider, "Sociologie et mythologie musicales," 13.

special sort of celebration); inseparable from municipal life: the bonfires of Saint John's Day, May feasts; or simply from life: 'a departure, the buying of a house . . . the happy outcome of a trial or bet.' It is a traveller from Basle [Thomas Platter] who speaks, and he forgets some: games of tennis (which was at the height of its popularity during the sixteenth century) are most often enhanced by the presence of instrumentalists; the many masquerades, 'bâtons,' 'réveils,' and divertissements of college students never took place without violins, cornets (with a mouthpiece), and oboes."[8]

In seventeenth-century Austria we also find an interesting example of the expression of a social reality in the arts: "in these presentations of tournaments and equestrian or naval feasts, even the places reserved for princes and dignified spectators were subject to the demands of the most tyrannical symmetry, symbol of Spanish ceremonial, and of the implacable hierarchy of the society. The coordinated parallelism of groups is the guiding principle of the 'entrées' in these ballets. Thus we are not surprised to see the Viennese J.H. Schmelzer base the orchestration of his dances for an open air ballet, on the figures of the choreography: an orchestra of brass and strings for centaurs, a second orchestra of strings alone for nymphs, and for the ensembles of nymphs and fauns, a third group of strings and woodwinds; and finally, for the choreographed ensembles, a pompous tutti of all three orchestras . . . This ballet was performed at the Schönbrunn in 1674."[9]

At this point we could mention another aspect dealt with by François Lesure in a particularly interesting way: namely, the position of music in society in light of the relationships between music and painting.[10] His work is not a "history of music in

---

[8]François Lesure, "Réflexions sur les origines du concert parisien," *Polyphonie* V (1949) 48.

[9]Paul Nettl, "L'évolution de la musique autrichienne au XVIIᵉ siècle: de la barcarole à la valse," *La revue musicale* CLV (1935) 259.

[10]François Lesure, *Musica e società* (Milan: Istituto Editoriale Italiano, 1966); Ger. tr. *Musik und Gesellschaft im Bild* (Kassel-Basel: Bärenreiter, 1966); Eng. tr. *Music and Art in Society* (Pittsburgh: Pennsylvania State U. Press, 1968).

pictures" of the type produced by Georg Kinsky in 1929, or more recently, from 1961 on, by others.[11] Lesure compares two types of evidence for the dependence of music on social life, one taken from the history of music itself and the other from paintings illustrating various aspects of social life in which music had a function. Choosing European art from the fourteenth to nineteenth centuries for this study, the author examines his subject, supporting his conclusions with some 100 reproductions of original paintings from that period (by Holbein, Giorgione, Carpaccio, Guardi, Laneret, Hogarth, Titian, Caravaggio, Vermeer, Canaletto and others). These paintings make clear how deeply music can be involved in social life at a given time.

II • MUSIC AS A SOCIAL PHENOMENON

These few illustrations of the tie between social and musical facts (as well as those that show the facts of music or musical life to be, at the same time, sociological facts) all show human groups—most importantly, "the public"—implicated in musical activity. On the other hand, as far as the problem of music as a social fact is concerned, in this matter too no simplification is permitted, and it is difficult to go along with proposals such as those offered by Alphons Silbermann: "We may say that music is chiefly a social phenomenon: social because it is a human product, and because it is a form of communication between composer, interpreter and listener. If music can be said to have an effect upon the individual in his social life, then this very relationship makes it a social phenomenon, and that is in many ways particularly noticeable in our own time. Firstly as a result of its mission: Music is no longer restricted to a small circle of cultivated listeners, but has cast off intimacy and reserve in order to become popular. Secondly as a result of its constitution:

---

[11]See Georg Kinsky, *Geschichte der Musik in Bildern* (Leipzig: Breitkopf & Härtel, 1929); and *Musikgeschichte in Bildern*. ed. Heinrich Besseler and Max Schneider (Leipzig: VEB Deutscher Verlag für Musik, 1961 and following).

The essence of music has become more and more social. While music was once the preserve of the individual, it now belongs to the masses, a fact which Taine, following Spinoza, was one of the first to recognize."[12] Though some aspects of these assertions are correct, others are oversimplified. It cannot be considered scientifically exact to say that any music is "chiefly a social phenomenon . . . because it is a human product," as there are human products that are not chiefly social phenomena. On the other hand, the idea of music as "a form of communication" is highly questionable and actually is questioned by many authors. Furthermore, whether it be more "popular" or, rather, "restricted to a small circle of cultivated listeners," it remains doubtful that music as music has really changed in its very essence. Finally, today as in the past, there exist different genres of music that belong respectively to the "masses" and to "individuals" (or to small circles of listeners). Every period has produced music for both large publics and limited groups, and both types are more or less socially and artistically relevant.

In some respects music is undoubtedly a social phenomenon and should be studied as such. Its extreme complexity, however, requires a careful investigation and accurate definition of the whole problem. The more so, as undesirable philosophical implications may easily interfere in the sociological examination of such a question. Social aspects of music should be investigated step by step, a kind of work that still remains to be done. However, music should never be reduced to these aspects alone, for they are but part of a larger whole. On the other hand, "We cannot, at the present time, form a usable concept of music as a world whole, and so cannot show wherein the relationship between such a one and world society consists or how it operates. Rather, we must, as members of a society in which science presumably takes precedence over criticism, deal first with particular musics and particular societies."[13]

---

[12]Alphons Silbermann, *The Sociology of Music.* Tr. Corbet Stewart. (London: Routledge and Kegan Paul, 1963) 38.

[13]Charles Seeger, "Music and Society: Some New-World Evidence of Their

III • TYPES OF RELATIONSHIPS
BETWEEN MUSIC AND PUBLIC

Various fundamental and characteristic relationships between music and the public, or attitudes of the public toward music, could be distinguished *grosso modo* but not without possibly risking some simplification. The oldest type is one in which music constitutes a collective act, as in primitive communities where the author is unknown and the performers comprise all—or almost all—of the members of the assisting community. There is no completely passive public.[14] These assistants sing, dance, clap hands or accompany the music with gestures; all of them are deeply affected by its rhythm. In this case music is linked to the social life of the community, to the whole ambiance of a village, for example, not specifically to a group of musicians. However, it would be simplistic to consider en masse all of the music of the early stages of humanity and the relationships that tied it to the social surroundings. In his work on "the four ages" of music, Walter Wiora remarked that "yet in early times there already was individual possession and even a sort of copyright, which reserved to an author the use of his own song."[15] On the other hand, as André Schaeffner wrote, the importance of performers, "while considerable in an evolved civilization, tends to increase as we approach less developed societies, with the limit, however, that the number of performers never equals that of a whole population: there are always categories of specialized individuals or categories of non-participants (women, for example). Inversely, the importance of the creative artist decreases; beyond a certain level, the question of first inventor

Relationship," in *Studies in Musicology 1935-1975* (Berkeley-Los Angeles-London: U. of California Press, 1977) 183.

[14]Jacques Chailley, "Problèmes de la musique contemporaine et de l'auditeur devant l'histoire du langage," *La revue internationale de musique* XIII (1952) 210.

[15]See Walter Wiora, *The Four Ages of Music* (New York: Norton, 1967) 39.

becomes unsolvable and should not even be asked."[16] In general, however, primitive music, like popular music, is an expression of a collective experience. It is not the well-defined work of a single individual, although an author of sorts might be found at the origin of a particular piece of music, and though a sort of "right of authorship" appears already here and there in primitive tribes. According to Béla Bartók's thesis, variability is one of the most significant and typical attributes of folk melody.[17] We could say the same for primitive music, since in both cases variations and improvisations are made from one performance to another. In primitive communities, musical performance is expressive and often creative. In these societies there are no musical works in the modern sense of the term, but only types, models or ways of singing and making music. Although the melodies might be more or less variable, the community however maintained control over them by imposing limits, thus encouraging their preservation over long periods of time.[18]

In a second type of relationship between the public and music, considered intermediary and called by Jacques Chailley a "collective stage by delegation",[19] music still expresses the collective experience of the assisting community. This type appears first in ancient civilizations and great empires of antiquity, in the Greek tragedies with their choruses, and then in European culture, in the offices of the Church and the medieval mystery plays. But here the listeners—by the very fact that they are only listeners—become musically passive and, as Jacques Chailley observed, their participation in the performance, or the singing, is only psychological, without accompanying,

[16]André Schaeffner, "Musique populaire et art musical," *Journal de psychologie* I-II (1951) 253.

[17]See Béla Bartók, "Pourquoi et comment recueille-t-on la musique populaire, Législation du folklore musical," *Archives internationales de musique populaire* (Geneva: A. Kundig, 1948) 4.

[18]See Walter Wiora, *The Four Ages of Music*, 40.

[19]See Jacques Chailley, "Problèmes de la musique contemporaine et de l'auditeur devant l'histoire du langage," 210.

more or less actively, the progress of the music.[20] Characteristic of this type of relationship is the involvement of a vast and yet undifferentiated public with music that is relatively accessible.[21] Although a distinction between composer, performers and public may already have been made, the composer often remains anonymous,[22] and is not separated from the others; all are powerfully united in what the music expresses. In this case, as in general, Alan P. Merriam correctly observed that "the listener responds socially in different ways to music, depending both upon the situation and his role in it. The primary question here is whether it is the music or the entire situation which shapes the listener's behavior."[23]

As to the activity or passivity of the public, one reservation must be made for the period of the first Christian centuries. The public is not musically passive during the Church offices; the simplicity of plainchant allows the public take an active part in it. Only the introduction of melismas and vocalizations requires the use of artists specially trained to sing them. From this moment participation starts to become passive.[24] In another sense, however, "church music during its first thousand years, at least, is an *active music*. One sings not to be heard, but to sing, offering one's song to God and going beyond oneself in singing. Even as there is no 'composer', neither are there listeners—only participants. The soloists are not artists before an audience, but delegates who express themselves in the name of all. The soloist's song, moreover, must be sanctioned by collective approval: this is the meaning of the final *Amen* of the faithful and of the primitive refrains that will become 'responsorial chant.' "[25]

---

[20]See *Ibid.,* 104.

[21]This type of relationship still exists today; it was particularly well established in times of romanticism and today concerns especially certain forms of popular music and its audiences.

[22]See below, p. 202-3.

[23]Alan P. Merriam, *The Anthropology of Music,* 144.

[24]See Lionel de La Laurencie, *Le Goût musical en France* (Paris: A. Joanin, 1905) 15, 37.

[25]Jacques Chailley, *40,000 ans de musique,* 90-91. See also *ibid.,* 196: "The

As we can see, the modern notion of a public is hardly applicable to these "publics" of former times.[26] The only heterogeneous form the medieval public takes to is religious, the church reuniting those whom society kept apart because of differences in social status.[27]

Nor was the public content to simply listen in early Oriental societies. The public took an active part in concerts by composing pieces of music and songs, by playing instruments, or showing its approval or disapproval by shouting out at opportune moments or using a drum called "for praise." In Vietnam, in the popular theater At Cheo, the public assisted in the progress of the plot. And even when the public did not participate actively in a concert or spectacle, a great sense of communion still existed between the performers and the public. In recent times, the Oriental public has adopted more and more the behavior of the West: silence observed during the performance, absence of comment or participation, applause at the end of a work.[28]

In the third type of relationship, the beginnings of which we find already in the Hellenistic age in Greece and the Middle Ages in Europe, the greater part of "learned" or "cultivated" music becomes more and more complex, and its execution even more difficult. Secular musical art addresses itself most often to the upper layers of society first (thus the royal courts of antiquity already formed one of the first passive audiences). The individuality of the musician as creator and interpreter imposes itself still more on the public. This public is completely passive musically (but not sociologically), not participating in the performance, which is reserved to artists who become always more specialized. In this sense, as François Lesure has stressed, in France at least the public starts to become passive at the

---

listener, here, is not a recipient, but one of the components of the collective inspiration."

[26]*Ibid.*, 76, 93.

[27]See Lionel de La Laurencie, *Le Goût musical en France*, 6; and also Jacques Chailley, *Histoire musicale du Moyen Age* (Paris: P.U.F., 1950) 43-44.

[28]See Tran Van Khê, "Le public de concert en Orient devant les changements d'ordre sociologique," *The World of Music* V/1-2 (1963) 17.

beginning of the seventeenth century. When we think of the "public" at this time, it is no longer the anonymous crowd of the sixteenth century, but a certain number of amateurs who gather together especially to listen to music. This signifies a transformation of musical life, which Curt Sachs characterized when he wrote that at this moment there became clear a division "between the active and passive in human culture, between the creators and the spectators, between the artist and public."[29] Or, as Kurt Blaukopf said, following Heinrich Besseler, "in the seventeenth century the way was paved in Europe for the replacement of participating audiences by the 'public.' This era shaped the transition from participation-oriented to performance-oriented music (in Besseler's terminology) and thereby to a performance where one was only required to listen[30]."[31] Besseler distinguished between "Umgangsmusik," which involved active participation of an attending public in the performance; and "Darbietungsmusik," in the performance of which the attending public did not take part. To these two terms Konrad Niemann added a third one, "Übertragungsmusik," to designate *grosso modo* music transmitted through the mass media.[32]

According to Hans Engel, it is even possible to distinguish two types of musicians: "There is an *Urtype* of artist, who is not bound to historical stages of development—an *Urtype* of the

[29]See François Lesure, "La naissance de l'orchestre en France au début du XVIIᵉ siecle," *Histoire de la musique* I. Ed. Roland-Manuel (Paris: Gallimard, 1960) 1562. See also F. Lesure, "Chambonnières, organisateur de concerts (1641)," *Revue belge de musicologie* III/3 (1949) 142-143.

[30]The reference is to Heinrich Besseler's *Das musikalisches Hören der Neuzeit*. Berichte über die Verhandlungen der sächsischen Akademie der Wissenschaft zu Leipzig, Philologisch-historisch Klasse, CIV/6 (Berlin, 1959).

[31]Kurt Blaukopf, "Historische Typen des musikalisches Hörens. Ein Beitrag zur Soziologie des musikalischen Verhaltens" *Jahresbericht der Akademie für Musik und darstellende Kunst in Wien*. Studienjahre 1955/56-1964/65 (Vienna, 1966) 354.

[32]See Konrad Niemann, "Mass Media—New Ways of Approach to Music and New Patterns of Musical Behaviour," *New Patterns of Musical Behaviour of the Young Generation in Industrial Societies*. Ed. Irmgard Bontinck. (Vienna: Universal Edition, 1974) 49.

extroverted or 'performing' artist. There is also an introverted type of musician, who is called not to 'performance' but to withdrawal into himself."[33]

If the refinement of music and shrinking of the public characterize the third type of relationship, which arises in the seventeenth century, it carries within itself the seed of a new type that involves the music and public in a relationship of collision and conflict. Beginning with the French Revolutionary era, and especially at the beginning of the nineteenth century, we observe a twofold characteristic movement. In its social functions, European art music tends to become more and more "democratic" and addresses itself to an ever-growing circle of listeners. Musical life is transformed and becomes more commercialized. Furthermore, the diffusion of music is accelerated by social, economic and general cultural evolution as much as, if not more than, by the technical progress of the twentieth century (radio, records, etc.). In the Orient also, the musical public enlarges considerably. Music of the court, formerly confined to the Imperial palaces, is now available to the public at large. As Tran Van Khê noted, the Japanese can listen to a Gagaku orchestra; the Vietnamese to Dainhar orchestra; the Cambodians, Thais and central Laotians to a Piphat or Seb Nai orchestra. In India, not only in the maharajas' palaces can one hear great music. In Vietnam, from the beginning of the nineteenth century, court actors have taught theatrical art to other actors who then play for the people. In Japan, the Noh theater ceases to be an amusement reserved for a very restricted public. The Kabuki theater also has conquered a public that has continued to grow since the beginning of the seventeenth century.[34]

Factors such as automation and a reduction in work hours have also contributed to the accessibility of music. In addition

[33]Hans Engel, *Musik und Gesellschaft. Bausteine zu einer Musiksoziologie* (Berlin-Halensee-Wunsiedel: Max Hesses Verlag, 1960) 306.

[34]See Tran Van Khê, "Le public de concert en Orient devant les changements d'ordre sociologique," *The World of Music* V/1-2 (1963) 16-17.

there are purely aesthetic factors, such as the widespread introduction into music of an expressive and illustrative element: the great development of "program" music, for instance, especially characteristic of the European Romantic Movement; and the birth of pieces called "polystratified,"[35] addressing themselves to both connoisseurs and amateurs (for example, those of Strauss, Honegger, Britten, Copland and Shostakovitch). On the other hand, in its refinement we see the inverse aspect of this double movement. One part of art music becomes less and less accessible to the totality of listeners, as publics become always more numerous, diversified and specialized. There is a divorce or—as some think—at least a lack of understanding[36] between the contemporary public and modern music. This divorce characterizes the fourth and last phase of a long history, the point at which we have now arrived in the twentieth century.[37]

On the other hand, as Kurt Blaukopf emphasized, "the behavior which listeners to entertainment music display after exposure to modern mass communications, and for which Adorno introduced the concept 'Regression des Hörens,'[38] is indeed a new sociological type, although its relationship to the passive listening of the Romantic Era has not been completely disavowed. For in the passive listening of the romantic type there exists an element of inner regression: the building of the

---

[35]See Walter Wiora, *The Four Ages of Music*, 164.

[36]See Claude Rostand, "La musique contemporaine et le public," *La Revue musicale* CCXLII (1958) 65-67.

[37]Robert Siohan, *Histoire du public musical* (Lausanne: Les Editions Rencontre, 1967. This is a timely work. While addressing a public of amateurs rather than specialists, it reminds the latter that a history of the musical public has yet to be written. Although elements of such a history already exist, scattered among numerous specialized works, it will require effort on the part of researchers before becoming solidly established within its limits and its essential aspects, before going beyond pure generalities too often repeated without deepening our understanding. Such a work could hold, for the sociology of music, considerable importance.

[38]This quote is from Theodor W. Adorno's, "Über den Fetischcharakter in der Musik und die Regression des Hörens," *Dissonanzen* (Göttingen, 1956): 28ff.

theme back to the motive, the restoration of 'thematic working-out' through the flow of sound to which the listener entrusts himself. When Adorno refers to the consumers of contemporary entertainment music [he says] they 'listen atomistically and disassociate [with] what they hear.' This characteristic perhaps partly relates to the broad Wagner-public of the nineteenth and the beginning of the twentieth century. Such atomistic listening has led to compositional consequences in the production of 'commercial' entertainment music."[39]

IV • TYPES OF MUSICAL PUBLICS

It is no longer possible to speak strictly of a single public—of *the public*—especially when we consider the contemporary situation. In fact we must speak of *the publics*, which we can then examine and classify according to different criteria. Rudolph Heinemann also states that therefore, we cannot speak simply of "the listeners"; it is more valuable to direct our attention to particular *groups* of listeners, who appropriate to themselves one particular type of music and refuse another.[40] We should not dwell here on the results of different inquiries, statistical studies and analyses attempted so far in this area, nor on the reports and discussions of congresses devoted to the problems of contemporary music and its publics.[41]

It is necessary to stress, rather, that the mentioned four types

---

[39]Kurt Blaukopf, "Historische Typen des musikalischen Hörens. Ein Beitrag zur Soziologie des musikalischen Verhaltens," 354-355.

[40]Rudolf Heinemann, "Der Hörer zwischen Musikwissenschaft, Soziologie und Kulturkritik," *Kölner Zeitschrift für Sociologie und Sozial-psychologie* XXI/3, (1969) 567.

[41]See, for example, the materials of the international congress on "Les Aspects Sociologiques de la Musique à la Radio"—Paris 1954, *Cahiers d'études de Radio-Télévision* III-IV (1955) 257-576; or the international congress on "La Musique et son Public"—Rome 1962, *The World of Music* V/1-2 (1963): 3-54; and, partly, of the second symposium of the IMS—Zagreb 1974, *IRASM* V/1 (1974) and VI/1 (1975).

of fundamental relationships do not exclude the existence of other types established according to other criteria. For all classification or typification is made with the understanding that only in the course of research can its worth be ascertained. That does not mean, of course, that a classification will necessarily be arbitrary or incoherent, but that it can and must be adjusted, made flexible and improved. Furthermore, there can be different types of relationships between the public and music even *within* one single era or one society, corresponding to these different types of publics. As Arnold N. Sochor pointed out, the compositional creativity of any land or any era reflects not only the general social structure of society, but also the structure of the public, of that part of society that is interested in and listens to music. This is the "public" in the broad sense of the word. At the same time we must speak of the public in a narrower sense. Then we can differentiate other meanings of this concept, depending upon the quantitative limits of the group under consideration, and the subject matter to be dealt with. So many different groups can stand under the concept of the "public." Therefore, the sociology of music must consider the multiplicity of the phenomena within this concept.

The public in each area can be structured not only in one single way but in many. According to Sochor, there are at least seven possible different structural layers for one and the same public: the social-demographic structure, the general psychological structure, the structure of music motivation, the musical activities structure, the music-knowledge structure, the music-orientation structure, and the music-qualification structure.[42] Hans Engel has likewise distinguished several types of musical public, always keeping in mind that "one may speak of a public only in so far as arrangements for admission are also available to the public."[43]

Finally, at least one more typology of musical public should

---

[42] Arnold N. Sochor, "Discussion," *IRASM* VI/1 (1975) 106.

[43] Hans Engel, *Musik und Gesellschaft, Bausteine zu einer Musiksoziologie* (Berlin-Halensee-Wunsiedel: Max Hesses Verlag, 1960) 302.

be mentioned, if only because of its wide reputation: that of Theodor Adorno.[44] This is a mixed typology, as it contains types of musical publics, musical audiences, and musical listeners—categories that should not be indiscriminately identified with each other. Furthermore, this typology does not have a unique criterion of typification, as was brilliantly shown by Jan Broecks in his excellent critical analysis.[45] In Adorno's distinctions (experts or specialists, good listeners, *Bildungskonsumenten*, emotional listeners, *ressentiment* listeners, jazz specialists or jazz fans, listeners for entertainment, etc.) historical, psychological and sociological criteria, applied in some cases only to particular music genres or areas, interfere with each other; thus this typology becomes scholarly untenable.

On the other hand, one of the most interesting processes to study from the sociological point of view is the *differentiation* of the social functions of music. This process gives birth to different forms of musical life, according to the stratifications of global societies, as expressed in the social composition and appurtenance of the particular publics—the consumers of music. Thus it is important not to view the public solely as an accidental agglomeration of individuals found in more or less the same situation, or as a simple collection of a given number of persons in a court, temple, church, theater, salon or concert hall; this in itself is of little interest and offers no great perspective for sociological studies. The public should be viewed as a social grouping integrated into global society and into different groups, strata and social classes, for inasmuch as the public reflects these groupings, it also represents in some way a manifestation of them.[46]

But obviously, to determine that a specific public constitutes a genuine group is in reality solely a question of fact, which can only be resolved by empirical study. This study must ascertain

---

[44]See Theodor W. Adorno, *Einleitung in die Musiksoziologie* (Frankfurt a. M.: Suhrkamp, 1962) 13-31.

[45]Jan Broecks, "Adorno sociologue," *Musique en Jeu* VII (1972) 44-56.

[46]See Georges Gurvitch, *La vocation actuelle de la sociologie* I (Paris: P.U.F., 1957) 133-135 and 302-303.

whether there has been transition of the audience from being a simple, occasional gathering of people, based on an affinity of tastes, interests, beliefs or doctrine, to a real group, a collective unity that is directly observable and is based on continuous and active attitudes—a collective unity which constitutes a macro-sociological body with a certain cohesion. In addition, a more thorough study of the history and sociology of musical audiences and publics should permit the presentation of an inventory of their types according to different criteria: for example, criteria of social composition or appurtenance, of internal cohesion, of structure or of organization, as well as the "consumption" of different musical genres.

In this regard, contemporary publics and audiences offer a particularly interesting area of study. On one hand, there are the mass audiences for popular music and other genres such as youth music, rock, jazz and all forms of "subcultural" music; on the other hand, there are the publics restricted to certain special forms of some of these musics; publics interested in certain currents of serious contemporary music (especially that called new, avant garde or experimental); and the public for "serious" music in general and especially for some of its particular genres, styles or periods. In this field, it seems that in order to understand some phenomena in contemporary musical life, two theses should be taken in consideration: "the reindividualization of cultural activities centered in the home, and the affirmation of an increasing uniformity in life-styles."[47] As to mass musical production, the industrialization of culture "in the musical domain, has given predictable results: rationalization of production and control of creativity by the economic sector, standardization, syncretization by recovery of various stylistic odds and ends, homogenization of these styles by actual musical rewriting done by arrangers whose role, as Adorno said, is to *predigest* music in order to increase sales."[48] All these conditionings, along with many others, act upon contemporary musical life.

---

[47]Paul Beaud and Alfred Willener, *Musique et vie quotidienne*, 11.

[48]Paul Beaud, "Musique, masses, minorités, marginaux," *IRASM* V/1 (1974) 159.

On the other hand, it is not only the reactions of the public that merit attention, important as they may be to the centers of musical activity. The active social role of the public extends beyond these particular centers into social spheres, economic or financial spheres, or spheres of politics and publicity that are sometimes equally or even more decisive in shaping the destiny of musical works. The public also exercises a more or less overt and important musical criticism.[49]

---

[49]See Armand Machabey, *Traité de la critique musicale*, 37-41.

CHAPTER TWO

SOCIAL ROLES OF VARIOUS AUDIENCES

I • THE MUSICAL PUBLIC AS A SOCIAL FACTOR

According to Jacques Handschin's formulation, each musical genre is always related and addressed to a certain type of man,[1] but this idea needs to be understood and enlarged in an anthropological and cultural direction. If this formula is to be accepted, it must be in terms of a public that, as instrument of reception, permits the activity of the composer to be measured and constitutes a sort of recording apparatus on which the history of music is inscribed.[2] In addition, the public belongs among the essential factors "which exert the necessary catalyzing functions on the composer."[3] The assertion that "the composer is dominated, even without his own knowledge, by his thinking about the public for which his work is destined"[4] could be examined to see how far and in what sense this domination may extend in any particular case. But it is indisputable that the destiny of musical works is fixed, across the ages, by the

---

[1] See Jacques Handschin, *Histoire de la musique,* printed in part in *Musica Aeterna* (Zürich-Lausanne-Brussels: M. S. Metz, 1948) 126.

[2] See Lionel de La Laurencie, *Le Goût musical en France,* 4.

[3] Jacques Chailley, *40,000 ans de musique,* 272.

[4] Armand Machabey, *Traité de la critique musicale,* 37.

"musical community" as a whole:[5] public[6] and musicians[7] taken together. There is no transmission of masterworks without a "collective testimony of previous generations."[8] Also, musical language "does not organize itself solely as a function of some sort of internal necessity; certain innovations achieve citizenship, others do not, according to whether the community admits them or not; the formation and the development of musical language depend at the same time on the innovations of composers, on a certain internal logic, and on acceptance, sooner or later, by the listener."[9]

---

[5]*Ibid.*, 37.

[6]As Jacques Chailley wrote, "It would be desirable to stop, once and for all, invoking at every turn a carefully selected, expurgated history stripped of all explanatory context, of these pseudo non–understandings of genius on the part of a public invariably presented as backward. This tendentious notion serves only to avoid the real problem. On the other hand, the lack of understanding has always been much greater, more serious and lasting on the part of professionals, critics, or colleagues of different aesthetic points of view, depending sometimes on the fatuity of a demi-culture, sometimes on a theoretical and practical formation which presented as eternal rules a factual state of affairs which the work at hand would then just proceed to surpass." ("La radio et le développement de l'instinct harmonique chez les auditeurs," *Cahiers d'études de Radio-Télévision* III-IV (1955) 403.)

[7]History furnishes numerous examples of this. Like many other composers, Campra wrote roles to show off the artists "by increasing the number of ariettes and dances which display the virtuosity of a singer or the agility of a dancer. It is not surprising that works of this time [1705-1722] are full of these pieces which attract the attention of the public and applause. Why did Campra write new airs for the reprise of *Hesione* in 1709, if not to show off the brilliance of an actress?. . . The success of his operas depend not only on their own value or the pleasure of the public, but on musicians, actors and their agents. . . To a large extent these conditions influenced his production during this very active period of his life." Maurice Barthélemy, *André Campra, sa vie et son oeuvre (1660-1744)* (Paris: Picard, 1957) 101-102.

[8]See Armand Machabey, *Traité de la critique musicale,* 37.

[9]Guy Hentsch, "Quelques réflexions sur la situation de la musique actuelle," *Feuilles musicales* I (1951) 6.

II • PRESENCE AND ABSENCE OF A MUSICAL PUBLIC

The simple presence or absence of a public already exerts a certain influence on music. It is known that Terpander of Lesbos, Thaletas of Gortynia, Xenodamos of Cythera, Xenocrites of Locris, Polymnestos of Colophon, and Sakadas of Argos were musically active at Sparta. "The foreign origin of most of these great artists (if it is not quite probable that Tyrteus was Athenian, Alcman seems indeed to have come from Sardis) testifies less to the creative impotence of Sparta than to its power of attraction (just as the career of a Händel or a Gluck attests, for their time, the power of London or Paris). If creators and virtuosi flowed into Sparta from all areas, it was because they were assured of finding there a worthy public and opportunities to make themselves known."[10]

Inversely, there is a simple reason why masterworks such as the Passions or Cantatas of Bach remained unnoticed. No public existed for them. The faithful at the church of St. Thomas came to the religious services mostly for religious reasons and not for music. In times when the public was unruly, as in the fifteenth century, the mysteries opened and were punctuated by pieces expressly entitled "*silete* (be quiet) and some of them were effectively sung with words such as *silete, silete, silentium habete*. The overtures of the first operas functioned only to silence the public (just as in today's music hall) and we can thus explain why it had, for Monteverdi, the character of a brilliant fanfare; for Lully, the stereotyped aspect of a solemn introduction in a pointed rhythm, and why it had to wait for Gluck and Mozart to give it a dramatic significance, which would become generalized from Wagner on."[11]

In seventeenth-century London and eighteenth-century Paris, respectively, John Banister and Anne Danican Philidor were able to establish their paying public concerts only thanks to the

---

[10]Henri-Irénée Marrou, *Histoire de l'éducation dans l'Antiquité*, 4th ed. (Paris: Seuil, 1958) 44.

[11]Jacques Chailley, *40,000 ans de musique*, 296.

presence of a potential public.[12] In the same way, the salons of La Pouplinière, Crozat, or the Prince of Conti could not have become centers of interest in music and its performance without the attention of a public of amateurs.[13] Likewise, the "transformations which appear at the end of the sixteenth century and which will fundamentally modify the conditions of musical life, and especially the social function of music in France,"[14] are due in part to the public. Until then, music was a part of a daily life in all social classes; now this entertainment music begins to decline. With rare exceptions, the court will be the focus for the evolution of French music, beginning with Louis XIII,[15] or more exactly, the evolution of its most developed, learned and artistic sector. For the art of music continues to be practiced elsewhere although it does tend to be less a part of everyday life. "It is also in the period of 1630–40 that the decline of the popular corporation (the 'players of instruments,' who were the only musicians of the previous century to exist outside the court) begins to set in."[16] Furthermore, a restricted public of privileged people partially explains, in a sociological way, the birth of chamber music. Initially, "chamber music was not intended to be heard by 'clients' as today, but for the pleasure of those who performed it."[17] This music is in opposition "to entertainment music, because it is only composed to be performed by a few chosen musicians, before an intimate audience."[18] As the French monarchy was no longer itinerant and was becoming centralized, the "predilection of the court for the dance easily explains the

---

[12]Cf. Ibid., 105-106 and 128; and Louis Striffling, Esquisse d'une histoire du goût musical en France au XVIIIᵉ siècle (Paris: Delagrave, 1912) 125-131.

[13]See Ibid., 122-124.

[14]François Lesure, La naissance de l'orchestre en France au début du XVIIᵉ siècle, 1561.

[15]See Ibid., 1562.

[16]François Lesure, "Chambonnières, organisateur de concerts (1641)," Revue belge de musicologie III/3 (1949) 143.

[17]Jacques Chailley, 40,000 ans de musique, 120.

[18]Lionel de La Laurencie, "Les débuts de la musique de chambre en France," Revue de musicologie XLIX (1934) 25.

rapid development of the dance suite."[19] This also explains the triumph of the *air de cour*, and especially the development of the *ballet de cour*.[20]

It is also in terms of the public that we can explain, sociologically, the birth of the concert. The concert brought about a reduction in the size of the public,[21] but the public, in the long run, assured the life of the concert. The intimate music played at the first concerts "delighted literary circles: a remarkable example is the Baïf Academy, established in 1570 by patents of Charles IX . . . Its success was such, according to Scévole de Sainte-Marthe, that the king and the princes of the court were eager to be present at these melodious concerts."[22] Thus, these and the first real concerts known to history were not accessible to just anyone. They were ceremonies for an initiated audience, and were originally of a somewhat religious character.[23] But their public did exist. About two centuries later, the French academies disappeared one after another, being unable to survive the Revolution, because they were deprived of their most ardent public—the aristocrats, and certain bourgeois milieus.[24] The presence or absence of a public depends, evidently, on socio-historical and socio-artistic conditions.

For now it will suffice to focus attention on the significance of this simple fact. Its importance designates it as a subject for study in the sociology of music, for this state of public presence or absence accordingly permits or discourages the practice of music, and orients it in a more or less determined direction.

---

[19]Francois Lesure, *La naissance de l'orchestre en France au début du XVIIe siècle*, 1563.

[20]See François Lesure, "Réflexions sur les origines du concert parisien," *Polyphonie* V (1949) 50.

[21]See *Ibid.*, 51.

[22]Lionel de La Laurencie, "Les débuts de la musique de chambre en France," *Revue de musicologie* XLIX (1934) 28. See also Michel Brenet, *Les Concerts en France sous l'ancien Régime*, 32; and Paul Loubet de Sceaury, *Musiciens et facteurs d'instruments de Musique sous l'ancien Régime*, 60.

[23]See Jacques Chailley, *40,000 ans de musique*, 121.

[24]See Humphrey Burton, "Les Académies de musique en France au XVIIIe siècle," *Revue de musicologie* CXII (1955) 142.

Today we cannot analyze the situation concerning contemporary music without considering the presence or absence of the public.

III • ATTITUDES OF THE PUBLIC

It is not only the presence of the public and its instantaneous reactions—its first attitudes, whether favorable or unfavorable, to musical works that are sociologically important. Numerous cases exist in which the public attached hardly any importance to works or to new artistic accomplishments that were, nonetheless, destined for a long future. The operas of Piccini, for example, had at the beginning more success with the Parisian public than those of Gluck;[25] this same public gave little attention to the appearance of the first piano in 1769;[26] it did not receive the symphonies of Haydn without mistrust, and later snubbed Berlioz (although he exaggerated the depth of his disgrace before the public).[27] The problem, then, goes beyond the immediate success or failure of a work.[28] As for the lack of success, sometimes "it is the insufficiency of the work which determines it; it may result as well from a disproportion between the conception of the artist and that which the public is capable of."[29] This does not foreclose the future for a work, but can even work in its favor, besides partly explaining the immediate failure. Thus, what is decisive to the future of a musical work, is a certain favorable *constancy* or *continuity* in the reactions and the interest of the whole musical community

[25]See Armand Machabey, *Traité de la critique musicale*, 53.

[26]See Michel Brenet, *Les Concerts en France sous l'ancien Régime*, 292-293, 334-335; Lionel de La Laurencie, "Les débuts de la musique de chambre en France," *Revue de musicologie* LII (1934) 204; Norbert Dufourcq, *La musique française* (Paris: Larousse, 1949) 210.

[27]See *Ibid.*, 196.

[28]See Etienne Souriau, "L'insertion temporelle de l'oeuvre d'art," *Journal de psychologie* I-II (1951) 38-62.

[29]Lionel de La Laurencie, *Le Goût musical en France*, 4.

(public and musicians), which is perpetuated within the given cultural and social ambiance in which the work has been performed. The dynamics of this continuity, more or less affirmed, ought to be studied along different scales, in order to follow the destinies of different works and genres of music up to the present. The absence of this continuity, like the pure and simple absence of the public, explains why most of the works of Schütz and Bach, for example, have for a long time remained unknown to a large audience.

The role of the public, however, is in no way reducible to a reaction *a posteriori*, which would only concern a work already performed in public. It doubles as a positive influence exerted on the creation and diffusion of musical works, as well as on future performance practice and musical interpretation. It not only confirms or rejects works, once realized, but also solicits their creation and performance.[30] In addition, this role of the public explains, many attitudes and actions of musicians, composers and interpreters.

The actions, reactions, and demands of the public are reflected in a great many aspects of musical life. In the sixteenth century the instruments appreciated above all others in cultivated milieus were the instruments with plucked or bowed strings: harpsichords, spinets, and viols. As reported by Sauval and Mersenne,[31] the concerts continuing the meetings of the Baïf Academy, held around 1590 by the musician Jacques Maudit, mirrored this definitive French fashion—an example of public's influence over the use of instruments. In the eighteenth century, the Parisian public favored competitions between virtuosi: violinists, such as Guignon and Anet, and later Guignon and Mondonville; or singers, such as Todi and Mara. At that time the interpreter sought to surprise and astonish the audience by the original and ingenious character of his performance; he was encouraged in

---

[30]We can find some illustrations of this for example already in Michel Brenet, *Les Concerts en France sous l'ancien Régime*, 343-345.

[31]See Lionel de La Laurencie, "Les débuts de la musique de chambre en France," *Revue de musicologie* XLIX (1934) 29.

this by a somewhat superficial and not very educated public; this situation was later pushed to an extreme, especially in Italy.[32] Campra and Danchet made numerous changes in their works from performance to performance, hoping to "retrieve the favor of the public which had given them a fairly cold reception for several years."[33] In Germany also, composers such as Johann Theile, Reinhard Keiser and others tried to anticipate the demands of the public in the composition of their operas.[34] And "as the huge aristocratic fortunes evaporated, a savage inflation and post-war depression after 1815 made the support of a paying audience essential to the satisfactory performance of opera and of large-scale orchestral music . . . The general public had to be invited because the special public to whom the court musician had addressed his communications assembled less and less frequently in princely salons and music rooms. Music and musicians turned to the general public for support because the traditional patrons were no longer able to play their traditional role in music . . . "[35]

The cutting up and pasting together of different fragments was a common practice in the eighteenth century. These patch works called *potpourris* were devised to vary the pleasure of the audience.[36] To satisfy the public of neophytes, entrepreneurs and composers were led to make concessions and accept compromises. In Paris, Legros took the same precaution with the *Carmen Seculare* of Philidor as he took with the *Stabat Mater* of Haydn: he cut it into fragments separated by different pieces of

[32]See Michel Brenet, *Les Concerts en France sous l'ancien Régime*, 320: Louis Striffling, *Esquisse d'une histoire du goût musical en France au XVIIIᵉ siècle*, 149-150.

[33]Maurice Barthélemy, *André Campra, sa vie et son oeuvre* (Paris: Picard, 1957) 108.

[34]See Marcel Beaufils, *Par la musique vers l'obscur* (Marseille; F. Robert, 1942) 180-185. New edition: *Comment l'Allemagne est devenue musicienne* (Paris: Laffont 1983).

[35]Henry Raynor, *Music and Society Since 1815* (New York: Schocken Books, 1976) 1.

[36]See Louis Striffling, *Esquisse d'une histoire du goût musical en France au XVIIIᵉ siècle*, 145. On the adaptations of the times, see also Léon Vallas, *Un siècle de musique et de théâtre à Lyon* (Lyon: P. Masson, 1932) 44.

a lighter genre, in order to make them acceptable to the public.[37] By means of such concessions, the audience accepted a little "learned music."[38] In the eighteenth century, small, light pieces were in the greatest vogue, and this influenced publication. Ballard printed whole volumes of them in Paris.[39] In the seventeenth century, music lived also from day to day, and knew only richnesses that were ephemeral.[40] The search of music for entertainment and dance in the twentieth century, never before so extensive, is in itself hardly a novelty.

The contemporary repertory of ancient music, serious and selected, and of an incontestable artistic value, often represented only an object of entertainment for the public of its time. Thus, at one point in the nineteenth century, Mozart and Beethoven would have been considered by the Viennese public as "old pedants," incapable of satisfying their desires, just like Johann Sebastian Bach, who, it seems, was once called "an old wig" by his own son Johann Christian.[41] However, both of them wrote music for "entertainment." Mozart composed *"divertimenti,* serenades, cassations, and night music, for the most varied instrumental combinations . . . ; these works of circumstance were then an obligatory part of musical and social life."[42] The public also influenced Chopin, as much in the genres he preferred to cultivate as in their actual character. It is "in the salons that Chopin found the atmosphere which most pleased him, the society which he appreciated the most: a restricted but understanding public whose loud and enthusiastic admiration counted only for him."[43] This is noticeable especially in waltzes and several mazurkas, but also to some degree in the nocturnes.

---

[37]See Michel Brenet, *Les Concerts en France sous l'ancien Régime,* 343.
[38]See *Ibid.,* 343-344.
[39]See *Ibid.,* 43-44 and 83.
[40]See *Ibid.,* 45.
[41]See Jacques Chailley, *40,000 ans de musique,* 63.
[42]Claude Rostand, *La musique allemande,* 72.
[43]Louis Bronarski, "La musique de Chopin et la musique de salon" *La Revue musicale* CLXVIII (1936) 236. See also: Louis Bronarski, *Etudes sur Chopin,* 2nd ed., (Lausanne: Ed. La Concorde, 1947) 83.

We could find many other examples of this kind of influence exerted on composers by the public.

IV • SOCIAL DEMAND

Immediate or direct social demand that assumes the form of a pure and simple command furnishes a special case of the action of the public on musical activity. One of the normal working conditions of the artist, engaged in the service of a particular individual, group or institution, has been to receive and execute commands for music. Music thus composed was intended most often for the individual or the group that issued the order, and thus bore dedications to them.[44] Social command does not characterize only certain global societies; it is linked to the socially inferior or subordinate position of the musician. This inferiority of position is pervasive except in certain tribal communities, and even there the musician's position often remains ambivalent.[45] In European history, only a few musicians profited from a privileged status—usually composers, such as Marenzio, Gesualdo, Lasso, Schütz or Händel. As to the heads of royal or princely courts, a prodigious amount of music was created for them and, in theory at least, exclusively for them. Their entourage and their guests benefited only as a surplus or almost through encroachment.[46] In several societies the commands addressed to musicians came from a public that belonged generally to an institution, class, or social group more privileged than the musician and thus able to exert pressure on him rather easily in order to obtain the desired result.

---

[44]See Manfred F. Bukofzer, *Music in the Baroque Era* (New York: Norton, 1947) 409.

[45]See p. 200-1.

[46]Jacques Chailley, *40,000 ans de musique*, 116. In addition, François Lesure introduces an appropriate term pertaining to this subject, distinct from that of "consumers" of music—i.e., that of "utilizers." The utilizers are presented, most importantly by the "mécènes" who ordered music, for whom it was written, or even dedicated, and who played it exclusively, or almost so. (See: *Musica e società*, 33-43.)

Thus, according to Hickmann, the first known musician of ancient Egypt, and possibly even the first in the entire history of music—Khoufou-'Ankh, singer head of the pharaoh's singers and overseer of the flutists, who lived near the end of the Fourth Dynasty (2563 B.C.)—had to say, even then, all sorts of nice things to his master every day. The pharaoh met with him daily, so great was his esteem for him.[47] His situation strongly recalls that of the composer to the Sun King, Michel-Richard Delalande, more than four thousand years later. He is not, like many others, a simple servant; Louis XIV lodges him in his château, visits him at work several times a day, and obliges him to touch up and redo his works until he, the king, is satisfied with them.[48] To fill up the programs at court, Delalande wrote numerous divertissements, pastorales, motets and symphonies, which were ordinarily played "at the king's supper."[49] Under these conditions, his creative work was necessarily produced on demand. An analogous situation existed between Heinrich Graun and Frederick the Great.[50] A book written about music "in the service of the king" in seventeenth-century France gives an extensive picture of musical life before and during the reign of Louis XIV, with special emphasis on operas and the centralization of music at the time.[51]

In Italy, at the Gonzaga court in Mantua, Jacques de Wert worked regularly on command. Much of his output was the normal product of his professional position as composer and *maître de chapelle*, and thus the official court musician. And so he

---

[47]See Hans Hickmann, *Le Métier de musicien au temps des Pharaons* (Cairo: Cahiers d'histoire égyptienne, 1954) series VI/5-6 pp. 257-258. See also J. Capart, and M. Werbrouck, *Memphis* (Brussels: 1930) 255 (cited in *ibid.*, 257-258).

[48]See Michel Brenet, *Les Concerts en France sous l'ancien Régime*, 64-65; and Norbert Dufourcq and others. *Notes et références pour servir à une histoire de Michel-Richard Delalande* (Paris: Picard, 1957) 150.

[49]See *ibid.*, 240, 255-269, 275 and 278; and Georges Cucuel, *La Pouplinière et la musique de chambre au XVIIIe siècle* (Paris: Fischbacher, 1913) 387.

[50]See Marcel Beaufils, *Par la musique vers l'obscur*, 34.

[51]See Robert M. Isherwood, *Music in the Service of the King. France in the Seventeenth Century* (Ithaca and London: Cornell U. Press, 1973).

puts into music the *Laudes of Santa Barbara*, patroness of the dynasty: "he receives precise instructions for this and agrees to follow them in beginning with the first ton on the invocation of the Trinity."[52] Campra also received many orders. The Duchess de la Ferté commanded a divertissement from him in 1698, and Arnoul, superintendant of the galleys and of commerce at Marseille, ordered another divertissement for the disembarkment of the Queen of Spain into that city in 1714; well before, Campra composed a divertissement ordered by the Duc de Sully.[53] With this work Campra wished to shine before the Duc de Chartres; he wanted to please the pleasure-loving society of Sully, the Contis and all those who looked to Versailles for entertainment. In this milieu, Campra is seeking protectors.[54] Well before this, Josquin des Pres himself composed polyphonic pieces at the command of Louis XII, where one part was likewise reserved for the *Vox Regis*.[55] To celebrate the Peace of Utrecht in July of 1713, the authorities ordered music for the occasion and paid Jean-Philippe Rameau, official musician of Lyons, to furnish it.[56] Buxtehude, Mozart, Beethoven, and many others have worked on command, bending themselves, in that way, to the demands of quite varied publics, whose social position, however, remained consistently dominant or privileged.

V • MOTIVATIONS FOR MUSIC

The desires of the public and its reactions and attitudes within given social frameworks, as well as beyond them, could be and

---

[52]Anne-Marie Bautier-Regnier, "Musiciens d'Oultremont à la Cour de Mantoue, Jacques de Wert (1535-1596)," *Revue belge de musicologie* IV/1-2 (1950) 63.

[53]See Maurice Barthélemy, *André Campra, sa vie et son oeuvre*, 21 and 114; and Id. "Le premier Divertissement connu d'André Campra," *Revue belge de musicologie* XI/1-2 (1957) 51-53.

[54] See *Ibid.*, 53.

[55]See Paul H. Lang, *Music in Western Civilization*, 299.

[56]See Léon Vallas, *Un siècle de musique et de théâtre à Lyon (1688-1789)*, 132.

in fact are differently motivated during different periods of history. These *motivations* can be classed in two fundamental categories (which often interpenetrate): *social* motivations and *aesthetic* motivations. The former concern the needs and conceptions predominating in a given social framework, and its social psychology and collective mentality. They raise first of all questions of sociohistorical conditionings. These will be illustrated in the following sections.[57] We will confine ourselves here to one example—that of the Parisian music public in the first half of the eighteenth century. At this time, people appreciate music more every day for the pleasures it can bring to fashionable society, a society where idleness continually gives rise to boredom. Fashion and conventions are mixed up together; everyone now prides himself for loving music and regaling his hosts with a concert. Music has become an art of pleasure, necessary to any distinguished education.[58]

But aesthetic motivations are no less interesting, because they can indicate the direction and development of taste and purely aesthetic judgments in different social groupings.[59] Reversing the question, we can say that "to study the behavior of social groups in regard to works of art, is . . . to discover the roots of artistic judgments,"[60] that is, to try to explain aesthetic conceptions and tastes on sociological grounds, even though we may not always be able to succeed.[61] According to Rudolph Heinemann, "taste is 'only a deeply rooted, ethnocentric rationalization

---

[57]See below p. 125 and following.

[58]Louis Striffling, *Esquisse d'une histoire du goût musical en France au XVIIIᵉ siècle*, 118. See also Michel Brenet, *Les Concerts en France sous l'ancien Régime*, 230.

[59]In the work by de La Laurencie on the history of musical taste in France, the author furnishes very few considerations of a properly sociological order.

[60]Gisèle Brelet, Report in *Revue d'esthétique* III/3-4 (1950) 437.

[61]In regard to the sociohistorical conditionings of musical taste, see the results of the interesting investigations done by Karl F. Schuessler, "Social Background and Musical Taste," *American Sociological Review* XIII/3 (1948) 330-335); and Paul R. Farnsworth, *Musical Taste, Its Measurement and Cultural Nature* (Stanford, California: Stanford U., 1950).

bearing habitual modes of thought,"[62] which is subject in most cases to social norms of behavior, and only for very few men depends on the quality of music itself."[63]

In this way we could explain the doctrine of the expressive value of music—of the *ethos* of different modes—that we find in ancient Greece (from Plato and Aristotle throughout the whole Hellenistic tradition). This was a belief in the psychological and moral efficacy of music, which arose perhaps from a belief in its material and magical efficacy. In archaic times, before the mode (or better, the *nomos*) became a certain type of abstract scale, it existed in the form of a certain number of typical works united by the sàme style, the same moral value and often the same social usage. The doctrine of music's innately expressive qualities was founded on the meaning or expressive significance of the mode, resulting from the consistency of its use. This expressive value was rather of a sociological order, as was, in part, the doctrine in question as well. This became absurd only when the structure of the modal scales was transformed, to the detriment of their expressive value, and when the nomenclature of the scales changed so that it was no longer clear which one referred to which expressive significance.[64]

The continued life of many works is due not only to artistic factors, but also, in part, to social factors: "if a work endures or is revived centuries later, it is because it is affected by a *constant* which persists in an identical relation with another, sociological, *constant*, immutable from one century to another or at least affected by a coefficient of infinitesimal change."[65] But we can

---

[62]Heinemann refers to John H. Mueller, *Fragen des musikalischen Geschmacks. Eine musiksoziologische Studie* (Cologne-Opladen: 1963) 114.

[63]Rudolf Heinemann, Der Hörer zwischen Musikwissenschaft, Soziologie und Kulturkritik, 563.

[64]See Henri-Irénée Marrou, *Histoire de l'éducation dans l'Antiquité*, 197-198; and Charles Lalo, *Eléments d'une esthétique musicale scientifique*, 17. See also Edward A. Lippman, *Musical Thought in Ancient Greece* (New York-London: Columbia U. Press, 1964) 45-86; and Warren D. Anderson, *Ethos and Education in Greek Music* (Cambridge, Mass.: Harvard U. Press, 1966) 31-36, 43-44, 46-50, 52-55.

[65]Armand Machabey, *Traité de la critique musicale*, 45.

also "envisage a second interpretation of the phenomenon and consider that the permanent favor which a work enjoys is due to a relationship which is progressively established between the music and another level of society as it evolves. Thus music would hold in its power different centers of attraction which would act successively, following the march of time, and all affected by the same potential, since it seems to be equally appreciated in different times and milieus. And it really is *equally* appreciated, but for *different* motives."[66] The independent existence of a body of music in spite of societal change is linked, one could say, to a "state of permanent flight before the perpetual aestheticization of its works by a market and a history of art which exposes and judges them;"[67] or, in other words, to a constant aesthetic, socioeconomic and scientific reevaluation. Many questions relating to these assertions, as well as the motives themselves, constitute an area of fruitful study for the sociology of music: not only questions of conscious motives, but especially of motivations that pass beyond individual personalized judgments and can show us the collective unconscious. Moreover, musicians participate in this as well as the public.[68]

VI • EVOLUTION OF MUSICAL TASTE

The active social role of the public in the history of music, however, should not mask the influence of musical art on the aesthetic and psychological evolution of the public. Here is an example: the length of Beethoven's symphonies was a considerable obstacle to their favorable reception by the public of that

---

[66]*Ibid.*, 45-46.

[67]Peter Gorsen, "Marxisme et esthétique: Perspectives d'une problématique nouvelle. *Les Sciences humaines et l'oeuvre d'art* (Brussels: La Connaissance, 1969) 209-244; p. 228 quoted in Paul Beaud and Alfred Willener, *Musique et vie quotidienne*, 38-39.

[68]See Maurice Halbwachs, "La mémoire collective chez les musiciens," *Revue philosophique* CXXVII (1939) 136-165; and Constantin Braïloïu, "Réflexions sur la création musicale collective," *Diogène* XXV (1959) 83-93.

day (and contemporary criticism cast this fact into clear relief). The Ninth, however, the last and the longest, did not meet with the same obstacle: The public was by then already prepared and accustomed to this characteristic.[69] "The effect of Beethoven's work was to make unprecedented demands not only on instrumentalists but on their audiences. The *Eroica*, written in 1803, lasts almost as long as any two symphonies by Haydn and Mozart; the Ninth Symphony lasts half as long again ... Such works, before the days of the long-playing gramophone record, could not become familiar, and familiarity is a necessary ingredient of devotion to any music. But Beethoven also demanded an unprecedented concentration and development of the musical memory ... "[70] Analogously, the French public, used to conciseness and brevity, grew but slowly accustomed to the length of the symphonies of Bruckner and Mahler.[71] And "today, our ears, assaulted constantly by the sharpness of new harmonies, are less sensitive to the differences in tuning of a piano in equal temperament and a violin, with Pythagorean intervals, playing together with a horn having natural intervals; the total capacity of attention is not less, it is only directed elsewhere."[72] These facts testify also to an evolution in music. An influence of this sort is sometimes considerable and involves sociologically important consequences. Thus in archaic Greece "there is a perfect equilibrium between musical art (still poor in means, sober and simple), culture, and education. This equilibrium is abruptly upset when the great composers—Melanippides, Cinesias, Phrynis and Timotheus—introduce into their musical writing a whole series of refinements ... accompanied by parallel improvements in instrument making. Very soon, under their influence, Greek music becomes complicated, its technique becomes so elaborated that amateurs can no longer master it, and its apprenticeship demands from then on an effort which

---

[69]See Armand Machabey, *Traité de la critique musicale*, 96-97.
[70]Henry Raynor, *Music and Society Since 1815*, 149.
[71]See Armand Machabey, *op. cit.*, p. 96-97.
[72]Jacques Chailley, *Histoire musicale du Moyen Age*, 63.

only few specialists can sustain. This evolution begun at the end of the fifth century continues throughout the fourth century.[73] It ends finally in a profound separation between professional art and popular art. The first disappeared without further development, while the latter, deprived of support from first-rate artists, falls in the hands of actors who bring it to Rome, and there it also disappears without any trace. It is only due to the Pythagoreans, who remained apart from this process, that the fruits of Hellenistic music theory have been preserved.[74]

But music can also create different tendencies within the public; some are expressed in specific attitudes that themselves display an active function with regard to music. Other, bursting forth spontaneously from the public itself, react upon the music and performance. Far from prevailing automatically, however, they can enter into conflict because of their reciprocal action. Historically, there is a progressive increase in the heterogeneity of tendencies within art music, which is also a result of its progressive enrichment, such that in the twentieth century we are witnesses to a phenomenon previously unknown in the history of music: an extraordinary expansion and differentiation of music. According to de La Laurencie, musical taste itself "is included in the law of passage from homogeneity to heterogeneity—in other words, from the simple to the composite. This law is expressed in three principal ways, affirming itself in three very clear directions: taste evolves from monody to polyphony; taste is expressed originally in a collective fashion and then leads toward individualism; taste, finally, bends itself to modes of expression more and more extensive, which go from anthropomorphism to love of nature."[75] It remains to be seen, however, whether history will not reveal many exceptions to these "laws". In reality, the problems of *musical taste* prove to be so complex that they cannot be discussed here in a specific and detailed manner, taking into consideration all aspects existing

---

[73]See Henri-Irénée Marrou, *Histoire de l'éducation dans l'Antiquité*, 195.

[74]See Jacques Chailley, "Vue sur les lendemains d'hier," *Polyphonie* III (1949/3) 65-66.

[75]Lionel de La Laurencie, *Le Goût musical en France*, 10.

from one case to another. These are not all of a strictly sociological order, but may be psychological, aesthetic, etc. The sociology of musical taste is only in its beginning stages, and works belonging within its proper domain are rare.[76]

Never have there been so many musicians, so many works composed, and such a diversity of orientation and aesthetics, as in the twentieth century. But neither has there been such a diversity of mass audiences (of race, class, nationality, mentality, age, culture and profession), with a volume as great as that today.[77] And this double differentiation of contemporary music taken in its totality on one hand, and of the public, on the other, is without doubt one of the artistic and sociological causes of the divorce apparent today between these composers and these publics.

It would be interesting to see to what extent, in different societies, we could confirm a hypothesis recently proposed for France: that for "cultural activities outside the home, individual consumption follows a progression proportionate to the rise in the standard of living, to the lowering of the average age of the population, to the advancement in schooling and its prolong-ation . . . and partially, to the development of urbanization," although this can also "include a diminution of time available for cultural activities, and even their disappearance, principally because of fatigue due to travel and the lack of collectively owned equipment."[78]

---

[76]See footnotes 61 and 62, p. 117-8.

[77]See Etienne Gilson, *La Société de masse et sa culture* (Paris: Vrin, 1967) 47-74, and the section "Das Musikpublikum in der industriellen Gesellschaft," in Walter Wiora, *Komponist und Mitwelt*, 69-73.

[78]Paul Beaud and Alfred Willener, *Musique et vie quotidienne*, 10.

CHAPTER THREE

MUSIC AND SOCIAL STRATIFICATIONS

I • SOCIAL DIFFERENTIATION AND MUSICAL PRACTICE

The question of the relationship between music and social groups—and more particularly, social classes—is in part only a refinement of the question of the relationship between music and the public. If by *social class* we mean "the totality of social groups having common economic interests, or groups whose members are, in a sense, in the same economic situation,"[1] we may note that there exists, in the history of music, a certain evolution corresponding to the rise and decline of social classes within global social structures. Each social class has its own universe of values, modes of thought, psychology and life-style. At the same time that it creates spheres of political and economic interest, it both takes part in them and flows from them.[2] As G. Gurvitch wrote, "no less known . . . are the differentiated roles played by various social classes, as well as by the groups and strata of which classes constitute the hierarchical macrocosms. It seems likely that not only at different moments or stages of its existence, but even under differing conditions, each class may

---

[1]Stanislaw Ossowski, "Les différents aspects de la classe sociale chez Marx," *Cahiers internationaux de sociologie* XXIV (1958) 67.

[2]See for example Henri Lefebvre, "Psychologie des classes sociales" *Traité de sociologie* vol. II (Paris: P.U.F., 1960) 364-386.

play roles which are far from being identical."[3] Evidently, the sociologist may elaborate various concepts of social classes: "the word class (*Klasse*) will, except for the propertied classes (*Besitzklassen*), have, in the broadest sociological sense, the same meaning as social layer (*Gesellschaftsschicht*) in general, as in the English *class* and the French *classe*."[4] Thus Walter Wiora prefers the terminology according to which "stratum (*Stand*) and class (*Klasse*) are two basic types of social layers, and this, the generalized main concept."[5] Clearly, the sociologist must define with care the words he uses. As for ourselves, we should prefer as our main general concept that of *social group*, because it covers social classes, layers, strata, and groupings. But in particular the evolution of social classes, their roles, their positions and their importance within the global society, can furnish interesting explanations of certain phenomena in the history of music: the inner bifurcation of musical art into popular music and learned music,[6] its division into two blocks, the one "uncultured" and the other "cultivated" or that which Charles Lalo has called the dualism of "popular" and "aristocratic" art which "is found in all civilisations, however little organized,"[7] and which has existed throughout history, offers an example of the greatest importance. We note, however that this division has not forced a complete or definite break in the artistic sphere, where—on the contrary—reciprocal influences have appeared and continue to appear with more of less frequency and intensity up to today: a striking example of an aesthetic commerce actuated sometimes under the pressures of purely artistic conditions, and sometimes under the pressure of sociohistorical conditionings that encourage

---

[3]Georges Gurvitch, "Sociologie du théâtre," *Les Lettres nouvelles* XXXV (1956) 198.

[4]Walter Wiora, "Der musikalische Ausdruck von Ständen und Klassen in eigenen Stilen," *IRASM* V/1 (1974) 94.

[5]*Ibid.* See also Walter Wiora, "Discussion," *IRASM* VI/1 (1975) 100-102.

[6]For lack of a better expression, we can employ that of learned or art music.

[7]Charles Lalo, *L'art et la vie sociale*, 140.

these points of contact.[8] Contrary cases do exist, however. Take that, for example, of the songs of the "little people," the laborers or workers of the thirteenth century. An almost insurmountable social barrier permitted almost no reciprocal influence between what they could sing and what was sung in the castle. The two "folklores developed simultaneously, in almost complete ignorance of each other."[9] Also, "in the historical context of eighteenth-century Paris, high culture was rather sharply distinguished from popular culture in the realm of musical entertainment. The two cultures differed basically in three ways. First, there was a clear distinction between classical and popular musical entertainments with respect to form, style, and content. Second, the two cultures appealed to different taste publics in part because they appeared in very divergent physical settings. Toward the end of the century, however, distinctions of taste and audience were not as great when popular culture captured the fancy of the high born. The third distinction involved the monopolistic privilege wielded by the older, prestigious musical and dramatic companies. Throughout the eighteenth century, low musical culture struggled to survive the repeated attacks of the privileged theaters who were determined to drive popular entertainment from existence, or to control it."[10]

Musical life takes its place in the life of social classes, strata, layers and groupings responding thus to their dynamics in various ways, and playing an active and more or less important role since antiquity. For example, in Egypt during the Ptolmaic period, as H. Hickman has shown, "the temples, the common districts of the towns and the countryside, continued to maintain a musical tradition without too much difficulty, while rich districts, the administrative centers in the provinces with their

---

[8]The relationships between popular music and art music deserve separate study from a sociological point of view. The principal question to examine would be that of reciprocal influences and of autonomous evolution under the pressure of extramusical social facts.

[9]Jacques Chailley, *Histoire musicale du Moyen Age*, 182.

[10]Robert M. Isherwood, "Popular Musical Entertainment in eighteenth-century Paris," *IRASM* IX/2 (1978) 295.

tradesmen and foreign officials, and some individuals of the Egyptian elite, took up the new musical culture spready by well known performers, cultivated at the court of the Ptolemys and taught in the schools."[11] In Greece, musical performance was forbidden to slaves in the public ceremonies, as music was considered a distinguishing mark of the free citizen and the status and education reserved for him.[12] In the Middle Ages, the horn "came to symbolize the feudal hero[13] . . . The oliphant was introduced into Western Europe in the tenth century; it came from Byzantium where it partly represented the insignia of a warrior or horseman, conforming to his oriental heritage[14]."[15] These two instruments became the exclusive property of kings, princes, nobles and chivalry; the feudal warrior always carried his horn with him. The accompaniment of the pipe, on the other hand, was especially popular among the lower classes, particularily in Provence. At the end of the Middle Ages a reaction set in against these two instruments because of their association with musicians of low estate—peasant amateurs, wandering minstrels and herdsmen.[16] According to Edmund A. Bowles, "throughout the Middle Ages bagpipes came to be associated with the humble, with shepherds and peasants, and later even with miserable people of all sorts. The instrument still benefited from its rustic heritage and was popular for accompanying rural festivities, dances and weddings . . . Little by little an image was born associating the bagpipes with wastrels and malefactors."[17]

---

[11]Hans Hickmann, *Musicologie pharaonique, études sur l'évolution de l'art musical dans l'Egypte ancienne* (Strasbourg: Heitz, 1956) 10-11.

[12]See Paul H. Lang, *Music in Western Civilization*, 13.

[13]This reference is from Edward Buhle, *Die musikalischen Instrumente in den Miniaturen des frühen Mittelalters* (Leipzig: 1903).

[14]Bowles refers to Curt Sachs' *The History of Musical Instruments* (New York: Norton, 1940) 280. In England, when a knight received a charge or a fief, his lord gave him an oliphant as a symbol of that transfer. Karl Geiringer, *Musical Instruments: Their History from the Stone Age to the Present Day* (London: 1943).

[15]E. A. Bowles, "La hiérarchie des instruments de musique dans l'Europe féodale," *Revue de musicologie* CXVIII (1958) 156-157.

[16]See *Ibid.*

[17]*Ibid.*, 168.

During the Renaissance the distinction was also made between "noble" and "plebeian" instruments, the instruments of a more intimate character being reserved for the first category.[18] These various examples show a certain diversity of result that the division of the global society into classes, strata and groupings can produce in musical life and in the very conception of music (or of certain of its elements). We will try here to expose in more detail some aspects of these phenomena, concerning especially the aristocratic and bourgeois milieus, though it must be kept in mind, as Walter Wiora emphasized, that the "scholarly sociology of music needs a sufficiently large number of concepts to correspond to the multiplicity of social layers, whereas one is often content with only too few labels, such as aristocracy and bourgeoisie. It is not logical that the most varied kinds of music since the *style galant* be derived from the same cause—'Bürgertum,' instead of investigating whether the multiplicity of results is not clarified by a multiplicity of causes."[19]

II • MUSICAL STYLE AND SOCIAL GROUPS

One of the aspects that can be examined here is the participation of the musical style of a given category of musical works in the lifestyle of a social class, and the extent to which, in other words, the lifestyle conditions musical style and the character of certain musical works in that style. In fact, "the concept of 'style' is finally, for the most part, a sociological one, for it always brings to expression the spirit of an epoch . . . And so we can never

---

[18]Robert Wangermée furnished some interesting examples of this in *Flemish Music and Society in the Fifteenth and Sixteenth Centuries* Tr. Robert Erich Wolf (New York: Praeger, 1968), concluding with this pertinent remark: "So musical instruments came to take their place on a social scale: the trumpet for the noble warriors, the organ for churchmen, the bagpipes for peasants. But such specialization was never rigid and time brought many changes." 210.

[19]Walter Wiora, "Der musikalische Ausdruck von Ständen und Klassen in eigenen Stilen," *IRASM* V/1 (1974) 93.

understand the artist so long as we separate him from the milieu in which he lived. One of the tasks of the sociology of music is to point out how musical style relates to this spiritual realm . . . "[20] If in a certain global society there prevails a certain mental structure and if, consequently, "different modes of thought correspond to different social types,"[21] then that fact also concerns the social classes, whose modes of thought are expressed in their life styles. And the public and the musician participate, of course, in social classes as well as in their global society. Musical styles, which are commonly called styles of given particular eras, reflect to some degree the lifestyle of a social group, layer or class. The Rococco or Galant style, for instance, expresses that of the aristocracy; other classes, such as the peasantry, remain more or less (or even entirely) estranged from this style. We are concerned here not with the style *of* an era but with styles *within* an era, primarily influenced by a given part of the society, but we can recognize also the parallel coexistence of several styles.[22]

In fact, the social trends, social groupings and particularly the social classes of an era permit, favor or adopt a preference for a particular style. The Romantic style, for example, coincides with the rise and expansion of the bourgeoisie in the nineteenth century; the values it advocates and realizes do not generally suit the aristocracy. Its most ardent representatives are found among the middle class: the works of Schubert, Schumann and many others furnish a striking example in this respect[23] (although Romanticism in fact had also anti-bourgeois connotations).[24] We find, in addition, that the great majority of musicians, composers and performers since the Middle Ages have been of

---

[20]Alphons Silbermann, *Empirische Kunstsoziologie* (Stuttgart: Ferdinand Enke, 1973) 75.

[21]Lucien Lévy-Bruhl, "Les fonctions mentales dans les sociétés inférieures," *Travaux de l'Année Sociologique* (Paris: P.U.F., 1910) 19.

[22]See Paul H. Lang, *Music in Western Civilization*, xx.

[23]See Guido Confalonieri, *Storia della musica*. Vol. II (Milan: Nuova Accademia editrice, 1958) 384.

[24]See Walter Wiora, "Der musikalische Ausdruck von *Ständen und Klassen*," 105.

bourgeois or common origin. The social position of the aristocrat did not allow a professional interest in music, but only one of amateur, listener or patron.[25]

The conditioning of musical style by the lifestyle of a social class extends as far as the actual creation of forms and musical genres that correspond (or are particularly well adapted) to the forms and customs of the social life of the class in question. "The common people, the bourgeoisie, and the nobility close themselves off into tight compartments, where musical forms adjusted to their milieu are born and develop . . . A musical translation of customs is thus established for each one . . . of these homogeneous and restricted publics, faithful to tradition and artistic customs," wrote de La Laurencie.[26] In addition to the *air de cour*,[27] we could propose, for example, the *ballet de cour*, which emerged in the sixteenth century as the preferred genre for entertainments and royal or aristocratic festivities, in which it played a central role. Paul H. Lang did not hesitate to call it a "state institution" in which the French king and his entourage did not disdain to take part before a large audience.[28] "No matter where the ballet was presented, the audience was almost always the same. Certainly at the Louvre the courtiers were in the majority

---

[25]See Marcel Beaufils, *Par la musique vers l'obscur*, 24-34. We should note that troubadours, came not always from the ranks of the nobility, but also from the bourgeoisie: for example, Fouquet de Marseille, a wealthy merchant; Pierre Vidal, son of a furrier from Toulouse; and Arnaud de Mareuil, a clerk or notary, who came from a poor family. See Henri Davenson, *Les Troubadours* (Paris: Seuil, 1961) 14.

[26]Lionel de La Laurencie, *Le Goût musical en France*, 6.

[27]See André Verchaly, "Air de cour et ballet de cour," *Histoire de la musique*, Vol. I (Paris: Gallimard, 1960) 1529-1560; Paul H. Lang, *Music in Western Civilization*, 377-378.

[28]See Paul H. Lang, *Music in Western Civilization*, 379; Lionel de La Laurencie, *Le Goût musical en France*, 107-110; Norbert Dufourcq, *La musique française*, 117-124; Pierre Mélèse, *Le théâtre et le public à Paris sous Louis XIV (1659-1715)* (Paris: E. Droz, 1934) 373-382; Manfred F. Bukofzer, *Music in the Baroque Era*, 141-147; and the series *Les Fêtes de la Renaissance* (Paris: C.N.R.S., 1956, 1960 and 1975).

and at the Hôtel-de-Ville, the bourgeoisie,"[29] but to dance in the ballet itself was not permitted to the latter.

We can also follow the evolution of popular dances that spring from the people and then, taken up by the aristocracy, change their style and become refined, pompous or precious. The pavane, the gavotte, the minuet and the sarabande, which have "their origin in certain popular dance-songs,"[30] are collected together into "suites" in the sixteenth century, while preserving their functional value—that of serving for dancing. At the beginning of the seventeenth century they become stylized and, in most spectacles in France, end in a purely instrumental presentation: no longer danced, but merely listened to.[31] "In the formal dance of any cultural group can be found the stylization of everyday movements and the emphasis of accepted expressions of feeling and emotion. In the Minuet was contained all that was inferred by the single word, 'complaisance.' 'Complaisance'—the mark of a courtier, the utmost in good breeding and refinement, inferring a morality where forbearance was considered a virtue, the attainment of complete self-control as truly noble, yet where the demeanour, in all appearances, was one of controlled vitality."[32] "The minuet was a purely French dance which, simplified and danced by a single couple, had a great success in the salons at the beginning of the eighteenth century. It began to go out of fashion, however, around 1750"[33] precisely during a time characterized more and more by the expansion of

---

[29]Henry Prunières, *Le Ballet de cour en France avant Benserade et Lully* (Paris: H. Laurens, 1913) 143.

[30]Norbert Dufourcq, *La musique française*, 45.

[31]See ibid., 45-46, 170-174, 182-183; Susanne Clercx, "La musique instrumentale en Europe du XIIIe au XVIIe siècle (1610)," *La musique des origines à nos jours* (Paris: Larousse, 1946) 164; Curt Sachs, *Eine Weltgeschichte des Tanzes* (Berlin: 1933)

[32]Margaret Mullins, "Dance and Society in the First Half of the Eighteenth Century," *Miscellanea musicologica. Adelaide studies in musicology* 7 (1975) 119.

[33]Georges Cucuel, *La Pouplinière et la musique de chambre au XVIIIe siècle* (Paris: Fischbacher, 1913) 395.

the musical public from the aristocracy toward a bourgeois milieu.[34]

III • A SOCIOHISTORICAL ASPECT: ARISTOCRACY AND MIDDLE CLASS

The middle class began to appear on the scene of music history at the end of the thirteenth century, but did not take it over until some five centuries later.[35] French chamber music from the first half of the eighteenth century still bears the mark of the aristocratic society for which it was destined: refinement, harmonic equilibrium, delicacy, and sobriety.[36] Charles H.H. Parry has observed that even Beethoven's position was paradoxical in that he adopted and brought to a peak a musical form (the sonata form) that was a typical example not only of the conventional tastes of his time, but also of the explicit preferences in those social circles to which he himself did not belong and which he opposed through his democratic convictions: the aristocracy.[37] Well before, Burgundian music was just as much "the very expression of its milieu: the music of a court where pleasure was the primary interest in life. There is no point in looking there for profound works. No doubt the offices of the church were faithfully followed, but these had to be brief; hence the religious compositions of Binchois characterized above all the desire to avoid boredom. Their style is lively, developments short; masses occasionally have the rhythm of a chanson. Little concerned with writing for the embellishment of religious ceremonies excepting Binchois, the Burgundian composers first and foremost dedicated themselves to a continuing program of

---

[34]The suite for example, figures, among the first instrumental pieces written for the programs of the Concert spirituel in Paris. See Lionel de La Laurencie, *Le Goût musical en France*, 212.

[35]See Jacques Chailley, *Histoire musicale du Moyen Age*, 197-198.

[36]See Louis Striffling, *Esquisse d'une histoire du goût musical en France au XVIII*e *siècle*, 162-163.

[37]See Charles H. H. Parry, *Style in Musical Art* (London: 1911) 93.

countless concerts and evenings of dancing. Thus their work is almost completely secular."[38] Even Binchois "did not altogether renounce the secular in his religious music. His sacred works are generally as florid, short and lively as his secular works."[39] According to André Pirro, the religious works of the Middle Ages generally were subject to secular influences, as the composers wished to please their lords, who were accustomed to listening to secular music.[40] "The most faithful submission to the taste of the nobility . . . appears in those compositions addressed to particular protectors. A few of these songs have come down to us, in which survive the hommages of minstrels, solicitors and eulogisers."[41] All these examples illustrate the influence that the lifestyle of a particular social milieu may exercise upon musical style.

We find another example in the origins of opera in the baroque era. As Bukofzer wrote, "the display of splendor" was one of the principal social functions of music in the aristocratic courts of that time.[42] "The opera remains a privilege of the wealthy upper classes, and remains geographically restricted to the capitals and larger cities, in which opera houses already exist. But the operas are financed from taxes on all the citizens."[43] The Roman aristocrats, for example, did not hesitate to adopt the opera, which was a new pleasure for them. "The spectacle of princes[44] with its voluptuous melodies, amorous intrigues, scenery and ballets, could not fail to seduce an elite whose artistic sensuality, no less than its intellectual refinement,

---

[38]Jeanne Marix, *Histoire de la musique et des musiciens de la cour de Bourgogne sous le règne de Philippe le Bon (1420-1467)*. (Strasbourg: Heitz, 1939) 218-219.

[39]André Pirro, *Histoire de la musique de la fin du XIVe siècle à la fin du XVIe* (Paris: H. Laurens, 1940) 93.

[40]*Ibid.*, 44-46.

[41]*Ibid.*, 36.

[42]See Manfred F. Bukofzer, *Music in the Baroque Era*, 394.

[43]Hans Engel, *Musik und Gesellschaft*, 28.

[44]Reference is to "Spettacolo veramente da Principi," preface of Gagliano's *Dafne*. This preface has been published in *Atti dell'Accademia del R. Ist. Musicale di Firenze* XXXIII (1895). "Commemorazione della Riforma Melodrammatica," 81.

had reached the highest point of development."[45] Born in aristocratic circles and conceived first for them, opera well expressed their spirit, both in the music and in the text. At the court, especially in France, wrote Bukofzer, opera employed huge choirs and orchestras, emphatic ensembles, the splendor of counterpoint. Heroes from mythology or ancient history were represented in stereotyped conflicts between honor and love, a theme dear to the hearts of the aristocracy. Often the principal hero personified the king; flattering allusions to him were not lacking, and no tragic endings offended propriety.[46]

Even at the height of the eighteenth century, the middle-class public was far from being as well informed and refined as the aristocracy. In spite of its interest in music, the middle class often displayed a taste that was only mediocre, if not bad. In Germany, for example, the opinion prevailed that music had the power to relieve the strains and boredom of a day spent (to be sure, by the middle-class) in working with figures and accounts and tending one's affairs—an opinion characteristic of this public's mode of thought.[47] In England too, similar ideas were current, as is testified by the *Daily Post* of 17 October 1724, which reported on the occasion of a concert as follows: "As musik must be allow'd to be the most innocent and agreeable Amusement, and a charming Relaxation to the Mind, when fatigued with the Bustle of Business, or after it has been long bent on serious Studies, this bids fair for encouraging the Science, and seems to be a very ingenious and laudable Undertaking."[48] About a half a century earlier, from 1673 on, it was still for moral edification, not for artistic reasons, that the commercial corporations of Lübeck demanded the *Abendmusik* concerts that Buxtehude had organized. The orientation toward more facile and accessible musical

---

[45]Henri Prunières, *L'Opéra italien en France avant Lulli* (Paris: Champion, 1913) 3.

[46]See Manfred F. Bukofzer, *Music in the Baroque Era*, 395-396.

[47]See Marcel Beaufils, *Par la musique vers l'obscur*, 59-94.

[48]Quoted in Percy M. Young, *The Concert Tradition from the Middle Ages to the Twentieth Century* (London: Routledge and Kegan Paul, 1965) 77.

genres was a normal reaction.[49] Another example is the *opéra comique*. It originated at about the same time—the beginning of the eighteenth century—in Italy, England, and at Hamburg[50] (especially during the fairs), and later received a more developed form in Paris.[51] The entire "history of opera through the centuries . . . shows a perpetual give-and-take between the severe aesthetic level which genius imposes, and the decadence imposed by an ever-growing public."[52] We have a typical example of that situation in eighteenth-century Germany, France, and Italy. The public wants scenery, always more machine effects and fantasy.[53] In Germany, Hamburg takes the lead in these developments.[54] Later on in Paris, in the same way, "the rich bourgeoisie of the *July Monarchy* give everyone proof of their bad taste.They favor with their applause the blossoming of a degraded lyric repertoire, and snub Berlioz."[55]

---

[49]At the time of the visit of Charles V to Cambrai, for example, we can ascertain already an analogous point: the bourgeois aspect of the reception. The prosperity of that town derived from bourgeois commercial activity. For that occasion the celebration was not confined within the palace, but flowed out into the streets. For the spectacles, biblical subjects had been chosen in preference to mythological legends, which were less accessible to the common people and the bourgeoisie. See Nanie Bridgman, "La participation musicale à l'entrée de Charles Quint à Cambrai le 20 janvier 1540," *Fêtes et cérémonies au temps de Charles Quint* (Paris: C.N.R.S., 1960) 243. See also Robert Wangermée, *Flemish Music and Society in the Fifteenth and Sixteenth Centuries*, 176-178.

[50]We note a curious detail: At that time the musical life of Hamburg was very open to outside influences; a result of its economic-geographic situation. As a Hanseatic town and maritime port, Hamburg had close relations, commercial and otherwise, with the rest of Europe. Its situation resembled that of St. Petersburg, which maintained musical relationships with the West, and was more influenced than Moscow, for example, which in the nineteenth century had, a more nationalistic orientation.

[51]See Louis Striffling, *Esquisse d'une histoire du goût musical en France au XVIIIe siecle*, 200-202; Norbert Dufourcq, *La musique française*, 200-201.

[52]Antoine Goléa, *La musique dans la société européenne*, 54.

[53]See Marcel Beaufils, *Par la musique vers l'obscur*, 185.

[54]See *Ibid.*

[55]Norbert Dufourcq, *La musique française*, 196.

But the *opéra comique,* whose characters and texts reflected principally the tastes of the bourgeois and petit-bourgeois public, provided a contrast to the aristocratic and court opera, with its heroic and mythological subjects. Extremely modest at first, the ordinary techniques of comic opera progressed step by step. The subjects were of especial interest to the middle classes, and sometimes even touched on current events. Often the nobility was ridiculed, and *opera seria* parodied. While the latter was an international affair, the *opéra comique* was national. Local dialects were even employed in it. It was a spectacle open to all without exception (provided they could pay), in contrast to the princely opera, which could be attended only by invitation.[56] This "paying" opera, made necessary and possible by the growth of the public, first appeared in Venice in 1637 at the theater of San Cassiano. It was followed in London in 1639 by Sir William d'Avenant, and then in 1669 in Paris by Cambert and Perrin.

On the other hand, one century later, the "period around 1770, which saw the birth of the light-hearted symphonie concertante and its rapid conquest of the concert rooms of Europe, saw, simultaneously, the intense emotional outburst in all the arts known as the Sturm und Drang. . . . The Sturm und Drang, which was nurtured in enclosed Germanic lands, was somber, turbulent, and introspective—and always in minor keys. The symphonie concertante, which flourished in accessible metropolises such as Paris and London, was light, decorative, and extroverted—and always in major keys,"[57] corresponding to the new, larger audiences of that time. The Sturm und Drang "was a symptom of an accelerating social upheaval—in particular, of a widespread middle-class disaffection with the dominance of aristocratic society. A sharp increase in public musical activities,

---

[56]See Manfred F. Bukofzer, *Music in the Baroque Era,* 395-399; and Theodor W. Adorno, "Bürgerliche Oper," *Klangfiguren, Musikalische Schriften I* (Berlin-Frankfurt am Main: Suhrkamp, 1959) 32-54.

[57]Barry S. Brook, "The Symphonie Concertante: Its Musical and Sociological Bases," *IRASM* VI/1 (1975) 19.

a creation of new genres and an expansion of the means of dissemination occured at this time."[58] Now all these indications of historical order open up yet another perspective for sociological study. "All cultural changes, including the birth, growth, and decline of forms and styles in music, are subject in varying degrees both to internal forces, governed by the genius of the creative mind, and to external ones, shaped by social, political and cultural imperatives. The symphonie concertante is a remarkable model of a musical genre in the creation of which *social* factors played the dominant role.... "[59] But in general, "neither the sociology nor the social history of musical genres has occupied scholars very much. The few exceptions . . . may be found in such fields as folk music, light music, and the hit song. The valiant effort by the Gesellschaft für Musikforschung at its Kassel Congress of 1962 to focus socio-historical attention upon major art-music genres has thus far remained without progeny[60]."[61]

We must see which typical dynamics of diverse social groups, within society as a whole, exert influences or have consequences typical for musical creativity and musical life. And conversely, we must see which phenomena, either musical or related to musical life, correspond best to certain social groups and attract their interest, and why. And finally, we must study how social facts and musical facts of this sort constantly interact with each other in such a way that a true interpenetration takes place. We

[58]Barry S. Brook, "Piracy and Panacea in the Dissemination of Music in the Eighteenth Century," *Proceedings of the Royal Musical Association* 102 (1975-1976) 13.

[59]*Ibid.*, 27.

[60]"Die musikalischen Gattungen und ihr sozialer Hintergrund" was one of the two general themes of the congress. Included were two principal papers by Hans Engel and Walter Wiora, and seven brief *Spezialreferate* by Georg von Dadelsen, Gibert Reaney, Franklin B. Zimmerman, Jaroslav Bužga, Percy M. Young, Friedrich W. Riedel, and Ludwig Finscher. See *Bericht über den Internationalen Musikwissenschaftlichen Kongress Kassel 1962*, Georg Reichart and Martin Just, ed. (Kassel: Bärenreiter, 1963) 3-39.

[61]Barry S. Brook, "The Symphonie Concertante: Its Musical and Sociological Bases," *IRASM* VI/1 (1975) 10.

could also approach the problem in the light of the social aspects of musical facts. In every case, the sociology of music must apply itself to typical data, while discarding accidental facts.

CHAPTER FOUR

MUSIC IN SOCIAL LIFE

I • SOCIAL DISTINCTION THROUGH MUSIC

There exists yet another important matter of a specifically social character: the function of *social distinction*. We find this function already at work in antiquity. Sometimes it applies not only to a class or social group, but also to individuals. In the time of the tribal competitions in Greece, each tribe "was represented by a chorus, recruited with care, and with training expenses paid by a wealthy citizen—the *chorege* . . . To be a *chorege* was considered most honorable: more than one winner desired to immortalize the memory of his victory by raising the monument to shelter the bronze tripod received as a prize."[1] The most famous of these was dedicated by Lysicrates in 335–334 B.C.

As André Pirro wrote, in the fifteenth century a large number of instrumentalists were supported by their masters as much from pride as through musical fervor. To the princes it seemed that the more noise their minstrels made, the more their majesty would be recognized.[2] This attitude was always evident when

---

[1]Henri-Irénée Marrou, *Histoire de l'éducation dans l'Antiquité*, 191.

[2]The magnificent sounds of wind instruments and the beating of drums especially pleased the nobility, always taken up as they were with pomp and solemnity. See Edmund A. Bowles, "La hiérarchie des instruments de musique dans l'Europe féodale," *Revue de musicologie* CXVIII (1958) 156.

princes and kings made entry into their palaces or the cities.[3] History gives us many references, among them the entry of Charles V into Cambrai.[4] When the ambassador of Philip the Good visited the court of Mantua in 1459, he received a magnificent welcome from Francesco Gonzaga, who had prepared a dinner for him. Several singers, trumpets, "clarons," lutes, harps, and other instruments of the duke's establishment played throughout the meal.[5] The concerts called *de table* were long an important element in presentations and dignified receptions at princely or lordly residences.[6] When the future "Joseph II arrived at Wallerstein in 1764, Prince Philip-Charles of Öttingen had clarinets and hunting horns played during the feast. This custom seems to have lasted longer in Germany than in France."[7] But in a certain sense it was part of the ceremonial etiquette, in which music and musicians participated in yet other ways. Thus, along with its purely artistic functions, the ducal choir of Galeazzo Maria Sforza of Milan had to fulfill a representative and decorative role as well. For certain official solemnities, such as the blessing of the Standards at the Cathedral, or on Saint George's Day, the choir became an integral part of the ceremony, joining with the staff personnel of the court.[8] Beyond any aesthetic interest (many princes, such as Ferdinand III and Leopold I, were musicians), the royal and princely courts of the R enaissance and baroque were concerned with matters of prestige and representation. Many examples of

---

[3] See André Pirro, *Histoire de la musique de la fin du XIVe siècle à la fin du XVIe*, 136-138.

[4] See Nanie Bridgman, *La participation musicale à l'entrée de Charles Quint à Cambrai*, 235-254.

[5] "ouquel disner ot pluseurs chantres, trompettes et clarons, lucz, harpes et autres instruments de l'hostel dudit duc, qui y juèrent durant ledit disner," Matthieu d'Escouchy. *Chronique*, Ed. G. du Fresne de Beaucourt (Paris: 1864) II, 376, cited in Edmund A. Bowles, "Musical instruments at the Medieval Banquet," *Revue Belge de Musicologie* (1958) 42.

[6] We find examples of *musique de table* from late antiquity on.

[7] Georges Cucuel, *La Pouplinière et la musique de chambre au XVIIIe siècle*, 393.

[8] See Gaetano Cesari, "Musica e Musicisti alla Corte Sforzesca" *Rivista musicale italiana* XXIX (1922) 11.

this attitude are to be found in the courts of Burgundy, Henry V of England, Emporer Maximilian, Charles VIII of France, and Matthew Corvinus, king of Hungary and Croatia. In Italy, the courts of the Medici, Gonzaga, Sforza and Este furnish numerous examples.[9]

For the aristocracy, as formerly for the class of feudal lords, music was part of the "decor" and the *lifestyle*. Music was a mark of social distinction, an activity that served to identify, especially among the aristocracy, its patrons as people of social importance and power; and as such it was progressively taken up by the middle class. More or less aware of the cultural advantages of the rival aristocratic class, the rising bourgeoisie attempted to imitate it in certain areas. But it did this according to its own *lifestyle* and modes of thought, in order to affirm its own personality and prestige. Here again music functioned as a social sign or emblem.

But if in its conquest of music the middle class evidenced a certain imitation of the aristocracy and even of the royal court,[10] the aristocrats themselves, in turn imitated the royal court as well. Their appropriation of the court *divertissements* offer us one example of this. At the time "of the reign of Louis XIV, the divertissements functioned to commemorate the happy event, a victory, a birth, an inauguration. The King offered one as a laurel crown to a victorious marechal or to a prince returning to court covered with the glory of battle. A little mythology, some dances, short action full of allusions—this was their substance."[11] The greatest names lent some prestige to these pieces: Lully, Boësset, Philidor, and Delalande. But soon the aristocracy reappropriated the genre, which was thus no longer practiced only at the court. Composed for a day or an evening, divertisse-

---

[9] See Paul H. Lang, *Music in Western Civilization*, 298-299.

[10] See Yolande de Brossard, "Musique et bourgeoisie au dix-septième siècle d'apres les gazettes de Loret et de Robinet," *"Recherches" sur la musique française classique (1960)*. Collection published under the direction of N. Dufourcq (Paris: Picard, 1960) 47; and Manfred F. Bukofzer, *Music in the Baroque Era*, 402.

[11] Maurice Barthélemy, *André Campra, sa vie et son ouvre*, 42.

ments were not destined to survive the persons they flattered,[12] being fulfillments of the social function of the moment. They are marked by superficially attractive surface characteristics, and predetermined form that was appropriate to their social function, but in general are of minor or ephemeral artistic value.

Following the example of the lords, the middle class sought to have minstrels available. The cities of Dijon and Orléans maintained skilled instrumentalists. The bourgeois sought to gather many minstrels for their feasts. In the fifteenth century, laws were enacted to reduce this practice and to limit expenses. Yet in Metz after 1480, there were weddings where more than thirty minstrels appeared, in the pay of the townsmen.[13] The same era supplies a curious instance of the thinking of the citizens townsmen of Dijon in regard to musical instruments. "The trumpeters of the Holy Roman Empire had to form fraternities (confréries) and these were subject to the head fraternity in Dresden. Only the Elector of Saxony was allowed to display a permit to trumpeters in all German territories. Up into the twentieth century 'Hoftrompeter' were in the service of the Saxon court."[14] According to Jeanne Marix, in Burgundy the trumpet "was, on the contrary, the instrument of the town par excellence. A document . . . from Dijon confirms the prestige of the trumpet. In the town register for 1433, there is a request to the Duke 'that he might be pleased to allow them to have a trumpet in place of the horn which they used for their announcements, because several lords and strangers ridicule the horn for not being respectable, and that it would be a greater honor for the city to have a trumpet than a horn'."[15] Philip the Good received this request favorably, allowing the town to make its announcements from then on by trumpet.[16] The use of

---

[12]See *Ibid.*, 42.

[13]See André Pirro, *Histoire de la musique de la fin du XIVe siècle à la fin du XVIe*, 141.

[14]Hans Engel, *Musik und Gesellschaft*, 223.

[15]Jeanne Marix, *Histoire de la musique et des musiciens de la cour de Bourgogne*, 100.

[16]See *Ibid.*, 100; and André Pirro, *Histoire de la musique de la fin du XIVe siècle à la fin du XVIe*, 141.

the trumpet took on a social dimension; the people of Dijon even attached to it the honor of the town. In Germany, the trumpet players were called *ritterliche Trompeter* and formed a separate category, as servants of princes or other distinguished persons, as opposed to the instrumentalists working for the cities or wandering the countryside. The trumpet players insisted that the cities should not have trumpets and drums in their pay, for the feudal lords alone had the right to be accompanied by the penetrating sound of these instruments.[17] In general, as Edward E. Lowinsky has stressed, "archives, chronicles, and paintings from all over Europe demonstrate that the town musicians were a universal social institution rooted in the Middle Ages but mainly developed in the Renaissance."[18]

In the seventeenth century a very important part of French musical life unfolded at the court. Louis XIII and Louis XIV "took up that art and practiced it themselves. Under the reign of Louis XIV no day passed without some concert or representation at the court: ballets, musical comedies, and later, operas, and concerts given in the King's apartments."[19] But French society then also included an enlightened bourgeoisie stimulated by music and trying to imitate what was done at court.[20] Certainly music-making among the bourgeoisie was neither as frequent nor as important than at court, but its presence indicates the need that class had for it. The *Mecure Galant* for May 1688 reports from Paris: "Nothing is so *à la mode* as music, and today it is the passion of most respectable men and persons of quality."[21] As Cousin wrote, "one was hardly a respectable man, in the well-known sense of the word, if, even in the bourgeoisie, one did not give from time to time a light meal with violins to the ladies, a little

---

[17]See Thédore Gérold, "Les instruments de musique au Moyen Age," *Revue des Cours et Conférences V* (Feb. 1928) 463. See below, p. 277.

[18]Edward Lowinsky, "Music in the Culture of the Renaissance," *Journal of the history of ideas* XV/4 (1954) 519.

[19]Yolande de Brossard, *Musique et bourgeoisie*, 47. See also Michel Brenet, *Les concerts en France sous l'ancien Régime*, 65.

[20]See Yolande de Brossard, *Musique et bourgeoisie*, 47.

[21]*Mercure galant* (May 1688) 204.

serenade in the garden, or, on the water, a more or less considerable concert."[22] We see that the taste for concerts expanded rapidly among the leisure classes of French society.[23] And this was true also of the bourgeoisie. As the material well-being of the middle class increased, it permitted the acquisition of leisure pastimes and distractions, in which music played a part.[24] In 1652, for example, "Loret tells us of a concert of two singers accompanied 'by a clavecin and two viols' which took place near Notre Dame, in the home of a certain Madame Payen; an interesting fact—the concert repeats every fortnight."[25]

With the increase in concert attendance and in musical evenings at home, or musical activity by amateurs, music gradually became, a social necessity and a distinctive mark of the middle-class family, especially toward the close of the eighteenth century. The piano, that symbol of bourgeois ease,[26] later penetrated into the homes of the bourgeoisie, and its study, especially for young women, became "a social imperative,"[27] a sign of a good education. That symbol and social judgment lasted well into the twentieth century; their origins, nevertheless, are well in the past. In France, as early as the seventeenth century we see the superiority of the clavecin defended in relation to other instruments "played" and not "touched," such as the organ, harp and lute. Conflicts of social and professional interests placed these instrumentalists in opposition to each other, even in legal litigation.[28] As a means of sociability, a fashion, a pretext for social encounters, and a sign of respectability, music would

[22]Victor Cousin, *La société française au XVIIe siècle*, 4th ed., II, 296, cited in Michel Brenet, *Les concerts en France sous l'ancien Régime*, 40.

[23]See *Ibid.*, 40.

[24]Whereas today leisure-time activities are more *mass phenomenon*, at that time and in the nineteenth century still, they were a function of *class*.

[25]Yolande de Brossard, *Musique et bourgeoisie*, 48.

[26]See Arthur Loesser, *Men, Women and Pianos, a Social History* (New York: Simon and Schuster, 1954) 314-318 and 386.

[27]See Robert Hoebaer, "L'intérêt pour l'art musical," *Bulletin de l'Institut de Recherches Economiques et Sociales* VII (1956) 705.

[28]See Paul Loubet de Sceaury, *Musiciens et facteurs d'instruments de musique sous l'ancien Régime*, 111.

carry out, more or less subtly, the same social function in the bourgeoisie of various European countries, and for several generations.

II • AMATEUR PERFORMANCES AND PUBLIC CONCERTS

A significant point, however, must be set in relief: music was not only the subject of public concerts, but of evenings at home— another example of the *function of distinction* that music can exert. Music gradually became part of social life, in the friendly atmosphere of the bourgeois home, just as it had previously in the aristocratic salon (in addition to the courtly spectacles).[29] Here we find one of the social roots of an important phenomenon that developed in the bourgeois milieus, especially in Germany: musical amateurism, deriving in part from the amateurism of the aristocracy.[30] This form of musical life had considerable social importance, and various musical ensembles, such as the *Convivia musica* and *Collegia musica*, provided a musical and social outlet for the German middle class. Organizations of this type appeared at the end of the sixteenth century. At first they were mainly choruses for sacred music. In the following century these were succeeded by groups of amateur instrumentalists. Along with the municipal bands these institutions were, in a way, bourgeois replies to princely and aristocratic institutions, the capella and orchestras of court or palace.[31] Most importantly, composers who until then had addressed themselves most often to the court and palace began to address the *Kenner und Liebhaber* (connoisseurs and amateurs). Even a periodical—*Der*

---

[29]A particularly rich and interesting documentation of this can be found in Walter Salmen, "Haus-und Kammermusik. Privates Musizieren im gesellschaflichen Wandel zwischen 1600-1900," *Musikgeschichte in Bildern*, Ed. Heinrich Besseler and Werner Bachmann. *Musik in der neuen Zeit.* Vol. IV/3. (Leipzig: VEB Deutscher Verlag für Musik, 1969).

[30]See Marcel Beaufils, *Par la musique vers l'obscur*, 24-34; 59-94.

[31]See Hans Engel, *Musik und Gesellschaft*, 233-237; and Paul H. Lang, *Music in Western Civilization*, 395 and 408.

musikalische Dilettante—was dedicated to them in 1769.[32] The *Lied* was a form cultivated essentially in this bourgeois environment. The music of the amateur aided the middle class toward self-awareness; it was a unifying social bond. This situation persisted throughout the eighteenth century and into the first part of the nineteenth.[33]

Today in the United States, choral societies of European immigrants present an altogether different example. Their existence and activity are explained in terms of ethnopolitics. Although the number of participants represents only a small part of the immigrant community, these societies perform an important social function—the preservation of national sentiments, symbols and memories. These specific functions are various, and Irving Babow, who has analyzed them in depth, groups them into four principal categories, which reflect four fundamental types of choral societies: societies with nostalgic tendencies (cherishing the memory of the Old Country); ceremonial societies (organizing competitions, banquets and speech-making); societies for cultural indoctrination (encouraging the young to learn the language and culture of their national origin); and protest societies (having an essential preoccupation not with the homeland, but with the social experience in the new country).[34] We could not find a more obvious example of social conditioning bearing on the formation and activity of an amateur musical group than this. It shows, one more time, the immersion of musical life in social life.

A solid example of empirical sociological research into musical amateurism, which could serve as a model for further

---

[32]See *Ibid.*, 723. On musical amateurism in England in the seventeenth and eighteenth centuries, see Walter L. Woodfill, *Musicians in English Society, from Elizabeth to Charles I*, 201-239.

[33]See Marcel Beaufils, *Par la musique vers l'obscur*, 59-94; and by the same author *Le Lied romantique allemand*, 7th ed. (Paris: Gallimard, 1956).

[34]See Irving Babow, "The Singing Societies of European Immigrants," *Phylon* XV/3 (1954) 289-295. See also his "Types of Immigrant Singing Societies," *Sociology and Social Research* XXXIX/4 (1955) 242-247.

study in the field, can be found in the study of Nicole Berthier. Among other things, she has examined the genesis of musical amateurism, musical amateurs in relationship to a global population, and a variety of musical activities of amateurs, arriving at some far-reaching conclusions of general interest.[35]

In France as in Germany, the eighteenth century was characterized by the growth of the bourgeois musical public. This had an important effect on musical life, leading to an increase in the number of public performances. Various concerts (or academies) were organized in the first half of the century. These academies existed in Paris, Marseille, Bordeaux, Nîmes, Lyon, Lille, and elsewhere.[36] At Amiens, the principal townsmen, forty in number, formed an association to establish a Public Concert.[37] The regulations of the Academy of Marseille specify that it was founded "to amuse the too-idle youth and give them something to do."[38] "The provincial academies, whose organization reflects . . . the influence of the learned academies as well as the social ambience of the *ancien Régime*, were primarily concert societies, of great importance to the expansion of musical culture in eighteenth century France."[39] But if they were not founded by the aristocrats, the academies almost always solicited the patronage of one or another of them. For in these gatherings the townsman could meet the aristocrat, and nothing flattered him

---

[35]See Nicole Berthier, *Mélomanes et culture musicale. Etude d'un statut socio-culturel* (Ph.D. dissertation, Troisième Cycle de Sociologie, U.E.R. des Sciences Sociales de Grenoble, 1975) 350 pp.

[36]The principal concerts of Paris in the eighteenth century with the founding dates are as follows: Concert Crozat (1724), Concert des Mélophilètes (1722-24), Concert spirituel (1725), Concert des Amateurs (1762), Concert d'Amis (1772), Concert des Enfants d'Apollon (1784), Concert de la Loge Olympique (1786), Concert de la Société d'émulation (1786), Concert Feydeau (1794), Concert de la rue de Cléry (1799?). See Norbert Dufourcq, *La musique française,* 196, and Jean Mongrédien, *La musique en France des Lumières au Romantisme (1789-1830),* 199-253.

[37]See Humphrey Burton, "Les Académies de musique en France au XVIIIe siècle," *Revue de musicologie* CXII (1955) 125.

[38]Cited in *ibid.,* 126.

[39]*Ibid.,* 124.

151

more. The audience at the salon of La Pouplinière, for example, was composed of both bourgeoisie and aristocrats.[40]

Another city of this time that deserves great attention along with the French capital which, "with half a million in population, second only to London, boasted: more concerts, more composers, more performers, engravers, and publishers of music than any other in Europe,"[41] was Leipzig: not only for its rich musical life and the great composers who lived there (in the first place J.S. Bach), but also because of the valuable research already done into its musical and sociomusical history by Arnold Schering. This work provides an excellent point of departure for any socio-logical investigation, and a model of what sources and aspects should be studied first,[42] in a sociological examination of the concert and other aspects of the musical life of a city.[43]

Among the aristocrats and the wealthy, there were many who organized concerts in their homes, where one could occasionally hear such remarkable musicans as Mozart. Trial, then Gossec, directed the concerts of the Prince de Conti, where appeared Schobert, Rodolphe, Janson, and others.[44] Baron de Bagge, Count d'Albaret, and the Duke d'Aiguillon were also patrons. But "the 'aristocracy of money' wished also to participate in the flattering role of patron surrounded by artists: the traditional position vested in the blooded aristocracy. A *fermier général* such as La Pouplinière, who had Rameau, Stamitz and Gossec at his court, played, in the eighteenth century, the same role

---

[40]See Georges Cucuel, *La Pouplinière et la musique de chambre au XVIIIe siècle*, 411-412.

[41]Barry S. Brook, "The Symphonie Concertante: Its Musical and Sociological Bases", 24.

[42]See Arnold Schering, *Musikgeschichte Leipzigs*, 3 vols, particularly the 3rd volume: *Johann Sebastian Bach und das Musikleben Leipzigs im 18. Jahrhundert* (Leipzig: Fr. Kistner & C.P.W. Siegel, 1941).

[43]See also Klaus Blum, *Musikfreunde und Musik. Musikleben in Bremen seit der Aufklärung* (Tutzing: Hans Schneider, 1965).

[44]See Michel Brenet, *Les concerts en France sous l'ancien Régime*, 349-351; and Lionel de La Laurencie, "Les débuts de la musique de chambre en France," *Revue de musicologie*, LII (1934) 230-231.

as a ruler of a German principality."[45] At that same time, in the pursuit of pleasure and amusement in music, the middle class finally joined hands with the aristocracy; but only after several centuries of existence. Although the struggle between the two classes was without mercy on a political and economic level, points of contact and solidarity can be ascertained in the general appreciation of musical art. Finally, even a "symbiosis of bourgeoisie and aristocracy was very important in the music life. This is already shown in the many court theaters, orchestras, *Kapellmeisters* and composers up to Richard Strauss. It is also seen, for example, in the persons to whom Beethoven dedicated his works, in the aristocratic traits of Chopin, or in the way of life of Wagner and Liszt. This was not a purely middle class epoch."[46] And little by little the aristocratic salons were opened to the bourgeois elite. Members of the two classes found themselves united in the listening: an incontestable result of music's power of sociability.

Citing a document of the times, Michel Brenet relates that the audience at the *Petits Concerts* in eighteenth century Paris was made up "of a large number of idle people and a small number of connoisseurs. The women are its ornament and rival the players . . . most come there to amuse themselves, to gossip or to show themselves off. Many inconsiderate young people, whose only object is to get together, come to be seen there and blame for the sake of appearance that which should be applauded."[47] And Brenet adds that "this description from 1757 remains true for the Paris of 1900, except that it applies, rather, to the audience at the Opera."[48] An analogous situation may be found in the middle of the nineteenth century,[49] and also in Germany at the same time, where much of the vast bourgeois

---

[45]Jacques Chailley, *40,000 ans de musique,* 118.

[46]Walter Wiora, *Der musikalische Ausdruck von Ständen und Klassen,* 106.

[47]Ancelet, *Observations sur la musique,* 38. Cited in Michel Brenet, *Les Concerts en France sous l'ancien Régime,* 230.

[48]*Ibid.,* 230.

[49]See Lionel de La Laurencie, *Le Goût musical en France,* 300.

public believed that "music is less an end in itself than a means of meeting good friends and acquaintances from time to time."[50] The opera in the nineteenth century was also viewed "as a social meeting-place. Liszt wrote in 1838: 'One goes to the theater to visit in the loges. The orchestra and the singers, who, mutually estranged from each other, receive no assistance from the public which either applauds or sleeps (in the fifth loge they eat and play cards), come here absent-minded, bored, sick—not as artists together, but as common people who will be paid for each hour of music-making . . . '[51] also, these days, the more expensive the opera is, the more the social interest it has, especially at holiday performances."[52] Another banal example is the Viennese classical waltz, which held, for the bourgeoisie during part of the nineteenth century, a place analogous to that of the aristocratic dances for the aristocracy.

As for the public concert, it became "a bourgeois ceremony which is enacted according to a particular ritual and almost never varies. Even for that reason, one could claim that the concert functionalizes the music in furnishing the pretext for a worldly meeting. It gathers together a chosen audience whose presence, one might suppose, is not determined exclusively by the desire to listen to music,"[53] an audience "taking pleasure to find itself in that circumstance and recognising itself especially in the correct enactment of the ritual."[54] But this is only one aspect of the matter. Before the appearance of the concert, music filled a social function as part of situations and events which were of prime importance; now music itself appears on the primary level, being also a possible pretext for extramusical social functions. But it is not necessary to confuse these two different and "reversed" aspects by insisting overmuch on the "ritual" of

---

[50]Testimony of the times cited by Marcel Beaufils, *Par la musique vers l'obscur*, 219.

[51]Hans Engel quotes from his own *Franz Liszt* (Potsdam: 1936) 221.

[52]Hans Engel, *Musik und Gesellschaft*, 29-30.

[53]Michel de Coster, *L'art mass-médiatisé*, 260-261.

[54]*Ibid.*, 261.

the concert of the nineteenth and twentieth centuries, as was perhaps done by Enrico Fubini and Michel De Coster.[55]

III • EARLY FORMS OF MUSICAL "MASS" CULTURE

In general, we speak about musical "mass" culture in terms of the music of the twentieth century and the phenomena associated with contemporary musical life; and even within this limited context, there is no shortage of viewpoints about the significance and meaning of the term. The term is usually applied to the field of entertainment and popular music, though nowadays it seems to be used with ever greater frequency in connection with "serious" or classical music, especially with respect to the diffusion and dissemination of such music through the mass media.[56] Not long ago, however, the question of early forms of musical "mass" culture was raised in a broader perspective—as to its significance, framework, and beginnings—and the concept was defined as the "performance or dissemination of music which does not rest upon personal relationships between musicians and public and for which obtaining—indeed, manipu-lating—a wide public is a primary goal. This is not just a matter of brute numbers of people buying music or going to concerts. What has characterized musical mass culture primarily has been rather the impersonality of relationships between listeners and performers and the active exploitation of a broad public by the music business."[57] So conceived, the early forms of musical

---

[55]See Enrico Fubini, "Implicazioni sociologiche nella creazione e fruizione della musica d'avanguardia," *IRASM* V/1 (1974) 169-176; and Michel De Coster, *L'art mass-médiatisé*, 255-267.

[56]See for example, Denis McQuail, *Towards a Sociology of Mass Communication* (London: 1969); G. Friedmann, "Rôle et place de la musique dans une société industrielle," *Diogène*, 72 (1970) 29–44; Helmut Rösing, "Zur Rezeption technisch vermittelter Musik. Psychologische, ästhetische und musikalisch-funktionsbezogene Aspekte," *Musik in den Massenmedien Rundfunk und Fernsehen*, ed. Hans-Christian Schmidt (Mainz: Schott, 1976), pp. 44–46.

[57]William Weber, "Mass Culture and the Reshaping of European Musical

"mass" culture would fall somewhere in the middle of the nineteenth century, at the time of the appearance and establishment of public interest in the music of the great Viennese classics, and at a time when the growth of publishing activities in the field of music assumed a new and important function in musical life.[58]

The problem of the "mass" character of a musical culture could be formulated still more broadly, not only by reference to some previous or contemporary "non-mass" phenomena in the musical culture under investigation—phenomena characterized by features that are different from or contrary to those that define the musical "mass" culture in question—but also by reference to the individual aspects of any musical "mass" culture, and not just to its mass character as a whole. In a certain sense, it could even be said that almost every age has had "mass" and "non-mass" forms of musical culture, at least in the sense that, on the one hand, there have been certain musical forms or genres that were performed and heard by small circles of the public, while on the other hand, other forms or genres belonged to a larger audience and to broader social strata, this irrespective of whether we are dealing with art or folk music, or with music that merely entertained (though the last two ordinarily belonged to a larger public). Where the "mass" or "non-mass" character of a musical culture or of one of its aspects begins and ends is a problem that can be solved only by analysis of specific data concerning a particular epoch and its cultural and social frameworks. Here a methodological question arises, namely whether it is possible or not to establish uniform criteria or common determinants of the "mass" character of a musical culture, either in its entirety or one of its parts, for all historical periods, or whether the criteria-determinants should be considered with flexibility and with reference to the various and variable historical conditions and to the elements they contain,

Taste, 1770–1870," *IRASM*, VIII (1977) 6–7.
[58]See Weber, "Mass Culture," 5–6.

in the frames of which—through their specific features—the more or less varied phenomena of the musical cultures of different social milieus can be designated as "mass" or "non-mass" phenomena.

This last rather pragmatic point of view seems to be more effective in historical research, as it permits a broadening of the problem across a greater number of historical periods as well as an insight into the "mass" or "non-mass" character of diverse spheres of musical life in all social strata and groups—from folk and popular music to art music, in the strict sense, and those of its genres and forms that were traditionally reserved for social minorities, and consequently, for more or less narrow audiences. Such a perspective would permit a historical study of the reception of particular musical compositions, whether by individual composers or of some musical genre in general, with reference to their success and "popularity" with the public; that is, their limited or "mass" acceptance. Such a consideration could be important and interesting in a social history of musical life and culture.

However, if one remains within the territory of European art music of recent centuries, it could be taken for granted that the first step toward a "mass" character appears with the development of public concerts. Contrary to the earlier private amateur performances and private concerts first known in court and aristocratic milieus and later in bourgeois houses, and contrary to the earlier intervening types of semi-public concerts, which were devoted mainly to chamber music, the public concerts of the second half of the eighteenth century denoted the first clear-cut movement toward what could be called, even then, an early "mass" form of musical life. Several pieces of evidence support this contention.

The years around 1770 witnessed a number of important turning-points in European musical life, some of which were linked in part to the flourishing activity in music publishing. At that time the middle class became more and more unsatisfied with its social status. Changes in the financial position of the musician became more pronounced. As Barry S. Brook has emphasized, "this period marked the culmination of a long process in which music was transformed from a semi-feudal craft serving church, town and court, into a free-enterprise profession supplying predominantly bourgeois markets."[59] The music profession followed the movements in other social spheres, and was increasingly penetrated by liberated entrepreneurship, which supplied the developing market according to the ever more pronounced laws of supply and demand, laws that also began to influence cultural life in specific ways. In the last quarter of the century, the role and the function of patronage started to decline. "An intensification of concert life and opera production all over Europe, as well as an unprecedented growth of commercial opportunities in aspects of music distribution such as copying, engraving, and printing, made it possible for countless composers and performers of independent spirit to practise their profession without recourse to traditional types of patronage."[60] The success of the musician and of the musical work were decided more and more within the framework of a musical life that was progressively more commercialized, organized for a predominantly new middle-class public, and of course, for the still-important aristocratic public; no longer was the musician and his work subject mainly to the fading importance of the private aristocratic residences in which the musician was only or almost a servant, as with Haydn at Esterháza or Mozart in Salzburg. Composers depended less and less on noble patrons.

The frequency and sometimes the quality of both concert and opera programs grew in general terms, along with the commercial entrepreneurship in the field of music distribution, which in turn became less dependent on copying and ever more closely associated with the growing young industry of engraving and printing. The abandonment of the shelter of traditional aristocratic patronage was accompanied by the evolution of a hitherto

---

[59]Barry S. Brook, "Piracy and Panacea in the Dissemination of Music in the Late Eighteenth Century," *Proceedings of the Royal Musical Association,* CII (1975–1976), 13.

[60]Barry S. Brook, "Piracy and Panacea," 13–14.

nonexistent freedom of choice in a whole series of professional musical activities. This freedom was exploited by a growing number of musicians. The mobility of the musical profession became more important, the social status of the musician was no longer so rigidly defined, and the "mobility" of music itself and of its effects and influences grew to a previously unknown extent. The expansion of printing and music publishing influenced not only the dissemination of and public acquaintance with music, through the publishing of musical works, but also was felt in broader social and geographical frames. Along with the greater movement of musicians from one country to another, more extensive music publishing helped to increase the influence of musical styles and individual composers upon each other, not only within their own countries, but across national boundaries as well. Increased publishing activity thus had important consequences at the musical-artistic level. In this expansion the leading roles were played by publishers in France, England and the Netherlands.

The great influence of music publishing at that time had several causes and can be considered an expression of larger events in the society and culture of the most developed countries of Europe. This epoch in music history was marked by a phenomenon that came to dominate it to an ever greater degree: *repetitiveness*, which Jacques Attali places at the end of the nineteenth century in terms of general social relationships,[61] though in musical life it appeared on the last decades of the eighteenth century. This repetitiveness is evident in, among other things, the field of music publishing. The unique quality of the musical event slowly disappeared; its limitation with respect to frequency began to decrease, and its restrictions to a special or unique occasion was undermined. The principle of repetitiveness in performance resulted in a movement away from the control of the composer (that is, away from performance under his leadership): his choice or even awareness of the place of

---

[61]Jacques Attali, *Bruits, Essai sur l'économie politique de la musique* (Paris: P.U.F., 1977), pp. 64–65.

performance, the circumstances of performance, and the performers themselves. Thus, for instance, Haydn lamented in 1768 that it was difficult for him to compose a cantata for a monastery in Austria since he did not know "either the persons, or the place."[62] If the quantitative growth of music and its dissemination had sociological causes—greater freedom for the composer, a larger public, and the economic stimulus from publishing, engraving, and printing—they also had definite consequences: further dissemination and broadening of the public, the increased repetitiveness of a musical presentation from one occasion to another, greater incentives for musical amateurism, and finally, stronger stimulus for commercial activities connected with music and musical life. Repetitiveness led step by step to the organization of a whole commercial net or chain of all those who played an active role in its further affirmation: printers, engravers, publishers, merchants and salesmen, manufacturers of instruments, organizers of musical life, and others.

In fact, as long as the creation and performance of art music had a strict and determined function for a specific extramusical occasion or motive along with satisfying the individual demand or command of employer or patron, particular musical works were not only performed, but often even composed expressly in terms of the function they had to assume and the occasion to which they were bent. Whether further performances occurred depended almost entirely on circumstances arising of the same or similar kind. Bach, for instance, would employ a previously performed cantata only if he had not composed a new one for a new occasion, and only if the one that he had previously composed was suitable for the new occasion or circumstances of performance. Thus one cannot say that there was a market—in the strict sense of the word—for the numerous liturgical works composed for the aristocracy and the churches during the

---

[62]Cited in Michel De Coster, "L'art mass-médiatisé. L'exemple de la musique classiquenregistrée," *IRASM* VI/2 (1975) 257.

Renaissance and Baroque periods. If, on the other hand, some secular genres, such as the French chanson, had a market—albeit a limited one—as early as the Renaissance, this was a result of both the existence of an amateur music public, which was pleased to hear and even sing the chanson, and of the transmission of the genre in printed editions that appeared from the beginning of the sixteenth century, at Ottaviano Petrucci in Venice, Pierre Attaingnant in Paris, Jacques Moderne in Lyons, and Tielman Susato in Antwerp.

If it is true, as was stressed by William Weber, that in the eighteenth century "relationships between performers and their patrons were . . . the central source of social order in musical life [and that] the key to success for musicians was not expanding the number of such ties but rather maintaining them with careful diplomacy in the small-group social context of the time,"[63] it is also true that in the last third of the century composers sought a broadening of their public and of their artistic affirmation outside the shelter of patronage and narrow social groups, something to which music publishing certainly contributed. This very development should be viewed as the beginning of the early forms of musical mass culture, which should be placed in this period, not—as Weber claims—in the middle of the nineteenth century. Neither should the phenomenon be related to that of repetitiveness in general social relationships as defined by Attali, who placed it at the end of the nineteenth century, though it might fairly contribute to his thesis that events in music are "forerunners" of events in general history.[64] Even if we accept Weber's definition of musical "mass" culture, it should be remarked that from the late eighteenth century on, music publishing was one of the essential elements of the "mass" character of musical culture: first of all, in the growing impersonality of the relationships between musicians and the public, in which printed music increasingly became the mediator; secondly, in composers' addressing a greater number

---

[63]William Weber, "Mass Culture," 8.
[64]See Jacques Attali, *Bruits*, 22.

of listeners, particularly musical amateurs, for whom music increasingly was intended; and finally, in the commercial exploitation of music, in almost the complete sense (that is, exploitation not only as investment in the music business in order to obtain profit, but also as influence exerted on the musical market, and the taste of the public, and as the composing and performing of works for the greatest profit).

When William Weber speaks of early forms of musical mass culture—thus utilizing a term which was invented in and for our time—[65] in European musical life from about 1770 to 1870, it is not a question of an unjustified retrospective use of the term, though some of his conclusions should be accepted with reservations. First, it would be more appropriate to use the term, when applying it to previous epochs, within quotation marks; for one cannot say that early forms of our own musical mass culture, at least as they concerned "serious" or "classical" music, could have constituted—in comparison with that of today— anything more than a musical "mass" culture that was severely limited with respect to its number of listeners, its commercial exploitation of music, and the impersonality of its relationships. Secondly, limited though they may have been, these phenomena existed, not only in the mid-nineteenth century, but in the last decades of the eighteenth century. Thus Weber's conception should be broadened and narrowed. For instance, although the relationship between musicians and their employers or patrons, who were at the same time the principal audience and the most privileged members of the public, remained personal throughout most of the eighteenth century, there was, with the development of the public concert and the appearance of a more or less anonymous public, a tendency for the relationship, whether public-performer or public-composer, to become depersonalized toward the end of that century. Inversely, the public-performer relationship remained personal in the sense that the public generally knew the musicians who played for it. If the public of the time knew the composer in most cases, the

---

[65]See William Weber, "Mass Culture," 6.

composer no longer knew his public as he had before: the greater the distance at which his compositions were performed, the less he knew his public. Finally, with respect to the question of the number of listeners as a criterion of the "mass" character of a musical culture, it may be taken into account in a double sense: with reference to a greater public in comparison with other contemporary centers of musical life (for example, public concert halls vs. aristocratic salons), or with reference to its lesser quantitative importance in former times. On the other hand, it would be an indefensible retrospective projection to conclude that the musical cultures of earlier periods had no "mass" features simply because those features were not similar to those present in the musical culture of the twentieth century, when the musical public is both absolutely and relatively more numerous than it has ever been before, or because in earlier times the technical mass media simply did not exist as they do today.

Before the development of the public concert, the personal character of the relationships between musicians and the public, particularly between musicians and their employers or patrons, was inescapable. For the musician these relationships meant responding to demands and commands, in accordance with the taste and wishes of either the people in whose service they were engaged or of those who could pay for both the composition and the performance for which the music was required. All of this was a function of personal, family, and court events, meetings, receptions, and celebrations within a restricted circle of people— and we are speaking of relatively small groups—in which music was especially appreciated, favored, and supported, not only for aesthetic and artistic motives, but also for reasons of social prestige, respect, and recognition. Musical amateurism in the middle-class milieu of the eighteenth century also existed in the nonanonymous circles of family and friends, where personal relationships between participants and audience were even closer and more direct, unburdened by official form and court etiquette.

When the size of audiences at public concerts began to grow during the eighteenth century, personal relationships were still essential in organizing performances. If it was almost impossible to arrange concerts for more than five hundred people,[66] this was so because typical public concerts of that period were organized under the auspices of various amateur societies and academies, often as benefit concerts founded essentially upon a basis of personal relationships and attended by a public made up of friends, colleagues, and relatives. Thus even the public concert of the eighteenth century rested to some extent upon personal relationships as its basis in musical life.

In the late eighteenth century things began to change. Early forms of musical "mass" culture manifested themselves first of all and to the highest degree in the largest European urban conglomerations, London and Paris, where the concentration of population was greatest. It is quite understandable that it was in these very cities that the principal conditions for both the early appearance of musical "mass" culture and the important development of music publishing were found. Furthermore, as was stressed by Cyril Ehrlich "the commercialisation of leisure, which was ultimately to become one of the world's great industries, providing employment for unprecedented numbers of musicians, was not an invention of the nineteenth century. J.H. Plumb has traced its origins in England to the century before 1770, 'when an affluent and growing middle class ... was willing to spend for the sake, not only of prestige, but also for enjoyment and self improvement'*. What was new in the century that followed was the wholly unprecedented scale of activity, as the desire and ability to pay for such pleasures. . . . One indicator is the number of professional musicians, which the census for England and Wales lists as increasing more than tenfold between 1841 and 1891 (from 3,600 to 38,600). By 1871 musicians came eighty-eighth in a league table of occupations, headed by 1,237,000 domestic servants. Slightly less numerous than the 18,886 law clerks, they were a larger group than the commercial travellers. By 1891 there were nearly twice as many

---

[66] See William Weber, "Mass Culture," 9.

*J.H. Plumb, *The Commercialisation of Leisure in Eighteenth-Century England* (Reading University, 1972) 19.

musicians as there were bank clerks."[67] This entire situation is a remarkable example of an important development in the musical life of an epoch, in which extramusical factors were at least of similar importance to proper musical factors.

IV • MUSICAL SUBCULTURES AND ACCULTURATION

In the middle of the twentieth century, the function of social distinction through music disappeared rapidly from the urban milieu. "The social layers of today are on the whole less differentiated from each other, and positions are less set apart than formerly. They are less separated from each other through their dress, hallmarks, status symbols and representative manners. There are no privileges associated with musical instruments, special sound-groups or dance-practices that would be reserved for one layer in order to characterize it musically."[68] On the other hand, among the middle classes music holds so much prestige that it "embodies the cultural values of the upper classes at the same time that it permits, particularly in its practice, a separation from the social layers which are economically and culturally less favored: children of the middle classes still have their private piano lessons"[69] (at least in some countries). In an industrial world, suffused with the spirit of technology, where music itself is put at the disposal of the consumer—that is to say, at the disposal of a great number of people—thanks to the mass media, the function of social distinction is therefore considerably demystified, even negated. In contemporary societies, the idea of social distinction through music can only be considered naive or as an outmoded remnant of certain conservative social milieus of a limited and more or less isolated nature.

---

[67]Cyril Ehrlich, "Economic History and Music," *Proceedings of the Royal Musical Association* 103 (1976-77) 194.

[68]Walter Wiora, "Der Musikalische Ausdruck von Ständen und Klassen," 106-107.

[69]Paul Beaud, "Musiques, masses, minorités, marginaux," *IRASM* V/1 (1974) 159.

However, "there are broad currents, among the young, which began with the youth movement. They make up a subculture of stamped idiosyncrasies in manner, dress and other areas— including dance and music. So far as they identify themselves with jazz or pop music, they find their musical expression and a means of self-realization."[70] This phenomenon, among others, was rightly stressed by Paul Beaud, who remarked that it is not sufficient to take into consideration only "the numerous contradictions, over which many authors support themselves, for seeing in popular music, for example, only an alien product, alienating them from the consumer society. Although it is legitimate in certain cases, this reductive analysis leads to a neglect of the socially and sociologically important aspects of these subcultural phenomena."[71] Emphasizing that "for reasons inherent in all hierarchical organizations, the tendency of adolescents towards marginalization is an almost universal phenomenon, observed as much by ethnologists as by sociologists,"[72] and that nowadays "the period of adolescence is prolonged ... : the subcultures of youth have thus an increased chance of becoming stabilized and autonomous systems",[73] Paul Beaud affirms that subcultural youth music tends to integrate itself, as a nonisolable element, into the subcultural youth movements: "it expresses, diffuses and reinforces at the same time the value systems belonging to these currents. It testifies to their development, in the same manner that the recent history of North-American jazz cannot be disassociated from the radicalization of black nationalism."[74] Furthermore, "a thesis set forth by Carl Belz[75] went so far as to ascribe the emergence of the rock-music movement in the United States to the autonomous activities of young people. This would indicate

---

[70]Walter Wiora, *Der musikalische Ausdruck von Ständen und Klassen,* 108.
[71]Paul Beaud, "Musiques, masses, minorités, marginaux," 165.
[72]*Ibid.,* 163.
[73]*Ibid.*
[74]*Ibid.* See also Howard S. Becker, *Outsiders. Studies in the Sociology of Deviance* (New York: The Free Press, 1963).
[75]Reference is to Carl Belz's *The Story of Rock* (New York: 1969) 21ff.

a genuine desire for spontaneous, joyful music-making in a clearly specified musical field."[76] In this new "musical mass movement . . . the electro-acoustic equipment offers entirely new possibilities for instrumental combination. More than ever before in this history of music the end result of a sound is dependent on and controllable by the technical equipment. Musical instruments and technical equipment have come to be regarded as inseparable."[77] On the other hand, it is necessary to consider here the subcultural musical phenomena, meaning by that "the cultural forms which are not defined by the size of the population which they concern, but by the radicalism of the new concepts and *patterns* which they place in opposition to both the elite and mass cultures. This is a culture which is in conflict with the dominant cultural system of the country in which it appears."[78]

As reported by Charles Seeger, the term *acculturation* was defined already in 1935 by a committee of the Social Research Council as follows: "Acculturation comprehends those phenomena which result when two groups of individuals having different cultures come into continuous firsthand contact, with subsequent changes in the original cultural patterns of either or both groups."[79] And Alexander L. Ringer suggests that not only our time but also "the nineteenth century produced a number of musical sub-cultures, each pursuing its own organic development in accordance with specific needs and functions"[80] and that even "*musica reservata* be treated as a sub-cultural phenomenon,"[81] though in another sense of the term subculture, i.e. "with

---

[76]Irmgard Bontinck, "Mass Media and New Types of Youth Music," *IRASM*, VI/1 (1975) 51.

[77]*Ibid.*

[78]Paul Beaud, "Discussion," *IRASM*, VI/1 (1975) 126.

[79]Charles Seeger, "Music and Society: Some New-World Evidence on Their Relationship," in *Studies in Musicology 1935-1975* (Berkeley-Los Angeles-London: U. of California Press, 1977) 193, and *American Anthropologist*, XXXVIII, 1 (January-March 1936).

[80]Alexander L. Ringer, *Musical Taste and the Industrial Syndrome, IRASM*, V/1 (1974) 143.

[81]Alexander L. Ringer, "Discussion," *IRASM*, VI/1 (1975) 126.

reference to relatively self-contained segments of the total culture that exist side by side. In other words, the prefix *sub* does not imply a stratified culture in which one stratum ranks higher than another."[82]

---

[82]*Ibid.*

CHAPTER FIVE

THE EXPANSION OF
MUSICAL "CONSUMPTION"

I • DEMOCRATIZATION OF MUSICAL LIFE

The enormous expansion of the musical public, begun in the last century, brought with it an enormous expansion in musical "consumption." But now, when in principle everyone can listen to art music or even take it up as amateurs, musical consumption ceases to be a sign of distinction. We note, with Etienne Gilson, that in the last fifty years the number of European symphonic concert societies has grown considerably. In the United States, "the increase in the production and consumption of traditional music—that of the lyric theatre and concerts—is most remarkable. Musical life has thus not suffered from its industrialization; some think that it has even gained. We could say as much for the number of amateurs who take up an instrument for their own pleasure. . . . The growth in the production and marketing of musical instruments in America proves at least that the mechanization of music does it no harm; on the contrary, it has never manifested such vitality."[1] And if in some European countries it is difficult to get an audience for some regional concert halls, in the United States that problem does not seem to exist. "When we put these facts together with the extremely positive youth

---

[1] Etienne Gilson, *La société de masse et sa culture,* 47.

responses to 'avant-garde' music, we obtain an overall picture that differs substantially from both the European scene and the usual European image of American musical life,"[2] as Alexander L. Ringer stated.

The "democratization" of learned music in the nineteenth century, however, concerned primarily the middle class, for it was in that milieu above all that musical consumption grew. Looking at that growth in the public from a sociological perspective, it is interesting to note a new trend of considerable importance in musical creativity: the full development of Romantic music, which, as expressive and program music, took on proportions never before attained, and reestablished contact between the composer and his era in a particularly profound manner. Even earlier, "the composers of the century of Louis XIV followed their tendencies and served the desires of the public by indicating with their precise titles the sentimental or imitative content of their pieces without words."[3] We need only think of the program compositions of Janequin, Couperin, or Rameau, in order to agree that "representative" music was not born in the nineteenth century. We need only remember the vocal music of Josquin, Marenzio, Gesualdo and Lassus, or the cantatas and Passions of J.S. Bach, to see that expressive music existed well before Beethoven. But these tendencies reached their apogee and their most spectacular fruition in the century of Romanticism. The essential characteristic of that music is that it is generally more accessible and understandable to a large audience, because of the extramusical element it communicates.[4] Thus we can appreciate the extraordinary success of this music not only with the middle-class public, but in the twentieth century, with a public made up of many social layers. It would be tempting to advance the hypothesis that the Romantic composers of the nineteenth century yielded, consciously or not, to a sociological tendency: to respond to a broad public by using a

---

[2]Alexander L. Ringer, "Discussion," *IRASM* VI/1 (1975) 163.

[3]Michel Brenet, *Les Concerts en France sous l'ancien Régime*, 102.

[4]See Ivo Supičić, *La Musique expressive* (Paris: P.U.F., 1957).

more accessible genre, while keeping to the technical and artistic requirements of the times.

In the nineteenth century, however, as well as in earlier times, secular learned music was always a minority affair: first, in respect to the listening public, and then to the artists who created and performed it.[5] The majority of the population was altogether uninvolved. In France, for example, the common people could attend musical performances (which most often presented works of little artistic value) in public places on festive occasions. In the seventeenth century, "public festivals continued to provide free concerts to the people. The Carousel of the Place Royale, for the marriage of Louis XIII in 1612, lasted two days."[6] The people also had "free access once a year to a grand concert of instrumental music which, since the end of the reign of Louis XIV, was given by the Royal Academy of Music in the garden of the Tuileries on August 24—the eve of St. Louis' Day."[7] In addition, the first Paris opera, that of Cambert and Perrin, had a popular franchise. After the Revolution, outdoor musical performances (of a generally lamentable value) began to multiply. Only in the twentieth century, thanks especially to the general social and economic development of many countries and also to the invention of radio and recordings, have many layers of society come in contact with secular learned music; not, however, without difficulties or problems that yet await solution.

We have referred several times to the dynamics of the growth or decline of a musical public or publics. At the close of the nineteenth century, we can see a movement toward the democratization of music; and in our day, its compartmentalization into more or less esoteric spheres—processes accompanied by parallel growth and shrinkage of the public. It is interesting to see an analogous phenomenon in the Hellenistic

---

[5]From a sociological point of view, this is also one of the criteria that differentiates learned music from ethnic music. The latter has never addressed itself to a social minority nor been practiced primarily on its behalf.

[6]Michel Brenet, *Les Concerts en France sous l'ancien Régime*, 19.

[7]*Ibid.*, 169.

period of Greece, and under the Roman Empire. As Walter Wiora remarked, at that time of expanding Hellenistic culture in large centers such as Rome and Alexandria, an essential characteristic of musical culture was the existence of music for the urban masses at the theater, the circus, in amusement and dances. Wealthy persons owned musician-slaves almost as one today a radio or record player; we have, as well, an entire genre of industrialized and commercialized music for the masses. Dion of Trosa in Bithynia traces an interesting picture of an artistic cult in the first century A.D.: the spectators are beside themselves, they acclaim the virtuoso as a savior or god, in their enthusiasm they jump from their seats higher than the dancers[8]— behavior altogether analogous to that one sees often today, especially in the field of popular music.

II • THE DISFUNCTIONALIZATION OF MUSIC

We recognize here yet another perspective for study and research in the sociology of music: the growth and decline of audiences for various musical genres. Moreover, it is appropriate in particular to study the phenomena of functionalization and disfunctionalization in music. Although these different musical functions appear in all their diversity throughout history, we discern today a *disfunctionalization* of music that, appearing at the close of the nineteenth century, sometimes seems to be an exceptional phenomenon, without precedent. According to Walter Wiora, "with the fall of the *ancien Régime*, the autonomy of art expanded and developed to an extent never before known in world history. This includes the disfunctionalization of music and the freeing of composers from commissions today."[9] One could speak rather of "a transformation of the social functions of music toward the end of the eighteenth century. With the birth of the Classical symphony, music became autonomous, forsaking

---

[8]See Walter Wiora, *The Four Ages of Music*, 85.
[9]Walter Wiora, "Der musikalische Ausdruck von Ständen und Klassen," 108.

its previous social function as accompaniment to particular circumstances. This is what Kurt Blaukopf demonstrated when he wrote that 'one of the innovations which the world of music owes to the classical Viennese school is the creation of works not destined for any particular occasion, place of performance, or predetermined musical ensemble, but living a life of their own.' [10]" [11] Here a special issue should also be taken into consideration: the *autonomization* of music which, as is generally so with art, is "correlated with the establishment of a distinct social category of professional artists, who are more and more inclined to follow no rules other than those of their own artistic tradition (rules passed down from their predecessors which furnish a point of departure or of rupture), and more and more able to free their production and products from all social servitude. . . . "[12]

To the conclusions of Robert Hoebaer[13] we may add that it is not only having to work hard, but also being unacculturated to learned music, and feeling removed from it, which still alienates a large portion of the public from music in the twentieth century. Although this phenomenon should not be generalized to apply to the whole world, this disfunctionalization concerns learned music primarily, not all music in general, or all genres of music. We hold also, with Robert Wangermée, that in the nineteenth century "there was a break between art which had ties with the past, and to which, in the genres recognized as noble—the symphony, chamber music, etc.—cultural ambitions are assigned: a gratuitous art which has no end other than itself; and, on the other hand, music 'for sale,' very 'functional,' which only

---

[10]Kurt Blaukopf, "Symphonie, concerts, public," *Le monde de la symphonie.* U. von Rauchhaupt et al. from Ger. by J. Fournier and D. Henry (Hamburg: Polydor, 1972) 9.

[11]Michel De Coster, "L'art mass-médiatisé: L'exemple de la musique classique enregistrée," *IRASM* VI/2 (1975) 257.

[12]Pierre Bourdieu, "Disposition esthétique et compétence artistique," *Les Temps modernes* 295 (Feb 1971) 1345-1378, quoted in P. Beaud and A. Willener, *Musique et vie quotidienne,* 34-35.

[13]See below p. 229.

intended to amuse." According to Wangermée, "in the 1830s an opposition is noted between that which was called 'light music' and, sadly enough, 'serious music.' "[14]

Having set these preliminary boundaries, we can now consider a first approach that may help explain this disfunctionalization sociologically: the study of social institutions that, compared to those of preceding century, have passed through profound changes in structure. At the end of the last century especially, professional musicians were no longer bound by the guilds, by service to the church, or by duties at court. The musician had other possible means of employment, and became ever more free in this respect. He stopped being so restricted by local limitations; contributing to this were more and more frequent competitions between virtuosi and composers, certain of whom resembled in their mobility the wandering musicians of the Middle Ages. Walter Salmen has traced an excellent social history of the latter, giving thereby an important model of the way to examine the social position of a group of musicians with a view to understanding as completely as possible the different aspects of their lives and the conditions laid down for them by society. Such a basic work, rich in historical documentation, provides an indispensable foundation for proper sociological research in the future.[15] The disappearance of the corporate guilds, the growth of the public, and the new organization of musical life, which was based more and more on commercial exploitation, all separated music from its former social function in restricted aristocratic

---

[14]Robert Wangermée, Preface to Jacqueline De Clercq, *La profession de musicien—Une enquête* (Brussels: Editions de l'Institut de Sociologie, 1970) 10. According to the same author, "the sixteenth-century polyphonic chanson must be considered what we call light music. Aesthetes would like to think that there is only one sort of music worthy of esteem, that music which, somewhat over-earnestly, they have labeled *serious*, the kind of music which today is confined to the concert hall. . . Its history is that of an art of high culture in which masterpieces of the past and present now exist side by side in an imaginary museum of the ear." *Flemish Music and Society in the Fifteenth and Sixteenth Centuries,* Tr. Robert Erich Wolf (New York: Praeger, 1968) 135.

[15]See Walter Salmen, *Der fahrende Musiker im europäischen Mittelalter* (Kassel: J. P. Hinnenthal, 1960).

milieus and presented it instead as a spectacle to be paid for, accessible to all in principle and independent of all extramusical occasions or circumstances (a status it has held from the nineteenth century until today).

A second area in which study can clarify the social disfunctionalization of music is that of social *models*, those more or less standardized images of collective behavior that are of considerable importance in social life. These cover a very wide range, from traditional clichés to fashions and passing fads; and they govern styles, proper behavior, and clothes, as well as political, legal, cultural, religious, and other aspects of social life. They also embody that which has been called, in respect to the public and its role in relation to music, the lifestyle of a social group or class, which is capable of exerting a strong influence on musical creativity, the orientation of the repertoire, and musical life in general. But it happens that changes brought about in the lifestyles of nineteenth-century society—and thus in the social models of certain milieus, especially the middle class—required music to be placed on a different level. Music ceased to be a decorative or ceremonial element or a matter of display, and became rather a sign of a good education. The emphasis became interior rather than exterior; music gradually ceased to perform a purely or predominantly ornamental function, and began to fulfill an autonomous aesthetic and cultural function.

Nevertheless, the whole process of social disfunctionalization of music would be neither comprehensible nor explicable without the establishment of certain new collective *behaviors,* which have a certain regularity, but are set outside society's organized musical institutions. Of this we have partly already spoken: the collective behavior of musicians as well as of the public.

To this we must add the conditioning of social *roles* played by musicians—as much structural social roles as symbolic social roles. Being freed from his ancient role as servant or wage earner and having obtained his emancipation, the musician changed his attitude. In his new role, facing a new public, he refused to have outdated social functions conferred on his works. Romanticism gave him, at the most, a symbolic role incompatible with its former social functions. In Romanticism the musical work contributes to the dissolution of that function in order to assume another—individualistic, and of a more psychological and aesthetic order. Music proposes to express the personal feelings of the musician and to establish a new contact with the listener. The latter no longer charges the musician with the expression of collective feelings, but meets him in the act of listening to the music presented to him. It will be the musician who must impose on the public his own manner of feeling. According to Theodor W. Adorno, on the other hand, the music market has often "refused that which was progressive, and thus stopped musical progress: without any doubt, many composers (and by no means only from the middle of the nineteenth-century) have been led to repress in themselves constrained to get adapted, that which, at heart, they greatly desired."[16]

Finally, we could mention the important aspect of ideas and collective *values* in the process of autonomization of learned music in the last two centuries, limiting the observation, however, to the strictly musical domain in which they are displayed. "This autonomization leads not only to the affirmation of the absolute primacy of the form, but also to a negation of the relationships of production in which the artist is situated when he composes: the creative act is that by which the musician escapes all social demands and is freed from these relationships while going beyond his own situation."[17] The formalist doctrine of music, which in the eighteenth century was the property of a few rare individuals such as Chabanon (who may be considered a precurser of Hanslick) became from that time and up to the present not only the appanage of an entire stream of musicians always more numerous, but also the appanage of a broad variety of listeners who refuse to look for anything extramusical in the musical work, who refuse to consider it, or better, to hear to it as expressing some aspects of the personality of the composer (be it on a psychological or a spiritual level). But the collective

---

[16]Theodor W. Adorno, "Sociologie de la musique," *Musique en jeu* II (1971) 8.
[17]P. Beaud and A. Willener, *Musique et vie quotidienne*, 35.

attitude among musicians and the public on this whole important issue brings up a profound difference in the ideas one has and the evaluations one makes in considering musical art. Here prevails a principally aesthetic understanding of a work evaluated in the purity of its artistic autonomy, which from now on is the only consideration—an idea Hanslick affirmed with enthusiasm, opposing this thesis of the specificity of music to the Hegelian idea of the unity of all the arts. But it is obvious that such a conception disfunctionalizes the musical work. It is disfunctionalized not only on a *social* level, but, up to a certain point, on a purely *human* level, because it is no longer considered as an expression of man, but more or less as a construction, a structure (a word sometimes *à la mode*), a sonorous arabesque, as Hanslick said, an architecture of sounds, in sum, as a universe apart, entirely autonomous and specific, whose total value resides in being harmoniously ordered according to formal principles which are variable and in evolution, but of a strictly technical nature. So "music will preserve the pre-eminence of that aesthetic finality until about the middle of the twentieth century, when an experimental music will be born, forcing art to return again to more definite social functions."[18] Within the body of that aesthetic conception, one could, it is true, attribute to music human functions other than expressive ones. But altogether, they are a long way from that functional aspect music assumes in many circumstances of community life, not only in former societies, but also in contemporary societies, especially rural ones. Such was the situation in the towns up until the last century. And such, in part, can be the new refunctionalization of certain recent musical works. "The problem of the functionalization and disfunctionalization of music . . . deserves, meanwhile, to be examined less from the point of view of a dichotomy than from that of a spread of diverse functions which take on, one after another, a certain relief."[19] The more so if, as Irmgard Bontinck stressed, referring to the qualitative change of the

---

[18]Michel De Coster, "L'Art mass-médiatisé," 258.
[19]*Ibid.*, 267.

message in music transmitted today through the mass media, "a factor originating from the characteristics of the technological transmission chain itself is far more important for music-sociological research than the new functional types of music."[20]

III • THE MASS MEDIA AND MASS MUSICAL CULTURE

Although the concept of the mass media can be understood more broadly—encompassing, for example, the press at large or even a specialized literature in the service of mass communication[21]—the following remarks will be limited to records, radio, and television, only as they relate to music.

According to Georges Friedmann, the "technical environment" that has created the mass media (and which is also partly produced by them) is formed by both the stimuli that emerge from it and by people's behavior and attitudes toward these stimuli. So the technical environment is a specifically social and human environment as well; the problems raised by the mass media in their relationship to music are not merely technical, but are also particularly sociological problems, and in some respects, cultural, psychological, and spiritual problems. Musical messages transmitted through the mass media act on several levels. They affect not only the aesthetic receptivity, but also the sensibility and the intellectual, physical, and moral spheres of man as a whole; consequently, it is necessary for all these aspects to be approached from as broad a base as possible. It is significant that musicians and sociologists themselves, in addition to philosophers, are beginning to see moral problems in the realm of music and its technical environment today; as Bergson already stated from a general philosophical standpoint, they consider that the development of the modern world, of modern techniques and modern art requires a "supplement of soul."[22]

---

[20]Irmgard Bontinck, "Mass Media and New Types of Youth Music," 49.

[21]See Barry S. Brook, "Music Literature and Modern Communication," *College music symposium* IX (1969) 48-59.

[22]See Theodor W. Adorno, "The Radio Symphony, an Experiment in

However, the mass media do not seem to have any automatic power to bring listeners closer to music in an authentic and enriching way, as was sometimes over-optimistically believed; they are able only to bring music closer to listeners, which is by no means the same thing. The fact that it is possible these days to hear or to listen to more music (good and bad) than before has not in itself proved sufficient. Social and especially educational influences seem to be the relevant, perhaps even decisive, forces in awakening the true interest of potential listeners and in making music a cultural "necessity" for them. The results of various studies in this area seem to be in concord. According to Paul Beaud, the mere possibility of hearing a piece of music many times, by means of the mass media, does not guarantee any real improvement in this area.[23] The findings of a relatively recent "Utrecht survey and other recent studies in the Netherlands may be said to have given strong support to the supposition that taste for fine music requires education, cultivation, and personal effort."[24] In analyzing the results of some inquiries made even earlier in the United States,[25] and more recently in Europe by the B.B.C., R.A.I., R.T.B., and Süddeutsche Rundfunk, Robert Wangermée comes to the conclusion that in spite of variations, statistics indicate indisputable correlations in all countries between the levels of education and the appreciation of serious music. But that does not indicate, in any way, that school in a proper sense can boast of molding musical character,[26]

Theory," *Radio research 1941*. P. Lazarsfeld and P. Stanton, ed. (New York: 1942); Etienne Gilson, *La société de masse et sa culture*, Ch. II, "Musique de masse," 47-74; Georges Friedmann, "Rôle et place de la musique dans une société industrielle," *Diogène* LXXII (1970) 43; Pierre Schaeffer, Discussion in "Musique et an-archie," *Bulletin de la Société française de Philosophie* III (1971) 108.

[23]See Paul Beaud, "Musiques, masses, minorités, marginaux," 158-159.

[24]Hugo de Jager, "Listening to the Audience," *Journal of Research in Music Education* XV/4 (1967) 299.

[25]Edward A. Suchman, "Invitation to Music: A Study of the Creation of New Music Listeners by the Radio," *Radio research 1941*. Ed. P. Lazarsfeld and P. Stanton. (New York: 1942) 140-311.

[26]Robert Wangermée, "La radio, la musique et les moralistes de la culture,"

at least in a number of West-European countries. "We must think, rather, that the social level is more important, and that raising it favors both general education and a certain conception of culture in which music takes its place."[27] And according to Hugo de Jager, it is essentially "a certain amount of cultivation that will decide the fate of music in modern society."[28]

If there is still controversy as to whether or not the mass media seriously affect the human "self" through real pressures at the three principal levels—information, formation of judgments, and personal activity—the listener to the mass media in the "optical age" (as Karel Pech put it[29]) seems to be exposed (though most likely to a lesser extent) to problems similar to those that beset the viewer watching television. Having so many sounds and images at our command overdevelops the corresponding ability to capture them, to the detriment of personal *activity* in both a general and a limited sense (i.e., in some particular fields—music, art, sport, etc.). In music, it was much more so in "Darbietungsmusik" than in "Umgangsmusik";[30] it is even more so in "Übertragungsmusik"[31] than in the two former categories. On the other hand, "the increasing differentiation between performers and receptors can be understood as a mark of a high musical culture: thus the irrevocable gulf without the least possibility of mutual contact between performers and

Publics et techniques de la diffusion collective. (Brussels: Ed. de l'Institut de Sociologie-Université Libre de Bruxelles, n.d.) 451-452.

[27]*Ibid.,* 452.

[28]Hugo de Jager, "Listening to the Audience," *Journal of Research in Music Education* XV/4 (1967) 299.

[29]See Karel Pech, *Hören im "optischen Zeitalter"* (Karlsruhe: G. Braun, (1969).

[30]See Heinrich Besseler, *Das musikalische Hören der Neuzeit,* Berichte über die Verhandlungen der sächsischen Akademie der Wissenschaften zu Leipzig, Philologisch-historische Klasse, CIV/6 (Berlin: 1959) 14.

[31]See Konrad Niemann, "Mass Media: New Ways of Approach to Music and new Patterns of Musical Behaviour," *New Patterns of Musical Behaviour of the Young Generation in Industrial Societies.* Irmgard Bontinck, ed. (Vienna: Universal Edition, 1974) 49.

receptors is a consequence of presentation through the mass media."[32]

Georges Friedmann's distinction[33] between free time ("temps libre") and freed time ("temps libéré"), insofar as the first concerns true *listening* (which alone permits "the engagement of the personality" and its "enrichment"), while mere *hearing* (which is often reduced to the reception of a "sonorous background accompanying the most diversified occupations") would fit the definition of freed time, could be accepted as the statement of a real problem. Preferably we might add that free time be understood not only as "entirely at our disposal for cultural *possibilities*," but also really focused by the human self in the function of its equilibrated inner growth. According to Friedmann, "hearing is the reception of a program heard by chance, admitted, sometimes even endured—in any situation and in any circumstances where the program is not *chosen*. Listening, on the contrary, involves a search for a program, a choice and maintained attention."[34] However, this is not necessarily always the case: a chosen radio program can be simply heard, while a program not chosen can be listened to.

In another sense it can be asked to what extent the mass media can be deleterious from the simple fact that they tend to take up ever greater quantities of time in human life (and also from their development and introduction of new devices and technical possibilities which successively capture the attention of the public and artificially produce new "consumer needs"). One might well ask, particularly with reference to the influence of television, what is happening to human "active" time, be it "free" or "freed." The mass media undoubtedly contribute to the "aggressiveness" of the contemporary acoustic environment

---

[32]Helmut Rösing, "Zur Rezeption technisch vermittelter Musik. Psychologische, ästhetische un musikalisch-funktionsbezogene Aspekte," *Musik in den Massenmedien Rundfunk und Fernsehen*. Ed. Hans-Christian Schmidt (Mainz: Schott, 1976) 47.

[33]See Georges Friedmann, "Rôle et place de la musique dans une société industrielle," *Diogène* LXXII (1970) 33-34.

[34]*Ibid.*, 30.

and to the fact that music is often heard against one's will. It was right for Blaukopf to speak of an intensified "social obtrusiveness of mass media music"[35] compared to that, according to Kant, of music as such. On the other hand, in spite of their unquestionable and well known advantages, the mass media seem to be able to stimulate and favor, more than live music performance, a sort of "aestheticist" attitude of "least resistance," of passive observation, which is the opposite of the true contemplation of and reaction to an artistic object created by others and communicated through a *natural channel.* Such an orientation of mind is apt not only to weaken the sense of total reality: it is also the result of that weakening. Preponderant or almost exclusive orientation to what has been said and created by others—that is, to artistic objects—is disproportionately reinforced by the intrusion of the mass media into daily life through their *artificial channels.* This kind of orientation can stimulate a unilateral development, in particular the development of a "television mentality" or a "spectator attitude" as a substitute for activities of a real social or spiritual nature. At the extreme lie two possibilities. One is the real enrichment of human lives through music, and the other creation, through music, of an alienating world of illusion, the latter being greatly encouraged by the mass media. However, both glorification and rejection of the mass media for their alleged action upon audiences should be carefully avoided, as such extreme conclusions are not justified by actual experience. As far as music is concerned, the mass media can be fully accepted and justified only to the extent that they serve the contents of its message, transmitted and transformed as it is by the mass media themselves. Thanks to the mass media, the old theories of art as a flight or escape from the realities of life to a higher world seem to have obtained further support, at least for some analysts who consider that they contribute to such a flight or escape.

---

[35]Kurt Blaukopf, "New Patterns of Musical Behaviour of the Young Generation in Industrial Societies," *New Patterns of Musical Behaviour of the Young Generation in Industrial Societies.* Ed. Irmgard Bontinck, 13.

According to some writers, the mass media would also create a "psychological illiteracy" providing a compensatory alternative for the failures people experience in life[36] and for the richness of life that they do not experience; the mass media would create a pseudoenvironment;[37] they would become a regular narcotic preventing any effective social activity and finally producing dependent individuals, not free human beings. As to their role in weakening the capacity for critical thought, as well as in the manipulation of opinion in general, the issue remains highly controversial.[38] It seems, however, that the mass media are less powerful than they sometimes appear: "People develop certain techniques of resistance which derive from their education, culture, environment, and a multitude of other influences. And at first, they make a preliminary choice in what is presented to them by the mass media."[39] The mass media have, rather, a first effect of reinforcing attitudes or (put more positively, perhaps) of exploiting certain predispositions.[40] [41] Perhaps thre is a kind of "preventive selection" made by listeners themselves, at least as far as music is concerned. Most listeners prefer to be confirmed in their tastes and preferences rather than challenged. In spite of their unquestionable power, the mass media act more as conditioning than as simple determinants. The extent of their final impact depends upon whom it falls. The mass media are not so responsible for the effects they produce as is the listener himself.

The specific question of whether records are preferable to radio or television lies perhaps in the less ephemeral character

[36]See C. W. Wills, *The Power Elite* (New York: Oxford U., 1956) 314.

[37]See T. Peterson, J. W. Jensen and W. L. Rivers, *The Mass Media and Modern Society* (New York: Holt, Rinehart and Winston, 1965) 23.

[38]See for example Denis McQuail, *Towards a Sociology of Mass Communication* (London: Collier-Macmillan, 1969) ch. II-3; and Kurt Blaukopf, "New Patterns of Musical Behaviour of the Young Generation in Industrial Societies," 22.

[39]Robert Wangermée, "La radio, la musique et les moralistes de la culture," 457.

[40]Wangermée refers to Edward A. Suchman, "Invitation to Music: A Study of the Creation of New Music Listeners by the Radio," 140-311.

[41]Robert Wangermée, "La radio, la musique et les moralistes de la culture," 459.

of their message, for what they transmit can be heard time after time, and in principle, can survive almost "forever"; this makes it possible to gain a deeper insight into its contents. Furthermore, radio and television shows could exercise a more formative influence on listeners, since they are to some extent "computed" according to time schedules that impose their own rhythm on those who use them, thus acquiring adaptive changes in behavior. Their function "is by no means limited to the dissemination of music; it also effects changes in the position of music within the society and in the musical practice."[42] Furthermore, the mass media make changes in patterns of musical behavior.[43] Thus, for instance, "live music is no longer the exclusive purveyor of musical culture. This is . . . dominated increasingly by the music of the technical media. Numerous titles are produced only in the recording studio, especially by means of playback techniques and special effects."[44] But records seem to offer a larger margin for free selection than do radio and television. This is a matter not only of time schedules, but of content. As was emphasized by Carl Belz, referring to rock music in the United States, it "has existed primarily on records. Records were the music's initial medium."[45] And as Günter Kleinen put it, Belz emphasizes that a disc recording is generally considered to be live performance, while a live performance attempts to reproduce the recording.[46]

The situation is quite different when we consider ethnic music, or musics in oral tradition: "those musics which we hear from the record player with a faultless material fidelity are only photographs in sound. They represent, in an image always like itself, a changing reality of nonwritten musical traditions, in

---

[42]Kurt Blaukopf, "New Patterns of Musical Behaviour of the Young Generation in Industrial Societies," 13-30.

[43]See Irmgard Bontinck, "Mass Media and New Types of Youth Music: Methodological and Terminological Problems," *IRASM* VI/1 (1975) 50-51.

[44]Günter Kleinen, *Jugend und musikalische Subkultur* (Regensburg: G. Bosse, 1973) 13.

[45]Carl Belz, *The Story of Rock* (New York: Oxford U., 1969) 2.

[46]Günter Kleinen, *Jugend und musikalische Subkultur*, 13.

which, on the field, the version of tomorrow will certainly have been different from that of yesterday . . . This music lives only in a context, and this context disappears in the record . . . We see with what care musicology must treat the precious and irreplaceable document in sound which the record provides."[47] Pre-Classical art music presents a similar problem. As its notation did not constitute a complete picture of its musical text (leaving out any information as to how it should be played), and as its interpretation has varied both then and now, the recording can be viewed here has more as a document of different styles of interpretation or various tastes that have governed its performance, than an "original."

Without going as far as Marshall McLuhan[48] and his view that the medium is the *message* and that, as reported by Michel De Coster, the appearance of new media transmitting Classical music modified the content itself of this music, we can accept the opinion that "new media shape a new culture or, better, determine first of all new ways of comprehending the old."[49] If the mass media condition musical content—the musical message itself—the environment in which music is performed also contributes to its functional transformation. Extracted from the social context in which it was once produced and performed, old music passes through a variety of environments and is, moreover, appreciated in a variety of new ways and for different reasons than formerly. Music as a rule has been written for a predetermined place of performance. Conceptions such as 'a cappella,"Sonata da chiesa,"chamber music,"Tafelmusik,' and even 'orchestral music' make that just as clear as the classification, common up until the end of the eighteenth century, into field, church, chamber and theatre music.[50] Thus "the more a work

---

[47]Jacques Chailley, "La musicologie et le disque," *Conférences des Journées d'études* (Paris: Chiron, 1965) 128.

[48]See Marshall McLuhan, *Understanding Media* (London: Routledge and Kegan Paul, 1964).

[49]Michel De Coster, "L'art mass-médiatisé," 263.

[50]See the appropriate headings in Riemann Musiklexikon, Sachteil. Ed. Hans Heinrich Eggebrecht (Mainz: 1967). Cf. Helmut Rösing, "Zur Rezeption technisch vermittelter Musik," 45.

belongs to the realm of *Gebrauchsmusik*, the closer its bond is to the actual occasion; the more a work belongs to the sphere of art music, the freer this bond is, especially since the beginning of the Classic era."[51] On the other hand, "art music itself, produced for a specific place of performance and performance milieu can, by means of separation from this performance milieu, lose force of statement: Bach's Passions in the concert hall instead of the church, Beethoven's symphonies in the open air instead of the concert hall, Schubert's string quartets in the gymnasium instead of a small recital hall."[52] But if the "here and now" of a work is lacking when transmitted through the mass media, nonetheless it is reshaped by them: there exists another "here and now" to replace it. As Gisèle Brelet has already pointed out, the radio, for instance, leads to an "abolition of frontiers in space and time";[53] it "achieves this despatialization of sound which music initiated";[54] thus the radiophonic universe, like the music universe, is one of pure sound, and the "recorded perform- ance . . . is a present which remains, an experienced time torn away from time."[55]

Listeners cannot enjoy and profit by something about which they have no opportunity to become informed. In this sense the dissemination of music through the mass media has a highly positive social impact. But the mass media favor and intensify communication on both an individual and a collective level, in only one direction (from those who transmit the message to those for whom it is intended, and from groups or societies having more developed communicative systems, or a monopoly of these, to those whose systems are less developed or nonexistent). For example, it is true that "the influence of the United States and England on the popular music scene of all industrialized countries went through recordings. These transmitted the

---

[51]*Ibid.*

[52]*Ibid.*, 46.

[53]Gisèle Brelet, "La radio purifie et confirme la musique," *Cahiers d'études de radio-télévision* III-IV (1955) 367.

[54]*Ibid.*, 369.

[55]*Ibid.*, 368.

repertoire as well as the sound of the leading groups."[56] And as the usual consequence in normal circumstances is the transmission of meaning and messages through the mass media, with the influence exerted in one direction only, in the end the question of cultural dissemination sometimes becomes more a question of both economic and technical power than of artistic quality. A case study of some musical genres or trends would probably confirm this assertion, which is here based upon observation.

In spite of the more or less developed variety and quality of particular radio and television music programs, these mass media seem to produce a uniformity in musical messages, creating commonly acceptable standards and a "universalization" of culture more than any earlier means of communication. They also seem to impose artistic values on the listeners by promoting certain particular genres of music more than the others. This type of musical culture could be considered an essentially urban one. On the other hand, music heard through the mass media may also contribute to the development of group "self-identification," if it affirms some group feelings or becomes characteristic or typical of a group (e.g., youth music). Symbols of technological culture, the mass media can thus serve as the means of social integration and assimilation, via music, for both groups and individuals; yet they can also play a negative role, as has happened mostly with television and radio, in the artificiality of their approach, creating an illusion of communication rather than promoting real sociability and interpersonal relationships. They may even break down relationships to some extent by isolating people, thus having an unfavorable effect on real and natural immediate communication. Also we might ask whether or not mass media audiences are the real public. Being in fact social groupings "at a distance," they can be recognized by their behavior, tastes, or specific attitudes toward a particular type or genre of music. It does seem that the mass media have reduced local audiences of music, or rather, have created new

---

[56]Günter Kleinen, *Jugend und musikalische Subkultur*, 13.

types of audiences, both national and international, that exist alongside those already extant.

Recognizing the enormous growth in the "objective" accessibility of music that the development of the mass media made possible, we might also ask to what extent they may be responsible for the decay of some types of music or even of particular musical works (which may be casually discarded as if they were used up and worn out). Because of the constant repetition of musical works in the mass media, they sometimes no longer touch the common sensibility, no longer excite either the emotions or the curiosity of a certain number of informed listeners. On the other hand, it would also be possible to regard this phenomenon as a counterpart to the growing interest in new music.[57] What could be cause and what effect here is a question for empirical inquiry. In any case, we can assume that in this respect the mass media have played a truly social function, or at least have led to some effects or consequences of sociological nature; i.e., the decline of interest in some compositions or music, and inversely, the contribution to the dissemination of contemporary serious music, and above all, popular music.

If the mass media change the behavior of musical audiences, they do not, however, seem to affect the so-called active and passive attitudes of listeners in a simply dichotomous way, as was sometimes believed. In reference to a survey made in Belgium, Gabriel Thoveron concluded that, while television is almost totally "active," the response to radio is divided nearly equally between active listening and passive hearing.[58] Without any doubt, responses vary from place to place among listeners. A more general problem remains: What are the particular tendencies inherent in different kinds of mass media, with regard to music transmitted through them? Would the special

[57]See Georges Friedmann, "Rôle et place de la musique dans une société industrielle," 37.

[58]See Gabriel Thoveron, *Radio et télévision dans la vie quotidienne* (Brussels: Editions de l'Institut de Sociologie, 1971) 391.

qualities of radio, rather than those of records, make it more appropriate for the creation of a bland musical decor, while television primarily maintains the role of the audiences as spectators of musical events, rather than transmitting the musical event alone with its specific message? First of all, Friedmann's and Thoveron's distinction between active listening and passive hearing is too simplistic. There is a variety of ways in which music can be heard or listened to. Empirical studies in this field confirm this assertion. As Robert Wangermée showed, these various degrees of attention and concentration apply not only in listening to the reception of music transmitted through the mass media, but also in listening to live performances. On the other hand, referring to an inquiry of budget-time made in 1964 by the R.T.B., Wangermée states that "active listening itself is not necessarily an exclusive listening. Indeed, the interviewees assert that they can listen attentively to the radio while carrying on other activities . . . In fact, listening to the radio thus doubles, for the most part, with the exercise of other activities."[59] Accordingly, at least three fundamental types of musical reception could be differentiated: exclusive listening, active listening accompanied by a secondary activity on the part of the listener, and passive hearing becoming secondary because accompanied by a primary activity and concentration on something other than music.

Regardless of this distinction, different types of amateur listeners could be also distinguished from other points of view. Thus, "for the tourist of waves (touriste des ondes[60]) music is above all a decor and diversion. He listens to what the radio offers, but with no particular curiosity. If he prefers that music and listens to it, it is because it seems more agreeable to hear

---

[59]Robert Wangermée, "La radio, la musique et les moralistes de la culture," 438-450.

[60]This term proposed by Jack Bornoff seems well adapted to this type of melomaniac. See "Technologie, techniciens et vie musicale," Cultures, UNESCO I (1973) 270.

than others (jazz or 'variety' music)."[61] Another type of listener, the product of mass media, is characterized primarily by the great interest in the communication techniques concerning music: large collection of records; sophisticated technical material (this type speaks most of stereo or magnetophone); intensive reader of specialized reviews, often several at once. Formed by the modern means of mass communication, this type of music-lover is evidently made sensible to productions of actuality; in the same way, his musical tastes reflect the homogenized culture diffused by the mass media.[62]

Another question concerning music in the mass media is whether or not general trends will confirm the assertion that the growth of broadcast and technically reproduced music has a harmful effect on the development, not only of musical amateurism, but of musical professionalism as well—just as, conversely, it seems to have a beneficial effect on the encouragement and extension of some categories of music making, regardless of their genre and cultural or subcultural character.[63] Particular inquiries in this field, however, cannot lead to a global answer. Here also, situations differ from place to place and from case to case, requiring very careful empirical analyses. As to the economic and commercial aspects of the mass-media industry, and its relationship to musical production and reproduction, this is an immense domain that still remains largely unexplored.[64]

---

[61]Nicole Berthier, "L'amateur de musique. Une approche sociologique," *IRASM* VIII/1 (1977) 33.

[62]See *Ibid.,* 34.

[63]See Georges Friedmann, *op. cit.,* 32, and Irmgard Bontinck, "Mass Media and New Types of Youth Music: Methodological and Terminological Problems," 50-51.

[64]As to records, see for example R. Reichardt, *Die Schallplatte als kulturelles und ökonomisches Phänomen. Ein Beitrag zum Problem der Kunstkommerzialisierung* (Zürich: 1962); Heinz Ott Luthe, "La musique enregistrée et l'industrie du disque," *Revue internationale des sciences sociales,* Vol. XX/4 (1968) 712-724; Michel De Coster, *Le disque, art ou affaires? Analyse sociologique d'une industrie culturelle* (Grenoble: Presses Universitaires de Grenoble, 1976).

CHAPTER SIX

THE SOCIAL STATUS AND ROLE
OF THE MUSICIAN

I • COLLECTIVE ATTITUDES TOWARD MUSICIANS

We cannot consider the social status of the musician without also taking into account the various interconnected aspects and levels of social reality upon which this status depends. To be understood, therefore, this status must be clarified from the point of view of all the socioartistic conditionings, and especially the sociohistorical conditionings, that are fundamental to its makeup.[1]

Sociological research on this subject should be oriented in several directions: first of all, toward investigation of the musician's status with regard to the whole web of relevant sociohistorical conditionings, including the dynamics of the social groupings to which the musicians belong and how these same groupings come into contact and conflict. Second, on the level of sociohistorical conditionings, sociological research should be oriented toward the study of the musician's status in a temporal perspective, in relation to collective values and ideas generated by society concerning the musician and his artistic work. Third, a sociological study of the musician's status should be oriented toward the existing artistic and musical inheritance provided by

---

[1]On the first of these see below, p. 319ff.

the traditions of the past and the customs of the musician's lifetime, and thus toward socioartistic conditionings. In addition, all these issues may be considered in the contexts of different global societies and the hierarchies of groups, strata, and classes therein. Finally, the social status of the musician could be studied from the point of view of different types of sociability— that is, the different ways in which the musician can be tied to and by a social whole, whether it be a professional or merely an amateur group, an extramusical social group, a social class, and so on.

Without being able to review even briefly all of these above-mentioned aspects, which to some degree determine the social status of the musician in all societies (and which would necessitate the prior account of a social history of music[2]), we propose here simply to break ground and to indicate some problems and perspectives for research, not without taking into consideration the different situations in which musicians can be found in various cultures and civilizations. Thus, for example, as Edith Gerson-Kiwi in a rather general way pointed out, "the social position of the ritual musician in the Orient is . . . very different from that in the West. He is classified as belonging to the priesthood and is to be compared only to the greatest of his secular colleagues . . . The human voice reigns supreme over all man-made musical instruments as the repository of the divine in Man. In the case of the cantor, where his singing is bound up with the message of holy texts, this fact elevates him to a class apart in his community, not comparable to other classes and decidedly not to the modest category of the Western cantor-schoolmaster."[3]

In society and for society, musicians are in fact specialized workers; they are treated this way both individually and as a group. Musical activity is regarded as just one type of work

---

[2]With regard to the composer, interesting aspects are discussed in Walter Wiora, *Komponist und Mitwelt* (Kassel-Basel: Bärenreiter, 1964).

[3]Edith Gerson-Kiwi, "The Musician in Society: East and West," *Cultures* I/1 (1973) 167.

among others, and in diverse global societies this work is usually paid for in the same way as any other socially useful work. Whether he is paid in kind or in cash, the musician is socially a worker. Consequently, his social status depends on the social conceptions—especially the conceptions of his potential employers—of the value of work in general, and artistic work in particular, prevalent in his time. The collective mentality thus exercises an important function here. The musician is classified in society according to the social hierarchy of predominant values in the milieu of his activity, or according to the currently accepted values of that socie y regarding artistic work—in the same way that the individual person is generally classified. His specific situation varies, however, not only from one era to another and from one society to another, but also from one country to another and from one category to another. The social status of the musician in each society and at each particular social juncture is a question of fact and only of fact, which, to be understood, demands continuously renewed efforts of investigation and interpretation.[4] We can never generalize about the status of the musician if we are to justify, even to a small degree, sociological analysis which could, in fact, only benefit from the reinforcement of historical confirmation. Although from a different point of view, the social status of the musician in different global societies might appear analogous, some differences are always present and must be pointed out.

Thus one of the important aspects of social reality affecting the status of the musician in society is that of collective attitudes. These imply a mentality comprising affective preferences and distastes, predispositions toward certain predetermined behavior and reactions, and tendencies to assume or to attribute to others precise social roles. They also imply a social framework in which social symbols manifest themselves and particular values are accepted or repudiated. Thus, in ancient Egyptian society for example, some of the high officials charged with the supervision

---

[4]On this topic, see Jacqueline De Clercq, *La profession de musicien—Une enquête* (Brussels: Editions de l'Institut de Sociologie, 1970).

of the royal music are known by name (as are several instrumentalists of the ancient empire), along with mention of their
specialties and their activities,[5] although musicians of that era
were generally anonymous—a proof of the minor importance
attributed to their position in society. Hans Hickmann also
mentions "the steles of several harpists and trumpeters as well
as that of a kettledrum player, which suggests the relatively high
social position of these artists,"[6] one of whom, the famous
Khoufou-'Ankh, has already been mentioned.[7] But it is not by
chance that we see the musicians of ancient Egypt in pictorial
documents kneeling before their masters and other high-
ranking personages.[8] Similarly, although it may have been an
honor to sing in the choruses of the Greek tragedies, musical
practice itself was not always held in honor in ancient Greece.
Jacob Burckhardt relates Antistene's judgement of the musician
Ismene, as given by Plutarch: "a man worthy of contempt for
being so excellent a flutist"; similarly, he relates how Philip of
Macedonia addressed his son Alexander after hearing him play
the kithara with skill: "Are you not ashamed to play so well?"
Thus Burkhardt concludes that at that time the Greeks, while
prizing the art of music, scorned the artists themselves because
of their manual and physical labor.[9] These attitudes were the
reflection of the collective views of that period. They implied a
certain mode of thought and a manner of judging the artist. This
mentality also explains why sculptors were less high prized than
painters: their work demanded more physical effort. We cannot
agree with Burckhardt, however, in one detail of vocabulary
which focuses on an important difference in meaning: we shall
not say that the Greeks, while scorning the artist, prized *art* itself,

---

[5]See Hans Hickmann, "Abrégé de la musique en Egypte," *Revue de musicologie* XCIII-XCIV (1950) 15.

[6]*Ibid.*, 15.

[7]See Hans Hickmann, "Le métier de musicien au temps des Pharaons," *Cahiers d'histoire égyptienne* VI/5-6 (1954) 257-258.

[8]See Jacques Chailley, *40,000 ans de musique*, 113-114.

[9]See Jacob Burckhardt, "Les Grecs et leurs artistes," in *Essais d'histoire grecque* (Tr. from the German).

but rather the *work of art.* The work of art must be distinguished from art, which designates precisely the operation or the activity of the artist which has as its goal the work of art itself.

During the Hellenistic era, one indeed admired the professional virtuosi "for their talent, and one never hesitated to pay well for their services, but at the same time, one disdained them: they did not normally belong to the worldly milieu where cultivated people were to be found. . . . the commercial character of their activity was sufficient to disqualify them: these were craftsmen—βάναυσοι. This disdain to which Aristotle already strongly testified asserted itself more and more clearly as the Hellenistic and Roman periods progressed. When Alexandrian spitefulness referred to Ptolemy XI (80–51 B.C.) by the surname aulos-player, this was not intented as a title of honor: the word meant something like "mountebank"; we are far removed from the time when Themistocles, that parvenu, was dishonored because he was found incapable of using the lyre which a dinner table companion at a banquet passed to him."[10] In Rome, despite the favors bestowed upon certain singers and aulos players, the female instrumentalists—*tibicinae* or *ambubaiae*—were ranked with the courtesans: In the Roman spectacles, the first fourteen rows of the orchestra were forbidden—that is inaccessible—to artists (actors and musicians) as well as to courtesans.[11] In one passage where he introduces the mother of Brutus, Sallust writes that she played the lyre and danced "even better than suited an honest woman" (*elegantius quam necesse probae*).[12] "This biased judgement clearly explains the position which Roman society finally seems to have adopted: the musical artists were well integrated into the culture as one of the elements necessary to luxury and elegant life, but more in terms of spectacles than as an art of amateurs."[13] Moreover, "not a word in all the Latin

---

[10]Henri-Irénée Marrou, *Histoire de l'éducation dans l'Antiquité,* 198-199.

[11]See Armand Machabey, "Etudes de musicologie pré-médiévale," *Revue de musicologie* LVI (1935) 225; LVII (1936) 2; and Jacques Chailley, *Histoire musicale du Moyen Age,* 7.

[12]See Henri-Irénée Marrou, *Histoire de l'éducation dans l'Antiquité,* 336.

[13]*Ibid.,* 336.

literature indicates that the musicians ever understood their art as a mission or that they exercised it as an apostolate. Thus it is a question of applause, favors, money—nothing more."[14] However, a deeper insight into Roman music, which has been until now largely neglected by scholarly research, reveals a fairly well developed professionalism and the outstanding importance of music in the social life of the Romans.[15]

In the collective mentality, the professional musician often acquired a rather ambiguous reputation. As Marius Schneider writes, the profession of musician is one of those that were late to receive recognition as a normal and honest profession. Overburdened with old superstitions and with all of the pecularities of the artistic mentality, it long remained both admired and scorned at the same time.[16] We can observe this in primitive societies. In various regions of Africa, the musician was sometimes "considered to be an elite being who sacrifices himself for the good of the community and deserves its esteem; he often enjoyed a privileged position. But this position is ambivalent, for in certain populations the esteem was tainted by a scornful nuance; thus among the Fulani, music was relegated to the Rimaybe slaves who cultivated the fields. A Fulani would be ashamed of singing or playing an instrument in the village: the women would make a mockery of him, for they themselves sing only for weddings ... Professional musicians form the caste of "griots" which holds precisely this ambivalent position, appropriate besides to people of caste."[17] In the Indies, most musicians belonged to the humblest of the oppressed classes, along with

[14]Jacques Chailley, *Histoire musicale du Moyen Age,* 10.
[15]See, in particular, Günther Wille, *Musica Romana. Die Bedeutung der Musik in Leben der Römer* (Ph.D. unpub. diss., Tübingen, 1951) 785; Alain Baudot, *Musiciens romains de l'Antiquité* (Montreal: U. de Montréal, 1973); and Alfred Sendrey, *Music in the Social and Religious Life of Antiquity* (Rutherford-Madison-Teaneck: Fairleigh Dickinson U., 1974) 369-438.
[16]See Marius Schneider, *Sociologie et mythologie musicales,* 19.
[17]G. Calame-Griaule, and B. Calame, "Introduction à l'étude de la musique africaine," *La revue musicale* CCXXXVIII (1957) 20-21.

the scavengers, the midwives, and the outcasts. In Ruanda in Africa, the musicians seem to have been divided into two principal classes: the tambourine players, who were free men, and musicians belonging to the inferior caste, who were often slaves.[18] "In the tripartite society of Touareg, the musicians likewise belonged to the slave class. With the Tommo of Sahel, the musicians were divided into two groups: the first includes the musicians who were counselors to the king; the second comprises slave-musicians who, during battles, mingle with the crowd in order to excite men to combat."[19] In Mesopotamia and ancient China, musicians—indeed, entire orchestras—were yielded up as war tribute. In medieval Arabic society, slave-musicians were sold publicly; this was also true in Japan. Kitab al-Agani reports that the great musician Ibn Mossadeh obtained his liberty, thanks to the generosity of a patron who discovered him at the marketplace.[20] Yet all these specific situations of musicians reflect the prevalent attitudes and collective mentality that shaped the hierarchy of social groups, as well as a hierarchy of values of a sociological nature. As for the social and material status of the musician today, which in itself constitutes an extremely large field of study, it has improved, but as Robert Wangermée observed, this musician "does not, in the final analysis, rise very high in the social hierarchy. Except for some orchestra conductors or soloists, necessarily few in number, the levels attained by musicians remain generally modest. . . . Also, despite the greater security and general improvement in their condition, musicians have not yet given up increasing their work and running after money. . . . Consequently, one is not surprised to find that well-off families do not willingly guide their children toward careers as musicians."[21]

---

[18]See Marius Schneider, *Sociologie et mythologie musicales*, 19-20.

[19]*Ibid.*, 21.

[20]*Ibid.*, 21.

[21]Robert Wangermée, Preface to De Clercq, *La profession de musicien-Une enquête*, 13.

II • THE MUSICAL PROFESSION

In the Middle Ages, the "first composers to consciously emerge from anonymity [in their own time[22]] were those for whom music, important as it was, was not the sole preoccupation: these were the *trouveurs*,[23] poet-musicians of the twelfth and thirteenth centuries."[24] The high social position of some of these musicians, such as Guillaume IX Count of Poitiers, or Thibault IV Count of Champagne, very probably facilitated this emergence.

As Ludwig Finscher has recently shown, "an interest in composers first manifested itself in a seemingly commonplace but historically important custom—: the attribution of work to a composer, by being designated with his name and by being collected under his name. This interest appears to have awakened surprisingly late in the history of Western music: even up to the fourteenth century, the fundamental tradition (fundamental understood here in the sense of ideal-typical)[25] is that of anonymity. The few contrary examples . . . confirm, in fact, the rule of anonymity."[26] Of course, there is a question here of composers who became known for reasons other than their higher social status, like some troubadours and trouvères, or Machaut in France. At the end of the fourteenth century in and around Florence, we find a "certain historical situation in which there arises an interest in the composer as a person. And this is reflected in the quite simple fact that the composer's name is handed down together with the works which are thought to be

---

[22]Author's remark.

[23]Remember that the word *trouveur* is a neologism embracing the *troubadours* of the South, the *trouvères* of the North, and the German *Minnesänger*.

[24]Jacques Chailley, *40,000 ans de musique*, 264.

[25]On the notion of the "ideal type," compare the methodology, above all, of Max Weber's "Die 'Objektivität' sozialwissenschaftlicher und sozialpolitischer Erkenntnis," in Max Weber, *Gesammelte Aufsätze zur Wissenschaftslehre* (Tübingen: (3/1968), 190ff. Moreover, in connection with our line of questioning, see Alfred von Martin, *Soziologie der Renaissance* (Munich: 1974), 11ff. [Finscher's note]

[26]Ludwig Finscher, "Die 'Entstehung des Komponisten,'" Zum Problem Komponisten-Individualität und Individualstil der Musik des 14. Jahrhunderts," *IRASM* VI/1 (1975) 31.

composed by him."[27] Finscher distinguishes, however, two other points: "The composer himself is trying to write the kind of music which can easily be associated with his personality, which means that he is developing what we are accustomed to call a personal style. And only the third part of the problem is that by means of such a personal style the composer does what we in colloquial terms describe as expressing himself."[28]

Here, we come upon a new perspective that opens a way to those sociological studies of music which consider the social status of the musican in terms of the diverse relationships he may entertain as a member of different social groups—not only professional groups of musicians, but also economic groups and extramusical professional groups. Here questions may be raised concerning both the different social roles the musician may play and the consequences that his social status and his various social roles may bring to musical creation and practice.

Most musicians of all categories throughout Europe during and well after the Middle Ages were people who served the Church or the princes, or later on, the towns—those "collective patrons" such as Venice, Dubrovnik, or the German Hanseatic towns. From the Middle Ages until the time of Haydn and Mozart, almost all composers of importance sought a position at court, at one of the larger churches, or wherever else a sufficient number of qualified performers were available—that is, in milieus of higher estates."[29] In the fourteenth century we find an entire list of musicians in the service of the court of Edward III of England.[30] In Italy, musicians also worked, for the most part, in the courts: Josquin des Prez for the Duke of Ferrara, Cypriano de Rore at the Farnese court in Parma; and, in the sixteenth century, Alexander Agricola, Jachet of Mantua, and Jacques de Wert at the musical chapel of the Gonzaga court in Mantua.[31] In

---

[27]Ludwig Finscher, "Discussion," *IRASM* VI/1 (1975) 135.

[28]*Ibid.*, 135-36.

[29]Walter Wiora, *Der musikalische Ausdruck von Ständen und Klassen*, 98.

[30]See Paul H. Lang, *Music in Western Civilization*, 165.

[31]Anne-Marie Bautier-Regnier, "Musiciens d'Oultremont à la cour de Mantoue, Jacques de Wert," *Revue belge de musicologie* IV/1-2 (1950) 42-46.

seventeenth-century Germany we still find at a court the musical ensemble considered to be the best in the land: that of the Italian musicians of the Elector of Saxony, Johann Georg II.

In France as elsewhere, "the sixteenth-century composer most often was a modest artisan engaged in the ministry. . . . Even the most celebrated did not always escape this rule: Pierre Certon and Claudin de Sermisy were fortunate to enjoy modest but stable positions at Sainte-Chapelle. Janequin had a less enviable lot: although his work had spread throughout Europe, he searched throughout his life for a prebend which would assure him decent revenues. Half a century later, we find Jacques Maudit comfortably installed in the magistracy, Eustache Du Caurroy the owner of herds of cows and sheep in Picardy (not to mention the advantages of all sorts which he obtained through his position at the Court), Pierre Guédron, 'seigneur de Harville,' possessing profitable lands in Dunois . . . But the following is most characteristic: when . . . Boësset dedicated his *eighth book of airs* to Cardinal Richelieu, in 1632, he says himself that he works *'for the elite more than for the masses*. I try to do so, my Lord, in order that my voice be able to hold some rank among the famous'."[32] Thus he demonstrates the inferior position held by the composer, that is, his dependence upon a social elite to which he did not belong. In fact, dependence upon a patron could give the musician a certain material security, but placed more or less strict conditions upon his work. The composers of Philip the Good produced no innovative work, doubtless because they "lived in a frivolous court more capable of enjoying the brilliant playing of a virtuoso than of appreciating the technical concerns of the composer"; that is why they composed so many "chansons designed for diversion, untiring in their celebrations of love,"[33] while, on the other hand, they did have the possibility of practicing their profession and

---

[32]François Lesure, "Réflexions sur les origines du concert parisien," *Polyphonie* V (1949) 49.

[33]Jeanne Marix, *Histoire de la musique et des musiciens de la cour de Bourgogne*, 219. It should be noted that the word "virtuoso" did not exist at that time, and has been adopted somewhat inappropriately in this context.

making a living at it. At the Burgundian court, as elsewhere, chaplains and minstrels formed two clearly distinct groups: the second held a socially inferior position.[34] The minstrels, who sang the praises of the nobles, never rose above their servile status; they sprang from the common people.[35] According to Marius Schneider, the traveling musician was descended from a line of tribal magicians; the temple singer and court musician of ancient times were, on the contrary, the beginning of a line of nonmigratory musicians. We meet these two types again in the Middle Ages.[36]

Another area must be considered, however, in order to understand the position of the musician as completely as possible. That is the organized levels or networks of social organizations, in all of their diversity and vitality, on which the social status of the musician (or of certain groups of musicians) may depend. For example, while the court musician, and especially the Church musician, was under the influence of an organized segment of social life for a long period of time, this was not true to the same degree for the traveling musician, who attempted over a long period to procure an organization for himself or to place himself under the protection of one or several institutions and finally succeeded. As Walter Salmen rightly observed, "at the height of the Middle Ages, musicians were in no way associated with a social class, caste or social station. They were simply a professional group united by the loosest professional bonds. Only in the case of a few musicians, who from the end of the 13th century joined together into corporations, can one even begin to speak of any sort of organization. Thus, the practicing musician did not enjoy the same prestige as was accorded to 'musica,' one of the 'septem artes liberales,' in the educational structure of the times."[37]

---

[34]See *Ibid.*, 88.

[35]See André Pirro, *Histoire de la musique de la fin du XIVe siècle à la fin du XVIe*, 15.

[36]See Marius Schneider, *Sociologie et mythologie musicales*, 18-19.

[37]Walter Salmen, *The Social Status of the Musician in the Middle Ages*, in: *ibid.*, ed. *The Social Status of the Professional Musician from the Middle Ages to the 19th Century* (New York: Pendragon, 1983) 7.

Traveling artists—first called actors, then jongleurs, mimes, minstrels,—persisted over the centuries because of their humble social status and the role which they played as entertainers throughout the wars, invasions, and revolutions that agitated European society. "The occupation of traveling musician in the Middle Ages is one of the less clearly definable professions. It represented no social state, nor even any closed social layer which could give the travelling musician an unambiguous ranking in the social hierarchy."[38] An ever-present repository of popular formulas, the traveling actor in France was an important popularizer of the music of the *trouvères* and troubadours. The favor he enjoyed can be explained by the similarity of his modes of thought and speech to those of the general population. And even if the traveling musician did not leave concrete historical traces of his activity, it was nonetheless intense and was perhaps of even greater importance to the citizenry as a whole than learned musicians instructed in polyphonic art[39] Moreover, the "light" music of that time—or to put it differently, songs and dance music—was presented and propagated chiefly by traveling musicians. The jongleurs and minstrels performed mainly at the fairs, in the monasteries, and in the castles. As Diego Carpitella observed, the two principal centers of medieval communal life were the castle and the monastery. Jongleurs and minstrels were most active at the fairs and, apparently, at the monasteries: at the former because there the jongleur found himself in his original ambiance (that is, the popular milieu from which he drew his literary and musical themes); at the latter because the monasteries were the cultural source that provided a certain stability and continuity, in contrast to the castle, where changes followed the uncertain course of political and social events.[40]

If the trumpet players in their turn, especially in Germany,

---

[38]Walter Salmen, *Der fahrende Musiker im europäischen Mittelalter*, 8.

[39]See Robert Wangermée, *Flemish music and society in the fifteenth and sixteenth centuries*, 182; Armand Machabey, *Genèse de la tonalité musicale classique* (Paris: Richard-Masse, 1955) 54-56; and Henri Davenson, *Les troubadours*, 5-7.

[40]See Diego Carpitella, "La monodie en Italie," *La revue musicale*, CCLV (1962) 21-22.

were appreciated as a category of musicians meriting a certain social esteem,[41] this was due to their social function, rather than to any virtue of their own, since they were attached to kings and feudal lords who retained them as symbols of dignity. The trumpeters "played the fanfares which proclaimed the entrance of their lord into the cities, announced his mealtimes, played during tournaments and military maneuvers, and announced decrees and ordinances."[42] Their salaries were generally higher than those of other musicians. In addition, they were ranked as officers in exchanges of prisoners of war. Their relatively high social position was symbolized even in musical scores, where the trumpet parts were generally written at the top—a practice still observed in Bach's cantatas. According to one view, the attribution of certain passages in musical compositions to these instruments sometimes had an allegorical meaning. In the works of Bach, it was intended to invoke God's supremacy.[43]

Up until about the thirteenth century, the composer of polyphonic music in effect did not exist. The "composer" only "found" the melody, and then the "discantor" "organized" it.[44] Besides, "the concept of a composer belongs to the overall concept of the music producer. From what historical time do we find musical producers who seek a particular style and are known by their own style? From a very early time indeed: on the one hand, in the person of the poet-musician, such as the Greek lyric poets, or later, Horace; and on the other hand, in productive instrumental musicians such as Timotheos and Phrynis, apostrophized by Aristophanes. The question to be clarified is how the position of composer in its narrower sense came about; this must also be considered in light of the history of musical production."[45] For a long time composer and interpreter were not distinguished from each other. The composer was generally

---

[41]See above, p. 146-147.
[42]Edmund A. Bowles, "La hiérarchie des instruments de musique dans l'Europe féodale" *Revue de musicologie* CXVIII (1958) 158.
[43]See Manfred F. Bukofzer, *Music in the Baroque Era*, 405-406.
[44]Jacques Chailley, *40,000 ans de musique*, 93.
[45]Walter Wiora, "Discussion," *IRASM*, VI/1 (1975) 138.

his own interpreter; he worked from day to day, according to prevailing demands and circumstances, performing or directing performances of his works. Secular music remained a sort of private property, which its composers safeguarded jealously. But it could easily be stolen unless the composer had a monopoly on its printing, as in the case of Lully in the seventeenth century. Even in this case such a privilege was at the time completely useless abroad.[46]

Throughout the Middle Ages, a large number of composers were priests. Their careers as musicians were often secondary or at least auxiliary. As a priest the composer might be head of the cathedral music school, director of the choir, or *precantor*.[47] He might also be engaged at court. Later, a new type of composer emerged, the opera composer, who traveled from court to court offering the fruits of his labors. At the Burgundian court, the position of *valet de chambre* was considered a high station for a minstrel to hold. At the French court, this title represented an honor: it was the standard position for a composer of quality.[48] At Esterháza, Haydn wore livery. Mozart, at the table of Arch-Bishop Colloredo, was seated between the valets and the cooks.[49] From the time of ancient civilizations up through the eighteenth century, the social status of most composers did change somewhat, but not in essence. It only assumed different forms of dependence, submission, and service. Some musicians of high rank had already acquired a certain independence as

[46]See Warren Dwight Allen, "Music and the Idea of Progress," *The Journal of Aesthetics and Art Criticism* III (1946) 168; and Manfred F. Bukofzer, *Music in the Baroque Era*, 410.

[47]The precantor was the highest dignitary of the cathedral after the bishop. (Chailley, *40,000 ans de musique*, 196.)

[48]See Jeanne Marix, *Histoire de la musique*, 88-89; Paul H. Lang, *Music in Western Civilization* 720; Norbert Dufourcq, *La musique française*, 105.

[49]A parallel going back to primitive societies may be found in the "dholi" (beggar-musicians of Ceylon) of the tribe of Bhil, who are by no means held in low esteem; the farmers consult them for all sorts of affairs; they are needed and honored with gifts. Yet the farmers will not eat at the same table with them nor will they even accept water from their hands. (Marius Schneider, *Sociologie et mythologie musicales*, 19-20).

early as the Renaissance, but in general, only "individual talent sometimes gave the artist great social distinction. Both Schütz and Lully are outstanding examples of composers who rose from a humble station to an aristocratic position. Telemann was greatly honored in Hamburg and Rudolph Ahle even rose to the highest circles in Italy only by virtue of his individual talent."[50] Not until the time of Händel and Bach (and after them Gluck, Mozart, and Beethoven) do we find a musician—one who is solely a musician—enjoying a considerably greater independence.[51] The rich development of new forms of musical life in approximately the second half of the eighteenth century, including the paying concert in particular, gave professional musicians additional opportunities for work besides those offered him by the Church, the court and the city. As Stig Walin noted, in several European countries average benefits increased and general conditions became more nearly the same. Thus the professional musician found himself freer to practice his profession by traveling from one city to another, but not without interacting with organizations such as amateur societies, professional academies, or public concerts. The itineraries drawn up by Leopold Mozart for his son's journeys involved organizations of this type.[52]

The travels of the virtuosi (which became increasingly frequent, especially in the nineteenth century, as transportation improved) recall, in fact, the trips of the traveling musicians of former times. These trips contributed to the progressive liberation of the musician from local and regional servitude. The very complex circumstances surrounding the liberation (in a musical and social sense) of the composer, the soloist, and the virtuoso are of a musical and social nature. We must include among noticeable causes the disappearance of the musicians' guilds, the growth of musical audiences, and the increasing organization

---

[50]Manfred F. Bukofzer, *Music in the Baroque Era*, 406.

[51]See *Ibid.*, 404.

[52]See Stig Walin, "Sur les conditions générales de l'internationalisme de Mozart," *Les influences étrangères dans l'oeuvre de W. A. Mozart*, coll. work edited by André Vérchaly (Paris: C.N.R.S., 1958).

of musical life in the form of commercial exploitation.[53] Describing the situation of the composer around 1770, a period that coincided with the *Sturm und Drang*, Barry S. Brook wrote that this was a time when the composer was thinking about himself in a new light. "At first, some musicians had to combine various methods of earning their living. For example, a composer might have an official post with a modest annual stipend, as a part-time *Kapellmeister* in a small German court; at the same time he might write an opera on a contractual basis, by *scrittura*, for an itinerant Italian opera company. He might present sets of trios or quartets, in half dozens, to a Polish prince and to the exiled Queen of Sweden and, in return for flowery dedicatory prefaces to be published with the works, receive a jewelled snuff box and a handful of gold coins respectively. He might sell manuscript copies of three of his symphonies to the Benedictine abbot of an Austrian monastery 'for his exclusive use'; and a week later, if his scruples permitted, resell the same compositions to publishers in both Amsterdam and Paris as works written 'especially for them'. If he preferred, however, he might become his own publisher, by buying himself about thirty copper plates, hiring an engraver to incise the notes, getting a local printer to run them off, and, after placing an advertisement in the local press, selling his compositions, singly or in sets, from his own house. He might give private lessons to the town physician's daughter, play for weddings and funerals, perform concertos for a fee with the orchestra of the local *concert des amateurs*, and enter into a contact with a London publisher to arrange popular operatic airs for some combination of instruments. Or he might organize a concert for his own benefit in a distant city; or open a shop selling instruments, music paper and his own works as well as those of other composers on commission. These were common activities for musicians in the 1770s, for the less as well as the more prominent figures. What made this era exciting, even

---

[53]See Kurt Blaukopf, *Les grand virtuoses* (Paris: Corrêa, 1955), 32-35, and Barry S. Brook, "Piracy and Panacea in the Dissemination of Music in the Late Eighteenth Century," *Proceedings of the Royal Musical Association* 102 (1975-1976) 14.

revolutionary, for many, was the new freedom of choice brought about by a greatly increased demand for their wares. Only a few decades earlier, the restraint imposed by society on musicians' activities had been far more stringent, the class status of musicians more rigidly defined and their career mobility more limited. In the early eighteenth century, only rare individuals, usually those associated with opera, were able to alter the course of their careers at will. By the end of the 1770s, however, any musician could, if he desired, free himself from the constraints of patronage by appealing to an 'anonymous community of audiences'."[54]

III • MUSICIANS IN OTHER PROFESSIONS

Quite often musicians were active in other professions at the same time. This suggests that by itself the musical profession, and above all the field of composition, was not always able to satisfy the professional, economic, or social aspirations of its members. In other respects the situation was sometimes the same as it is now. As Robert Wangermée noted, "the musician today, who fancies himself a man of culture, is restless and discontent when he discovers that the school does not really provide the means for gaining access to the higher circles where he wishes to be."[55] Hans Hickmann noted that already some of the female singers of Amon and some of the "divine spouses" played a role in the political and social life of ancient Egypt. He mentions singers and harpists who were temple officials as well as musicians.[56] The "trouveurs" of the twelfth and thirteenth centuries were not always musicians only. Adam de la Halle was the official poet of Charles d'Anjou; he must have played a substantial role in the French court at Naples. In the fourteenth

---

[54]Barry S. Brook, "The Symphonie Concertante: Its Musical and Sociological Bases," *IRASM* VI/1 (1975) 19-20.

[55]Robert Wangermée, Preface to De Clercq's *La profession de musicien-Une enquête*, 11.

[56]See Hans Hickmann, *Le métier de musicien au temps des Pharaons*, 271 and 286.

century, an analogous situation must have impelled the contemporaries of Guillaume de Machaut to pay attention to the compositions of this illustrious musician, who in his time was not simply a composer but a distinguished poet and diplomat as well.[57] In the sixteenth century, Jacques Maudit, Eustache Du Caurroy, and Pierre Guédron, for example, had occupations other than music.[58] These cases are not isolated: many others exist. Later, Agostino Steffani was to serve in an important diplomatic mission.[59] Cardinal Mazarin constantly employed musicans and singers (Atto Melani, for example) as spies and diplomatic agents.[60] Minstrels were also given missions with no connection with their usual profession; being assigned "sometimes a position as mediator or, more frequently, to carry out a secret mission . . . The role of spy as well, and perhaps even like that of the harpist Vaulthier l'Anglois—three years in the service of Philip the Bold—who was charged, by Charles the Bad, King of Navarre, with penetrating the kitchens of the king of France and other princes, supplied with a poisonous powder."[61] We know also that at the beginning of the fifteenth century the English Parliament accused the minstrels of Wales of being partially responsible for the rebellions that occurred there.[62] Earlier in France, after the revolt of the Maillotins, all of the royalties and trade masterships including the minstrels' royalty

[57]Jacques Chailley, *40,000 ans de musique*, 265.

[58]See above p. 204.

[59]See Manfred F. Bukofzer, *Music in the Baroque Era*, 406.

[60]See Henri Prunières, *L'Opera italien en France avant Lulli*, 55.

[61]André Pirro, *La musique à Paris sous la règne de Charles VI (1380-1422)* (Strassburg: Heitz, 1930) 9-10.

[62]The following denunciation is cited by J. Jusserand (*English Wayfaring Lives in the Middle Ages*, New York: 1920, 212): "No westours and rimers, minstrels or vagabonds, be maintained in Wales to make kymorthas or quyllages on the common people, who by their divinations, lies and exhortations, are partly cause of the insurrections and rebellion now in Wales." (As cited by P. H. Lang in *Music in Western Civilization*, 166.) These musicians, like the music which they performed, became subversive elements. Evidently, the activity of which they were accused could not claim to be a profession but it points out at least the social role which the musicians assumed under the circumstances.

were abolished (to be reinstated, however, in 1392).[63] In general, the traveling musician worked in other professions as well, and only in rare cases exclusively as a musician. Most often he was master of yet other skills or traveled about in the company of those who plied other trades.[64]

In England, Thomas Tallis and William Byrd obtained a monopoly on music printing and publishing. And some of Henry VIII's musicians were involved in business. Among these "merchant-musicians," the most active was William Crane, who in 1509 became the tax collector for harbor rights in the city of Dartmouth. In Bristol, John Lloyd was in charge of the custom-house and handled most of his affairs from there.[65] John Banister was the first musician to organize commercially based concerts (as recounted in the London Gazette of 30 December 1672).[66] In France, Guillaume Chastillon de la Tour devoted himself in part to the book trade, for from 1604 on we find him at the annual royal book fair.[67] With regard to Lully, it is known that he was businessman and entrepreneur.[68] And, in Neuchâtel, over a long period of time, we find in the Protestant churches "regent-cantors" who "directed the singing of psalms by intoning and then carrying them. . . . These regent-cantors received a modest salary. To provide for their upkeep, they found it necessary to look for additional resources: we find regent-cantors who, at the same time, are notaries, carpenters, watchmakers, etc."[69]

Speaking of musicians involved in Italian theater production

---

[63]See Paul Loubet de Sceaury, Musiciens et facteurs d'instruments de musique sous l'ancien Régime, 37.

[64]See Walter Salmen, Der fahrende Musiker im europäischen Mittelalter, 9.

[65]See Hugh Baillie, "Les musiciens de la Chapelle Royale d'Henri VIII au camp du Drap d'Or," Fêtes et cérémonies au temps de Charles Quint (Paris: C.N.R.S., 1960) 150-151.

[66]See Paul H. Lang, Music in Western Civilization, 721.

[67]See Antoine Bloch-Michel, "Chastillon de la Tour," in "Recherches" sur la musique française classique (1960) (Paris: Picard, 1960) 8.

[68]See Edmond Radet, Lulli, homme d'affaire, propriétaire et musicien (Paris: L. Allison, n.d.).

[69]Edouard-M. Fallet, La vie musicale au pays de Neuchâtel du XIIIe à la fin du XVIIIe siècle (Leipzig-Strasbourg-Zürich: Heitz, 1936) 75.

during Vivaldi's lifetime, Lorenzo Bianconi points out that no one could live from theater work only: "The situations differ, but the basic condition is identical: there are many varied jobs, all inadequately or badly paid. The preferred combination is a theatrical position as well as an institutional charge. In Venice, for example, only the chapel master of St. Mark's approaches the status of a musician-functionary supported exclusively by an institution (and in fact, Monteverdi, Cavalli, Legrenzi, Partenio, Lotti, never produced—or only with reluctance and in exceptional conditions—theatrical works during their service at St. Marks's). For all others, from the assistant chapel-master on down, there is no incompatibility between the job in basilica and composing for public scenes."[70] On the other hand, in treating of the origin and social status of the court orchestral musicians in the eighteenth and early nineteenth century in Germany, Christoph-Hellmut Mahling emphasized that even as late as the nineteenth century "the court orchestral employee was at the same time musician *and* servant. This dual function was a primary factor in determining his social status. While the larger courts could waive the obligations for musicians to perform additional duties, the smaller ones were dependent upon this dual role. Only in exceptional cases did a smaller court have sufficient funds to maintain an orchestra whose musicians only fulfilled musical duties."[71] In the nineteenth century, for example, Rimsky-Korsakov, Borodin, and Mussorgsky also pursued extramusical professions. And today also many composers are still obliged to work, as they did formerly, in teaching or administrative positions or elsewhere. On the other hand, most composers were to double their creative activity of another sort of musical activity. Thus Mozart and later Chopin,

---

[70]Lorenzo Bianconi, "Condizione sociale e intellettuale del musicista di teatro ai tempi di Vivaldi," in *Antonio Vivaldi. Teatro musicale, cultura e società* (Firenze: Olschki, 1982) 387.

[71]Christoph-Hellmut Mahling, "The Origin and Social Status of the Court Orchestral Musician in the 18th and early 19th Century in Germany," in Walter Salmen, ed., *The Social Status of the Professional Musician from the Middle Ages to the 19th Century* (New York: Pendragon Press, 1983) 249.

Liszt, Brahms, and Saint-Saëns, for example, were also concert performers, as were many others before and after them. Bach, Beethoven, Schubert, Franck, Massenet, and d'Indy all taught music. Schumann, Weber, Berlioz, Dukas, Debussy, d'Indy, and Fauré were critics.[72] And during his first trip to Paris (1839–1842) Wagner was forced to become a "transcriber" and "arranger of operas" in order to survive.[73] But this already touches upon another aspect—the economic one—of the socio-historical conditionings of the musical profession.

IV • PROFESSIONAL ORGANIZATIONS OF MUSICIANS

Economic conditions played an important function in the development of the profession. This formative process in itself constitutes an interesting question that deserves investigation. For example, "one of the oldest *inscriptions*, that of king Telepinu (of the second half of the seventeenth century B.C.), already makes mention, with regard to a religious ceremony, of singers from the town of Hattous . . . The wording of this inscription permits us to conclude that in the large cities there existed, if not guilds, at least groups of singers, who were associated with religious practices or who perhaps specialized in ceremonial chant."[74] In addition, Greco-Roman Egypt witnessed "a growth in professionalism unknown until that time, explainable by the atmosphere in the city of Alexandria (whose inhabitants knew only one god—money—according to a letter of the Emperor Hadrian), without giving up an amateurism which never completely disappeared."[75] During Greece's Hellenistic period, around the time of Alexander, troups of professional artists appeared grouped into "trade-guilds." From

---

[72]See Jim Cork, "Society versus the Composer" *The Antioch Review* XI (1951) 50; and M. Daubresse, *Le musicien dans la société moderne* (Paris: Le Monde musical, 1914) 192-95.

[73] See *Ibid.*, 199.

[74]Armand Machabey, *La musique des Hittites* (Paris: Fischbacher, 1945) 7–8.

[75]Hans Hickmann, *Le métier de musicien au temps des Pharaons*, 296.

then on, the choruses for tribal competitions were entrusted to them, not to the amateurs.[76] The Romans created "colleges" that corresponded to the "trade-guilds" of the Greeks. Instrumentalists figured in a number of these colleges, for instance the *collegium tibicinum* (aulos players) dating back to the earliest antiquity, the *collegium aeneatorum* (horn players), the *collegium liticinum* (trumpet and horn players), the *stadium orchestrophales* (mimes), etc.[77] In the Roman army, traces of associations of military musicians have also been found, as is evidenced by inscriptions at Lambese in Algeria, dating from the time of Emperor Caracalla.[78] For the most part Roman military musicians were not treated simply as soldiers, but as officers: "the right of association which will develop in the camps (from the time of Septimus Severus will be given first to officers or to specialists of similar rank: such is, indeed, the case of the musicians, who will receive, in effect, the authorization to organize themselves into colleges, with solid financial management and detailed statutes."[79]

But the important period in the development of the profession of the musical performer was the Middle Ages. The birth of the medieval guilds of minstrels can be explained by economic reasons, in addition to the ethical motives their statutes frequently invoked.[80] Besides moral prescriptions, these statutes included clauses concerning the distribution of benefits, the introduction and departure of members, the continuation of the association, the prohibition against appearances with other troups, the illness of members, and other issues. The oldest of these medieval guilds was the *Nicolaibruderschaft* of Vienna (1288), followed by the company of trumpeters of Lucca, the brotherhood of jongleurs and instrumentalists of Fécamp, and by the

---

[76]See Henri-Irénée Marrou, *Histoire de l'éducation dans l'Antiquité*, 191-192.

[77]See Paul Loubet de Sceaury, *Musiciens et facteurs d'instruments de musique sous l'ancien Régime*, 1.

[78]See Théodore Reinach, "Un cercle de musique militaire dans l'Afrique romaine," *Revue de musicologie* XXV (1928) 12-14.

[79]Alain Baudot, *Musiciens romains de l'Antiquité*, 33.

[80]See Armand Machabey, *La musicologie* (Paris: P.U.F., 1962) 111–112.

Brotherhood of St. Julien of the Minstrels of Paris—this last even had a hospital for its members.[81]

At the beginning of the seventeenth century, we find in Paris a curious example of a professional association set up for economic reasons: "On February 26, 1602, twelve master instrumentalists and royal violinists entered into association for 40 years! . . . The contract was declared valid for 'their present and future male offspring' when they will have reached the age of 20.[82] These new arrangements were typical of the political and social climate of the time: this was an important period of political reversals, and of transmission of services. Everything was being transferred: in 1596, Jean Perrichon sold his commission as the king's oboist to Michel Henry.[83] Before long, the court composers themselves were to choose their successors, a practice which continued at least up until the time of Louis XIV. We see here the handful of privileged masters who assured the future of their children even within the popular brotherhood."[84] In the second half of the sixteenth century, new clauses appeared in the instrumentalists' contracts, giving precise details concerning the internal organization of ensembles to which these players belonged. "Previously, the particular instrumental part that such and such a player was supposed to play was never specified. However, from about 1580 on,[85] the members adopted the habit of distributing before a notary the respective parts which they had to play in the small orchestra."[86] At the royal

---

[81]See Paul H. Lang, *Music in Western Civilization*, 166; Jacques Chailley, *Histoire musicale du Moyen Age*, 110; and Paul Loubet de Sceaury, *Musiciens et facteurs d'instruments sous l'ancien Régime*, in toto.

[82]Contract of 13 November 1607, which reprints the resolutions of the contract of 1602 (which is not preserved): Min. cent. LXI. 16. (=Minutier central des notaires des Archives nationales.)

[83]Min. centr. XCI, 153 bis.

[84]François Lesure, "Les orchestres populaires à Paris vers la fin du XVIe siècle" *Revue de musicologie* XXXVI (1954) 48–49.

[85]V. Leblond cites three such members in 1580, in *Les associations de musiciens à Beauvais au XVIe siècle* (1925) 50–51.

[86]François Lesure, "Les orchestres populaires à Paris vers la fin du XVIe siècle," *Revue de musicologie*, 36 (1954) 50.

French court, on the other hand, there was a detailed hierarchy of instrumentalists.[87]

But let us return for a moment to the status of the musician. While we have already dealt with the problems of collective attitudes toward musicians within a society, we must not forget to consider the collective attitudes of the musicians themselves, without mutually opposing them, since the two are found in numerous intense relationships, sometimes complementary, sometimes contradictory, sometimes ambiguous, sometimes polarized, or finally, sometimes even reciprocal in their perspective. Individual musicians often changed their attitudes according to the groups to which they belonged and the social roles they assumed. Thus we can ascertain different collective attitudes, for example, regarding music itself or its various genres, or toward certain groups of musicians according to their social appurtenances. Class distinctions and differences in social status and appurtenance are also reflected in the ranks of musicians. It is interesting that the use of various designations for musicians, especially in the Middle Ages, reflects not only a difference in conception of the artistic importance or dignity of the musician, but reflects also the inequality of his social status.[88] The conflict in Paris at the end of the seventeenth century and through the eighteenth century between the "harmonists" and te instrumentalists' guild (the so-called Corporation de joueurs d'instruments) had economic and professional causes as well as it was a matter of social prestige. These differences were

---

[87]See Norbert Dufourcq, La musique française, 105–107, and Marcelle Benoît, Les musiciens du Roi de France (1661–1733) (Paris: Presses Universitaires de France, 1982) 95–110.

[88]See Edgar De Bruyne, Etudes d'esthétique médiévale (Bruges: De Tempel, 1946) Vol. I, 32–34; Vol. II, 118–119; Carl Anthon, "Some Aspects of the Social Status of Italian Musicians During the Sixteenth Century," Journal of Renaissance and Baroque Music I/2 (1946) 111–23 and I/3 (1946) 222–234; Guillaume de Van, "La pédagogie musicale à la fin du Moyen Age" Musica Disciplina II/1–2 (1948) 75–97; Paul Loubet de Sceaury, Musiciens et facteurs d'instruments de musique sous l'ancien Régime, 103–153; Walter L. Woodfill, Musicians in English Society from Elizabeth to Charles I (Princeton: Princeton U., 1953) 56–57; Hans Engel, Musik und Gesellschaft, 197–256.

extended even to the instrument makers, the *facteurs* (manufacturers) of organs and *faiseurs* (makers) of flutes, oboes, and
certain other instruments; such distinctions in designation were
even established officially in France by decree in 1692.[89] Toward
the end of the sixteenth century, the French guild system was
arranged according to five classes, with the guild of minstrels
occupying the middle position. An edict of Turgot in 1776
ended the history of all guilds. Thereafter, all the arts and trades
were free.[90]

---

[89]See Paul Loubet de Sceaury, *Musiciens et facteurs d'instruments de musique sous l'ancien Régime,* 165.
[90]See *Ibid.,* 153.

CHAPTER SEVEN

MUSIC AND ECONOMICS

Musical creation and practice are conditioned not only by the public, by the internal divisions of global societies, and by the social conditions affecting the musician; they are also—and more deeply—affected by the economy, by the technical means of production and labor, and by the situation of labor itself. They are conditioned by political, cultural, ideological, and religious factors as well. Some of these sociohistorical conditionings of music must now be dealth with. "Provided they do not attempt to impose socioeconomic straitjackets, economic historians can contribute something to the history of music because, as Denis Arnold has demonstrated, 'music does not exist *per se*, but only in its relationship to man.' . . . 'Context' should be examined more systematically than hitherto, for even those musicians who recognise its importance tend to be vague about its content."[1] An example of interdisciplinary collaboration in this field, needed in some analyses of economical aspects of musical life, can be found in a work such as that published by Mark

---

[1]Cyril Erlich, "Economic History and Music," *Proceedings of the Royal Musical Association* 103 (1976–1977) 199. Erlich quotes Denis Arnold, *God, Caesar and Mammon: a Study of Patronage in Venice 1550–1750* (Nottingham University, 1970) 3.

Blaug, although it goes beyond the borders of music alone.[2] In this collective work we find among others studies about subsidizing and cultural accounting in recent times.[3]

First of all, we shall try here to clarify several aspects of the functional integration of musical facts with social facts, at a level of observation, i.e. the economical level, which implies an important material aspect of social and musical life, but which is nevertheless inconceivable without the simultaneous intervention of several other levels of social reality. Once more, we will not sketch here a social history of music, but will rather attempt to show, through several examples in areas concerning global societies (above all those areas of labor, economy, means of production, and political life), how problems can be presented and in which directions they could be further investigated. To do this, it is clearly necessary to take into account not only the structure of global societies, but also the social groups concerned, the various levels linked to that of the facts studied, and other variables eventually brought into play.

I • TYPES OF SOCIETIES AND MUSICAL FUNCTIONS

From the sociological point of view, the emancipation of musical art was made possible only as a result of the social division of labor. As far back as the division of labor goes, as early as the so-called primitive or archaic societies, its importance in making possible the later autonomous evolution of music cannot be overemphasized. In these societies, music was constrained for a twofold reason: first, the general human condition in these societies; second, more specifically, the lack of musical traditions

---

[2]See Mark Blaug, ed., *The Economics of the Fine Arts* (Boulder, Colorado: Westview Press, 1976)

[3]See T. Moore, "Reasons for Subsidizing American Theater (1968)," A.T. Peacock, "Welfare Economics and Public Subsidies to the Arts (1969)," A.T. Peacock, and C. Godfrey, "Cultural Accounting," in *ibid.,* 25–41, 70–83, 87–100.

that were sufficiently developed technically. According to Karl Marx, as long as human labor was still so unproductive that it furnished little in excess of the necessary means of subsistence, the accumulation of productive forces, the extension of trade, the development of the state and of law, and the foundation of art and science were not possible except by means of an enforced division of labor, which must necessarily have meant a division between the masses (who provided simple manual labor) and the privileged few (who were assigned to the direction of labor, commerce, affairs of state, and to artistic and scientific occupations).[4] Compared to the situation in so-called primitive or archaic societies where the division of labor was minimal, we find in the societies of the oldest civilizations of the Near East (where labor was already highly diversified[5] a profound difference in the situation of music and musical activities. It is only in more developed global societies that certain professional groups, such as musicians, are freed from the need to participate in material production. While in primitive societies "primitive music" was at the same time "folk music," mostly entrusted to a large circle of performers, and was found from its beginning to be in a syncretic state, we see in the music of these ancient civilizations (the Egyptian and Babylonian, for example) the rise of a differentiation betwen folk music and music intended for special social functions other than those involving a large percentage of the population (e.g., specific court, temple, and military music). In other words, there already existed a division of artistic labor within the realm of musical activity itself.[6] And if through a lack of adequate documents we can know little of its importance in the specifically artistic

---

[4]Karl Marx, and Friedrich Engels, *Sur la littérature et l'art* (Paris: Editions sociales, 1954) 177–178.

[5]See André Aymard, and Jeannine Auboyer, *L'Orient et la Grèce antique*, Vol. I (Paris: P.U.F., 1953) 40–46, 132–138.

[6]Charles Lalo gives but a single page (35) of observations (and those fairly mediocre) in his work, *L'art et la vie sociale*, in the middle of a chapter entirely given over to the division of labor in art in general.

domain,[7] we can be sure that this division reflects a social situation, effected accordingly to social exigencies that derive from the global structure of these societies. Thus, it takes a place according to the social functions that are assumed by music and dictated by these global societies.

Now, it is important to note that the same types of *social functions* of music correspond to the same types of *global societies*. In the ancient civilizations of Egypt, Mesopotamia, India, and China, all characterized by the same global social structure— with a predominance of the state on a territorial basis, a division into classes or strata (or even, as in India, into castes), a clearly pronounced hierarchy of social groups, a well-determined set of social regulations, and an extensive division of labor in the accumulation of goods—music assumes noticeably analogous social functions. We see everywhere a ceremonial music that is part of the court apparatus, an institutionalized music sometimes already extremely diversified functionally (such as Babylonian music), and a specifically military music (such as Egyptian and Assyrian music), to mention only a few examples. In addition, music in these civilizations becomes more independent. It takes on a value of its own, and while assuming definite social functions, it offers entertainment of an aesthetic order, which also assumes its own function. It passes from being a secondary element to having a cultural domain of its own by, among other ways, the construction and maintenance of instruments that are specifically musical and serve no other purpose.[8] But—and here once more the necessity arises of not separating sociological analysis from historical analysis, while at the same time distinguishing them—the same types of global societies and civilizations that have come to an analogous degree of cultural development can exhibit very different phenomena on the

---

[7]See Armand Machabey, "Musique égyptienne" and "Musique suméro-chaldéenne" *La Musique des origines à nos jours* (Paris: Larousse, 1946) 59–62, Id. "L'Antiquité orientale" *Précis de musicologie* (Paris: P.U.F., 1958) 59–72, and Hans Hickmann, *Abrégé de l'histoire de la musique égyptienne* (Paris: Fischbacher, 1950).

[8]See Walter Wiora, *The Four Ages of Music*, 64–65.

purely *artistic* and *technical* levels of music.[9] The importance of these differences is, again, a question of historical verification.

In all ways, the sociology of music brings to this point a perspective for the study of all global societies, including those of today. It also provides a perspective for studying the social functions of music and their differentiations which give birth to musical genres and different forms of musical life, according to the global societies and their internal stratifications, and which are expressed also in the social composition and appurtenance of the public—the "consumer" of music. As was emphasized, "music represents, for the sociologist, an aspect which is lesser met in the other traditional arts, and which is introduced only in such new arts as the cinema: that of 'collective' work and the division of labor. In this sense, models of musical production may be considered as models that have developed from the social organization itself. The musician, in order to disseminate the product of his creation, is obliged (except in very special cases) to go through a smaller or larger number of mediations which are not, as in painting for example, of an essentially mercantile order, but which may well belong to the very process of that creation—orchestra conductor, performer, sound engineer, and so forth."[10]

But in order to return to that first fundamental division of labor within musical art (followed by other divisions, such as that between the creative and the interpretative activities), it is necessary to establish that the division itself, and logically, the development of learned music,[11] have also been a consequence of improvements brought about in musical technique, improvements that presupposed and enforced more intensified musical activity. On the other hand, this was made possible precisely by the general division of labor in society, as well as by the social

---

[9]See Roman I. Gruber, *Istorija musykaljnoj kuljtury* (Moscow-Leningrad: Gosizd, 1941-1959) I, 235.

[10]P. Beaud, and A. Willener, *Musique et vie quotidienne*, 28.

[11]See p. 225.

demand for a music with definite social functions, since the time of the great ancient civilizations. Thus this demand was a result of general developments as well. It was due to internal differentiations in the global societies within these civilizations, due to their structuring into professions, groups, or hierarchical castes. Their upper layers were quite capable of sustaining such a demand: being delivered from the common yoke of heavy labor, they had the necessary leisure and disposition of spirit to pursue the musical arts. Nevertheless, musical professionalism and amateurism should not be confused with learned and folk musical activity. In almost all periods folk music had its professionals, as learned music had its amateurs, and vice versa.

II • LABOR AND MUSICAL RECEPTION

Another consequence of the general social division of labor was that it favored the blossoming of some musical talents, while suppressing others, in the general population. This is relevant not only to the division of labor, but also to the internal differentiations of global societies into groups, classes, layers, strata, or castes. As has been recently shown, "the taste for learned music, the attendance at concerts and finally the practice of music increase as a function of the following variables: social origin, how early one begins to go to concerts, and the fact that one goes to concerts first with one's parents. These factors, added together, permit the verification of Pierre Bourdieu's and Alain Darbel's statement that cultural need tends to increase as far as it is satisfied; as well as inversely: the absence of this need is accompanied by the lack of awareness of its absence."[12] On the other hand, labor can prevent those subjected to it from having access to the enjoyment of music of higher quality, and from becoming interested in it. If musical talents can be favored or suppressed, the same is true for the talents of the audience, and labor is one of the explanations for it. Yet as Arnold N. Sochor

---

[12]Paul Beaud, "Musique, masses, minorités, marginaux", 158.

has put it, "The concept of the 'developmental level of the listener' is relative. This level, can, in each case, be determined only in relation to the concrete spheres of musical life. A less well developed listener to symphony or opera may prove to be a highly developed listener to jazz or folk music, and inversely."[13] A glance over the history of music permits us to realize that learned music, especially secular "serious" music, has most often had a "leisure" public, a public became "bored," a public, for the most part, well-off. (While religious music generally brought together much larger audiences.)[14]

Subjection to daily manual labor, a common condition in much of the world, does not favor the acquisition of the values of learned music of a deeper, more serious nature and of a higher quality. A study done in Belgium shows the burning actuality of the problem even in the middle of the twentieth century. It confirms a situation that dates, in Europe, as far back as the origins of the development of secular learned music, and for which we can find the equivalent in the civilizations of antiquity. It is "the very milieu where the manual laborer lived which seems to be the determining cause of the lack of interest in serious music. Not often after hard, monotonous, and concentrated labor on material objects can the spirit produce an effort to which it is not accustomed. Serious music requires a certain capacity for attention in order to be appreciated. . . . If the life-milieu does not furnish the conditions necessary for the awakening of musical sensibility, the succession of sounds the ear perceives remains without interest to the listener. . . . A certain degree of liberation from the subjugation which manual labor involves is necessary to attain this favourable disposition which every culture requires."[15] In addition, "leisure, in the modern economy, has become more and more an integral part of the labor system. It is even recognized and defended by law.

---

[13]Arnold N. Sochor, "Discussion," *IRASM* VI/1 (1975) 107.

[14]See Michel Brenet, *Les Concerts en France sous l'ancien Régime*, 39–40 and 230; and Marcel Beaufils, *Par la musique vers l'obscur*, 59–94 and 219.

[15]Robert Hoebaer, "L'intérêt pour l'art musical," *Bulletin de l'Institut de Recherches Economiques et Sociales* VII (1956) 730.

This fact . . . aims at the clean separation of labor on one hand and rest on the other."[16] Now, "the distance of so-called serious music from day-to-day life bears witness to the loss of its social function, inherent nevertheless in music from its beginnings. Thus the emphasis with which the 'serious' side of music is underlined could be considered a tactic admission that it has lost contact with its roots in the immediate communication of men."[17] While in the past music was often performed in the midst of daily life, irrespective of any division of "leisure" and "labor" time, it became later connected only with the first.

In effect, we return here to the problem of the disfunction-alization of learned or "cultivated" music. There is no doubt that the separation that always exists between many people and music of high artistic standing is an unfortunate state of affairs, and that the access of vast publics to the true values of musical art is a long-term task to be realized one step at a time. This poses immense and extremely complex problems of education and acculturation, which demand enormous large-scale, organized efforts.

Nonetheless, we should not forget that the disfunctionalization of learned music, begun in the nineteenth century, concerned not a "mass-public," but a "class-public." On the other hand, the largest contemporary publics enjoy music that is fairly functional, albeit commercialized, "industrial," most often transmitted through the mass media and of a particular genre, and pertaining to "mass culture." When truly listened to, serious music, music of high artistic standing, remains reserved for single moments of aesthetic contemplation, isolated not only in time and space, but also set apart from all other activities or extramusical social functions. This must not, however, be seen as a negative phenomenon in itself. On the contrary, according to Etienne Gilson, "precisely because music implies a personal man-to-man relationship, it is an essentially social art. In this regard, the

---

[16]René König, "Sur quelques problèmes sociologiques de l'émission radio-phonique musicale," *Cahiers d'études de radio-télévision* III–IV (1955) 358.
[17]*Ibid.*, 358–359.

perfect musical experience takes the form of a concert. . . . The attention of the solitary listener undergoes fluctuations to which it would not be subjected in a concert hall."[18] In a concert there is also, so to speak, a sort of purification of the act of listening, as it is removed from extramusical social functions. But the radio, as Gisèle Brelet remarked, contributes perhaps more to this process, since it places the listener alone, face to face with music. According to Brelet's own expression, radio "purifies and confirms music."[19] That this approach to music and this way of experiencing it may have until now effectively interested a social minority, is not an exceptional situation. It is found at other times in connection with a lack of education or disposition toward a highly cultured music in the masses: problems to study and resolve not only through the sociology of music, but also through social psychology and a proper cultural and educational policy. For music of high value could perhaps find its proper function—that of contributing to the interior equilibrium of man, and while not becoming merely utilitarian, of delivering to each man, whatever his station, the purity and transparency of a spiritual and aesthetic joy and delectation—in daily life in the future.

III • MUSIC FOR WORK

Today many people find themselves far removed from the function music once had in connection with labor in the countryside; not only in archaic societies, but also in civilized societies. This functionalism could be found in music that was directly conditioned by work, especially so-called primitive music in which songs have been in part influenced by the cadences of collective manual labor that required a large common effort, and from which some, Karl Bücher, for instance,

---

[18]Etienne Gilson, *La société de masse et sa culture*, 65, 64.
[19]See Gisèle Brelet, "La Radio purifie et confirme la musique," *Cahiers d'études de radio-télévision* III–IV (1955) 367–378.

have wished even to derive the very origins of music. Bücher's theory[20] has already received a valid criticism in Charles Lalo's observation that the idea of labor itself was inadequately presented: in the over-large sense in which Bücher took it, the idea of labor is reduced to that of activity in general. Labor has been a developmental factor in, not the origin of, the rhythmic arts.[21] In addition, the idea of rhythm itself was not well defined by Bücher. His concern was meter, a succession of strong and weak beats; this alone was generally sufficient to facilitate movements, especially collective movements. But rhythm itself was not always and everywhere necessarily determined by labor.[22] In addition, the flaw in Bücher's theory, like that in the no-less-famous theory of Jules Combarieu about music and magic, is that it limits observation solely to work songs or magical chants—to their rhythm and melodic design, the onomatopeia of the words, and their sense and allusions[23]— while forgetting instrumental music. Another flaw is his searching for the origins of music in the characteristics it possesses at more developed level, not at an elementary one. Moreover, Bücher's observations are better applied to the global societies of ancient civilizations rather than to those of primitive peoples.

While the question of the origins of music remains rather unsolved, that of music that aids labor, or of work-music itself, can be dealt with more fruitfully. The music of this genre was very widespread; it is also often linked to magical rites and beliefs.[24] For example, among the Dogon of the Cliffs of Bandiagara, at the mouth of the Niger, we find songs for the

---

[20]See Karl Bücher, *Arbeit und Rhythmus* 3rd ed. (Leipzig: Teubner, 1902).

[21]See Charles Lalo, *L'art et la vie sociale*, 22.

[22]See *Ibid.*, 22. See also Jules Combarieu, *La musique et la magie* (Paris: Picard, 1909) 314–316.

[23]André Schaeffner, *Origine des instruments de musique*, 95.

[24]The attribution of medical qualities to music is also often founded on magical beliefs. See Jules Combarieu, *La musique et la magie*, 69–88; Armand Machabey, "La musique et la médicine," *Polyphonie* VII–VIII (1951) 40–47; and Dorothy M. Schullian, Max Schoen, et. al. *Music and Medicine* (New York: Henry Schumann, 1948).

crushing of onion stalks. Music, particularly song, "is here the practically inseparable accompaniment to all kinds of work. The weaver of his craft hums work songs in an ancient tongue; words and music are caught up in the threads of the work, impregnating them with water and oil. . . . The songs which accompany the different agricultural operations, the playing of flutes or horns when going to the field, have the effect not only of assuring the farmers' return, but of procuring for the man abundant harvest."[25] In Africa again, as S.D. Cudjoe reports, the preparation of the food called *foufou* is accompanied by fascinating rhythms.[26] And as Jules Combarieu already related, when it is time to unbeach a boat, the divers in the Congo swim around it singing together. At a certain point in their ritual song they dive together, then continue to sing mentally in order, at another point in the song, to give the simultaneous underwater effort sufficient strength to accomplish their task. A perfect simultaneity of song and movement is necessary here.[27] Zygmunt Estreicher has made some interesting observations on the songs of the Eskimo-Caribou. These observations lead to an explanation of a purely musical phenomenon by means of the social function assumed by music. The preponderance of monody in the songs of the Eskimo-Caribou is due "to factors foreign to music. . . . Singing the *magic song* is a sacred act: any change in it could destroy its supernatural force. The *dance song*, like all dance, must allow the vocal soloist, often a shaman, to enter into an ecstatic trance . . . . The attention of all participants must be concentrated and turned toward the same goal: their song must hypnotize. This concentration of the spirit on an extra-musical object, excluding all artistic preoccupation, evidently renders unison obligatory . . . But when nothing imposes monody, that is, when the song is executed without this practical goal, the attention of

---

[25]G. Calame-Griaule, and B. Calame, "Introduction à l'étude de la musique africaine," *La revue musicale* CCXXXVIII (1957) 16.

[26]See S.D. Cudjoe, "The Techniques of Ewe Drumming and the Social Importance of Music in Africa," *Phylon* III (1953) 281–282.

[27]See Jules Combarieu, *La musique, ses lois, son évolution* (Paris: Flammarion, 1907) 147–148.

the singers turns to the musical phenomenon itself: it is then that polyphony can be born."[28] And Estreicher concludes: "Monody is logically a more simple phenomenon; but, realized by a group of performers, it requires of them a certain discipline. Heterophony, one of the most rudimentary polyphonic forms, does without it; thus, according to the sociologist, heterophony would be more 'simple' "; yet it is necessary to make "a clear distinction between 'involuntary' polyphony, which one would be tempted to attribute to the inability to sing in unison which certain singers experience . . . and voluntary polyphony (polyphony proper)."[29] To these formulae, we could compare that of Curt Sachs: "Heterophony is any manner of sounding tones together based on tradition and improvization: 'contrappunto alla mente' as opposed to 'res facta.' "[30]

Just as it is necessary to distinguish *work* songs (those sung during work itself) and *trade* songs (those that relate to work and to crafts, but are not sung during work), it is necessary to distinguish work songs that are linked by their rhythm to the rhythm of work, from work songs that "are not linked to the rhythm of the work but, on the contrary, must be freely emitted, often improvised, and which can be adjusted to unexpected contingencies arising in the course of the work . . . Under this [latter] type one may classify the song of the muleteer . . . who inhabits the slopes of the Sierra Nevada in Andalusia. The song is very ornate and seemingly free, but is actually built on improvised strophes. Exhortations to the mule as well as long silences separate or interrupt the strophes and coincide with the demands of work in a country where the rough terrain makes the task difficult."[31] As for work songs in which the rhythmic structure is dependent on the rhythm of the work in process, we

---

[28]Zygmunt Estreicher, "La polyphonie chez les Esquimaux," *Journal de la Société des Américanistes* XXXVII (1948) 268.

[29]*Ibid.,* 259.

[30]Curt Sachs, "Heterophonie" *MGG*, VI, 327.

[31]Claudie Marcel-Dubois, *Nature et fonction de la musique ethnique,* Cours à l'École Pratique des Hautes Etudes, *Ethnomusicologie* (Paris: 21. XI, 1961) 14-15.

find an example in the "song that aids the making of *tapa* [cloth] in Oceania. The last step in making *tapa* consists in beating the strips of conveniently anchored mulberry bark for a long time with a paddle of wood or stone . . .; the rhythm of the song is already laid out by the scansion of the beaters; the song will be, in this circumstance, the stimulus, the required aid."[32] In Venezuela, on the island of St. Marguerite in the sea of the Antilles, we find a song that accompanies the grinding of maize and has a rhythm absolutely conditioned by the movement of the work.[33] Yet in work songs the essential function of music was not always to accompany rhythmically or by metrical cadences the physical movement required by the work, but was also to simply maintain the ebb and flow of energy concentrated in the action.[34]

Pictorial documents show that music accompanied agricultural work in ancient Egypt.[35] We can also see in the Louvre that Theban group, where bakers knead dough to the playing of a flute; much work, with the Greeks, was done to the sound of music.[36] In Greek music, "the work songs were: the *ptistic*, for threshing wheat; the *igdis*, or morterer's song, which made his millstone seem less heavy, and the *mactrimos*, sung by bakers, stirring pastry."[37] Jean-Jacques Rousseau mentions also the songs of cattle drivers, reapers, millers, weaver, and flax workers in ancient Greece: the bucolic and pastorale, the *lytierse*, the hymn, the yule, and other songs.[38] "When Epaminondas had Messena rebuilt, he thought that the masons would find their task easier and more noble if accompanied by music, and had musicians brought in to execute the airs of *Pronomos*. And in *The*

---

[32]*Ibid.*, 15.

[33]See *ibid.*, 16.

[34]Marius Schneider, *Sociologie et mythologie musicales*, 21.

[35]Hans Hickmann, "Abrégé de l'histoire de la musique en Egypte," *Revue de musicologie* XCII–XCIV (1950) 11.

[36]Jules Combarieu, *La musique, ses lois, son évolution*, 148.

[37]Marcel Belvianes, *Sociologie de la musique*, 122.

[38]Jean-Jacques Rousseau, *Dictionnaire de musique* (Paris: Veuve Duchesne, 1768) 80–81.

Acharnians, Aristophanes has one of his characters say: 'In the arsenal, one drives plugs in with a great noise, one makes reams, one attaches them with straps, one hears nothing but whistles, the sound of flutes and fifes which animate the workers.' "[39]

In the Middle Ages also it was the custom to sing while working. "Just as they have their songs and their passwordcries, the different crafts possess . . . their own steps and rhythms: here is the *shoemaker's branle,* the *washer-women's branle,* and the *vine trellis dance.*"[40] But the practice of singing while working gradually disappeared later, especially in the towns; maybe we can find a reason in the generally growing passivity among the city dwellers with regard to song, probably due to the mechanization of labor, and much later, to the ever-growing diffusion of recorded music.[41] Julien Tiersot cited, even in his time, many examples concerning, it is true, the countryside: in Normandy the "reaping" songs and the "gathering" songs, the names of which alone indicate their usage, and in the workshops of Flanders, the "tellingen."[42] In Corsica, even in our time, for example, one sings while driving the cattle that pull the stone that grinds corn. In this work there is a mixture of song and shouts of encouragement to the cattle. In the Hebrides, on the other hand, in milking, the sound of the jet of milk squirting in the bucket regulates the rhythm of the song. Here also music aids in arranging, coordinating, or stimulating the motions of work, and we could amass more of such examples.

Now, work and craft songs (which must be distinguished) are

---

[39]Marcel Belvianes, *Sociologie de la musique,* 127–128. See also Jules Combarieu, *La musique, ses lois, son évolution,* 149.

[40]Norbert Dufourcq, *La musique française,* 44.

[41]Vige-Langevin, "Causes de la régression de la chanson populaire," *Deuxième Congrès international d'Esthétique et de Science de l'Art,* Vol. I (Paris: Alcan, 1937) 318–22, and Lewis Mumford, *Technique et Civilisation* (Paris: Ed. du Seuil, 1950) 185.

[42]Julien Tiersot, *Histoire de la chanson populaire en France* (Paris: Plon-Heugel, 1889) 147, 149. We can find a collection of French craft and work songs in Paul Olivier, *Les chansons de métiers* (Paris: Fasquelle, 1910).

the expression of a phenomenon already mentioned: the differentiation of the social functions of music. Labor conditions the birth of an appropriate genre, the work song, which stimulates the worker by making his task easier or more agreeable. And not only work and crafts express themselves in music[43] (we find an echo of them in certain compositions by Honegger, Mossolov, Meytus, Villa-Lobos, Prokofiev, and others).[44] Not only can a group united by the same work or craft find in music a group symbol, a social sign, or an exalting emblem,[45] but above all, here music serves as a "social control[46] for specific ends: the sociopsychological unification of indi-

---

[43]Let us note, however, that "certain songs have been appropriated by defined occupations without seeming to have anything, either in sense or in form, that relates to their functions: so, such a trade song, because sung at peeling or gathering, or during common labor during the watches of winter, without there being to this any motive other than long tradition which has consecrated the usage." Julien Tiersot, *Histoire de la chanson populaire en France*, 148. See also Jacques Charpentreau, "La chanson contemporaine," *Esprit* CCLXXXVII (1960) 1404–1407, where the author indicates numerous contemporary songs having for their subject matter work and the worker.

[44]Also the cinema, in its presentation of documentaries and certain factual situations, solicits musical translations of wheels, pistons, turbines, steam hammers, spirals in movement, etc. This conjugation, ordinarily without great artistic range, is characteristic. Many compositions evoke the factory and foundry. See Maurice Faure, "La Machine, source de l'inspiration musicale," *Revue internationale* VI (1946) 577.—If a sociohistorical conditioning can explain the appearance or existence of a work or musical genre, it can also explain—and here its deepest action is manifest—such and such a properly musical trait, more or less characteristic of the work or the genre in question. The action of the extramusical on the musical is often a source of descriptive music. See Charles W. Hughes, "Music and machines" *The Journal of Aesthetics and Art Criticism* V/I (1946) 28–34; and Michel P. Philippot, "La Musique et les machines," *Cahiers d'études de radio-télévision* XXVII-XXVIII (1960) 274–292.

[45]Such as the songs of companions and trade guilds. See Julien Tiersot, *Histoire de la chanson populaire en France*, 140.

[46]Georges Gurvitch, "Contrôle social," *La sociologie au XXᵉ siècle*, Vol. I (Paris: P.U.F., 1947) 296–297.

viduals and the facilitation of work.[47] "Functional" music[48]—as some have agreed to call it—is applied today in the factory for psychological and productive ends; it can, knowingly measured out, influence worker productivity and the returns of certain industrial work.[49] This application brings up many aesthetic, psychological, sociological, and human questions.

IV • INFLUENCE OF ECONOMIC SOURCES ON MUSIC

Music also exerts a social and sociologically important influence in the sense that it gives rise to a whole series of jobs in society. This economic aspect would require a study by itself; never systematically approached, it includes all the professions, industries, and the activities that assist in and render possible the dissemination of music, from printing and publishing to the manufacture of instruments, and the radio and recording industries, as well as the organization of musical life. Inversely, economic support also conditions the dissemination of music. To say, "if the economic question is never sufficient to explain why masterpieces are created, it occasionally suffices to prevent them from happening, and consequently it directs to some degree the development of art"[50] surely is not enough. In musical creation and practice, in musical life as a whole, economic conditions have not only a negative, but also a positive function, in the sense that certain forms of artistic musical activity and of its "socialization" cannot exist without economic support. Since music is not of itself an activity of economical potential, its realization in society demands either that it somehow develop

---

[47]Examples: songs of the unskilled laborers and the washerwomen in France. See Julien Tiersot, *Histoire de la chanson populaire en France*, 159–162.

[48]Jacques Descotes, "La musique fonctionnelle," *Polyphonie* VII–VIII (1951) 71–92.

[49]Paul R. Farnsworth, *The Social Psychology of Music* (Ames, Iowa: Iowa State U., 1969) 2nd ed., 209–219; and Wheeler Beckett, and Lee Fairley, "Music in Industry: a Bibliography," *MLA Notes* I/4 (1944) 14–20.

[50]Charles Lalo, *L'art et la vie sociale*, 68.

such potential, or else that it be sustained by a social factor that can provide the necessary resources. The first case is illustrated by the commercialization of musical life in Europe from the seventeenth and eighteenth centuries, especially the eighteenth, until today; patronage supplies an example of the second.

In civilized societies, extensive development of musical activity generally occurs in social milieus that are well endowed economically. As for the action of economic conditions in general, it has already been demonstrated that in ancient India and ancient Egypt "the simultaneous presence in these two countries of the same instruments is the fruit of commercial exchanges which took place between them, at first with the Phoenicians, the Sabaeans, and the Indian colonists on the shores of Arabia as intermediaries, then directly under the Ptolemies and later under the Roman emperors."[51] In the twelfth century, "the success of the first Crusade, through its economic and moral consequences, opened a path to an era of prosperity in which the arts also profited. Mediterranean traffic in the hands of the Italian cities of Genoa, Pisa, Venice, established a broad current of interchange between East and West; a vast industrial and commercial renaissance took place in continental Europe. . . . Curiosity about the arts and literature, until then a prerogative of few specialized monks, spread to the upper classes, and in the following century won over the bourgeois. The progressive 'secularization' of the literary and musical arts issuing from the Church . . . will now proceed at an accelerated pace."[52] As for the positive action of economic conditions upon music, we find another interesting example in Switzerland at the beginning of the fifteenth century, where a committee of bishops made a visit to the churches of the Diocese of Lausanne (1416–1417): "With some exceptions, religious music is cultivated where power and wealth are found united. It is practiced mainly in chapters and in the convents benefitting from the

[51]Claudie Marcel-Dubois, *Les instruments de musique de l'Inde ancienne* (Paris: P.U.F., 1941) 198.

[52]Jacques, Chailley, *Histoire musicale du Moyen Age*, 112-118.

support, if not the protection, of rich and noble families. That means that the social milieu and economic conditions influenced even the development of sacred music to a considerable extent."[53] On the other hand, during the Thirty Years' War, Switzerland was inundated with poor refugees who, lacking stable and regular employment, applied themselves to making music, for better or worse.[54] In a somewhat later period—the second half of the same century—there exists an anonymous contemporary piece of evidence, according to which the poor students of Burgundy, Franche-Comté, Lorraine, and Flanders sang litanies in the streets of Cologne at the doors of houses "to have something to eat"[55]—this represents an analogous situation.

Burgundy at its height possessed the most populous cities and the richest territories of the West. Benefiting also from an exceptional location at the entrance to the North Sea, with Bruges and Antwerp as the most frequented commercial markets in Europe, it offered a fertile ground for musical culture. The large commercial ships, some of which even carried organs, could provide themselves with their own musicians as well. In Burgundy musicians were well paid; knowing that they would be well received in this country where music was appreciated, many were drawn to it. We even find in Bruges, in 1318, a school of minstrels. And Flemish instrument makers, well known abroad also, could expand their activity to full capacity.[56] "Well before 1420, the musicians of Mons, Bruges, and Brussels were famous, and the most beautiful organs of the time were made at Ghent."[57] All these developments depended on a solid financial situation. Among various theories, there is one that accounts for

[53]Edouard-M. Fallet, *La vie musicale au pays de Neuchâtel du XIIIᵉ à la fin du XVIIIᵉ siècle* (Leipzig-Strasbourg-Zürich: Heitz, 1936) 5.

[54]*Ibid.*, 114.

[55]See André Pirro, "Remarques de quelques voyageurs sur la musique en Allemagne et dans les pays du Nord de 1634 à 1700" *Riemann Festschrift* (Leipzig: Max Hesses Verlag, 1909) 332.

[56]Jeanne Marix, *Histoire de la Musique et des Musiciens de la Cour de Bourgogne*, 10-13.

[57]*Ibid.*, 11.

the appearance of the Renaissance on the basis of the concomitant rise of capitalism.[58] "In particular, this emergence of
capitalism in the early 16th century proved to be of importance
for the late Renaissance developments in German painting and
music, through the influence of Flemish musicans and artists,
who made important stylistic contributions in both fields. In the
first six decades of the 16th century Antwerp emerged as the
commercial and financial center of Europe . . . It developed a
machinery of international finance that made it the main money
market of Europe. The effect of new capitalism, arising from
Antwerp's thriving commerce, upon music, and in particular
church music, within the city of Antwerp itself can be illustrated
from data taken from records of the Cathedral of Our Lady in the
archives of the City Hall of Antwerp, examined and transcribed
by E.E. Lowinsky."[59] They show that at that time a great number
of lay congregations were founded in Antwerp. The members
were wealthy merchants, bankers, and industrialists of the town,
and especially for them a number of church services, with
singing, were organized.[60] To take another example, in two
German towns, in the sixteenth century, "was an opulence and
prosperity representative of the emergent capitalism of the
time. The wealth of the mining engineers of Nuremberg and the
financiers of Augsburg . . . was reflected in the proliferation of
civic culture; the rapid spread of lay education in the towns; the
founding of universities; the rise of linguistic disciplines;
humanism and Roman law; painting and music . . . In the early
16th century Nuremberg became the representative center of
Meistersinger activity. The Meistersinger art was stimulated by
increasing prosperity and the resultant increased social status of

---

[58]Cf. Herbert Weismger, "The English Origins of the Sociological Interpre-
tations of the Renaissance," *Journal of the History of Ideas* XI (1950) 321–338.
Edward E. Lowinsky: "Music in the Culture of the Renaissance," *Journal of the
History of Ideas* XV (1954) 511.

[59]John Wesley Barker, "Sociological Influences Upon the Emergence of
Lutheran Music," *Miscellanea musicologica. Adelaide Studies in Musicology* 4
(1969) 160.

[60]Cf. *ibid.*, 161.

the merchants and tradesmen of the town. Just as strict laws regulated the activities of the burghers engaged in any form of industry, through various guilds, so music was strictly organised with regard to the form and styles of word-setting."[61]

The presentation of operas required at times fabulous sums, as for example the production of Cavalli's *Ercole* in Paris and Cesti's *Pomo d'Oro* in Vienna.[62] We know of the enormous amounts of money spent by Mazarin for Luigi Rossi's *Orfeo;* indeed, this served as a welcome pretext to excite the Parisian people against him, for the contrast between his lavish expenditures on opera and the appalling public destitution was too striking to ignore.[63] The importance of funds necessary to maintain an opera house and the economic burden this represented is also illustrated in the case of the Duke of Brunswick, in Germany (where there were many small court operas). In order to finance his opera productions he coupled direct and indirect taxes with a kind of slave traffic, selling his subjects as soldiers.[64] Nor is it by chance that the first traces of commercial public concerts appeared in the seventeenth century in England, the most economically developed country in Europe at the time.[65] The institution of these concerts was only possible in a country where the public for which they were conceived could pay admission. The organization of the academies or concerts in France may be explained also, in part, by economic conditions. The academies offered a joint concert organization that cost much less than maintenance by a patron of an individual professional orchestra.[66] The participation of amateurs contributed considerably here. The "Concerts d'émulation" (1786) in Paris, for example, comprised both professionals and amateurs. Similarly, "one third of the orchestra in Mme de Pompa-

---

[61]*Ibid.*, 162-3.

[62]Manfred F. Bukofzer, *Music in the Baroque Era,* 400.

[63]Henry Prunières, *L'Opéra italien en France avant Lulli,* 141-42.

[64]Bukofzer, *Music in the Baroque Era,* 398.

[65]*Ibid.*, 403.

[66]Humphrey Burton, "Les Académies de musique en France au XVIIIe siècle," *Revue de musicologie* CXII (1955) 124.

dour's theater, in the Petits Appartements of Versailles, was made up of amateurs, happy to put their talent to the service of the marquise, and not afraid of competing with professionals."[67]

The academies, those "fortresses of courtliness of the ancien Régime,"[68] did not survive the Revolution; there are many reasons to explain their decline, economic as well as social.[69] On the other hand, the enormous popularity of music during the first half of the eighteenth century was a somewhat artificial passing fashion. As symbols of privilege and of all that was represented by the ancien Régime, the academies could not survive this period, but their decline, which in many cases was well under way before 1789, was also a consequence of monetary difficulties following the deterioration of the French economy in the course of the eighteenth century. The academies were also the victims of wars, particularly the Seven Years' War.[70] The hypothesis has been advanced that Delalande contrived to write more simply, giving the soloist a larger part, when in 1706, in the middle of the War of Succession in Spain, he launched in Versailles the Second Psalm, *Quare fremuerunt gentes*; the reason being that he would have lacked the means in la Chapelle—the finances were no longer available to him.[71] As for J.S. Bach, who lived almost entirely on his salary as a cantor, the sale of *The Art of the Fugue*, published when he died, did not even cover the expenses of the copper engraving. We should not be surprised that he published so few of his masterpieces

---

[67]Louis Striffling, *Esquisse d'une histoire du goût musical en France au XVIIIe siècle,* 119. See also Michel Brenet, *Les Concerts en France sous l'ancien Régime,* 143; and Barry S. Brook, *La Symphonie Française,* 28-35. Cf. below note 77.

[68]Burton, "Les Académies," 140.

[69]The king did not want to grant any more letters patent to the academies. In refusing a "patent letter" to the city of Caën in 1757, he explained that music prevented youth from applying itself to studies, which would be much more useful to the state than music. See *ibid.,* 140.

[70]See *ibid.,* 140-42. Here are some closing dates for academies in the provinces: Nantes, 1758; Lyon and Moulin, c. 1775; Bordeaux, Montpelier, Marseille, and Aix-en-Provence, c. 1789.

[71]See Norbert Dufourcq et al., *Notes et références pour servir à une histoire de Michel-Richard Delalande* (Paris: Picard, 1957) 32.

during his lifetime. Later music possibly suffered the consequences of this unfavorable economic situation: it took almost one hundred years for the public at large to rediscover Bach and to feel his influence directly. But other reasons contributed to this. Also, according to Jacques Chailley, it is to the "forced unemployment of a London violinist that we owe the most monumental transformation of musical customs of all time. For, in order to make some money, which was not otherwise forthcoming, Banister, beginning in 1672, conceived the idea of giving musical soirées at his home, open to anyone who could pay. This was an unprecedented innovation."[72] But as was pointed out by Barry S. Brook, music attains a socioeconomic status as a valuable consumer product only in the Romantic era, during the rapid industrialization of Europe.[73]

In the twentieth century, the musical community in the French provinces enjoyed a period of prosperity that ended with the war of 1914; after the war, restoration of ruins and new acquisitions necessitated expenses that were often prohibitive.[74] But in the decade before this war, more and more rapid communications, and the provincial bourgeois custom of making frequent and prolonged sojourns in the capital, took a part of their clientele away from provincial opera houses.[75] Diego Carpitella has been able to show, on the other hand, that musical folklore in Italy has maintained "its own archaic traits, especially in the central, southern and island regions (Umbria, Latium, Campania, Apulia, Basilicata, Calabria, Molise, Sicily, Sardinia), a fact which is very understandable since we are dealing with economically and socially less developed regions."[76] As for the

---

[72]Jacques Chailley, *40,000 ans de musique,* 128.

[73]Barry S. Brook, "Discussion," *IRASM* VI/1 (1975) 128.

[74]See Arthur Manouvrier, "Des orphéons aux grandes sociétés musicales en France," *Polyphonie,* V (1949) 101.

[75]See René Dumesnil, "La décentralisation musicale en France," *Polyphonie,* V (1949) 83.

[76]Diego Carpitella, "Considérations sur le folklore musical italien dans ses rapports avec la structure sociale du pays," *Journal of the International Folk Music Council,* XI (1959) 67.

influence of economic conditions on musical composition itself, we notice it, for instance, with the French symphonies of the eighteenth century. To take into account their publisher's market, composers had to write the kind of scores that could work for the small as well as the large orchestras of the time and had to be careful in using wind instruments, because a large number of small orchestras were composed only of strings.[77] The exigencies of publishing, as a business activity, had a negative effect on "symphonic orchestration in France in the eighteenth century, a period during which the intentions of the composer were generally secondary and during which performers and publishers permitted themselves all sorts of . . . liberties."[78]

V • COPYING, PRINTING AND PUBLISHING

Even as late as the eighteenth century, composers indicated very few details in the scores they intended for publication. In accordance with the artistic traditions and conventions of the times, the performers (unknown to the composers) were sufficiently free with their interpretations, and for ensemble works, even in their choice of instruments. The introduction of printing into the musical domain presented from the start both advantages and inconveniences to composers. With regard to the inconveniences, we can mention first the situation in which the composer was placed of not knowing, through immediate contact, his whole audience, which was growing, and whose reactions he could learn only indirectly and after the fact; then, the difficulties in choosing his publisher, that new social factor in musical life, who could, on the one hand, offer the composer a more independent economic situation than that of service to the

---

[77]See Barry S. Brook, *La Symphonie française dans la seconde moitié du XVIIIe siècle*, Ph.D. dis. (Paris: Sorbonne, 1959) 25. Printed edition (Paris: Morin-Institut de Musicologie de l'Université de Paris, 1962) 3 vols.

[78]*Ibid.*, 26.

aristocracy, but who could, on the other hand, tie him down by other bonds of a commercial and economic order. Without a doubt, the printing of musical works contributed to their dissemination. As Robert Wangermée remarked, it also stimulated composers and in fact increased their number. In the fifteenth century there were not many composers; one finds the same names in the manuscripts again and again. But in the sixteenth century there were hundreds who devoted themselves to the chanson and who succeeded in publishing and selling their compositions. That indicates that a market existed for this genre. Changes in the spirit and form of the chanson of this period can be explained in the same way by the considerably increased interest of a larger and more diverse audience. And the publishing of music took park in these transformations. In the first half of the century, there were three great centers of chanson publication in Western Europe: Paris, with Attaingnant; Lyons, with Jacques Moderne; and Antwerp, with Tielman Susato. Nevertheless, the polyphonic chanson remained tied to a certain culture and affected the bourgeoisie without reaching the lower classes of society.[79]

From its beginnings, the publishing of chansons represented a good source of income for the publishers. Proof of this is in the fact that certain books of music were quickly published in several editions. The rights of the author could be neither guaranteed nor effectively assured, especially abroad; on the contrary, these rights were often violated. The sixteenth century thus saw, in Venice, the first disputes between publishers over the rights of authors.[80]

At the outset of music publishing, the publisher did not represent the composer; he was simply a businessman who chose authors and their works according to the demands of the market. In the early eighteenth century, however, publishers started to publish more upon the demand of the composers

---

[79]See Robert Wangermée, *Flemish Music and Society in the Fifteenth and Sixteenth Centuries*, in toto.

[80]See François Lesure, *Pour une sociologie historique des faits musicaux*, 341.

themselves. Even later on it also happened that "often the composer was his own publisher: he hired an engraver, chose a printer, corrected the proofs and sold in his own house the copies on which he put his signature as a guarantee. Sometimes the engraver or publisher was a member of the composer's family. The whole operation was controlled, from the beginning to the end, on the spot. If, however, the composer preferred not to publish his works himself, he had at his disposal not only a great number of professional publishers, but also all of those composers and artists who were also publishers. Some of these were his friends, or at least his colleagues, sitting near him in the orchestra."[81] On the other hand, there is a "moment in the eighteenth century, when publishing a musical work, instead of being an expense, became profitable. This is a key moment, since the composer could possibly make a living from his production. Previously, only the dedication procedure presented an indirect means of obtaining money. A new individual thus inserted himself into musical life—the publisher of music. . . . The composers learn then to play the game of the simultaneous publication of their works in London, Paris, and elsewhere, in order to be paid not once, but two, three, or four times. And this is also the moment when copyright begins to appear."[82] Around 1700, the preeminence of France, Italy, and Germany in musical publishing, passed on to England and the Low Countries, with the activities of John Walsh and Estienne Roger in London and Amsterdam, respectively. But between 1750 and 1770 the very active Parisian publishing business again took first place, stimulated by the rich musical life in the twenty or so concert halls in Paris (in 1782 there were already forty-four music publishers in Paris). Circulation varied considerably, from thirty copies (of *The Art of Fugue* by Bach) up to about 1500 copies.[83]

---

[81]Barry S. Brook, *La Symphonie française dans la seconde moitié du XVIIIe siècle*, 3 vol. (Paris: Institut de Musicologie de l'Université de Paris, 1962).

[82]François Lesure, "Discussion," *IRASM* VI/1 (1975) 124-125.

[83]See François Lesure, *Pour une sociologie historique des faits musicaux*, 343.

In the nineteenth century, a new development took place. To the greater number of small publishers were added large, well-organized publishing houses such as Breitkopf & Härtel.[84] In addition, "the pertinent role of publisher was surely reinforced by that of instrument manufacturers who regarded public concerts as part and parcel of their sales campaigns. The extent to which publishing and instrument-making interests coincided is demonstrated not only by the monopolies held often in both fields by the same individual (Clementi in England and Pleyel in France) but also by the flood of published arrangements of entire operas, not to speak of Beethoven sonatas, for flute, piccolo or other incongruous instruments."[85] However, to evaluate properly this aspect of economic influence on the musical culture of a period, it would be necessary to consider not only the quantity and frequency of musical publication, but also the consumers and purchasers of publications, the changes introduced in music publishing by the development and enforcement of copyrights, and the influence exerted by the publishers on the musical taste of the public—questions that still await thorough exploration.[86]

VI • EARNINGS AND ROYALTIES

The economic conditioning of musical activity does not generally explain the artistic quality of musical works and is not responsible for it. On the contrary, it is more directly responsible for the quantity of works produced, and their genre, as well as for the material well-being of the composer. Until about the eighteenth century, the artistic rights of the composer were neither recognized nor guaranteed (no more than were his monetary rights). Sometimes mention of the composer's name was omitted in a

---

[84]Jacques Chailley, 40,000 ans, 282.

[85]Alexander L. Ringer, "Discussion," IRASM VI/1 (1975) 122.

[86]See the studies devoted to musical publishing in Musik und Verlag. Karl Vötterle zum 65. Geburtstag am 12. April 1968. Richard Baum und Wolfgang Rhem, ed. (Kassel-Basel: Bärenreiter, 1968).

concert program when that composer was young and unknown; but famous and respected works were all the more exposed to alteration—they belonged to the public. The composer did not generally get a contract; he was offered a fee. The minstrels financed their travels from castle to castle by playing before the nobility, and the composers offered these same noblemen their works, expecting compensation. Binchois, who stayed in the service of Philip the Good until his death; Dunstable, who served the Duke of Bedford; and Ockeghem, who was in the service of Charles VII, were all paid in cash and kind. Josquin de Prez, who served, among others, Galeazzo Maria Sforza, Duke of Milan; then Cardinal Ascanio Sforza; and also Louis XII, would have been attracted by promises of high salary which the Duke of Ferrara made him: "CC ducati de provisione, la casa e le spese e anche beneficii per bona somma."[87] In contrast to the stinginess of Ascanio Sforza, Galeazzo Maria Sforza offered his musicians high salaries, since he considered this the best way to make them come from other courts and from their homes, which were often far away.[88] In the eighteenth century, many musicians gained interesting positions in Dijon: "Michel, music master of Sainte-Chapelle, saw himself provided with a canonry. The count of Tavannes, Lieutenant-General of Burgundy, obtained lodgings in the royal palace for Capus. Bourgeois was given room and board with the Steward of Province. De Montigny, Treasurer-General of the States, protected Lacombe and obtained a canonry for his music master, the Abbé Patelin; while Chartraire de Bourbonne, 'Président à mortier,' sent Guillemain to Italy at great expense and provided for him in his will."[89] All these musicians accepted these advantageous conditions. The fact that musicians were always remunerated in one

---

[87]Cited without reference in Anne-Marie Bautier-Regnier, "Musiciens d'Oultremont à la Cour de Mantoue, Jacques de Wert," *Revue belge de musicologie* IV/1-2 (1950) 43. See also André Pirro, *Histoire de la musique de la fin du XIVᵉ siècle à fin du XVIᵉ*, 171-172.

[88]Gaetano Cesari, "Musica e Musicisti alla Corte Sforzesca," *Rivista musicale italiana* XXIX (1922) 10.

[89]Maurice Barthélemy, "La vie et la culture musicale en France vers 1762,

way or another does not need further demonstration. Numerous examples exist.[90] We will refer to only a few. Brenet cited the case of Eloy d'Amerval, master of the children's chorus at Sainte-Croix in Orléans, dating from the end of the fifteenth century: "A sum of '104 Parisian *solz*, valued at four *escus d'or*' was paid him, said the accounts of the city 'in compensation and renumeration for having put down words and music for a motet in Latin and French . . . ' "[91] Referring to the letters of Mozart, he also shows that the Concerts des Amateurs in Paris paid composers "five *louis d'or* for a symphony."[92] Beethoven, on the other hand, proposed to Ignace Pleyel in a letter dated 26 October 1807 to entrust him, for the "moderate price of 1200 Augsburg florins," with the publication of six works, including a symphony, a concerto, three quartets and the *Coriolan* overture.[93] And "Gounod transferred to the publisher Choudens 'the full and entire rights without any restrictions or reserve, for France and Belgium,' of his opera *Faust*, for the sum of 10,000 francs."[94] As far as teaching was concerned,[95] Rameau took eight pounds per lesson, and in 1778 in Paris Mozart took three pounds per lesson. Professors with lesser reputation took under one

d'après un manuscrit du Musée de Condé," *"Recherches" sur la musique française classique (1960)* (Paris: Picard, 1960) 142.

[90]They can be found in abundance in works such as Carl Anthon, "Some Aspects of the Social Status of Italian Musicians during the Sixteenth Century," *Journal of Renaissance and Baroque Music*, I/2 (1946) 111-123 and I/3, 222-234; Walter Woodfill, *Musicians in English Society from Elizabeth to Charles I*, (Princeton: Princeton U. Press, 1953).

[91]Michel Brenet, *Les Concerts en France sous l'ancien Régime*, 15-16.

[92]*Ibid.*, 359.

[93]M. Daubresse, *Le musicien dans la société moderne* (Paris: Le Monde musical, 1914) 162.

[94]*Ibid.*

[95]It is interesting to note that the music master was sometimes treated particularly well in ancient Greece, as with Teos in the 2nd century. His annual salary was 700 drachmas, whereas that of his colleagues was between 500 and 600. See Henri-Irénée Marrou, *Histoire de l'éducation dans l'Antiquité*, 194-195.

pound.[96] But generally the composers had to adapt to the existing economic conditions, not the other way around. Normally it fell to the patrons, employers or publishers to dictate their conditions to the composer.

It is often the same in our day. The commercialization of musical life has invaded all sectors; it is also responsible for the immense musical inflation caused both by the mechanization of production and the industrialization of the musical dissemination. A study, however succinct, of economic conditions reigning in the actual world of music, which are certainly complex and variable from country to country although essentially similar everywhere, would widely exceed, of course, the limits of this work.[97]

---

[96]Marc Pincherle, "La musique dans l'éducation des enfants au XVIIIᵉ sièle," *Mélanges d'histoire et d'esthétique musicales offerts à Paul-Marie Masson* V. II, (Paris: Richard-Masse, 1955) 121.

[97]For the situation some time ago in Belgium, for example, in respect to the earnings of musicians, see Jacqueline De Clercq, *La profession de musicien—Une enquête*, 25, 92-94.

CHAPTER EIGHT

MUSIC AND TECHNIQUE

I • PRODUCTION OF INSTRUMENTS

There are several aspects to the conditioning of music by production techniques. One of the most important is the influence exerted by techniques of production on the manufacture of instruments, and through this on the creation, performance, and interpretation of music. This aspect is probably the most interesting to study in the primitive phase of the evolution of music, because at that stage music is closely linked to all the fundamental (religious, magical, and economical) aspects of social life. It is also fruitful to consider it in the era following the great development of industry in Europe, from the sixteenth century onward.

While the technical level of certain other arts did not advance appreciably over very long periods, music experienced an evolution that was linked to technical advances, one of which was the construction of instruments.[1] "Throughout the history of Western music, the technology of instrument building has had an effect on how music was performed and written. The availability of a keyboard instrument with a completely chromatic

---

[1]See Theodore Caplow, "The Influence of Radio on Music as a Social Institution," *Cahiers d'études de radio-télévision* III-IV (1955) 280.

scale prompted composers to write passages they could and would not otherwise had done; the more sonorous and easily played stringed instruments built in the Baroque period contributed to the flood of compositions for strings characteristic of this time; wind instruments with completely accurate and usable chromatic scales and brass instruments with valves (making it possible for them to play full chromatic scales also) changed the character of orchestral sound in the late eighteenth and nineteenth centuries. . . . "[2] Thus we can even say "that each instrument has engendered its own specific style, in the history of musical thought. And this style is related not only to the spiritual, but also to the technical aspect of the instrument."[3] This aspect is strictly dependent upon the means of production that have served in the construction of the instruments in any given era. Composers have always created with a view to the instruments they had available. As a result, the possibilities of instruments have conditioned, and still condition today, if not their thought, then at least its possible expression. It has thus been asserted that diverse "facts of our modern music owe their existence only to the habit of composing at the piano. How would the more or less archaic musics have escaped the pressure of instruments more successfully? We are even in a position to assert that the effects particular to a specific instrument have been transfered, by transposing themselves to other instruments. . . . Today, for example, is it not evident that our string instruments have acquired the timbral characteristics of wind instruments, if not an accentuation typical of percussion instruments?"[4]

In primitive or archaic music, timbre and rhythm generally predominate as essential elements. This is due not only to the artistic level of primitive man, considered from a cultural and psychological point of view, but also to the means he employs to

---

[2]Charles Hamm, "Technology and Music: The Effect of the Phonograph," Charles Hamm, Bruno Nettl, and Roland Byrnside, *Contemporary Music and Music Cultures* (Englewood Cliffs: Prentice-Hall, 1975) 270.

[3]Gisèle Brelet, *L'interprétation créatrice* Vol. 1 (Paris: P.U.F., 1951) 32.

[4]André Schaeffner, *Origine des instruments de musique*, 352.

express his musical emotions. In order to produce different timbres, primitive man first makes use of various objects, utensils, and tools that are basically extraartistic in nature. These are principally working and fighting implements. We could mention, as an example, the boomerangs of the Australian aborigines, weapons of war and implements of the hunt. They are knocked together to make music. According to André Schaeffner, the blacks of the Cameroons produce rhythms by striking the edges of their boats with the tops of their oars; while in other countries the ploughshare is utilized as a musical instrument. In some Indochina countries the troughs for husking rice serve, when not used for working purposes, to accompany singing. Various tribes of Black Africa also use gourds as instruments.[5] Almost everywhere analogous usages have been observed.

The use of such objects for musical purposes partially explains one of the already mentioned characteristics of primitive instrumental music in general: the predominance of rhythm and timbre—an extensive use of noises. As for musical instruments in their proper sense, many of the most primitive probably developed from nonmusical objects such as working tools and hunting implements. Thus string instruments, according to Marcel Mauss as cited by André Schaeffner, were developed from various strands or from the bow and arrow: "At the origin of string instruments simple strands could probably be found. Their tension revealed to primitive man the sonorous property of strings. . . . Similarly, there undoubtedly was a relationship between traps and instruments with resonating pits (ground zither, ground bow, etc.)"[6] Likewise, it "is possible that a certain number of whistles and ocarinas also had a utilitarian origin. In order to attract pigeons, certain peoples of Borneo use a special instrument made of a narrow and long bamboo which carries the player's breath to the edge of a notch made on the surface of another wider and shorter bamboo. Its beveled

---

[5] *Ibid.,* 97 ff.
[6] *Ibid.,* 100.

extremity calls to mind a kind of pipe of *angkloun*.'"[7] Whether produced by instruments as such or by the utilization of other objects, nonvocal music in its primitive stage is dominated by the means available; means that depend themselves on primitive production techniques. However, "the[se] techniques are applied not only in the construction of instruments (instruments of clay, of bronze) but they also are employed in various other circumstances. Thus the instruments are mainly linked to techniques of hunting, breeding and agriculture, and possess, therefore, a sound with a well-defined utilitarian role. Such are, for example, the bird-calls whose purpose is to constitute sonorous traps; such is the play of seesaw pipes which serve as a scarecrows in the rice-fields of Madagascar."[8]

Nevertheless, the instruments themselves could not have been invented, developed, utilized, adopted, or handled, without the intervention of other factors or levels of the collective life that permit, favor or require them. This clearly material base of music—the instruments themselves—would not be a social one if it were not profoundly penetrated and transformed by collective human action. Everything that is appropriated by society in one way or another (instruments included) is thus imbued with social impulses that are inconceivable without the simultaneous intervention of several levels of life in the global societies. This also holds true for musical works: we will now attempt to describe the technical and material aspect of the manufacture of instruments by placing the problem in the social and historical context of European music.

Indeed, a complex relationship appears in the evolution of the European instrumental art-music. Instrumental musical work in a given milieu depends upon the level of technical processes at the time of its creation. In Europe instrumental music, especially

[7]*Ibid.*, 100. Schaeffner refers to Hose and MacDougall, *The Pagan Tribes of Borneo* Vol. 1, 149, fig. 25. Identical instrument in the Pitt-Rivers museum at Oxford.

[8]Claudie Marcel-Dubois, "Instrument de musique," *Encyclopédie de la musique* II (Paris: Fasquelle, 1959) 562-563.

ensemble music, did not blossom until the seventeenth century.[9] In the fourteenth century and perhaps even earlier toward the end of the thirteenth century, the individualization of instruments began. Not, however, the rational utilization of one timbre rather than another. That will come with modern orchestration and we must await Giovanni Gabrieli to witness its first rough drafts. We also know that even Couperin himself still demonstrated a certain indifference in this matter. We can only see, in the fourteenth century, the individualization of instruments in general with regard to voices, but without specifying which ones.[10] The great evolution of instrumental music does not begin, therefore, until three centuries later, in the seventeenth century, made possible in part by the development of new techniques of production upon which the manufacture of certain instruments depended.[11] Vocal music had for a long time been predominant over instrumental music, both in quantity and in quality, and had influenced it as late as the sixteenth century.[12] Instruments, hardly yet perfected, still held only secondary and rather limited artistic significance. The construction of string instruments, which as a process of craftsmanship alone, led to the more rapid perfection and individualization of these instruments. This can be observed in the steadily increasing number of works written for them, as well as in their central position in the instrumental ensembles of the Baroque era. Nevertheless, it would be a mistake to imagine, by simplifying the issue, that all the technical improvements in

---

[9]See Robert Hoebaer, "L'intérêt pour l'art musical," *Bulletin de l'Institut de Recherches Economiques et Sociales,* 702. Also from a more general view point, Pierre Francastel "Technique et Esthétique," *Cahiers internationaux de sociologie* V (1949) 97-116.

[10]See Jacques Chailley, *Histoire musicale du Moyen Age,* 220. On the situation in this regard, in the sixteenth century, see Michel Brenet, *Les Concerts en France sous l'ancien Régime,* 34-35, and in eighteenth century Louis Striffling, *Esquisse d'une histoire du goût musical en France au XVIIIᵉ siècle,* 146-147 and Norbert Dufourcq, *La musique française,* 163 et 173.

[11]See Lewis Mumford, *Technique et Civilisation* (Paris: Ed. du Seuil, 1950) 185.

[12]See Lionel de La Laurencie, *Le Goût musical en France,* 112-113.

instrument construction immediately found a practical application and instrumentalists capable of profiting by them. At times, the performance possibilities of string instruments greatly exceeded what performers expected or demanded from them.[13] Sometimes a considerable period of time elapsed before a technical advance was put to artistic use. It is, indeed, in that way that we can explain, at certain stages, the temporary advance of particular forms intended for wind instruments, in comparison to those reserved for string instruments. In the long run, nevertheless, a technical improvement in an instrument always brought about favorable consequences in artistic practice.

If we wish to find, for example "a more profound explanation for the vogue of the lute, we have first to search for it in the history of instrument-building. In contrast to the violin and the clavichord, and even more so to wind instruments, the lute was, around 1620–1630, an instrument which instrument-makers had brought in some ways to the height of its perfection in France. The daily commerce between instrument-makers and instrumentalists most likely had much to do with the result of these efforts, which, at the end of the century, resulted in the birth of a lute school both in the domain of instrument-building and in that of composition. . . . Antoine Francisque, Jacob Reys, René Mésangeau, Luis de Briceno, for example, lived intimately with lute makers such as Robert Denis, Gervais Rebans, Claude Lesclop, Jean Jacquet—in the same way that organists lived for almost two centuries very close to the builders of keyboard instruments."[14]

In this example we find a concrete illustration of social intervention of another level, whose general character we have already established: the collaboration, in this case, of two social groups of different professions—instrument-makers and lutenists—which contributed to the perfecting of the instrument. In order to give the problem a full and properly sociological study,

---

[13]See Max Weber, *The Rational and Social Foundations of Music,* 108-111.

[14]François Lesure, "Recherches sur les luthistes parisiens à l'époque de Louis XIII" *Le luth et sa musique* (Paris: C.N.R.S., 1958) 211.

a specialist in this time and area ought to ask himself: what was the intensity and the importance of that collaboration; what was the social demand for lute music; whether it influenced efforts toward perfecting the instruments; and if so, to what extent. He would then examine whether this demand had aesthetic motivations only, or had social ones as well, and from which precise milieus or social groups it came. He would still need to determine typical phenomena, to indicate the social roles played by professional and amateur lutenists, to discover the collective ideas current in the global society (or only in certain classes and social groups) about lute music and the instrument itself that contributed to its perfection. Finally, he ought to ask himself whether these technical improvements were merely the result of a personal fascination with the lute and its music on the part of the lute-players and -makers.

To close this parenthesis, let us say, on the other hand, that until the eighteenth century, the bowed instruments were charged with the differentiation of timbre in ensemble works. Even in the seventeenth century, the instrumental body of an ensemble work could be arbitrarily modified. One could substitute wind instruments for strings, and vice-versa: evidence that the element of timbre still had only a minimal importance.[15] The sense of timbre and sound color was awakened only slowly and rather late in the history of European music; it became well-developed only in the nineteenth century, and even more in the twentieth. The element of timbre became increasingly more interesting in musical creation itself, especially with Beethoven and the Romantics; and an increasingly important element in musical style, especially with Debussy.[16] Although the Baroque orchestra was based on the sonority of string instruments, new mechanical inventions permitted the classic orchestra to modify the quality of its sonority. All instruments gradually became

---

[15]See Zofia Lissa, Prilog proučavanju sociologije muzike (Contribution to research in the sociology of music), *Muzika 3* (1949) 18. See also: Norbert Dufourcq, *La musique française*, 108.

[16]See Gisèle Brelet, *L'interprétation créatrice*, Vol. I, 105; and Norbert Dufourcq, *La musique française*, 101-105.

scientifically calibrated. Sound production became determined, standardized, predictable. With the increase in the number of instruments in the orchestra, the division of labor in the orchestra corresponded to that of the factory.[17] The leader of the orchestra appeared somewhat like a director of production in charge of the manufacture and assembly of a product—a piece of music; and the composer corresponded to the inventor, the engineer and builder who had calculated on paper, with the aid of instruments such as the piano, the nature of the final product, determining its slightest details before it ever reached the manufacturing stage.[18]

Throughout the eighteenth and especially the nineteenth centuries, the development of technical and industrial means of production of many instruments—especially wind instruments, or more precisely the "brass," but also instruments such as the piano and organ—brought many changes. First, they made possible the perfecting of preexisting types of instruments, and the creation of entirely new instruments. They also facilitated performance by renewing or expanding its possibilities.[19] This has a subordinate but important consequence—a further emancipation of instrumental music, and in particular, the expansion of orchestral music. Having at its disposal a timbre ever richer and more differentiated, more subtle dynamic possibilities, and a larger register (thanks to the number of instruments becoming ever more perfected), instrumental music advanced beyond purely vocal music in quantity and quality. The function and the position of instruments with the ensemble also became formalized.

Among all the instruments of the twentieth century, only the violin group and the trombone have undergone no important transformation since the start of the great industrial revolution in Europe.[20] A few examples will suffice to illustrate that the

---

[17]See Lewis Mumford, *Technique et civilisation*, 185.

[18]*Ibid.*, 185-186.

[19]See Louis Striffling, *Esquisse d'une histoire du goût musical en France au XVIII* siècle, 132-135.

[20]See André Schaeffner, "Les instruments de musique," *La Musique des*

perfecting of existing instruments and the invention of new instruments takes place, for the most part, in the period that follows the development of industry and the appropriate techniques to which it gives birth. This is easy to understand if we bear in mind that metallic parts—for example, the pins of wood instruments—as well as several parts of brass instruments (thus the wind instruments) are turned on a lathe.[21] Even in 1785 there were metalworkers who built instruments of brass.[22] But in the industrial era, machines and instrument-makers, ever more specialized, took over the manufacture of instruments. In France "as the Revolution had dissolved the Guilds and the inventors, since the last years of the eighteenth century, having sanctioned keys and values, the freed artisanship became complex and industrialized; this resulted in a multiplicity of instrumental types built by large firms whose competition is expressed in improvements of the brass instruments."[23] But starting with the universal lathe, specialized lathes were gradually created (the screw-cutting lathe, for example, in 1800)[24] As a secondary result, the mechanization of production brought about the production of mechanical instruments, for which even such composers as Mozart and Beethoven sometimes wrote.[25]

---

origines à nos jours (Paris: Larousse, 1946) 43, and Jacques Chailley, *40,000 ans de musique,* 225.

[21]See M. A. Soyer, *Des instruments à vent, de leur principe,* in *Encyclopédie de la musique,* de Lavignac, 2ᵉ partie (Paris: Delagrave, 1927) 1478-1479.

[22]See Constant Pierre, *Les facteurs d'instruments de musique, les luthiers et la facture instrumentale* (Paris: Sagot, 1893) 294-302; Paul Loubet de Sceaury, *Musiciens et facteurs d'instruments de musique sous l'ancien régime,* 190-191, et Armand Machabey, "Aperçus historiques sur les instruments de cuivre," *La Revue musicale,* CCXXVI 23-24.

[23]*Ibid.,* 24. Paul Loubet de Sceaury, *Musiciens et facterurs d'instruments de musique sous l'ancien régime,* 198-199.

[24]See Georges Friedmann, and Jean-Daniel Reynaud, "*Sociologie des techniques de production et du travail,*" *Traité de sociologie.* Vol. I (Paris: P.U.F., 1968) 418.

[25]See Charles-Marie Boncourt, "La Fantaisie mécanique de Mozart," *Polyphonie,* VI (1950) 140-143, René König "Sur quelques problèmes sociologiques de l'émission radiophonique musicale," *Cahiers d'études de radio-télévision* III-IV (1955) 353.

Some important transformations also occurred in the making and use of ordinary instruments.

The transverse flute, for instance, "which became in the nineteenth century simply the flute, after taking the place of all the other flutes, had had a quite modest existence until the eighteenth century ... Little by little, however ... we see it introduced into the salon and called on to take part in chamber music."[26] "The valve trumpet was born at the beginning of the nineteenth century. ... The invention of valves permitted the construction, during the nineteenth century, of various types of wind instruments, which figured at first in military music. ... The first tubas were built in Germany by Moritz and Wieprecht around 1835."[27] Toward the end of the seventeenth century the modern clarinet was born; it was introduced into the orchestra at the beginning of the following century and was perfected during that century.[28] It "engendered a series of instruments of different registers, which came into existence in the nineteenth century (with the exception of the bass clarinet and the basset horn, both of which appeared around 1770). The saxophone, with tube of conical bore, dates from 1840."[29] The modern contrabassoon of metal also dates from the nineteenth century, as does also the keyed trumpet (although the keyed horn dates from the end of the eighteenth century).[30]

However, the greater sonorous possibilities offered by these instruments and so many others, both new and already perfected,[31] have influenced not only the composers who wrote for

---

[26]M. A. Soyer, *Des instruments à vent, de leur principe,* 1429. See also Lionel de La Laurencie, "Les débuts de la musique de chambre en France," *Revue de musicologie,* (1934) 224-223; and Norbert Dufourcq, *La musique française,* 189.

[27]André Schaeffner, *Les instruments de musique,* 48-49.

[28]See Constant Pierre, *Les facteurs d'instruments de musique, les luthiers et la facture instrumentale,* 294-362; M. A. Soyer, *Des instruments à vent, de leur principe,* 1415. See also other bibliographical references. See also Jacques Chailley, *40,000 ans de musique,* 273, where there are other bibliographical references.

[29]André Schaeffner, *Les instruments de musique,* 44.

[30]*Ibid.,* 45.

[31]The sociology of music has not taken sufficient note of the artistic value of particular instruments, be they ancient or modern. From the aesthetic point of

them and introduced them, step-by-step, into the orchestra. That the nineteenth century is the golden century of instrumental, orchestral and symphonic music, is too well known a fact for us to belabor. These increased instrumental possibilities have also conditioned musical performance.[32]

Above all, the development of ever-more refined instruments permitted the expansion of virtuoso techniques as never before, and at the same time, the birth of "virtuoso" music. The nineteenth century marked the debut of that important item particularly for the piano. The development of virtuosity ran parallel to (if not contemporary with) the progress in instrumental improvements.[33]

During the era of the organ "with hard-to-manage keys in the form of slides worked by full hands,[34] there was no question of creating an emancipated organ music, or of virtuosity. From the moment when Pepin the Short received the first pneumatic organ known in Europe from Emperor Constantine Copronymus, in the eighth century, the construction of the organ conditioned the creation of its music, and at the same time the development of organ performance practices.[35] The hypothesis has even been advanced that a detail in the construction of the keyed organ in the eleventh century would have been able to exert an influence over a long period of music history—from the development of organum to the chorale of J.S. Bach.[36] The influence of instrumental construction on techniques of production—on the development of possibilities for performance, is again illustrated

---

view, however, it is fortunate (as Handschin wrote) that a prejudgment was not made, according to which modern instruments, as products of evolution, would automatically be better than the ancient. But it would be equally unreasonable to place ancient instruments above new ones. See Jacques Handschin, *Musikgeschichte* Lucerne: Räber, 1948) 390.

[32]See the interesting facts on this subject in Jacques Chailley, *40,000 ans de musique,* 224-226.

[33]For the violin, up to improvements in the bow itself, see *ibid.,* 226.

[34]Chailley, *Histoire musicale du Moyen Age,* 110.

[35]See Jean Perrot, "Les origines de l'orgue carolingien," *La Revue musicale* CCXXVI (1955) 7-15.

[36]See Jacques Chailley, "Un Clavier d'orgue à la fin du XIe siècle," *Revue de musicologie* XVIII (1937) 5-11.

by the following: "Until the middle of the nineteenth century, French organists used only a rudimentary pedal-board with tuning pegs, which doomed all virtuosity. They only adopted the German pedal-board around 1845. The English organ had no pedal-board until the middle of the eighteenth century. Italy had no organs with multiple keyboards until the end of the seventeenth century . . . It was a Frenchman who applied electricity to the organ (1865), and Americans are the ones who for fifty years have taken better advantage of this invention. The mechanism used until the middle of the nineteenth century, and which continues to be used in the restoration of old instruments—namely, *traction* . . . after passing through a pneumatic stage, tends to become completely *electric*: a system permitting many combinations which from day to day add to the possibilities of the instrument."[37]

But the style of interpretation is perhaps due also to the quality of instruments, as well as to the aesthetic sensibility formed, in its turn, in relation to them.

In this way, mechanization has been partly responsible for the dryness and inflexibility of interpretation found at the beginning of the twentieth century; at that time composers voluntarily entrusted their "objective" music to mechanical instruments, which assured them as "objective" a performance as could be desired. And many were the pianists held up as rivals to the "objectivity" of the pianola.[38] We find a similar example in the evolution of interpretative style in older music for keyboard instruments, which at one time could be played on either the clavichord, the harpsichord, or the organ; later on, music for each of the three instruments was gradually differentiated. According to Gisèle Brelet, "since the piano has replaced the harpsichord for us, a work originally intended for harpsichord appears to us at the same time more accessible and more alive

[37]Norbert Dufourcq, "L'Orgue" *La Musique des origines à nos jours* (Paris: Larousse, 1946) 46.

[38]See Gisèle Brelet, *L'interprétation créatrice.* I, 106.

when we hear it performed on the piano."[39] But it is also for the piano's sonorous resources, especially the possible variation in dynamic nuance, that one plays it today. These dynamic nuances, made possible by the modern construction of the piano, conditioned the modern style of performance of older music, and encouraged the creation of expressive music for the piano, especially since Beethoven and the Romantic composers. This expressive character was due not only to the fact that their music already belonged to a new style, but also to the sonorous possibilities offered by the instrument itself. In addition, the new technical methods of piano-building permitted its wide distribution. The piano became the prefered instrument in bourgeois milieus, and for a long time enjoyed a veritable supremacy over other solo instruments. Its new qualities contributed to the development of large forms intended for it, such as the sonatas of Beethoven; and even more to the refinement of a virtuoso technique and the trend toward orchestral dimensions found in the music of Liszt. "The close connection between the rapid development of the orchestra and piano as the romantic solo instrument *par excellence* requires little comment. Already Liszt . . . characterized the piano style inspired by Beethoven's later sonatas as 'orchestration of the piano'."[40]

II • MUSIC AND ARCHITECTURE

In presenting the piano as a middle-class instrument, Max Weber noted that it was not equally practiced in all climates. Peoples living in more northern climates are, in fact, the foremost practitioners of the pianistic art, and this is not

---

[39]*Ibid.,* 104.

[40]Alexander Ringer, "Musical Taste and the Industrial Syndrome," *IRASM* V/1 (1974) 145. Reference is made to Adolph Bernhard Marx, *Die Musik des neunzehnten Jahrhunderts,* 2nd edition (Leipzig: 1873) 91.

accidental. Their climate imposes on them an indoor life, centered around home and hearth. Piano practice in the South—as in Southern Europe—where the comfortable indoor life has been restricted by climatic and historical factors, did not expand as rapidly as in the North (in Germany, for example). And neither did it reach to the same degree in the South that honorable position it held in the North for the middle classes as an important piece of beautiful furniture as well.[41] But its wide popularity was also favored by new acoustic conditions in the great halls where paying concerts were given, which were open to the public at large as opposed to those of the aristocratic salons reserved for a few invited guests. The place of the piano in musical life has thus been conditioned by technical factors, both social and architectural. It was perfectly adapted to the new acoustic conditions, being, along with the organ, a single instrument easily heard in the great halls. The "failure" (if one can speak of it as failure, pure and simple) of chamber music in the twentieth century—which Arthur Honegger lamented—is undoubtedly due to that element opposing the intimate ambience in which chamber music ought to be performed and for which it was written.[42] Besides, "to each architectural era corresponds a way of writing music, a standard sonority which has been classified, and which is inspired with care for eliciting the best sound of the halls where these works were intended to be played . . . The observations of Johann Sebastian Bach on the acoustical qualities of Saint-Thomas Church in Leipzig are known; the Holywell Music Room at Oxford was especially arranged for the performance of works by Händel in 1748. . . . Mozart wrote some of his music to be performed in the palace of the Prince of Salzburg. Praise of the theatre at Bayreuth leaves nothing more to be said. Berlioz noted, at the top of the score of his *Requiem,* the placements of the different instruments and

---

[41]See Max Weber, *The Rational and Social Foundations of Music,* 124.

[42]See Arthur Honegger, "Le musicien dans la société moderne," *L'artiste dans la société contemporaine* (Liège: UNESCO. H. Vaillant-Carmane, 1954) 64.

fanfares in the *Chapelle des Invalides*."[43] Spacious halls also favored the widespread use of orchestral music, of course.

A characteristic relationship of dependence can be established between the development of production techniques and the state of instrumental music, with instrument-making as an intermediary; this instrument-making also found, on the other hand, a source of activity in the greater and greater demands created by the diffusion of instrumental music.[44] It was thus conditioned by the social demand for music, and developed under the influence of a growing interest in musical art. If it has conditioned instrumental music, it has itself been conditioned by musical "consumption," by the presence of an ever-growing musical public. This in turn encouraged the construction of concert halls of grander dimensions. "The rapid expansion of sonorous resources generally went hand in hand with the broadening of the social base on which music and art was destined to flourish throughout the nineteenth century.... Since there is a direct relationship between box office receipts and the number of tickets sold for any given performance, the commercialization of musical life prompted the use of ever bigger halls for ever larger audiences, requiring in turn ever greater volumes of sound."[45] This provides an idea of the complexity of the sociohistorical conditionings of music in this area. However, to understand the importance of the influence of production techniques on music, it is not enough to take a dynamic point of view regarding historical *change* by appreciating only the impact that a technical invention could have on music upon its first appearance, which arouses the curiosity of the public and the interest of the musician. We must also consider the position occupied by a technical advance or invention for a shorter or

---

[43]José Bernhart, "Des salles de concerts et de leurs problèmes acoustiques," *Polyphonie* V (1949) 58.

[44]Constant Pierre, *Les facteurs d'instruments de musique, les luthiers et la facture instrumentale*, 403.

[45]Alexander Ringer, "Musical Taste and the Industrial Syndrome," *IRASM*, V/1 (1974) 140-141.

longer time, as the basis or as a certain condition of instrument-making upon which depend the qualities of an instrument and through these, in part, the quality of the instrumental music itself.[46]

---

[46]See the interesting reports, on a broader level, given at the colloquium "Music and Technology" organized by UNESCO (Stockholm, 8-12 June 1970), and published in *La revue musicale* (1971).

CHAPTER NINE

SOCIOPSYCHOLOGICAL CONDITIONS

I • MUSIC AND SOCIAL SYMBOLIZATION

In order to gain a better understanding of the full complexity of the sociohistorical conditionings of music, we must also take into consideration the symbolic aspect of social reality as it relates to music and the musician. This is so vast and important, so all-pervading, that it is rather difficult to delimit. The symbols, conditioning and conditioned terms of social reality represent at times the "quintessence" of society, and function within it as elements of connection and communication. Linked to collective ideas and values concerning music, they give, however, an inadequate, incomplete, but still real expression of these through music. National hymns, patriotic and revolutionary songs of all eras, the early national operas, Wagnerian leit-motivs and the musical dramas they are part of, the Masonic music of Mozart (his *Magic Flute*, for example),[1] the various types of religious works, as well as certain instruments and their usage—all of these depend on a more or less pronounced symbolism. Individual as well as collective feelings express themselves in a vast symbolic array through music. Thus some musical works—

---

[1]See on that subject Jacques Chailley, *Musique et ésotérisme: "La Flûte enchantée," Opéra maçonnique* (Paris: Robert Laffont, 1968).

273

while expressing only partially, and within the specific delimita-
tions of their own language, the significant contents that have
been entrusted to them—have served as mediators between
these contents and the individual and collective subjects who
formulated them. This mediation consists of pushing toward the
active and mutual participation of subject with content, and
content with subject. The ambiguity of the expressive and
symbolic possibilities of musical language, which is not a
conceptual language,[2] represents no difficulty insofar as the
symbolic sphere itself is essentially ambiguous. We may add
that the social symbols with which music can deal are mainly
emotional in nature, that they can express a variety of points of
view, and that they can arise even without the composer or the
performer having thought to form or introduce them (as, for
example, in the case of Verdi's opera, *Nabucco*). Here again, the
immersion of musical life in the life of society needs no further
demonstration. According to John Shepherd, "any significance
assigned to music must be ultimately and *necessarily* located in
the commonly agreed meanings of the group or society in which
the particular music is created . . . The meaning of music is
somehow located in its function as a social symbol. It is the word
'meaning' which creates the greatest problem in this context. For
most people a symbol has meaning because it refers to something
outside itself."[3] And it is in just this sense that music can assume
a symbolic function in society.

It is a notable and positive fact that many times when a small
cultural group, ethnic group, or sometimes even a political
group has been struggling to preserve a particular spiritual
patrimony, it seeks refuge in the arts and finally in music,
because there some of the roots of its spiritual principles exist.[4]
We have seen this in the choral societies of groups of European

---

[2]See Enrico Fubini, "Linguaggio e semanticità della musica," *Rivista di
estetica*, II (1961) 249-262.

[3]John Shepherd, "Media, Social Process and Music," in *Whose Music? A
Sociology of Musical Languages* (New Brunswick-London: Transaction Books,
1977) 7.

[4]See Etienne Souriau, *"Allocution"* to the International Congress on the

immigrants in the United States. Also, when the Moslems in Spain were reduced to a minority, and their civilization finally crumbled, it was the arts that preserved their ancient patrimony for the last Moslems, newly become Christians, to the point that in the end one could destroy the social minority that they represented only by attacking their arts, which survived and fulfilled a symbolic function. A particular royal regulation of 1666 prohibited the new Christians from engaging in a given number of activities, such as working the earth and assembling together to sing "Leila."[5] Similarly, as stated by Edgar R. Clark, the music of the blacks in North America has survived because of discrimination and segregation. Without civil rights, economic security, or social status equal to that of the whites, the blacks were forced to turn to artistic expression and to reach for "cultural self-determination."[6] This is why many of their songs are songs of protest (for example, *Go Down, Moses*).[7] It is interesting to note also the case of the popular songs in the Hawaiian Islands during World War II, when there was an abrogation of self-government, and an institution of curfew and martial law. Linton C. Freeman was able to establish that changes in the words of certain popular songs, notably "Lei Ana Ika," were due to the fact that the local community was deprived of its means of expression and its usual activities, and that therefore the people expressed themselves in a symbolic manner through song. Long frustrated, the community rose up against the prevailing conditions of life. Freeman concluded that, in this case, the popular song is not only a form of recreation, but, depending on social conditions, also an integrating element of society, a technique for the maintenance of

---

Sociological Aspects of Music for the Radio, Paris, 27-30 October 1954, *Cahiers d'études de radio-télévision* III-IV (1955) 271.

[5]*Ibid.*, 271.

[6]See Edgar Rogie Clark, "Negro Folk Music in America," *Journal of American Folklore* CCLIII (1951) 282.

[7]*Ibid.*, 286; and Russel Ames, "Protest and Irony in Negro Folksong," *Science and Society* III (1950) 193-213.

social order.[8] On the reservations of the Blood Indians in Canada, on the other hand, the different communities are constantly competing in ceremonies and social activities. Social dances represent one of the principal points of rivalry; in these, one tribe strives to surpass the other, thus affirming and symbolizing its own individuality and value.[9]

We must not believe that such cases occur only in more-or-less primitive societies. We could relate several instances involving social classes in more evolved societies.[10] Analogous cases are also found on the international level, as for example in the Austrian Court of the seventeenth century, where "it is a question of creating in Vienna an analog, a counterpart to the famous Divertissements and Comédies-Ballets. Do we not see— reading the correspondance of Ambassador Pötting—the Emperor Leopold, altogether fed up with the triumphant success of a French ballet presented at the French embassy by Ambassador Grenonville?"[11] In this instance music participates in the realm of political prestige. It is not, however, only in the small social groups of a global society, but even in an entire society or political community, in comparison with another society or in comparison with its own members, that we find this recourse to music as a symbol or means of social affirmation, and even of political prestige.

In addition, one of the particular functions that music has often assumed is the glorification or symbolic celebration of political power and the persons who wield it. Music is often a more particular sign of social distinction or valorization.[12] We can agree, with André Pirro, that it would be tedious to recall all "the numerous festivities [in the French court] where one could

---

[8]See Linton C. Freeman, "The Changing Functions of a Folksong," *Journal of American Folklore* CCLXXVII (1957) 215-220.

[9]See Hugh A. Dempsey, "Social Dances of the Blood Indians of Alberta, Canada," *Journal of American Folklore* CCLXXI 271 (1956) 47-52.

[10]See above, p. 145-148.

[11]Paul Nettl, "L'évolution de la musique autrichienne au XVIIe siècle de la barcarole à la valse," *La revue musicale* CLV 155 (1935) 258.

[12]See above, p. 143.

admire the prowess of musicians. There were no weddings, no tournaments, no solemn processions without them."[13] For the coronation of Charles VI at Reims in 1380, there were "more than 30 trumpets which rang out with astonishing clarity."[14] It "was appropriate that there be only vigor and brilliance in fanfares which glorified the power of the nobility. Received in London in 1363, 'with great celebration of trumpets and a host of other instruments,'* Pierre de Lusignan was saluted a little later by his troops, *tubis omnis exercitus insonantibus***. . . . When the king of France welcomed emperor Charles IV in 1377, there resounded silver trumpets with embroidered banners".[15] As we know, "all during the Middle Ages, the brass instruments were associated with kings, princes and nobles . . . In a princely court the trumpeters were the most important of the upper order of minstrels; they formed for a long time a caste proud of its role, one that refused to mingle with other musicians. They accompanied the prince on his travels and sounded their instruments as they entered a town. They also were used in making the proclamations, announcing mealtimes, and marking different phases of a tournament. Their presence was a sign of distinction that, for a long time, the nobility wished to preserve for itself and that cities borrowed from them in order to demonstrate both their independence and power."[16] Similarly, at the court of Philip the Good of Burgundy, there were trumpets to announce victories and symbolize the might of the sovereign by the power and brilliance of their sound. Trumpeters were in the personal service of the prince,[17] and the pomp of the Burgundian court was famous in all Europe.[18]

---

[13]André Pirro, *La musique à Paris sous le règne de Charles VI*, 10-11.

[14]Froissart, *Croniques* X (G. Raynaud, 1897) 10, cited in *ibid.*, 4.

*Froissart, *Croniques*, VI (Simeon Luce, 1876) 283.

**De Mézières, Philippe. *Vita Sancti Petri Thomasii*. (G. Henschen, 1659) 155.

[15]André Pirro, *Histoire de la musique de la fin du XIVᵉ siècle à la fin du XVIᵉ*, 7.

[16]Robert Wangermée, *Flemish Music and Society* . . . , 198-200.

[17]Jeanne Marix, *Histoire de la Musique et des Musiciens de la Cour de Bourgogne*, 60.

[18]Robert Wangermée has shown well the place which music held there. See

The entry of Louis XII in Paris, July 2, 1498, was also accompanied by a great musical array. Josquin des Prez had written the chanson "Vive le Roi et sa puissance" for Louis XII, although we do not know with certainty for what occasion.[19] And Clemens non Papa celebrated the power of the imperial fleet ("Caesar habet naves validas") and Charles V himself ("Quis te victorem dicat").[20] Moreover, "in the realm of Charles V music had always held an important place in the commemoration of political events ... A motet by Gombert was sung in Barcelona on June 29, 1529 to celebrate the reconciliation of the Emperor with the Pope. His is also the motet sung when two sovereigns met in Bologna in 1533, as well as one that was heard at Cambrai at the festivities in honor of the *Paix des Dames*; the Truce of Nice in 1537, was celebrated with a motet by Morales, who also had several compositions performed in Mexico in 1559 at a commemorative ceremony for Charles.[21] In the seventeenth century, Campra is charged with the role of conducting the "numerous *Te Deums* sung on the occasion of royal victories. The capture of Gerona (July, 1694), of Palamos, and Barcelona (August, 1697), the signing of treatises such as that at Rijswick (1698), became pretexts for singing the glory of the sovereign."[22] In 1701, Marin Marais "was called upon to compose a *Te Deum* for the convalescence of the Dauphin, and, according to Titon du Tillet, the work would have been sung by the acolytes and the priests of the oratory in the course of an office presided over by Bossuet."[23] In 1745, Rameau composed a piece on command for the occasion of the marriage of the

---

the section "Les fêtes bourguignonnes" in his work *Flemish Music and Society in the Fifteenth and Sixteenth Centuries*, 149-155.

[19]Paule Chaillon, *"Les musiciens du Nord à la cour de Louis XII,"* La Renaissance dans les Provinces du Nord (Paris: C.N.R.S., 1956) 64-66.

[20]See André Pirro, *Histoire de la musique . . .* , 261.

[21]Nanie Bridgman, *"La participation musicale à l'entrée de Charles Quint à Cambrai,"* Fêtes de la Renaissance II (Paris: C.N.R.S., 1960) 235.

[22]Maurice Barthélemy, *André Campra, sa vie et son oeuvre*, 15.

[23]François Lesure, "Marin Marais, sa carrière—sa famille," *Revue belge de musicologie* VII/2-3-4 (1953) 133.

Dauphin. Several years later, to celebrate the birth of the Duke of Burgundy, the same composer wrote *Acante et Céphise,* also on command.[24] In England, the great success of Händel's oratorios, during his lifetime, stemmed partly from political reasons. His glorification of liberty corresponded well to the aspirations and optimistic conceptions of the contemporary audience, which saw its views confirmed in his works.[25] Händel was also concerned with music of pomp and display. He was an extraordinary organizer of pleasures for the king and the court.[26] There are, of course, earlier examples of musical celebration of political personalities. Thus, "after his victory over Syagrius, Clovis rushed to ask Theodoric the Great, who ruled in Ravenna over the Ostrogoths, to send him a poet to sing his glory. We 'send you the poet and performer on the cithara for whom you have asked, answered Theodore. He is skillful in his art. May he please you in celebrating ... your glory and your power. We have confidence in his success especially since it is you who will have inspired him.' "[27]

During the French Revolution, the organization of national festivities, in which music played an important part, was one of the constant preoccupation of legislators.[28] And "the fashion demanded bruyant effects, a pompous grandiloquence: military music, fanfares and cannonades, made a terrible uproar and politics invaded the theatres."[29] Even the masses were drawn into musical participation by the commissioning of choral works for this purpose; occasional pieces, both vocal and instrumental, grew in number.[30] "When the first anniversary of the capture of

[24]See Paul Berthier, Réflexions sur l'Art et la Vie de Jean-Philippe Rameau (Paris: Picard, 1957) 17 and 56.

[25]See Manfred F. Bukofzer, *Music in the Baroque Era,* 404.

[26]Antoine Goléa, *La musique dans la société européenne* (Paris: Bibliothèque de l'Homme d'action, 1960) 64.

[27]See also Armand Machabey, *Genèse de la tonalité musicale classique,* 54.

[28]See Lionel de La Laurencie, *Le Goût musical en France,* 222.

[29]*Ibid.,* 222-223.

[30]See *Ibid.,* 223-224. *L'Offrande à la Liberté, Serment républicain, Chant du départ, Hymne du 10 Août, Carmagnole, Ça ira, Marseilleuse,* etc.

the Bastille rang out, Gossec had only to augment the instrumentation of his *Te Deum* with a military band, a group of drumers, and an artillery piece, to make it appropriate for the outdoor performance of the festivity of the Federation (14 July 1790)".[31] Above all, Revolutionary musical taste is characterized by mass participation. Obedient to popular taste, musical performances tended toward vast ensembles and the imposing deployment of sonority, customarily employing rather thick and brutal effects and projecting an image of military force and patriotic impetus.[32] The execution of Louis XVI was "commemorated" by gigantic music festivals in which singers took part by the hundreds.[33] Several years later, J.F. Reichardt remarked on the exaggerations of dynamic nuance in the performance of serious symphonic music, in the interpretations of the Concerts des Amateurs in Paris. It was impossible, according to him, not to see there a consequence of the pompous fracas of national festivities to which the French were accustomed.[34]

In addition to music that had a political function, without, however, being expressly conceived for this purpose, music composed deliberately to fill a symbolic political function developed, in general, certain specific characteristics. The first type is well illustrated by Verdi's *Nabucco*, and to a certain degree, by the national opera of the nineteenth century. National opera was not, however, devoid of patriotic feelings (as, for example, in *Porin* by the Croatian composer Vatroslav Lisinski). The second type of phenomenon is not new either. Already in the praises addressed by the medieval minstrels to their lords, André Pirro was able to discover a certain intelligibility, regularity, and simplicity that testifies not only to a poverty of inspiration but proves itself necessary and appropriate

---

[31]Michel Brenet, *Les concerts en France sous l'ancien Régime*, 325.

[32]Cf. Lionel de La Laurencie, *Le Goût musical en France*, 224-225.

[33]See Paul H. Lang, *Music in Western Civilization*, 787-789.

[34]See Jean Mongrédien, *La musique en France des Lumières au Romantisme*, 208-215.

in that it does not lead the listener into confusion.[35] At the time of the absolute monarchy, Nicolas Lebègue, organist to Louis XIV, gives evidence in his two offertories (in C major) of the *Troisième Livre d'Orgue*, of a pompous and vigorous breadth of style, a certain grandiose accent and vulgarity inspired by the worship of royalty.[36] Music with political goals is often of a special musical character; it requires a mode of expression adapted to its function: it is solemn, pompous or exalted; it is most often linked to words in order to better accomplish its function; finally, it is almost always of an inferior artistic quality; it willingly assumes simple forms, easily recognizable melodies, and accessible content. That is a logical consequence of its "pedagogical" and functional role, because it often addresses itself to musically uninformed audiences.

II • MUSIC, POLITICAL LIFE, AND IDEOLOGIES

Political conditionings only add to the complexity of sociohistorical conditionings that affect the place of music in global societies. Charles Lalo could conclude that "the most important and most incontestable action that political regimes exert on the arts is primarily negative: it consists in doling out to them a greater or less degree of liberty, in permitting or restraining their spontaneous development."[37] A more moderate view however is more realistic: "Political regimes can condition the arts to a certain degree, by favoring or thwarting their development, by giving them a certain stimulus. Pericles, Augustus, the

---

[35]See André Pirro, *Histoire de la musique de la fin du XIVᵉ siècle à la fin du XVIᵉ*, 38.

[36]See André Pirro, *Nicolas Lebègue*, XVI.

[37]Charles Lalo, *L'art et la vie sociale*, 209. Lalo adds: "there is some truth in the argument, however mediocre, that the poet Laprade displays in his book *Contre la musique*. . .Since it is not offensive to any government, scarcely having any ideas to express, music, he says, is the art of enslaved peoples: it is favorable to despotism." *Ibid.*, 212.

Medici, took positive measures in favor of the arts."[38] Undoubtedly political conditioning has produced very varied consequences in the musical domain. And for the sociology of music, it is not a question of knowing whether their influence could have been positive or negative for musical activity in a particular instance, but of revealing the whole variety and complexity of this influence and of the function that music could have had in political life itself.

In early Sparta, the regulations of Lycourgos arranged for the utilization of musical education for political motives. These regulations were justified by the example of Crete, where musical practice was said to have given rise to a remarkable devotion to the gods and to have made the Cretans a law abiding people.[39] Here we can see the important influence of "the πόλις: the artistic life of Sparta (and the athletic life as well) was embodied in collective manifestations that were state institutions: the great religious holydays."[40] In the philosophy of Plato and Aristotle also, music assumes an educational and political importance.[41] After the second war with Messena (645–628), Sparta, now rid of its external enemies, could foster "a more graceful art. In the midst of political changes which occurred at the time, military orchestric no longer occupied the great masters so much . . . Of all the poetic and musical productions which appeared during the stormy years when the future of the Lacedemonian state was being decided, the only ones to last through the centuries were the songs of Tyrtheus; their universal character . . . enabled them to survive the circumstances from which they came . . . A few years after the end of the war, we see, in Sparta, the flourishing of a choral music foreign to politics and education, brilliant rather by grace than strength and concentrated almost entirely in the hands of the female part

---

[38]Robert Hoebaer, "L'intérêt pour l'art musical," *Bulletin de l'Institut de Recherches Economiques et Sociales*, 702.

[39]See Paul H. Lang, *Music in Western Civilization*, 13.

[40]Henri-Irénée Marrou, *Histoire de l'éducation dans Antiquité*, 44-45.

[41]See Evanghélos Moutsopoulos, *La Musique dans l'oeuvre de Platon* (Paris: P.U.F., 1959) 157-226 and 296-304.

of the population."[42] The representative of this new school was Alcman, active between 628 and 600 B.C.

Two millenia later, the culture at the end of the Middle Ages and the beginning of the Renaissance had its own strong sense of ostentatious display, a sense strictly associated with the requirements of political life. "Under these conditions, art can truly prosper, without being relegated to the level of mere filigree, without becoming a scarcely tolerated accessory. The deep culture of the *Chapelle de la Musique* [in Paris] and its manifestation in the framework of the state's political activity demonstrated this kind of spirit in living fashion. This is particularly evident at the very beginning of the reign of François I, at the time of the Concordat of Bologna signed in 1516, and at the time of the official visit of Henry VIII to the Field of the Cloth of Gold in 1520."[43] We realize however, that compared to ancient Greece, there is a considerable narrowing in the use of music related to politics. Music only surrounds sovereigns, it is not used for political purposes in the general population. We can say as much for official music in the centralized monarchy of Louis XIV, for Lully's music, and for the organization of that era's musical life in Paris.[44] A political function in the life of society was assigned to the "Musique du Roi." Its limits were defined by the sovereign; its goals were in accordance with the ceremonial rules that served to glorify the monarchy and the monarch himself.[45] Under Richelieu, Mazarin, and Colbert, music was to become, perhaps more than ever before, a malleable political instrument that the regime would use for its own specific ends.[46]

And even in ancient Egypt we find more or less direct political

[42]François Auguste Gevaert, *Histoire et théorie de la musique de l'Antiquité* (Ghent: C. Annoot-Braeckman, 1881) Vol. II, 381.

[43]Paul Kast, "*Remarques sur la musique et les musiciens de la Chapelle de François 1er au Camp du Drap d'Or*," *Fétes de la Renaissance II* (Paris: C.N.R.S., 1960) 135.

[44]See Norbert Dufourcq, *La musique française*, 139-142.

[45]Norbert Dufourcq et al., *Notes et références pour servir à une histoire de M. R. Delalande*, 14.

[46]Manfred F. Bukofzer, *Music in the Baroque Era*, 142.

intervention in the musical scene. During the Ramesid Dynasty music was saturated with foreign elements as a consequence of commercial and political relationships with Asia. Immigration increased, and a strong Semitic current was soon in evidence in the nobility and inhabitants of the cities. At this moment the high priests, who had a strong political influence, intervened. The distinction between the sacred national music reserved for the high priests alone and the secular music of the foreigners was accentuated.[47] The former "remained practically closed to outside influences; the latter was performed by women, slaves, and guilds of foreign musicians. Thus, in contrast to the Greeks, the Egyptians taught their children to despise an art performed by slaves and prostitutes."[48] In France, on the other hand, from the middle of the seventeenth century, political intervention affected the introduction of instruments (other than the organ) into the church. In the use of motets with instruments, the royal chapel set the example. Instruments were allegedly added to voices at the "express command" of Louis XIV; until then this was exceptional in the church. Thus the *Te Deums*, with which all churches in Paris were obliged to celebrate public events (for example in 1672, for the ratification of the true with Germany; or in 1682, for the birth of the Duke of Burgundy), were the occasion, wished-for or not, of introducing instruments in the church. At this time also the spirit and style of opera penetrated French religious music, giving it a character of pomp and majesty.[49]

When music takes on an official character, surrounding the representatives of political power, musicians themselves follow

---

[47]See Hans Hickmann, *Le métier de musicien au temps des Pharaons*, 291-2; and Francesco Pasini, "A propos d'une contradiction de Diodore de Sicile," *Riemann-Festschrift* (Leipzig: Max Hesses Verlag, 1909) 188.

[48]*Ibid.*, 188.

[49]See Michel Brenet, "Notes sur l'introduction des instruments dans les églises de France," *Riemann-Festschrift* (Leipzig: Max Messes Verlag, 1909) 277-286. Louis Striffling, *Esquisse d'une histoire du goût musical en France au XVIIIe siecle*, 33; Norbert Dufourcq, *Notes et références pour servir à une histoire de M. R. Delande*, 75.

in the same direction. The displacements of musicians in the course of the official journeys of these representatives are known from the time of ancient Egypt. Musicians in the service of the pharaoh accompanied his boating tour of the Nile, an honor due to the fact that he wished to have them at his side.[50] The same was true in the fifteenth century when minstrels accompanied Philip the Good on his travels. He always had a musical escort with a full display of military trumpeters.[51]

In the Middle Ages, princes did not travel without their minstrels. When the English knight, Peter Courtenay, came to France to fight La Trémoille, his jongleurs came with him. And when the Count of Derby visited northern Germany in 1390–1391, he took trumpeters and pipers with him.[52] It was also presupposed that ten *conductus* of the thirteenth century, occasional pieces of the last eight of which refer to the crusade to Egypt, were perhaps sung before Saint Louis on the boat that carried him to the Orient in 1248.[53] In eighteenth-century Germany, an ever-present threat hung over musicians and musical life—that of public mourning on the occasion of the death of a prince. When there was a *Landestrauer* there could be no music. This forced musicians to move from one city or region to another like true nomads. Kuhnau wrote at that time that "no one prayed with more devotion for the long life of their sovereigns than the instrumentalists."[5] Mozart himself had to interrupt the composition of his singspiel *Zaïde* because of a similar circumstance.[55] Grétry adapted himself with skill, versatility and even enthusiasm to the political regimes under which

---

[50]See Hans Hickmann, *Le métier de musicien au temps des Pharaons*, 271.

[51]See Jeanne Marix, *Histoire de la Musique et des Musiciens de la Cour de Bourgogne*, 59-60.

[52]See André Pirro, *Histoire de la musique de la fin du XIV siècle à la fin du XVI*, 14.

[53]See Yvonne Rokseth, "Le contrepoint double vers 1248," *Mélanges de musicologie offerts à M. Lionel de La Laurencie* (Paris: E. Droz, 1933) 6.

[54]See Marcel Beaufils, *Par la musique vers l'obscur*, 35-58; and Manfred F. Bukofzer, *Music in the Baroque Era*, 406.

[55]See Jacques Chailley, *40,000 ans de musique*, 268.

he lived in Paris;[56] Le Sueur, on the other hand, was imprisoned for having "made music for Jesus Christ."[57] In the last movement of his Ninth Symphony, Beethoven himself was compelled under Metternich's regime of police terror to write in the words "Alle Menschen werden Brüder" instead of the original text "Bettler Werden Fürstenbrüder," of Schiller's *Ode to Joy*.[58] In those times the censor too had a strong hold: in 1823, in Vienna, Schubert had to change the title of his opera *Die Verschworenen* to *Der häusliche Krieg*. The original title seemed rebellious.[59]

Music has served political ends in many eras. In Rome, Suetonius preserved some of the couplets directed at the emperors that people dared to sing.[60] And Diodorus of Sicily wrote: "The Gauls also have poets whom they call Bards and who sing praises and blames while accompanying themselves on instruments."[61] In the Middle Ages, one of the innovations of the heretics was to set their ideas into couplets, and this 'sung' propaganda met with disquieting success. The Gnostics were the first to engage in this powerful means of reaching the populace. Arius used this with even greater mastery.[62] The *sirventes*, works of the 'sirven,' were political or satirical songs intended to insult the adversary.[63] This function has something in common with the *conductus*, which were a sort of 'sung newspaper,' a commentary on events.[64] Bertrand de Born "greatly contributed to arousing the sons of Henri II Plantagenet against each other. And Richard the Lionhearted deeply insulted the Dauphin of Auvergne with

---

[56]See Albert Van Der Linden, "Réflexions bibliographiques sur les 'Mémoires de Grétry," *Revue belge de musicologie*, III/2 (1949) 82; and Id. "Broutilles au sujet de Grétry," *Revue belge de musicologie* XII/1-4 (1958) 74-7.

[57]See Paul H. Lang, *Music in Western Civilization*, 783.

[58]See Jacques Chailley, *40,000 ans de musique*, 269.

[59]Hans Engel, *Musik und Gesellschaft*, 29.

[60]See Armand Machabey, "Etudes de musicologie pré-médiévale," *Revue de Musicologie* LX (1935) 217.

[61]Cited in Paul Loubet De Sceaury, *Musiciens et facteurs d'instruments de musique sous l'ancien Régime*, 11.

[62]Jacques Chailley, *Histoire musicale du Moyen Age*, 36.

[63]See Marcel Belvianes, *Sociologie de la musique*, 183-184.

[64]See Jacques Chailley, *Histoire musicale du Moyen Age*, 168-169.

songs to which the latter responded in kind with the voice (and means) of his poet-musicians."[65] In Paris toward the end of the fourteenth century, a *ballade* abusive to Parisians was making the rounds; a harpist was arrested in Melun for circulating it. At the Peace of Arras (1414) songs of political character were prohibited.[66] This kind of song was considered subversive to the political regime and the established order. In the United States, on the other hand, even the "nineteenth-century popular music was an instrument for social and political reform. Abolition, prohibition, women's suffrage, anti-war sentiments, political satire, child labor, destruction of the natural environment, and many other causes were fit and frequent topics for song texts. Many famous performers were aware of their potential role as reformers through song."[67]

As early as the ninth century, however, Charlemagne was attracted to the use of music for political ends. He favored and defended Gregorian chant, seeing in it an extremely powerful tool for preserving the unity of his kingdom, which was then threatened by internal strife. "In fact, Charlemagne appears to have been the one who truly carried on the work of Saint Gregory. Most certainly, he did not intervene in the setting of the liturgy but, like Gregory, he was an apostle of musical unification, creating the means of preserving tradition."[68] Much later, Mazarin would utilize music as a political tool with singular skill. The political designs of Mazarin upon the opera could seem like a childish Machiavellianism to those who

---

[65]Marcel Belvianes, *Sociologie de la musique*, 184.

[66]André Pirro, *La Musique à Paris sous le règne de Charles VI (1380-1422)*, 31. As a matter of fact, a prescription of 14 September 1395 forbade the singing of "dits" and songs which made mention of the Pope, the king, and the lords. The "dit" which later became the "diction" or "blason" was a short work in satirical verse. At the end of the fourteenth century, satirical songs, which until then were few, burst into life. See Paul Loubet De Sceaury, *Musiciens et facteurs d'instruments de musique sous l'ancien régime*, 38-39.

[67]Charles Hamm, "The Acculturation of Musical Styles: Popular Music, U.S.A.," in Charles Hamm, Bruno Nettl, and Ronald Byrnside, *Contemporary Music and Music Cultures* (Englewood Cliffs: Prentice-Hall, 1975) 127.

[68]Jacques Chailley, *Histoire musicale du Moyen Age*, 56.

ignored the function of music in the Roman society of the seventeenth century: "It was a fact known to everyone that the Italian princes had encouraged its development for political interests, for reasons of state. The composer Kuhnau verified this, not without bitterness, in his *Musicalischer Quack-Salber:* 'The music,' he wrote, 'creates a diversion in people's thoughts, distracting them from scrutinizing the plans of their rulers. Italy is an example of this; its princes and ministers have allowed it to come under the spell of musicians to ensure that their own affairs will not be disturbed.'*"[69] Hence Mazarin saw in the opera "a marvelous instrument of seduction and domination. In order to win to his side those hostile noblemen who were already agitated by the stirrings of the Fronde, in order to divert them from public affairs, he believed that it would be sufficient to give them better amusements than they had ever had before. Sure of his motto, *qui a le coeur, a tout* [who wins the heart wins everything], he hoped to win them over by offering them the most magnificent of divertissements. He understood, as well, the effect of spectacles on the people and though to appease the complaints of the bourgeois, crushed with taxes, by providing them with entertainments."[70] But just the opposite occurred. The sets of Luigi Rossi's *Orfeo* cost a great deal of money; Mazarin's adversaries used this against him, and soon patriotic arguments against Italian musicians also arose. The Italians were then to be victims of the Fronde: the Italianate divertissements were to be banished as were the Italian artists themselves.[71]

The history of music has also known the formation of true musical "parties," which sometimes became political "parties"; and inversely, appreciation often bestowed upon works and

---

*The Kuhnau's reference is in *Der Musicalische Quack-Salber* (Leipzig: 1700) ch. 43. This is a commonplace in the XVIIth century: "I have heard it said in the theatre that politics needs music. . . " declared a character in the dialogues of Bordelon. *Les Malades en bel humeur* (1696) 35.

[69]Henry Prunières, L'Opéra italien en France avant Lulli, 43-44.
[70]*Ibid.*, 43.
[71]See *Ibid.*, 141-150.

composers for political reasons. There were also various groups in which ideas about taste and aesthetics were mixed with political attitudes. Such were, specifically: the quarrels about French and Italian music, between Lullists and Ramists, between the followers of Gluck and Piccini; and in the nineteenth century, those surrounding Verdi, for example, and the musical national schools. Such situations caused not only an explosion of conflicts in the musical public as such, but they reached as well the broader strata of the public, which would not otherwise have been interested in music (with all of the advantages and inconveniences this consequence could have for musical art). At the beginning of the eighteenth century, the debate about French and Italian music intensified. Italian music enjoyed the favor of the nobility, and the first French composers of the Italian-born sonata generally dedicated their works to the Duke of Orléans, a declared partisan of the Italian tide. Perhaps we can see also in this infatuation a means of opposing the inclinations of the court; contemporaries also noted this tendency of the nobility.[72] On the other hand, the quarrel of the Bouffons made people forget the quarrels of parliament and the clergy, which until then had been the object of public curiosity; and this shift in public attention, according to Grimm, even prevented a civil war.

The question of the relationship between music and political life continues today.[73] Political conditionings are not the only organized level of social life needing study in relationship to music, but they are certainly among the most useful in explaining many phenomena of musical life itself. The sociology of music should be concerned with ideologies, political or otherwise. "Nevertheless, the interest that the sociology of music brings to

---

[72]See Maurice Barthélemy, *André Campra, sa vie et son oeuvre*, 88-89.

[73]Two works have been especially dedicated to it: Berta Geissmar, *Musique et politique* (Paris: Albin Michel, 1949); and Paul Riesenfeld, *Politik und Musik. Von grossen Zeitaltern zu kleinen Gleichschaltern* (Tel Aviv: Lidor, 1958). See also Hans Engel, *Musik und Gesellschaft* (Berlin-Halensee-Wunsiedel: Max Hesses Verlag, 1960) 257-278, and Rudolf Stephan, ed., *Über Musik und Politik* (Mainz: B. Schott's Söhne, 1971).

ideologies is not exhausted by their formulation and analysis. We should observe with the same attention how ideologies take over in actual musical life, thus becoming ideologies on music. There is a possibility that ideology in our day is entangled with an exasperating naivety. Music is received, insofar as it is a consumer good, in a noncritical manner, just as is the cultural sphere in general: approved of because it is there, without much reference to its concrete nature. The duty falls to empirical research to verify such theses. This control would be a partial aspect of the much broader task of research, which is to establish in which measure that which is called 'the taste of the masses' is manipulated, to what extent it is indeed the taste of the masses, and to what degree, on the contrary, it reflects (in those instances where it is indeed attributable to the masses) whatever, through the centuries, has been stuffed into their heads—and yet reflects, even more, something which, sociopsychologically, the general state foists upon them."[74]

Another sociohistorical conditioning of a political nature has influenced the development of military music. As far back as the great civilizations of antiquity, where powerful armies existed, military musical ensembles were present. Here also a social reality initiated a musical reality. "The military music which was known to the Egyptians, at least at the beginning of the new Empire, had to rest on simple forms and march rhythms which we see punctuated by drum and cymbals."[75] A trumpet of this era has been found and is preserved in the Louvre. The Assyrian empire also had military music, as extant bas-reliefs prove. Here we can see musicians of Ashurbanipal's army playing the frame drum, harp, kithara, cymbals, and lute. Corroborating documents are also kept in the Louvre.[76] The Greeks had the *pyrrhic,* a war dance mentioned by Aristotle and Tacitus. But they also used instruments in military combat.[77] Maneuvers to the sound of the

[74]Theodor W. Adorno, "Sociologie de la musique," *Musique en jeu* II (1971) 11.

[75]Armand Machabey, "Musique égyptienne," *La Musique des origines à nos jours* (Paris: Larousse, 1946) 61.

[76]See Id., *Musique suméro-chaldéenne,* in *ibid.,* 60-61.

[77]See Marcel Belvianes, *Sociologie de la musique,* 174-175.

horn were the key to victories of the Roman army, and the battle of Pydna, which marked the collapse of the Greek world in the face of the Roman world, was also a victory of horns. It can also be stated that the victories of the Moslems in Spain were victories of the Arab drum. In the eleventh century, the Almoravides attacked in Spain, with separate units maneuvering individually and joining together as soon as their enormous drums began to sound.[78] We recognize also as war instruments the trumpets of the Celts, the horns of the Gauls, and the "nakers" (kettledrums) of the Saracens.[79] Besides being a stimulating and tactical factor in combat until approximately the fifteenth century, the employment of instruments was intended to provoke fear and spread panic in the enemy's ranks.[80]

At times war and other military activities had additional impact on music. Wars by themselves "exert no profound influence on technique, substance, or incentives to aesthetic activity."[81] But the economic disruptions that they generally cause, and occasionally the changes in the collective mentality, play a definite role. During the Hundred Years' War and the Thirty Years' War, a "disturbing and often mournful mysticism was manifested in mass grave's macabre dances, in ascetic works of an exalted piety, or in the meditative music of a Heinrich Schütz."[82] In addition to the appearance of music that was specifically military and martial (and thus utilitarian, like marches), sociohistorical conditionings of this type brought about the creation of a certain number of compositions whose object was the musical description of war. Such are the *Bataille de Marignan*, the *Siège de Metz*, and the *Guerre de Renty* by Janequin, Mathias Herman's *Battle of Pavia*, Christopher Demant's *Tympanum*

---

[78]See Etienne Souriau, "Autorité humaine de la musique," *Polyphonie* VII-VIII (1951) 26.

[79]See Joachim Rouiller, "La musique instrumentale de cuivres," *Musica Aeterna*, II (Zürich-Brussels-Lausanne: A.S. Metz, 1949) 226.

[80]See *ibid.*, 226-227.

[81]Charles Lalo, *L'art et la vie sociale*, 267.

[82]*Ibid.*, 266.

militaire, and Thomas Macinus' *Battle of Sievershausen.*[83] But competitions of this kind occur sporadically in music history; only Janequin's *Bataille de Marignan* has become widely known.

Just as we were previously able to note the function of social distinction that was fulfilled by music, we will observe here that frankly utilitarian music assumes, on the contrary, a levelling function. By its nature it simplifies, concentrates and communicates a collective feeling. That is what military music proposes to do, in addition to awakening combative feelings in the listeners. In this respect the primary function of music has scarcely changed since the days of the ancient Greeks. In Europe, military music began to develop at the time of the Renaissance. With the birth of large and well-organized armies in the eighteenth century, especially in Germany and Russia, the importance of military music increased.[84] Lully wrote military marches, preserved by the composer and librarian André Danican Philidor, and reprinted in J.G. Kastner's *Manuel Général de Musique Militaire,* which was published in 1848.[85] The practical value of military music decreased in proportion to the increasing mechanization of the military arts. The formerly extensive use of instruments for tactical military purposes has virtually disappeared today.

Moreover, military music, like all "official" music, is conditioned by a socially determined function bound to a given social or political institution. This is sometimes also the case with music that assumes a social function similar to that of a play.[86] Like military music but with altogether different characteristics, religious music, when it is linked to worship, is also an

---

[83]See François Lesure, "La chanson française au XVIe siècle," *Histoire de la musique* I (Paris: Gallimard, 1960) 1050 and Marcel Belvianes, *Sociologie de la musique,* 185.

[84]See Jacques-Gabriel Prod'homme, "Les musiques militaires," *La musique des origines à nos jours* (Paris: Larousse, 1946) 559.

[85]See Warren Dwight Allen, "Music and the Idea of Progress," *The Journal of Aesthetics and Art Criticism* IV/3 (1946) 178.

[86]See Johan Huizinga, *Homo Ludens, Vom Ursprung der Kultur im Spiel* (Hamburg: Rowohlt, 1958) 153-61. Trans. from the Dutch.

"institutional" music. Patriotic songs and national hymns regularly serve as specific social symbols, while the political significance of revolutionary music, important as far back as the European peasant rebellions, continues up to our day. In proportion to their social and artistic importance, different types of "institutional" music (of which only a few have been touched upon here) need a special study in relation to the evolution of social institutions; this provides the sociology of music with a vast field for exploration. In his study, which rests firmly on a rich bibliography, Tibor Kneif rightly includes the institutions of musical life within the field of exploration of the sociology of music; at the same time he points out that the influences of the institutions of musical life on the life of music itself are multiple and cannot be reduced to a single formula.[87] This also concerns in part religious and sacral music, the special sociological aspects of which exceed the boundaries of this general study and can be only briefly approached here.[88]

III • MUSIC, CEREMONY AND RITUAL

What could be seen as paradoxical at first is the evidence, throughout history, of the close relationship between music and ceremony: "The most interior of all arts" is connected with what seems to be most exterior, *par excellence.* However, the distinction might be made from the very outset between ceremony and ritual.[89] Ceremony might be seen in a somewhat pejorative way

---

[87]See Tibor Kneif, "Gegenwartsfragen der Musiksoziologie," *Acta musicologica* XXXVIII/2-4 (1966) 110. See also Hans Engel, *Musik und Gesellschaft,* 17-100.

[88]See Karl Gustav Fellerer, *Soziologie der Kirchenmusik* (Cologne: Westdeutscher Verlag, 1963).

[89]Our definitions are, of course, far from complete. The richness of the phenomena in question and the variety of different theories about them are enormous. To mention a few examples: *"Ritus* nennen wir die sozial stereotypisierte zur Regelform gewordene Ablaufganzheit eines als korrekt geltenden Verhaltens. In diesem Sinne mehr oder weniger ritualisiert ist das ganze Brauchtum des Menschen (E. E. Mühlmann, "Ritus," in: *Die Religion in Geschichte und Gegenwart,* hrsg. von Kurt Galling, J.C.B. Mohr (Paul Siebeck),

as a rather superficial procedure deprived of deeper spiritual or practical sense, except that of fulfilling a more or less symbolic and conventional social or sociocultural function. It could be also considered a substitute for a lack of human consciousness, an attempt to reach by a short-cut a goal that would otherwise require much more psychological and spiritual energy to be properly attained. Ceremony can also sometimes be thought of as magic not only in the usual sense: as a means of conveying social suggestions, imposing social behavior and even of exercising social control, through which a society or a social group assembles or integrates its members around a determined, often collective, purpose or design. Defined as a sociocultural phenomenon, ceremony could be, additionally, a kind of mask on the face of society, a repetitive and mechanical way of acting, denaturing authentic approaches to things and persons, and alienating true relationships between men and God or men themselves. At one level, ceremonies could be a means of communication between individuals or groups, and at the other a means of pseudomediation, an artificial substitute for real relationships.

Ritual differs from ceremony, as defined above, in its meaning and content. Insofar as it is not only destined to keep its bearers and its "public" in a sort of social and emotional trance,[90] but is rather an attempt to encounter a sociocultural or transcendental reality that would otherwise escape us, a ritual—even when

---

Tübingen 1961, 1127; "un rite semble être une action qui se répète selon des règles invariables et dont on ne voit pas que son accomplissement produise des effets utiles"; however "le rite est une action qui est suivie de conséquences réelles; c'est peut-être une sorte de langue, mais c'est autre chose aussi." Jean Cazeneuve, *Sociologie du rite*, (Paris: P.U.F., 1971, 16, 10); "il termine 'rito' vienne a volte usato per esprimere in generale un meccanismo ripetitivo con funzione regolatrice psicologica o sociale." (Rizzi, Armido, "Rito," in *Dizionario teologico interdisciplinare*, Torino 1977, vol. III, p. 136); the rite is "un acte qui. . . vise toujours à abolir une forme du temps et à imaginer une nouvelle manière d'être à soi-même et au monde"; it is "une réalité proprement fondatrice, dans la mesure où c'est d'elle que s'engage, pour une large part, l'expérience et la diction du sens." (Pierre-Jean Labarrière, "Le rite et le temps," in *Le rite* (Paris: Beauchesne, 1981, 24, 31).

[90]Gilbert Rouget, *La musique et la transe* (Paris: Gallimard, 1980).

solely symbolic in nature—has not only subjective value for those who practise it, but also objective meaning in the life of the individuals and societies who participate in it.[91]

If ceremony and ritual can be terminologically and essentially distinguished in this way, this distinction is obviously a schematic and pragmatic one, inasmuch as in reality a multitude of their components can overlap or permeate each other on a number of levels and in many ways. Thus, scholars could probably describe situations in which elements of both mere ceremony and vital ritual were mixed; or trace, for instance, a whole history of instances in which meaningful rituals, losing their original sense, gradually became pale and empty ceremonies. Still, our distinction seems to make sense both when ritual and ceremony alone are concerned and when music is connected with one of them; the more so as it can help us to better understand another aspect of the purely exterior, phenomenological, and "historical" music-ceremony connection: i.e., the music-ritual relation, the roots of which are much deeper and tied not only to some extramusical and sociocultural bases, but to some extent to musical fundamentals as such.

Furthermore, the essential question to which the whole problem can lead us is not so much that of music *and* ceremony, or that of music *and* ritual, but much more that of music *as* ceremony, and even more that of music *as* ritual. This second aspect of the question does not eliminate, however, the first one. In the sociology of music, though, in a general way, the opposition of "society," on the one hand, and "music," on the other, does not always lead to satisfactory results. "A revised methodological approach" would need to study music itself as a "social fact."[92] The same, *mutatis mutandis,* applies in our case. Briefly, music itself can become more or less "ceremonial" or "ritual," "magic" or "spiritual," and should be studied as such. It

---

[91] Cf. for example Jean Cazeneuve, *Le rite et la condition humaine* (Paris: P.U.F., 1962).

[92] Cf. Irmgard Bontinck, "Mass Media and New Types of Youth Music," *IRASM* VI/7 (1975) 48.

can express spiritual meaning and show formal purity delivered from ceremonial or ritual traits, or it can do the same in spite of possessing such traits. The spirituality of a work resides in its intrinsic musical characteristics, and in no way simply in its connections with extrinsic nonmusical phenomena such as ceremony or ritual.

If Shuhei Hosokawa's distinction between two types of ritual, "rite *accompaned by* music and rite *accompanying* music,"[93] is pertinent, it still does not cover the whole question. It is a truism that one of the "purest" presentations of music, that of the concert as a public form of musical life that developed from the seventeenth century on, is still a "ritual" one or, as Hosokawa rightly had it, "*quasi*-ritual."[94] Thus, according to Michel De Coster, "the public concert is a bourgeois ceremony which develops according to a particular ritual and which varies almost never. Even just on this ground, we can claim that a concert functionalizes music furnishing the pretext for a fashionable meeting."[95] The concert hall in itself would be capable of favoring and imposing this new, ritualized listening, upon music of the present as well as of the past. Listening to music becomes a collective rite to be celebrated in the most absolute silence.[96] For Etienne Gilson, "the concert is a social ceremony of a complexity to confound the imagination",[97] but, as Hosokawa observes, "all representations of music, not only those of concert music, are 'ritual'."[98]

Much has been said about *Umgangsmusik, Darbietungsmusik* and *Übertragungsmusik*,[99] and when Hosokawa goes further in

---

[93]Shuhei Hosokawa, "Considérations sur la musique mass-médiatisée," *IRASM* 12/1 (1981) 26.

[94]Cf. *ibid.*

[95]Michel De Coster, "L'art mass-médiatisé," *IRASM* VI/2 (1975) 260.

[96]Cf. Enrico Fubini, "Implicazioni sociologiche nella creazione e fruizione della musica d'avanguardia," *IRASM* V/1 (1974) 172.

[97]Etienne Gilson, *La société de masse et sa culture* (Paris: Vrin, 1967) 66.

[98]Shuhei Hosokawa, *op. cit.,* 26.

[99]Cf. Heinrich Besseler, *Das musikalische Hören der Neuzeit,* Berichte über die Verhandlungen der sächsischen Akademie der Wissenschaften zu Leipzig,

order to affirm that "the rituality of musical representation is not a new phenomenon. . . . It would be more exact to say that this rituality is understood since the origins of music as a support of any musical representation", [100] he is right, although he remains within the limits of the question of the rituality of musical representation and not of music itself. On the other hand, the question of function appears insofar as both music and ritual are concerned, regardless of whether music accompanies a ritual or is itself accompanied by a ritual. It is impossible, in fact, to deal with any question concerning the ritual or ceremonial dimensions of music as well as its connections with ritual or ceremony without taking into consideration their functional aspect. This aspect alone constitutes a whole universe in the history of music.

But as far as listening to music at a concert is concerned, it belongs much more to an intermediate sphere, located between ritual and custom, than to ritual *stricto sensu*. As Jean Cazeneuve correctly emphasized, to identify rite and custom "would be manifestly to divert the words from their usual signification," [101] and "in calling profane ceremonies rituals, one does not employ the term in its most precise sense," for it is a question here rather of "acts, attitudes, formulas, pretty often stereotyped, which are half-way between habits and rites." [102] The way of speaking proper to E. Fubini and M. De Coster is, consequently, not quite precise. [103]

Another still deeper question deserves full attention: that of the common traits of ritual and music, of the ritual elements in

---

Philologisch-historische Klasse, Band 104, Heft 6, Berlin 1959, 14, and Konrad Niemann, "Mass Media—New Ways of Approach to Music and New Patterns of Musical Behaviour," in Irmgard Bontinck, ed., *New Patterns of Musical Behaviour of the Young Generation in Industrial Societies* (Vienna: Universal Edition, 1974) 49.

[100] Shuhei Hosokawa, *op. cit.,* 26.

[101] Jean Cazeneuve, *Sociologie du rite,* 15.

[102] Pierre-Jean Labarrière, *op. cit.,* 16.

[103] Cf. p. 155, footnote 55.

music, and of the proximity of music and ritual taken in the proper sense.

The common basic traits of music and ritual are their essentially temporal character and, in connection with this, their repetitiveness. Both music and ritual exist and develop in the temporal flow, emerge from it and identify themselves with it. Music's character is essentially temporal. Time is at the heart of music, just as it is of ritual. Temporarily determined, music and ritual cannot but follow their temporal destiny, order determined in advance, according to inherent temporal rules. For music, deviation from temporal determination would be a diversion from its very nature just as, for ritual, it would be a step away from its very meaning, purpose and function. If in music, as was stressed by G. Brelet, "there are reprises, it is so because the musical work, which is perceived only by fragments and which follows the flow of real duration, has no other means to deliver us its total form and its being except like abridged . . . The musical time wants its repetition, far from being afraid of it: because, far from destroying it, it affirms it in confirming it. Because it develops in time . . . the musical work delivers its being only dispersed in a series of instants: we have to construct it little by little, to conquer it in time and on time, perpetually wring it from arising which originates and carries it."[104]

Similarly, repetition is in the essence of ritual itself.[105] If a ritual is an act that repeats itself, the resulting "rigidity of the ritual, its conformity of principle to rules,"[106] cannot but find a parallel in musical structures, which cannot escape their inherent repetitive laws and rules, despite their variety and their more or less flexible applications in different styles. If rituals aim at a departure from ordinary time in order to enter a differently qualified time,[107] music aims at the same. By the "ensemble of words, attitudes and gestures through which ritual tries to

---

[104]Gisèle Brelet, *Le temps musical* (Paris: P.U.F., 1949) t. II, 584.
[105]Cf. Jean Cazeneuve, *Sociologie du rite*, 13.
[106]*Ibid.*, 13.
[107]Pierre-Jean Labarrière, *op. cit.*, 19.

structure the experience of man"[108] it leads him also toward another experience of time and of its sense.

There is another important aspect common to ritual and music: although music as well as ritual can be utilized in various directions and, consequently, can have a variety of functions, they are both, in themselves, intrinsically nonutilitarian. Music-making and the practice of rituals are not in themselves utilitarian activities aiming at a productive result of a practical nature, visible immediately. In the practical world, every activity is intended to produce a more or less immediate result. In arts, as well as in ritual, what is instead of prominent importance is the activity itself, the immanent "productive" activity as such. Still, there are important differences between various arts. Music, for instance, is directed rather toward a sort of *celebrating* activity, and as such—and in this sense—is much closer to ritual than, for example, the art of writing novels or of painting. Music is much closer than any other art to a kind of celebration, festivity, or feast, and this feature brings it close to a ritual.

One of the most profound reasons why music has always attracted the human soul is not only, or maybe even not so much, because of its *social* functions, however real, but because of its *aesthetic* functions[109] and of its possibilities for elevating man from the everyday world of constraint, determinism, and utility to a world of beauty and celebration and of freedom from the practical sphere and everyday life. The listener to music, as well as the spectator or participant in rituals or the watcher of a play, is more or less delivered from the constraints of practical life and its burdens, and is able to enter a world where the possibilities of surpassing delight become real on an infinite scale.

If ritual is to some extent spectacle and play, as music itself can be, it is also, and even more, a celebration in itself. This aspect stems from its distance from the practical world and from labor

---

[108]*Ibid.,* 13.
[109]See Robert Wangermée, "Auditeurs de musique et comportement musical," *Revue belge de musicologie* XXXV (1981) 263.

and work, as well as from its proximity to the "leisure" time of festivity and play, of freedom that celebration presupposes. In this respect, its nearness to music is evident. Ritual acts just as music does, and especially as music used to do. Before being a product, music was a production. As Walter Wiora remarked, before being a composer, the musician was a producer of music.[110] According to Zofia Lissa and Patricia Carpenter, before becoming an object, music was a process.[111] If it was necessary to wait till the sixteenth century to find a theorist, Nicolaus Listenius, to expound in his treatise *Musica* (1537) the viewpoint of the composer as a producer of lasting products, of an *opus perfectum et absolutum*,[112] even after Listenius musical practice continued to confirm the concept of music as a productive activity.

This could be connected with another aspect of ritual, found by Roger Caillois: that of *play*.[113] He has distinguished between four principal types of play in the complex history of ritual: *agon* (competition), *alea* (chance), *mimicry* (imitation), and *illinx* (vertigo); and these can be found in music too, even at an elementary structural level. Throughout its history music has known different styles of competition between voices and instrumental groups or individual instruments within the musical work, as in Baroque music, where procedures of opposition in the solo concerto and the *concerto grosso* were usual. The element of chance is present in almost all improvisational works, especially those from before the Classical era and in the aleatoric music of our time. The principle of imitation of one voice by another or within the same part appeared early in European polyphony and remained a fundamental compositional technique. And that dizzying element known as brilliance or virtuosity, which has invaded music in many ways, appeared as

---

[110]Cf. Walter Wiora, "Discussion," *IRASM* VI/1 (1975) 31.

[111]Cf. Patricia Carpenter, "The Musical Object," *Current Musicology* 5 (1967) 56–87, and Zofia Lissa, "Die Prozessualität der Musik," *Aufsätze sur Musikästhetik. Eine Auswahl* (Berlin: Henschelverlag, 1969) 37–47.

[112]Cf. Frits Noske, "Forma formans," *IRASM* VIII/1 (1976) 43–62.

[113]Cf. Roger Caillois, *Les jeux et les hommes* (Paris: Gallimard, 1958).

early as the Franco-Flemish school and survived different vocal and instrumental styles in composition and in performance.

However, it could be said that the aspect of play emerges much more in ritual procedures in which "in the course of a very long history, the rites domesticated themselves and pacified themselves, so that their link with the founding violence is more or less well dissimulated. But the more one returns toward the origin, the more one finds violence in the fold of the rite."[114]

In this regard, the interesting approach of Jacques Attali to music *and* ritual, and even more to music *as* ritual, deserves full attention, though at first glance it might appear strikingly distant from the usual concerns of traditional musicology. Attali transfers to music the anthropological postulates of René Girard of "the role of sacrificial ritual as a political channeling of and a substitute for general violence"[115] in society. He states: "*Noise is a weapon and music is, from its origins, the shaping, the domestication, the ritualisation of the use of that weapon in a simulacre of ritual murder.*"[116] In fact, Girard elaborated a whole theory[117] and an audacious hypothesis concerning the existence and identity of a *principle of violence* in society,[118] which is the origin of the rite.[119] The ritualization would have been a sort of limiting issue of the violence, directing it toward particular victims instead of leaving it generalized, as it had been before ritual appeared in the history of mankind and thus before organized life in society was possible. As with every ancestral sacrificial ritual, so, according to Attali, "every music, every organization of sound is

---

[114]Cf. Jean Greisch, "Une anthropologie fondamentale du rite: René Girard," in *Le rite* (Paris: Beauchesne, 1981) 107.

[115]Jacques Attali, *Bruits. Essai sur l'économie politique de la musique* (Paris: P.U.F., 1977) 53.

[116]*Ibid.*, 49.

[117]Cf. René Girard, *Mensonge romantique et vérité romanesque* (Paris: Grasset, 1972); *La violence du sacré* (Paris: Grasset, 1972); *Des choses cachées depuis la fondation du monde*. Recherches avec J.P. Oughourdian et Guy Lefort (Paris: Grasset, 1978).

[118]Cf. J. Greisch, *op. cit.*, 90.

[119]Cf. J. Attali, *op. cit.*, 53.

then a tool for the creation or consolidation of a community, of a totality; it is a bond between power and its subjects and thus, more generally, an attribute of power, whatever that is."[120] Music is a *ritual* tool of power "when it is a question of making us forget the fear and violence".[121] "Music... channeler of violence, creator of differences, sublimator of noise, attribute of power, it first created, in the feast and the ritual, order from the noises of the world. Then, listened to, repeated, dressed, framed, and sold, music went on to announce the establishment of new totalizing social order, made of spectacle and exteriority."[122] "Music is the fragile order of the ritual and of the prayer, an unstable order on the edge of danger, harmony on the edge of violence."[123] "Its first function... is ritual; namely, before any mercantile exchange, music is the *creator of political order for it is a minor form of sacrifice. In the realm of noise, it signifies symbolically the channeling of violence and of the imagery, the ritualisation of a murder substituted for general violence, the affirmation that society is possible....* "[124] Obviously, "this little function of music will be dispersed little by little when the position of music changes".[125] Still, *"noise is violence*: it disturbs.... *Music is the channeling of noise* and hence a simulacre of sacrifice."[126]

Attali's theory, taken independently of general anthropological views and other presuppositions on which Girard's and Attali's observations are based, could offer a fruitful perspective for

---

[120]*Ibid.*, 14.
[121]*Ibid.*, 39.
[122]*Ibid.*, 46-47.
[123]*Ibid.*, 47.
[124]*Ibid.*, 52.
[125]*Ibid.*
[126]*Ibid.*, 53. Cf. also Kurt Blaukopf's remark: "Music was called an 'obtrusive art' by the German philosopher Immanuel Kant. Recordings and broadcasts, music boxes and functional music have contributed to a growing obtrusiveness of music in a more general and social sense... By dint of its technical omnipresence music can exercise a 'power of external coercion upon the individual'." *New Patterns of Musical Behaviour of the Young Generation in Industrial Societies,"* in: Irmgard Bontinck, ed., *New Patterns of Musical Behaviour* (Vienna: Universal Edition, 1974) 13-14.

research, especially if reinterpreted and developed in a broader way: first, its too-narrow linking with sacrificial murder should be abandoned; secondly, its too-restrictive political aspect should be broadened. Furthermore, the idea of a development from the aggressiveness of noises to more or less "cultivated" sounds, which presupposes self-control and discipline, if not at the same time a search for beauty, also involves a "sacrificial" attitude on the part of those who took part in this development. Besides, in primitive societies musicians were sometimes regarded as beings who sacrificed themselves for the good of the community, but in spite of that, they enjoyed an ambivalent situation just as sacrificial victims themselves did: they were at the same time "rejected and worshipped."[127]

On the other hand, the affirmation, however elementary, of an order of sounds, implies ineluctably though often unconsciously a recognition of order and of meaning as such, and not only of a specifically political and social order. Thus it could be said that the existence of ordered musical thought was not an affirmation "that society is possible," but rather a confirmation that something meaningful could be found in life, that *sense* does in fact exist. Even if in practice the political and social orders were imposing and oppressive powers, the search for "musical order" at a relatively early stage in civilization undoubtedly surpassed these limitations to reach for a broader sphere of human life; gradually opposing, later on, by its own specific nature the utilitarian and frequently violent social and political spheres. Early on in ancient civilizations a belief in the psychological and *moral* efficacy and influence of music was added to the conviction of its *magical* effect, and elaborated on afterwards in various philosophical theories.

But it should not be forgotten that in its long history music itself sometimes became, at another level, a tool of violence and power: as an instrument of collective suggestion, pressure, and social control, as a means of indoctrination and as a symbol of power it was used in many rituals and ceremonies, both sacred

---

[127]Cf. p. 200.

and secular. Sociologically speaking, in the history of music there appear a variety of genres and currents that, under various social and cultural or political conditions, themselves contributed, as a subordinate but important auxiliary force, to many sorts of power and violence. Of course, here it is not only a question of tribal chants and of social dances,[128] military music, and patriotic, subversive and revolutionary songs from all periods expressing various social forces openly engaged in competition and conflict; but also of the use of music as a subtle instrument encouraging the integration of people into various social groups, as happens today among young people, for instance, or as happened in the past within different professional and other groups. Moreover, the true nature of this use of music in rituals and ceremonies, sacred and secular, was often hidden from the eyes of those who were submitted to its influence—as it was, sometimes, even for those who supported it.

IV • A NOTE ON COURT MUSIC

In the epoch of the absolute monarchies of Baroque times, music occupied an important and integral place in both the social and cosmic worlds. In that society, which eschewed sacrificial rituals, the rituals that survived were rituals of prestige; it was precisely in these that secular and sacral music played a prominent role. But its real function in social life as a means and symbol of power was not revealed as such in most of the theoretical writings of the time. Still, court music, for instance, seems to have buttressed whole centuries the power of a court, its way of life, its ambitions, and its ceremonies and rituals. But inversely, music itself was also greatly supported by the courts' commissions and commands, and above all by the power of *patronage* that court power and its rulers had over music and musicians. Court power was a force that permitted and favoured

---

[128]See Hugh A. Dempsey, "Social Dances of the Blood Indians of Alberta, Canada," *Journal of American Folklore,* 271 (1956) 47-52.

the creation, performance, and finally the survival of a marvelous corpus of musical works. Therefore, these two opposing aspects should both be taken into consideration. How, on the other hand, could music's functions of symbolization vis-à-vis power be explained?

When we speak of power in connection to court music, we mean a sort of cumulative power that includes the political, economic, military and, depending on time and place, more or less psychological aspects of grandeur and prestige. To concur with Iain Fenlon, the arts and music had an important function in the construction of an entire "mythology," the primary function of which was to furnish religious justification or political authority as well as proof of the merits, virtues and magnificence of particular rulers, to whom increasingly professionalized and bureaucratic courts had to contribute via official rituals and ceremonies.[129] If this was definitely so in sixteenth-century Italy, at least some elements of the situation had existed much earlier. And all of these ceremonies and rituals had, among others, the function of creating distance, accentuating differences, and monopolizing what was considered of special value for rulers and their courts—beginning with power itself, and embracing also (perhaps last, but not least) a particularly suitable type of music. In Jacques Attali's words, "the monopolization of the emission of messages, the control of noise and the institutionalization of the silence of others are everywhere the conditions of the perpetuity of power".[130] Musical life at the court of Louis XIV, with its series of well-known privileges, the so-called *lettres patentes*, and special permissions that had to be obtained for performing or printing music, are an example of this.

Yet through the centuries the retention of one's power implied the absence of power for others.[131] More often, through

[129]Cf. Iain Fenlon, *Music and Patronage in Sixteenth-Century Mantua* (Oxford: Oxford University Press, 1981) 6.

[130]Jacques Attali, *op. cit.*, 17.

[131]Cf. René Girard, *op. cit.* Cf. footnote 27.

whole ages, political power was less in the service of the common good than of particular goods and interests. And even when it did serve common interests, political power always served its particular interests as well: those of larger or smaller groups, families, dynasties, and courts, of course. The service of particular interests is always the sacrifice of other interests. We could state that the court music, involved with the monarchical and princely power of past centuries, served the courts' particular interests much more than the common interests of the time. From a sociological point of view, it was functional and subservient; we could say, more generally, as is stated in the title of Robert M. Isherwood's book, that it was *Music in the Service of the King*.[132] Nevertheless, in serving court interests, music as an art was itself served by the court that supported it, and at least in part, preserved for future generations. In other words, court power did a great deal for the power of the music. Even more, music at courts became at times a sort of *counterpower,* or at least was interpreted as such. To give only a few examples, in early Baroque times we can see a series of authors who attribute to music the power of elevating the souls of kings, princes, and rulers from their worries, of giving them the necessary *delectatio,* as said Tomas Lodovico da Vitoria or of relieving them from "le gravi cure del regno," according to Tarquinio Merula. Or as Angelo Berardi wrote in his *Ragionamenti musicali* in 1681: "Finalmente la Musica è necessaria á Principi grandi, ritrovandosi in questi la giustizia e la misericordia; adolcisce l'animo loro, distogliendolo dall'ira, e dalla vendetta, con mentenerlo placido per l'esercizio della clemenza."[133]

But it should be seen under which circumstances and conditions music can be called "court music." It could be argued that not all musical works composed at courts and by court musicians, even those written for a court, can necessarily be termed court music. Bach's Brandenburg Concertos were written

---

[132]Cf. Robert M. Isherwood, *Music in the Service of the King* (Ithaca and London: Cornell University Press, 1973).

[133]Angelo Berardi, *Ragionamenti musicali,* Bologna, 1681, 110.

at the Court of Cöthen, by a court musician, and addressed to the ruler of another court, with the intention that they be performed there. As the performance apparently never happened, can these concertos be considered court music? Although composed at a court and for a court, they were not utilized by a court for its interests and purposes. If they are to be considered court music, then that can be based only on their artistic or stylistic characteristics, or purely on Bach's intentions and dedications, and not on a function that they failed to fulfill at the time of their creation.

To come closer to our problem of establishing what court music actually is, and how it could be better delimited, an additional approach could be foreseen—that of court music understood in a whole series of meanings. Just as we cannot think of court music as separate from various historical periods and different cultural milieus, neither can be ignored the fact that court music can comprise rather unequal types of music and fall into a number of diverse categories. Very schematically, we can try to formulate an elementary classification of five categories of court music, in which from one category to the next there will be a movement toward a more specific "court" character in the music, as follows: a) music simply performed at a court; b) music composed at court by a court musician and performed there; c) music commissioned by a court or its ruler, actually composed for the court and performed at court; d) music composed and performed specifically for official court rituals and ceremonies; e) music that bears the characteristics of a courtly taste and style, irrespective of the previously mentioned factors.

Obviously, many other classifications are possible. But these delimit somewhat the relationship between courtly power and music and the interplay between their subtle functions of symbolization and signification, especially in the Renaissance and Baroque eras in Europe. Similar phenomena certainly existed in other cultures and periods. However, the institutionalization of sacred and secular rituals and ceremonies led to one of the peaks of Western court music in Renaissance and Baroque times. In these periods, courtly power gave music a high social status. Music itself functioned as a status symbol. In Baroque times the sacred and the secular were not as clearly separated as they became later on, least of all in the minds of the ordinary people. According to views of those times, the status of music, and its position in the universe, the cosmos, and the social and political hierarchy, derived from two principal sources: the divine and the earthly.

If kings and princes attribute to themselves, or let others attribute to them, qualities such as grandeur and magnificence, majesty, power, and—of course—all kinds of virtues, this is partly due to a usurpation from the sacral sphere, in which, however, originally the divine attributes of glory and greatness meant something quite different and had only a spiritual sense. But as a sacral sphere was invaded by secular elements, along with the concept of courtly power came decorum, display of splendor, social dignity, and ornament—in brief, prestige: all emanations of might. If music in itself is a sort of celebrating activity, it was as such much closer to courtly ceremonies and rituals than some of the other arts. And as is very well known, some kinds of celebrations, feasts, and festivities were at the center of the courtly life. According to the queen Cristine of Sweden, music in itself was already the "ornament of princes and the delight of residences," as reported in 1656 by Priorato Galeazzo Gualdo ("ornamento de' Principi, e diletto delle camere").[134] The magnifying of the monarch—also through music—was a logic consequence of the cult of the king, which developed so greatly in the seventeenth century.[135] It is perhaps particularly interesting that the courts of Baroque times, which saw a peak in the institutionalized sacred and secular music of their ceremonies and rituals, put both sacred and secular music to the service of secular purposes. *Te Deums*, for instance, sometimes even when they were performed out of the court

---

[134]Cf. Priorato Galeazzo Gualdo, *Historia della S.R.M. di Christina Alessandra Regina di Svetia*, Roma, 1656, p. 144.

[135]"Magnifico, è il maggior titolo, che si possa donare ad un Principe." (Emanuele Tesauro, *Il cannocchiale aristotelico/O sia dell'arguta et ingeniosa elocutione*, Torino, 1670, 166.)

setting, in churches such as Notre Dame in Paris, belonged nonetheless to the ceremonies of the court and for the court.

If in a certain sense it could be said that almost every age has had mass and non-mass forms of musical culture, at least in the sense that there have been musical forms or genres performed and listened to by small segments of the public, as well as those enjoyed by a larger audience and a broader social strata, then court music was obviously a non-mass form of musical culture. In its time it was more or less a "closed" type of music. The abandonment of the shelter of traditional court patronage was accompanied by the evolution of hitherto nonexistent freedom of choice in a whole series of professional musical activities. Then the mobility of the musical profession became more important, and the social status of the musician was no longer so rigidly defined. It cannot be said that there was, in the strict sense of the word, a market for the musical works performed in courts and aristocratic residences during the Renaissance and Baroque periods. The goal of court musicians was not to expand their public, but rather to maintain their position within the small, intimate circles of the court. When in the last third of the eighteenth century composers sought to broaden their audiences and artistic recognition outside of the system of court patronage, an effort aided by the expansion in music publishing as well, court music and its power as well as (somewhat later) courtly power itself had already begun to decline. A radical change appeared, the transition from the courtly small-group context to the large-group context of public musical life. A new era began, that of the great development of public concerts.

V . SACRED AND SECULAR MUSIC

A superficial historical view, ignoring other ancestral and ancient religions and the original sacrificial nature of the social organization, could consider Christian sacred music from its very beginnings at the time of the downfall of the ancient world and through the Middle Ages, Renaissance, and Baroque as the typical example of the music-ritual connection and of sacred ritual music in general. Instead, as R. Girard strongly emphasized, the advent of Judaeo-Christianity coincided historically with the *way out* of the sacral and the "realm of rite."[136] According to Girard, one of the deepest messages of the Bible, already announced by the prophets, is that of judgment passed upon the injustice of the world and its order, which is nothing less than a sacrificial institution, with its logic of violence, power, and might, and which is definitively confounded through the passion of Christ, the supreme victim of the world. Beginning with this crucial event, the world's sacrificial institutions, both sacred and secular, and the principle of violence that governs them, were once and for all manifestly condemned. This event revealed their radical absurdity, although they had to continue to exist,[137] not only through those who reject the essential message of this event or do not understand it but also through those who accept it theoretically, but often betray it in practice. From then on, anyway, the sacral character of violence had been unmasked: a murder is a murder, a victim a victim, violence is violence.[138]

On the other hand, the nature of Christian religious rites differed essentially from those of other religions that practiced the sacrifice of people, animals, and goods. Although some aspects of the old sacrificial rites, emerging from the unconscious and the irrational, reappeared here and there with their usual external manifestations of repetitiveness and mimicry, Christian religious rites directed themselves from the very beginning, in their essence, to the spiritually interior and simple. This very aspect had a decisive influence on church music from its beginnings. The shift in emphasis from the exterior to the interior is well illustrated by many facts.[139]

Later on, besides the musical works for the church that preserved their religious character and purity of style, there were a still larger number of ecclesiastical compositions influ-

---

[136]Cf. R. Girard, *Des choses cachées depuis la fondation du monde*, 168-202.
[137]Cf. J. Greisch, *op. cit.*, 113-114.
[138]Cf. *ibid.*, 121.
[139]Cf. below p. 312-315.

enced by secular music, as, for example, a music of the seventeenth and eighteenth centuries, which was invaded by the secular spirit with its ceremonial characteristics. Undoubtedly contributing to this were not only the political influences existing in France under Louis XIV, but also the negligence of the clergy in allowing inappropriate elements to enter the music of the church.[140]

Secular rituals and ceremonies quite logically existed wherever power was present, with all of its typical techniques of collective suggestion, symbolic mimicry, and gestures of festivity and grandeur, which mask its essential aspect of sacrificial violence and conflict inherent in society and the human world. As R. Girard put it, "the rites consist, paradoxically, of a transformation of disintegration through conflict of the community into an act of social collaboration."[141] Captured by society, music contributed to these functions and techniques, remaining at the same time, however, a symbol of something else; i.e., preserving its ambivalent position, which was due on the one hand to its specific artistic nature—a nature of beauty and purity, incompatible as such with its role as an obscure servant of power and might—and on the other hand to its development in simple and innocent dance and song forms, where it assumed (as it did in sacred forms) a quite opposite function aimed essentially at spiritual purity and simplicity, not "in the service of the King,"[142] but for the glory of God.

The history of Western music had to witness, however, both the collision and the overlapping of the two forms of musical intent. It was not only a matter of the reciprocal influence and mutual exclusivity of two different worlds of thought, feeling, and existence on the artistic level, each of which supposed

---

[140]Cf. Michel Brenet, *Notes sur l'introduction des instruments dans les églises de France*, in *Riemann-Festschrift* (Leipzig: Max Hesses Verlag, 1909) 277-286, and Norbert Dufourcq, *Notes et références pour servir à une histoire de M. R. Delalande* (Paris: Picard, 1957) 75.

[141]R. Girard, *op. cit.*, 29.

[142]See Robert M. Isherwood, *Music in the Service of the King* (Ithaca and London: Cornell University Press, 1973).

different purposes and functions of various musical genres and forms, but also a matter of two different and in themselves incompatible rituals, sacred and secular, which, though influencing each other and corresponding at times in their exterior features, remained essentially unlike and aimed at radically different goals. The inheritor and successor of old pre-Christian ceremonies and rituals aimed at the exterior magnifying of power and political might, European secular court music could only be opposed, in its stylistic and expressive characteristics, to a Christian sacred music in search of simplicity, even poverty, of expression.[143] The two were radically different in spirit. Nevertheless, an intrusion of secular into sacred, and the reverse, can be observed. Two main currents were born: one that accepted, for various reasons, the permeating realities of mixture and mutual influence, and another that preserved the purity of forms and the specificity of the respective domains.

The lesser position of instrumental music in church throughout whole centuries has an explanation: music without words was incapable of filling a pedagogical function; thus vocal music could become a virtual monopoly and succeed in relegating instrumental music to a secondary role.[144] Moreover, the early Christian moralists took care to forbid the use of musical instruments in liturgy, for they were used in pagan sacrifices and orgies; on the other hand, since the destruction of the temple of Jerusalem in 70 A.D., they knew nothing more of Old Testament worship musical practices than the a capella chant of the synagogue.[145]

Through the centuries, as stressed by Safford Cape, it was worship itself that the Church authorities wished above all to shelter from secular invasion. On the whole, the Church's disfavor was aimed not at instruments or secular music *per se*, but rather at their introduction into sacral music. In effect, the

---

[143]Cf. e.g. Solange Corbin, *L'Eglise à la conquête de sa musique* (Paris: Gallimard, 1960), 50-51.

[144]See Lionel de La Laurencie, *Le Goût musical en France*, 39.

[145]See Jacques Chailley, *Histoire musicale du Moyen Age*, 30-31.

churchmen who created Western European polyphony actually welcomed all the principal contributions of secular music, developed these contributions in their turn, and returned them, ripened and perfected, to their secular source. Although we can notice two fundamental attitudes that have characterized Christians (Catholic as well as Protestant) since their origins: one favorable to music (the Benedictines of Cluny and the Lutherans, for example) and the other unfavorable (the disciples of Saint Bernard and the Calvinists), the Church has never been opposed to instrumental and secular music as such. Objections to the wandering minstrel, as an agent of social trouble and occasional disseminator of immoral texts, were directed against the musician to a much lesser degree.[146] The conclusions of the Council of Trent, which within its extensive texts devoted only a few lines to music, emphasized only that the bishops should take care that no secular elements be introduced by way of organ and choir into the church, which is, first of all, a house of prayer.[147]

Moreover, the promotion of vocal music, as well as the pursuit of simplicity and search for well-known formulas, is necessary from the moment one seeks to reach the congregation: while the hymns of Prudentius and Hilarius—being too classical in rhythm—had but little success, the songs of Saint Ambrose and his disciple Saint Augustine—which were much more accessible and had regular verse—spread and took root.[148] As early as the third century, in Edessa, the gnostic Bardesan attracted people to his heresy by replacing psalms with songs, which had well-marked beats so that they were easy for everyone to sing. As he had considerable success, those of orthodox faith, as in the case of Ephraim, had no other recourse

---

[146]See Safford Cape, "Thèse et histoire," *Revue belge de musicologie* II/2 (1948) 35-36.

[147]See Felix Raugel, "Palestrina," *Histoire de la musique* I (Paris: Gallimard, 1960) 1193, and Edith Weber, *Le Concile de Trente et la musique, de la Réforme à la contre-Réforme* (Paris: Champion, 1982).

[148]See Armand Machabey, *Genèse de la tonalité musicale classique*, 56. About the active aspect of Christian Church music see above, p. 91-92.

but to compose in their turn readily accessible chants with texts conforming to Church doctrines.[149] Thus were born the versified hymns of the fourth century, whose essential features can be considered as relatively well preserved examples of the popular songs of the time.[150]

The search in the Christian church for simplicity of expression and clarity of meaning in the words gives undeniable evidence of the influence of sociohistorical conditionings on musical creation, but with a basic difference in quality compared with politically inspired music: much religious music, including that of the Christian church, has lasted beyond the period of its creation and is distinguished by high artistic quality.

We can say that, in contrast to so much of the *levelling* music (whether produced for this purpose or not) from so many musical genres, which was destined to fulfill socially determined functions, there exists also a *surpassing* music. This surpassing implies two aspects: a sociological one, because this music has been able to surpass the limitations of place and original surroundings and the social functions of the moment, and a spiritual aspect because it has been able to carry to man a message of purity and transparency of content of which it alone is capable, thus transcending in great measure all social conditionings and restraints.

On the other hand, a certain "disembodiment of music must be viewed as a specific accomplishment of the occidental-Christian civilization. The crucial steps toward this development was taken when liturgical singing was separated from its physical accentuation. After that, monasticism succeeded in gradually directing organized polyphony. To separate singing from body movement or dance had already been an aspiration of early Christianity . . . From the writings of Max Weber we gather that he already realised the connection between disembodying asceticism and musical rationalization . . . " to be "ini-

---

[149]*Ibid.*, 30.

[150]See Jacques Chailley, *La Musique médiévale* (Paris: Ed. du Coudrien, 1951) 13-14.

tially directed against the religious rites of late antiquity, which were accompanied by instrumental music."[151]

Sacred and secular principles, however different and distinguished, were never strictly delimited or totally separated. As W. Wiora pointed out, "the spiritual and the temporal, the sacred and the profane were never set upon the same level . . . A lasting tension existed between them, as between Church and State, that 'inner dynamic in which Western culture had the advantage over every sort of pure theocracy or purely secular state,' as Eduard Spranger expresses it. Only because they were fruitful solution of such tensions, above the extremes of purism and secularization, could the great works of Christian musical art—of Dufay and Josquin, Lassus and Schütz, Bach and Bruckner—come into being. They form a peak in the history of the West and over and above this in the history of the human spirit. In Hegel's words, 'this fundamental religious music belongs to the most profound and the most influential that any art can produce'."[152] In other words, the meeting of sacred and secular gave music, above all, most fruitful results. The radical change in the religious sphere began with an interiorization of the consciousness which had to "surpass the formalism of the ritual mediation",[153] and had a decisive impact on the new sacred ritual practices, which were deeply purified and delivered from the old sacrificial burdens of the ancestral and pagan religions of the Ancient World. Christian sacral rites exerted a determining influence on the character of the new music that sprang up in connection with them. At a later stage, these rites were institutionalized; they became a framework. However, in their case, as Ephrem Dominique Yon observed, "the fact that the cult be an objective *given* does not contradict either the demand for or the possibility of spiritualization or of freedom; it does mean that it is no longer simply an exterior prescription

---

[151]Irmgard Bontinck, "Mass Media and New Types of Youth Music," 54-55.

[152]Walter Wiora, *The Four Ages of Music* (New York: Norton, 1967) 138-139.

[153]Ephrem-Dominique Yon, "Deux figures du rite dans le christianisme," in: *Le rite* (Paris: Beauchesne, 1981) 206.

without a link with the relationship of love which it has a function to set up and support; the cult—though institutional— appeals to the act of consciousness which finds in it support for offering itself to the infinite."[154] In precisely this stage of institutionalization, the Christian rites became an important conditioning for music throughout most of its history in Europe. On the other hand, the institutionalization of secular—social and political—ritual and ceremony led to one of the peaks of profane "ritual" music—the court music of Renaissance and Baroque times.

In this schematic survey one more aspect can be mentioned, that of the greater or less vitality and presence of the musical works that were linked to sacred and secular rituals in the past. Although only a detailed historical study could give us a totally satisfactory answer on this point, it seems however that a hypothesis can be presented: though deeply tied to their particular contexts, musical works linked to *sacral* rites may be considered, on the whole, to have been able to surpass the limitations of place and their original milieu in much greater numbers and to a much more considerable extent than those musical works that were tied in many ways to *secular* rituals were able to. Although no generalization can be made here, another hypothesis, to be verified through specialized research, could also be proposed, that, in the history of European music, works linked to sacral rites have been able to transmit a message of sublimity of which they alone were capable and which transcended to a considerable extent, till now, all sociological contingencies and limitations of space and time. If Helmut Rösing's thesis that "the place of performance, i.e. the occasion of performance and musical function often stand in direct mutual relationship . . . The more a work appertains to the domain of utilitarian music, the closer is its link to the particular occasion; the more a work belongs to the sphere of art music, the more free this linkage is, especially from the beginning of musical classic"[155]—is correct,

---

[154]*Ibid.*, 210.

[155]Helmut Rösing, "Zur Rezeption technisch vermittelter Musik. Psycholo-

it could also be argued that musical works connected to sacred rituals were, throughout the history of European music, much less dependent on their ritual context and were much more autonomous artistically. This is proved by their survival and frequent performance to this day. They still have a large, educated public and are marked *grosso modo* by highly distinguished and artistic qualities. On the contrary, the majority of music linked to secular rituals and ceremonies seems to have been much more dependent on its function, and thus limited in a sociological and sometimes even an artistic sense. Contrary to the sort of *levelling* music that was produced to fulfill socially limited functions in a series of secular ceremonies and rituals, the music linked to sacral rituals can much more be spoken of as a *surpassing* or transcending one.

gische, ästhetische und musikalisch-funktionsbezogene Aspekte," in: Hans-Christian Schmidt, ed., *Musik in der Massenmedien Rundfunk und Fernsehen. Perspektiven und Materialien* (Mainz: Schott, 1976) 45.

CHAPTER TEN

SOCIOARTISTIC ASPECTS
OF MUSIC

The socioartistic aspects of music itself pose the problem of its socioartistic conditionings. The latter embrace several questions, of which the most important is that of musical creation. Whereas our preceding considerations dealt with the extramusical social aspects of music and its relationships with social facts other than those implied specifically by music itself, the problem that we will approach now consists in the significance, the place, and the importance that must be attributed to the influence of sociological conditions upon musical creation functioning within the musical artistic order alone. Whereas until now the question involved the *sociohistorical* conditioning of music, the investigation will from now on examine its *socioartistic* conditionings.[1] Some of the elements that will be briefly examined on level of the artistic creation concern only Western musical culture, which, taken as a whole, has not been characterized by stagnation, as is the case in certain other cultures, but on the contrary by a dynamism that let it from one discovery to another, from one innovation to another.

According to L.H. Correa De Azevedo, "up until now, Oriental music has remained utterly faithful to its traditional sources. Remaining historically pure, it has prolonged its rich

---

[1]See above, p. 47-56.

past and kept itself alive,"[2] but "the traditional music of Asia has always evolved, and will continue to do so, albeit more slowly than Western music."[3] As we know, Max Weber considered "rationalization" to be one of the essential traits of this music and its dynamism.[4] In response to the question of why polyphonic and harmonic-homophonic music developed beyond the pre-conditions of widespread polyvocality only in the West, Max Weber answered that the specific conditions of music development in the West involved first and foremost the invention of notation.[5] The availability of a standardized notation led to an overall change in the destiny of music. This return of notation to music induces us to see in it a social fact, a normative system that would control therewith the structure of musical conduct. It could be said not only that polyphony appeared with notation, that it was born from it, but even that 'it is notation.'[6]Therefore, compared to other cultures, Western music is distinguished, among other things, by the importance it gives to the notation of its learned music. We should observe, however, that musical notation was quite indispensable to the survival of tradition as to the development of innovations. Only the adoption of notation permitted the conservation of an increasingly important musical output and the introduction into this output of innovations that, by their presence, modified it while prolonging it.

---

[2]Luis Heitor Corrêa de Azevedo, "Contemporary Music and Musical Tradition," *Bulletin of the International Music Council* 1 (1975) 1.

[3]*Ibid.*, 2.

[4]For the significance of the term "rational" in Max Weber's works, compare the introductory study in the American edition of his book *The Rational and Social Foundations of Music*, XVIII-XIX, entitled "Max Weber's Sociology of Music," by Don Martindale and Johannes Riedel. On the importance of Weber's other sociological views on music, see Kurt Blaukopf, "Tonsysteme und ihre gesellschaftliche Geltung in Max Weber's Musiksoziologie," *IRASM*, I/2 (1970) 156-167.

[5]Max Weber, *The Rational and Social Foundations of Music*, 83.

[6]Cf. Kurt Blaukopf, *Musik im Wandel der Gesellschaft* (München-Zürich: Piper and Co., 1982) 236, and Francoise Escal, *Espaces sociaux, espaces musicaux* (Paris: Payot, 1979) 144.

I • TRADITION, INVENTION, AND INNOVATION

From the sociological point of view, the whole history of Western music seems to be a matter of continuity and discontinuity. A dialectic of sequences and ruptures, of traditions and of inventions, depending on the social as much as on the personal, constituted the evolution of the musical as such. Invention, which for Gabriel Tarde was already an important factor of progress and an achievement of the individual, did not become the object of many studies in sociology.[7] It was, sometimes however, envisioned on the artistic level. Charles Lalo believed that the "alleged *personality* . . . is only a superior manner of understanding technique, of making it one's own, of identifying it with one's activity and thought."[8] According to Max Radin, "if one excepts some of the innovations that each age creates for itself (phenomena of *invention*) and some elements that come from other groups by the process of diffusion (phenomena of *borrowing*), all the elements of social life are traditional."[9] In fact, the ideas of invention and tradition are closely connected and it is impossible to validly consider one without the other.[10]

According to Charles Seeger, "tradition comprehends those phenomena exhibited in the inheritance, cultivation, and transmission of a body of practice, or way of doing something, in a society. I shall view a music tradition as operating in three dimensions: in extent, throughout the geographical area occupied by a society; in depth, throughout the social mass; and in duration, throughout its span of life."[11] Still, musical tradition

---

[7]See Gabriel Tarde, *Les lois de l'imitation* (Paris: Alcan, 1890) and *L'Opinion et la Foule* (Paris: Alcan, 1901).

[8]Charles Lalo, *Les sentiments esthétiques* (Paris: Alcan, 1901) 223.

[9]Max Radin, "Tradition," *Encyclopaedia of the Social Sciences*, ed. by E. Saligman and A. Johnson (New York-London: 1930-1935) 62.

[10]See for example Mikel Dufrenne, "Note sur la Tradition," *Cahiers internationaux de sociologie* III (1947) 158-69; and Henry Raynor, "Tradition and innovation," *Monthly Musical Record* 85/970 (1955) 207-211, and 85/971 (1955) 227-231.

[11]Charles Seeger, "Music and Society: Some New-World Evidence of Their

is not necessarily made up of the totality of results of all inherited musical activities within the framework of the social and cultural environment. It is formed by those elements that are active in this environment and maintain an influence upon it. Tradition implies both the totality of extant works and human artificats and the totality of accepted conceptions, attitudes, inclinations, tastes, and habits. This is why it must be defined dynamically, not statically, as a living reality, changing and in motion, in which new elements arise while others decline in the course of history. What is tradition in one social and cultural environment is not tradition in another, in the same way that what is tradition at one historical moment is not necessarily so during a later one. The rediscoveries of forgotten musical works such as those of Schütz and Bach, which were later integrated into the living tradition, offer appropriate examples in connection with this. The durations and positions of particular elements within the musical tradition are then variable and diverse. Consequently we may say, with Zofia Lissa, that tradition itself becomes a place for certain changes. And to the extent it survives as tradition it can also operate in the current era quite differently than it did in previous historical periods. Although it remains rather questionable that "in Western music, however, only the countries having a great musical past bear the imprint of a national tradition,"[12] "at the outset of the 20th century, [in] those countries which had hitherto been eclipsed by musically stronger ones . . . it became important to create a kind of music

---

Relationship," in *Studies in Musicology 1935-1975* (Berkeley-Los Angeles-London: U. of California Press, 1977) 184.

[12]See Zofia Lissa, "Prolegomena to the Theory of Musical Tradition" *IRASM*, I/1 (1970); and Hans Heinrich Eggebrecht, *"Traditionskritik,"* Studien zur Tradition in der Musik ed. H.H. Eggebrecht, and M. Lütolf (Munich: Emil Katzbichler, 1973, 2. See in the same volume particularly: Joseph Smits van Waesberghe, *Gedanken über den inneren Traditionsprozeß in der Geschichte der Musik des Mittelalters*, 7-30; Carl Dahlhaus, *Traditionszerfall im 19. und 20. Jahrhundert*, 177-190; Rudolf Stephan, *Zum Problem der Tradition in der neuesten Musik*, 191-200.

from which one could determine a country of origin; but today, this once generalized preoccupation has disappeared."[13] And, as it was put by Andrej Rijavec, more developed and quantitatively stronger milieus bear, from their sheer quantity, *via facti* more quality and thus set up criteria in the fields of musical production, performance and musicology.[14]

What is, then, the presence of tradition in musical creation? In order to answer this question both a source and an essential method are required: the musical works, and their comparative study. This study reveals that throughout the history of Western and Oriental art, music tradition has played an essential and inescapable role in musical creation. The former has conditioned the latter during all periods and under all circumstances, with the exception of its absolute beginnings, which, however, do not necessarily coincide with the birth of primitive art. Here is an example: The liturgical drama was born out of the Christian "office, born spontaneously, born without a model or a precursor, with all religious, musical, and ritual characteristics of the Dionisiac theater at its beginnings; but without imitating it."[15] If one form or musical genre can originate without an analogous musical tradition and without socioartistic conditionings (which happens only rarely), it is never born without any relation to an extramusical tradition, or sociohistorical conditions. In the case above, liturgical drama's relationship was Christian office, which, however, actually incorporated a musical element. The constancy and the regularity of this phenomenon permit us to see in it the expression of a sociological law. Ever since the times of the oldest known document of Christian music—the Oxyrhynchos fragment—(leaving aside certain phenomena where new music breaks with tradition), this fact has been confirmed. And this implies the relativity of creative originality. Musicologists have generally agreed on the fundamental socioartistic position

---

[13]*Ibid.*, 1.

[14]Andrej Rijavec, "Notes towards the National and International in Music," *IRASM* VII/1 (1976) 86.

[15]Jacques Chailley, *Histoire musicale du Moyen Age*, 68.

of the composer in his creative work. They sometimes express themselves on this subject in almost identical terms. Thus, according to Gisèle Brelet, Jacques Handschin, and Zofia Lissa, the composer does not create *ex nihilo*, from nothing, but his work always attaches itself more or less to tradition.[16] According to Armand Machabey, "all innovation is contained in a germinal pre-existant formula, or motivated by concomitant conditions."[17] Asking the question of how innovators in musical composition proceeded until now, Jacques Challey answers: "First by assimilating the theory of their predecessors and by writing, more or less submissively, in the same way. Later, as they grew in experience, they began to forget the theory, and little by little, their instinct dictated what should be discarded and what should be modified or added to. This is how Beethoven developed from Haydn, Wagner from Meyerbeer, Debussy from Massenet."[18] Also, "neither Fauré nor Ravel could be explained without Saint-Saëns, any more than Grigny or Couperin can be understood without Lebègue."[19] This "flow" of creators, one after another, supposes a tradition that always implies a passage through a social channel or a mediate way. This explains why, in the majority of composers, we find originality developing in a way such that historians of music sometimes believed it valuable to divide a composers' creative span—Beethoven's for example—into several creative periods. However, it is necessary to distinguish two aspects of the presence of social reality (represented by tradition) in the creation of musical works: a *negative* aspect, relating to the affirmation of elements opposed to it, and a *positive* aspect, relating to its traces in the work that can have themselves either

---

[16]See Gisèle Brelet, *Esthétique et Création musicale,* 18; Jacques Handschin, "Musicologie et musique," *La revue internationale de musique,* (winter 1950-1951) 230; Zofia Lissa, "Prilog proučavanju sociologije muzike" (Contribution to research in the sociology of music), *Muzika* 3 (1949) 24.

[17]Armand Machabey, *Traité de la critique musicale,* 95-96.

[18]Jacques Chailley, "La Radio et le développement de l'instinct harmonique chez les auditeurs," *Cahiers d'études de radio-télévision,* III-IV (1955) 403-404.

[19]Norbert Dufourcq, *Nicolas Lebègue* (Paris: Picard, 1954) 4.

a universal or a residual character, the composer not wanting or not being able to liberate himself from them. We must likewise distinguish the socioartistic conditioning *in* musical creation from the socioartistic conditioning *of* musical creation; the logical (and important) consequence here is the distinction between the socioartistic conditioning *of* musical works and the socio-artistic conditioning *in* musical works. The second aspect implies the action of socioartistic conditions that have influenced the creation of these works. The first aspect implies the manifestation and the presence of these conditions in the works; that is, the presence of all the integrating elements that are neither original nor new, but that have already been realized in other previous works, and which have acted as socioartistic conditions in the creation of these new musical works.

Historical analysis indicates that these constituent elements may all become part of a musical work, with a single exception: *specific musical content.* [20] This element substantially differentiates these works from one another, even within the same style or musical language. But within musical content one can follow other elements contained in a musical work. Specific musical content is the result of the personal innovation of the creator, a unique and objectively new reality, subjectively original, that gives an unmistakable mark of uniqueness to the musical work. Of course, it is not only the specific musical content of a work that carries the imprint of the creative musical personality. Neither is it content alone that must or can make the sole difference between different musical works. The difference may also consist in characteristics of style and technique; but these characteristics do not necessarily create the difference. The specific musical content, on the contrary, has to create this difference in order to give the work its aspect of individuality

---

[20] We are not unaware of the fact that ancient composers sometimes borrowed their musical material from the works of other composers, or from their own earlier works; however, they never reached the state of identification that would, if such be the case, result in a plagiarism or in unnecessary repetition. See Armand Machabey, *La Musicologie*, 112-113.

and particularity, and in order to be truly the content of the work, that is, the actualization of a musical thought as a thought.

The difference in the specific musical content of different works by the same composer does not demand that the compositions be different in style, as is the case with Stravinsky, or that they be characterized by eclecticism, as are those of Richard Strauss. They can very well possess identical fundamental stylistic characteristics, as do the works of Palestrina, Bach, Haydn, or Chopin, and still differ in their specific musical content. This content (even within a single era or one composer's style) must necessarily vary, be always different, subjectively and objectively original, in order to prevent the work from expressing what has already been said. On the other hand, the specific stylistic characteristics of this content, as well as the other integrating elements of the musical work, can be common to a whole series of compositions that differ in their specific musical content. There are no socioartistic conditionings *in* this content: there are only socioartistic conditionings *of* the content (with these elements and their stylistic and technical characteristics as an intermediary); the content cannot be separated from them, although it is distinguished from them as an actualization of a musical thought. The socioartistic conditionings exercise an influence, therefore, only on these elements and on these characteristics. And these elements and characteristics are precisely the ones that extend from one musical work to another and constitute an aspect of musical tradition.

II • ORIGINALITY AND HISTORICAL RELATIVITY

These observations permit the introduction of greater clarity into the problem of originality in musical creation, a problem closely linked to the effect of socioartistic conditionings on creation. First of all, it is necessary to make a distinction between the *objective* originality of the musical work and the *subjective* originality of the musical creation (both of the terms being taken in their fullest sense). A musical work cannot be objectively original without being the result of the subjective originality of creation. The latter, however, is not sufficient for the creation of an objectively original work. For the objective originality of the created work implies the introduction of some new and previously nonexistent contributions, either absolute, or relative to a given artistic-cultural environment. In this case, it is only a question of "reduced" or incomplete originality, although the created work might be a result of an incontestable subjective originality. The subjective originality of the musical creation does not necessarily result (although this may most often be the case) in a musical work which is objectively original, especially in the absolute sense. Hence the output of lesser composers is borrowed and adopted from a language, style, or technique that these composers themselves neither created nor helped to create, but within which framework they compose. Their works sometimes contain nothing objectively original by way of spirit, style, technique, or language, but only a separate specific musical content. Nevertheless, the objective originality of the musical work is inconceivable without the subjective originality of musical creation.

Originality in musical creation does not require the negation of socioartistic conditionings. On the contrary, it presupposes a partial acceptance of the legacy of musical tradition and the perseverance of some of its elements. At the same time however,—and this is essential—creative musical originality implies a break with musical tradition through the introduction of original, novel, and hitherto nonexistent musical contributions. Now, the history of music shows that, while objectively supplying something formerly nonexistent, musical creation is always original *in relation* to a given tradition, in relation to preexistent musical works. The originality of musical creation, profoundly rooted in music history itself, is therefore historically relative. It is also affected, up to a certain point, by socioartistic conditions. What is original for one social and artistic-cultural environment is not necessarily so for another. Certainly, *absolute* originalities do exist, in the sense that their contributions are without precedent anywhere. *Total* originalities do not exist, however— a subject to which we shall return later.

The objective originality of the musical work is doubly relative: not only in the sense already mentioned (by the contribution of innovations, which can be absolute on a world-wide level, or valid solely for one artistic-cultural environment—in relation to which the work represents an objective innovation from the point of view of its musical tradition), but also because no musical work can be, or is, objectively original in *all* its aspects and elements. That is why there is no total objective originality, if by that one means an innovation in *all* the elements a musical work contains or can contain. No composition of such originality has yet been written in the history of music. And this fact confirms the degree to which the musician-creator is dependent on the past, the extent to which he thinks and acts historically (even without knowing it), how closely he is tied to tradition and rooted in the social (even when he claims the most radical changes). And this is understandable: the opposite would signify the negation of the existence of socioartistic conditionality *in* musical creation, as well as *in* musical works. We will confine ourselves to only two illustrations of the temporal scope of this conditionality: the function exerted by the monastic office, revised and augmented by the use of tropes, in the birth of the European theater,[21] and representative symbolism of liturgical chant as the "initial principle from which had to derive the use of the leitmotif, heralding a personage or associated with a general idea in dramatic music,"[22] especially in the works of Wagner. The greatest innovators in the history of music were not totally original, even in their most mature and most objectively and absolutely original works. This is true of the most outstanding composers, such as Palestrina, Bach, and Beethoven, who always were great continuers, skillful in summarizing and in synthesizing tradition while transforming it creatively in their works.[23]

---

[21]Jacques Chailley, *Histoire musicale du Moyen Age,* 90.

[22]Lionel de La Laurencie, *Le Goût musical en France,* 42.

[23]See for example, Jacques Chailley, "Atavismes musicaux de J. S. Bach," *La revue internationale de musique* VII (1950) 25-32.

Outside of specific musical content, the other elements that the work involves, implies, and presupposes can only be *partially* (and not totally) original. Musical works are always original, when they are so, in ónly some of their elements or their aspects, never in their totality. This partial lack of originality is an inevitable consequence of the socioartistic conditionings present in the work. There only exists a total objective originality of the specific musical content as such, but not a total objective originality of the musical work in all its aspects. A brief historical analysis could show this; a systematic analysis of the whole history of music could prove it in detail. A few examples, however, suffice to illustrate it in a convincing manner.

The metrics of European learned music, much simpler than those of Oriental music, is one of those constitutive elements that have slowly evolved in the course of history and consequently have conditioned the output of many generations of composers. In the fourteenth century, European learned music added the *tempus imperfectum* to the *tempus perfectum,* itself admitted in the twelfth and thirteenth centuries. It was necessary to await the nineteenth century to observe (besides the technical and stylistic changes of the preceding centuries) the introduction of the first profound and durable changes in classical system of measures. Many remarkable composers did not touch this received tradition, notwithstanding the diverse originalities in other domains of their creations. The measure comprising five beats will only be employed by Boïeldieu, Wagner, Gounod, d'Indy, Tchaikowsky, Ropartz and Debussy; the seven-beat measures by Berlioz, Wagner, Elgar and again Debussy; the nine-beat measure by d'Indy; and that of eleven beats by Rimski-Korsakov.[24] And polymetrics will be utilized considerably in European learned music only in the twentieth century. Even Schönberg employed the most classical measures in spite of the breaks he provoked on the level of tonal language.

Similarly, modality reigned for entire centuries in European music, and during entire eras classical tonality appeared to

---

[24]See Edgar Willems, *Le rythme musical* (Paris: P.U.F., 1954) 188.

composers as fundamental (even "natural" in the eyes of some), and not as something momentary or relative. In other words, the question of musical language did not come up in the actual practice of composition; from one generation to another the traditional solution was accepted. The classical tonal language as a factor and socioartistic condition was utilized by all the masters of the Baroque, Classical and Romantic eras. Classical tonality profoundly conditioned their creation and is one of the essential characteristics of their works. This testifies equally to the constant socioartistic conditioning exerted on musical creation and to the roots of its originality in the musical tradition. It also leads us to conclude that socioartistic conditioning in musical creation does not permit a total, objective originality of the musical work in all its aspects and elements. Every musical work necessarily contains some elements previously provided by tradition.

Throughout music history, the specific content of the socioartistic conditioning of musical creation has varied; it is always being modified to a greater or less extent, in spite of the greater or lesser constancy of its particular factors. This is the source of differences in the fundamental position of the composer with regard to socioartistic conditioning. If socioartistic conditioning of musical creation represents certain limitations for the artist-creator, it also can affect his creation positively and in a profitable way. Tradition gives him indispensable material that serves as a starting point for his creation. It also contributes to the formation, enrichment, and deepening of his artistic experience. The richer and more diverse the tradition is that reaches the composer, the more extensive and diversified is the manner in which it conditions him in his musical creation. Likewise, it offers the composer a greater choice of the sources that he will be able to bring to his creation, and according to which he will be able to advance his creative endeavors. Conversely, the poorer and more unvaried the musical tradition is, the fewer are the socioartistic factors that condition his creation. But the composer does not become freer thereby nor does he have greater creative possibilities at his disposal. On the contrary, the less rich and differentiated are the materials provided by tradition, the more the composer's creative possibilities are limited. Thus there might be a paradox here; the socioartistic conditioning comprises two different aspects: limitation and enrichment. It is, nevertheless, for a composer as a social being and creative personality, an inevitable and normal fact.[25]

Still, the value of musical tradition in musical creation does not depend solely on what it provides for a composer, but also on what he will be able to find in it. To the extent that the knowledge of the composer is more limited—when his talent and ability to penetrate the legacy of tradition is less significant, and when his subjective originality is less important—to that same extent he has less liberty in creation, he is more conditioned, more subject to socioartistic conditionings. The scope of his creative initiative narrows and is reduced to the domain delimited by these conditionings, within which, consequently, he creates. Inversely, to the extent that his abilities have more depth and amplitude and his subjective originality and talent expand, the composer is much less conditioned, much freer in creative abilities and in the choice of sources upon which he can draw. In the intersecting of the creative personality and socioartistic conditionality, and in the dialogue that unfolds within the creative process and manifests itself in the created work, exists the essential solution to the problem of the composer's position within the history of music itself. This problem extends, however, into that of sociohistorical conditionings, which we have already attempted previously to survey.

III • CHANGE, EVOLUTION AND PROGRESS IN MUSIC

The question of change, evolution, and progress in music, as well as that of tradition, was present at least implicitly long

---

[25]For the contemporary situation see the interesting discussion and criticism of the conceptions of four distinguished authors (J. Chailley, W. Wiora, R. L. Crocker, and L. B. Meyer), by Leo Treitler, "The Present as History," reprint from *Perspectives of New Music*. Princeton U. Press VII/2 (1969) 1-58.

before it found explicit expression in different theories. Until the seventeenth century, musicians felt spontaneously that music was progressing. The music of their own time was the most widely performed and the most appreciated.[26] In the seventeenth century the idea of progress in music expressed itself in the disputes between the "Ancients" and the "Moderns," especially in French music. The music of the past was often regarded as obsolete, and during this and the following century a more or less clearly defined theory of progress was formulated, according to which only *new* music was *good* music. Sethus Calvisius, Pierre Maillart, Wolfgang Caspar Printz, Sébastian de Brossard, Charles Burney, and many other believed in the progress of music. Even Johann Sebastian Bach found himself considered, in the eyes of the younger generation (e.g., Adolph Scheibe), a retrograde composer.

During the well-known *querelles des Anciens et des Modernes,* contemporary artists were compared with those of antiquity, and—in a broader sense—the concept of historical progress also appeared.[27] In fact, early Christianity, particularly from St. Augustine on, had abandoned the Greek theory of the cyclic movement of time and history. But even in the seventeenth and eighteenth centuries the historical awareness of ancient music was not sufficiently developed. During earlier centuries people had even less a sense of history and devoted less attention and consideration to the music of the past. Before the theory of progress in music was clearly formulated, it was believed, in

---

[26]However, as Thomas Munro stressed, the theory of progress, which emerged during the Baroque era and the period of the Enlightment, "had been obstructed in the Renaissance by too much humanistic worship of the classics, as superior to Gothic art. See "Do the Arts Progress?" *The Journal of Aesthetics and Art Criticism* XIV/2 (1955) 189.

[27]"The famous 'Quarrel of the Ancients and the Moderns,' which agitated seventeenth and eighteenth century scholars, was mostly limited to a comparison between the moderns of the time and the classics of Greece and Rome. The question was often phrased in terms of whether progress existed in the arts; but no one seriously disputed that classical art was better than savage or barbarous art." *Ibid.,* 189.

practice, that progress in music exists, thus implying that change, development, and evolution also exist. The medieval theorists dealt with theoretical questions about music mostly in an abstract and general way, not with a historical perspective. Even as the theorist was considered as musician *par excellence,* so music itself was included in the quadrivium among other scientific disciplines. Thus it is not surprising that as early as the Middle Ages there appeared opinions that, in accordance with music's standing as science, not art, dealt with it at least implicitly as capable of progress by accumulation. In his treatise *De Musica,* Johannes Affligemensis wrote in the twelfth century: " ... Moderni autem subtilius omnia atque sagacius intuentes, quia, ... quanto juniores, tanto perspicaciores." (" ... The moderns, however, ... being so much younger, they are so much more perspicatious.") On the level of musical practice, Squarcialupi's *Codex,* of the fifteenth century, was an exception in that it contained compositions created one hundred years earlier. The theorist Tinctoris held that music more than forty years old was not worth listening to—an evaluation clearly attributable to a sense of progress. The German humanist Nicolaus Listenius, in his treatise *Musica* of 1537, expressed a new and significant view of the composer's task: his duty was to produce an *opus perfectum et absolutum,* which would live after his death. As Walter Wiora and Frits Noske rightly stressed, that was the first time in history that musicians had been considered as creators of lasting products. In accordance with this and similar statements, which reflected a new spirit, from approximately 1600 on composers began to indicate with the expression *opus* the ordinal number of their compositions.[28] The emergence of the composer as personality, preceded the "transition" of musical work from process to product, and its identification as such. As Ludwig Finscher remarked, interest in the composer first manifested itself in a way that was apparently banal, but rich

---

[28]See the discussion of Walter Wiora at the second symposium of the IMS, in *IRASM,* VI/1 (1975) 70, and Frits Noske, "Forma formans," *IRASM* VII/1 (1976) 43.

in historical consequences: in the attribution of particular compositions to a definite composer, in their designation by his name. With rare exceptions, which can be explained by special reasons, European composers as a rule were anonymous until the end of the fourteenth century. Only then, first in Italy, in and around Florence, in a middle-class milieu, did they begin to emerge gradually from anonymity, at the point when the developed bourgeois society of the Italian cities was already declining and completing its first "cycle."[29] The excepts to this, Leoninus and Perotinus, and after them de Vitry and Machaut, were not known as a result of having their names mentioned on the manuscripts of their musical works, but were known via other sources and circumstances. Otherwise, Finscher correctly distinguishes three phases of the artist's becoming known in connection with his musical works: first, the appearance of his name on musical manuscripts; second, his endeavor to compose in a personal, individual style; and third, his effort to express himself in his musical work.[30]

Implicitly or explicitly most musical theorists of the seventeenth and eighteenth centuries considered that only the music of their own time was good or best, thus sustaining the idea of progress. Such an attitude was also reflected in musical life. At the time of Palestrina, for example, works by Leoninus, Perotinus, Machaut, or Dufay were not performed, as were contemporary works. In the short supplement to his treatise, *Exercitationes musicae duae*, which bears the indicative subtitle *De origine et progressu musices*, Sethus Calvisius gave, in 1600, the first brief summary of music history, but—typically, and quite logically for that period—his main purpose was to describe the music of his own time. In 1610, in *Les tons ou discours sur la musique*, Pierre Maillart states explicitly: if it is true that time brings us always something new, it seems certain that this should be applied

[29]See Ludwig Finscher, "Die 'Entstehung des Komponisten.' Zum Problem Komponisten-Individualität und Individualstil in der Musik des 14. Jahrhunderts," *IRASM* VI/1 (1975) 31; and his discussion, p. 136.
[30]*Ibid.*, 139-141.

above all to music, in which nothing is considered good unless it is new. The idea of progress in music was even more developed in *Historische Beschreibung der edelen Sing- und Klingkunst* . . . ,from 1690, by Wolfgang Caspar Printz, in the long title of which the progress of music is explicitly mentioned as an object of that work. The idea of progress in music appears in one way or another in a whole series of eighteenth-century treatises, for example in the well-known *Dictionnaire de la musique* (1703), by Sébastian de Brossard who considered that modern music had perfected the ancient one and that it was in better accordance with the requirements of reason. In this work it is already possible to discern the influence of the early rationalism of the Enlightenment. In Bach's era, as Enrico Fubini emphasized, the ideal of *galant* music was proposed and defended in almost all theoretical treatises, for the most part by musicians themselves. The concept of progress not only predominates in all these treatises but also represents one of the major criteria of evaluation. The compositions of modern musicians supersede those of previous ones; music reaches always new peaks and advances in its expressive and imitative possibilities; and those contemporary composers who did not accomodate themselves to new times are irrevocably condemned. Such aesthetic and historiographic perspectives are found, for example, in the writings of Bach's contemporary Johann Mattheson.[31] In this light it is also quite easy to understand the famous attack of Adolph Scheibe against Bach, which was an expression of the thinking and attitudes of a younger generation of composers who were no longer oriented toward the ideals of the Baroque, but rather toward new stylistic phenomena and tendencies.

But as early as the eighteenth century, along with dominant ideas of progress in music appear different, even opposite views. It was noted that music had also passed through periods of decadence and degeneration. While for Charles Burney the history of music was a continuous progress, and the music of his

---

[31]See Enrico Fubini, *L'estetica musicale dal Settecento a oggi* (Turin: Einaudi, 1968) 67.

time the apogee (as it abandoned for ever "gothic" harmony for a more free melodism), John Hawkins pointed to the decline of polyphony and counterpoint after Händel and Bach, considering that music had reached its peak of perfection with the polyphony and counterpoint of these two composers and had definitely degenerated after them. Burney conceived of music as interwoven with the general course of civilization, and therefore with continuing progress. Through his beliefs Burney gave music its full dignity, considering it to be an important element of human civilization, not a secondary one.[32]

At the time of Romanticism the idea of progress in music, otherwise so close to rationalist optimism, had not been completely abandoned. Romanticism transformed the idea considerably, however, and brought in a new point of view, one which attached a high value to music of the past. On the other hand, Romantic music itself led to deeply divided views on the subject; the polemics about Wagner's music contributed greatly to this, though he himself was convinced that music progresses and that, of course, his own music had reached the highest point in all of music history. Thus Wagner himself regarded his work in the light of the idea of progress, considering it not only as a peak in the historical evolution of art—its last word—but also as "the art of the future," which became, however, as long as any art remained afterwards, whatever its value, an art of the past. And this fact, as many others on the level of musical production, clearly speaks not only in favor of changes, but of progress too, both of which do exist; for until now no art had ever presented itself as an unchangeable model for artistic works to come.

But Romanticism held less and less to the belief that progress in music existed, although in another sense. The Romantic orientation toward history and the past, and with it the rediscovery of old masters and the values of their music, demonstrated that contemporary music was in no sense absolute. The autonomous, even topical, current value of past music was recognized.

---

[32]*Ibid.*, 63-64.

Besides, it became more and more evident that all contemporary music was not, as had been thought, valuable for the sole reason that it was contemporary, since it did not find any more of a unanimous acclaim among contemporary critics and public. To this new outlook, musical criticism of the time surely contributed. In the nineteenth century criticism developed more than ever before, and reflected all the richness and variety of its authors' concepts, tastes, and points of view. So Romanticism did not attribute exclusive importance to contemporaneity. Instead, under Rousseau's influence, it projected "the golden age" of art into past ages. In that complex time the 'Umwertung aller Werten" (Nietzsche) was performed almost completely in art, though not so much as one might suppose. As ever, breaks and continuity, novelty and tradition were all present. Particular periods of music history were regarded more and more as periods of degeneration and decadence; thus it was recognized at least indirectly that historical advancement does not bring only progress. Even more than the eighteenth century, the nineteenth century witnessed decadence in church music, the decline of polyphony, and in the climate of emerging positivism, the decadence of later Romantic music itself, to which can be added "the decay of forms" and even "pathological aspects" about which Hanslick wrote so much, in attacking Wagner.

In the twentieth century the ideas of progress in music have been revived again. Considerations of the definitive decline of tonal music—even more about all the traditions of the past in contemporary creative orientations, and finally, fears about the end or ruin of music as such, have been expressed and still exist. Such views, sometimes based on extreme interpretations of one part of reality, are often integrated into artistic movements that regard themselves either as progressive or, on the contrary, as opposed to the concept of progress in art. In the twentieth century both progress and tradition are questioned, but they are also both reaffirmed in many ways. As P.E. Carapezza stressed, never so much as in our own time has tradition in all the arts been so vivid. It has autonomous vitality; works of long past or recent tradition are present in human life to an endlessly greater quantity and frequency than those of contemporary radical

339

art.[33] No era has been so thoroughly penetrated by tendencies toward novelty and innovation as the present one, no music has made such a break with traditional (or past) musical art as has contemporary music. Nevertheless, no period in the history of music has been so well informed about the music of the past, and no age has appreciated traditional music so fully, as has our own.

However, Hanslick already emphasized that no art wears out its forms as quickly and as often as music does. Modulations, cadences, interval movements, and harmonic progressions are so exhausted in fifty, even thirty years, that an ingenuous composer, forced to use new musical devices, cannot employ them any longer. According to Hanslick, it can be said of a number of musical works considered outstanding in their own time that they *were* beautiful.[34]

Such views, clearly under positivist and historicist influence, brought a radical relativization that is hardly acceptable. It is true that changes and evolution in the musical language and its technique exist, that in their usage there are points of saturation as well as necessary renovations. In music there are no absolute or permanent models of beauty. Styles depart more or less from each other in various aspects. Still such differences do not necessitate the downfall of musical works that at the time of their production were not only considered beautiful by a specific public, but also contained real features of beauty. Their beauty can be differently experienced and evaluated, in various ways and from different points of view, or because of diverse motives. But not all nor even most beautiful musical works of the past can be considered as if they used to be beautiful, and are not beautiful any longer.

In his views on this matter Hanslick approached the idea of progress in music in just one of its less acceptable aspects. The

[33]See P. E. Carapezza, "La costituzione della nuova musica," *Aut aut*, 79-80, (1964) 36.

[34]See Eduard Hanslick, *Vom Musikalisch-Schönen. Ein Beitrag zur Revision der Asthetik der Tonkunst* (Leipzig: Barth, 1891, 8th ed.) 93.

historical character of musical technique and language is a fact that cannot be denied. As E. Fubini stressed, these concepts, which are in perfect accordance with Hanslick's formalist aesthetic viewpoints, have until now served many critics as a methodological basis for their interpretation of music history and its evolution, taken just as a gradual "expenditure" of technical forms and procedures, thus imposing on it a continuous renewal and regeneration.[35]

According to Gerald Abraham, "the true essence of tradition . . . is perpetual life and change, very often slow and organic, yet often modified—sometimes quite violently modified—by external circumstances."[36] Tradition is not an obstacle to progress: progress is based on it. Progress does not imply demolition of all traditions, but rather their selection. Tradition and traditionalism are not the same thing. Tradition is a historical fact, and traditionalism is a conservative aesthetic attitude, contesting or opposing not only progress, but also evolution and change.

Now the question arises: What is progress? First of all, the term "progress" historically has taken various meanings. The idea of progress in music is at present often unclear, even to musicians themselves. In order to clarify it, it is necessary to distinguish progress exclusively in a *musical* sense from progress in the *extramusical* functions of music embracing its cultural, historical, social, and other aspects. In the latter sense one can speak of the greater or less progress in music of a given style, musical genre, or particular work, to the extent that they succeed more or less in fulfilling or satisfying those cultural, historical, psychological, social, or other extramusical functions to which their time and the moment of their appearance or performance invited them. This is an aspect which could be called *progress of music*. On the other hand, the *progress in music* consists in the amelioration and new achievements of inner qualities, characteristics and features of music itself. However, these two

---

[35]See Enrico Fubini, *L'estetica musicale dal Settecento a oggi*, 140.

[36]Gerald Abraham, *The Tradition of Western Music* (Berkeley-Los Angeles: University of California Press, 1974) 1.

essential aspects of progress related to music can be more or less connected, and consequently viewed from different but complementary sociological and musicological points of view. The progress *of* music is an indisputable fact that appears in the course of all music history in a variety of ways, and is especially interesting in sociological research. The aesthetic and historical study of music is, on the contrary, more concerned with progress *in* music. We can distinguish *technical* and *stylistic* progress in music, which concerns the enrichment of its expressive possibilities or characteristics, and is connected with the evolution of musical instruments, the enlargement of instrumental ensembles, the improvement of performance practice, and the change in particular structural devices of music—for instance, its form, rhythmic elements, harmonic language, etc.

IV • SOCIOLOGICAL PERSPECTIVES AND HUMAN HORIZONS

The problems that arise today in music are, for the most part, analogous to those that arise in art, science, and culture. It happens that a humanistic conception of music is opposed by other conceptions with which certain currents of contemporary development concur. It is frequently said that contemporary music, at least in its extremist fringe, became less accessible to the every-growing body of listeners, that it became more and more alienated from the traditions of *musica humana*, and that in this way it lost its close ties to human life. Not that this assertion is untrue: on the contrary, it derives from a perfectly accurate evaluation. It is unacceptable only if it is restricted to its purely negative aspect, since all negativism, even if it rightly condemns or destroys, is not constructive. As we have already mentioned, there is a gulf, or as some people think, a lack of comprehension on the part of the vast public about much of contemporary music. Nevertheless, when it is a question of the relationship between the composer and the public (even outside the contemporary context, which is charged with particular complications), we must say, with Walter Wiora, that even if in most cases the composer is not at the same time his own interpreter, the mediation of his relationship with the listener through an interpreter has been completely developed in the musical art of the West alone. All previous cultures, as well as contemporary cultures in the Orient, have differentiated much less between musical creation and performance, so that the possibility of a distance or break between production and listening was greatly reduced. When the composer is unable to place himself in a direct relationship with the listener, his communication with the listener is less easily established than that of an orator or a singer with their publics.[37] Incidentally, often the music played or sung—which is now called *reproduction*—socially preceded the *production* or actual creation of music itself.[38] Nevertheless, the problem of the relationship between music and its public is only the sociological dimension, although an important and a real one, of a more profound problem—that of the relationship between man and music.

The traditional aim of *musica humana* consisted in the ennoblement and purification of man, in his humanization: music had a human as well as an aesthetic function. This concept was widespread. Also, humanization and dehumanization are not confined to a certain time or era; they are inseparable from human and social life. Dehumanization is only one aspect of this "natural tendency toward denaturization"[39] and of man's alienation, both of which manifest themselves on different levels and never leave him. It would be quite surprising if art in general and music in particular did not reflect this. According to Aristotelian and Thomist philosophical tradition, the objective of art is not a perfection of the acting subject, the artist, but rather a work to be produced, hence, an "inhuman" aim or objective—a concept

---

[37]See Walter Wiora, *Komponist und Mitwelt,* 15.

[38]See Theodor W. Adorno, "Sociologie de la musique," *Musique en jeu,* II (1971) 9.

[39]See Paul Chauchard, *Vices des vertus, vertus des vices* (Paris: Mame, 1963) 24.

that Stravinsky also accepted in his *Poetics of Music*. Even so, in spite of the fact that the final objective of an artistic activity is to produce a work, the activity still remains a human one, and is thus imbued with human characteristics. The creator, whether he wants to or not, betrays himself through the spirit of his work, its atmosphere, and its artistic subject. In this sense every musical work possesses a profoundly tendentious character. It tends—inevitably, but with different nuances according to circumstances and to the human subjects who contemplate it— toward the humanization and ennoblement of man, or toward the opposite.

One could say that purely technical concepts of music have nothing to do with ethics, which could, perhaps, be true. But even mathematicism in music, the "pure cerebrality" of constructivist processes, has been built on some "ethics" and has called upon a true one. This may be regarded as a significant indication that in art one does not depart so easily from the human element. There have also been a whole series of compositions that have acted upon the listener in a generally enervating and depressing manner, hence in an extramusical way. As Gisèle Brelet remarked, atonality, for example, deserved at the outset to be called "the technique of anguish and despair." Atonality, destroyer of tonality (that symbol of equilibrium, health, and serenity), seemed to be truly pathological. Even if atonality could prove the depth and the intensity of its expressive powers, it was mainly by appealing to the gloomy and morbid side of the human soul, as the themes from Schönberg's *Pierrot Lunaire* and *Erwartung* as well as Berg's *Wozzeck* and *Lulu* indicate.[40]

From a purely aesthetic perspective, the musical work certainly has only itself as an objective. It is subject only to the law of aesthetics, to the intrinsic laws of music. But from an ethical and sociological perspective, the musical work enters into a relationship with the very goal and good of man and humanity. Thus it can be legitimately judged in this regard, although its human and moral character shoud remain a spontaneous product of the

---

[40]See Gisèle Brelet, "Serijelna muzika" (Musique sérielle), *Zvuk*, LXI (1963) 1-2.

creator's spirit rather than a specific response to an ethical imperative. To neglect this perspective would be to cut the work of art from its natural links with the life of a person and of a society, and to forgo understanding it in its *total* meaning and significance. What matters most in the quality of an art and a musical work is therefore not only their artistic value, but also their *spirit*, which depends on that of their creator. And it is this very simple but essential fact that sometimes seems to be forgotten by the contemporary composer. Nevertheless, the composer is a man: "nonartistic motives fatally precede and accompany his effort ... He belongs to a social group whose beliefs and traditions cannot exist at his side without touching or impregnating him, even if they have nothing directly to do with art."[41] What largely characterizes some contemporary composers, especially avant-garde composers, is precisely this lack of perspective on the totality, of the whole picture, of this wisdom of the human objectives belonging to art, which can only be authentically conceived as the integrating objectives of the human being.[42]

The composer of today lives in an age of specialization and technicalization. But given this state of affairs, composers will also have to surpass it. The technique of composition today often goes further than the power of the musical thought itself, further than the very substance of the work, and sometimes occupies too exclusively the attention of the composer who is more interested in *how* he will compose than in *what* he has to say. Too much technique is applied to the music. Music is also technicalized by the procedures used in its reproduction; not without consequences for musical performance and interpretation. There unquestionably exists a certain "imperialism" of the technical element, under its various forms and meanings. "Generally speaking, one could say that the flood of mechanical music necessarily modifies the listener's attitude toward the art of music ... The mechanization of art dehumanizes it and

---

[41]Maurice Nédoncelle, *Introduction à l'esthétique* (Paris: P.U.F., 1960) 7.
[42]See Jacques Maritain, *La responsabilité de l'artiste* (Paris: Fayard, 1961) 13-40.

replaces it with something else, which can abound in qualities of all sorts, but which is only a phantom of a real art."[43]

Moreover, the present great diffusion of music in developed countries has led to a sort of musical "satiety" or "inflation" while producing at the same time "a lassitude from which music probably suffers, rather than benefits."[44]

A certain complexity of expression can be added to this over-abundance of the technical element as an explanation of why musical works are inaccessible to a vast audience. This inaccessibility likewise stems partially from the absence of predominant, clearly audible constructive elements: first, from the absence of melody (in favor of which Stravinsky pleaded in his time, at least theoretically) as well as from the breakdown of tonality, without the substitution of other equally important elements. This state of affairs arises also from a certain formalism that regards music as an autonomous play of sounds or as sonorous "architecture," and not as an art capable of expressing anything extramusical. A good part of contemporary music has become considerably alienated from authentic expressive tendencies; it views sound only as sound itself, and sometimes even tries to abandon that aspect. Expressive music, however, has always been an area where communion between the public and the composer were likely to take place. Formerly, expressive music seemed "natural" to both listeners and musicians. Today, however, expression is frequently considered an aesthetic impurity. What seems even more serious, on an artistic and aesthetic level, is the relegation to a secondary place of a perceptible and audible order, and the substitution of a conceptual, extramusical order—for example, numerical order—which is impervious to auditory perception; something to which the serial technique has already led. Composers whose works lean in this direction are mainly preoccupied with the fascination of abstract combinations, rather than with the transmission of a truly musical content to their listeners. It is not surprising, therefore, that the genuine

---

[43]Etienne Gilson, *La société de masse et sa culture*, 63-64.
[44]*Ibid.*, 59.

dialogue between composer and the public has virtually stopped, since the interest of those constructions is not audibly perceptible to the public.[45] There is a strong tendency to abandon almost everything that music traditionally meant in order to make it different. And in doing this, as soon as one encounters the absurd, the question of sense is posed again, quite logically. Finally, we must add to the negative balance of contemporary music this dehumanization, already mentioned, which manifests itself in the various ways; a dehumanization which, aside from some possible purely technical or experimental interest, offers an example of distortion and deformation affecting the human being himself.

In the majority of contemporary tendencies, we have to distinguish clearly between authentic and valid particularities of new techniques, experiences, and researches, and the aberrations of principle and matter, always possible, of which music history offers numerous examples and to which our age is not immune either. We cannot refrain from considering that in these aberrations a certain totalitarianism and a certain nihilism are expressed, and these are two consequences of the collapse of an authentic scale of values. In music, as elsewhere,[46] we can see a dogmatization of half-truths and partial truths, be they of long standing or newly risen, rather than the search for union, for an integration into the hierarchy of real values, including ethical and human values. Much avant-garde music offers the image of an absolutization of relative values and of a relativization of those values that the traditional *musica humana* considered as absolute.

On the other hand, if it is unfortunate to proclaim outmoded things as eternal, it is also vexatious to try to accomplish the acceptance of any fresh innovations as supreme values. It is quite easy to say, by playing with words, that everything people do is human, in order to make acceptable everything some dare

---

[45]See Jacques Chailley, *40,000 ans de musique,* 146-147.

[46]See Igor A. Caruso, *Psicanalisi e sintesi dell'esistenza* (Torino: Marietti, 1953) 13. Translated from the German.

to do with and to music today. What seems surprising, however, is the facility with which so many people, musicians included, let themselves be captivated by sophisms, the only effect of which lies in their ability to obscure essential truths.

For the contemporary composer, an important means of professional and artistic affirmation is undoubtedly to innovate, to make progress in a musical world; but that has become very difficult. That is why the composer sometimes writes for a narrow circle of connoisseurs rather than for a large audience. A music critic could write quite openly: "We must build ivory towers. We must once more form small groups of the initiate who thrive on over-refined intellectual problems . . . I see among European youth a few creative musicians who have recognised that a highly exclusive experience of music is indispensable to the evolution of a culture."[47]

It happens quite frequently, under these conditions, that many contemporary compositions—especially those of some avant-garde trends—are more important or interesting to their composers themselves than they are aesthetically agreeable to the majority of listeners.

Some avant-garde music today does not fulfill a definite social function, as art music generally did in the past. Sociologically, one hardly knows why and for what such music is written. In older times the public was not always interested in musical innovations, which were destined nevertheless for a great later success. In our times, however, one occasionally has the impression that some avant-garde music could very well be dispensed with; not only the general public, but also the public initiated into traditional musical culture seems to have no need for it. Obviously, these remarks do not concern all modern music, but only certain trends within it. The general trends of cultural and social evolution today lead, for their part, toward a conception of music as a humanistic art, in the integral sense of the word. The trends of much avant-garde music lead, however, toward a particular artistic universe that recognizes only its own

---

[47]Hans Heinz Stuckenschmidt, quoted in Walter Wiora, *The Four Ages of Music*, 167.

needs and secludes itself within strictly professional preoccupations. It is true, this situation hardly represents a problem for the public, but rather for the composer, who is caught between trying to meet the needs of the former and his wish to follow some current trends of his profession.

This situation is analogous to that at the dawn of the Hellenistic era, when Greek music incorporated a whole series of refinements, became an elaborate technique for the exclusive enjoyment of specialists (and which listeners and amateurs followed with great difficulty), and toward which criticisms of corrupt taste were leveled from several directions.

That the majority of the contemporary avant-garde music would have, in the whole world, a minority public is a foregone conclusion. That its authors might generally consider this public insufficient is also understandable. And that they find themselves in a paradoxical situation is absolutely true. This situation stems from the desire to reach a larger public, while pursuing ends that are for the most part foreign to it. The public has never been interested in such technical problems as preoccupy the composer; it should not surprise us that it has no such interest today. The public senses that many modern composers wish to serve, first and foremost, not the public, but art (or sometimes a pseudoart) with its technical progress, its new conquests, and its own demands, whereas the traditional composer served both his art and his public at the same time.

The traditional composer observed values inherited from his musical ancestry and considered them more or less untouchable; he changed them only a little, or bit by bit. The contemporary composer, on the contrary, often thinks that he himself can reverse everything, embody and create the highest values, and, as far as he is concerned, decide about them infallibly. For Bach, as for his predecessors, the purpose of music was to glorify God and to serve man. Otherwise, he considered it "a devillish *Geplerr* and *Geleyer.*"[48] But for certain contemporary musicians, the purpose of music resides only in establishing order in

---

[48]Quoted in Albert Schweitzer, *J. S. Bach, le musicien-poète* (Lausanne: Ed. Foetisch, 1958) 6th ed., 102.

temporal succession, or in a formal organization of the raw material of sound, or again in an ordered relationship between man and duration. Until the nineteenth century, to a greater or lesser extent all music was functional (in the human and social sense of the word). Today its disfunctionalization is often considered necessary for its emancipation. The composer, who formerly acknowledged inherited artistic values, is transformed into a being who constructs and defines new ones, while breaking with those of the past.

This subjectivism also manifests itself in research and in the choice of expressive traits that are of secondary significance, or even accidental or extravagant, that have become independent, and that are erected as absolute. In these procedures and this behavior (which does not concern all of today's composers) some psychologists have seen symptoms of a neurotic attitude characterized precisely, among other things, by making the relative absolute, and the absolute, relative.[49] And as Gisèle Brelet remarked, now that no system of aesthetics manages to prevail or to pull the composer away from his insatiable desire for research; now that each composer wishes to ask and resolve for himself the problems of musical thought (which the classics held as solved before creating their works, and whose traditional solution they accepted, with little modification)[50]—it is especially important for contemporary music to find again its universality and its place in the authentic hierarchy of human values.

It has been said that humanizing and dehumanizing movements are inseparable from human life and social life; even more, that they coexist simultaneously. This is only one aspect of the fact that, throughout human history, all authentic achievements are accompanied by losses, or by contrary and parasitic movements. Thus the legitimate and authentic "specialization" of contemporary music; the achievements of its complete autonomy in relation to other artistic domains (for which

---

[49]See Igor A. Caruso, *Psicanalisi e sintesi dell'esistenza*, 1-3.

[50]See Gisèle Brelet, *Chances de la musique atonale* (Alexandria, Ed. du Scarabée, 1947) 4.

Hanslick already fought when he opposed the Hegelian principle of the unity of all the arts); its emancipation from the diverse social functions which it had assumed for centuries; and the immense growth in self-awareness of the musician, who has become more reflective and lucid than ever before, have unfortunately been accompanied by the more or less complete disregard for the fact that music has no raison d'être in and of itself. It does not create itself, and it is not played in order to satisfy one knows what internal need of its intrinsic laws and their evolution. As a human creation, music must serve man, in the most noble sense of the word 'serve.' Certainly this means it must serve in many ways, while being respected and served itself. And it must serve not only in those musical genres of a somewhat problematical nature so prevalent today, which succeed in reaching (at the price of compromise, as did, once, a certain genre of opera) the largest audience, especially young people; but also, and primarily, in accordance with its highest possibilities and hopes. We could say, with Adorno, that "the question of truth and non-truth in music is closely linked to that of the relationship between its two spheres: serious music, and music which is wrongly called light—of an inferior sphere. This division probably had its sources in the division of social work and in the most archaic conditions of class, which arranged the choice [of music] for rulers and [its] use by the populace; cultural differences have been inserted into aesthetic difference. Little by little the division hardened, solidified and finally was institutionalized, and found its echo in the opinion of listeners who, as it seems, insist on the one or the other ... A critical sociology of music will have to explore in detail why light music today (differently from a hundred years ago) is bad, without exception—is inevitably bad ... Without knowing it, the masses, who are submerged in it, relish the level to which they are reduced. The proximity to which light music pushes them offends human dignity as well as aesthetic distance."[51]

Mistress of silence and contemplation, music is called, on the

---

[51]Theodor W. Adorno, "Sociologie de la musique," *Musique en jeu* II (1971) 12.

contrary, to bring us to ourselves or rather, to contribute to this. According to Gisèle Brelet, it is invited to help us realize within ourselves that inner denouement, that profound peace, and that perfect detachment that allows us to hear the pure voice of the spirit. Musical asceticism should predispose toward higher accomplishments of the spiritual life, by guiding us to the threshold of authentic contemplation; and, *mutatis mutandis*, the soul of the musician should strive to resemble that of the contemplative—a soul purified and made peaceful, which is fulfilled in solitude far from earthly tumult, finds again its lightness and the ingenuity of its vision and discovers in the nakedness of total renunciation the fullness of supreme possession.[52]

In a time of tremendous technological development such as ours, which calls imperatively for a "supplement of soul" (Henri Bergson), music has its own mission: to contribute to the inner equilibrium of contemporary man and, without becoming utilitarian, to deliver to each one the purity and the joy of a higher aesthetic delectation of which he has, perhaps without knowing it, a greater need than ever before. Contemporary man needs to find in music a real joy and quietude, consciously and actively received, not an excitation and daily narcotic, which blunts and enervates. Music should not be an idol devouring human substance, but a universe of beauty and profound, enriching meaning. Its principal social and human mission is to contribute to the humanization and personalization of both society and man.

It could be said, perhaps, that today this is too much to ask of it in as much as a great part of contemporary music appears to succumb to temptations that keep it from fulfilling such a lofty and elevated task. It has also been said that the truth is too difficult, too heavy in its totality for man in his weakness to carry. The same is true of the task that those who practice the art of music would assign themselves. Nevertheless, we must not forget that if one deprives oneself of higher delectations, one passes quickly

---

[52]Gisèle Brelet, "Art et Sagesse," *La Table ronde* CLXX (1962) 37.

to lower ones, inasmuch as man can not live without enjoyment. Although the task may be difficult, it is absolutely necessary that someone devote themselves to it. In raising questions concerning the relationship between art and ethics one always risks, it is true, setting the whole world against oneself . . . Nevertheless, if we see today a rush to the facile, it is because the serious and the difficult (as well as what passes for such) are partly responsible themselves for their poor reception by many listeners. Far from pleading about a musical purism (which is not, however, to be confounded with disembodied pettiness), music must remain, on the contrary, integrally human. Its problems today rejoin, in the end, the problems of contemporary man.

Without sharing the pessimism of A. Honegger, who believed, it seems, in the profound and definitive decadence of music—fearing it would leave us and begin to disappear, that it would disengage itself from its very destination, from that charm, those marvels, that solemnity that must surround artistic revelation—it is nevertheless tempting to think that "in music there are no longer infinite stretches of new territory open to conquest, that its expansions have come up against boundaries or must pass over these boundaries into neighboring realms of noise."[53]

At the same time we must understand that the problem of old and new, of tradition and originality, of past and future, is not the basic problem of music, as long as beyond this one there exists another fundamental problem, that of its human significance and mission, which reside in the ennobling of man. The question is not so much to know whether music can evolve further, but if it can continue on its way while remaining on a sufficiently elevated level. The basic problem does not reside so much in the purely artistic and technical side as on the human and spiritual side. If certain composers, in spite of the complete honesty of their artistic efforts, do not succeed in passing over the apparently insurmountable wall that blocks their way on an aesthetic and technical level, it is perhaps because the time approaches when they could be led, gradually, to change their

---

[53]Walter Wiora, *The Four Ages of Music*, 134.

perspective and to turn their attention to the essence of things. Then the musician will probably be able to overcome this rather distressing aspect of "specialization," which is customarily called—in other fields also—professional deformation.

In fact, it would be dangerous for composers to forget their essential responsibility to the spirit and the human function of their music and to forget the public at large, as it would be inadmissible for them to cease being faithful to the most profound imperatives of their art. Even the most appropriate utilization of every possible means of communication and information, even the application of the most general efforts to educate the public, even the most refined use of technical methods of rapprochement between the public and new music will be only a superficial and facile solution—or better, a half-solution—without the essential and substantial contribution of the composer on the level of the musical content and spirit of his creation. Let us say once again, with Arthur Lourié, that often "music, in its modern conception, has come to represent only a technique . . . But if the technique remains without substance, if it lacks musical material and reality, it would then be nothing but an illusion."[54] According to him, "not only contemporary aesthetics has suffered a spiritual bankruptcy, but the world in which we live has fallen into a cynicism without precedence . . . The most characteristic phenomenon of our times is that art always manifests itself under an aspect of evil and ugliness."[55] Nevertheless, "the fight for humanism is also the fight for music."[56] Thus, a completely genuine solution to the problem of the composer-public relationship cannot only be technical and imposed from without. It depends fundamentally on the use to which society (especially its most organized and competent sectors) will wish to put music as an integral element of the culture, but it also depends on the composer, who will have to

---

[54]Arthur Lourié, *Profanation et sanctification du Temps* (Paris: Desclée De Brouwer, 1966) 184.
[55]*Ibid.*, 185, 186.
[56]*Ibid.*, 189.

rediscover and recreate by himself, as much as possible, a new function for his art, placing the spirit and content of his works not at the periphery of the most profound and human preoccupations of contemporary man, but at their very center—and high enough.

With these considerations, however, we leave strictly sociological perspectives and approach broader horizons concerning the philosophy and aesthetics of music.

CONCLUSION

The facts and ideas presented in these pages allow us to open the way to some new perspectives for a sociology of music. Music has always had its points of social reference, and because of this, its social functions. The social functions of music evolve, diversify, and are transformed, reflecting different aspects according to the global societies from which they emerge. But certain social functions of music and certain conditionings maintain their essential character in diverse forms and modalities in many global societies. Thus, throughout music history, secular learned music has been directed primarily to a social minority, and this minority especially has most directly bene-fitted from it.

The social functions of music, which are imposed by a global society and more or less linked to it, to a given civilization, or to a historical era, demonstrate relevant *typological* laws. The social functions of music that show, on the contrary, a certain historical stability, thus expressing certain fundamental relationships extending beyond different global societies or historical eras, demonstrate *supertypological* laws. The social functions of music demonstrating typological laws presuppose, to a greater or lesser degree, social functions of music demonstrating super-typological laws, and are based upon them. The same is true, respectively, of social conditionings. The dependence of musical life on economic life exemplifies a supertypological law, while the commercialization of musical life in Europe from the seventeenth century on demonstrates an example of a typological law operating in one particular society.

The social functions and references of music derive from its social conditionings. Musical facts may be functional with respect to social reality as well as with respect to other musical facts. This functioning (functionality) concerns, respectively, sociohistorical and socioartistic conditionings. While the former have the greatest influence on musical activity in different times and places, the latter depend on a much freer play of circumstances, which may be spread across time and space. However, even if particular global societies do influence in a decisive way the evolution and transformation of the social functions of music, there is nothing to prove that every global society has created all of the musical art—all the works—which it needed or could need to satisfy the artistic demands of its social life. There is no absolutely determinant conditioning that automatically produces results on a musically artistic level according to the requirements crystallized within a global society. There is only a socially conditioning action that *permits* the musical activity to be expressed and to be realized in the society, according to the social functions possible within the given social context, through response to the "provocations" of the ambience, or that *favors* it in this direction. It always remains to be seen, however, what the character and the quality (especially on a purely artistic level) of these responses will be.

In responding to the requirements of a special social function, many musical works acquire characteristics, in their purely artistic quality, that better correspond to those social functions. In a general way, in their formations and transformations, the social functions of music will condition musical expression. We may observe this particularly in the formation and characteristics of different musical genres and various musical productions, or even in individual compositions; from work music or "magic" music to martial and military music, from music for dance, for entertainment, or for concerts, to music for religious purposes.

But certain musical works surpass, in a sense, the social functions imposed on them by a global society at a given

360

moment. They surpass them through their artistic quality (destined to survive particular social milieus or entire societies) and through their tendency toward autonomous evolution. This is manifested in the appearance of individual works, forms, and genres that, while subject to the conditionings of the times, free themselves from them to a considerable extent and are not wholly or partly "utilitarian" or functional. These works preserve a value and interest beyond their social functions of the time of their creation. Their social functions give way to other social functions or simply weaken and disappear before their aesthetic functions, which remain in the everchanging interplay and interaction of social and musical forces.

The least we can say is that there is a great deal of musical works and facts for which the precise social conditionings of their origins have not until now (no more within the limits of this work than in others) been demonstrated in detail or with certainty. In Part II of this book, however, it has been possible to establish a whole series of facts demonstrating the existence of these conditionings; joined with others, these facts would be susceptible to classification using a more detailed and subtle typification or typology. This would prove the interaction and the interpenetration of various social functions of music concerning typological and supertypological laws in more detailed way. The very existence of these facts confirms both the necessity for a sociological study of music and, thereby, the cogency of that point of view proposed in Part I, which points to the need for an autonomous elaboration of the sociology and social history of music.

CONTENTS OF THE BIBLIOGRAPHY

The Sociology of Art   363
Approaches to the Sociology of Music,
    Fundamental Works   367
Subject, Problems and Methods   373
Sociology of Music and Related Disciplines   377
Social Psychology of Music   382
Social History of Music   385
Social Functions of Music   391
Musical Public   400
Reception of Music. Musical Taste   404
Social Status and Role of Musicians   409
Musical Institutions   417
Music, Social Life and Culture   423
Music and Economics   434
Music and Technique   438
Music and the Mass Media   442
Musical Styles. Musical Genres   447
Music and Politics   453
Music and Ideologies   458
Music and Education   462
Music and the Arts   467
Tradition and Innovation   470
Acculturation in Music. Musical Sub-cultures   472

BIBLIOGRAPHY

SOCIOLOGY OF ART

ABRUZZESE, Alberto, *Arte e pubblico nell'età del capitalismo. Forme estetiche e società di massa*, Marsilio, Venezia 1973.

ADORNO, Theodor Wiesengrund, »Kunst- und Musiksoziologie,« in »Soziologische Exkurse,« *Frankfurter Beiträge zur Soziologie*, 1956, IV, pp. 93—105.

— »Thesen über Kunstsoziologie,« in *Ohne Leitbild*, Frankfurt/M. 1967.

ALBRECHT, Milton C., J. H. BARNETT and M. GRIFF, »Art as an Institution,« *American Sociological Review*, 1968, 33, pp. 383—397.

— *The Sociology of Art and Literature. A Reader*, Praeger, New York 1970.

ANTAL, F., *Florentine Painting and its Social Background*, Kegan Paul, London 1947.

BALDWIN, James A., »Mass Culture and the Creative Artist: Some Personal Ideas,« *Daedalus*, 1960, 89, pp. 373—376.

BALET, L., *Die Verbürgerlichung der deutschen Kunst, Literatur und Musik im 18. Jahrhundert*, Heitz, Leipzig—Strasbourg—Zurich 1936.

BARBU, Z., »Sociological Perspectives in Art and Literature,« in J. CREEDY, ed., *The Social Context of Art*, Tavistock, London 1970.

BARNETT, J. H., »Research Areas in the Sociology of Art,« *Sociology and Social Research*, 1958, XLII/6, pp. 401—405.

BARNETT, J. H., »The Sociology of Art,« in MERTON, BROOM and COTTRELL, eds., *Sociology Today*, Basic Books, New York 1958.

BASTIDE, Roger, »Les problèmes de la sociologie de l'art,« *Cahiers internationaux de sociologie*, 1948, IV, pp. 160—171.

BAXANDALL, Michael, *Painting and Experience in Fifteenth Century Italy: A Primer in the Social History of Pictorial Style*, Clarendon Press, 1972, pp. VIII+165.

BLASS, Joseph Herring, *Indeterminacy as a Factor in Scientific and Artistic Attitudes of the Twentieth Century*, Ph. D. Thesis (Humanities), Florida State University, 1968.

BLAUG, Mark, ed., *The Economics of the Arts*, Westview Press, London 1976, pp. 272.

BLAUKOPF, Kurt, ed., *The Phonogram in Cultural Communication*, Springer-Verlag, Wien—New York 1982, pp. 181.

BOURDIEU, Pierre, »Eléments d'une théorie sociologique de la perception artistique,« *Revue internationale des sciences sociales*, 1968, 20/4, pp. 640—644.

— *Sociologie de la perception artistique*, in *Les sciences humaines et l'oeuvre d'art*, Ed. La Connaissance, Bruxelles 1969 pp. 161—176.

CORVISIER, André, *Arts et sociétés dans l'Europe du XVIII* siècle*, P. U. F., Paris 1978, pp. 248.

DASNOY, H., »L'art et le public,« *La revue nouvelle*, 1958, 28/10, pp. 265—274.

DEINHARD, Hanna, *Meaning and Expression. Toward a Sociology of Art*, Beacon Press, Boston 1970, pp. 120.

DUVIGNAUD, Jean, »Problèmes de sociologie de la sociologie des arts,« *Cahiers internationaux de sociologie*, 1959, XXVI, pp. 137—148.

— *Sociologie du théâtre*, P. U. F., Paris 1965.

— *Sociologie de l'art*, Paris 1967.

EGBERT, Donald Drew, *Social Radicalism and the Arts: A Cultural History from the French Revolution to 1968*, Knopf, New York 1970.

ESCARPIT, Robert, *Le littéraire et le social. Eléments pour une sociologie de la littérature*, Flammarion, Paris 1970.

— *Sociologie de la littérature*, P. U. F., Paris 1958.

ETZKORN, K. Peter, »A Sociological Look at African Art,« in *The Traditional Artists in West African Societies*, Warren d'Azevedo, ed., Indiana University Press, Bloomington 1972.

— »Non-Rational Elements in the Sociology of Arts,« *Indian Sociological Bulletin*, 1966, 3/4, pp. 279—285.

FALLICO, Arturo B., *Art and Existentialism*, Prentice-Hall, Englewood Cliffs, N. J. 1962.

FINKELSTEIN, Sidney, *Art and Society*, International Publishers, New York 1947.

FRANCASTEL, Pierre, »Problèmes de la sociologie de l'art,« G. Gurvitch, ed., in *Traité de sociologie*, 2. vol., P. U. F., Paris 1960.

GAERTNER, J. A., »Art as the Function of an Audience,« *Daedalus*, 1955, LXXXVI/1, pp. 80—93.

GERSCHKOWITSCH, S., »Die Kunst und der Fortschritt in der Massenkommunikationstechnik,« *Kunst und Literatur*, 1971, XIX/1, pp. 45—59.

GOTSHALD, D. W., *Art and the Social Order*, University of Chicago Press, Chicago 1947.

GRANA, Cesar, *Fact and Symbol: Essays in the Sociology of Art and Literature*, Oxford University Press, New York 1971, pp. XII+212.

HARAP, Louis, *Social Roots of the Arts*, International Publishers, New York 1949.

HARRIS, Neil, *The Artist in American Society: The Formative Years 1790—1860*, Braziller, New York 1966.

HASKELL, Francis, *Patrons and Painters: A Study in the Relations between Italian Art and Society in the Age of the Baroque*, Knopf, New York 1963.

HATTERER, Lawrence J., *The Artist in Society: Problems and Treatment of the Creative Personality*, Grove, New York 1965.

HAUSER, Arnold, *The Social History of Arts*, 3 vols, Vintage Books, New York 1958. 1st ed. Routledge and K. Paul, London 1951.

HERBERT, Robert L., ed., *Modern Artists on Art*, Prentice-Hall, Englewood Cliffs (N. J.) 1968.

HERRING, Paul D. and James E. MILLER, Jr., *The Arts and the Public*, University of Chicago Press, Chicago 1967.

HERRMANN, Rolf-Dieter, *Der Künstler in der modernen Gesellschaft*, Athenäum, Frankfurt/M. 1971.

— »Über das gesellschaftliche Sein des Künstlers,« *Zeitschrift für Ästhetik und allgemeine Kunstwissenschaft*, 1968, 13, pp. 113—139.

HOKE, H. G., »'Gemeinschaft'-Musik,« in *Beiträge zur Musikwissenschaft*, 1960, 2, 3/4, pp. 104—109.

HONIGSHEIM, Paul, »Soziologie der Kunst, Musik und Literatur,« in *Die Lehre von der Gesellschaft. Ein Lehrbuch der Soziologie*, Stuttgart 1958, pp. 338—373.

HUACO, George A., *The Sociology of Film Art*, Basic Books, New York 1965.

KARBUSICKY, Vladimir, »L'interaction réalité-œuvre d'art-société,« *Revue internationale des sciences sociales*, 1968, XX/4, pp. 698—711.

KAVOLIS, Vytautas, *Artistic Expression: A Sociological Analysis*, Cornell University Press, Ithaca (N. Y.) 1968.

KEMPERS, P. B., »Soziale und asoziale Kunst,« in *Internationaler Musikkongreß Wien 1952 — Bericht*, Vienna 1953.

KNEIF, Tibor, »Kunst- und Musiksoziologie,« in *Soziologische Exkurse nach Vorträgen und Diskussionen*, Frankfurt/M. 1956, pp. 93—105.

KNEPLER, Georg, *Über Wechselbeziehungen der Künste in der Massenkommunikation*, Hauptkommission Musikwissenschaft des Verbandes Deutscher Komponisten und Musikwissenschaftler, Berlin 1970, pp. 133—135.

LALO, Charles, *L'art et la vie sociale*, Doin, Paris 1921.

LENK, K., »Zur Methodik der Kunstsoziologie,« *Kölner Zeitschrift für Soziologie und Sozialpsychologie*, 1961, XIII/3, pp. 413—425.

LEWIS, G. H., *Side-Saddle on the Golden Calf: Social Structure and Popular Culture in America*, Goodyear Publishing, Pacific Palisades (California) 1972.

— »The Sociology of Popular Culture«, *Current Sociology*, 1978, 26/3, pp. 1—160.

— »Mass, Popular, Folk and Elite Cultures,« *Media Asia*, 1979, 6/1, pp. 34—52.

MARTIN, Frank, »Le rôle de l'art dans la Société d'aujourd'hui«, *Schweizerische Musikzeitung*, 1976, 5, pp. 329—344.

MARTIN, F. David, »The Sociological Imperative of Stylistic Development,« *The Bucknell Review*, Lewisburg (Penn.) 1963, XI/4, pp. 54—80.

MERRILL, Francis E., »Art and the Self,« *Sociology and Social Research*, 1968, 52, pp. 185—194.

MERSMANN, Hans, *Freiheit und Bindung im künstlerischen Schaffen — Ein Vortrag*, Kassel 1960.

MIERENDORF, M., »Über den gegenwärtigen Stand der Kunstsoziologie in Deutschland,« *Kölner Zeitschrift für Soziologie und Sozialpsychologie*, 1957, IX/3, pp. 397—412.

MIERENDORF, M., and H. TOST, *Einführung in die Kunstsoziologie*, Cologne-Opladen 1957.

MUKARJEE, Radhakamal, *The Social Function of Art*, Philosophical Library, New York 1954.

MÜLLER-FREIENFELS, R., »Künstlertum und Kunstpublikum,« *Kölner Vierteljahrshefte für Soziologie*, 1931/1932, 10, pp. 67—86.

NEWTON, E., »Art as Communication,« *The British Journal of Aesthetics*, London 1961, I/2, pp. 71—85.

NKETIA, J. H. Kwabena, »The Arts in Traditional Society,« *Ghana News*, Embassy of Ghana, Washington (D. C.) 1970, 2/5, pp. 4—6.

OSBORNE, Harold, »Primitive Art and Society,« *The British Journal of Aesthetics*, 1974, 14/4, pp. 290—306.

PAREYSON, Luigi, »Personalità e socialità dell'arte,« *Rivista di Estetica*, Torino 1959, IV/2, pp. 197—218.

SCHÜCKING, L. L., *The Sociology of Literary Taste*, Routledge & Kegan Paul, London 1950.

SEDLMAYR, H., *Die Revolution der modernen Kunst*, Rowohlt, Hamburg 1955.

SILBERMANN, Alphons, *Empirische Kunstsoziologie. Eine Einführung mit kommentierter Bibliographie*, F. Enke Verlag, Stuttgart 1973.

— »Situation et vocation de la sociologie de l'art,« *Revue internationale des sciences sociales*, 1968, 20/4, pp. 617—639.

SOURIAU, Etienne, »L'art et la vie sociale,« *Cahiers internationaux de sociologie*, 1948, 5, pp. 66—96.

— »L'insertion temporelle de l'œuvre d'art,« *Journal de psychologie*, 1951, 1—2, pp. 38—62.

TAINE, Hyppolite, *Lectures on Art*, Holt, New York 1883.

TOMARS, Adolph Siegfried, *Introduction to the Sociology of Art*, Mexico City 1940.

TOOZE, R., and B. PERHAM-KRONE, *Literature and Music as Resources for Social Studies*, Prentice-Hall, Englewood Cliffs (N. J.) 1955.

VRIESEN, G., »Die Frau in der Kunst,« in *Die Frau in unserer Zeit*, Stalling, Hamburg 1954.

BIBLIOGRAPHY

WEBER, A., *Kulturgeschichte als Kultursoziologie*, Piper, Munich 1950.

WILSON, Robert N., *The Arts in Society*, Prentice-Hall, Englewood Cliffs (N. J.) 1964.

— *Man made Plain: The Poet in Contemporary Society*, Howard Allen, Cleveland 1958.

APPROACHES TO THE SOCIOLOGY OF MUSIC. FUNDAMENTAL WORKS

ADORNO, Theodor Wiesengrund, *Einleitung in die Musiksoziologie* — *Zwölf theoretische Vorlesungen*, Suhrkamp Verlag, Frankfurt/M. 1962; Rowohlt, Frankfurt/M. 1968, pp. 253.

— »Zur gesellschaftlichen Lage der Musik,« *Zeitschrift für Sozialforschung*, 1932, 1, pp. 102—124 and 356—378.

— «Ideen zur Musiksoziologie,« *Schweizer Monatshefte*, 1958, 38, pp. 679— —691; in *Klangfiguren* — *Musikalische Schriften*, 1959, 1, pp. 9—31.

— *Klangfiguren* — *Musikalische Schriften, I*, Berlin-Frankfurt/M. 1959.

ADORNO, Theodor W., *Introduction to the Sociology of Music*, Seabury Press, New York 1976.

— »Sociologie de la musique«, *Musique en jeu*, Seuil, 1971, 2, pp. 5—14.

ALLEN, Warren Dwight, *Our Marching Civilization: An Introduction to the Study of Music and Society*, Stanford 1943.

BECKER, Howard, ed., *Whose Music? A Sociology of Musical Languages*, Transaction Books, New Brunswick — London 1977, pp. XIV-300.

BELLAIGUE, Camille, »La musique au point de vue sociologique«, in *Etudes musicales*, Delagrave, Paris 1898.

— »Die Musik vom soziologischen Standpunkt,« *Allgemeine Musik-Zeitung*, 1901, 28, pp. 506, 523—525, 543—545, 559—561, 579—581, 595—597, 611—613, 627—629 and 651—653.

BELVIANES, Marcel, *Sociologie de la musique*, Payot, Paris 1951.

BERTEN, W., »Musikpolitik — Musiksoziologie — Musikdramaturgie. Begriffsbestimmungen und Zielsetzungen,« in *Festschrift für P. Raabe*, 1942, pp. 52ff.

BLAUKOPF, Kurt, »Der Gegenstand musiksoziologischer Forschung,« *Musik und Bildung*, 1972, IV/2, pp. 67—68.

— »Musiksoziologie — Bindung und Freiheit bei der Wahl von Tonsystemen,« in *Soziologie und Leben* — *Die Soziologische Dimension der Fachwissenschaft*, Tübingen 1952, pp. 237—257.

— *Musiksoziologie: Eine Einführung in die Grundbegriffe mit besonderer Berücksichtigung der Soziologie der Tonsysteme*, Zollikopfer, St. Gallen 1950; G. Kiepenheur Vienna — Cologne 1950; 2nd ed.: A. Niggli, Niederteufen 1972.

— *Werktreue und Bearbeitung. Zur Soziologie der Integrität des musikalischen Kunstwerks*, G. Braun, Karlsruhe 1968, pp. 44.

BLAUKOPF, Kurt, »Tonsysteme und ihre gesellschaftliche Geltung in Max Webers Musiksoziologie,« *The International Review of Music Aesthetics and Sociology*, 1970, 1/2, pp. 159—168.

— *Musik im Wandel der Gesellschaft*, Piper, München—Zürich 1982, pp. 383.

BLOMSTER, W. V., "Sociology of Music: Adorno and Beyond," *Telos*, 1976, 28, pp. 81-112.

BORRIS, Siegfried, »Soziologische Musikbetrachtung — Vom Wesen der Musik,« in *Das Musikleben*, 1950, 3, pp. 5—9.

BUCHHOFER, Bernd, Jürgen FRIEDRICHS, and Harmut LÜDTKE, *Musik und Sozialstruktur. Theoretische Rahmenstudie und Forschungspläne*, Arno Volk Verlag-Hans Gerig KG, Cologne 1974.

CAPPUCCIO, G., *L'arte della Musica e la Sociologia*, Siracuse 1895.

DAHLHAUS, Carl, "Das musikalische Kuntswerk als Gegenstand der Soziologie," *International Review of the Aesthetics and Sociology of Music*, 1974, V/1, pp. 11-24.

ELSCHEK, Oskár, »Hudba — človek — spoločnost,« *Slovenska hudba*, 1971, XV/9—10, pp. 348—355.

ELSTE, M., *Verzeichnis deutschsprachiger Musiksoziologie* (Teil A und B, 1848—1973), Wagner, Hamburg 1975.

ENGEL, Hans, »Musik, Gesellschaft, Gemeinschaft,« *Zeitschrift für Musikwissenschaft*, 1935, 17, pp. 175—185.

— »Grundlegung einer Musiksoziologie,« in *Der Musik-Almanach*, Munich 1948, pp. 253—296.

— *Musik und Gesellschaft — Bausteine zu einer Musiksoziologie*, M. Hesse, Berlin-Halensee 1960.

— »Soziologie der Musik,« in *MGG*, Vol. 12, pp. 948—967.

— »Music and Society,« in *International Encyclopedia of the Social Sciences*, 1968, X, pp. 566—575.

ETZKORN, K. Peter, »Georg Simmel and the Sociology of Music,« *Social Forces*, 1964, 43/1, pp. 101—107.

— *Music and Society; The Later Writings of Paul Honigsheim*, John Wiley and Sons, New York 1973.

— *Sociologists and Music*. in P. Etzkorn, ed., *Music and Society. Tne later Writings of Paul Honigsheim*, John Wiley and Sons, New York—London—Sydney—Toronto 1973, pp. 3—40.

— »On Music, Social Structure and Sociology«, *International Review of the Aesthetics and Sociology of Music*, 1974, V/1, pp. 43—51.

FELLERER, Karl Gustav, *Soziologie der Kirchenmusik — Materialen zur Musik und Religionssoziologie*, Schriften zur Kunstsoziologie und Massenkommunikation, 9, Westdeutscher Verlag, Cologne-Opladen 1963

FUKAČ, Jiři, Ladislav MOKRY and Vladimir KARBUSICKY, *Die Musiksoziologie in der Tschechoslowakei*, Tschechoslowakisches Musikinformationszentrum, Prague 1967.

HANSEN, B., »Soziologie der Musik,« in *Riemann Lexikon*, 12.

HASELAUER, Elisabeth, *Handbuch der Musiksoziologie*, Hermann Böhlaus, Wien—Köln—Graz 1980, pp. 232.

HÖCKNER, H., »Musik und Gemeinschaft,« in *Die Musikantengilde*, 1924; in *Deutsche Musikpflege*, Frankfurt/M. 1925, pp. 1—7.

HONIGSHEIM, Paul, »Musik und Gesellschaft«, in *Kunst und Technik*, Volksverband der Bücherfreunde, Wegweiser-Verlag, Berlin 1930.

— »Musikformen und Gesellschaftsformen,« in *Die Einheit der Sozialwissenschaften*, W. Bernsdorff and G. Eisermann, eds., Enke Verlag, Stuttgart 1955, pp. 214-225.

— »Musiksoziologie,« in *Handwörterbuch der Sozialwissenschaften*, VII, 1961, pp. 485-494.

— »Soziologie der Kunst, Musik und Literatur,« in *Die Lehre von der Gesellschaft — Ein Lehrbuch der Soziologie*, G. Eisermann, ed., Enke Verlag, Stuttgart 1958, pp. 338—373.

JAGER, Hugo de, »Enige beschouwingen over de muzieksociologie van Paul Honigsheim,« *Mens en Maatschappij*, 1961, 36/5, pp. 394—399.

JARDANYI, P., »Music in Modern Society,« *The New Hungarian Quarterly*, 1964, V/13, pp. 162—167.

JELINEK, E., F. ZELLWECKER and W. ZOBL, *Materialien zur Musiksoziologie*, Vienna-Munich 1972.

JÖDE, F., »Musik und Gesellschaft,« *Musik und Gesellschaft*, 1930/1931, pp. 1—3.

KALISCH, Volker, »Zur Rezeption der Max Weberschen Musiksoziologie aus musiksoziologischer Sicht,« *International Review of the Aesthetics and Sociology of Music*, 1981, 12/2, pp. 165—180.

KARBUSICKY, Vladimir, "Zur empirisch-soziologischen Musikforschung," in *Bieträge zur Musikwissenschaft*, Berlin, 1966, 8/3-4, pp. 215-240.

— *Empirische Musiksoziologie. Erscheinungsformen, Theorie und Philosophie des Bezugs »Musik-Gesellschaft,«* Breitkopf und Härtel, Wiesbaden 1975.

— *Significato antidogmatico e antiideologico della sociologia empirica della musica*, in *La sociologia della musica*, EDT, Torino 1980, pp. 139—148.

— *Alcuni problemi metodologici della sociologia empirica della musica*, in *La sociologia della musica*, EDT, Torino 1980, pp. 149—154.

KISIELEWSKI, Stefan and Boguslaw SCHÄFFER, *Socjologia muzyki wspolczesnej*, Polskie Wydawnictwo Muzyczne, Cracow 1971, pp. 40.

KLÜPPELHOLZ, Werner, »Zur Soziologie der neuen Musik«, *International Review of the Aesthetics and Sociology of Music,* 1979, 10/1, pp. 73—87.

KNEIF, Tibor, »Gegenwartsfragen der Musiksoziologie,« *Acta musicologica,* 1966, XXXVIII/2—4, pp. 72—118.

— »Kunst und Musiksoziologie,« in *Soziologische Exkurse nach Vorträgen und Diskussionen,* Frankfurt/M. 1956, pp. 93—105.

— »Gegenwartsfragen der Musiksoziologie,« *Acta musicologica,* 1966, XXXVIII/2—4, pp. 72—118.

— »Zeichen und Gleichnis. Über zwei Anschauungsmodelle der Musiksoziologie, *Neue Zeitschrift für Musik,* 1968, CXXIX, pp. 444-446.

— »Musiksoziologie,« *Melos,* 1971, XXXVIII/12, pp. 529—530.

— *»Musiksoziologie,«* Gerig, Cologne 1971, pp. 152.

— *Musiksoziologie,* in *Einführung in die systematische Musikwissenschaft,* ed. C. Dahlhaus, Gerig, Cologne 1971.

KNEIF, Tibor, ed., *Texte zur Musiksoziologie,* Volk-Gerig, Cologne 1975

KUHN, Dieter, *Musik und Gesellschaft,* Tsennas, Bad Homburg 1971, pp. 86.

KUNST, Jaap, *Some Sociological Aspects of Music. Lectures on the History and Art of Music,* The Louis Charles Elson Memorial Lectures at the Library of Congress, Washington 1958; De Capo Press, New York 1968, pp. 139—165.

LAUNSPACH, J. A., »Muzieksociologische Notities,« in *Mens en Maatschapij,* 1964, 39/2, pp. 81—89.

LE BRAS, G., »Sur la sociologie de la musique sacrée,« *Archives de sociologie des religions,* 1963, VIII/16, pp. 139—140.

LESURE, François, *Musik und Gesellschaft im Bild,* Bärenreiter, Kassel-Basle 1966.

— »Pour une sociologie historique des faits musicaux, in *International Musicological Society — Report of the Eighth Congress, New York 1961,* Kassel-Basle-London-New York 1961, Vol. 1, pp. 333—346.

— »Sociologia della musica,« *La Musica,* 1966, IV/1, pp. 425—428.

— *Musica e società,* Istituto editoriale italiano, Milan 1966.

— *Music and Art in Society,* Pennsylvania State University Press, Pittsburgh 1968, pp. 300.

LEVY, Ernest, *Des rapports entre la musique et la société,* La Baconnière, Neuchâtel — Payot, Paris, 1979, pp. 68.

LING, Jan, »Två musikprojekt i Göteborg,« *Nutida musik,* 1968/1969, XII/1, pp. 25—28.

— »Music-sociological projects in Gothenburg,« *The International Review of Music Aesthetics and Sociology,* 1971, II/1, pp. 119—130.

BIBLIOGRAPHY

LUNACZARSKI, A. W., *Woprosy sociologii muzyki*, Moscow 1927.

MAHLING, Christoph-Hellmut, »Soziologie der Musik und musikalische Sozialgeschichte,« *International Review of Music Aesthetics and Sociology*, 1970, I/1, pp. 92—94.

MANNHEIM, Karl, »Musik und Gesellschaft,« in *Arbeitsblätter für soziale Musikpflege und Musikpolitik*, Wolfenbüttel-Mainz 1930/1931.

MARK, Desmond, »John H. Mueller und sein Beitrag zur Musiksoziologie,« *International Review of the Aesthetics and Sociology of Music*, 1976, VII/2, pp. 185—203.

MELLERS, Wilfrid H., »Music and Society Now,« in *Music and Western Man*, London 1958, pp. 312—317.

MERSMANN, Hans, »Soziologie als Hilfswissenschaft der Musikgeschichte,« *Archiv für Musikwissenschaft*, 1953, X, 1, pp. 1—15.

MEYER, Ernst H., *Musik im Zeitgeschehen. Grundprobleme der Musiksoziologie*, Henschel, Berlin 1952.

MOKRÝ, Ladislav, »Otázky hudebnì sociologie,« *Hudebnì věda*, 1962, pp. 2—4.

MOLNÁR, A., »A zene szociológiajához,« *Valóság*, 1961, 4/6, pp. 65—70.

MOSER, Hans J., »Zuständigkeitsgrenzen der Musiksoziologie,« in *Festschrift Hans Engel zum siebzigsten Geburtstag*, Kassel 1964, pp. 245—249.

OEHLMANN, Werner, »Musik und Gesellschaft,« *Musica*. 1949, 3/5, pp. 161-164.

OFFER, John, »An Examination of Spencer's Sociology of Music and Its Impact on Music Historiography in Britain,« *International Review of the Aesthetics and Sociology of Music*, 1983, 14/1, pp. 33—52.

PIERSIG, J., *Beiträge zu einer Rechtssoziologie der Kirchenmusik*, Bosse, Regensburg 1972.

PISK, P. A., »Zur Soziologie der Musik,« in *Kampf*, Vienna 1925, 18/5, pp. 184—187.

PORENA, Boris, *Musica/Società*, Einaudi, Torino 1975, pp. 223.

RAMON Y RIVERA, L. F., »Musica y sociedad,« *Revista nacional de cultura*, 1959, XXI/135, pp. 113—117.

REICH, Willi, »Musik und Gesellschaft heute,« *Melos*, 1971, XXXVIII/11, pp. 476—478.

REININGHAUS, F. Cristoph, J. H. TRABER, »Musik als Ware — Musik als Wahre. Zum politischen Hintergrund des musiksoziologischen Ansatzes von T. W. Adorno,« *Zeitschrift für Musiktheorie*, 1973, IV/1, pp. 7—14.

REINOLD, Helmut, »Die Bedeutung musiksoziologischen Denkens für die Musikgeschichte,« in *Festgabe zum fünfzigsten Geburtstag von K. G. Fellerer*, Cologne 1952.

RUMBELOW, Allan Stuart, *Music and Social Groups: An Interactionist Approach to the Sociology of Music*, Ph.D. Thesis (Musicology-Sociology), University of Minnesota, 1969, pp. 262.

371

BIBLIOGRAPHY

RUMMENHÖLLER, Peter, *Einführung in die Musiksoziologie*, Heinrichshofen, Wilhelmshaven 1978, pp. 280.

SALAZAR, A., *Musica y sociedad en el siglo XX. Ensayo de critica desde el punto de vista de su funcion social*, Mexico City 1939.

SCHUBERT, Giselher, »Aspekte der Bekkerschen Musiksoziologie,« *International Review of Music Aesthetics and Sociology*, 1970, I/2, pp. 179—186.

SAMKO, Jozef, *Hudba a hudobnost v spoločnosti*, K. Jaroň, Bratislava 1947.

SEEGER, Charles, *Music and Society. Some New World Evidence of their Relationship*, Washington 1953.

SERRAVEZZA, Antonio, ed., *La sociologia della musica*, Edizioni di Torino, Torino 1980, pp. 316.

— *Musica, filosofia e società in Th. W. Adorno*, Dedalo, Bari 1976, pp. 255.

SIEGMEISTER, Elie, *Music and Society*, Critics Group Press, New York 1938, Germ. transl. *Musik und Gesellschaft*, Dietz, Berlin 1948.

SIEGMUND-SCHULTZE, W., »Grundprobleme der Musikforschung — Musikwissenschaft als Gesellschaftswissenschaft,« in *Wissenschaftliche Zeitschrift der Martin-Luther-Universität Halle-Wittenberg*, 1960, IX/1, pp. 37—46.

— »Musikwissenschaft als Gesellschaftswissenschaft,« in *Deutsches Jahrbuch der Musikwissenschaft*, 1957, 2.

SILBERMANN, Alphons, *Introduction à une sociologie de la musique*, P. U. F., Paris 1955.

— »Max Webers musikalischer Exkurs — Die rationalen und soziologischen Grundlagen der Musik,« *Kölner Zeitschrift für Soziologie und Sozialpsychologie*, Sonderheft 7, Max Weber zum Gedächtnis — Materialien und Dokumente zur Bewertung von Werk und Persönlichkeit, Westdeutscher Verlag, Cologne-Opladen 1963, No 7, pp. 448—469.

— *Of Musical Thing*, Grahame, Sidney 1949, pp. 233.

— »Theoretische Stützpunkte der Musiksoziologie,« *Musik und Bildung*, 1972, IV/2, pp. 61—67.

SOCHOR, Arnold N., *Muzyka i obščestvo*, Znanie, Moscow 1972, pp. 48.

— *Die Entwicklung der Musiksoziologie in der Sowjetunion. Eine musiksoziologische Untersuchung*, Arno Volk Verlag, Cologne 1973, pp. 197.

STAHL, Henri H., »Constantin Brailoïu și sociologia vieții muzicale,« *Cercetari Muzicol*, 1970, II, pp. 37—49.

SUMIKAWA, Tomoko, »Ongaku — shakaigaku no hôhô,« *Ongaku-gaku*, 1974/ /1975, 20, pp. 84-97.
— »Der musiksoziologische Unfug,« *Österreichische Musikzeitschrift*, 1956, II.

SUPIČIĆ, Ivo, »Neki problemi sociologije muzike,« *Zvuk*, 1960, 39—40, pp. 433—439.

— *Elementi sociologije muzike*, JAZU, Zagreb 1964, pp. 160.

372

— »Problèmes de la sociologie musicale,« *Cahiers internationaux de sociologie*, 1964, XXXVII, pp. 119—129.

— »Umjetničko-historijska uvjetovanost u muzičkom stvaranju,« *Rad JAZU*, No. 337, Zagreb 1965, pp. 221—239.

— »Pour une sociologie de la musique,« *Revue d'esthétique*, 1966, 19/1, pp. 66—77.

— »Sociologija glasbe in muzikologija,« *Muzikološki zbornik*, Ljubljana 1966, 2, pp. 116—123.

— *Wstęp do socjologii muzyki*, Panstruove Wydawnictvo Naukove ,Warsaw 1969, pp. 184.

— »Instead of an Introductory Word,« *The International Review of Music Aesthetics and Sociology*, 1970, I/1, pp. 3—14.

— *Round table: Sociology in Music — Results and Perspectives of Current Research*, Bärenreiter/University of Ljubljana, Kassel-Ljubljana 1970, pp. 405—423.

— *Musique et société. Perspectives pour une sociologie de la musique*, Institute of Musicology — Academy of Music, Zagreb 1971, pp. 208.

TESSAROLO, Mariselda, *L'espressione musicale e le sue funzioni*, Giuffrè, Milano 1983, pp. XI-336.

VALLS, M., *Musica i societat*, Barcelona 1963.

VOICANA, Mircea, »Premisele sociologiei muzicii,« *Muzica*, 1974, XXIV/9, pp. 26-27.

WARD, Benjamin F., »The Muted Strain: Adorno's Approach to a Sociology of Music,« *Journal of the Indian Musicological Society*, March 1977, 8/1, pp. 22—45.

WEBER, Max, *Die rationalen und soziologischen Grundlagen der Musik*, Drei Masken Verlag, Munich 1921; reprint: Mohr, Tübingen 1972; Engl. transl. *The Rational and Social Foundations of Music*, Southern Illinois University Press, Carbondale 1958.

WEITZMAN, Ronald, »An Introduction to Adorno's Music and Social Criticism,« *Music and Letters*, 1971, LII/3, pp. 287—298.

WILLENER, Alfred, »Music and Sociology,« *Cultures*, 1973, I/1, pp. 233——249.

ZWEERS, W., »Muzikale differentiatie en sociale stratifikatie,« *Mens en Maatschappij*, 1964, 39/2, pp. 90—106.

SUBJECT, PROBLEMS AND METHODS

ADORNO, Theodor Wiesengrund, »Ideen zur Musiksoziologie,« *Schweizer Monatshefte*, 1958, 38, pp. 679—691; also in *Klangfiguren — Musikalische Schriften*, I, Berlin—Frankfurt/M. 1959, pp. 9—31.

— »Sociologie de la musique«, *Musique en jeu*, 1971, 2, pp. 7—15.

BIBLIOGRAPHY

BLAUKOPF, Kurt, »Der Gegenstand musiksoziologischer Forschung,« *Musik und Bildung*, 1972, IV/2, pp. 67—68.

— »Werktreue und Bearbeitung. Zur Soziologie der Integrität des musikalischen Kunstwerk,« in Schriftenreihe *Musik und Gesellschaft*, 3, Braun, Karlsruhe 1968, pp. 44.

BLOMSTER, W. V., »Sociology of Music: Adorno and Beyond,« *Telos*, 1976, 28, pp. 81—112.

BURDE, W., »Was ist eine musiksoziologische Tatsache?,« *Musik und Bildung*, 1972, 2, pp. 57—61.

CAPE, Safford, »Thèse et histoire, quelques réflexions à propos de l'ouvrage du Dr. Ernst Meyer,« *English Chamber Music«, Revue belge de musicologie*, 1948, II/1—2, pp. 31—37.

DADELSEN, Georg, »Die Vermischung musikalischer Gattungen als soziologisches Problem,« in *Bericht über den internationalen musikwissenschaftlichen Kongreß Kassel 1962*, Bärenreiter, Kassel 1963, pp. 23—25.

DAHLHAUS, Carl, »Soziologische Dechiffrierung von Musik. Zu Theodor W. Adornos Wagnerkritik,« *The International Review of Music Aesthetics and Sociology*, 1970, I/2, pp. 137—147.

DAUM, H., *Soziologie der Musik, Ansätze und Probleme*, Graz 1958.

EISLER, H., »Gesellschaftliche Grundfragen der modernen Musik,« *Aufbau*, 1948, 4, pp. 550—558.

ELSSNER, Mechthild, »Zu Fragen der Musiksoziologie,« *Wissenschaftliche Beiträge der Universität Halle*, Reihe G, Halle 1968, VIII/1, pp. 249—266.

ENGEL, Hans, »Grundlegung einer Musiksoziologie,« in *Der Musik-Almanach*, Munich 1948, pp. 253—296.

— »Grundprobleme der Musiksoziologie,« in *Bericht über den Internationalen Musikkongreß Wien 1952*, Vienna 1953, pp. 96—100.

— »Musiksoziologie mit Fragezeichen,« *Neue Zeitschrift für Musik*, 1957, 118, pp. 176—177.

— »Was ist eigentlich Musiksoziologie?,« *Das Musikleben*, 1955, 8, pp. 124—125.

FELLERER, Karl Gustav, »Soziologische Fragen um die religiöse und liturgische Musik,« in *Kirchenmusikalisches Jahrbuch*, LII, Cologne 1968, pp. 131—144.

FRIEDLÄNDER, Walther, »Musik und Gesellschaft — Probleme und Methoden der Musiksoziologie,« *Frankfurter Allgemeine Zeitung*, 1954, Nr. 100, p. 129.

— »Probleme und Methoden der Musiksoziologie,« *Das Musikleben*, 1954, 4, pp. 161—164.

HONIGSHEIM, Paul, »Musikformen und Gesellschaftsformen,« in *Die Einheit der Sozialwissenschaften*, W. Bernsdorff and G. Eisermann, eds., Enke Verlag, Stuttgart 1955, pp. 214—225.

JAGER, Hugo de, »De sociologische benaderingswijze van de muziekgeschiedenis,« *Mens en Maatschappij*, 1957, XXXII/1, pp. 22—31.

374

KAPUSTA, Jan, »Hudba ve zmizelé společnosti. K metodologii studia sociálních hudebních jevú,« *Opus musicum,* 1971, III/3—4, pp. 67—74, 101—106.

KARBUSICKÝ, Vladimir, »Teoreticke predpoklady empiricko-sociologickeho vyzkumu hudby,« *Hudební věda,* 1965, 3, pp. 372—418.

— »Zur empirisch-soziologischen Musikforschung,« in *Beiträge zur Musikwissenschaft,* Berlin 1966, 8, 3/4, pp. 215—240.

— *Empirische Musiksoziologie: Erscheinungsformen, Theorie und Philosophie des Bezugs »Musik-Gesellschaft«,* Breitkopf und Härtel, Wiesbaden 1975, pp. 490.

KNEIF, Tibor, »Der Gegenstand musiksoziologischer Erkenntnis,« *Archiv für Musikwissenschaft,* 1966, 23/3, pp. 213—236.

— »Gegenwartsfragen der Musiksoziologie,« *Acta musicologica,* 1966, XXXVIII/2—4, pp. 72—118.

— »Zeichen und Gleichnis — Über zwei Anschauungsmodelle der Musiksoziologie,« *Neue Zeitschrift für Musik,* 1968, CXXIX, pp. 444—446.

KRAUS, Egon, »Bibliographie. Zur Soziologie und Musiksoziologie,« *Musik und Bildung,* 1972, IV/2, pp. 88—89.

KUNST, Jaap, »Some Sociological Aspects of Music,« *Lectures on the History and Art of Music,* The Louis Charles Elson Memorial Lectures at the Library of Congress, Washington 1958; Da Capo Press, New York 1968, pp. 139—165.

LASKE, Otto E., »Verification and Sociological Interpretation,« *International Review of the Aesthetics and Sociology of Music,* 1977, VIII/2, pp. 211—237.

LAUNSPACH, J.A., "Muzieksociologische Notities.", *Mens en Maatschappij,* 1964, 39/2, pp. 81-89.

LESURE, François, »Pour une sociologie historique des faits musicaux,« in *International Musicological Society — Report of the Eighth Congress,* Bärenreiter New York 1961, Vol. 1, pp. 333-347.

— »Sociologia della musica,« *La Musica,* 1966, IV/1, pp. 425—428.

MAHLING, Christoph-Hellmut, »Soziologie der Musik und musikalische Sozialgeschichte,« *International Review of Music Aesthetics and Sociology,* 1970, I/1, pp. 92—94.

— *Difficoltà dell'interpretazione sociologica dell'opera lirica,* in *La sociologia della musica,* EDT, Torino 1980, pp. 267—274.

MALER, W., »Ästhetisch oder soziologisch?«, *Musica,* 1949, pp. 7—8.

MAYER, G., »Zur musiksoziologischen Fragestellung,« in *Beiträge zur Musikwissenschaft,* 1963, 5, pp. 311—322.

375

BIBLIOGRAPHY

MERSMANN, Hans, »Soziologie als Hilfswissenschaft der Musikgeschichte,« *Archiv für Musikwissenschaft*, Trossingen 1953, X/1, pp. 1—15.

MEYER, Ernst H., *Musik im Zeitgeschehen. Grundprobleme der Musiksoziologie*, Henschel, Berlin 1952.

MEYER SERRA, O., »Problemas de una sociología de la música,« *Revia Mexicana de Sociología*, 1951, 13/1, pp. 23—34.

MOKRÝ, Ladislav, »Hudební sociologie již bez otazníků?,« *Hudební rozhledy*, 1964, 8.

MOSER, Hans J., »Zuständigkeitsgrenzen der Musiksoziologie,« in *Festschrift Hans Engel zum siebzigsten Geburtstag*, Kassel 1964, pp. 245—249.

NATHAN, Ernst, »Musiksoziologie — wozu und wie?,« *Musik und Bildung*, 1970, II/12, pp. 536—538.

NETTL, Bruno, »Change in Folk and Primitive Music. A Survey of Methods and Studies,« *Journal of the American Musicological Society*, Summer 1955, 8, pp. 101—109.

NIEMANN, Konrad, *Experimentelle und soziologische Methoden zur Ermittlung des Musikniveaus. Ein Beitrag zur Methodik empirischer Musiksoziologie*. Ph.D. Thesis, Humboldt University, Berlin 1968, pp. 230.

— »Soziologische Analyse der Musikgespräche 1966,« *Neue Musik*, Berlin 1969, pp. 263—294.

SCHNEIDER, Marius, »Sociologie et mythologie musicales,« Les Colloques de Wégimont, III-1956, in *Ethnomusicologie*, II, Les Belles Lettres, París 1960, pp. 13—22.

SERAUKY, Walter, »Wesen und Aufgaben der Musiksoziologie,« *Zeitschrift für Musikwissenschaft*, 1934, XVI/4, pp. 232—244.

SIEGMUND-SCHULTZE, W., »Musikwissenschaft als Gesellschaftswissenschaft,« in *Deutsches Jahrbuch der Musikwissenschaft*, 1957, 2.

SILBERMANN, Alphons, »Was will der Hörer überhaupt hören. Sinn und Unsinn der Musikstatistik,« *Das Musikleben*, 8, 1955.

— *Wovon lebt die Musik. Die Prinzipien der Musiksoziologie*, Bosse, Regensburg 1957. Engl. transl. *The Sociology of Music*, Routledge & Kegan Paul, London 1963. French transl. *Les principes de la sociologie de la musique*, Droz, Genève 1968, pp. 193.

— »Musiksoziologisches Akrostichon,« in *Musikerkenntnisse und Musikerziehung*, Dankesgaben für Hans Mersmann zu seinem 65. Geburtstag, Kassel-Basle 1957, pp. 135—142.

— »Die Stellung der Musiksoziologie innerhalb der Soziologie und der Musikwissenschaft,« *Kölner Zeitschrift für Soziologie und Sozialpsychologie*, 1958, X/1, pp. 102—115.

— »Die Ziele der Musiksoziologie,« *Kölner Zeitschrift für Soziologie und Sozialpsychologie*, 1962, XIV/2, pp. 322—335.

— »Die Pole der Musiksoziologie,« *Kölner Zeitschrift für Soziologie und Sozialpsychologie*, 1963, XV/3, pp. 425—448.

— »Anmerkungen zur Musiksoziologie. Eine Antwort auf Theodor W. Adornos 'Thesen zur Kunstsoziologie',« *Kölner Zeitschrift für Soziologie und Sozialpsychologie*, 1967, XIX/3, pp. 538—545.

— *La sociologia empirica della musica come ricerca evalutativa*, in *La sociologia della musica*, EDT, Torino 1980, pp. 133—138.

SOROKIN, Pitirim, *La musica nella dinamica socio-culturale*, in *La sociologia della musica*, EDT, Torino 1980, pp. 66—76.

SOCIOLOGY OF MUSIC AND RELATED DISCIPLINES

ADORNO, Theodor Wiesengrund, *Philosophie der neuen Musik*, Mohr, Tübingen 1949, Frankfurt/M. 1958.

ALBERSHEIM, Gerhard, »Reflexionen über Musikwissenschaft und Soziologie,« *International Review of Music Aesthetics and Sociology*, 1970, I/2, pp. 200—208.

ALBRECHT, Ján, »Leverkühn oder die Musik als Schicksal,« *Deutscher Vierteljahrsschrift für Literaturwissenschaft und Geistesgeschichte*, 1971. XLV/2, pp. 375—388.

BARTENIEF, Irmgard, and Forrestine PAULAY, »Research in Anthropology: A Study of Dance Styles in Primitive Cultures,« in *Research in Dance: Problems and Possibilities, Proceedings of the Preliminary Conference on Research in Dance*, Richard Bull, ed., New York 1967; New York University, New York 1968, pp. 91—104.

BRIEGLEB, Ann, »Ethnomusicological Collections in Western Europe — A Selective Study of Seventeen Archives,« *Selected Reports*, 1968, 1/2, Institute of Ethnomusicology of the University of California, Los Angeles, pp. 77—148.

BROERE, Bernard J., and Sylvia MOORE, »Ethnomusicology in the Netherlands,« *Recorded Sound*, 1969, 36, pp. 545—559.

BROOK, Barry S., »Music, Musicology and Related Disciplines: On Perspective and Interconnectedness,« in *A Musical Offering. Essays in Honor of Martin Bernstein*, ed. by Edward H. CLINKSCALE and Claire BROOK, Pendragon Press, New York 1977, pp. 69-77.

BUHOCIU, Octavian, »Folklore and Ethnography in Rumania,« *Current Anthropology*, 1966, 7/3, pp. 295—314.

CAPLOW, Theodor, *The Sociology of Work*, University of Minnesota Press, Minneapolis 1954.

CARPITELLA, Diego, »Gli studi sul folklore musicale in Italia,« *Società*, 1952, 8, pp. 539—549.

CHAPPLE, E. D., and C. S. COON, *Principles of Anthropology*, Holt, New York 1942.

CHASE, Gilbert, »American Musicology and the Social Sciences,« in *Perspectives in Musicology*, ed. by Barry S. Brook, Edward O. D. Downes and Sherman Van Solkema, Norton, New York 1972, pp. 202—220.

BIBLIOGRAPHY

COURT, Raymond, *Le musical. Essai sur les fondements anthropologiques de l'art*, Klincksieck, Paris 1976, pp. 320.

Adorno et la nouvelle musique. Art et modernité, Klincksieck, Paris 1981, pp. 155.

DANIÉLOU, Alain, »Values in Music,« in *Artistic Values in Traditional Music: Proceedings of a Conference*, Berlin, July 14 to 16, 1965, Peter Crossley, ed., International Institute for Comparative Music Studies and Documentation, Berlin 1966, pp. 10—21.

DUNCAN, Hugh Dalziel, »Sociology of Art, Literature and Music: Social Contexts of Symbolic Experience,« in *Modern Sociological Theory in Continuity and Change*, Howard Becker and Alvin Boskoff, eds., The Dryden Press, New York 1957.

ENGEL, Hans, »Musiksoziologie und musikalische Volkskunde,« in *Bericht über die musikwissenschaftliche Tagung der Internationalen Stiftung Mozarteum in Salzburg vom 2. bis 5. August 1931*, Leipzig 1932, pp. 304—312.

— »Der Standort der Musiksoziologie im Umkreis der Wissenschaftsdisziplinen,« *Melos*, 1931, 10, pp. 238.

ERDELY, Stephen, *Methods and Principles of Hungarian Ethnomusicology*, Uralic and Altaic Series, Vol. 52, Indiana University Publications, Bloomington 1965.

FREEMAN, Linton D., and Alan P. MERRIAM, »Statistical Classification in Anthropology: An Application to Ethnomusicology,« *American Anthropologist*, June 1956, 58/3, pp. 464—472.

GILLIS, Frank, and Alan P. MERRIAM, *Ethnomusicology and Folk Music: An International Bibliography of Dissertations and Theses*, Wesleyan University Press for the Society of Ethnomusicology, Middeltown (Conn.) 1966.

HANEY, James E., *Ethnomusicology: The World of Music Cultures*, (Research News, Vol. 21, No. 2), University of Michigan, Office of Research Administration, Ann Arbor 1970 (August).

HAUSER, Arnold, *The Philosophy of Art History*, Routledge and Kegan Paul, London 1958.

HEINEMANN, Rudolf, »Der Hörer zwischen Musikwissenschaft, Soziologie und Kulturkritik. Ein musiksoziologisches Akrostichon.« *Kölner Zeitschrift für Soziologie und Sozialpsychologie*, 1969, XXI/3, pp. 560—568; *Musik und Bildung*, 1970, II/3, pp. 105—108.

HERTZLER, Joyce O., *A Sociology of Language*, Random House, New York 1965.

HERZOG, George, »Music at the Fifth International Congress of Anthropological and Ethnological Sciences, Philadelphia, U.S.A.,« *Journal of the International Folk Music Council*, 1957, 9, pp. 71—73.

HIBBERD, Lloyd, "Musicology Reconsidered," *Acta Musicologica*, 1959, XXI/1, pp. 25-31.

HONIGSHEIM, Paul, *Sociology of Literature, Theater, Music, and the Arts: A Working Outline*, Michigan State University, East Langsing 1962 (Mimeographed).

— »Soziologie der Kunst, Musik und Literatur,« in *Die Lehre von der Gesellschaft: Ein Lehrbuch der Soziologie*, Gottfried Eisermann, ed., Enke Verlag, Stuttgart 1958, pp. 338—373.

HOOD, Mantle, *The Ethnomusicologist*, McGraw Hill, New York 1971.

— »The Quest for Norms in Ethnomusicology,« *Inter-American Music Bulletin*, May 1963, 35, pp. 1—5.

HOWES, Frank, *Man, Mind and Music; Studies in the Philosophy of Music and in the Relations of the Art to Anthropology, Psychology and Sociology*, Secker & Warburg, London 1948.

JAGER, Hugo de, »De sociologische benaderingswijze van de muziek geschiedenis,« *Mens en Maatschappij*, 1957, XXXII/1, pp. 22—31.

JENSEN, Jorgen Pauli, »Om musikkenspsykologi og sociologi som en del af den totale musikvidenskab,« *Svensk tidskrift för musikforskning*, 1970, LII, pp. 57—63.

KARBUSICKÝ, Vladimir, *Podstata umění. Sociologicky přípěvek do diskuse o gnoseologismu v estetice a teorii umění*, Horizont, Prague 1969, pp. 104.

KUNST, Jaap, *Ethnomusicology: A Study of its Nature, its Problems, Methods and Representative Personalities to which is Added a Bibliography*, 3rd ed., Nijhoff, The Hague 1959.

LALO, Charles, *Eléments d'une esthétique musicale scientifique*, 2nd ed., Vrin, Paris 1939.

— »Méthodes et objets de l'esthétique sociologique,« *Revue internationale de philosophie*, 1949, 7, pp. 5—41.

— *L'estetica sociologica e l'arte musicale*, in *La sociologia della musica*, EDT, Torino 1980, pp. 55—64.

LEICHTENTRITT, Hugo, *Music, History and Ideas*, Cambridge 1941.

LESURE, François, »Musicologie et sociologie,« *La Revue musicale*, 1953, 221, pp. 4—11.

LÉVI-STRAUSS, Claude, *Structural Anthropology*, Trans. by Claire Jacobson and Brooke Grundfest Schoepf, Basic Books, New York 1967.

McALLESTER, David P., »Ethnomusicology, the Field and the Society,« *Ethnomusicology*, 1963, 7/3, pp. 182—186.

MERRIAM, Alan P., *The Anthropology of Music*, Northwestern University Press, Evanston (Ill.) 1964.

— »Ethnomusicology Revisited,« *Ethnomusicology*, May 1969, 13/2, pp. 213—229.

— »Ethnomusicology,« in *International Encyclopedia of the Social Sciences*, David L. Sills, ed., Macmillan and Free Press, New York 1968, Vol. 10, pp. 562—566.

379

— »Ethnomusicology,« *The Review*, Indiana University, Alumni Association of the College of Arts and Sciences — Graduate School, 1967, 9/3, pp. 1—9.

— »The Arts and Anthropology,« in *Horizons of Anthropology*, Sol Tax, ed., Aldine, Chicago 1964, pp. 224—236.

— »The Purposes of Ethnomusicology, An Anthropological View,« *Ethnomusicology*, 1963, 7/3, pp. 206—213.

— »Ethnomusicology — Discussion and Definition of the Field,« *Ethnomusicology*, 1960, 4/3, pp. 107—114.

— »Ethnomusicology in Our Time,« *American Music Teacher*, 1959, 8, pp. 6—7, 27—32.

MEYER, Leonard B., »Meaning in Music and Information Theory,« *Journal of Aesthetics and Art Criticism*, 1957, 15, pp. 412—424.

MUNRO, Thomas, *Toward Science in Aesthetics*, Liberal Arts Press, New York 1956.

NATTIEZ, Jean-Jacques, »Sur les relations entre sociologie et sémiologie musicales«, *International Review of the Aesthetics and Sociology of Music*, 1974, V/1, pp. 61—77.

NETTL, Bruno, »Historical Aspects of Ethnomusicology,« *American Anthropologist*, 1958, 60, pp. 518—532.

— *Reference Materials in Ethnomusicology. A Bibliographic Essay*, 2nd rev. ed., Information Coordinators, Detroit 1967.

— *Theory and Method in Ethnomusicology*, Free Press, New York 1964.

NIEMANN, Konrad, »Mehrdimensionale Musikurteile in der soziologischen Forschung,« in *Bericht über den Internationalen Musikwissenschaftlichen Kongreß*, Leipzig 1966, pp. 490—498.

PARMAR, Shyam, »Prelude to Ethnomusicology in India,« *Folklore*, 1971, 12/1, pp. 20—29.

PETROVIĆ, Radmila, »Ethnomusicology in Yugoslavia,« *Zvuk*, 1967, 77—78, pp. 20—30.

POLUNIN, Ivan, »Visual and Sound Recording Apparatus in Ethnographic Fieldwork,« *Current Anthropology*, 1970, 11/1, pp. 3—22.

PORENA, Boris, »Musica/società: una questione semiologica?,« *Proceedings of the 1st International Congress on Semiotics of Music*, Beograd 17—27 Oct. 1973, Centro di iniziativa culturale, Pesaro 1975, pp. 173—183.

RAMSEYER, Urs, *Soziale Bezüge des Musizierens in Naturvolkkulturen, Ein ethnosoziologischer Ordnungsversuch*, Francke, Bern-Munich 1970, pp. 128.

REINOLD, Helmut, »Die Bedeutung musiksoziologischen Denkens für die Musikgeschichte,« in *Festgabe zum fünfzigsten Geburtstag von K. G. Fellerer*, Cologne 1952.

— »Grundverschiedenheiten musikwissenschaftlichen und soziologischen Denkens und Möglichkeiten zu ihrer Überwindung,« in *Kongreßbericht Hamburg 1956*, Kassel 1957.

RUMBELOW, A. S., »Sociology of Music & Musical Aesthetics,« *Journal of the Indian Musicological Society*, 1976, 7/2, pp. 5—44.

RUWET, Nicolas, »Musicology and Linguistics,« *International Social Science Journal*, 1967, 19/1, pp. 79—87.

SEEGER, Charles, »Toward a Unitary Field Theory for Musicology,« in *Selected Reports*, Institute for Ethnomusicology of the University of California, Los Angeles 1970, 1/3, pp. 172—210.

SILBERMANN, Alphons, »Das Chaos der Neuen Musik. Zur Verwischung der Grenzen zwischen Philosophie und Soziologie,« *Musica*, 1956, pp. 30——32.

— »Die Stellung der Musiksoziologie innerhalb der Soziologie und der Musikwissenschaft,« *Kölner Zeitschrift für Soziologie und Sozialpsychologie*, 1958, 10/1, pp. 102—115.

SIMMEL, Georg, »Psychologische und ethnologische Studien über Musik,« *Zeitschrift für Völkerpsychologie und Sprachwissenschaft*, 1882, 13, pp. 261—305.

SODERBERG, Bertil, »Field Research in Ethnomusicology,« *Ethnos*, Stockholm 1966, 31, pp. 83—88.

SUPIČIĆ, Ivo, »Esthétique musicale et sociologie de la musique,« *Revue d'esthétique*, 1960, IV/13, pp. 392—402.

— »Positive Musikwissenschaft und Wertprobleme der Musik,« in *Festschrift der Akademie für Musik und darstellende Kunst, Wien 1817——1967*, Vienna 1967, pp. 61—64.

— »Science on Music and Values in Music,« *The Journal of Aesthetics and Art Criticism*, 1969, XXVIII/1, pp. 71—77.

THIEME, Darius L., »Ethnomusicology — The Discipline and its Objective,« *Musart*, 1965, 18/2, pp. 14—15, 38—40.

TITON, Jeff Todd, *Ethnomusicology of Downhome Blues Phonograph Records, 1926—1930*, University of Minnesota, 1971, pp. 302.

VAN DEN BOREN, Charles, »Musicologie et géographie,« in *La Renaissance dans les Provinces du Nord*, C. N. R. S., Paris 1956, pp. 19—25.

VIG, Rudolf, *Indian Folk Music Ethnomusicology: Comparative Study of Indian Folk Music and the Music of European Gypsies by Recording Indian Folk Music on Tape*, Hungarian Academy of Science, Budapest 1968.

VOLEK, Tomislav, »Razprava o huaební antropologii,« *Hudebni rozhledy*, 1969, XXII/1, pp. 4—7.

WACHSMANN, Klaus P., »Recent Trends in Ethnomusicology,« Proceedings of the Royal Musical Association, London 1958—1959, 85, pp. 65—80.

WILZIN, L., *Musikstatistik — Logik und Methodik gesellschaftsstatistischer Musikforschung*, Deuticke, Vienna 1937.

381

WINCKEL, Fritz, »Aspects of Information Theory in Relation to Comparative Music Studies,« in *Artistic Values in Traditional Music: Proceedings of the Conference, July 14 to 16, 1965,* P. Crossley-Holland, ed., Berlin, International Institute for Comparative Music Studies and Documentation, 1966, pp. 124—127.

WIORA, Walter, »Musikwissenschaft und Universalgeschichte,« *Acta musicologica,* 1961, XXIII/2—4, pp. 84—104.

— »Ethnomusicology and the History of Music,« *Studia Musicologica,* 1965, 7, pp. 187—193.

SOCIAL PSYCHOLOGY OF MUSIC

ADORNO, Theodor Wiesengrund, »Über den Fetischcharakter und die Regression des Hörens,« *Zeitschrift für Sozialforschung,* 1939, 7, pp. 321—356; also in *Dissonanzen — Musik in der verwalteten Welt,* Göttingen 1958, pp. 9—45.

BIMBERG, Siegfried, and Wolfgang KÖHLER, »Zur Methodik von Untersuchungen musikalischer Interessen,« *Wissenschaftliche Zeitschrift Universität Halle,* 1968, XVII/4, pp. 107—114.

BRAÏLOÏU, Constantin, »Réflexions sur la création musicale collective,« *Diogène,* 1959, 25. pp. 83—93.

DAVIES, Evan, »The Psychological Characteristics of Beatle Mania,« *Journal of the History of Ideas,* 1969, XXX/2, pp. 273—280.

DISERENS, Charles M., *The Influence of Music on Behavior,* Princeton University Press, Princeton 1926.

EDWARDS, John S., and M. C. EDWARDS, »A Scale to Measure Attitudes Toward Music,« *Journal of Research in Music Education,* 1971, XIX/2, pp. 228—233.

FARNSWORTH, Paul R., *The Social Psychology of Music,* The Dryden Press, New York 1958; reprint: Iowa State University, Ames (Iowa) 1969.

FISHER, S., and R. L. FISHER, »The Effects of Personal Insecurity on Reactions to Unfamiliar Music,« *Journal of Social Psychology,* 1951, 34, pp. 265—273.

FRIEDMAN, Estelle R., »Psychological Aspects of Folk Music,« in *Proceedings of the 76th Annual Convention of the American Psychological Association,* 1968, pp. 449—450.

GORDON, Edwin, »Third-Year Results of a Five-Year Longitudinal Study of the Musical Achievement of Culturally-Disadvantaged Students,« *Experimental Research in the Psychology of Music,* 1972, 8, pp. 45—64.

GRAF, Max, *From Beethoven to Shostakovich — The Psychology of the Composing Process,* Philosophical Library, New York 1948.

HELMS, Siegmund, »Umfrage nach musikalischen Verhaltensweisen,« *Musik und Bildung,* 1969, I/10, pp. 531—533.

382

HOEBAER, R., »L'intérêt pour l'art musical. Essai d'analyse sociologique,« in *Bulletin de l'Institut de Recherches Economiques et Sociales*, 1956, 7.

HONIGSHEIM, Paul, »Die soziologischen und soziopsychologischen Grundlagen des Rundfunks und der Radiomusik,« in *Discours au Congrès de musique radiogénique*, Göttingen May 1928; Berlin 1929.

INGLEFIELD, Howard Gibbs, *The Relationship of Selected Personality Variables to Conformity Behavior Reflected in the Musical Preferences of Adolescents when Exposed to Peer Group Leader Influences*, Ph. D. Thesis (Music), Ohio State University 1968.

JOLLY, Howard Delcour, *Popular Music: A Study in Collective Behavior*, Ph. D. Thesis (Sociology), Stanford University 1967.

JOST, Ekkehard, *Sozialpsychologische Faktoren der Popmusik — Rezeption*, B. Schott's, Mainz 1976, pp. 99.

KAPLAN, Max, »A Sociological Approach to Music and Behavior,« *The American Journal of Occupational Therapy*, January-February 1950.

KARBUSICKY, Vladimir, and J. KASAN, *Erforschung des gegenwärtigen Standes der Musikalität*, Prague 1964.

KESTON, M. J., »An Experimental Investigation of the Relationship Between the Factors of the Minnesota Multiphasic Personality Inventory and Musical Sophistication,« *American Psychologist*, 1956, 11, pp. 434 ff

KLYMASZ, Robert B., »Social and Cultural Motifs in Canadian Ukrainian Lullabies,« *Slavic and East European Journal*, 1968, 12/2, pp. 176—183.

KNEIF, Tibor, »Der prädikative Mensch-Bemerkungen zum musikalischen Snobismus,« in *Über das Musikleben der Gegenwart*, Merseburger, Berlin 1968, pp. 52—60.

KURTH, Ernst, *Musikpsychologie*, Hesse, Berlin 1931.

MALETZKE, G., *Der Rundfunk in der Erlebniswelt des heutigen Menschen--Untersuchungen zur psychologischen Wesenseigenart des Rundfunks und zur Psychologie des Rundfunkshörer*, Diss., Hamburg 1950.

MICHEL, André, *Psychanalyse de la musique*, P.U.F., Paris 1951.

MOWINCKEL, L.J. Jr., *Bidrag til publikums psykologi — Belyst ved undersøkelser i Oslo*, Oslo 1937; in *Musik um Wandel von Freizeit und Bildung*, Kassel 1957.

MUELLER, John H., *The American Symphony Orchestra — A Social History of Musical Taste*, Bloomington 1952; London 1958.

— »A Sociological Approach to Musical Behavior,« *Ethnomusicology*, 1963, 7/3, pp. 216—220.

MÜLLER-FREIENFELS, R., *Psychologie der Musik*, Vieweg, Berlin 1936.

MURESIL, James L., »Psychology and the Problem of Scale,« *The Musical Quarterly*, 1946, 32, pp. 564—573.

— *The Psychology of Music*, 1937. Reprint: Johnson Reprint, New York 1970.

NASH, Dennison, *The American Composer: A Study in Social-Psychology*, Ph. D. Thesis (Sociology), Pennsylvania, 1954.

NETTL, Bruno, »Infant Musical Development and Primitive Music,« *Southwestern Journal of Anthropology*, 1956, XII/1, pp. 87—91.

PECH, Karel, *Hören im »optischen Zeitalter«*, G. Braun, Karlsruhe 1969.

PHILIPPOT, M. P., »Aspects psycho-sociologiques de la haute fidélité,« in *Conférences des Journées d'Etudes*, Chiron, Paris 1963, pp. 3—13.

PRATT, Caroll C., *The Meaning of Music: A Study in Psychological Aesthetics*, 1931; Johnson Reprint, New York 1968.

— »Music as the Language of Emotion,« in *Lectures on the History and Art of Music: The Louis Charles Elson Memorial Lectures at the Library of Congress, 1946—1963*, Da Capo Press, New York 1968, pp. 41—64.

REIK, Theodor, *The Haunting Melody. Psychoanalytic Experience in Life and Music*, Farrar, Straus and Young, New York 1953.

REINECKE, Hans-Peter, »Sozialpsychologische Hintergründe der Neuen Musik,« in *Das musikalisch Neue und die Neue Musik*, Schott, Mainz 1969, pp. 73—92.

RÉVÉSZ, Géza, *Einführung in die Musikpsychologie*, Amsterdam 1946; London 1953.

REYNOLDS, Roger, *Mind Models; New Forms of Musical Experience*, Praeger, New York 1975, pp. 238.

RITTENHOUSE, C. H., *Masculinity and Femininity in Relation to Preferences in Music*, Ph. D. Thesis, Stanford 1952.

ROBERSTON-DECARBO, Carol E., »Music as Therapy: A Biocultural Problem,« *Ethnomusicology*, 1974, 18/1, pp. 31-42.

ROGERS, V. R., »Children's Musical Preferences,« in *The Adolescent*, J. M. Seidmann, ed., New York 1960, 2. ed., pp. 510—515.

ROSENMAYR, Leopold, Eva KÖCKEIS, and Henrik KREUTZ, *Kulturelle Interessen von Jugendlichen. Eine soziologische Untersuchung an jungen Arbeitern und höheren Schülern*, Hollinek/Juventa, Vienna-Munich 1966.

SANDVOSS, Joachim, *A Study of the Musical Preferences, Interests, and Activities of Parents as Factors in Their Attitude Toward the Musical Education of Their Children*, Ed. D. Thesis (Music), University of British Columbia, 1969.

SCHNEIDER, Marius, »Les fondements intellectuels et psychologiques du chant magique,« Les Colloques de Wégimont, I, Elsevier, Brussels 1956, pp. 56—63.

SCHOEN, Max, *The Effects of Music*, Harcourt, Brace, New York 1927.

SEASHORE, Carl, *Psychology of Music*, McGraw-Hill, New York 1938.

SILBERMANN, Alphons, »Réflexions sur les conflits des groupes dans les milieux musicaux,« in *Soziologische Arbeiten*, P. Atteslander and R. Girod, eds., Verlag Hans Huber, Bern 1966, pp. 1—19.

SIMMEL, Georg, »Psychologische und ethnologische Studien über Musik,« *Zeitschrift für Völkerpsychologie und Sprachwissenschaft*, 1882, 13, pp. 261—305. Trans. in K. Peter Etzkorn, *Georg Simmel: The Conflict in Modern Culture*, Teachers College Press, New York 1968, pp. 98—140.

WATERMAN, Richard A., »Music in Australian Aboriginal Culture. Some Sociological and Psychological Implications,« *Music Therapy*, 1956, 5, pp. 40—49.

— »Sozialpsychologische Aspekte im Wandel des Chopin-Idols,« in *The Book of the First International Congress Devoted to the Works of Fr. Chopin, Warsaw 16. — 22. 2. 1960*, Warsaw 1963.

WILLIAMS, Robert Otis, *A Study of the Effects of Socio-Economic Status, Musical Aptitude and Instruction upon Attitudes Held Toward Various Types of Music*, University Microfilms, Ann Arbor 1970, pp. 128.

YOUNG, K., *Handbook of Social Psychology*, Routledge & Kegan Paul, London 1951.

SOCIAL HISTORY OF MUSIC

ADKINS, Aldrich Wendell, *The Development of the Black Art Song*, University of Texas, Austin 1972, pp. 170.

BALET, Leo, *Die Verbürgerlichung der deutschen Kunst, Literatur und Musik im 18. Jahrhundert*, Heitz, Leipzig-Strasbourg-Zurich 1936.

BARKER, John W., »Sociological Influences upon the Emergence of Lutheran Music,« *Miscellanea Musicologica*, Adelaide Studies in Musicology, 1969, 4, pp. 157—198.

BARZUN, Jacques, *Music in American Life*, Garden City (N. Y.) 1956.

BEAUFILS, Marcel, *Par la musique vers l'obscur — Essai sur la musique bourgeoise et l'éveil d'une conscience allemande au XVIIIᵉ siècle et aux origines du XIXᵉ siècle*, F. Robert, Marseille 1942.

BECKER, Carl Ferdinand, *Die Hausmusik in Deutschland in dem 16., 17. und 18. Jahrhunderte*, Fest, Leipzig 1840.

BEHN, F., *Musikleben im Altertum und frühen Mittelalter*, Stuttgart 1954.

BERNHARD, B., »Recherches sur l'histoire de la corporation des Ménétriers ou joueurs d'instruments de la ville de Paris,« *Bibl. de l'Ecole des Chartes*, 3, 1842, p. 377; 1843, pp. 525-548.

BESSELER, Heinrich, *Musik des Mittelalters und der Renaissance*, Potsdam 1931.

— »Umgangsmusik und Darbietungsmusik im 16. Jahrhundert,« *Archiv für Musikwissenschaft*, 1959, 16, pp. 21—43.

BLUM, Stephen, »Towards a Social History of Musicological Technique,« *Ethnomusicology*, 1975, XIX/2, pp. 207-231.

BRENET, Michel, *Les concerts en France sous l'ancien régime*, Fischbacher, Paris 1900.

— »Notes sur l'introduction des instruments dans les églises de France,« in *Riemann-Festschrift*, Max Hesses Verlag, Leipzig 1909, pp. 277—286.

BRIDGMAN, Nanie, »Charles-Quint et la musique espagnole,« *Revue de musicologie*, Paris 1959, XLIII/119, pp. 44—60.

— »La participation musicale à l'entrée de Charles Quint à Cambrai le 20 janvier 1540,« in *Fêtes et cérémonies au temps de Charles Quint*, Centre National de la Recherche Scientifique, Paris 1960, pp. 235—254.

— *La vie musicale au Quattrocento et jusqu'à la naissance du madrigal (1400—1530)*, Gallimard, Paris 1964.

BRION, Marcel, *Daily Life in the Vienna of Mozart and Schubert*, Macmillan, New York 1962.

BROOK, Barry S., *La symphonie française dans la seconde moitié du XVIIIᵉ siècle*, Institut de Musicologie de l'Université de Paris, Paris 1962, 3 vol., pp. 684 + 726 + 231.

BUKER, A., *A Social Approach to Music Appreciation, Music and History from Stone Age to Steel Age*, Palo Alto 1963.

BURTON, Humphrey, »Les Académies de musique en France au XVIIIᵉ siècle,« *Revue de musicologie*, Paris 1955, XXXVII/112, pp. 122—147.

CHAILLEY, Jacques, »Un clavier d'orgue à la fin du XIᵉ siècle,« *Revue de musicologie*, 1937, 18/61, pp. 5—11.

— *Histoire musicale du Moyen Age*, P. U. F., Paris 1950.

— Problèmes de la musique contemporaine et de l'auditeur devant l'histoire du langage. Essai d'explication technique d'un divorce,« *La Revue internationale de musique*, 1952, 13, pp. 209—220.

— *40.000 ans de musique*, P. U. F., Paris 1950.

— *40 000 Years of Music: Man in Search of Music*, Da Capo Press, Reprint of the 1964 edition, New York 1975, pp. XIV—229.

COMBARIEU, Jules, *Histoire de la musique*, A. Colin, Paris 1913—1919, 3 vol.

— *La musique, ses lois, son évolution*, Flammarion, Paris 1907.

CVETKO, Dragotin, »Sociološki i nacionalni uvjeti promjena u položaju glazbe Južnih Slavena u XIX stoljeću,« *Zvuk*, 1974, 2, pp. 102—110.

DAHNK, E., »Musikausübung an den Höfen von Burgund und Orléans während des 15. Jahrhunderts,« *Archiv für Kulturgeschichte*, 1934, 25, pp. 184—215.

DARBELLAY, Etienne, »La musique à la cour de Maximilien I (1459-1519),« *Schweizerische Musikzeitung*, 1978, I, pp. 1-10.

DENT, E. J., *Foundations of English Opera — A Study of Musical Drama in England during the Seventeenth Century*, The University Press, Cambridge 1928.

DOMP, J., *Studien zur Geschichte der Musik an westfälischen Adelshöfen im XVIII Jahrhundert*, Regensburg 1934.

DONAKOWSKI, Conrad L., *A Muse for the Masses. Ritual and Music in an Age of Democratic Revolution (1770—1870)*, The University of Chicago Press, Chicago and London 1977.

DÖRFFEL, Alfred, *Geschichte der Gewandhaus Concerte zu Leipzig*, Breitkopf & Härtel, Leipzig 1881—1884.

DUNNING, Albert, »Die 'aktuelle' Musik im Zeitalter der Niederländer,« in *Bericht über den Internationalen Musikwissenschaftlichen Kongreß*, Leipzig 1966, pp. 181—186.

EGBERT, D., *Social Radicalism and the Arts — A Cultural History from the French Revolution to 1968*, Knopf, New York 1970.

FALLET, Edouard Marius, *La vie musicale au pays de Neuchâtel du XIIIe à la fin du XVIIIe siècle*, Heitz, Leipzig—Strasbourg—Zurich 1936.

FARMER, Henry George, *Concerts in Eighteenth-Century Scotland*, Hinrichsen, Glasgow 1945.

FINSCHER, Ludwig, *Studien zur Geschichte des Streichquartetts*, Bärenreiter Verlag, Kassel 1974, pp. 301.

FINSCHER, Ludwig, *Per una storia sociale del quartetto d'archi*, in *La sociologia della musica*, EDT, Torino 1980, pp. 204—208.

GOLEA, Antoine, *La Musique, de la nuit des temps aux aurores nouvelles*, Leduc, Paris 1977, 2 sv., pp. 954.

GÜLKE, Peter, *Mönche, Bürger, Minnesänger: Musik in der Gesellschaft des europäischen Mittelalters*, Böhlau, Vienna 1975, pp. 283.

HARMAN, R. A., A. MILNER and W. MELLERS, *Man and His Music: The Story of Musical Experience in the West*, 4 vols., Barrie and Rockliff, London 1969.

HEMPEL, G., »Die bürgerliche Musikkultur Leipzigs im Vormärz,« in *Beiträge zur Musikwissenschaft*, 1964, 6, pp. 3—14.

— »Das Ende der Leipziger Ratmusik im 19. Jahrhundert,« *Archiv für Musikwissenschaft*, 1958, XV/3, pp. 187—197.

HOLLANDER, Hans, *Die Musik in der Kulturgeschichte des 19. und 20. Jahrhunderts*, Arno Volk, Cologne 1967, pp. 171.

JOHNSON, David. *Music and Society in Lowland Scotland in the Eighteenth Century*, Oxford University Press, Oxford 1972, pp. 233.

JUNGHEINRICH, Hans-Klaus, Luca LOMBARDI, eds., *Musik im Übergang. Von der bürgerlichen zur sozialistischen Musikkultur*, Damnitz Verlag, Munich 1977, pp. 182.

KAHL, W., »Soziologisches zur neueren rheinischen Musikgeschichte,« *Zeitschrift für Musik*, 1939, 106.

KATZ, B., *The Social Implications of Early Black Music in the United States*, Arno Press, New York 1969.

KNEPLER, Georg, *Musikgeschichte des XIX Jahrhunderts*, Band II: Österreich-Deutschland, Henschelverlag, Berlin 1961.

KOS, Koraljka, »Style and Sociological Background of Croatian Renaissance Music,« *International Review of the Aesthetics and Sociology of Music,* 1982, 13/1, pp. 55—82.

LANG, Paul Henry, *Music in Western Civilization,* Norton, New York 1941.

LASTER, Arnaud, »Musique et peuple dans les années 1830,« *Romantisme,* 1975, 9, pp. 77—83.

LOWINSKY, Edward, »Music in the Culture of the Renaissance,« *Journal of the History of Ideas,* 1954, XV/4, pp. 509—553.

MACKERNESS, Eric David, *A Social History of English Music,* Greenwood Press, Westport (Conn.) 1976, c1964; Reprint, London: Routledge and K. Paul, Issued in series Studies in social history.

MARIX, Jeanne, *Histoire de la musique de la cour de Bourgogne sous le régne de Philippe le Bon (1420—1467),* Heitz, Strasbourg 1939.

MELLERS, Wilfred Howard, *François Couperin and the French Classical Tradition,* D. Dobson, London 1950.

— *Music and Society: England and the European Tradition,* D. Dobson, London 1946; 2nd ed. 1950. Germ. transl. *Musik und Gesellschaft,* 2. vols., Frankfurt/M. 1964 and 1965.

MELLERS, W. H., R. A. HARMAN and A. MILNER, *Man and His Music: The story of Musical Experience in the West,* Barrie and Rockliff, London 1969, 4 vols.

MERSMANN, Hans, *Musikgeschichte in der abendländischen Kultur,* Menck, Frankfurt/M. 1956.

MEYER, E., *Musik im Zeitgeschehen,* Berlin 1952.

MUELLER, John Henry, *The American Symphony Orchestra — A Social History of Musical Taste,* Indiana University Press, Bloomington 1952; 2nd. ed., London 1958.

MÜLLER-BLATTAU, J., »Zur Geschichte der musikalischen Gesellschaftsformen,« *Die Musikpflege,* 1930, 1, pp. 134—148.

MULLINS, Margaret, »Dance and Society in the First Half of the Eighteenth Century,« *Miscellanea Musicologica,* Adelaide Studies in Musicology, 1975, 7, pp. 118—141.

MUSSULMAN, Joseph A., *Music in the Cultured Generation, 1870—1900,* Northwestern University, Evanston 1971, pp. 298.

NETTEL, Reginald, *The Orchestra in England — A Social History,* J. Cape, London 1946; 2nd ed. London 1956.

— *Sing a Song of England: A Social History of Traditional Song,* Alan Swallow, Denver 1954.

— *Seven Centuries of Popular Song: A Social History of Urban Ditties,* London 1956.

— *A Social History of Traditional Song,* Reprint: Adams and Dart/Augustus M. Kelley, London-New York 1969.

NETTL, Paul, »Zur Geschichte der kaiserlichen Hofmusikkapelle 1636—1680,« in *Studien zur Musikwissenschaft,* Gesellschaft zur Herausgabe von Denkmälern der Tonkunst in Österreich, vols. 16—19, Vienna 1929——1932.

NORTH, Louise McCoy, *The Psalms and Hymns of Protestantism from the Sixteenth to the Nineteenth Century,* The University, Madison (N. J.) 1936.

NOWAK, Leopold, »Das deutsche Gesellschaftslied in Österreich von 1480 bis 1550,« in *Studien zur Musikwissenschaft,* Gesellschaft zur Herausgabe von Denkmälern der Tonkunst in Österreich, vol. 17, Vienna 1930.

PINTHUS, Gerhard, *Das Konzertleben in Deutschland. Ein Abriß seiner Entwicklung bis zum Beginn des 19. Jahrhunderts,* Heitz, Strasbourg-Leipzig-Zurich 1932.

PIRRO, André, *Histoire de la musique de la fin du XIVe siècle à la fin du XVIe,* H. Laurens, Paris 1940.

— *La musique à Paris sous le règne de Charles VI* (1380—1422), Heitz, Strasbourg 1930.

POUGIN, Arthur, *L'Opéra-Comique pendant la Révolution de 1788 à 1801,* Minkoff Reprint, Geneva 1973, pp. 337.

PREUSSNER, Eberhard, *Die bürgerliche Musikkultur,* Hanseatische Verlagsanstalt, Hamburg 1935; 2nd ed., Bärenreiter Verlag, Kassel-Basle 1950.

PRITCHARD, Brain W., *The Musical Festival and the Choral Society in England in the 18th and 19th Centuries: A Social History,* University of Birmingham, Birmingham 1968, 3 vol., pp. 927.

— *Societies in Society: A Case Study in the Historical Sociology of Music,* M. A. Thesis (Folklore), Indiana University, 1965.

PRÖSLER, H., *Hauptprobleme der Sozialgeschichte,* Plam & Enke, Erlangen 1951.

PRUNIÈRES, Henry, *Le Ballet de cour en France avant Benserade et Lully,* H. Laurens, Paris 1913.

— *L'Opera italien en France avant Lulli,* Champion, Paris 1913.

RABIN, Marvin J., *History and Analysis of the Greater Boston Youth Symphony Orchestra from 1958 to 1964,* University of Illinois, 1968, pp. 500.

RAUPACH, H., *J. S. Bach und die Gesellschaft seiner Zeit,* Callwey, München 1973.

RAYNOR, Henry, *A Social History of Music from the Middle Ages to Beethoven,* Barrie & Jenkins, London 1972, pp. viii+373.

— *Music and Society since 1815,* Schocken Books, New York 1976, pp. VIII+213.

RIEDEL, F. W., »Der 'Reichsstil' in den deutschen Musikgeschichte des 18. Jahrhunderts,« in *Bericht über Internationalen Musikwissenschaftlichen Kongreß Kassel 1962,* Bärenreiter, Kassel 1963, pp. 34-36.

RUHNKE, M., *Beiträge zur Geschichte der deutschen Hofmusikkollegien im 16. Jahrhundert*, Berlin 1963.

RUSSEL, Theodore C., *Theodore Thomas: His Role in the Development of Musical Culture in the United States, 1835—1905*, University of Minnesota, 1969, pp. 225.

RUST, Frances, *Dance in Society: An Analysis of the Relationship between the Social Dance and Society in England from the Middle Ages to the Present Day*, Routledge and Kegan Paul, London 1969.

SACHS, Curt, *Musikgeschichte der Stadt Berlin bis zum Jahre 1800*, Gebr. Paetel, Berlin 1908, pp. 325.

— *Musik und Oper am Kurbrandenburgischen Hof*, J. Bard, Berlin 1910, pp. 299.

— *Die Musikinstrumente des alten Ägyptens, Mitteilungen aus der ägyptischen Sammlung der Staatlichen Museen zu Berlin*, vol. 3, K. Curtius, Berlin 1921, pp. 92.

— *Musik des Altertums*, Ferdinand Hirt, Breslau 1924, pp. 96.

— »Die Musik der Antike,« in *Handbuch der Musikwissenschaft*, Athenaion, Wildpark 1928, pp. 34.

— *The History of Musical Instruments*, Norton, New York 1940.

— *The Rise of Music in the Ancient World East and West*, Norton, New York 1943.

— *The Wellsprings of Music*, Da Capo Press, New York 1977 (Reprint of the Hague ed., 1962), pp. XI-228.

SALAZAR, Adolfo, *La música como proceso histórico de su invención*, Mexico City-Buenos Aires 1950.

— *La música en la sociedad Europea*, El Colegio del Mexico, Mexico City 1942.

SALMEN, Walter, *Musikleben im 16. Jahrhundert*, VEB Deutscher Verlag für Musik, Leipzig 1976, vol. III, pp. 212.

SCARAMUZZI, Francesco, *Per dilettatione grande et per utilità incredibile. Musica ed esperienze sociali tra Rinascimento e Barocco*, Laterza, Bari 1982, pp. 133.

SCHOLES, P. A., *The Puritans and Music in England and New England — A Contribution to the Cultural History of Two Nations*, Oxford University Press, London 1934; New York 1962.

SENDREY, Alfred, *The Music of the Jews in the Diaspora (up to 1800). A Contribution to the Social and Cultural History of the Jews*, A. S. Barnes, Cranbury 1970, pp. 483.

— *Music in the Social and Religious Life of Antiquity*, Dickinson University Press, Rutherford-Madison-Teaneck Fairleigh 1974.

STRIFFLING, Louis, *Esquisse d'une histoire du goût musical en France au XVIIIᵉ siècle*, Delagrave, Paris 1912.

STUMPF, Carl, *Die Anfänge der Musik*, Leipzig 1911.

SZABOLCSI, Bence, »Die ungarischen Spielleute des Mittelalters,« in *Gedank-schrift H. Albert*, Halle 1928, pp. 154—164.

VALLAS, Léon, *Un siècle de musique et de théâtre à Lyon (1688—1789)*. P. Masson, Lyon 1932.

WALLASCHEK, R., *Die Anfänge der Tonkunst*, Leipzig 1903.

WANGERMÉE, Robert. *La musique flamande dans le société des XVe et XVIe siècles,* Arcade, Brussels 1966, 2nd ed.

WEBER, William, »Mass Culture and the Reshaping of European Musical Taste 1770—1870,« *International Review of the Aesthetics and Sociology of Music*, 1977, 8/1, pp. 5—22.

WIER, Albert Ernst, *The Piano: Its History, Makers, Players, and Music*, Longmans, London 1940.

WIORA, Walter, *Die vier Weltalter der Musik*, Stuttgart 1961. French transl *Les quatre âges de la musique*, Payot, Paris 1963. Engl. transl. *The Four Ages of Music*, Norton, New York 1967.

WOLFF, Helmuth Christian, *Die Venezianische Oper in der zweiten Hälfte des 17. Jahrhunderts. Ein Beitrag zur Geschichte der Musik und des Theaters im Zeitalter des Barocks*, O. Elsner, Berlin 1937.

WOODFILL, Walter, *Musicians in English Society, from Elizabeth to Charles I*, Princeton University Press, Princeton 1953.

YOUNG, Percy, *The Concert Tradition from the Middle Ages to the 20th Century*, Routledge and Kegan Paul, London 1965.

ZACCARO, Gianfranco, *Storia sociale della musica*, Newton Compton Editori, Roma 1979, pp. 207.

ZEMP, Hugo, *Musique dan. La musique dans la pensée et la vie sociale d'une société africaine*, Mouton, Paris-La Haye 1971, pp. 320.

ŽAK, S., *Musik als »Ehr und Zier« im mittelalterlichen Reich. Studien zur Musik im Höfischen Leben, Recht und Zeremoniell*, Verlag Dr. Päffgen, Neuss 1979, pp. IX-347.

SOCIAL FUNCTIONS OF MUSIC

ADORNO, Theodor Wiesengrund, »Zur gesellschaftlichen Lage der Musik,« *Zeitschrift für Sozialforschung*, 1932, I, pp. 103—124 and 356—378.

ALLEN, Warren Dwight, »Music and the Idea of Progress,« *The Journal of Aesthetics and Art Criticism*, 1946, IV/3—4, pp. 166—179.

ANDERSON, Simon V., »Adolescent Musical Preferences: Two Comentaries. The Role of Rock,« *Music Journal Educators*, 1968, V/54, pp. 37, 39, 41, 85—87.

BIBLIOGRAPHY

ASHSON, Joseph Nickerson, *Music in Worship*, The Pilgrim Press, Boston 1943.

AZBILL, Henry, »Native Dances: A Basic Part of Culture, Tradition, Religion,« *Indian Historian*, 1967, I/1, pp. 16—17, 20.

BECKET, Wheeler, *Music in Warplants*, War Production Board, War Production Drive Headquarters, Washington (D. C.), August 1943.

BERGER, K., *Die Funktionsbestimmung der Musik in der Sowjetideologie*, Berlin 1963.

BLACKING, John, »The Value of Music in Human Experience,« *Yearbook of the International Folk Music Council*, 1969, 1, pp. 33—71.

BLEGEN, Theodore Christian, and Martin B. RUUD, *Norwegian Emigrant Songs and Ballads*, University of Minnesota Press, Minneapolis 1936.

BOBILLIER, Marie, *La musique militaire*, H. Laurens, Paris 1917.

BOWLES, Edmund A., »La hiérarchie des instruments de musique dans l'Europe féodale,« *Revue de musicologie*, Paris 1958, XLII/118, pp. 155—169.

— »Musical Instruments at the Medieval Banquet,« *Revue belge de musicologie*, Brussels 1958, XII/1—4, pp. 41—51.

— »Musical Instruments in Civic Processions During the Middle Ages,« *Acta musicologica*, Basel 1961, XXXIII/2—4, pp. 147—161.

BRELET, Gisèle, »Art et Sagesse,« *La Table Ronde*, 1962, 170, pp. 27—37.

BRENET, Michel, »Notes sur l'introduction des instruments dans les églises de France,« in *Riemann-Festschrift*, Max Hesses Verlag, Leipzig 1909, pp. 277—286.

BRUNNER, A., *Wesen, Funktion und Ort der Musik im Gottesdienst*, Zurich 1960.

BUCCI, Jerry Michael, *Love, Marriage, and Family Life Themes in the Popular Song: A Comparison of the Years 1940 and 1965*, Ph. D. Thesis, Columbia University, New York 1968.

BÜCHER, Karl, *Arbeit und Rhythmus*, Teubner, Leipzig 1892, 2nd ed. 1892, 3rd ed. 1902.

BUMPUS, John Skelton, *A History of English Cathedral Music 1549—1889*, Pott, New York 1908.

BURDE, Wolfgang, »Über gesellschaftliche Vermittlung von Musik,« *Neue Zeitschrift für Musik*, 1970, CXXXI/11, pp. 558—561.

BURGE, William, *On the Choral Service of the Anglo-Catholic Church*, G. Bell, London 1844.

CALAME-GRIAULE, G., and B. CALAME, »Introduction à l'étude de la musique africaine,« *La revue musicale*, 1957, 238, pp. 5—21.

CAMUS, Raoul F., *Military Music of the American Revolution*, The University of North Carolina Press, Chapel Hill 1977, 2nd ed., pp. XII——218.

CAPLOW, Theodor, »The Influence of Radio Music as a Social Institution,« *Cahiers d'études de Radio-Télévision*, 1955, 3/4, pp. 279—291.

CARADEC, Fr., and WEILL, A., *Le café-concert*, Atelier Hachette-Massin, Paris 1980, pp. 342.

CARDINELL, R. L., »Music in Industry,« in *Music and Medicine*, D. M. Schullian and M. Schön, ed., Schumann, New York 1948.

CARPITELLA, Diego, »Considérations sur le folklore musical italien dans ses rapports avec la structure sociale du pays,« *Journal of the International Folk Music Council*, 1959, 11, pp. 66—70.

CLARK, K. S., *Music in Industry*, New York 1929.

CLEARING, Carl, *Music and Jägerei*, Bärenreiter-Verlag, Kassel 1937.

COLES, Robert, »The Words and Music of Social Change,« *Daedalus*, 1969, 98, pp. 684—689.

COLLINS, J. J., *The Social and Economic Value of Music in Industry*, East St. Louis (Illinois) 1937.

COMBARIEU, Jules, *La musique et la magie. Etude sur les origines populaires de l'art musical, son influence et sa fonction dans les sociétés*, Picard, Paris 1909; reprint: Minkoff, Genève 1971.

CRESSEY, Paul Goalby, *The Taxi-Dance Hall; A Sociological Study in Commercialized Recreation and City Life*, Greenwood Press, New York—Chicago 1968; Patterson Smith, Montclair (N. J.) 1969.

CSIPAK, Károly, »Zur Stellung der Musik in der gegenwartigen Gesellschaft,« in *Das Argument — Berliner Hefte für Probleme der Gesellschaft*, Juli 1963, 26, pp. 22—26.

CUDJOE, C. D., »The Techniques of Ewe Drumming and the Social Importance of Music in Africa,« *Phylon*, 1953, XIV/3, pp. 280—291.

DANIÉLOU, Alain, »Values in Music,« in *Artistic Values in Traditional Music: Proceedings of a Conference*, Berlin, July 14 to 16, 1965, Peter Crossley--Holland, ed., International Institute for Comparative Music Studies and Documentation, Berlin 1966, pp. 10—21.

DAVID, H. T., »The Cultural Functions of Music,« *Journal of the History of Ideas*, 1951, XII/3, pp. 423—439.

DAVIS, Martha Ellen, »The Social Organization of a Musical Event: The Fiesta de Cruz in San Juan, Puerto Rico,« *Ethnomusicology*, 1972, XVI/1, pp. 38—62.

DAVISON, A. T., *Church Music — Illusion and Reality*, Cambridge (Mass.) 1952.

DENISOFF, R. Serge, »Popular Protest Song; The Case of Eve of Destruction,« *Public Opinion Quarterly*, 1971, XXXV, pp. 117—122.

— »Protest Movements: Class Consciousness and the Propaganda Song,« *Sociological Quarterly*, 1968, IX, pp. 228—247.

— »Protest Songs: Those on the Top Forty and Those on the Street,« *American Quarterly*, 1970, XXII/4, pp. 807—823.

— *Sing a Song of Social Significance*, University Popular Press, Bowling Green 1972.

DENISOFF, R. Serge and R. A. PETERSON, *The Sounds of Social Change*, Rand McNally, Chicago 1972.

DESCOTES, Jacques, »La musique fonctionnelle,« *Polyphonie*, 1951, 7—8, pp. 71—92.

DISERENS, Charles M., *The Influence of Music on Behavior*, Princeton University Press, Princeton 1926.

DOBBS, Jack Percival Baker, *Music and the Dance in the Multi-Racial Society of West Malaysia*, University of London, 1972, pp. 559.

DOMP, J., *Studien zur Geschichte der Musik an westfälischen Adelshöfen im XVIII Jahrhundert*, Regensburg 1934.

DONAKOWSKI, Conrad L., *A Muse for the Masses. Ritual and Music in an Age of Democratic Revolution, 1770—1870*, The University of Chicago Press, Chicago and London 1972, 1977, pp. 435.

DORŮŽKA, Lubomír, »Protest durch U-Musik,« *The World of Music*, 1970, XII/2, pp. 19—31.

DOWNEY, James Cecil, *The Music of American Revivalism*, Ph. D. Thesis, Tulane University, 1968.

— »Revivalism, the Gospel Songs, and Social Reform,« *Ethnomusicology* 1965, 9/2, pp. 115—125.

EGGEBRECHT, Hans Heinrich, »Funktionale Musik,« *Archiv für Musikwissenschaft*, 1975, 30, pp. 1-25.

EICHENSEER, Adolf J., *Volksgesang im Inn-Oberland. Die Funktion des Singens in einem oberbayrischen Dorf der Gegenwart*, Historischer Verein Rosenheim, Rosenheim 1969, pp. 365.

ESCHMANN, Wolfgang, »Musik — ein Medium der Persönlichkeitsbildung,« *Rheinische Philharmonie*, Koblenz 1970, pp. 44—49.

FENDRYCH, L., »K otácze spoločenske funkce masových hudebních žanrů a jejich estetickeho hodnosení,« *Hudebni věda*, 1967, IV/4, pp. 665—680.

FENLON, Iain, »Music and Spectacle at the Gonzaga Court, c. 1580—1600,« *Proceedings of the Royal Musical Association*, 1976-77, 103, pp. 90——105.

FOX, Lilla M., *Instruments of Religion and Folklore*, Roy Publishers, New York; Lutterworth Press, London 1969.

FRANCÈS. Robert, »La langue musicale dans la société contemporaine,« *Sciences de l'Art*, 1964, 1, pp. 29—46.

FREEMAN, L. C., »The Changing Functions of a Folksong,« *Journal of American Folklore*, 1957, LXX/277, pp. 215—220.

FRIEDMANN, Georges, »Rôle et place de la musique dans une société industrielle,« *Diogène*, 1970, 72, pp. 27—44.

FUKS, Marian, »Muzyka w gettach,« *Muzyka*, 1971, XVI/1, pp. 64—76.

GAERTNER, J. A., »Art as the Function of an Audience,« *Daedalus*, 1955, LXXXVI/1, pp. 80—93.

GARON, Paul, »Blues and the Church: Revolt and Resignation,« *Living Blues*, Chicago 1970, 1/1, pp. 18—23.

GILSON, Etienne, *La société de masse et sa culture*, Vrin, Paris 1967.

GLADDING, B. A., »Music as a Social Force During the English Commonwealth and the Restoration (1649—1700)«, *Musical Quarterly*, 1929, 15, pp. 506—512.

GÖTLIND, Erik, »Some Functions of Music,« in *Fylkingen International Bulletin*, No. 2, 1969.

GREENBIE, M. B., *The Art of Leisure*, Mc-Graw-Hill, New York 1935.

GREENWAY, John, *American Folksongs of Social and Economic Protest*, Ph. D. Thesis, University of Pennsylvania 1951.

GRIGOROVICI, Lucian, »Socialist Politmusic — Viewed Sociologically,« *Musik und Bildung*, 1970, IX/2, pp. 367—369; *The World of Music*, 1970, XII/1, pp. 6—18.

GUILD, Elliott William, *The Sociological Role of Music in Primitive Cultures*, M. A. Thesis, Stanford University 1931.

HALPIN, D. D., »Industrial Music and Moral,« *The Journal of the Acoustical Society of America*, 1943, 15, pp. 77—78.

HAMBLY, W., *Tribal Dancing and Social Development*, London 1926.

HARRISON, Frank, »Music and Cult: the Functions of Music in Social and Religious Systems,« in *Perspectives in Musicology*, New York 1972, pp. 307-334.

HASSAN, S. Q., *Les instruments de musique en Irak et leur rôle dans la société traditionelle*, Mouton/Ed. de l'Ecole des hautes études en sciences sociales, Paris 1980, pp. 258.

HAWEIS, Hugh Reginald, *Music and Morals*, Harper, New York 1900.

HAYBURN, Robert F., *Papal Legislation on Sacred Music. 95 A. D. to 1977 A. D.*, The Liturgical Press, Collegeville (Minnesota) 1979, pp. XIV-619.

HEILFURTH, Gerhard, *Das Bergmannslied — Wesen, Leben und Funktion*, Ein Beitrag zur Erhellung von Bestand und Wandlung der sozialkulturellen Elemente im Aufbau der industriellen Gesellschaft, Kassel 1954.

HIRSCH, Jean-François, »La dé-fête urbaine I,« *Musique en jeu*, 1976, 24, pp. 45-54.

HONIGSHEIM, Paul, »Die Ähnlichkeit von Musik und Drama in primitiven und totalitären Gesellschaften,« *Kölner Zeitschrift für Soziologie und Sozialpsychologie*, 1964, XVI/3, pp. 481—490.

HONOLKA, K., »Die soziale Funktion der Neuen Musik,« *Musica*, 1953, 7, pp. 243—246.

HOSOKAWA, Shuhei, »Considérations sur la musique mass-médiatisée,« International Review of the Aesthetics and Sociology of Music, 1981, 12/1, pp. 21—50.

HUSKISSON, Yvonne, »The Social and Ceremonial Music of the Pedi,« Journal of Social Research, 1959, 10, pp. 129—130.

JACKSON, Anthony, »Sound and Ritual,« Man, 1968, 3/2, pp. 143—145.

JEUDY, Henri-Pierre, »Fêtes, musique et morcellement de la ville,« Musiaue en jeu, 1976, 24, pp. 55-64.

JUNGHEINRICH, Hans-Klaus, »Hörmassage. Musik in der Werbung,« Musica, 1969, XXIII/6, pp. 559—561.

KAPLAN, Max, Music in the City, First Mimeographed Edition, Pueblo 1944.

KESTING, Marianne, »Happenings. Analyse eines Symptoms,« Melos, 1969, XXXVI/7—8, pp. 307—319.

KLAUSMEIER, Friedrich, Jugend und Musik im technischen Zeitalter, Bonn 1963.

— »Musik als Mittel sozialer Integration in Israel. Bericht nach einer Studienreise,« Musik und Bildung, 1972, IV/1, pp. 20—24.

— »Über die Wirkung der Musik,« in Musik im Unterricht, 1966, 7/8.

— »Singen und Lied in unserer Gesellschaft. Ein Beitrag zu ihrer Motivation,« in Schriftenreihe der Bundeszentrale für politische Bildung, Vol. 76, n. d., pp. 3—12.

KLEINHEKSEL, John R., »The Role of the Choir in Reformed Church Worship: Past, Present and Future,« Reformed Review, 1964, 17, pp. 13—24.

KLUSEN, Ernst, »Musik zur Arbeit heute,« Arbeit und Volksleben, Schwarz, Göttingen 1967, pp. 306—317.

KONZ, Stephen and David McDOUGAL, »The Effect of Background Music on the Control Activity of an Automobile Driver,« Human Factors, 1968, 10/3, pp. 233—244.

KOTEK, Josef, »Die Rezeption der Funktionalen Musik als gesellschaftlicher Aneigungsprozeß,« International Review of the Aesthetics and Sociology of Music, 1978, 9/2, pp. 183—218.

KRESANEK, J., Sociálna funkcia hudby, Bratislava 1961.

»Die gesellschaftliche Funktion der Musik,« Beiträge zur Musikwissenschaft, 1963, 5, pp. 304-306.

LAADE, Wolfgang, »The Situation of Music and Music Research in the Pacific — A Call for Increased Activity,« Bulletin of the International Committee on Urgent Anthropological and Ethnological Research, 1968, 10, pp. 53—60.

LEFEBVRE, Henri, »La musique et la ville, avec Henri Lefebvre,« Musique en jeu, 1976, 24, pp. 75-81.

LESSER, Wolfgang, »Die soziale Funktion unserer Kunst bei der Entwicklung einer sozialistischen Volkskultur,« *Musik und Gesellschaft*, Berlin (GDR) 1968, XVIII, pp. 743—814.

LORTAT-JACOB, Bernard, *Musique et fêtes au Haut-Atlas*, Publications de la Société française de Musicologie, Paris 1982, pp. 154.

MACHAYÉKHI, A., »Musique dans la ville,« *Musique en jeu*, 1976, 24, pp. 29-32.

MADSEN, Clifford K., and Charles H. MADSEN Jr., »Music as a Behavior Modification Technique with a Juvenile Delinquent,« *Journal of Music Therapy*, 1968, 5/3, pp. 72—76.

MALCOLM, Charles Alexander, *The Piper in Peace and War*, J. Murray, London 1927.

MALLEY, François, »En Amerique Latine: les trouvères rebelles chantent la révolte,« in *Croissance des jeunes nations*, 1972, 140, pp. 28—29.

MANHEIM, Henry L., and Alice CUMMINS, »Selected Musical Traits among Spanish, Negro, and Anglo-American Girls,« *Sociology and Social Research*, 1960, 45/1, pp. 56—64.

MASS, Edgar, »Montesquieu und Jean-Jacques Rousseau. Die politische Funktion der Musik,« *Zeitung für französische Sprache und Literatur*, 1969, LXXIX, pp. 289—303.

McALLESTER, David P., »The Role of Music in Western Apache Culture,« in *Selected Papers of the Fifth International Congress of Anthropological and Ethnological Sciences, 1956*, University of Pennsylvania Press, Philadelphia 1960, pp. 468—472.

McKISSICK, Marvin Leo, *A Study of the Function of Music in the Major Religious Revivals in America since 1875*, MM. Thesis, University of Southern California 1957.

McLEOD, N., *The Social Context of Music in a Polynesian Community*, M. A. Thesis, London School of Economics, London 1956—1957.

MERRIAM, Alan P., *The Anthropology of Music*, Evanston (Ill.) 1964.

— »The Use of Music as a Technique of Reconstructing Culture History in Africa«, in *Reconstructing African Culture History*, C. Gabel and N. R. Bennett, eds., Boston University Press, Boston 1967, pp. 83—114.

MEYER, Ernst H., »Die aktive gesellschaftliche Rolle der Musik,« *Aufbau*, Berlin 1951, 7, pp. 349—352.

MOBERG, Carl-Alan, »The Function of Music in Modern Society,« *Svensk Tidskrift for Musikforskning*, 1954, XXXVI, pp. 84—93.

MUSEL, Albrecht, »Das politische Massenlied in der DDR. Funktion, Pflege, Verbreitung und Wirkung,« in *Deutsche Studium*, 1968, VI/23, pp. 264—278.

MUKERJEE, Radhakamal, *The Social Function of Art,* Philosophical Library, New York 1954.

— »Musik im Wandel von Freizeit und Bildung,« in *Musikalische Zeitfragen,* Vol. 2, Kassel 1957.

NETTEL, R., *Music in Five Towns 1840—1914. A Study of Social Influence of Music in an Industrial District,* 3rd ed., Oxford 1945.

NUNES, Geraldo, I. STOIANOVA and E. VERON, »Musique-en-ville,« *Musique en jeu,* 1976, 24, pp. 34-44.

ODUM, Howard Washington, *Negro Workaday Songs,* Oxford University Press, H. Milford, London 1926.

PARKER, H. W., *Music and Public Entertainment,* Boston 1911.

PIETZSCH, G., *Die Musik im Erziehungs- und Bildungsideal des ausgehenden Altertums und frühen Mittelalters,* Halle 1932.

PISCHNER, Hans, »Brecht und die gesellschaftliche Funktion der Musik. Zum 70. Geburtstag des Dichters am 10. Februar,« *Musik und Gesellschaft,* Berlin 1968, XVIII/2, pp. 75—86.

PODVIN, Mary Grace, »The Influence of Music on the Performance of a Work Task,« *Journal of Music Therapy,* 1967, 4/2, pp. 52—56.

REINECKE, Hans-Peter, »Musische Bildung und soziale Funktion,« in *Perspektiven kommunaler Kulturpolitik,* pp. 410-421.
— »Zehn Thesen zum Thema »Musik in Arbeitswelt und Freizeit,« *Musikbildung,* 1974, VI/11, pp. 589-591.

RHODES, Willard, »Music as an Agent of Political Expression,« *African Studies Bulletin,* 1962, 5, pp. 14—22.

RICKS, George Robinson, *Some Aspects of the Religious Music of the United States Negro: An Ethnomusicological Study with Special Emphasis on the Gospel Tradition,* Ph. D. Thesis (Anthropology), Northwestern University, 1960.

RÖSING, Helmut, »Funktion und Bedeutung von Musik in der Werbung,« *Archiv für Musikwissenschaft,* 1975, 32, pp. 139—155.

Thesen zur Funktionsnivellierung massenmedial dargebotener Musik, in *Symposium Musik und Massenmedien,* H. Rösing, ed., München 1978, pp. 95—104.

SALAZAR, Adolfo, *Música y sociedad en el siglo XX, ensayo de critica desde el punto de vista de su funcion social,* Mexico City 1939.

— *La música en la sociedad Europea, El Colegio de México,* Mexico City 1942.

SCARAMUZZI, Francesco, *Per dilettatione grande et per utilità incredibile. Musica ed esperienze sociali tra Rinascimento e Barocco,* Laterza, Bari 1982, pp. 133.

SCHAEFFNER, André, »Musique et structures sociales,« *Revue française de sociologie,* 1962, III/4, pp. 388—395.

SCHAFER, Murray, *The Tunning of the World*, Knopf, New York 1977.

SCHAUFFLER, Robert Haven, *Music as a Social Force in America*, The Caxton Institute, New York 1927.

SCHENDA, Rudolf, »Noch einmal: Triviallyrik — Küchenlieder,« *Kölner Zeitschrift für Soziologie und Sozialpsychologie*, 1970, XXII, pp. 129—134.

SCHLOEZER, B., »La fonction sociale du compositeur,« in *Atti del secondo Congresso internazionale di Musica*, F. le Monnier Florence 1940, pp.9-13

SCHNEIDER, Marius, »Le rôle de la musique dans la mythologie et les rites des civilisations non-européenes,« in *Histoire de la musique*, Gallimard, Paris 1960, Vol. I, pp. 131—214.

SCHOPP, J., *Das deutsche Arbeitslied*, Ph.D. Thesis, Heidelberg 1935.

SCHUTZ, Alfred, »Making Music together: A Study in Social Relationship,« in *Collected Papers, Studies in Social Theory* A. Brodessen, ed., Martinus Nijhoff, The Hague 1964, Vol. 2, pp. 159—178.

SCHWAB, Heinrich W., »Unterhaltendes des Musizieren im Industriegebiet des 19. Jahrhunderts,« in *Studien zur Trivialmusik des 19. Jahrhunderts*, G. Bosse, Regensburg 1967, pp. 151—158.

SCHWAEN, K., *Tonweisen sind Denkweisen. Beiträge über die Musik als eine gesellschaftliche Funktion*, Lied der Zeit, Berlin 1949.

SEEGER, Charles, »Music and Class Structure in the United States,« *American Quarterly*, 1957, IX/3, pp. 281—294.

— »Music as a Tradition of Communication, Discipline, and Play,« *Ethnomusicology*, 1962, 6/3, pp. 156—163.

— »The Music Process as a Function in a Context of Functions,« *Yearbook*, Inter-American Institute for Musical Research, 1966, II, pp. 1—36.

— »The Music Compositional Process as a Function in a Nest of Functions and in Itself a Nest of Functions,« in *Studies in Musicology, 1935-1975*, University of California Press, Berkeley-Los Angeles-London 1977. pp. 139-167

SELLERS, Mary Josephine, *The Role of the Fine Arts in the Culture of Southern Baptist Churches*, Ph.D. Thesis (Humanities), Syracuse University, 1968.

SHAY, Frank, *American Sea Songs and Chanteys from the Days of Iron Men and Wooden Ships*, Norton, New York 1968.

SMALLEY, William A., »Music, Church, and Ethnocentrism,« *Practical Anthropology*, 1962, 9, pp. 272—273.

SMITH, Michael G., »The Social Functions and Meaning of Hausa Praise-Singing,« *Ibadan*, 1965, 21, pp. 81—92.

SOIBELMAN, D., *Therapeutic and Industrial Uses of Music. A Review of the Literature*, Columbia University Press, New York 1948.

STAPLES, Sylvia M., »A Paired-Associates Learning Test Utilizing Music as the Mediator: An Exploratory Study,« *Journal of Music Therapy*, 1968, 5/2, pp. 53—57.

399

STEELE, Anita Louis, »Effects of Social Reinforcement on the Musical Preference of Mentally Retarded Children,« *Journal of Music Therapy*, 1967, 42/2, pp. 57—62.

STEFANI, Gino, »Hören, Sprechen, Singen in der Gruppe,« *Musik und Altar*, 1970, XX/4, pp. 166—177.

STEGNER, S. Page, »Protest Songs from the Butte Mines,« *Western Folklore*, 1967, XXVI/3, pp. 157—167.

STOCKHAUSEN, Karlheinz, »Musik in Funktion,« *Melos*, 1957, 24/9, pp. 249——251.

STÜRZBECHER, Ursula, »Das große Fragezeichen hinter einer gesellschaftspolitischen Funktion der Musik,« *Melos*, 1972, XXXIX/3, pp. 142—149.

SUPIČIĆ, Ivo, »Music and Ceremony. Another Aspect,« *International Review of the Aesthetics and Sociology of Music*, 1982, 13/1 pp. 21—38.

TALLON, Roger, »La musique utilitaire, avec Roger Tallon,« *Musique en jeu*, 1976, 24, pp. 68-74.

TAUT, Kurt, *Beiträge zur Geschichte der Jagdmusik*, Radelli & Hille, Leipzig 1927.

TESSAROLO, Mariselda, *L'espressione musicale e le sue funzioni*, Giuffrè, Milano 1983, pp. XI-336.

TRAORÈ, Bakary, *The Black African Theatre and its Social Functions*, Ibadan University Press, 1972, pp. XVII+130.

— UNESCO, *Music in Education, International Commission on the Role and Place of Music in the Education of Youth and Adults*, Brussels, June 29 — July 9, 1953, Paris 1955.

VALLS, N., *Musica i societat. Notes per un etudi de la funcio social de la musica*, Barcelona 1963.

ŽAK, S., *Musik als »Ehr und Zier« im mittelalterlichen Reich. Studien zur Musik im Höfischen Leben, Recht und Zeremoniell*, Verlag Dr. Päffgen, Neuss 1979, pp. IX-347.

MUSICAL PUBLIC

ADORNO, Theodor Wiesengrund, »Neue Musik, Interpretation, Publikum,« in *Klangfiguren — Musikalische Schriften I*, Berlin — Frankfurt/M. 1959.

— »Typen musikalischen Verhaltens,« in *Einleitung in die Musiksoziologie — Zwölf theoretische Vorlesungen,* Luhrkamp, Frankfurt/M. 1962, pp. 13—31.

ALEXANDRESCU, Lucia, and Vladimir POPESCU - DEVESELU, »Probleme actuale ale publicului muzical,« in *Studii şi cercetări de istoria artei, teatru, muzica, cinematografie*, 1971, XVIII/2, pp. 215—222.

BACHMANN, Claus-Henning, »Rundfunk, neue Musik, Publikum: Fragen und Versäumnisse«, *Schweizerische Musikzeitung*, 1977, 5, pp. 253—260.

BARRAUD, Henri, »La musique et son public en France,« *Age nouveau*, 1955, X/92, pp. 42—47.

BECKER, Howard S., »The Professional Dance Musician and His Audience,« *The American Journal of Sociology*, Chicago 1951, LVII/2, pp. 136—144.

BECKER, H., »Komponist und Mitwelt — Ein Plädoyer für das Publikum,« *Musica*, 1969, 23, pp. 1-4.

BESSELER, Heinrich, »Umgangsmusik und Darbietungsmusik im 16. Jahrhundert,« *Archiv für Musikwissenschaft*, 1959, 16, pp. 21—43.

BEVILLE, H. M., *Social Stratification of the Radio Audience*, New York 1939.

BONTINCK, Irmgard, »The Public of the Music Theatre. A Preliminary Bibliography,« in *IMDT Progress Report No. 5*, Vienna 1971.
»Das Publikum des Musiktheaters und die technischen Medien,« in *IMDT Progress Report No. 3*, Vienna 1970.

BOUYER, R., »Le public des concerts et la composition des programmes,« *Revue politique et littéraire*, 1905, 2, pp. 857—859.

CHAILLEY, Jacques, »Problèmes de la musique contemporaine et de l'auditeur devant l'histoire du langage. Essai d'explication technique d'un divorce,« *La revue internationale de musique*, 1952, 13, pp. 209—220.

— »La radio et le développement de l'instinct harmonique chez les auditeurs,« *Cahiers d'études de Radio-Télévision*, 1955, 3/4, pp. 401—412.

CLERCQ, Jacqueline de, »Le public des concerts à Bruxelles,« *International Review of the Aesthetics and Sociology of Music*, 1972, III/1, pp. 43—60.

* * *, *Composer, Performer, Public: A Study in Communication*, IMC, 1970, pp. 212.

COOPER, Martin, »La musique moderne et l'auditeur,« *Polyphonie*, 1949, 5, pp. 108—112.

DASNOY, H., »L'art et le public,« *La revue nouvelle*, 1958, 28/10, pp. 265—274.

DEKANY, Emile, »Une forme 'élémentaire' de la vie sociale: le public,« *Revue internationale de sociologie*, 1936, XLIV/5—6, pp. 263—277.

DUFRENNE, Mikel, »Pour une sociologie de public,« *Cahiers internationaux de sociologie*, 1949, VI, pp. 101—112.

DURAND, Jacques, *Le cinéma et son public*, Sirey, Paris 1958.

DURGNAT, Raymond, »Art and Audience,« *The British Journal of Aesthetics*, 1970, X/1, pp. 11—25.

EISLER, Hanns, »Hörer und Komponist,« *Aufbau*, 1949, pp. 200—208.

ELKIN, Robert, *The Old Concert Rooms of London*, Edward Arnold, London 1955.

401

FURTWÄNGLER, Wilhelm, *Der Musiker und sein Publikum*, Atlantis, Zurich 1955

GEORGESCU, Corneliu Dan, »Aspectul estetic si 'de consum' al muzicii in societatea contemporanâ (The Aesthetic Aspect and the Performance of Music in Contemporary Society),« *Muzica*, 1974, XXIV/4, pp. 5—7.

GIULIANI, Elizabeth, »Le public de l'Opéra de Paris de 1750 à 1760. Mesure et définition,« *International Review of the Aesthetics and Sociology of Music*, 1977. VIII/2, pp. 159—183.

GÜNTHER, S., »Die Oper und ihr Publikum,« *Musica*, 1967, 21/3, pp. 97-101.

HARDING, D. W., »The Social Background of Taste in Music,« *The Musical Times*, 1938, LXXIX, pp. 333—335 and 417—419.

HELM, Everett, *Composer, Performer, Public*, Leo S. Olschki, Florence 1970.

HRDÝ, Ladislav, »Kolik Pražanů navštěvuje koncerty umělecké hudby?,« *Hudební rozhledy*, 1973, 26/7, pp. 330—334.

— »Mladí lidé a koncerty«, *Opus Musicum*, 1974, VI/8, pp. 257-263.

HELM, Everett, *Composer, Performer, Public*, Leo S. Olschki, Florence 1970.

HERRMANN, H., »Struktur und Funktion des Publikums. Eine grundsätzliche Frage,« *Musica*, 1958, 6.

HILLER, F., *Die Musik und das Publikum. Vortrag, gehalten zu Gunsten der Veteranen in Köln*, Cologne 1864.

HIRSCH, P., *The Structure of the Popular Music Industry. An Examination of the Filtering Process by which Records are Preselected for Public Consumption*, University of Michigan, 1970.

HONOLKA, K., »Hat das Publikum versagt? Eine notwendige Richtigstellung,« *Musica*, 1956, 7—8.

* * *, *De Houding van het publiek tegenover de opera, Verslag van een psychologisch en statistisch onderzoek, ingesteld in opdracht van de Amsterdamse Kunstraad*, Amsterdam 1963.

JAGER, Hugo de, *Cultuuroverdracht en concertbezoek*, Leiden 1967.

— *Listening to the Audience. A Survey among Regular Concertgoers of the Utrecht Symphony Orchestra*, Utrecht 1963.

— »Listening to the Audience,« *Journal of Research in Music Education*, 1967, XV/4, pp. 293—299.

KARKOSCHKA, Erhard, »Neue Musik und ihr Publikum — gestern, heute und morgen,« *Musik und Bildung*, 1968, I/7—8, pp. 317—322.

* * *, *Komponist - Interpret - Publikum*, *Musik und Gesellschaft*, 1962, 12, pp. 329—330.

KONEČNÁ, Helena, »Publikum & opera ve svetle jednoho výzkumu,« *Opus Musikum*, 1970, ii/4, pp. 97—104.

BIBLIOGRAPHY

KOTEK, Josef, »Hudbení publikum — iluze a realite,« *Hudební rozhledy,* 1966, 19/5, pp. 129—133; 19/7, pp. 195—198.

— »Das Musik-Publikum,« *Musik und Gesellschaft,* 1967, XVII/2, pp. 81—87.

MARSOP, P., »Theater. Konzertsaal, Zuhörerschaft,« *Wissen und Leben,* 1922, 17, pp. 1339—1347.

MAYER, Jacob Peter, *British Cinemas and Their Audiences: Sociological Studies,* D. Dobson, London 1948.

MÖWINCKEL, L. J. Jr., *Bidrag til publikums psykologi — Belyst ved undersøkelser i Oslo,* Oslo 1937.

MUELLER, John Henry, »The Aesthetic Gap between Consumer and Composer,« *Journal of Research in Music Education,* 1967, XV/2, pp. 151—158.

MÜLLER-FREIENFELS, R., »Künstlertum und Kunstpublikum,« *Kölner Vierteljahrshefte für Soziologie,* 1931/1932, 10, pp. 67—86.

* * *, *Music and its Public,* Special number of *The World of Music,* 1963, 5.

NÜHLEN, K., »Das Publikum und seine Aktionsarten,« *Kölner Zeitschrift für Soziologie und Sozialpsychologie,* 1952/1953, 5, pp. 446—474.

PAULI, Hansjörg, *Für wenn komponieren Sie eigentlich?,* Fischer, Frankfurt//M. 1971, pp. 154.

PETERSON, Richard A., »Artistic Creativity and Alienation: The Jazz Musician vs. his Audience,« *Arts in Society,* 1965, 3, pp. 244—248.

POLLMAN, J., »Notities over muziek en publiek,« in *Volksopvoeding,* 1966, 15/6, pp. 372—378.

PORTE, J., »Une enquête par sondage sur l'auditoire radiophonique,« in *Bulletin mensuel de statistique,* Suppléments trimestriels, Institut national de la statistique, Paris 1954.

RAUHE, Hermann, *Popularität in der Musik,* G. Braun, Karlsruhe 1974, pp. 63.

ROSTAND, Claude, »La musique contemporaine et le public,« *La Revue musicale,* 1958, 242, pp. 65—67.

RUTZ, H., »Musik und Publikum,« *Musica,* 1950, 4, pp. 369—371.

SAVA, Iosif, »Muzica si publicul,« *Muzica,* 1972, XXII/2, pp. 6—8.

SCHERING, Arnold, »Künstler, Kenner und Liebhaber der Musik im Zeitalter Haydns und Goethes,« in *Jahrbuch Peters,* 1931, 38, pp. 9—23.

SESSIONS, Roger, *The Musical Experience of Composer, Performer, Listener,* University of Princeton Press, Princeton 1950.

SILBERMANN, Alphons, »Die Musik und das Publikum von morgen. Bericht und Gutachten zu einem Forschungsprojekt des internationalen Musikrats«, *Musikbildung,* 1975, VII/2, pp. 73-77.

SINGER, K., »Das Publikum,« *Musik und Leben,* 1929, 5, pp. 81ff.

SIOHAN, Robert, *L'histoire du public musical,* Editions Rencontre, Lausanne 1967.

SUPIČIĆ, Ivo, »L'auditeur contemporain et la musique moderne,« *The World of Music*, 1963, V/1—2, pp. 34—35.

— »Music and the Mass Audience in Yugoslavia Today,« in *Papers of the Yugoslav-American Seminar on Music*, Malcolm H. Brown, ed., Indiana University, Bloomington 1970, pp. 62—66.

— »Music with or without a Public,« *The World of Music*, 1968, X/1, pp. 13—21.

— »La musique et son public,« *Schweizerische Musikzeitung*, 1963, CIII/6, pp. 343—348.

TAUBMAN, Howard, »Music Today and the Mass Audience in the United States,« in *Papers of the Yugoslav-American Seminar on Music*, Malcolm H. Brown, ed., Indiana University, Bloomington 1970, pp. 67—72.

TAYLOR, D., *The Well Tempered Listener*, New York 1940.

TRAN VĂN KHÊ, »Le public de concert en Orient et les changements d'ordre sociologique,« *The World of Music*, 1963, 5; in *France-Asie/Asia*, 1967, 191, pp. 549—562.

WEIL, Rudolf, *Das Berliner Theaterpublikum unter A. W. Ifflands Direktion, (1796—1814)*, Selbstverlag der Gesellschaft für Theatergeschichte, Berlin 1932.

ZWEERS, Willem, and L. A. WALTERS, *Tonnel en publiek in Nederland*, Rotterdam-Utrecht 1970.

RECEPTION OF MUSIC. MUSICAL TASTE

ADORNO, Theodor Wiesengrund, »Anweisungen zum Hören neuer Musik,« in *Der getreue Korrepetitor. Lehrschriften zur musikalischen Praxis*, Frankfurt/M. 1963.

— *Schwierigkeiten in der Auffassung neuer Musik*, Bärenreiter, Kassel 1968, pp. 9—20.

— »Über den Fetischcharacter und die Regression des Hörens,« *Zeitschrift für Sozialforschung*, 1939, 7, pp. 321—356.

ARVIDSON, Peter, »On Interest, Activity and Taste in Music,« *New Patterns of Musical Behaviour*, Universal Edition, Vienna 1974, pp. 142—159.

BAGENAL, Hope, »Musical Taste and Concert Hall Design,« in *Proceedings of the Royal Musical Association*, 1951—1952, 78, pp. 11—229.

BERNER, H., »Untersuchungen zur Begriffsbestimmung und zu einigen Fragen der Rezeption von Programm-Musik. Ein Beitrag zur Musikerziehung und zur musikalischen Populärwissenschaft,« *Die Musikforschung*, 19, 1966; Leipzig 1964, pp. 54.

BESSELER, Heinrich, »Grundfragen des musikalischen Hörens,« *Jahrbuch Peters*, 1925, 32, pp. 35—52.

— *Das musikalische Hören der Neuzeit*, Berlin 1959.

BIBLIOGRAPHY

BIMBERG, Siegfried, »Entwurf einer Rezeptionslehre für die Musik,« in *Wissenschaftliche Beiträge der Universität Halle*, 1968, VIII/18, pp. 155—222.

BIMBERG, Siegfried, and Wolfgang KÖHLER, »Zur Methodik von Untersuchungen musikalischer Intereßen,« in *Wissenschaftliche Zeitschrift Universität Halle*, 1968, XVII/4, pp. 107—114.

BLAUKOPF, Kurt, »Probleme der Raumakustik und des Hörverhaltens,« *Musikalische Zeitfragen*, 19, Vol. XII, pp. 61—71.

— Über die Veränderung der Hörgewohnheit — Aktuelle Bemerkungen zum akustisch-technischen Einfluß auf den musikalischen Geschmack,« *Schweizerische Musikzeitung*, 1954, 94, pp. 60—61.

— »Zur Bestimmung der klanglichen Erfahrung der Musikstudierenden,« in Schriftenreihe *Musik und Gesellschaft*, G. Braun, Karlsruhe 1968, Vol. 2.

CHAILLEY, Jacques, »Problèmes de la musique contemporaine et de l'auditeur devant l'histoire du langage. Essai d'explication technique d'un divorce,« *La revue internationale de musique*, 1952, 13, pp. 209—220.

CONYERS, James E., »An Exploratory Study of Musical Tastes and Interests of College Students,« *Sociological Inquiry*, Winter 1963, 33/1, pp. 58—66.

CYRUS, Andrew, »Music for Receptive Release,« *Journal of Music Therapy*, 1966, 3, pp. 45-52.

EBERHARD, F., *Der Rundfunkhörer und sein Programm — Ein Beitrag zur empirischen Sozialforschung*, Berlin 1962.

EHRENZWEIG, A., *The Psycho-Analysis of Artistic Vision and Hearing*, Routledge & Kegan Paul, London 1953.

FALTIN. P.. and H.-P. REINECKE, *Musik und Verstehen. Aufsätze zur semiotischen Theorie, Ästhetik und Soziologie der musikalischen Rezeption*, Gerig, Köln 1973.

FARNSWORTH, Paul Randolph, *Musical Taste. Its Measurement and Cultural Nature*, Stanford University Press, Stanford (California) 1950, University Series, Education-Psychology, Vol. 2, no. 1.

— »The Phenomenon of Musical Taste,« *Psychology Today*, Stanford University, 1967, I/4, pp. 14—19, 40—43.

— »Ratingscales for Musical Interests,« *The Journal of Psychology*, 1949, 28, pp. 245—253.

FEDERHOFER, Hellmut, »Zur Rezeption Neuer Musik,« *International Review of the Aesthetics and Sociology of Music*, 1972, III/1, pp. 5—34.

FISHER, R. L., »Preferences of Different Age and Socio-Economic Groups in Unstructured Musical Situations,« *Journal of Social Psychology*, 1951, 33, pp. 147—152.

FISHER, S., and R. L. FISHER, »The Effects of Personal Insecurity on Reactions to Unfamiliar Music,« *Journal of Social Psychology*, 1951, 34, pp. 265—273.

FRANCÈS, Robert, *La perception de la musique*, Vrin, Paris 1958.

405

BIBLIOGRAPHY

GEIGER, T., »A Radio Test of Musical Taste,« *Public Opinion Quarterly*, 1950, 14, pp. 453—460.

GÜLKE, Peter, »Interpretation und die Wandlungen des musikalischen Hörens,« in *Bericht über den Internationalen Musikwissenschaftlichen Kongreß*, Leipzig 1966, pp. 487—489.

GÜNTHER, S., »Hörer und Hören in unserer Zeit. Versuch einer psychologischen Typologie der Konzertbesucher von heute,« *Schweizerische Musikzeitung*, 1958, pp. 7—8.

HAASE, Rudolf, *Über das disponierte Gehör*, Fragmente als Beiträge zur Musiksoziologie, 4, Vienna 1977, pp. 52.

HARDING, Denys W., »The Social Background of Taste in Music,« *The Musical Times*, 1938, 79, pp. 333—335, 417—419.

HEINEMANN, Rudolf, »Der Hörer zwischen Musikwissenschaft, Soziologie und Kulturkritik. Ein musiksoziologisches Akrostichon,« *Kölner Zeitschrift für Soziologie und Sozialpsychologie*, 1969, XXI/3, pp. 560—568.

— »Der Hörer zwischen Musikwissenschaft, Soziologie und Kulturkritik,« *Musik und Bildung*, 1970, II/3, pp. 105—108.

HOEBAER, Robert, »L'intérêt pour l'art musical. Essai d'analyse sociologique,« *Bulletin de l'Institut de recherches économiques et sociales*, 1956, 7, pp. 699—730.

JARUSTOVSKY, Boris Mikhailovitch, »Persönlicher Geschmack verbunden mit staatsbürgerlichem Standpunkt,« *Kunst und Literatur*, 1971, XIX/6, pp. 650—668.

JOHNSON, H. Earle, »Musical Interests of Certain American Literary and Political Figures,« *Journal of Research in Music Education*, 1971, XIX/3, pp. 22.

JOHNSTONE, J., and E. KATZ, »Youth and Popular Music: A Study in the Sociology of Taste,« *The American Journal of Sociology*, 1957, LXII/6, pp. 563—568.

JOST, Ekkehard, *Sozialpsychologische Faktoren der Popmusik-Rezeption*, B. Schott's Söhne, Mainz 1976, pp. 99.

KARBUSICKY, Vladimir, »Sociální faktory estetického vnímání. Příspěvek ke vztahu sociologického a estetického experimentu,« *Estetika*, Prague 1967, 3.

— »Electronic Music and the Listener,« *The World of Music*, 1969, XI/1, pp. 32—44.

— »Die Musikerziehung zwischen Geschmack, Verhalten und Bedürfnis,« in *Forschung in der Musikerziehung*, 1970, 3—4, pp. 56—63.

GÜLKE, Peter, »Interpretation und die Wandlungen des musikalischen Hörens,« in *Bericht über den Internationalen Musikwissenschaftlichen Kongreß*. Leipzig 1966, pp. 487—489.

KLAUSMEIER, F., »Radio-Hören und Musikpflege. Ein Beitrag zur geistigen Situation der höheren Schule,« *Kulturarbeit*, 1954, 6/1.

KLAUSMEIER, F., »Das Musikinteresse der höheren Schüler in Köln und sein Bezug zur Konfession,« *Kölner Zeitschrift für Soziologie und Sozialpsychologie*, 1959, 11/3, pp. 460—495.

— »Vorurteile in den Einstellungen zur Musik,« *Musik und Bildung*, 1972, IV/2, pp. 69—75.

KRUGMAN, H. E., »Affective Response to Music as a Function of Familiarity,« *Journal of Abnormal and Social Psychology*, 1943, 38, pp. 388—392.

LEVENTMAN, Seymour, »Sociological Analysis of Musical Taste,« M. A. Thesis (Sociology), Indiana University 1953.

LEWIS, George H., »Taste Cultures and Culture Classes in Mass Society,« *International Review of the Aesthetics and Sociology of Music*, 1977, VIII/1, pp. 39—49.

MERSMANN, H., *Musikhören*, Menck, Frankfurt/M. 1954.

MEYER, Leonard B., »On Rehearing Music«, *JAMS*, Richmond, Philadelphia 1961, XIV/2, pp. 257—267.

MICHEL, Paul, »Das historische Hören,« *Parlando*, 1969, XI/11, pp. 13—22.

MOLES, Abraham, »Facteurs physiques influençant l'écoute musicale et la cristallisation du groupe auditif,« *Cahiers d'Etudes de Radio-Télévision*, 3—4.

MOONEY, H. F., »Popular Music since the 1920s: The Significance of Shifting Taste,« *American Quarterly*, 1968, 20/1, pp. 67—85.

MUELLER, John Henry, *The American Symphony Orchestra — A Social History of Musical Taste*, Indiana University Press. Bloomington 1952; London 1958.

— *Fragen des musikalischen Geschmacks; eine musiksoziologische Studie*, Westdeutscher Verlag, Cologne 1963.

— »Methods of Measurement of Aesthetic Folkways,« *American Journal of Sociology*, 1945/1946, 51, pp. 276—282.

— »The Social Nature of Musical Taste,« *Journal of Research in Music Education*, 1956, 4/2, pp. 113—122.

MUELLER, John Henry, and Kate HEVNER, *Trends in Musical Taste*, Indiana University Press, Bloomington 1942.

NASH, D. J., »The Alienated Composer,« in *The Arts in Society*, R. N. Wilson, ed., Englewood Cliffs 1964.

* * *, »Na putah issledovania muzykalnih vkusov,« *Sovetskaja muzyka*, 1973, 1, pp. 59—69.

PAVLOV, Evgeni, »Musical Interests of 5th to 8th-Graders in Pleven,« *New Patterns of Musical Behaviour*, Universal Edition, Vienna 1974, pp. 135—140.

PECH, K., *Hören im »optischen Zeitalter«*, G. Braun, Karlsruhe 1969.

PERGER, Richard von, and Robert HIRSCHFELD, *Geschichte der K. K. Gesellschaft der Musikfreunde in Wien*, Kaiserlich-Königliche Gesellschaft der Musikfreunde, Vienna 1913.

PHILIPPOT, Michael P., »Observations on Sound Volume and Music Listening,« *New Patterns of Musical Behaviour*, Universal Edition, Vienna 1974, pp. 54—60.

PREUSSNER, E., »Der Hörer im Wandel der Zeiten,« *Das Musikleben*, 1951, 9.

RANKE, O. F., and H. LULLIES, *Gehör, Stimme, Sprache*, Berlin 1953.

REINOLD, H., »Zur Problematik des musikalischen Hörens,« *Archiv für Musikwissenschaft*, 1954, 11/2.

RICHTER, H. P., »Zur Soziologie und Psychologie des Hörens,« *Rufer und Hörer*, 1952/1953, 7.

RINGER, Alexander L., »Musical Taste and the Industrial Syndrome. A Socio-musicological Problem in Historical Analysis,« *International Review of the Aesthetics and Sociology of Music*, 1974, 5/1, pp. 139—153.

RITTENHOUSE, C. H., *Masculinity and Femininity in Relation to Preferences in Music*, Ph.D. Thesis, Stanford 1952.

ROGERS, V. R., »Children's Musical Preferences,« in *The Adolescent*, J. M. Seidmann, ed., 2. ed., New York 1960, pp. 510—515.

RÖSING, Helmut, »Zur Rezeption technisch vermittelter Musik. Psychologische, ästhetische und musikalisch-funktionsbezogene Aspekte,« in *Musik in den Massenmedien Rundfunk und Fernsehen, Perspektiven und Materialen*, Schott, Mainz 1976, pp. 44—66.

—— »Musik und ihre Wirkungen auf den Rezipienten. Versuch einer Standortbestimmung,« *International Review of the Aesthetics and Sociology of Music*, 1981, 12/1, pp. 3—20.

SANDVOSS, Joachim, *A Study of the Musical Preferences, Interests, and Activities of Parents as Factors in Their Attitude Toward the Musical Education of Their Children*, Ed.D. Thesis (Music), University of British Columbia, 1969.

SCHOEN, Max, *The Effects of Music*, Harcourt, Brace, New York 1927.

SCHUESSLER, Karl F., »Social Background and Musical Taste,« *American Sociological Review*, 1948, 13, pp. 330—335.

SILBERMANN, Alphons, *Musik, Rundfunk und Hörer. Die soziologischen Aspekte der Musik am Rundfunk*, Westdeutscher Verlag, Cologne—Opladen 1959.

—— *La musique, la radio et l'auditeur. Etude sociologique*, P.U.F., Paris 1954.

SLUSS, J. H., *High School Senior Attitudes toward Music*, Ph.D. Thesis, Colorado State Cóllege, Ann Arbor 1968, pp. 146.

SNYDERS, G., »Une révolution dans le goût musical au 18ᵉ siècle; l'apport de Diderot et Jean-Jacques Rousseau,« in *Annales*, 1963, 18, pp. 20—43.

STEPHANI, H., *Zur Psychologie des musikalischen Hörens*, Regensburg 1956.

SUPIĆIĆ, Ivo, »L'auditeur contemporain et la musique moderne,« *The World of Music*, Kassel, 1963, pp. 1-2.

STRIFFLING, Louis. *Esquisse d'une histoire du goût musical en France au XVIIIe siècle*, Delagrave, Paris 1912.

SIMEK, Milan, »Musical Interests of the Czech Youth in the Light of Research Findings,« *New Patterns of Musical Behaviour*, Universal Edition, Vienna 1974, pp. 140—142.

TAYLOR, D., *The Well Tempered Listener*, New York 1940.

TAYLOR, Gene Fred, *Culturally Transcendent Factors in Musical Perception*, Ph.D. Thesis (Music), Florida State University, 1969.

THORPE, L. P., »The Orchestral Type Preferences of Students,« *The Journal of Applied Psychology*, 1937, 20, pp. 778—784.

VERNON, P. E., »The Decline in Musical Taste,« *The Musical Times*, 1938, 79, pp. 253—255.

WANGERMÉE, Robert, »Auditeur de musique et comportement musical,« *Revue belge de musicologie*, 1981, pp. 251—268.

WATSON, Thomas William, *A Study of Musical Attitudes and Their Relationship to Environment among Rural Socio-Economically Deprived Students in Central Oklahoma*, University Microfilms, Ann Arbor 1968, pp. 117.

SOCIAL STATUS AND ROLE OF MUSICIANS

ADORNO, Theodor Wiesengrund, »Kritik des Musikanten,« in *Dissonanzen — Musik in der verwalteten Welt*, Göttingen 1958, pp. 62—101.

— »Strawinsky — Ein dialektisches Bild,« in *Quasi una fantasia — Musikalische Schriften II*, Frankfurt/M. 1963, pp. 201—242.

— *Versuch über Wagner*, Berlin — Frankfurt/M. 1952.

— *Mahler — Eine musikalische Physiognomik*, Frankfurt/M. 1960.

ALTAR, C. M., »Wolfgang Amadeus Mozart im Lichte osmanisch-österreichischer Beziehungen,« *Revue belge de musicologie*, 1956, X/3—4, pp. 138—148.

ANDERSON, William Robert, *Music as a Career*, Oxford University Press, London 1939.

ANGLÈS, Higinio, »Cantors und Ministrers in den Diensten der Könige von Katalonien-Aragonien im 14. Jahrhundert,« in *Kongreßbericht*, Basel 1924; Leipzig 1925, pp. 56—66.

ANTHON, Carl, »Some Aspects of the Social Status of Italian Musicians during the 16th Century, *Journal of Renaissance and Baroque Music*, 1946, 1, pp. 111—123 and 222—234.

APPLETON, Jon, »A New Role of the Composer,« *Musical Journal*, 1969, XXVII/3, pp. 59—61.

AUBRY, Pierre, *La musique et les musiciens d'Eglise en Normandie au XIIIe siècle*, H. Champion, Paris 1906.

BIBLIOGRAPHY

BECKER, Howard S., »The Professional Dance Musician and His Audience,« *The American Journal of Sociology*, Chicago 1951, LVII/2, pp. 136—144.

— »Some Contingencies of the Professional Dance Musician's Career,« *Human Organization*, 1952, 12/1.

BECKWITH, J., and U. KASEMETS, ed., *The Modern Composer and His World. A Report from the International Conference of Composers 1960*, Toronto 1961.

BENOIT, Marcelle, »Versailles et les Musiciens du Roi, 1661—1733. Etude institutionnelle et sociale,« in *La vie musicale en France sous les rois Bourbons*, A. et J. Picard, Paris 1971, pp. 474.

BERGMANN, Leola N., *Music Masters of the Middle West*, University of Minnesota Press, Minneapolis 1944.

BIMBERG, S., »Gesellschaftlicher Auftrag und Komponist,« *Musik und Gesellschaft*, 1963, 13, pp. 562—563.

BLAUKOPF, Kurt, *Die Endkrise der bürgerlichen Musik und die Rolle Arnold Schönbergs*, Vienna 1935 (Pseudonym: Hans E. Wind).

BÖHME, E. W., »Zur sozialen Lage unserer Musiker,« *Neue Musikzeitschrift*, 1949, 3/4, pp. 50.

BOHE, Walter, *Richard Wagner im Spiegel der Wiener Presse*, K. Triltsch, Würzburg 1933.

BOUQUET, Marie-Thérèse, *Musique et musiciens à Annecy. Les maîtrises (1630—1789)*, Académie Salésienne, Annecy, Picard, Paris 1970.

BRION, M., *Schumann and the Romantic Age*, Macmillan, New York 1956.

BRITTEN, Benjamin, »The Artist and Society,« *Records and Recording*, November 1964, pp. 14—17, 90.

BROCKHAUS, Heinz Alfred, »Die Bedeutung der Oktoberrevolution für das Schaffen Hanns Eislers,« *Musik und Gesellschaft*, 1968, XVIII/3, pp. 168—172.

BUŽGA, Jaroslav, »Die soziale Lage des Musikers im Zeitalter des Barocks in den böhmischen Ländern und ihr Einfluß auf seine künstlerische Möglichkeiten,« in *Kongreßbericht Kassel 1962*, Kassel 1963, pp. 28—32.

CAMBOR, Glenn C., G. M. LISOWITZ, and M. D. MILLER, »Creative Jazz Musicians: A Clinical Study,« *Psychiatry*, 1962, 25/1, pp. 1—15.

CARSALADE DU POND, H., »Les conditions de vie des musiciens en France,« *Etudes*, 1961, CCCXI/10, pp. 78—91.

CASAGRANDE, C., and VECCHIO, S., »Clercs et jongleurs dans la société médiévale (XII—XIIIᵉ siècles),« *Annales*, 1979, XXXIV/5, pp. 913—923.

CATTIN, Giulio, *Church Patronage of Music in Fifteenth-Century Italy*, in Iain Fenlon, ed., *Music in Medieval & Early Modern Europe. Patronage, Sources and Texts*, Cambridge University Press, Cambridge 1981, pp. 21—36.

CESARI, Gaetano, »Musica e musicisti alla corte Sforzesca,« *Rivista musicale italiana*, 1922, XXIX, pp. 1—53.

CLERCQ, Jacqueline de, *La profession de musicien*, Institut de sociologie de l'Université libre de Bruxelles, Brussels 1970, pp. 165.

CORK, J., »Society Versus Composer,« *The Antioch Review*, 1963, XI/26, pp. 49—56.

DANIÉLOU, A., *The Situation of Music and Musicians in Countries of the Orient*, Olschki, Florence 1971.

DAUBRESSE, M., *Le musicien dans la société moderne*, Le Monde musical , Paris 1914.

DAVENSON, Henri, *Les troubadours*, Le Seuil, Paris 1961.

DAVIES, Hunter, *The Beatles; The Authorized Biography*, McGraw-Hill, New York 1968, pp. 357.

DELIÈGE, Célestin, »Une incidence d'Adorno. Quelques déterminations sociologiques de la création beethovenienne,« *Arc*, 1970, 40, pp. 96—108.

DIBELIUS, Ulrich, Gesellschaft als Partner und Modell, Zum Komponieren von Nicolaus A. Huber,« *Musica*, 1972, XXVI/4, pp. 338—341.

DORIAN, F., *L'atelier du musicien*, P. U. F., Paris 1962.

DUFOURCQ, Norbert, *Une Association de symphonistes en France au XVIIe siècle*, in »Recherches«, XX, Picard, Paris 1981, pp. 255—260.

EINEM, Gottfried von, *Komponist und Gesellschaft*, Verlag G. Braun, Karlsruhe 1967.

EINSTEIN, Alfred, *Schubert. A Musical Portrait*, Oxford University Press, New York 1951.

EISLER, H., »Hörer und Komponist,« *Aufbau*, 1949, pp. 200—208.

ENGEL, Hans, »J. S. Bach — Ein soziologisches Portrait,« *Das Musikleben*, 1950, 3, pp. 193—199.

— »Soziologisches Portrait Johann Sebastian Bachs,« in *Kongreßbericht Lüneburg 1950*, Kassel, n. d., pp. 222—226.

»Der Musiker — Beruf und Lebensformen,« in *Von deutscher Tonkunst, Festschrift zu P. Raabes 70. Geburtstag*, Leipzig 1942, pp. 180—204.

ENGEL, Hans, H. HICKMANN, W. SALMEN, »Musiker,« in *MGG*, 9, pp. 1081—1105.

ETZKORN, K. Peter, »On Esthetic Standards and Reference Groups of Popular Songwriters,« *Sociological Inquiry*, 1966, 36/1, pp. 39—47.

— »Die Verwundbarkeit von Berufen und der soziale Wandel: das Beispiel der Schlagerkompositionen,« *Kölner Zeitschrift für Soziologie und Sozialpsychologie*, 1969, XXI/3, pp. 529—542.

FALLET, Edouard Marius, *La vie musicale au pays de Neuchâtel du XIIIe à la fin du XVIIIe siècle*, Heitz, Leipzig—Strasbourg—Zurich 1936.

FALVY, Zoltán, »Spielleute im mittelalterlichen Ungarn,« *Studia musicologica*, 1961, 1, pp. 29—64.

FAULKNER, Robert Roy, *Studio Musicians: Their Work and Career Contingencies in the Hollywood Film Industry*, Ph. D. Thesis, University of California, Los Angeles 1968.

FARNSWORTH, P. R., »The Effects of Role-Taking on Artistic Achievement,« *Journal of Aesthetics and Art Criticism*, 1960, 18, pp. 345—349.

FEDERHOFER, Hellmut, »Der Musikerstand in Österreich von cca. 1200 bis 1520,« *Dt. Jahrbuch der Musikwissenschaft*, 1959, III, pp. 92—97.

FENLON, Iain, *Music and Patronage in Sixteenth-Century Mantua*, Cambridge University Press, Cambridge—London—New York—New Rochelle—Melbourne—Sydney 1980, pp. XIV-233.

FINKELSTEIN, Sidney, *Composer and Nation — The Folk Heritage of Music*, Lawrence and Wishart, London 1960; New York 1960.

FISHER, R. L., »Preferences of Different Age and Socio-Economic Groups in Unstructured Musical Situations,« *Journal of Social Psychology*, 1951, 33, pp. 147—152.

FOX, Daniel M., »Artists in the Modern State: The Nineteenth-Century Background,« *Journal of Aesthetics and Art Criticism*, 1963, 22, pp. 135—148.

FREEDMAN, Alex S., »The Folksinger: A Note on Ethnocentrism,« *Ethnomusicology*, 1965, 9/2, pp. 154—156.

GERSON-KIWI, Edith, »The Musician in Society: East and West,« *Cultures*, 1973, I/1, pp. 165—193.

GIANNARIS, George, *Mikis Theodorakis: Music and Social Change*, Allen & Umvin, London 1973, pp. XIX+322.

GRAF, Max, *Composer and Critic*, Norton, New York 1946.

GRIFF, Mason, *The Commercial Artist: A Study in Role Conflict and Career Development*, University of Chicago Press, Chicago 1958.

— »The Recruitment and Socialization of Artist,« in *International Encyclopedia of the Social Sciences*, D. L. Sills, ed., Macmillan and Free Press, New York 1968, vol. 5, pp. 447—455.

GRUHN, Wilfried, »Richard Strauss aus soziologischer Sicht. Bemerkungen zu einzelnen Ausführungen Theodor W. Adornos über Strauss,« in *Mitteilungen der Internationalen Richard-Strauss-Gesellschaft BRD*, 1968, 1, pp. 11—14.

GURLITT, Wilibald, »Johann Sebastian Bach in seiner Zeit und heute,« in *Bericht über die Wissenschaftliche Beachtagung der Gesellschaft für Musikforschung*, Leipzig 1950, pp. 51—80.

HALBWACHS, Maurice, »La mémoire collective chez les musiciens,« *Revue philosophique*, 1939, Vol. 127, pp. 136—165.

HARRISON, Frank L., »The Social Position of Church Musicians in England, 1450—1550,« in *Report of the Eighth Congress of IMS*, Vol. 1, Bärenreiter, Kassel 1961, pp. 346—356.

HARTLEY, J., »Music and Musicians in Restoration London,« *The Musical Quarterly*, 1954, 40, pp. 509—520.

412

BIBLIOGRAPHY

HEER, Josef, *Der Graf von Waldstein und sein Verhältnis zu Beethoven*, Quelle & Meyer, Leipzig 1933.

HELM, Everett, *Composer, Performer, Public*, Olschki, Florence 1970.

HERIOT, A., *The Castrati in Opera*, Secker & Warburg, London 1956.

HERZEFELD, Friedrich, *Königsfreundschaft, Ludwig II und Richard Wagner*, W. Goldmann, Leipzig 1941.

HICKMANN, Hans, »Le métier de musicien au temps des Pharaons,« *Cahiers d'histoire égyptienne*, 1954, VI/5—6, pp. 253—335.

HINDEMITH, Paul, *A Composer's World*, Harvard University Press, Cambridge (Mass.) 1952.

IHLENFELD, Kurt, »Sebastiana. Lebensdokumente des Thomaskantors,« *Der Kirchenmusiker*, 1971, XXII/3, pp. 81—94.

ILLIASIEWICZ, Elzbieta, »Polish Composers as a Social Group,« *International Review of the Aesthetics and Sociology of Music*, 1980, 11/2, pp. 239—251.

JAGER, Hugo de, »Muzieksociologische kanttekeningen rond het auteursrecht van de componist,« *Mens en Maatschappij*, 1960, pp. 256—265.

— »De componist in sociologisch perspectief,« *Mens en Maatschappij*, 1964, 39/2, pp. 107—116.

KAPLAN, Max, *The Musician in America: A Study of His Social Roles*, Ph. D. Thesis (Sociology), University of Illinois 1951.

KLAUSMEIER, Friedricn, »Zur Stellung des Musikers in unserer Gesellschaft,« *Orchester*, 1967, XV/7—8, pp. 283—290.

KLEMENT, Udo, »Carl Orff und seine Grenzen,« *Musik und Gesellschaft*, 1970, XX/7, pp. 465—471.

KOBALD, Karl, *Beethoven, seine Beziehungen zu Wiens Kunst und Kultur, Gesellschaft und Landschaft*, Amalthea-Verlag, Zurich 1927; Vienna 1964.

KOMMA, Karl Michael, *Johann Zach und die Tschechischen Musiker im deutschen Umbruch des 18. Jahrhunderts*, Bärenreiter Verlag, Kassel 1938.

KRACAUER, Siegfried, *Orpheus in Paris: Offenbach and the Paris of his Time*, Knopf, New York 1938.

KRAFT, Günther, »Das mittelthüringische Siedlungszentrum der Familien Bach und Wilcken,« in *Vetter Festschrift*, VEB Deutscher Verlag für Musik, Leipzig 1969, pp. 153—164.

KRICKEBERG, Dieter, »Beobachtungen zum sozialen Selbstverständnis der deutschen Spielleute im 17. und 18. Jahrhundert, in *Jahrbuch für Volksliedforschung*, 1970, XV, pp. 140—144.

LEIBOWITZ, René, *Impegno artistico e impegno sociale del compositore*, in *La sociologia della musica*, EDT, Torino 1980, pp. 155—163.

LESURE, François, »La communauté des 'joueurs d'instruments' au XVIe siècle,« *Revue historique de droit français et étranger*, 1953, 1, pp. 79—109.

LESURE, François, *Musique et musiciens français du XVIᵉ siècle*, Minkoff Reprint, Geneva 1976, pp. 283.

LEWINSKI, W.-E. v., »Der junge Interpret im heutigen Musikleben«, *Musica*, 1963,`17/5, pp. 203—206.

LIESS, Andreas, *Beethoven und Wagner im Pariser Musikleben*, Hamburg 1938.

LOCKWOOD, Lewis, *Strategies of Music Patronage in the Fitfeenth Century: the cappella of Ercole I d'Este*, in Iain Fenlon, ed., *Music in Medieval & Early Modern Europe. Patronage, Sources and Texts*, Cambridge University Press, Cambridge 1981, pp. 227—248.

MALHERBE, Henry, *Richard Wagner révolutionnaire*, A. Michel, Paris 1938.

MARSOP, P., *Die soziale Lage der deutschen Orchestermusiker*, Berlin-Leipzig 1905.

— *Zur »Sozialisierung« der Musik und der Musiker. Ein Vortrag mit einem Anhang: Musiker und Musikagent*, Regensburg 1919.

MARTYNOV, Ivan I., *Dimitri Shostakovich, the Man and his Work*, Philosophical Library, New York 1947.

MASSIN, Brigitte, and Jean MASSIN, »Beethoven et la Révolution française,« *Arc*, 1970, 40, pp. 3—14.

MASSIP, Catherine, *La vie des musiciens de Paris au temps de Mazarin*, Picard, Paris 1976, pp. 186

MATERNE, Gerd, *Die sozialen und wirtschaftlichen Probleme des Musikers*, Ph. D. Thesis, Mannheim-Munich 1953.

MICHEL, P., »Lage und Ausbildung des Musikers im 19. Jahrhundert,« in *Musik in der Schule*, 1963, 14/3, pp. 95—105.

MITTAG, Erwin, *Aus dem Geschichte der Wiener Philharmoniker*, Gerlach, Wiedling, Vienna 1950.

MÖNCKEBERG, A., *Die Stellung der Spielleute im Mittelalter, Spielleute und Kirche im Mittelalter*, Ph. D. Thesis, Freiburg i. Br. 1910.

* * *, *Muziek*, special number of *Mens en Maatschappij*, 1964, 39/2.

NASH, Dennison J., »The Alienated Composer,« in *The Arts in Society*, R. N. Wilson, ed., Englewood Cliffs 1964.

— »The Socialization of an Artist: the American Composer,« *Social Forces*, 1957, XXXV/4, pp. 307—313.

— »The Role of the Composer,« *Ethnomusicology*, 1961, 5, pp. 81—94, 187—205.

ONION, Charles Clary, *The Social Status of Musicians in Seventeenth Century France*, Ph. D. Thesis (History), Minnesota 1959.

PASTENE, Jerome, *Three Quarter Time: The Life and Music of the Strauss Family of Vienna*, Abeland Press, New York 1951.

PETZOLDT, R., »Zur sozialen Stellung des Musikers im 17. Jahrhundert,« in *Kongreßbericht Köln 1958*, Cologne 1958, pp. 216.

PETZOLD, Richard, »Die Stellung des Musikers in der Bach-Händel-Telemann--Epoche,« *Musik und Gesellschaft*, 1967, XVII/10, pp. 667—675.

— »Zur sozialen Stellung Telemanns und seiner Zeitgenossen,« in *Rat der Stadt*, Magdeburg 1969, pp. 5—12.

POHLMANN, H., *Die Frühgeschichte des musikalischen Urheberrechts (ca. 1400—1800). Neue Materialien zur Entwicklung des Urheberrechtsbewußtseins der Komponisten*, Bärenreiter, Kassel 1962.

RATCLIFFE, H., »Social and Economic Position of the Performing Musician,« *The World of Music*, 1961, 3, pp. 61—64.

RAUPACH, H., J. S. *Bach und die Gesellschaft seiner Zeit*, Callwey, München 1973.

REDLICH, H. F., *Claudio Monteverdi, Life and Works*, Oxford University Press, London 1952.

REINECKE, Hans-Peter, »Zur Situation des Musikers im gegenwärtigen Musikleben,« in *Deutscher Musikrat*, Referate, Informationen, 1972, 20, pp. 2—6.

RINGER, Alexander L., »Mozart and the Josephian Era: Some Socio-Economic Notes on Musical Change,« *Current Musicology*, 1969, 9, pp. 158—165.

RODNITZKY, Jerome L., *Minstrels of the Dawn. The Folk Protest Singer as a Cultural Hero*, Nelson-Hall, Chicago 1976, pp. XX-192.

SAKUMA, Arline Fuju, *Education and Styles of Innovation: The Socialization of Musicians*, Ph.D. Thesis (Sociology), University of Washington, 1968.

SALMEN, Walter, *Die Schichtung der mittelalterlichen Musikkultur in der ostdeutschen Grenzlage*, Bärenreiter, Kassel 1954.

— »Die Auslandsfahrten ungarischer Spielleute im Mittelalter,« in *Musikwissenschaftliche Studien*, 1957, 6, pp. 751—754.

— »Die fahrenden Berbmusikanten im mitteldeutschen Musikleben des 17. und 18. Jahrhunderts,« *Der Anschnitt*, 1958. 10, pp. 11—13.

— »Die Beteilung Englands am irternationalen Musikantverkehr des Mittelalters,« *Die Musikforschung*, 1958, XI/3. pp. 315—320.

— »Der Musiker in der mittelalterlichen Gesellschaft,« in *Bericht über den Siebenten internationalen musikwissenschaftlichen Kongreß, Köln 1958*, Kassel-Basle 1959, pp. 354—357.

— *Die fahrende Musiker im europäischen Mittelalter*, Hinnenthal, Kassel 1960.

— »Zur sozialen Schichtung des Berufsmusikertums im mittelalterlichen Eurasien und im Africa,« Colloques de Wégimont, III—1956, *Ethnomusicologie*, II, Paris 1960, pp. 23—32.

— »Die soziale Geltung des Musikers in der mittelalterlichen Gesellschaft,« in *Studium Generale*, 1966, 19, pp. 92—103.

— *Haus- und Kammermusik. Privates Musizieren im gesellschaftlichen Wandel zwischen 1600 und 1900*, VEB Deutscher Verlag für Musik, Leipzig 1969, pp. 203.

415

SALMEN, Walter, ed., *Der Sozialstatus des Berufsmusikers vom 17. bis 19. Jahrhundert. Gesammelte Beiträge*, Auftrag der Gesellschaft für Musikforschung, Bärenreiter-Verlag, Kassel 1971, pp. 146.

SALMEN, Walter, ed., *The Social Status of the Professional Musician from the Middle Ages to the 19th Century*, Pendragon Press, New York 1983, pp. III-281.

SAß, H., and Walter WIORA, *Musikberufe und ihr Nachwuchs. Statistische Erhebungen 1960/1961 des Deutschen Musikrates*, Mainz 1962.

SCHAAP, J., »De materiele positie van de dirigent,« *De dirigent*, 1967, 7/3, pp. 5—8.

SCHAPIRO, Meyer, »On the Relation of Patron and Artist. Comments on a Proposed Model for the Scientist,« *American Journal of Sociology*, 1964, 70, pp. 363—369.

SCHAEFFNER, André, »Situation des musiciens dans trois sociétés Africaines,« Colloques de Wégimont, III—1956, *Ethnomusicologie*, II, Paris 1960, pp. 33—49.

SCHLŒZER, Boris de, »La fonction sociale du compositeur,« in *Atti del secondo Congresso internazionale di Musica*, Florence 1940.

SCHNEIDER, Frank, »Zur Situation der jungen Komponisten in der DDR,« *Musik und Gesellschaft*, 1970, XX/8, pp. 505—510.

SCHOLLUM, R., »Zur Situation der Komponisten in Österreich,« *Österreichische Musikzeitschrift*, 1964, 19/4, pp. 181—185.

SCHOOLFIELD, G. C., *The Figure of the Musician in German Literature*, Chapell Hill 1956.

SCHREIBER, U., *Mahler: il musicista delle contraddizioni sociali*, in *La sociologia della musica*, EDT, Torino 1980, pp. 275—287.

SCHUTZ, A., »Making Music Together. A Study in Social Relationship,« *Social Research*, 1951, 18/1, pp. 76—97.

SITTNER, Hans, »Zur sozialen Lage des Berufsmusiker,« *Österreichische Musikzeitschrift*, 1954, 9, pp. 48—52.

STEBBINS, Robert A., »Class, Status, and Power among Jazz and Commercial Musicians,« *The Sociological Quarterly*, 1966, 7/2, pp. 197—213.

STOSCH, J., *Der Hofdienst der Spielleute im deutschen Mittelalter*, Berlin 1881.

SZABOLCSI, Bence, »Die ungarischen Spielleute des Mittelalters,« in *Gedankschrift H. Abert*, Halle 1928, pp. 154—164.

TAPPOLET, W., »De quoi vit le compositeur suisse?,« *Schweizerische Musikzeitung*, 1961, 4, pp. 246—248.

THIELECKE, Richard, *Die soziale Lage der Berufsmusiker in Deutschland und die Entstehung, Entwicklung und Bedeutung ihrer Organisation*, Ph.D. Thesis, Frankfurt/M. 1921.

VANCEA, Zeno, »Libertatea de creatie si responsabilitatea sociala a compozitor rului,« *Studii de muzicologie*, 1972, 8, pp. 41—48.

WALTZ, H., *Die Lage der Orchestermusiker in Deutschland mit besonderer Berücksichtigung der Musikgeschäfte (Stadtpfeifereien)*, Karlsruhe 1906.

416

WARD, John Owen, *Careers in Music*, H. Z. Walck, New York 1968, pp. 127.

WERNER, A., *Vier Jahrhunderte im Dienste der Kirchenmusik. Geschichte des Amtes und Standes der evangelischen Kantoren, Organisten und Stadtpfeifer seit der Reformation*, Leipzig 1933.

WESTBY, D. L., »The Career Experience of the Symphony Musician,« *Social Forces*, 1960, XXXVIII/3, pp. 223—229.

WHITE, H. C., »The Professional Role and Status of Music Educators in the United States,« *Journal of Research in Music Education*, 1967, XV/1, pp. 3—10.

WILLIAMS, John Graham, *The Influence of English Music and Society on G. F. Handel*, University of Leeds, Leeds 1969, pp. 82.

WIORA, Walter, *Komponist und Mitwelt*, Bärenreiter, Kassel-Basle 1964.

WOODFILL, Walter, *Musicians in English Society, from Elizabeth to Charles I*, Princeton University Press, Princeton 1963.

WRIGHT, Craig, *Antoine Brumel and Patronage at Paris*, in Iain Fenlon, ed., *Music in Medieval & Early Modern Europe. Patronage, Sources and Texts*, Cambridge University Press, Cambridge 1981, pp. 37—60.

MUSICAL INSTITUTIONS

ADRIO, Adam, *Die Anfänge des geistlichen Konzerts*, Junker, Berlin 1935.

ANDERSON, John, *The American Theatre*, Dial Press, New York 1938.

ARIAN, Edward, *Bach, Beethoven and Bureaucracy: The Case of the Philadelphia Orchestra*, University of Alabama Press, Alabama 1971.

BABOW, Irving, »The Singing Societies of European Immigrants,« *Phylon*, Atlanta 1954, XV/3, pp. 289—295.

— »Types of Immigrant Singing Societies,« *Sociology and Social Research*, 1955, XXXIX/4, pp. 242—247.

BASSO, Alberto, *Il teatro della città dal 1788 al 1936*, »Storia del Teatro Regio di Torino«, vol. II, Cassa di Risparmio, Torino 1976, pp. 856.

BIEBER, Margarete, *The History of the Greek and Roman Theatre*, Princeton University Press, Princeton 1939.

BING, Rudolph, *Five Thousand Nights at the Opera*, Doubleday and Co., New York 1972.

BLAUKOPF, Kurt, »Musical Institutions in a Changing World,« *International Review of the Aesthetics and Sociology of Music*, 1972, III/1, pp. 35—42.

BLUMNER, Martin, *Geschichte der Sing-akademie zu Berlin*, Horn & Raasch, Berlin 1891.

BOLLERT, Werner, *Sing-Akademie zu Berlin*. Rembrandt Verlag, Berlin 1966.

BONNASSIES, Jules, *Les Spectacles Forains et la Comédie Française*, E. Dentu, Paris 1875.

417

BORCHERDT, Hans Heinrich, *Das Europäische Theater im Mittelalter und in der Renaissance*, J. J. Weber, Leipzig 1935.

BORGERHOF, Joseph Leopold, *Le Théâtre anglais à Paris sous la Restauration*, Hachette, Paris 1912.

BORNOFF, Jack, *Music Theatre in a Changing Society*, UNESCO, Paris 1968, pp. 144.

BOUQUET, Marie-Thérèse, *Il teatro di corte dalle origini al 1788*, »Storia del Teatro Regio di Torino«, vol. I, Cassa di Risparmio, Torino 1976, pp. 561.

BRENET, Michel, *Les concerts en France sous l'ancien régime*, Fischbacher, Paris 1900.

BRODT, G., »Von der Entwicklung der Konzerte,« *Neue Musikzeitschrift*, 1950, 4, p. 314.

BRUSH, Gerome, *Boston Symphony Orchestra*, Printed for the Orchestra, Boston 1936.

BURTON, Humphrey, »Les Académies de musique en France au XVIIIe siècle,« *Revue de musicologie*, Paris 1955, XXXVII/112, pp. 122—147.

CAIN, Georges, *Anciens théâtres de Paris*, Charpentier et Fasquelle, Paris 1920.

CAMPARDON, Emile, *L'Académie royale de musique au XVIIIe siècle*, Berger--Levraut, Paris 1884.

CARSE, Adam, *The Orchestra in the Eighteenth Century*, Heffer, Cambridge 1950.

CAZALET, William Wahab, *The History of the Royal Academy of Music*, T. Bosworth, London 1854.

CHAMBERLAIN, Houston Stewart, *Die ersten zwanzig Jahre der Bayreuther Bühnenfestspiele, 1876—1896*, L. Ellwanger vorm. T. Burger, Bayreuth 1896.

CHEVALLEY, Heinrich, *Hundert Jahre Hamburger Stadt-Theater*, Broschek & Co., Hamburg 1927.

CHRYSANDER, Friedrich, »Geschichte der Braunschweig-Wolfenbüttelschen Capelle und Oper vom 16. bis 18. Jahrhundert,« in *Jahrbücher für musikalische Wissenschaft*, 1863, 1, pp. 147—286.

CONRAD, Michael Georg, *Wagners Geist und Kunst in Bayreuth*, E. W. Bonsels, Munich 1906.

CORDER, Frederick, *A History of the Royal Academy of Music*, F. Corder, London 1922.

CRESSEY, Paul Goalby, *The Taxi-Dance Hall: A Sociological Study in Commercialized Recreation and City Life*, Greenwood Press, New York—Chicago 1968; Patterson Smith, Montclair (N. J.) 1969, pp. 300.

CREUZBURG, Eberhard, *Die Gewandhaus-Konzerte zu Leipzig*, Breitkopf & Härtel, Leipzig 1931.

CROSTEN, William Loran, *French Grand Opera. An Art and a Business*, King's Crown Press, New York 1948.

CUVELIER, Michel, »Les jeunesses musicales dans le monde,« *La Revue musicale*, 1958, 242, pp. 33—40.

DAVIS, Ronald G., »Radical Theatre Versus Institutional Theatre,« in *Studies on the Left*, 1964, 4, pp. 28—38.

DANDELOT, A., *La société des concerts du Conservatoire 1828-1923*, Paris 1923.

DÖRFFEL, Alfred, *Geschichte der Gewandhaus Concerte zu Leipzig*, Breitkopf & Härtel, Leipzig 1881—1884.

DUFOURCQ, Norbert, *Contribution à l'histoire du Concert Spirituel dans la seconde moitié du XVIIIᵉ siècle*, in »Recherches,« XIX, Picard, Paris 1979, pp. 195—211.

ELKIN, Robert, *Royal Philharmonic*, Rider, London 1946.

ELLMAN, V., »Das Musikleben in den deutschen Universitäten,« in *Musik im Volk*, Stumme, C. F. Vieweg, Berlin 1939.

ENGELBRECHT, Christiane, *Die Kasseler Hoffkapelle im 17. Jahrhundert*, Bärenreiter, Kassel 1958.

ERSKINE, John, *The Philharmonic-Symphony Society of New York*, Macmillan, New York 1943.

FARMER, Henry George, *Concerts in Eighteenth Century Scotland*, Hinrichsen, Glasgow 1945.

FOSS, Michael, *The Age of Patronage: The Arts in England 1600—1750*, Cornell University, Ithaca (N. Y.) 1971, pp. 234.

GEER, William James, *The Artist as a Member of a Formal Organization*, Ph. D. Thesis, University of Minnesota, 1969.

GERBOD, P., »L'institution orphéonique en France du XIXᵉ au XXᵉ siècle«, *Ethnologie française*, 1980, 10/1, pp. 27—44.

GERSON, Robert A., *Music in Philadelphia*, Theodore Presser, Philadelphia 1940.

GILLHOFF, Gerd Aage, *The Royal Dutch Theatre at the Hague, 1804—1876*, M. Nijhoff, The Hague 1938.

GRANT, Margaret, and Herman S. HETTINGER, *America's Symphony Orchestras and How They Are Supported*, Norton, New York 1940.

GREGOR, Joseph, *Geschichte des österreichischen Theaters*, Donau-Verlag. Vienna 1948.

HABEL, Heinrich, »Das Odeon in München und die Frühzeit des öffentlichen Konzertsaalbaus,« in *Neue Münchner Beiträge zur Kunstgeschichte*, De Gruyter, Berlin 1967,

HACKETT, Karleton Spalding, *The Beginning of Grand Opera in Chicago, 1850—1859*, The Laurentian Publishers, Chicago 1913.

HANSLICK, Eduard, *Geschichte des Concertwesens in Wien*, W. Braunmüller, Vienna 1869—1870.

HENNEBERG, Fritz, *The Leipzig Gewandhaus Orchestra*, Dennis Dobson, London 1966.

419

HODERMANN, Richard, »Geschichte des Gothaischen Hoftheaters 1775—1779,« in *Theatergeschichtliche Forschungen*, Berthold Litzmann, L. Boss, Hamburg 1894, No. 9, pp. 183.

HOGWOOD, Christopher, *Music at Court*, Victor Gollancz Ltd, London 1980, pp. 128.

HOWE, Mark Antony de Wolfe, *The Boston Symphony Orchestra: An Historical Sketch*, Houghton Mifflin, Boston 1914, pp. 279.

INDY, Vincent d', *La Schola cantorum: son histoire depuis sa fondation jusqu'en 1925*, Bloud & Gay, Paris 1927.

KAPLAN, Max, *Music in the City*, First mimeographed edition, Pueblo 1944.

— »Teleopractice: A Symphony Orchestra as it Prepares for the Concert,« *Social Forces*, 1955, 33/4, pp. 352—355.

KAPP, Julius, *Geschichte der Staatsoper Berlin*, M. Hesse, Berlin 1937.

KARLSSON, Henrik, *Statens försöksverksamhet med rikskonserter. Enstudie av ett statligt musikdistributionssystem*, Accent 3, Institut för rikskonserter, Stockholm 1971, pp. 116.

KOLODIN, Irving, *The Metropolitan Opera, 1883—1935*, Oxford University Press, New York 1936.

KRALIK, Heinrich, *Die Wiener Philharmoniker*, W. Frick, Vienna 1938.

KREHBIEL, Henry, *The Philharmonic Society of New York*, Novello, Ewer & Co. Ltd., London and New York 1892.

LA GORCE, Jérôme de, »L'Académie Royale de Musique en 1704, d'après des documents inédits conservés dans les archives notariales,« *Revue de Musicologie*, 1979, 2, pp. 160—191.

LEBLOND, Richard Emmett Jr., *Professionalization and Bureaucratization of the Performance of Serious Music in the United States*, Ph. D. Thesis (Sociology), University of Michigan, 1968.

LEICHTENTRITT, Hugo, *Serge Koussewitzky, the Boston Symphony Orchestra and the New American Music*, Harvard University Press, Cambridge (Mass.) 1946.

LESURE, François, »Chambonnières, organisateur de concerts,« *Revue belge de musicologie*, 1949, III/3, pp. 140—144.

— »Réflexions sur les origines du concert parisien,« *Polyphonie*, 1949, 5, pp. 47—51.

— »Les orchestres populaires à Paris vers la fin du XVIe siècle,« *Revue de musicologie*, 1954, 36, pp. 39—54.

— »Naissance de l'orchestre en France au début du XVIIe siècle,« in *Histoire de la musique*, vol. I, Gallimard, Paris 1960.

LIEBERMANN, Rolf, »Oper in der Demokratie,« *Musica*, 1964, pp. 98—103.

MARK, Desmond, *Zur Bestandaufnahme des Wiener Orchesterrepertoires. Ein Soziographischer Versuch nach der Methode von John H. Mueller*, Universal Edition, Wien 1979.

MARTORELLA, Rosanne, *Negotiating Conflict: The Case of Opera,* 71st Annual Meeting of the American Sociological Association, San Francisco 1976.
— *The Performing Artist as a Member of an Organization: A Sociological Study of Opera Performers and the Economics of Opera Production,* Ph. D. Thesis, New School for Social Research, New York 1974.

MEE, John Henry, *The Oldest Music Room in Europe: A Record of Eighteenth Century Enterprises of Oxford,* J. Lane, London 1911.

MESSITER, Arthur Henry, *A History of the Choir and Music of Trinity Church, New York,* E. S. Gorham, New York 1906.

MEYER—SIAT, P., »Administration et musique au milieu du XIXᵉ siècle,« *Istra,* Paris 1970. pp. 197—242.

MITTAG, Erwin, *Aus dem Geschichte der Wiener Philharmoniker,* Gerlach, Wiedling, Vienna 1950.

MUELLER, John H., *The American Symphony Orchestra — A Social History of Musical Taste,* Indiana University Press, Bloomington 1952; London 1958.
— *Music Theatre in a Changing Society,* UNESCO, New York 1968, pp. 144.

NETTEL, R., *The Orchestra in England. A Social History,* J. Cape, London 1946, London 1956.

NETTL, Paul, »Zur Geschichte der kaiserlichen Hofmusikkapelle 1636—1680,« in *Studien zur Musikwissenschaft,* Gesellschaft zur Herausgabe von Denkmälern der Tonkunst in Österreich, vols. 16—19, Vienna 1929——1932.

PEYSER, Ethel Rose, and Marion BAUER, *How Opera Grew,* Putnam and Sons, New York 1925.

PIERRE, Constant, *Histoire du concert spirituel, 1725—1790,* Publications de la Société française de musicologie, sér. 3, Heugel et Cie., Paris 1975, pp. 372.

PRITCHARD, Brian W., *The Musical Festival and the Choral Society in England in the 18th and 19th Centuries: A Social History,* Musicology, Vol. 3, University of Birmingham, 1968, pp. 927.

— »The Provincial Festivals of the Ashley Family,« *Galpin Society Journal,* 1969, XII, pp. 58—77.

RABIN, Marvin J., *History and Analysis of the Greater Boston Youth Symphony Orchestra from 1958 to 1964,* Music Education, University of Illinois, 1968, pp. 500.

RENTON, Edward, *The Vaudeville Theater, Building, Operation, Management,* Gotham Press, New York 1918.

RICH, Maria, »Opera on the Map,« *Opera News,* 22 December 1973, pp. 14-18.
— ed., *Opera Companies in the United States,* Central Opera Service, New York 1966.
— ed., *Opera Repertory in the United States, 1966-1972,* Central Opera Service, New York 1973.

ROBINSON, Ray E., *A History of the Peabody Conservatory of Music,* Indiana University, 1969, pp. 706.

RUHNKE, M., *Beiträge zur Geschichte der deutschen Hofmusikkollegien im 16. Jahrhundert*, Merseburger, Berlin 1963.

SALEM, Mahmoud, *Organizational Survival: The Case of the Seattle Opera Company*, Praeger Books, New York 1976.

SALMEN, Walter, *Musikleben im 16. Jahrhundert*, (Musikgeschichte in Bildern III/9), VEB Deutscher Verlag für Musik, Leipzig 1976, pp. 214.

SANDBERGER, Adolf, *Beiträge zur Geschichte der bayerischen Hof-Kapelle unter Orlando di Lasso*, Breitkopf & Härtel, Leipzig 1894.

SCHIEDERMAIR, Ludwig Ferdinand, »Die Blütezeit der Öttingen-Wallerstein'schen Hofkapelle,« in *Sammelbände der internationalen Musikgesellschaft*, 1907—1908, 9, pp. 83—130.

SCHLESINGER, Janet, *Challenge to the Urban Orchestra. The Pittsburgh Symphony*, 1971.

SCHMITZ, Hans Heinrich, »Sinfoniekonzert im Jahre 2000,« *Musik und Gesellschaft*, June 1967, XVII/6, pp. 366—378.

SCHOTT, S., »Theater und Orchester,« *Statistisches Jahrbuch der deutschen Städte*, 1931, 5, pp. 279—308.

SELTZER, George, comp., *The Professional Symphony Orchestra in the United States*, Scarecrow Press, Metuchen (N. J.) 1975, pp. 486.

SHANET, Howard, *Philharmonic: A History of New York's Orchestra*, Doubleday and Co., Garden City (N. Y.) 1975, pp. 788.

SMIJERS, Albert, »Die Kaiserliche Hofmusik-Kapelle von 1543—1619,« in *Studien zur Musikwissenschaft*, Gesellschaft zur Herausgabe von Denkmälern der Tonkunst in Österreich, Vols. 6—9, Vienna 1920.

SONNECK, Oscar George Theodore, *Early Concert Life in America, 1731——1800*, Breitkopf & Härtel, Leipzig 1907.

TITTERTON, William Richard, *From Theatre to Music Hall*, Stephen Swift, London 1912.

* * *, UNESCO, *Music Theatre in a Changing Society*, Paris 1968.

VALLAS, L., *Un siècle de musique et de théâtre à Lyon (1688—1789)*, P. Masson, Lyon 1932.

WESTBY, David Leroy, *The Social Organization of a Symphony Orchestra, with Special Attention to the Informal Associations of Symphony Members*, M. A. Thesis, University of Minnesota 1957.

WISTER, Frances Anne, *Twenty Five Years of the Philadelphia Orchestra*, Philadelphia 1925.

WOLFE HOWE, M. A. de, *The Boston Symphony Orchestra: A Historical Sketch*, Miflin & Co., Houghton 1914.

BIBLIOGRAPHY

MUSIC, SOCIAL LIFE AND CULTURE

ABRUZZESE, Alberto, *Arte e pubblico nell'età del capitalismo. Forme estetiche e società di massa*, Marsilio, Venezia 1973.

ADAMS, John Clarke, »The Verdi Tenor and the Modern Culture,« in *Atti del I° congresso internazionale di studi verdiani*, 1968, pp. 298—308.

ADORNO, Theodor Wiesengrund, *Dissonanzen. Musik in der verwalteten Welt*, Vandenhoeck & Ruprecht, Göttingen 1956.

— »Soziologische Anmerkungen zum Musikleben in Deutschland,« *Frankfurter Allgemeine Zeitung*, 11. 3. 1967, p. 60.

ANDREWS, E. D., *The Gift to be Simple: Songs, Dances and Rituals of the American Shakers*, Dover, New York 1962.

ATTALI, Jacques, *Musica e musicista nell'era della »rappresentazione«*, in *La sociologia della musica*, EDT, Torino 1980, pp. 177—187.

AZBILL, Henry, »Native Dances: A Basic Part of Culture, Tradition, Religion,« *Indian Historian*, 1967, I/1, pp. 16—17 and 20.

BAILBÉ, Joseph Marc, *Le Roman et la Musique en France sous la Monarchie de juillet*, Lettres Modernes, Paris 1969, pp. 446.

BAILBÉ, Joseph Marc, »Le Bourgeois et la Musique au XIX° siècle,« *Romantisme*, 1977, 17—18. pp. 123—136.

BARZUN, J., *Music in American Life*, New York 1956.

BASCOM, W. R., and M. J. HERSKOVITS, *Continuity and Change in African Cultures*, University of Chicago Press, Chicago 1959.

BEKKER, Paul, *Das deutsche Musikleben*, Berlin 1916.

BERRIEN, William, *Report of the Committee of the Conference on Inter--American Relations in the Field of Music*, U. S. Department of State, Washington (D. C.) 1940.

BERTEN, W. M., *Musik und Musikleben der Deutschen*, Hamburg 1933.

BESSELER, Heinrich, »Umgangsmusik und Darbietungsmusik im 16. Jahrhundert,« *Archiv für Musikwissenschaft*, 1959, 16/1-2, pp. 21—41.

BHATTACHARYA, Sudhibhushan, »Role of Music in Society and Culture,« *Folklore*, Calcutta 1970, 11/6, pp. 202—211.

BLAUKOPF, Kurt, »Strukturanalyse des Musiklebens. Erfahrungen, Modelle, Aufgaben,« *Musik und Bildung*, 1971, III/1, pp. 11—15.

— »Tonalität und Soziologie,« in *Bericht über den Internationalen Musikkongreß Wien 1952*, Vienna 1953, pp. 104-107.

BONTINCK, Irmgard, »New Patterns of Musical Behaviour of the Young Generation in Industrial Societies,« *International Review of the Aesthetics and Sociology of Music*, 1972, III/2.

— »Report on New Patterns of Musical Behaviour of the Young Generation in Industrial Societies,« *International Review of the Aesthetics and Sociology of Music*, 1972, III/2.

BORRIS, Siegfried, »Einfluß und Einbruch primitiver Musik in die Musik des Abendlandes,« *Sociologus*, 1952, 2/1, pp. 52—72.

BOWLES, Edmund A., »Eastern Influences on the Use of Trumpets and Drums during the Middle Ages,« *Annuario Musical*, 1971, 26, pp. 3—28.

BREVAN, Bruno, »Vie musicale et société parisienne de 1774 à 1799,«
Ethnopsychologie, 1979, 36/1, pp. 109—147.
— *Les changements de la vie musicale parisienne de 1774 à 1799*, Presses Universitaires de France, Paris 1980.

BRIDGMAN, Nanie, *La vie musicale au Quattrocento et jusqu'à la naissance du madrigal (1400—1530)*, Gallimard, Paris 1964.

BRUFORD, W. H., *Culture and Society in Classical Weimar, 1775—1806*, Cambridge University Press, London 1962.

BURNEY, Charles, *The Present State of Music in Germany, the Netherlands and United Provinces*, T. Becket, London 1773.

BUTLER, Janet W., and Paul G. DASTON, »Musical Consonance as Musical Preference: A Cross-Cultural Study,« *Journal of General Psychology*, 1968, 79/1, pp. 129—142.

CARADEC, Fr., and WEILL, A., *Le café-concert*, Atelier Hachette-Massin, Paris 1980, pp. 342.

CASAGRANDE, C., and VECCHIO, S., »Clercs et jongleurs dans la société médiévale (XII—XIIIe siècles),« *Annales*, 1979, XXXIV/5, pp. 913—923.

CATTIN, Giulio, *Church Patronage of Music in Fifteenth-Century Italy*, in Iain Fenlon, ed., *Music in Medieval & Early Modern Europe. Patronage, Sources and Texts*, Cambridge University Press, Cambridge 1981, pp. 21—36.

CAULLIER, Joëlle, »Les chefs d'orchestre allemands à Paris entre 1894 et 1914,« *Revue de Musicologie*, 1981, 67/2, pp. 191—210.

COMBARIEU, Jules, *La musique et la magie — Etude sur les origines populaires de l'art musical, son influence et sa fonctions dans les sociétés*, Picard, Paris 1909.

CONRAD, Michael Georg, *Wagners Geist und Kunst in Bayreuth*, E. W. Bonsels, Munich 1906.

CORVISIER, André, *Arts et sociétés dans l'Europe du XVIIIe siècle*, P. U. F., Paris 1978, pp. 248.

CVETKO, Dragotin, »Sociološki i nacionalni uvjeti promjena u položaju glazbe Južnih Slavena u XIX stoljeću,« *Zvuk*, 1974, 2, pp. 102—110.

DANIÉLOU, Alain, *Inde du Nord*, Les traditions musicales, 1, Buchet-Chastel, Paris 1966.

DARBELLAY, Etienne, »La Musique à la cour de Maximilien I (1459—1519),« *Schweizerische Musikzeitung*, 1978, 118/1, pp. 1—10.

DAVID, Haus T., »The Cultural Functions of Music«, *Journal of the History of Ideas.* Lancaster-New York 1951, Vol. 12, N⁰ 3, pp. 423—439.

DE LEEUW, Ton, »Music in Orient and Occident — A Social Problem,« *The World of Music*, Paris 1969, 11/4, pp. 6—17.

DE LERMA, Dominique-René, *Black Music in our Culture: Curricular Ideas on the Subjects, Materials and Problems*, Kent State University Press, Kent (Ohio) 1970.

DENISOFF, R. Serge, »Popular Protest Song; The Case of Eve of Destruction,« *Public Opinion Quarterly*, 1971, XXXV, pp. 117—122.

DJURIĆ-KLAJN, Stana, »Gesellschaftsformen und Musikentwicklung,« in *Bericht über den Internationalen Musikkongreß Wien 1952*, Vienna 1953, pp. 136-139.

DONAKOWSKI, Conrad L., *A Muse for the Masses. Ritual and Music in an Age of Democratic Revolution, 1770—1870*, The University of Chicago Press, Chicago and London 1972, 1977, pp. 435.

DUSE, Ugo, *Musica e cultura*, Marsilis Edition, Padova 1967, pp. 157.

ECHANOVE, T., »La Radiodifusion, y la Cultura,« *Revista International de sociología*, 1958, 16/64, pp. 589—615.

EHINGER, H., »Vom Föderalismus zum Regionalismus. Gedanken zum heutigen Musikleben,« *Schweizer Rundschau*, 1964, LXIII/2—3, pp. 96—102.

ENGEL, Hans, »Soziologie des Musiklebens,« *Musica*, 1949, 3, pp. 265—268.

FALLET, Edouard Marius, *La vie musicale au pays de Neuchâtel du XIII* à la fin du XVIII* siècle*, Heitz, Leipzig—Strasbourg—Zurich 1936.

FALTIN, Peter, »Die Bedeutung von Musik als Ergebnis sozio-kultureller Prozesse«, *Die Musikforschung*, 1973, XXVI/4, pp. 435—445.

FARREL, Joseph, »Culture and Curriculum: A Note on the Gathering of an Idea Whose Time Has Come,« in *Council for Research in Music Education Bulletin*, 1971, 25, pp. 1—11.

FEDERMANN, Maria, *Musik und Musikpflege zur Zeit Herzog Albrechts*, Bärenreiter-Verlag, Kassel 1932.

FELLERER, Karl Gustav, *La musica liturgica come problema sociologico*, in *La sociologia della musica*, EDT, Torino 1980, pp. 223—228.

FENLON, Iain, »Music and Spectacle at the Gonzaga Court, c. 1580—1600,« *Proceedings of the Royal Musical Association*, 1976-77, 103, pp. 90—105.
——, *Music and Patronage in Sixteenth-Century Mantua*, Cambridge University Press, Cambridge—London—New York—New Rochelle—Melbourne—Sydney 1980, pp. XIV-233.

FENLON, Iain, ed., *Music in Medieval & Early Modern Europe. Patronage, Sources and Texts*, Cambridge University Press, Cambridge 1981, pp. XIII-409.

FINELL, Judith Greengerg, comp., *The Contemporary Music Performance Directory: A Listing of American Performing Ensembles, Sponsoring Organizations, Performing Facilities, Concert Series, and Festivals of europäischen Mittelalters*, Koehler und Amelang, Leipzig 1975, pp. 283.

FINKELSTEIN, Sidney, *Composer and Nation*, International Publishers, New York 1960.

FLOTZINGER, Rudolf, »Zum Topos von der Völker und Stände verbindenden Wirkung der Musik,« *International Review of the Aesthetics and Sociology of Music*, 1981, 12/2, pp. 91—101.

FRANCÈS, Robert, »La langue musicale dans la société contemporaine,« *Sciences de l'Art*, 1964, 1, pp. 29—46.

GIERLICHS, W., »Soziologische Grundlagen des Kölner Musiklebens,« *Rheinische Blätter*, 1943, 20/6.

GILSON, Etienne, *La société de masse et sa culture*, Vrin, Paris 1967.

GIROD, R., »Recherches sociologiques et développement de la culture musicale,« *Cahiers d'études de Radio-Télévision*, Paris 1955, 3—4, pp. 338—343.

GORDON, Edwin, »Third-Year Results of a Five-Year Longitudinal Study of the Musical Achievement of Culturally-Disadvantaged Students,« in *Experimental Research in the Psychology of Music*, 1972, 8, pp. 45—64.

GROSSO DESTRERI, Luigi del, *Europäisches Hit-Panorama*, G. Braun, Karlsruhe 1972, pp. 51.

GUIGNARD, Michel, *Musique, honneur et plaisir au Sahara. Etude psycho--sociologique et musicologique de la société maure*, Paul Geuthner, Bibl. d'Etudes Islamiques, Paris 1975, pp. 232.

GULKE, Peter, *Mönche, Bürger, Minnesänger: Musik in der Gesellschaft des europäischen Mittelalters*, Koehler und Amelang, Leipzig 1975, pp. 283.

GÜNTHER, S., »Musik in der verwalten Welt. Die gesellschaftliche Situation der Musik in Deutschland seit dem Ende des 1. Weltkrieges, *Kölner Zeitschrift für Soziologie und Sozialpsychologie*, 1964, 16, pp. 491—506.

GRUBER, Roman I., *Istorija muzykaljnoj kuljtury*, Gosizd, Moscow-Leningrad 1941—1959, 3 Vols.

GÜNTHER, S., »Die Musik in der pluralistischen Massengesellschaft. Über die soziale Mobilität im deutschen Musikleben des 20. Jahrhunderts,« *Kölner Zeitschrift für Soziologie und Sozialpsychologie*, 1967, 19/1, pp. 64—86; 19/2, pp. 283—305.

HAMEL, F., »Musik und Zeitgeist,« in *Bericht über den internationalen Musikkongreß Wien 1952*, pp. 28-32.
HIRSCH, Jean-François, »La dé-fête urbaine I,« *Musique en jeu*, 1976, 24, pp. 45-54.

HAMM, Charles, *Changing Patterns in Society and Music: The U. S. Since World War II*, in *Contemporary Music and Music Cultures*, Prentice--Hall, Englewood Cliffs (New Jersey) 1975, pp. 35—70.

426

BIBLIOGRAPHY

HAMM, Charles E., Bruno NETTL, Ronald BYRNSIDE, *Contemporary Music and Music Cultures*, Prentice-Hall, Englewood Cliffs (N. J.) 1975, pp. 270.

HANSLICK, Eduard, *Vienna's Golden Years of Music*, Simon and Schuster, New York 1950.

HARDING, D. W., »The Social Background of Taste in Music,« *The Musical Times*, 1938, LXXIX, pp. 333—335 and 417—419.

HASSAN, S. Q., *Les instruments de musique en Irak et leur rôle dans la société traditionelle*, Mouton/Ed. de l'Ecole des hautes études en sciences sociales, Paris 1980, pp. 258.

HITCHCOCK, H. Wiley, *Music in the United States*, Prentice-Hall, Englewood Cliffs (N. J.) 1969.

HORKHEIMER, Max, »Neue Kunst und Massenkultur,« *Internationale Revue Umschau*, 1948, III.

HORNBOSTEL, Erich Maria von, »Die Massnorm als Kulturgeschichtliches Forschungsmittel,« in *Festschrift. Publication d' hommage, offerte à Paul Wilhelm Schmidt*, Vienna 1928, pp. 303—323.

KATZ, B., *The Social Implications of Early Black Music in the United States*, Arno Press, New York 1969.

KELDANY-MOHR, Irmgard, »*Unterhaltungsmusik« als soziokulturelles Phänomen des 19. Jahrhunderts*, Gustav Bosse Verlag, Regensburg 1977, pp. 143.

KISHIBE, Shigeo, »Means of Preservation and Diffusion of Traditional Music in Japan,« *Asian Music*, 1971, 2/1, pp. 8—13.

KNEPLER, Georg, »Entwicklungstendenzen der sowjetischen Musikkultur,« *Musik und Gesellschaft*, Berlin 1968, XVIII/3, pp. 163—167.

KOPECZEK-MICHALSKA, Krystyna, »Jawne i tajne zycie koncertowe w Warszawie w latach okupacji hitlerowskiej,« *Muzyka*, 1970, XV/3, pp. 47—64.

KOTEK, Josef, »Die Rezeption der Funktionalen Musik als gesellschaftlicher Aneigungsprozeß,« *International Review of the Aesthetics and Sociology of Music*, 1978, 9/2, pp. 183—218.

LAADE, Wolfgang, *Neue Musik in Afrika, Asien und Ozeanien: Diskographie und historisch-stilistischer Überblick*, Heidelberg 1971, pp. 463.

LALO, Charles, *L'art loin de la vie*, Vrin, Paris 1939.

LASTER, Arnaud, »Musique et peuple dans les années 1830,« *Romantisme*, 1975, 9, pp. 77—83.

LEBLOND, Richard E., Jr., *Professionalization and Bureaucratization in the Performance of Serious Music in the United States*, Ph. D. Thesis, University of Michigan, 1968.

LEFEBVRE, Henri, »La musique et la ville, avec Henri Lefebvre,« *Musique en jeu*, 1976, 24, pp. 75-81.

LEVI-STRAUSS, Claude, *Mythologiques. Le cru et le cuit*, Plon, Paris 1964,

LEVY, Ernst, *Des rapports entre la musique et la société*, La Baconnière, Neuchâtel 1979, pp. 66.

LEWIS, George H., »Taste Cultures and Culture Classes in Mass Society,« *International Review of the Aesthetics and Sociology of Music*, 1977, VIII/1, pp. 39—49.

LIEBERMAN, Fredric, »Relationships of Musical and Cultural Contrasts in Java and Bali,« *Asian Studies*, Quezon City 1967, 5/2, pp. 274—281.

LISSA, Zofia, »Povijesna glazbena svijest i njena uloga u savremenoj muzičkoj kulturi,« *Zvuk*, 1973, 4, pp. 375—388.

LIST, George, and Juan ORREGO-SALAS, eds., *Music in the Americas*, Indiana University Research Center in Anthropology, Folklore and Linguistics, Bloomington 1967.

LOMAX, Alan, *Folk Song Styles and Culture: A Staff Report on Cantometrics*, American Association for the Advancement of Science, Washington (D. C.) 1968, pp. 308.

LORTAT-JACOB, Bernard, *Musique et fêtes au Haut-Atlas*, Publications de la Société française de Musicologie, Paris 1982, pp. 154.

MACHAYEKHI, A., »Musique dans la ville,« *Musique en jeu*, 1976, 24, pp. 29-32.

MADEIRA, Louis Cephas, *Annals of Music in Philadelphia and History of the Musical Fund Society*, J. B. Lippincott, Philadelphia 1896.

MALMROS, Anna-Lise, »Organisational Set-up and Politico-Cultural Aspects of Beat in Copenhagen,« in: I. Bontinck, ed., *New Patterns of Musical Behaviour*, Universal Edition, Vienna 1974, pp. 114—119.

MANNHEIM, Karl, *Essays on the Sociology of Culture*, Routledge & Kegan Paul, London 1956.

MARK, Desmond, *Zur Bestandaufnahme des Wiener Orchesterrepertoires. Ein Soziographischer Versuch nach der Methode von John H. Mueller*, Universal Edition, Wien 1979.

MARX, A. B., *Denkschrift über Organisation des Musikwesens im preußischen Staate*, Berlin 1948.

McALLESTER, David P., *Enemy Way Music. A Study of Social and Esthetic Values as Seen in Navaho Music*, Peabody Museum, Cambridge (Mass.) 1954.

McCUSKER, Honor, *Fifty Years of Music in Boston*, Published by the Trustees of the Public Library, Boston 1938.

MEAD, M., *Cultural Patterns and Cultural Change*, New American Library, New York 1955.

MEE, John Henry, *The Oldest Music Room in Europe: A Record of Eighteenth Century Enterprises of Oxford*, J. Lane, London 1911.

MERRIAM, Alan P., »Music and the Origin of the Flathead Indians — A Problem in Culture History,« in *Music in the Americas*, George List and Juan Orrego—Salas, eds., Indiana University Research Center in Anthropology, Folklore and Linguistics, Bloomington 1967, pp. 129—138. (Inter—American Music Monograph Series, Vol. 1)

MERRIAM, Alan P., »Music in American Culture,« *American Anthropologist*, 1955, 59/6, pp. 1173—1181.

— »The Use of Music as a Technique of Reconstructing Culture History in Africa,« in *Reconstructing African Culture History*, Creighton Gabel and Norman R. Bennett, eds., Boston University Press, Boston 1967, pp. 83—114.

MERRILL, F. E., *Society and Culture*, Prentice-Hall, New York 1957.

MIES, P., *Sinn und Praxis der musikalischen Kritik*, Butzon & Bercker, Kevelaer 1950.

MORTON, David, *The Traditional Music of Thailand: Introduction, Commentary, and Analyses*, UCLA Institute of Ethnomusicology, Los Angeles 1968.

MUELLER, John H., »The Aesthetic Gap between Consumer and Composer,« *Journal of Research in Music Education*, 1967, XV/2, pp. 151-158.

MÜLLER-BLATTAU, J., »Zur Geschichte der musikalischen Gesellschaftsformen,« *Die Musikpflege*, 1930, 1, pp. 134—148.

MUMFORD, Lewis, *Technics and Civilisation*, Harcourt, New York 1934.

— *The Culture of Cities*, Harcourt, New York 1938.

MÜSEL, Albrecht, »Das politische Massenlied in der DDR. Pflege, Verbreitung und Wirkung,« in *Deutsche Studium*, 1968, VI/23, pp. 264—278.

* * *, *Music in Canada, its Resources and Needs*, Canadian Music Council Conference 1966, Ottawa 1966.

MUSSULMAN, Joseph A., *Music in the Cultured Generation, 1870—1900*, Northwestern University, Evanston 1971, pp. 298.

* * *, *Muze aan de Maas*, Enquête over muziek en het muziekleven bij de bevolking van Rotterdam en omgeving, Nederlandse Stichting voor Statistiek, The Hague 1965.

NAGEL, W., *Die Musik im täglichen Leben. Ein Beitrag zur Geschichte der musikalischen Kultur unserer Tage*, Langensalzach 1907.

NANRY, Charles, ed., *American Music: From Storyville to Woodstock*, Dutton, New Brunswick (N. J.) 1972.

NETTL, Bruno, *Music in Primitive Culture*, Harvard University Press, Cambridge 1956.

NETTL, Bruno, *The Western Impact on World Music: Africa and the American Indians*, in *Contemporary Music and Music Cultures*, Prentice-Hall, Englewood Cliffs (New Jersey) 1975, pp. 101—124.

429

NETTL, Bruno, ed., *Eight Urban Musical Cultures: Tradition and Change*, Urbana, University of Illinois Press, 1978.

OSMAN, Mohd Taib, »Some Observations on the Socio-Cultural Context of Traditional Maly Music,« *Tenggara*, 1969, 5, pp. 121—128.

OWE, Roger C., Nancy E. WALSTROM, and Ralph C. MICHELSEN, »Musical Culture and Ethnic Solidarity: A Baja California Case Study,« *Journal of American Folklore*, 1969, 82/324, pp. 99—111.

* * *, *The Performing Arts, Problems and Prospects*, Rockefeller Panel Report on the Future of Theatre, Dance, Music in America, McGraw-Hill, New York 1965.

PINTHUS, Gerhard, *Das Konzertleben in Deutschland. Ein Abriß seiner Entwicklung bis zum Beginn des 19. Jahrhunderts*, Heitz, Strasbourg-Leipzig-Zurich 1932.

PIRRO, André, *La musique à Paris sous le règne de Charles VI (1380—1422)*, Heitz, Strasbourg 1930.

PREUSSNER, Eberhard, *Die bürgerliche Musikkultur. Ein Beitrag zur deutschen Musikgeschichte des 18. Jahrhunderts*, Hanseatische Verlagsanstalt Hamburg 1935; Bärenreiter, Kassel - Basel 1950; Hamburg 1954.

RAYNOR, Henry, *Music & Society Since 1815*, Schocken Books. New York 1976, pp. VIII-213.

REINECKE, Hans-Peter, »Zum Forschungsprojekt einer Strukturanalyse unseres Musiklebens,« *Orchester*, 1970, XVIII/2, pp. 55—56.

— »Zur Strukturanalyse des deutschen Musiklebens,« *Musik und Bildung*, 1971, III/1, pp. 4—11.

REINHOLD, H., »Musik im Rundfunk. Ein kultursoziologisches Problem unserer Zeit,« *Kölner Zeitschrift für Soziologie und Sozialpsychologie*, 1955, 7, pp. 55—69, 233—246.

ROSENBERG, Bernard, and David M. WHITE, eds., *Mass Culture: The Popular Arts in America*, Free Press, Glencoe 1957.

RUSSEL, Theodore C., *Theodore Thomas: His Role in the Development of Musical Culture in the United States, 1835—1905*, University of Minnesota, 1969, pp. 225.

SACHS, Curt, *Musikgeschichte der Stadt Berlin bis zum Jahre 1800*, Gebr. Paetel, Berlin 1908, pp. 325.

— *Musik und Oper am Kurbrandenburgischen Hof*, J. Bard, Berlin 1910, pp. 299.

SALMEN, Walter, *Haus- und Kammermusik: Privates Musizieren im gesellschaftlichen Wandel zwischen 1600 und 1900* (Musikgeschichte in Bildern IV/3), VEB Deutscher Verlag für Musik, Leipzig 1969, pp. 203.

— *Die Schichtung der mittelalterlichen Musikkultur in der ostdeutschen Grenzlage*, Kassel 1954.

— *Musikleoen im 16. Jahrhundert* (Musikgeschichte in Bildern III/9), VEB Deutscher Verlag für Musik, Leipzig 1976, pp. 214.

— *Höfische Kultur im Hoch- und Spätmittelalter*, in *Musikgeschichte Österreichs*, Bd. I, Rudolf Flotzinger and Gernot Gruber, eds., Verlag Styria, Graz-Vienna-Cologne 1977, pp. 117—142.

SCHAEFER, H., »Über Glanz und Elend des bürgerlichen Musiklebens,« *Musik und Gesellschaft*, 1962, 12, pp. 216—220.

SCHAEFFNER, A., »Musique et structures sociales (sociétés d'Afrique noire),« *Revue française de sociologie*, 1962, III/4, pp. 388-395.

SCHERING, Arnold, »Künstler, Kenner und Liebhaber der Musik im Zeitalter Haydns und Goethes,« *Peters Jahrbuch*, 1931, 38, pp. 9—23.

SCHMIDT, Franz, *Das Musikleben der bürgerlichen Gesellschaft Leipzigs im Vormärz (1815—1848)*. Langensalza 1912.

SCHNEIDER, Constantin, *Geschichte der Musik in Salzburg von der ältesten Zeit bis zur Gegenwart*, R. Kiesel, Salzburg 1935.

SCHNEIDER, Marius, »Le rôle de la musique dans la mythologie et les rites des civilisations non-européennes,« in Roland-Manuel, ed. *Histoire de la musique*, Gallimard, Paris 1960, Vol. I, pp. 131—214.

SCHOLES, P. A., *The Puritans and Music in England and New England. A Contribution to the Cultural History of Two Nations*, Oxford University Press, London 1934; New York 1962.

SCHOLL, Sharon, and Sylvia WHITE, *Music and the Culture of Man*, Holt, Rinehart and Winston, New York 1970.

SEEGER, Charles, »Music and Culture,« *Proceedings of the Music Teachers National Association*, 35th series, 1941, pp. 112—122.

SCHWAB, Heinrich W., »Unterhaltendes des Musizieren im Industriegebiet des 19. Jahrhunderts,« in H. de la Motte, ed., *Studien zur Trivialmusik des 19. Jahrhunderts*, Bosse, Regensburg 1967, pp. 151—158.

SELLERS, Mary Josephine, *The Role of the Fine Arts in the Culture of the Southern Baptist Churches*, Ph. D. Thesis (Humanities), Syracuse University 1968.

SENDREY, Alfred, *The Music of the Jews in the Diaspora (up to 1800). A Contribution to the Social and Cultural History of the Jews*, A. S. Barnes, Cranbury 1970, pp. 483; New York 1970.

SENDREY, Alfred, *Music in the Social and Religious Life of Antiquity*, Fairleigh Dickinson University Press, Rutherford-Madison-Teaneck 1974.

SERAUKY, Walter, »Musikgeschichte der Stadt Halle,« in *Beiträge zur Musikforschung*, Max Schneider, Waisenhaus, Halle 1932.

SESSIONS, Roger, *The Musical Experience of Composer, Performer, Listener*, University of Princeton Press, Princeton 1950.

SEYMOUR, Margaret R., *Music in Lincoln, Nebraska in the Nineteenth Century: A Study of the Musical Culture of a Frontier Society*, M. A. Thesis, University of Nebraska, 1968.

SHEPHERD, John, »Music and Social Control: An Essay on the Sociology of Musical Knowledge,« *Calalist*, 1979, 13, pp. 1—54.

SILBERMANN, Alphons, »Gruppenberührung und Gruppenkonflikt in der Musik,« in *Schriftenreihe des Instituts für neue Musikerziehung Darmstadt*, 1959, 1, pp. 12—32.

SMIJERS, Albert, »Die Kaiserliche Hofmusik-Kapelle von 1543—1619,« in *Studien zur Musikwissenschaft,* Gesellschaft zur Herausgabe von Denkmälern der Tonkunst in Österreich, vols. 6—9, Vienna 1920.

SOCHOR, Arnold N., *Music and Life. Music and Musicians of Leningrad* (in Russian), Sovetskij Kompozitor, Moscow 1972, pp. 239.

SONNECK, Oscar George Theodore, *Early Concert-Life in America, 1731——1800,* Breitkopf & Härtel, Leipzig 1907.

SOROKIN, Pitirim, *La musica nella dinamica socio-culturale,* in A. Seravessa, ed., *La sociologia della musica,* EDT, Torino 1980, pp. 66—76.

SPALDING, Walter Raymond, *Music at Harvard,* Coward-McCann, New York 1935.

STANISLAV, Jozef, *Hudebni kultura, uměni a život,* n. p., 1940.

STEFANI, Gino, *Musica e religione nell'Italia barocca,* Flacovio, Palermo 1975, pp. 261.

STEVENSON, R., *La musica colonial en Colombia,* Publicaciones del Instituto popular de Cultura de Cali, Departemento de investigaciones folcloricas, Cali 1964.

STONE, J. H., »Mid-Nineteenth-Century American Beliefs in the Social Values of Music,« *The Musical Quarterly,* 1957, XLIII, pp. 38—49.

SUPIČIĆ, Ivo, »Music and Ceremony. Another Aspect,« *International Review of the Aesthetics and Sociology of Music,* 1982, 13/1, pp. 21—38.

SUPPAN, Wolfgang, *Bürgerliches und bäuerliches Musizieren in Mittelalter und früher Neuzeit,* in *Musikgeschichte Österreichs,* Bd. I, Rudolf Flotzinger and Gernot Gruber, eds., Verlag Styria, Graz-Vienna-Cologne 1977, pp. 143—172.

SZWED, John F., »Musical Style and Racial Conflict,« *Phylon,* 1966, 27/4, pp. 358—366.

TAYLOR, Clifford, »Music, The Design of Culture and the Afro-Asian Revolution,« *Encounter,* 1968, XXXI/5, pp. 41—48.

TUCKER, Archibald Norman, *Tribal Music and Dancing in the Southern Sudan (Africa) at Social and Ceremonial Gatherings,* William Reeves, London 1933.

THOVERON, Gabriel, »Leisure Time Behaviour and Cultural Attitude of Youth. Subjects of an International Research Project,« in: I. Bontinck, ed., *New Patterns of Musical Behaviour,* Universal Edition, Vienna 1974, pp. 226—231.

VALENTIN, Caroline, *Geschichte der Musik in Frankfurt am Main vom Anfang des XIV. bis zum Angange des XVIII. Jahrhunderts,* Voelcker, Frankfurt 1906.

VALENTIN, E., »Zur Soziologie des Musiklebens,« in *Kongreßbericht,* Gesellschaft für Musikforschung, Lüneburg 1950, pp. 220—222.

VERNILLAT, Fr., »Chanson et société: l'orientation de l'opinion par la chanson,« *Les Amis de Sèvres,* 1980, 99/3, pp. 7—15.

VIRDEN, Ph., and T. WISHART, *Some Observations on the Social Strati-fication of the Twentieth-Century Music*, in *Whose Music? A Socio-logy of Musical Languages*, Transaction Books, New Brunswick—London 1977, pp. 155—178.

VULLIAMY, Graham, *Music as a Case Study in the 'New Sociology of Education'*, in *Whose Music? A Sociology of Musical Languages*, Transaction Books, New Brunswick—London 1977, pp. 201—232.

——, *Music and the Mass Culture Debate*, in *Whose Music? A Socio-logy of Musical Languages*, Transaction Books, New Brunswick--London 1977, pp. 179—200.

WALTER, Don C., *Men and Music in Western Culture*, Appleton-Century-Crofts, New York 1969, pp. 244.

WANGERMÉE, Robert, »La radio, la musique et les moralistes de la culture,« Institut de Sociologie de l'Université libre de Bruxelles, Brussels 1971, pp. 435—464.

WARREN, Fred, and Lee WARREN, *The Music of Africa: An Introduction*, Prentice-Hall, Englewood Cliffs 1970, pp. 88.

WATERMAN, Richard A., »Music in Australian Aboriginal Culture. Some So-ciological and Psychological Implications,« *Music Therapy*, 1956, 5, pp. 40—49.

WEBER, William, *Music and the Middle Class. The Social Structure of Con-cert Life in London, Paris and Vienna*, Croom Helm, London 1975, pp. 172.

— »Mass Culture and the Reshaping of European Musical Taste, 1770——1870,« *International Review of the Aesthetics and Sociology of Mu-sic*, 1977, VIII/1, pp. 5—23.

WEGNER, Max, *Das Musikleben der Griechen*, W. Gruyter und Co., Berlin 1949, pp. 232 + 32.

WEISMANN, Adolf, *Berlin als Musikstadt*, Schuster & Loeffler, Berlin 1911.

WESTRUP, Jack A., »Domestic Music under the Stuarts,« in *Proceedings of the Royal Musical Association*, London 1942, 68, pp. 19—53.

YOUNG, Percy M., *The Concert Tradition from the Middle Ages to the 20th Century*, Roy Publishers, New York-London 1965, pp. 278.

ZACCARO, Gianfranco, *Storia sociale aella musica*, Newton Compton Edi-tori, Roma 1979, pp. 207.

ZANZIG, Augustus Delafield, *Music in American Life, Present and Future*, Oxford University Press, London 1932, pp. 560.

ZEMP, Hugo, *Musique Dan: La musique dans la pensée et la vie sociale d'une société africaine*, Mouton, The Hague 1971.

ŻAK, S., *Musik als »Ehr und Zier« im mittelalterlichen Reich. Studien zur Musik im Höfischen Leben, Recht und Zeremoniell*, Verlag Dr. Päff-gen, Neuss 1979, pp. IX-347.

BIBLIOGRAPHY

MUSIC AND ECONOMICS

ADORNO, Theodor Wiesengrund, »Musikalische Warenanalysen,« *Neue Rundschau*, 1955, 66, pp. 59—70.

ANDERLUH, Anton, »Das Lied der Arbeit im deutschen Alpenland,« *Arbeit und Volksleben*, 1967, pp. 325—330.

ARTARIA, Franz, and Hugo BOTSTIBER, *Joseph Haydn und das Verlagshaus Artaria*, Artaria, Vienna 1909.

* * *, »Aspekte des internationalen Musikkonsums,« *Österreichische Musik-Zeitschrift* (special number), 1964, 19, 10.

ATTALI, Jacques, *Bruits. Essai sur l'économie politique de la musique*, P. U. F., Paris 1977, pp. 304.

BAUM, Richard, and Wolfgang REHM, eds., *Musik und Verlag*, Bärenreiter, Kassel-Basle 1968, pp. 624.

BAUMOL, William J., and William G. BOWEN, *Performing Arts: The Economic Dilemma: A Study of Problems Common to Theatre, Opera, Music and Dance*, Twentieth Century Fund, New York 1966.

BLAUG, Mark, ed., *The Economics of the Arts*, Westview Press, London 1976, pp. 272.

BOOSEY, William, *Fifty Years of Music Publishing*, Benn, London 1931.

BROOK, Barry S., *La symphonie française dans la seconde moitié du XVIIIᵉ siècle*, Institut de Musicologie de l'Université de Paris, Paris 1962, 3 vol., pp. 684+726+231.

——, »Piracy and Panacea in the Dissemination of Music in the Late Eighteenth Century«, *Proceedings of the Royal Musical Association*, Vol. 102 (1975—1976), London 1979, pp. 13—36.

BÜCHER, Karl, *Arbeit und Rhythmus*, Teubner, Leipzig 1892, 2nd ed. 1899, 3rd ed. 1902.

CAHN-SPEYER, R., »Beiträge zur Vorgeschichte und zu den Grundlagen des musikalischen Urheberrechtes,« in *Geistiges Eigentum*, 1936/37, 2, pp. 227—251.

CASTELAIN, R., »Histoire de l'édition musicale ou du droit d'éditeur au droit d'auteur (1501—1793),« Lemoin Paris, 1957.

COLLINS, J. J., *The Social and Economic Value of Music in Industry*, East St. Louis (Illinois) 1937.

COONTZ, S., *Population Theories and the Economic Interpretation*, Routledge and Kegan Paul, London 1957.

CROSTEN, William Loran, *French Grand Opera, An Art and a Business*, King's Crown Press, New York 1948.

DORIAN, Frederick, *Commitment to Culture, Art Patronage in Europe — Its Significance for America*, University of Pittsburgh Press, Pittsburgh 1964.

DRUCKER, F., *Die Praxis des Management*, Econ, Düsseldorf 1956.

EHRLICH, Cyril, »Economic History and Music,« *Proceedings of the Royal Musical Association*, 1976-77, 103, pp. 188—199.

EHRMANN, Albert, »Aspect moral et économique des sociétés d'amateurs de musique,« *La revue musicale*, 1958, 242, pp. 53—57.

ENGLERT, H., *Der Markt für musikalische Kompositionen*, Diss., Cologne 1971.

FAULKNER, Robert Roy, *Studio Musicians: Their Work and Career Contingencies in the Hollywood Film Industry*, Ph. D. Thesis, University of California, Los Angeles 1968.

FISHER, R. L., »Preferences of Different Age and Socio-economic Groups in Unstructured Musical Situations,« *Journal of Social Psychology*, 1951, 33, pp. 147—152.

***, *The Finances of the Performing Arts*, Ford Foundation, New York 1974.

FRISIUS, Rudolf, »Musik als Konsumartikel? Wandlungen des musikalischen Materials, Wandlungen musikalischen Verhaltens,« in *Perspektiven kommunaler Kulturpolitik*, pp. 442-453.

GAMBLE, William, *Music Engraving and Printing*, Pitman, London 1923.

GERICKE, H., *Der Wiener Musikalienhandel von 1700 bis 1778*, Graz-Cologne 1960.

GOLDSCHMIDT, Sylvie, *Les aides à la création musicale dans quelques pays d'Europe*, Conseil de l'Europe, Education et culture, Strasbourg 1980.

GRIMM, B., »Die sozial-ökonomische Lage der Weimarer Hofkapellisten in der ersten Hälfte des 19. Jahrhunderts, dargestellt am Beispiel J. Ch. Lobes,« *Die Musikforschung*, 1966, 19, pp. 55—56

GÜLKE, Peter, »Edition Peters: 175 Jahre Musikverlag im Leipzig,« *Musik und Gesellschaft*, 1975, XXV/12, pp. 749-752.

HALPIN, D. D., »Industrial Music and Moral,« *The Journal of the Acoustical Society of America*, 1943, 15, pp. 77—78.

HARWELL, Richard Barksdale, *Confederate Music*, University of North Carolina Press, Chapel Hill 1950.

HASE, Hermann, *Joseph Haydn und Breitkopf & Härtel*, Breitkopf & Härtel, Leipzig 1909.

HELMS, S., ed., *Schlager in Deutschland. Beiträge zur Analyse der Popularmusik und des Musikmarktes*, Wiesbaden 1972.

HOFFMANN-ERBRECHT, Lothar, »Johann Sebastian und Carl Philipp Emanuel Bachs Nürnberger Verleger,« in *Die Nürnberger Musikverleger und die Familie Bach*, pp. 5-10.

HORTSCHANSKY, Klaus, »Pränumerations- und Subskriptionslisten in Notendrucken deutscher Musiker des 18. Jahrhunderts,« *Acta Musicologica*, 1968, XL/2—3, pp. 154—174.

KAVOLIS, V., »Economic Correlates of Artistic Creativity,« *American Journal of Sociology*, Chicago 1964, 70, N⁰ 3, pp. 332—341.

KING, A. Hyatt., *400 Years of Music Printing*, British Museum, London 1964.

LESURE, François, *Cinq catalogues d'éditeurs de musique à Paris (1824— —1834): Dufaut et Dubois, Petit-Frère, Delahante-Erard, Pleyel*, Minkoff, Genève 1976, 1, multiple pagination.

LUCIUS, Joachim, »Das Geschäft mit dem Schlager,« *Volksmusik*, XII/1, 1967, pp. 6—7; 1967, XII/2, pp. 18—20; 1967, XII/3, pp. 8—9; 1967, XII/7, pp. 22—23.

LUTHE, Heinz Otto, »La musique enregistrée et l'industrie du disque,« *Revue internationale des sciences sociales*, 1968, XX/4, pp. 712—724.

— »Recorded Music and the Record Industry: A Sector Neglected by Sociological Research,« *International Social Science Journal*, 1968, 20/3, pp. 656—666.

MAC-DOUGALD, D., »The Popular Music Industry,« *Radio Research*, New York 1941, pp. 92.

MATERNE, Gerd, *Die sozialen und wirtschaftlichen Probleme des Musikers*, Diss., Mannheim 1953.

MATZKE, H., *Musikökonomik und Musikpolitik — Grundzüge einer Musikwirtschaftslehre — Ein Versuch*, Quader, Breslau 1927.

McPHEE, William N., »When Culture Becomes a Business,« in *Sociological Theories in Progress*, Joseph Berger, ed., Houghton Mifflin, New York 1966, pp. 227—243.

MINUS, Johnny, and William Storm HALE, *The Managers', Entertainers' and Agents' Book; How to Plan Plot, Scheme, Learn, Perform, Avoid Dangers and Enjoy Your Career in the Entertainment Industry*, Seven Arts Press, Hollywood (Calif.) 1971, pp. 29.

MOORE, Thomas Gale, *The Economics of the American Theater*, Duke University Press, Durham (N.C.) 1968.

* * *, *Musik und Wirtschaft*, Special number of *Musica*, 1951, 5, 7/8.

NETTEL, R., *Music in Five Towns 1840—1914. A Study of Social Influence of Music in an Industrial District*, Oxford 1945, 3rd ed.

PEACOCK, Alan, »Public Patronage and Music: An Economist's View,« *Welsh Music*, 1968, III/3, pp. 24-38.

PEACKOCK, Alan, and Ronald WEIR, *The Composer in the Market Place*, Faber Music, London 1975, pp. 172.

PETERSON, Richard A., and David G. BERGER, »Entrepreneurship in Organizations: Evidence from the Popular Music Industry,« *Administrative Science Quarterly*, March 1971, 16, pp. 97—106.

PODVIN, Mary Grace, »The Influence of Music on the Performance of a Work Task,« *Journal of Music Therapy*, 1967, 4/2, pp. 52—56.

PROKOPOWICZ, Maria, »Wydawnictwo muzyczne Klukowskich 1816-1858,« *Rocznik Warszawski*, 1975, XIII, pp. 135-159.

RADET, Edmond, *Lulli homme d'affaire, propriétaire et musicien*, L. Allison, Paris n. d.

RATCLIFFE, H., »Social and Economic Position of the Performing Musician,« *The World of Music*, 1961, 3, pp. 61—64.

REICHARDT, R., *Die Schallplatte als kulturelles und ökonomisches Phänomen. Ein Beitrag zum Problem der Kunstkommerzialisierung*, Zurich 1962.

REININGHAUS, F. Christoph, J. H. TRABER, »Musik als Ware — Musik als Wahre. Zum politischen Hintergrund des musiksoziologischen Ansatzes von T. W. Adorno,« *Zeitschrift für Musiktheorie*, 1973, IV/1, pp. 7—14.

RINGER, Alexander L., »Mozart and the Josephian Era: Some Socio-Economic Notes on Musical Change,« *Current Musicology*, 1969, 9, pp. 158—165.

RINGER, Alexander L., »Musical Taste and the Industrial Syndrome. A Socio-musicological Problem in Historical Analysis,« *International Review of the Aesthetics and Sociology of Music*, 1974, 5/1, pp. 139—153.

ROTH, Ernst, *The Business of Music*, Cassell, London 1965.

ROTH, Ernst, *Musik als Kunst und Ware. Betrachtungen und Begegnungen eines Musikverlegers*, Atlantis, Zurich 1966.

ROUT, Leslie B., Jr., »Economics and Race in Jazz,« in *Frontiers of American Culture*, B. B. Browne, R. H. Crowder, V. L. Lokke, and W. T. Stafford, eds., Purdue University Studies, West Lafayette 1968, pp. 154—171.

SARAMAKI, Martii, and Jukka HAARMA, *The International Music Industry*, Finnish Broadcast Company, Planning Research, Helsinki 1979.

SCHAAL, Richard, *Musiktitel aus fünf Jahrhunderten. Eine Dokumentation zur Typographischen und künstlerischen Gestaltung und Entwicklung der Musikalien*, Quellenkatalogue zur Musikgeschichte, 5, Heinrichshofen, Wilhelmshaven 1972, pp. iv-250.

SCHAEFER, Hartmut, *Die Notendrucker und Musikverleger in Frankfurt am Main von 1630 bis 1720: eine bibliographisch-drucktechnische Untersuchung*, Kassel-Basel-Tours-London, Bärenreiter, 1975, pp. 711.

SCHOTT, S., »Theater und Orchester,« *Statistisches Jahrbuch der deutschen Städte*, 1931, 5, pp. 279—308.

SCHUMANN, M., *Zur Geschichte des deutschen Musikalienhandels seit der Gründung des Vereins der Deutschen Musikalienhändler*, Leipzig 1929.

***, *A Study of the Non-Profit Arts and Cultural Industry in New York State*, Cranford Wood, Inc., New York 1973.

SUPIČIĆ, Ivo, »La musique et les techniques de production,« *Schweizerische Musikzeitung*, 1961, CI/4, pp. 241—245.

* * *, UNESCO, *Music Theatre in a Changing Society*, Paris 1968.

WAHL-ZIEGER, E., *Theater und Orchester zwischen Marktkräften und Marktkorrektur*, Göttingen 1978.

WANGERMÉE, Robert, »Notes sur l'économie des institutions musicales non-lucratives,« *International Review of the Aesthetics and Sociology of Music*, 1982, 13/2, pp. 141—160.

— »Notes sur l'économie des institutions musicales non-lucratives,« *International Review of the Aesthetics and Sociology of Music*, 1982, 13/2, pp. 141—160.

WARSCHAUER, Frank, »Technisierung und die Folgen,« *Melos*, 1970, XXXVII /7—8, pp. 279—281.

WEBER, Max, *Wirtschaft und Gesellschaft*, Tübingen 1956.

WEDGEWOOD, Mary, »Avant-garde Music: Some Publication Problems,« *Library Quarterly*, 1976, XLVI/2, pp. 137-152.

WEINMANN, Alexander, *Der Alt-Wiener Musikverlag im Spiegel der »Wiener Zeitung«*, Hans Schneider, Tutzing 1976, pp. 71.

WRIGHT, Craig, *Antoine Brumel and Patronage at Paris*, in Iain Fenlon, ed., *Music in Medieval & Early Modern Europe. Patronage, Sources and Texts*, Cambridge University Press, Cambridge 1981, pp. 37—60.

ZINGEL, Hans Joachim, *Harfe und Harfenspiel vom Beginn des 16. bis in zweite Drittel des 18. Jahrhunderts*, M. Niemeyer, Halle 1932.

ZOSEL, Johannes M., »Zur industriellen 'Revolution' in der Musik,« *Melos*, 1969, XXXVI/9, pp. 353—357.

MUSIC AND TECHNIQUE

ADORNO, Theodor Wiesengrund, »Musik und Technik,« in *Klangfiguren — Musikalische Schriften* I, Berlin—Frankfurt/M. 1959.

— »Musique et technique, aujourd'hui,« *Arguments*, 1960, 19, pp. 50—58.

BAGENAL, Hope, »Musical Taste and Concert Hall Design,« in *Proceedings of the Royal Musical Association*, 1951/52, 78, pp. 211—229.

BLAUKOPF, Kurt, »Raumakustische Probleme der Musiksoziologie,« *Gravesaner Blätter*, 1960, 5, pp. 171—176.

— »Raumakustische Probleme der Musiksoziologie,« *Die Musikforschung*, 1962, XV/3, pp. 237—246.

— »Probleme der Raumakustik und des Hörverhaltens,« *Musikalische Zeitfragen*, XII, pp. 61—71.

BONTINCK, Irmgard, »Das Publikum des Musiktheaters und die technischen Medien,« in *IMDT Progress Report No. 3*, Vienna 1970.

BRUN, Herbert, »Technology and the Composer,« in Music and Technology, Stockholm Meeting June 8—12, 1970, organized by UNESCO, *La Revue musicale*, Paris 1971, pp. 181—192.

BRUNNER, Hans, *Das Klavierklangideal Mozarts und die Klaviere seiner Zeit*, Dr. B. Filser Verlag, Augsburg 1933.

CARDINELL, R. L., »Music in Industry,« in *Music and Medicine*, D. M. Schullian and M. Schön, ed., Schumann, New York 1948.

CHAILLEY, Jacques, »Un clavier d'orgue à la fin du XIᵉ siècle,« *Revue de musicologie*, 1937, 18/61, pp. 5—11.

CIAMAGA, Gustav, »The Training ot the Computer in the Use of New Technological Means,« in Music and Technology, Stockholm Meeting June 8—12, 1970, organized by UNESCO, *La Revue musicale*, Paris 1971, pp. 143—150.

COLLINS, J. J., *The Social and Economic Value of Music in Industry*, East St. Louis (Illinois) 1937.

CONKLIN, H. C., and W. C. STURTEVANT, »Seneca Indian Singing Tools at Coldspring Longhouse. Musical Instruments of the Modern Iroquois,« in *Proceedings of the American Philosophical Society*, 1953, XCIII/3, pp. 262—290.

DE COSTER, Michel, »Le monde des éditeurs phonographiques. Résultats et réflexion critique à propos d'une démarche,« *Communications*, 1977, vol. 2, pp. 201-211.

DOLGE, Alfred, *Pianos and Their Makers*, Covina Publishing Company, Covina (Calif.) 1911—1913.

DRÄGER, Hans Heintz, *Die Entwicklung des Streichbogens und seine Anwendung in Europa (bis zum Violinbogen des 16. Jahrhunderts)*, Bärenreiter-Verlag, Kassel 1937.

DUFOURCQ, Norbert, *Documents inédits relatifs à l'orgue français*, E. Droz, Paris 1934.

EHRLICH, Cyril, *Social Emulation and Industrial Progress: The Victorian Piano*, Queen's University of Belfast, Belfast 1975, pp. 20.

FARMER, Henry George, *Turkish Instruments of Music in the Seventeenth Century*, The Civic Press, Glasgow 1937.

— *Studies in Oriental Musical Instruments*, I. Series, H. Reeves, London 1931; II. Series, The Civic Press, Glasgow 1939.

FENWICK, J. W., *Instruction Book for the Northumbrian Small-pipes*, Northumberland Press Limited for the Northumbrian Pipers' Society, Newcastle upon Tyne 1931.

FRIEDMANN, Georges, »Role et place de la musique dans une société industrielle,« *Diogène*, 1970, 72, pp. 27—44.

HELMS, Hans, »Neue Musik unter den Zwängen einer monopolisierten Musikindustrie,« *Hi-Fi Stereophonie*, 1973, XII/6, pp. 583-587.

HENRY, Otto Walter, »The Electro-Technology of Modern Music,« *Arts in Society*, 1970, VII/1, pp. 20—26.

— »Music and the New Technology,« *Arts in Society*, 1972, IX/2, pp. 305—306.

HIRSCH, P. Morris, *The Structure of the Popular Music Industry: The Filtering Process by which Records are Preselected for Public Consumption*, Institute for Social Research, The University of Michigan, Ann Arbor 1969, 1973, pp. 72.

HOFFMANN, Wilrich, *Komponist und Technik. Die Bedeutung naturwissenschaftlicher Forschung für die Musik*, G. Braun, Karlsruhe 1975, pp. 61.

HUGHES, Ch. W., »Music and Machines,« *The Journal of Aesthetics and Art Criticism*, 1946, V/1, pp. 28—34.

IYER, M. Subramania, »Classical Music Under the Impact of Industrial Change,« in *Music East and West*, Roger Ashton, ed., Indian Council for Cultural Relations, New Delhi 1966, pp. 143—145.

KAEGI, Werner, »Music and Technology in the Europe of 1970,« in Music and Technology, Stockholm Meeting June 8—12, 1970, organized by UNESCO, *La Revue musicale*, Paris 1971, pp. 11—31.

KARBUSICKÝ, Vladimir, »Electronic Music and the Listener,« *The World of Music*, 1969, XI/1, pp. 32—44.

KLAUSMEIER, Friedrich, *Jugend und Musik im technischen Zeitalter*, H. Bouvier und Co. Verlag, 2nd ed., Bonn 1968.

KOENIG, Gottfried, »The Use of Computer Programmes in Creating Music,« Music and Technology, Stockholm Meeting June 8—12, 1970, organized by UNESCO, *La Revue musicale*, Paris 1971, pp. 93—115.

KRAUS, Egon, ed., *Der Einfluß der technischen Mittler auf die Musikerziehung unserer Zeit*, Vorträge der Siebten Bundesschulmusikwoche, Hannover 1968, B. Schott's Söhne, Mainz 1968.

LESURE, François, »La facture instrumentale à Paris au seizième siècle,« *The Galpin Society Journal*, 1954, VII, pp. 11—52.

— »Notes sur la facture du violon au XVIᵉ siècle,« *La Revue musicale*, 1955, 226, pp. 30—34.

— »Recherches sur les luthistes parisiens à l'époque de Louis XIII,« in *Le Luth et sa musique*, C.N.R.S., Paris 1958, pp. 209—223.

LOUBET DE SCEAURY, Paul, *Musiciens et facteurs d'instruments de musique sous l'Ancien régime; status corporatifs*, A. Pedone, Paris 1949.

LÜTGENDORFF, Willibald Leo Freiherr von, *Die Geigen- und Lautenmacher vom Mittelalter bis zur Gegenwart*, Hans Schneider, Frankfurt 1922, 2 vols.

MARTORELLA, Rosanne, »The Relationship between Box Office and Repertoire: A Case Study of Opera,« *Sociological Quarterly*, 1977, 18, pp. 354-366.
— »Music and Technology,« *La Revue Musicale*, 1971, pp. 208.

MATZKE, H., *Grundzüge einer musikalischen Technologie*, Breslau 1931.

— »Vom Schicksal der Musik im Zeitalter der Technik,« in *Festschrift der Technischen Hochschule zu Breslau*, Breslau 1935.

McVEIGH, J., »La musique dans l'industrie (musique fonctionnelle), in *La musique dans l'éducation*, UNESCO, Paris 1955, pp. 200—204.

MEAD, M., *Cultural Patterns and Technical Change*, New American Library, New York 1955.

MUMFORD, Lewis, *Technics and Civilisation*, Harcourt, New York 1934.

PHILIPPOT, M.-P., »Aspects psycho-sociologiques de la haute fidélité,« in *Conférences des Journées d'Etudes*, Chiron, Paris 1963, pp. 3—13.

— »La musique et les machines,« *Cahiers d'études de Radio-Télévision,* 1960, 27—28, pp. 274—292.

PRIEBERG, F. K., *Musik des technischen Zeitalter,* Atlantis, Zurich 1956.

RICHARDS, James, »The Organ in the Parlor,« *Clavier,* 1969, VIII, pp. 16——20.

RUPP, Emile, *Die Entwicklungsgeschichte der Orgelbaukunst,* Benzinger, Einsiedeln 1929.

SACHS, Curt, *The History of Musical Instruments,* Norton, New York 1940.

— *Les instruments de musique de Madagascar,* Institut d'Ethnologie, Paris 1938.

SCHAEFFER, Pierre, »Music and Computers,« Music and Technology, Stockholm Meeting June 8—12, 1970, organized by UNESCO, *La Revue musicale,* Paris 1971, pp. 57—92.

SCHAEFFNER, André, *Les Kissis, une société noire et ses instruments de musique,* Hermann, Paris 1951.

— *Origine des instruments de musique,* Payot, Paris 1936.

SHIBATA, Minao, »Music and Technology in Japan,« in Music and Technology, Stockholm Meeting June 8—12, 1970, organized by UNESCO, *La Revue musicale,* Paris 1971, pp. 173—179.

SIMBRIGER, Heinrich, »Gong und Gongspiele,« in *Internationales Archiv für Ethnographie,* No. 36, Brill, Leiden 1939, pp. 180.

SITTNER, Hans, »Technische Medien im Dienst der Musik,« *Österreichische Musikzeitschrift,* 1968, XXIII/3, pp. 121—122.

SPILLANE, Daniel, *History of the American Pianoforte, Its Technical Development and the Trade,* D. Spillane, New York 1890.

STELLFELD, J. A., *Bronnen Tot de Geschiedenis der Antwerpsche Clavecimbelen Orgelbouwers in XVI en XVII eeuwen,* Drukkerij Resseler, Antwerp 1942.

STOCKHAUSEN, Karlheinz, *Texte zur elektronischen und instrumentalen Musik I,* DuMont Schauberg, Cologne 1963.

SUPIČIĆ, Ivo, »La musique et les techniques de production,« *Schweizerische Musikzeitung,* 1961, CI/4, pp. 241—245.

SZLIFIRSKI, Krzysztof, »New Technology and the Training of Composers in Experimental Music,« in Music and Technology, Stockholm Meeting June 8—12, 1970, organized by UNESCO, *La Revue musicale,* Paris 1971, pp. 151—156.

WARSCHAUER, Frank, »Technisierung und die Folgen,« *Melos,* 1970, XXXVII /7—8, pp. 279—281.

WEBER, M., *I problemi tecnici della musica, oggetto di indagine storica e sociologica,* in *La sociologia della musica,* EDT, Torino 1980, pp. 77—80.

— *La fortuna storica del pianoforte e le sue motivazioni sociali,* in *La sociologia della musica,* EDT, Torino 1980, pp. 217—222.

WIER, Albert Ernst, *The Piano: Its History, Makers, Players, and Music*, Longmans, London 1940.

WIESCHHOFF, Heinrich Albert, *Die Afrikanischen Trommeln und ihre außerafrikanischen Beziehungen*, Strecker & Schroeder, Stuttgart 1933.

ZINGEL, Hans Joachim, *Harfe und Harfenspiel vom Beginn des 16. bis in zweite Drittel des 18. Jahrhunderts*, M. Niemeyer, Halle 1932.

ZOSEL, Johannes M., »Zur industriellen 'Revolution' in der Musik,« *Melos*, 1969, XXXVI/9, pp. 353—357.

MUSIC AND THE MASS MEDIA

ADLER, A. F., »Presuppositions of and Design for a Quantitative Study in the Sociology of Radio Music,« *Cahiers Internationaux d'Etudes de Radio-Television*, 3—4.

ADORNO, Theodor Wiesengrund, *Der getreue Korrepetitor — Lehrschriften zur musikalischen Praxis*, Frankfurt/M. 1963.

— *The Radio Symphony; Radio Research*, 1941.

— »A Social Critic of Radio Music,« *The Kenyon Review*, 1945, 7, pp. 208—217 (Reprinted in Berelson, Bernard and Morris Janovitz, eds., *Reader in Public Opinion and Communication*, Free Press, Glencoe 1950, pp. 309—316.

ALVARES, A. L., »Le disque et la musique contemporaine,« *Esprit*, 1960, XXVIII/280, pp. 124—130.

AMBROŽIĆ-PAIĆ, Arlette, »Mass Media and Pop Groups in Yugoslavia,« in Irmgard Bontinck, ed., *New Patterns of Musical Behaviour*, Universal Edition, Vienna 1974.

BACHMANN, Claus-Henning, »Rundfunk, neue Musik, Publikum; Fragen und Versäumnisse,« *Schweizerische Musikzeitung*, 1977, 5, pp. 253—260.

BAIRD, Jo Ann, *Using Media in the Music Program*, Center for Applied Research in Education, New York 1975.

BAKOŠ, Oliver, and Ivan PREDANOCY, »Prieskum počuvanosti a hodnotenia rozhlasoveho vysielania,« *Českolovensky rozhlas*, Bratislava 1968, pp. 255.

BERTEN, W. M., *Musik und Mikrophon — Zur Soziologie und Dramaturgie der Musikweitergabe durch Rundfunk, Tonfilm, Schallplatte und Fernsehen*, Schwann, Düsseldorf 1951.

BEVILLE, H. M., *Social Stratification of the Radio Audience*, New York 1939.

BLAUKOPF, Kurt, *The Function of the Disc in Contemporary Musical Life*, Niggli, Niederteufen 1968, pp. 164.

— »Hudba, mládež a tehnické médiá,« *Slovenská Hud*, 1968, XII/1, pp. 13—17.

— »Die qualitative Veränderung musikalischer Mitteilung in den technischen Medien der Massenkommunikation,« *Kölner Zeitschrift für Soziologie und Sozialpsychologie*, 1969, XXI/3, pp. 510—516.

— »Zur Bestimmung der klanglichen Erfahrung der Musikstudierenden,« Vol. 2, in Schriftenreihe *Musik und Gesellschaft*, G. Braun, Karlsruhe 1968.

BLAUKOPF, Kurt, *Massenmedium Schallplatte. Die Stellung des Tonträgers in der Kultursoziologie und Kulturstatistik*, Breitkopf & Härtel, Wiesbaden 1977, pp. 92.

— »The Sociography of Music Life in Industrialised Countries. A Research Task,« *The World of Music*, 1979, 21/3, pp. 78—86.

— *L'approccio sociologico ai problemi della musica*, in *La sociologia della musica*, EDT, Torino 1980, pp. 87—93.

— »Democratisation of the Musical Theatre of Our Days«, *International Review of the Aesthetics and Sociology of Music*, 1982, 13/2, pp. 199—200.

— *Musik im Wandel der Gesellschaft*, Piper, München—Zürich 1982, pp. 383.

BLAUKOPF, Kurt, ed., *The Phonogram in Cultural Communication*, Springer-Verlag, Wien—New York 1982, pp. 181.

BOHNSTEDT, Werner, »Erwägungen zum Thema Film und Radio als Gegenstände soziologischer Erkenntnis,« in *Reine und angewandte Soziologie* (Festausgabe für Ferdinand Tönnies zu seinem 80. Geburtstage), Leipzig 1936.

BONTINCK, Irmgard, »Mass Media and New Types of Youth Music. Methodological and Terminological Problems,« *International Review of the Aesthetics and Sociology of Music*, 1975, VI/1, pp. 47—56.

BORNOFF, Jack, *Music and the Twentieth Century Media*, Olschki, Florence 1972.

BRANIŠ, František, »Vychovne poslanie hudebného rozhlasu,« *Broadcast Bratislava*, Bratislava 1970, pp. 91.

BRELET, Gisèle, »La Radio purifie et confirme la musique,« *Cahiers d'études de Radio-Télévision*, 1955, 3-4, pp. 367-378.

DE COSTER, Michel, *Le disque, art ou affaires? Analyse sociologique d'une industrie culturelle*, Presses Universitaires de Grenoble, Grenoble 1976.

DONOSE, Vasile, »Televiziunea și definirea valorilor artistice în conștiinta maselor,« *Muzica*, 1971, XI/7, pp. 10—11.

EBERHARD, F., *Der Rundfunkhörer und sein Programm — Ein Beitrag zur empirischen Sozialforschung*, Berlin 1962.

ECHANOVE, T., »La Radiofusion, y la Cultura,« *Revista International de sociologia*, 1958, 16/64, pp. 589—615.

ERNST, Georg, and Bernhard MARSHALL, *Film und Rundfunk. 2. Internationaler kath. Filmkongreß. 1. Internationaler kath. Rundfunkkongreß*, Verlag Leohaus, Munich 1929, pp. 432.

FASSET, J., *What Radio is Doing for Serious Music*, Pittsburgh 1940.

CANTRILL, H., and G. W. ALLPORT, *Psychology of Radio*, New York—London 1935.

BIBLIOGRAPHY

CAPLOW, Theodor, »The Influence of Radio Music as a Social Institution,« *Cahiers d'études de Radio-Télévision*, 1955, 3/4, pp. 279—291.

CHAILLEY, Jacques, »La musicologie et le disque,« in *Conférences des journées d'études*, Paris 1965, pp. 126—130.

— »La radio et le développement de l'instinct harmonique chez les auditeurs,« *Cahiers d'études de Radio-Télévision*, 1955, 3/4, pp. 401—412.

CHARPENTREAU, Jacques, *Nouvelles veillées en chansons. Des disques et des thèmes*, Editions ouvrières, Paris 1970, pp. 208.

CHASE, Gilbert, *Music in Radio-Broadcasting*, McGraw Hill, New York 1946.

GAISBAUER, Dieter, »Musikalische Selbsttätigkeit der Jugend im Kraftfeld der technischen Medien,« *Musik und Bildung*, 1972, IV/6, pp. 301—303.

GEIGER, T., »A Radio Test of Musical Taste,« *Public Opinion Quarterly*, 1950, 14, pp. 453—460.

GEORGESCU, Lucilia, »L'Internationale dans le plus ancien enregistrement sur disque roumain,« *Muzica*, 1971, XXI/4.

GERSCHKOWITSCH, S., »Die Kunst und der Fortschritt in der Massenkommunikationstechnik,« *Kunst und Literatur*, 1971, XIX/1, pp. 45—59.

GÖNNENWEIN, W., »Die Schallplatte im gesellschaftlichen Leben unserer Zeit,« *Musica Phonoprisma*, Mai/Juni 1966, pp. 69—74.

HAGEMANN, W., *Fernhören und Fernsehen*, Vowinckel, Heidelberg 1954.

HOSOKAWA, Shuhei, »Considérations sur la musique mass-médiatisée,« *International Review of the Aesthetics and Sociology of Music*, 1981, 12/1, pp. 21—50.

JACOBS, Norman, ed., *Culture for the Millions: Mass Media in Modern Society*, Beacon, Boston 1964.

KLAPPER, J. T., *The Effects of Mass Media*, Columbia University Press, New York 1949.

KLAUSMEIER, F., »Radiohören und Musikpflege. Ein Beitrag zur geistigen Situation der höheren Schule,« *Kulturarbeit*, 1954, 6/1.

— *Jugend und Musik im technischen Zeitalter*, Bonn 1963.

KNEPLER, Georg, *Über Wechselbeziehungen der Künste in der Massenkommunikation*, Hauptkommission Musikwissenschaft des Verbandes Deutscher Komponisten und Musikwissenschaftler, Berlin 1970, pp. 133—135.

KOCH, Ludwig, »Schallplatte, Sprachmaschine und ihre kulturelle Mission,« in *Funkalmanach*, 1930.

KÖNIG, René, »Sur quelques problèmes sociologiques de l'émission radiophonique musicale,« *Cahiers d'études de Radio-Télévision*, 1955, 3-/5, pp. 348—365.

LAZARSFELD, P. F., and F. N. STANTON, eds., *Radio Research 1941*, Duell, Sloan & Pearce, New York 1941.

LENZ, Friedrich, *Einführung in die Soziologie des Rundfunks*, Lechte, Emsdetten 1953.

LIST, Kurt, »Zur Soziologie der Schallplatte,« *Österreichische Musikzeitschrift*, Wien Mart 1968, XXIII/3, pp. 140—145.

LUTHE, Heinz Otto, »La musique enregistrée et l'industrie du disque,« *Revue internationale des sciences sociales*, 1968, XX/4, pp. 712—724.

MALETZKE, G., *Der Rundfunk in der Erlebniswelt des heutigen Menschen — Untersuchungen zur psychologischen Wesenseigenart des Rundfunks und zur Psychologie des Rundfunkshörer*, Diss., Hamburg 1950.

MATSUMAE, Norio, »A Study of the European Musical Program at the Tokyo Broadcasting Station (March 1925 — August 1926) that Existed Prior to the Establishment of N.H.K.,« in *Nomura Festschrift*, Ongakuno-Tomo Sha, Tokyo 1969, pp. 407—419.

MEISTERMAN-SEEGER, E., »Rundfunkhören und Fernsehen als Funktion früher Objektbeziehungen,« *Kölner Zeitschrift für Soziologie und Sozialpsychologie*, 1969, 3, pp. 645—656.

NEWMAN, E., E. SCHOEN, and A. BOULT, »Music for Broadcasting,« in *B. B. C. Annual*, London 1935.

NIEMANN, Konrad, »Mass Media — New Ways of Approach to Music and New Patterns of Musical Behaviour,« in: I. Bontinck, ed., *New Patterns of Musical Behaviour*, Universal Edition, Vienna 1974, pp. 44—54.

PECH, Karel, *Hören im »optischen Zeitalter«*, G. Braun, Karlsruhe 1969.

PHILIPPOT, M. P., »Aspects psycho-sociologiques de la haute fidélité,« in *Conférences des Journées d'Etudes*, Chiron, Paris 1963, pp. 3—13.

PORTE, J., »Une enquête par sondage sur l'auditoire radiophonique,« *Bulletin mensuel de statistique*, Suppléments trimestriels, Institut national de la statistique, Paris 1954.

* * *, *Radio, musique et société*, Actes du Congrès sur les aspects sociologiques de la musique à la Radio (Paris 27—30 Oct. 1954), *Cahiers d'Etudes de Radio-Télévision*, 1955, 3—4, pp. 259—575.

RAMACHANDRAN, N. S., »Classical Music and the Mass Media (with Special Reference to South India),« in *Music East and West*, R. Ashton, ed., Indian Council for Cultural Relations, New Delhi 1966, pp. 166—170.

REICHARDT, R., *Die Schallplatte als kulturelles und ökonomisches Phänomen. Ein Beitrag zum Problem der Kunstkommerzialisierung*, Zurich 1962.

REINOLD, Helmut, »Musik im Rundfunk. Ein kultursoziologisches Problem unserer Zeit,« *Kölner Zeitschrift für Soziologie und Sozialpsychologie*, 1955, 1/2, pp. 55—69; 1955, 7, pp. 233—246.

— »Rundfunk als soziales Phänomen,« *Kölner Zeitschrift für Soziologie und Sozialpsychologie*, 1957, 9, pp. 413—423.

— »Rundfunkhören als musikwissenschaftliches Problem,« *Musikforschung*, 1955, 8, pp. 212—215.

* * *, Research Department of the Czechoslovakian Radio: »Výskum hudebných záujmov poslucháčov rzhlasu júna 1966. I časť',« *Československý rozhlas,* Bratislava 1967, pp. 216.

RÖSING, Helmut, »Zur Rezeption technisch vermittelter Musik. Psychologische, ästhetische und musikalisch-funktionsbezogene Aspekte,« in *Musik in den Massenmedien Rundfunk und Fernsehen, Perspektiven und Materialen,* Hans-Christian Schmidt, ed., Schott, Mainz 1976, pp. 44—66.

— *Thesen zur Funktionsnivellierung massenmedial dargebotener Musik,* in *Symposium Musik und Massenmedien,* H. Rösing, ed., München 1978, pp. 95—104.

— »Musik und ihre Wirkungen auf den Rezipienten. Versuch einer Standortbestimmung,« *International Review of the Aesthetics and Sociology of Music,* 1981, 12/1, pp. 3—20.

ROSTAND, Claude, »Mozart et le disque. Un phénomène de sociologie musicale,« *Table ronde,* 1956, 101, pp. 91—95.

RUHNKE, M., *Rundfunk und Hausmusik — Gegensatz oder Ergänzung?,* Kassel 1958.

SCHMIDT, Hans-Christian, ed., *Musik in den Massenmedien Rundfunk und Fernsehen. Perspektiven und Materialen,* Schott, Mainz 1976, pp. 340.

SCHRAMM, W., ed., *The Process and Effects of Mass Communication,* University of Illinois Press, Urbana 1954.

SHEPHERD, John, *Media, Social Process and Music,* in *Whose Music? A Sociology of Musical Languages,* Transaction Books, New Brunswick--London 1977, pp. 7—51.

SILBERMANN, Alphons, *Musik, Rundfunk und Hörer. Die soziologischen Aspekte der Musik am Rundfunk,* Cologne-Opladen 1959.

— »Musiksoziologie im Dienste des Rundfunks,« *Das Musikleben,* 1952, 5, pp. 241—245.

— *La musique, la radio et l'auditeur. Etude sociologique,* P. U. F., Paris 1954.

— »Schallplatte und Gesellschaft,« in *Bertelsmann Briefe,* 1963, 24, pp. 1—8.

— »Schallplatte und Gesellschaft. Ketzerein eines Soziologen — Kritische Außerungen zu Fragen unserer Zeit,« Vienna-Düsseldorf 1965, pp. 165—187.

— »Schwächen und Marotten der Massenmedienforschung,« *Kölner Zeitschrift für Soziologie und Sozialpsychologie,* 1972, 24, pp. 118—131.

— »Sociological Aspects of Radio Music,« in *Transactions of the 2nd World Congress of Sociology,* Vol. 1, 1953, pp. 129—131.

— »Die soziologischen Aspekte der Musik und Rundfunk,« *Schweizerische Musikzeitung,* 1954, XCIV, pp. 133—138.

— *Vorteile und Nachteile des kommerziellen Fernsehens. Eine soziologische Studie,* Econ, Düsseldorf 1968.

BIBLIOGRAPHY

SILBERMANN, Alphons, and Ernest ZAHN, *Die Konzentration der Massmedien und ihre Wirkungen*, Econ, Düsseldorf 1970.

SITTNER, Hans, »Technische Medien im Dienst der Musik,« *Österreichische Musikzeitschrift*, 1968, XXIII/3, pp. 121—122.

SMITH, Don Crawmer, »Music Programming of Thirteen Los Angeles AM Radio Stations,« *Journal of Broadcasting*, 1964, 8/2, pp. 173—184.

SØNSTEVOLD, Gunnar, and Kurt BLAUKOPF, *Musik der 'einsamen Masse'. Ein Beitrag zur Analyse von Schlagerschallplatten*, G. Braun, Karlsruhe 1968, pp. 36.

SUPIČIĆ, Ivo, »Glazba i masovni mediji — neki osnovni problemi,« *Zvuk*, 1977, 3, pp. 10—16.

* * *, *Technik, Wirtschaft und Ästhetik der Schallplatte* (Symposion auf der »hifi '68 Düsseldorf«), G. Braun, Karlsruhe 1970, pp. 61.

TEINER, Manfred, »The Influence of the Mass Media on Children between the Age of Six and Eight,« in: I. Bontinck, ed., *New Patterns of Musical Behaviour*, Universal Edition, Vienna 1974, pp. 192—201.

TITON, Jeff Todd, *Ethnomusicology of Downhome Blues Phonograph Records, 1926—1930*, University of Minnesota. 1971. pp. 302.

WANGERMÉE, Robert, »La Radio, la musique et les moralistes de la culture,« in *Publics et techniques de la diffusion collective*, Editions de l'Institut de Sociologie, Université Libre de Bruxelles, Bruxelles 1971, pp. 435—464.

— *Rundfunkmusik gegen die Kulturmoralisten verteidigt: Versuch zur künstlerischen Kommunikation*, G. Braun, Karlsruhe c1975, pp. 40.

WERBA, Erik, »Das Musikleben und die Schallplatte,« *Wiener Figaro*, 1969, pp. 1—6.

WIDECKI, T., »Plyta gramofanowa w obrockie ksiegarskim,« *Ksiegarz*, 1967, XI/3, pp. 21—27.

WINZHEIMER, Bernhard, *Das musikalische Kunstwerk in elektrischer Fernübertragung*, Dr. B. Filser, Augsburg 1930, pp. 120.

MUSICAL STYLES. MUSICAL GENRES

BANGERT, Mark Paul, »Franz Liszt's Essay on Church Music (1834) in the Light of Felicité Lammenais's System of Religious and Political Thought,« in *Student Musicologists at Minnesota*, 5, University of Minnesota, Minneapolis 1972, pp. 182—219.

BARKER, John Wesley, »Sociological Influences upon the Emergence of Lutheran Music,« *Miscellanea Musicologica*, Adelaide Studies in Musicology, 1969, 4, pp. 157—198.

BARO, Claude, »Le jazz et la société française,« *Revue Internationale de Musique Française*, 1982, 3/8, pp. 65—86.

BERGHAHN, W., »In der Fremde — Sozialpsychologische Notizen zum deutschen Schlager,« in *Frankfurter Hefte*, 1962, 17/3, p. 193ff.

BERNARD, Yvonne, »La chanson, phénomène social,« *Revue française de socio-logie*, 1964, V/2, pp. 166—174.

BIE, O., »Oper und Gesellschaft,« *Musik*, 1911/12, 18, pp. 331—348.

BLACKIE, John Stuart, *Scottish Song: Its Wealth, Wisdom, and Social Significance*, AMS Press, New York 1976.

BONTINCK, Irmgard, »The Public of the Music Theatre. A Preliminary Bib-liography,« in *IMDT Progress Report No. 5*, Vienna 1971.

BRECHT, Bertold, »Zur Soziologie der Oper — Bemerkungen zu 'Mahagonny',« *Musik und Gesellschaft*, 1930/31, pp. 105—112.

BROOK, Barry S., »Koncertantna simfonija — njezini glazbeni i sociološki temelji,« *Zvuk*, 1974, 2, pp. 81—94.

— »The Symphonie Concertante: Its Musical and Sociological Bases« *In-ternational Review of the Aesthetics and Sociology of Music*, 1975, VI/1, pp. 9—28.

— *La Symphonie française dans la seconde moitié du XVIIIᵉ siècle*, In-stitut de Musicologie de l' Université de Paris, Paris 1962, 3 vols.

CAMUS, Raoul F., *Military Music of the American Revolution*, The University of North Carolina Press, Chapel Hill 1977, 2nd ed., pp. XII— 218.

CARAWAN, G., and C. CARAWAN, *Freedom is a Constant Struggle: Songs of the Freedom Movement*, Oak Publications, New York 1968.

CHARPENTREAU, Jacques, »La chanson contemporaine,« *Esprit*, XXVIII/287 1960, pp. 1404—1417.

COHEN, Norman, »John T. Scopes and Evolution in Hillbilly Songs,« in *John Edwards Memorial Foundation Quarterly*, 1970, VI/4, pp. 174—181.

COLES, Robert, »The Words and Music of Social Change,« *Daedalus*, 1969, 98, pp. 684—689.

CROSTEN, W. L., *French Grand Opera: An Art and a Business*, King's Crown Press, New York 1948.

CUCUEL, G., *La Pouplinière et la musique de chambre au XVIIIᵉ siècle*, Fischbacher, Paris 1913.

DADELSEN, Georg, »Die Vermischung musikalischer Gattungen als soziologi-sches Problem,« in *Bericht über der internationalen musikwissenschaft-lichen Kongreß Kassel 1962*, Bärenreiter, Kassel-Basel 1963, pp. 23—25.

DENISOFF, R. Serge, »Popular Protest Song; The Case of Eve of Destruction« *Public Opinion Quarterly*, 1971, XXXV, pp. 117—122.

— »Protest Movements: Class Consciousness and the Propaganda Song,« *Sociological Quarterly*, 1968, IX, pp. 228—247.

— »Protest Songs: Those on the Top Forty and Those on the Street,« *American Quarterly*, 1970, XXII/4, pp. 807—823.

— *Sing a Song of Social Significance*, University Popular Press, Bowling Green 1972.

DEVA, Indra, »Modern Social Forces in Indian Folk Songs,« *Diogenes*, 1956, 15, pp. 58—65.

DOWNEY, James Cecil, »Revivalism, the Gospel Songs, and Social Reform,« *Ethnomusicology*, 1965, 9/2, pp. 115—125.

ENGEL, Hans, »Das Chorwesen in soziologischer Sicht,« *Zeitschrift für Musikwissenschaft*, 1952, 113, pp. 433—439.

— »Die musikalischen Gattungen und ihr sozialer Hintergrund,« in *Kongreß-bericht Kassel 1962*, Bärenreiter, Kassel-Basel 1963, pp. 3—14.

— »Die soziale Grundlagen der Chorgeschichte,« *Neue Zeitschrift für Musik*, 1956, 117, pp. 267—271.

ETZKORN, K. Peter, »On Esthetic Standards and Reference Groups of Popular Songwriters,« *Sociological Inquiry*, 1966, 36/1, pp. 39—47.

— »The Relationship between Musical and Social Patterns in American Popular Music,« *Journal of Research in Music Education*, 1964, 12, pp. 279—286.

FARMER, Henry George, *The Rise and Development of Military Music*, W. Reeves, London 1912.

FELLERER, Karl Gustav, *Soziologie der Kirchenmusik. Materialen zur Musik- und Religionssoziologie*, Schriften zur Kunstsoziologie und Massenkommunikation, Westdeutscher Verlag, 9, Cologne/Opladen 1963.

FELLERER, Karl Gustav, »Soziologische Fragen um die religiöse und liturgische Musik,« *Kirchenmusikalisches Jahrbuch*, Cologne 1968, LII, pp. 131—144.

FINSCHER, Ludwig, *Hausmusik und Kammermusik*, Bärenreiter, Kassel 1968, pp. 67—76.

— »Zur Sozialgeschichte des klassischen Streichquartets,« in *Kongreß Berichte Kassel 1962*, Kassel 1963, pp. 37—39.

FREEDMAN, Alex S., »The Sociology of Country Music,« *Southern Humanities Review*, 1969, 3/4, pp. 358—362.

FRITH, Simon, *The Sociology of Rock*, Constable, London 1978.

FUBINI, Enrico, »Implicazioni sociologiche nella creazione e nella fruizione della musica d'avanguardia,« *International Review of the Aesthetics and Sociology of Music*, 1974, V/1, pp. 169—181.

GAER, Joseph, ed., *The Theatre of the Gold Rush Decade in San Francisco*, Library Research, California 1935.

GARDNER, Emelyn Elizabeth, and Geraldine Jencks CHICKERING, *Ballads and Songs of Southern Michigan*, University of Michigan Press, Ann Arbor 1939.

GILBERT, Douglas, *American Vaudeville, Its Life and Time*, McGraw-Hill, New York 1940.

GIULIANI, E., »Retour à l'opéra, retour à l'utopie,« *Etudes*, 1979, 351/6, pp. 631—645.

GLASS, Paul, *Songs and Stories of Afro-Americans*, Grosset & Dunlap, New York 1971, pp. 61.

HALL, James W., »Concepts of Liberty in American Broadside Ballads, 1850 —1870: A Study of the Mind of American Mass Culture,« *Journal of Popular Culture*, 1968, 2/2, pp. 252—277.

HAMM, Charles, *The Acculturation of Musical Styles: Popular Music, U. S. A..* in *Contemporary Music and Music Cultures*, Prentice-Hall, Englewood Cliffs (New Jersey) 1975, pp. 125—158.

HAYBURN, Robert F., *Papal Legislation on Sacred Music. 95 A. D. to 1977 A. D.*, The Liturgical Press, Collegeville (Minnesota) 1979, pp. XIV-619.

HEILFURTH, Gernard, *Das Bergmannslied — Wesen, Leben, Funktion. Ein Beitrag zur Erhellung von Bestand und Wandlung der sozialkulturellen Elemente im Aufbau der industriellen Gesellschaft*, Kassel 1954.

HEMPEL, G., »Das Ende der Leipziger Ratmusik im 19. Jahrhundert,« *Archiv für Musikwissenschaft*, 1958, XV/3, pp. 187—197.

HENNENBERG, Fritz, *Paul Dessaus politische Chorkantaten 1944—1968*, Hauptkommission Musikwissenschaft des Verbandes deutscher Komponisten und Musikwissenschaftler, Berlin 1970, pp. 91—129.

HENNING, N., »Patronage and Style: Some Reflections on Their Relationship,« in Milton C. ALBRECHT, H. JAMES and Mason GRIFF, eds., *The Sociology of Art and Literature*, Praeger Publishing Co., New York 1970.

HIRSCH, Paul, »Sociological Approach to the Pop Music Phenomenon,« *American Behavior Scientist*, 1971, 14, pp. 371—388.

ISTEL, Edgar, *Die Entstehung des deutschen Melodramas*, Schuster & Löffler, Berlin 1906.

— *Revolution und Oper*, G. Bosse, Regensburg 1919.

JACKSON, George Pullen, *White Spirituals in the Southern Uplands*, University of North Carolina Press, Chapel Hill (N. C.) 1933.

JAGER, Hugo de, De componist in sociologisch perspectief, *Mens en Maatschappij*, 1964, 39/2, pp. 107—116.

— »Muzieksociologische kanttekeningen rond het auteursrecht van de componist,« *Mens en Maatschappij*, 1960, pp. 256—265.

KARBUSICKÝ, Vladimir, »Electronic Music and the Listener,« *The World of Music*, 1969, XI/1, pp. 32—44.

— »Tradični hornické pisne na Kladensku,« *Československi Etnograf*, 1959, VII/1, pp. 14—28.

— »Zur Entwicklung des tschechischen und slowakischen Bergmannsliedes,« in *Deutsches Jahrbuch für Volkskunde*, 1959, V/2, pp. 361—377.

— *Ideologie im Lied. Lied in der Ideologie; Kulturanthropologische Strukturanalysen*, Hans Gerig Verlag, Cologne 1973, pp. 207.

KELDANY-MOHR, Irmgard, *Unterhaltungsmusik als soziokulturelles Phäno-men des 19. Jahrhunderts*, Gustav Bosse Verlag, Regensburg 1977, pp. 143.

KNEPLER, Georg, »Epochenstil?,« *Beiträge zur Musikwissenschaft*, 1969, XI/3—4, pp. 213—233.

— »Musical Style Changes and General History,« in *IMS Report of the Tenth Congress*, Bärenreiter/University of Ljubljana, Kassel-Ljubljana 1970, pp. 251—270.

HEMPEL, G., »Das Ende der Leipziger Ratmusik im 19. Jahrhundert,« *Archiv für Musikwissenschaft*, 1958, XV/3, pp. 187—197.

KOS, Koraljka, »Style and Sociological Background of Croatian Renais-sance Music,« *International Review of the Aesthetics and Sociology of Music*, 1982, 13/1, pp. 55—82.

LACOMBE, A., and Ch. ROCHE, *La musique du film*, Van de Velde, Pa-ris 1979, pp. 516.

LA LAURENCIE, Lionel de, »Les débuts de la musique de chambre en France,« *Revue de musicologie*, 1934, pp. 25—34, 49—52, 86—96, 159—167, 204—231.

LAHR, John, »The American Musical; The Slavery of Escape,« *Evergreen ·R*, September 1968, XII/58, pp. 23—25, 73—76.

LAMMEL, Inge, *Das Arbeiterlied*, Reclam, Leipzig 1970, pp. 266.

— »Einige Gedanken zu theoretischen und praktischen Aspekten des Ar-beiterliedes,« *Musik in der Schule*, 1972, XXIII/11, pp. 425—429.

LE BRAS, G., »Sur la sociologie de la musique sacrée,« *Archives de sociolo-gie des religions*, 1963, VIII/16.

LEE, E., *Music of the People: A Study of Popular Music in Great Britain*, Barrie and Jenkins, London 1970.

LOBACZEWSKA, Stefania, *Zarys historii form muzycznych. Próba ujęcia socjologicznego*, Cracow 1950.

LOMAX, Alan, »Folk Song Style,« *American Anthropologist*, 1959, 61/6, pp. 927—954.

LONGYEAR, R. M., »The Ecology of 19th-Century Opera«, in *Bericht über den Internationalen Musikwissenschaftlichen Kongreß Bonn 1970, 1971*, pp. 497-499.

MAHLING, Christoph-Helmut, »Selbstdarstellung und Kritik der Gegenschaft in der Opern. Bemerkungen zu Opern von Mozart bis Dessau,« in *Bericht über den Internationalen Musikwissenschaftlichen Kongreß Bonn 1970, 1971*, pp. 232-236.

— »Zur Soziologie des Chorwesens,« *Saarbrücker Studien zur Musikwissen-schaft*, Kassel

MARK, Desmond, »Pop and Folk as a Going Concern for Sociological Re-search,« *International Review of the Aesthetics and Sociology of Mu-sic*, 1983, 14/1, pp. 93—98.

MARTORELLA, Rosanne, »The Relationship Between Box Office and Reper-toire: A Case Study of Opera,« *Sociological Quarterly*, 1977, 18, pp. 354-366.

451

MAURER, Friedrich, »Zu den frühen politischen Liedern Walthers,« in *Früh-mittelalterliche Studien*, 1969, III, pp. 362—366.

MENDOZA DE ARCE, Daniel, »On Some of the Sociocultural Factors Affecting the General Characteristics of the Western Musical Styles During the Low Middle Ages,« *International Review of the Aesthetics and Sociology of Music*, 1981, 12/1, pp. 51—63.

MIDDLETON, Richard, and David HORN, eds., *Folk or Popular? Distinctions, Influences, Continuities* (Popular Music 1), Cambridge University Press, Cambridge 1981, pp. VII-222.

MUSEL, Albrecht, »Das politische Massenlied in der DDR. Funktion, Pflege, Verbreitung und Wirkung,« in *Deutsche Studium*, 1968, VI/23, pp. 264——278.

MUELLER, John Henry, »Baroque — Is it Datum, Hypothesis or Tautology?,« *The Journal of Aesthetics and Art Criticism*, 1954, 12/4, pp. 421—437.

NOISETTE DE CRAUZAT, Cl., *L'orgue dans la Société française*, Champion, Paris 1979, pp. 135.

NOSKE, Frits, »'Art Music' and 'Trivial Music': Anatomy of a False Argument,« *International Review of the Aesthetics and Sociology. of Music*, 1973, IV/2, pp. 287—293.

NOWAK, Leopold, »Das deutsche Gesellschaftslied in Österreich von 1480 bis 1550,« in *Studien zur Musikwissenschaft*, Gesellschaft zur Herausgabe von Denkmälern der Tonkunst in Österreich, Vol. 17, Vienna 1930.

PETERSON, R. A., and P. DIMAGGIO, »From Region to Class: The Changing Focus of Country Music,« *Social Forces*, 1975, 53, pp. 497—506.

PIERSIG, Johannes, *Beiträge zu einer Rechtssoziologie der Kirchenmusik*, Bosse, Regensburg 1972, pp. 198.

POUGIN, Arthur, *L'Opéra-Comique pendant la Révolution de 1788 à 1801*, Minkoff Reprint, Geneva 1973, pp. 337.

REANEY, G., »The Isorhythmic Motet, and its Social Background,« in *Kongreßbericht Kassel 1962*, Bärenreiter, Kassel- Basel 1963.

REINECKE, Hans-Peter, »Sozialpsychologische Hintergründe der Neuen Musik,« in *Das musikalisch Neue und die Neue Musik*, Schott, Mainz 1969, pp. 73—92.

RIJAVEC, Andrej, »Notes towards the National and International in Music,« *International Review of the Aesthetics and Sociology of Music*, 1976, Vol. VII, No. 1, pp. 83—87.

RINGER, Alexander L., »The Political Uses of Opera in Revolutionary France,« in *Bericht über den Internationalen Musikwissenschaftlichen' Kongreß Bonn 1970*, Bärenreiter, Kassel-Basle 1971, pp. 237-242.

RUFF, Lillian M., and Arnold D. WILSON, »The Madrigal, the Lute Song, and Elizabethan Politics,« *Past and Present*, 1969, 44, pp. 3—51.

SACHS, Kurt, *The Commonwealth of Art Style in the Fine Arts, Music and Dance*, New York, n. d.; D. Dobson, London 1955.

SALMEN, Walter, *Haus- und Kammermusik. Privates Musizieren im gesellschaftlichen Wandel zwischen 1600 und 1900,* VEB Deutscher Verlag für Musik, Leipzig 1969, pp. 203.

SCHWAB, Heinrich W., »Unterhaltendes des Musizieren im Industriegebiet des 19. Jahrhunderts,« in *Studien zur Trivialmusik des 19. Jahrhunderts,* Bosse, Regensburg 1967, pp. 151—158.

SOCHOR, Arnold N., »Die Theorie der musikalischen Genres: Aufgaben und Perspektiven,« in *Beiträge zur Musikwissenschaft,* 1970, XII/2, pp. 109—120.

SOLOMON, M., *Beethoven: la dimensione utopica della sonata,* in A. Seravessa, ed., *La sociologia della musica.* EDT, Torino 1980, pp. 237—255.

STAHMER, Klaus, *Musikalische Formung in soziologischen Bezug, dargestellt an der instrumentalen Kammermusik von Johannes Brahms,* Ph. D. Thesis, Christian-Albrechts-Universitv. Kiel 1968, pp. 222.

STEINBECK, Dietrich, »Soziologische Aspekte der Operninszenierung,« in *Bericht über den Internationalen Musikwissenschaftlichen Kongreß Bonn 1970, 1971,* pp. 242-247.

STROH, Wolfgang Martin, *Zur Soziologie der elektronischen Musik,* Amadeus Verlag. Zurich 1975, pp. 200.

VELTEN, Rudolf, *Das ältere deutsche Gesellschaftslied unter dem Einfluß italienischer Musik,* C. Winter, Heidelberg 1914.

VERNILLAT, Fr., »Chanson et société: l'orientation de l'opinion par la chanson,« *Les Amis de Sèvres,* 1980, 99/3, pp. 7—15.

WANGERMÉE, Robert, »Introduction à une sociologie de l'opéra,« *Revue belge de musicologie,* 1966, XX/1—4, pp. 153—166.

WAWRZYKOWSKA-WIERCIOCHOWA, Dionizja, *Polska piesn rewolucyjna,* Wydawnictwo Związkowe, Warsaw 1970, pp. 438.

WECKERLIN, Jean Baptiste Théodore, *L'ancienne chanson populaire en France XVIᵉ—XVIIIᵉ siècles,* Garnier, Paris 1877.

WENDEL, Hermann, *Die Marseillaise: Biographie einer Hymne,* Europa-Verlag, Zurich 1936.

WESTERMEYER, Karl, *Die Operette im Wandel der Zeitgeistes: von Offenbach bis zur Gegenwart,* Drei Masken Verlag, A. G., Munich 1931.

WIORA, Walter, »Die musikalischen Gattungen und ihr sozialer Hintergrund,« in *Kongreßbericht Kassel 1962,* Bärenreiter. Kassel-Basel 1963, pp. 15—23.

WORBS, H. C., *Soziologische Studien an der Instrumentalmusik Haydns,* Berlin 1952.

MUSIC AND POLITICS

ADORNO, Theodor Wiesengrund, *Die gegängelte Musik. Bemerkungen über die Musikpolitik der Ostblockstaaten,* Frankfurt/M. 1954.

ALLEN, Warren Dwight, *Our Marching Civilisation: An Introduction to the Study of Music and Society,* Stanford 1943.

ALTAR, C. M., »Wolfgang Amadeus Mozart im Lichte osmanisch-österreichischer Beziehungen,« *Revue belge de musicologie*, 1956, X/3-4.

AMES, R., »Protest and Irony in Negro Folksong,« *Science ana Society*, 1950, XIV/3, pp. 193—213.

ATTALI, Jacques, *Bruits. Essai sur l'économie politique de la musique*, P.U.F., Paris 1977, pp. 304.

AUBRY, G. J., *La musique et les nations*, Paris 1922.

BANGERT, Mark Paul, »Franz Liszt's Essay on Church Music (1834) in the Light of Felicité Lamennais's System of Religious and Political Thought,« in *Student musicologists at Minnesota*, 5, University of Minnesota, Minneapolis 1972, pp. 182—219.

BEAUFILS, Marcel, *Par la musique vers l'obscur. Essai sur la musique bourgeoise et l'éveil d'une conscience allemande au XVIIIᵉ siècle et aux origines du XIXᵉ siècle*, F. Robert, Marseille 1942.

BLEGEN, Theodore Christian, and Martin B. RUUD, *Norwegian Emigrant Songs and Ballads*, University of Minnesota Press, Minneapolis 1936.

BOEHMER, Konrad, »Anmerkungen zu einem politischen Musiktheater,« *Oper*, 1969, pp. 63—67.

— »Karlheinz Stockhausen oder: Der Imperialismus als höchstes Stadium des kapitalistischen Avantgardismus,« *Musik und Gesellschaft*, 1972, XXII/3, pp. 137—150.

BONDY, Curt, *Die proletarische Jugendbewegung in Deutschland*, Adolf Saal, Lauenburg 1922.

BORRIS, Siegfried, »Luigi Nono — Zur Problematik engagierter Musik,« *Musik und Bildung*, 1972, IV/6, pp. 289—291.

BRINKMANN, Reinhold, »Ästhetische und politische Kriterien der Kompositionskritik,« *26. internationale Ferienkurse für Neue Musik*, Schott, Mainz 1973, pp. 28—41.

BRIX, Lothar, »Anmerkungen zu einer sich politisch verstehenden Musikerziehung,« *Musik und Bildung*, 1972, IV/6, pp. 292—297.

BROCKHAUS, Heinz Alfred, »Die Bedeutung der Oktoberrevolution für das Schaffen Hanns Eislers,« *Musik und Gesellschaft*, 1968, XVIII/3, pp. 168—172.

CAMUS, Raoul F., *Military Music of the American Revolution*, University of North Carolina Press, Chapel Hill (N. C.) 1976, pp. 218.

CARAWAN, G., and C. CARAWAN, *Freedom is a Constant Struggle: Songs of the Freedom Movement*, Oak Publications, New York 1968.

CARLES, Philippe, and Jean-Louis COMOLLI, *Free Jazz, Black Power*, Champ libre, Paris 1971, pp. 328.

CERVONI, G., »Politique et chanson,« *Humanisme*, 1980, 136, pp. 109—133.

BIBLIOGRAPHY

CLAUSEN, Karl, »Es können passieren... Es sind vorzuenthalten... Zensur deutscher und dänischer Lieder in Tondern 1830—1847. Ein Beitrag zur- deutschdänischen Nachbarschaft im Liede,« *Jahrbuch für Volkslied- forschung,* 1970, XV, pp. 14—56.

COLES, Robert, »The Words and Music of Social Change,« *Daedalus,* 1969, 98, pp. 684—689.

CUTTER, Charles, »The Politics of Music in Mali,« *African Arts,* 1968, 1/3, pp. 38—39, 74—77.

DENISOFF, R. Serge, »Protest Songs: Those on the Top Forty and Those on the Street,« *American Quarterly,* 1970, XXII/4, pp. 807—823.

DENISOFF, R. Serge, *Folk Consciousness. The People's Music and American Communism,* University of Illinois Press, Urbana 1971.

— »Folk Music and the American Left: A Generational-Ideological Compar- ison,« *British Journal of Sociology,* 1969, XX, pp. 427—442.

— »Protest Movements: Class Consciousness and the Propaganda Song,« *Sociological Quarterly,* 1968, IX, pp. 228—247.

DENISOFF, R. Serge, and R. A. PETERSON, *The Sounds of Social Change,* Rand McNally, Chicago 1972.

DONAKOWSKI, Conrad L., *A Muse for the Masses. Ritual and Music in an Age of Democratic Revolution, 1770—1870,* The University of Chicago Press, Chicago and London c1972, 1977, pp. 435.

DUNNING, Albert, *Die Staatsmotette (1480—1555),* A. Oosthoek's Uitge- versmaatschappij N. V., Utrecht 1970.

EBERT-OBERMEIER, Traude, *Das Verhältniß der deutschen Arbeitklasse zur Instrumentalmusik, dargestellt bis zum Jahre 1933,* Humboldt Univer- sity, Berlin 1972, pp. 302.

ELDER, J. D., »Color, Music and Conflict. A Study of Aggression in Trinidad with Reference to the Role of Traditional Music,« *Ethnomusicology,* 1964, 8/2, pp. 128—136.

ENGELMANN, Günther, »Orchester — Mechanismen geistiger Unterdrück- ung?,« *Orchestra,* 1970, XVIII/2, pp. 53—55.

FOWKE, Edith, »Labor and Industrial Protest Songs in Canada,« *Journal of American Folklore,* 1969, 82/323, pp. 34—50.

HENNENBERG, Fritz, *Paul Dessaus politische Chorkantaten 1944—1968,* Hauptkommission Musikwissenschaft des Verbandes Deutscher Kom- ponisten und Musikwissenschaftler, Berlin 1970, pp. 91—129.

HENZE, Hans Werner, *Musik und Politik: Schriften und Gespräche 1955—1975,* Deutscher Taschenbuch Verlag, Munich 1976, pp. 273.

HOLST, Gail, *Theodorakis: Myth and Politics in Modern Greek Music,* Adolf M. Hakkert, Amsterdam 1980, pp. XV-262.

HONIGSHEIM, Paul, »Die Ähnlichkeit von Musik und Drama in primitiven und totalitären Gesellschaften,« *Kölner Zeitschrift für Soziologie und Sozialpsychologie,* 1964, XVI/3, pp. 481—490.

ISTEL, Edgar, *Revolution und Oper*, G. Bosse, Regensburg 1919.

JOHNSON. H. Earle, »Musical Interests of Certain American Literary and Political Figures,« *Journal of Research in Music Education*, 1971, XIX/3, pp. 22.

JUNGHEINRICH, Hans-Klaus, Luca LOMBARDI, eds., *Musik im Übergang. Von der bürgerlichen zur sozialistischen Musikkultur.* Damnitz Verlag, Munich 1977, pp. 182.

KAPLAN, Arthur Abraham, *Popular Music as a Reflection of the Depression Era*, M. A. Thesis (Music), University of Southern California 1949.

KNEIF, Tibor, *Politische Musik?*, Doblingcr, Vienna 1977, pp. 60

KÜHN, Dieter, »Musik und Revolution,« *Melos*, 1970, XXXVII/10, pp. 394—401.

LAWRENCE, Vera Brodsky, *Music for Patriots, Politicians and Presidents: Harmonies and Discords of the First Hundred Years*, Macmillan, New York 1975, pp. 480.

LEHMANN-HAUPT, H., *Art under Dictatorship*, Oxford University Press, New York 1954.

LIEBERMANN, Rolf, »Oper in der Demokratie,« *Melos*, 1964, pp. 98—103.

LOMBARDI, Luca, »Réflexions sur le thème 'Musique et politique'«, *Schweizerische Musikzeitung*, 1978, 118/1, pp. 15—20.

MALLEY, François, »En Amerique Latine: les trouvères rebelles chantent la révolte,« in *Croissance des jeunes nations*, 1972, 140, pp. 28—29.

MALMROS, Anna-Lise, »Organisational Set-up and Politico-cultural Aspects of Beat in Copenhagen,« *New Patterns of Musical Behaviour*, Universal Edition, Vienna 1974, pp. 114—119.

* * *, »Musique et politique,« *Musique en jeu*, Seuil, 1971, 3, pp. 85—117.

MAROTHY, Janos, *Zene és polgar — zene és proletar*, Akademiai Kiado, Budapest 1966.

MARTORELLA, Rosanne, »The Relationship Between Box Office and Repertoire: A Case Study of Opera,« *Sociological Quarterly*, 1977, 18, pp. 354-366.

MASS, Edgar, »Montesquieu und Jean-Jacques Rousseau. Die politische Funktion der Musik,« *Zeitung für französische Sprache und Literatur*, 1969, LXXIX, pp. 289—303.

MATZKE, H., *Musikökonomik und Musikpolitik — Grundzüge einer Musikwirtschaftslehre — Ein Versuch*, Quader, Breslau 1927.

MAURER, Friedrich, »Zu den frühen politischen Liedern Walthers,« in *Frühmittelalterliche Studien*, 1969, III, pp. 362—366.

MEYER, Eve R., »Joseph II: The Effect of His Enlightened Apsolutism on Austrian Music,« in *Enlightenment Essays*, 1971, II/3—4, pp. 149—157.

MÜLLER, Georg Herman, *Richard Wagner in der Mai-Revolution 1849*, O. Laube, Dresden 1919.

NOLI, Bishop Fan Stylian, *Beethoven and the French Revolution*, International Universities Press, New York 1947.

NOTOWICZ, N., »Über die Entwicklung unseres musikalischen Schaffens zu einer sozialistischen Kunst,« *Musik und Gesellschaft*, 1960, 10, pp. 259——271.

POPOVICI, Doru, »Prezenta tematicii istorice şi patriotice,« *Studii de muzicologie*, 1971, 7, pp. 91—111.

PREUSSNER, Eberhard, »Musikpolitik. Ihr Aufgabenkreis und ihre Grundzüge,« *Musik und Gesellschaft*, 1930—1931, pp. 21—22.

RHODES, Willard, »Music as an Agent of Political Expression,« *African Studies Bulletin*, 1962, 5, pp. 14—22.

RIESENFELD, P., *Politik und Musik, von großen Zeitaltern zu kleinen Gleichschaltern*, Lidor Printing Press, Tel Aviv 1958.

RINGER, Alexander L., »The Political Uses of Opera in Revolutionary France,« in *Bericht über den Internationalen Musikwissenschaftlichen Kongreß Bonn 1970*, Bärenreiter, Kassel-Basle 1971. pp. 237-242.

RUFF, Lillian M., and Arnold D. WILSON, »The Madrigal, the Lute Song, and Elizabethan Politics,« *Past and Present*, 1969, 44, pp. 3—51.

SCHAEFER, Hansjürgen, »Musik in der entwickelten sozialistischen Gesellschaft,« *Musik und Gesellschaft*, 1967, XVII/6, pp. 361—365.

— *Musik in der sozialistischen Gesellschaft*, Tribüne, Berlin 1967, pp. 92.

SCHWAEN, K., »Der gefesselte Orpheus,« *Musik und Gesellschaft*, 1959, 9, pp. 338—340.

SHANK, Theodore, »Political Theater: The San Francisco Mime Troop,« *The Review*, 1974, 18, pp. 110-117.

SHAPIRO, Theda, *Painters and Politics: The European Avant-Garde and Society, 1900-25*, Elsevier, New York 1976.

* * *, *Singing Soldiers: A History of the Civil War in Song*, Paul Glass and Louis C. Singer, eds., Da Capo, New York, Paperback ed., 1975, pp. 300.

STAFFORD, Peter, »Rock as Politics,« *Crawdaddy*, New York 1968, 19, pp. 31—33.

TUKSAR, Stanislav, »Glazba i politika u renesansnom Dubrovniku,« in *Zbornik radova o Pavlu Markovcu*, JAZU, Zagreb 1979, pp. 99-109.
— »Musique et politique à Dubrovnik à l'époque de la Renaissance,« *International Review of the Aesthetics and Sociology of Music*, 1979, X/1, pp. 99-111.

STEPHAN, Rudolf, *Über die Musik und Politik*, Schott, Mainz 1971, pp. 99.

STÜRZBECHER, Ursula, »Das große Fragezeichen hinter einer gesellschaftspolitischen Funktion der Musik,« *Melos*, 1972, XXXIX/3, pp. 142—149.

VANCEA, Zeno, »Libertatea de creatie si responsabilitatea sociala a compozitor rului,« *Studii de muzicologie*, 1972, 8, pp. 41—48.

VUČKOVIĆ, Vojislav, »Hudba jako propagační prostředek,« *Klič*, 1932—1933, 3.

WANG, B., »Folk Songs as Regulators of Politics,« *Sociology and Social Research*, 1935, 20/2, pp. 161—166.

MUSIC AND IDEOLOGIES

BEAUFILS, Marcel, *Par la musique vers l'obscur. Essai sur la musique bourgeoise et l'éveil d'une conscience allemande au XVIIIe siècle et aux origines du XIXe siècle*, F. Robert, Marseille 1942.

BECK, Hermann, »Das Konzil von Trient und die Probleme der Kirchenmusik,« *Kirchenmusikalische Jahrbuch*, 1964, 48.

BENSMAN, Joseph, *Dollars and Sense (Ideology, Ethics and the Meaning of Work in Profit and Non-Profit Organizations)*, Macmillan and Co., New York 1967.

BETZ, Albrecht, *Hanns Eisler. Musik einer Zeit, die sich eben bildet*, Munich 1976, pp. 252.

BLAUKOPF, Kurt, *Arnold Schönberg und die Endkrise der bürgerlichen Musik*, Wien 1935 (Pseudonym: Hans E. Wind).

BOEHMER, Konrad, »Karlheinz Stockhausen oder: Der Imperialismus als höchstes Stadium des kapitalistischen Avantgardismus,« *Musik und Gesellschaft*, 1972, XXII/3, pp. 137—150.

— »Zwischen Reihe und Pop. Musik und Klassengesellschaft,« *Jugend und Volk*, Wien 1970.

BORRIS, Siegfried, »Luigi Nono — Zur Problematik engagierter Musik,« *Musik und Bildung*, 1972, IV/6, pp. 289—291.

BROCKHAUS, Heinz Alfred, »Die Bedeutung der Oktoberrevolution für das Schaffen Hanns Eislers,« *Musik und Gesellschaft*, 1968, XVIII/3, pp. 168—172.

— *Probleme der Realismustheorie*, Hauptkommission Musikwissenschaft des Verbandes Deutscher Komponisten und Musikwissenschaftler, Berlin 1970.

CARAWAN, G., and C. CARAWAN, *Freedom is a Constant Struggle: Songs of the Freedom Movement*, Oak Publications, New York 1968.

CARLES, Philippe, and Jean-Louis COMOLLI, *Free Jazz, Black Power*, Champ libre, Paris 1971, pp. 328.

COLES, Robert, »The Words and Music of Social Change,« *Daedalus*, 1969, 98, pp. 684—689.

COLLET, Henri, *Le mysticisme musical espagnol au XVIe siècle*, F. Alcan, Paris 1913.

DORŮŽKA, Lubomír, »Protest durch U-Musik,« *The World of Music*, 1970, XII/2, pp. 19—31.

ELDER, J. D., »Color, Music and Conflict. A Study of Aggression in Trinidad with Reference to the Role of Traditional Music,« *Ethnomusicology*, 1964, 8/2, pp. 128—136.

FOWKE, Edith, »Labor and Industrial Protest Songs in Canada,« *Journal of American Folklore*, 1969, 82/323, pp. 34—50.

FRISIUS, Rudolf, and Ulrich GÜNTHER, »Politische und soziologische Bezüge im Musikunterricht, dargestellt an einem Ausschnitt aus den *Hymnen* von Karlheinz Stockhausen,« in *Musikunterricht an Gesamtschulen*, Klett, Stuttgart 1971, pp. 42—65, 143—180.

GARON, Paul, »Blues and the Church: Revolt and Resignation,« *Living Blues*, Chicago 1970, 1/1, pp. 18—23.

GEIGER, Th., »Kritische Bemerkungen zum Begriff der Ideologie,« in *Gegenwartsprobleme der Soziologie*, Athenaion, Potsdam 1949.

GEISSMAR, Berta, *Musik im Schatten der Politik*, Freiburg 1951.

GEORGESCU, Lucilia, »L'Internationale dans le plus ancien enregistrement sur disque roumain,« *Muzica*, 1971, XXI/4.

GERLACH, Caroline, »Zum Problem des sozialistichen Realismus im Schlager,« in *Hauptkommission Musikwissenschaft des Verbandes Deutscher Komponisten und Musikwissenschaftler*, Berlin 1970, pp. 113—119.

HAAKE, Claus, *Der Beitrag des Chorsingens zur ästhetischen Erziehung und Bildung der Arbeiterklasse in der Deutschen Demokratischen Republik*, Universität Halle, 1971, pp. 320.

HAGELWEIDE, Gert, *Das publizistische Erscheinungsbild des Menschen im kommunistischen Lied. Eine Untersuchung der Liedpublizistik der KPD (1919—1933) und der SED (1945—1960)*, Westfälische Wilhelms-Universität, Münster 1968.

HEMPEL, G., »Die bürgerliche Musikkultur Leipzigs im Vormärz«, *Beiträge zur Musikwissenschaft*. 1964, 6, pp. 3—14.

HRUŠOVSKY, I., »Ideologie a hudba,« in *Otazky marxistickej filozofie*, Bratislava 1962, 6.

IMAI, Michio, »Shina-tetsugaku ni okeru kayôto ongaku (Folk music, folk songs, and music in general, as conceived in Chinese philosophy),« *Nippon Tôyô Ongaku Ronkô*, Ongaku-no-tomosha, Tokyo 1969, pp. 497—516.

* * *, »Jazz and Revolutionary Black Nationalism — A Panel Discussion,« *Jazz*, New York April 1966, 5/4; July 1967, 6/7.

KADEN, Werner, »Der Einfluß der KPD auf die musikalische Entwicklung in Deutschland vor 1933,« *Musik in der Schule*, 1968, XIX, pp. 400—408.

— *Die Entwicklung der Arbeitersängerbewegung im Gau Chemnitz des Deutschen Arbeitergebundes von den Anfängen bis 1933*, Pädagogisches Institut, Zwickau 1966, pp. 389.

KNEIF, Tibor »Der Bürger als Revolutionär,« *Melos*, 1969, XXXVI/9, pp. 372—374.

KOFSKY, Frank, *Black Nationalism and the Revolution in Music*, Pathfinder Press, New York 1970, pp. 280.

KOPECZEK-MICHALSKA, Krystyna, »Jawne i tajne zycie koncertowe w Warszawie w latach okupacji hitlerowskiej,« *Muzyka*, 1970, XV/3, pp. 47—64.

KORALL, Burt, »The Music of Protest,« *Saturday Review*, November 16, 1968, 51/46, 126, pp. 36—39.

* * *, *Krizis buržuaznoj kuljturi i muzyka*, Sbornik statej, Muzyka, Moscow 1972, pp. 288.

LADNER, Robert Jr., »Folk Music, Pholk Music and the Angry Children of Malcolm X,« *Southern Folklore Quarterly*, 1970, 34/2, pp. 131—145.

459

LEJTES, Ruf', »The Song of Revolutionary Struggle,« *Sovetskaja muzyka,* 1972, 8, pp. 122—130.

LESSER, Wolfgang, »Die soziale Funktion userer Kunst bei der Entwicklung einer sozialistischen Volkskultur,« in *Musik und Gesellschaft,* Berlin (G.D.R.) 1968, XVIII, pp. 743—814.

LETELIER, Alfonso, »La música y el cristianismo,« *Rivista musical chilena,* Santiago de Chile 1961, XV/77, pp. 15—23.

LOVEJOY, Arthur O., *On the Discrimination of Romanticism,* in *Essays in the History of Ideas,* The John Hopkins Press, Baltimore 1948.

MUZET, Denis, »Socio-Idéologie de l' »Etat Musical«: le cas d'une »propagande musicale,« *Communications,* 1975. 3, pp. 393-403

NOLI, Bishop Fan Stylian, *Beethoven and the French Revolution,* International Universities Press, New York 1947.

NOWAK, Adolf, »Wagners Parsifal und die Idee der Kunstreligion,« in *Richard Wagner — Werk und Wirkung,* Bosse, Regensburg 1971, pp. 161—174.

NURSE, George T., »Popular Songs and National Identity in Malawi,« *African Music,* 1964, 3/3, pp. 101—106.

OANA-POP, Rodica, »Semnificatii socialpatriotice în creaţia de operă si balet,« *Studii de muzicologie,* 1971, 7, pp. 221—236.

ORDZONIKIDZE, Givi, »Zur Dialektik der Idee des Kampfes in Beethovens Musik«, *Beethoven-Kongreß 1970,* Berlin 1971, pp. 365—371.

MARCKHL, Erich, *Engagement, Protest, Provokation und das Konservative,* Vortrag gehalten am 13. 1. 1971, Hochschule für Musik und darstellende Kunst, Graz 1971, pp. 26.

MAROTHY, Janos, *Zene és polgar — zene és proletar,* Akademiai Kiado, Budapest 1966.

MARX, Karl, and Friedrich ENGELS, *Über Kunst und Literatur — Eine Sammlung aus ihrer Schriften,* Berlin 1953.

— *Sur la littérature et l'art,* Paris 1954.

MAYER, Günter, *Die Kategorie des musikalischen Materials in den ästhetischen Anschauungen Hanns Eislers. Zur Entwicklung der Theorie und Geschichte des sozialistischen Realismus im Bereich der marxistischen Musikästhetik,* Humboldt Universität, Berlin 1970, pp. 343.

MEYER, Eve R., »Joseph II: The Effect of his Enlightened Apsolutism on Austrian Music,« in *Enlightenment Essays,* 1971, II/3—4, pp. 149—157.

MEYER, Leonard B., *Music, the Arts, and Ideas,* University of Chicago Press, Chicago 1967.

MICHEL, Paul, »Der Systemcharakter der sozialistischen Musikerziehung,« *Beiträge zur Musikwissenschaft,* 1969, XI/3—4, pp. 259—267.

MICHELS, Robert, »Die Soziologie des Nationalliedes,« in *Der Patriotismus,* Munich-Leipzig 1929.

MÜLLER, Georg Herman, *Richard Wagner in der Mai-Revolution 1849,* O. Laube, Dresden 1919.

PAUL, Charles B., »Rameau, d'Indy, and French Nationalism,« *Musical Quarterly*, 1972, LVIII/1, pp. 46—56.

PEACOCK, James L., *Rites of Modernization, Symbolic and Social Aspects of Indonesian Proletarian Drama*, University of Chicago Press, Chicago 1968.

PLAVŠA, Dušan, »Društveno-istorijska uslovljenost muzike,« *Zvuk*, 1977, 3, pp. 31-39.

POPOV, Innokentij, *Some Features of Socialist Realism in Soviet Music* (in Russian), Muzyka, Moscow 1971, pp. 199.

PRACHT, Erwin, *Zu einigen philosophisch-weltanschaulichen Grundfragen der Theorie des sozialistischen Realismus*, Hauptkommission Musikwissenschaft des Verbandes Deutscher Komponisten und Musikwissenschaftler, Berlin 1970, pp. 57—75.

PRIEBERG, Fred K., »Skriabin und die Sowjetmusik. Ein Überblick über die Wandlung der offiziellen Sowjetmeinung hinsichtlich Skriabin und dessen Musik,« *Hi-Fi Stereophonie*, 1972, XI/1, pp. 14—16.

RACKWITZ, Werner, »Beitrag der Musik und des Theaters zu sozialistischen Persönlichkeitsentwicklung,« *Musik in der Schule*, 1972, XXIII/1, pp. 1—8.

REINECKE, Hans-Peter, »Sozialpsychologische Hintergründe der Neuen Musik,« *Das musikalisch Neue und die Neue Musik*, Schott, Mainz 1969, pp. 73—92.

RIESENFELD, P., *Politik und Musik, von großen Zeitaltern zu kleinen Gleichschaltern*, Lidor Printing Press, Tel Aviv 1958.

RODNITZKY, Jerome L., »The Evolution of the American Protest Song«, *Journal of Popular Culture*, 1969, 3/1, pp. 35—45.

ROZENSILD, Konstantin, »Lenin und die ästhetischen Probleme heutigen Musik«, *Kunst und Literatur*, 1971, XIX/3, pp. 314—331, 423—440.

RICHTER, Raoul Hermann Michael, *Kunst und Philosophie bei Richard Wagner*, Quelle & Meyer, Leipzig 1906.

RUBIN, Ruth, »A Comparative Approach to a Yiddish Song of Protest,« *Studies in Ethnomusicology*, 1965, 2, pp. 54—74.

SCHIEDERMAIR, Ludwig Ferdinand, *Die Gestaltung weltanschaulicher Ideen in der Vokalmusik Beethovens*, Veröffentlichungen der Beethovenhauses in Bonn, No. 10, Quelle & Meyer, Leipzig 1934, pp. 56.

SCHMIDT, Franz, *Das Musikleben der bürgerlichen Gesellschaft Leipzigs im Vormärz, 1815—1848*, Langensalza 1912.

SCHUHMACHER, Gerhard, »Free Jazz und Engagement,« *Schallplatte und Kirche*, 1970, 1, pp. 60—66.

SIEGMUND-SCHULTZE, Walther, *Zu Fragen des sozialistischen Realismus in der Instrumentalmusik*, Hauptkommission Musikwissenschaft des Verbandes Deutscher Komponisten und Musikwissenschaftler, Berlin 1970, pp. 90—98.

— »Die Rolle der Tradition in der Musik des sozialistischen Realismus,« *Musik in der Schule*, 1959, 10, pp. 4—10.

SOCHOR, Arnold Naumovič, »Die Leninsche Widerspiegelungstheorie und die Musik,« *Kunst und Literatur*, 1970, XVIII/3, pp. 258—269.

SORIANO, M., »Les problèmes de la musique et le marxisme,« *La pensée*, Nouvelle série, 1954, 56, pp. 77—88.

STANISLAV, Jozef, »Ideologie a hudba,« *Rytmus*, 1936—1937.

STONE, J. H., »Mid-Nineteenth-Century American Beliefs in the Social Values of Music,« *The Musical Quarterly*, 1957, XLIII, pp. 38—49.

SYCHRA, A., *Parteiliche Musikkritik als Mitschöpferin einer neuen Musik. Eine Einführung in die Musikästhetik des sozialistischen Realismus*, Berlin 1953.

SZATMARI, Antal, »A szovjet Vörös Hadseregben harcolt magyar internacionalista vöröskatonák dalai (1917—1921),« *Magyar zene*, 1967, VIII/5, pp. 475—486.

SZWED, John F., »Musical Style and Racial Conflict,« *Phylon*, 1966, 27/4, pp. 358—366.

TAYLOR, Clifford, »Music — The Design of Culture and the Afro-Asian Revolution,« *Encounter*, 1968, XXXI/5, pp. 41—48.

THIBAUT, Walter, *François-Joseph Gossec, chantre de la Revolution française*, Institut Jules Destrée, Gilly 1970, pp. 79.

THURMAN, Howard, *Deep River: Reflections on the Religious Insight of the Negro Spirituals*, 1955, Reprint: Kennikat Press, Port Washington (N. Y.) 1969.

URBANO, J., »La musica y la Révolucion francesa,« *Revista musical chilena*, 1955, X/49, pp. 8—17.

VASSBERG, David E., »Villa-Lobos. Music as a Tool of Nationalism,« *Luso--Brazilian Review*, 1969, VI/2, pp. 55—65.

VUČKOVIC, Vojislav, »Hudba jako propagační prostředek,« *Klič*, 1932—1933, 3.

WAWRZYKOWSKA-WIERCIOCHOWA, Dionizja, *Polska piesn rewolucyjna*, Wydawnictwo Związkowe, Warsaw 1970, pp. 438.

WEITZMAN, »An Introduction of Adorno's Music and Social Criticism,« *Music and Letters*, 52/3, 1971, pp. 287—298.

MUSIC AND EDUCATION

BERNER, H., *Untersuchungen zur Begriffsbestimmung und zu einigen Fragen der Rezeption von Programm-Musik — Ein Beitrag zur Musikerziehung und zur musikalischen Populärwissenschaft*, Leipzig 1964; in *Die Musikforschung*, 1966, 19, pp. 54.

BIRGE, Edward Bailey, *History of Public School Music in the United States*, Oliver Ditson Co., Philadelphia 1937.

BLAUKOPF, Kurt, »Musiksoziologie im Unterricht,« *Musikerziehung*, 1953/54, 7, pp. 252—255.

BONTINCK, Irmgard, »Die Instrumentenwahl in der volkstümlichen Musizierpraxis der Großstadt unter Berücksichtigung der Geige,« in *Forschung in der Musikerziehung* (Beiheft der Zeitschrift *Musik und Bildung*), 1971. 5/6.

BRIX, Lothar, »Anmerkungen zu einer sich politisch verstehenden Musikerziehung,« *Musik und Bildung*, 1972, IV/6, pp. 292—297.

CAMPEANU, Pavel, »The Implications of Light Music for a Group of Apprentices in Bucarest,« *New Patterns of Musical Behaviour*, Universal Edition, Vienna 1974, pp. 103—108.

CHEN, Marjory Liu, »Music Education and Community Life in Taiwan China,« *Musart*, Washington (D. C.) 1968, 20/5, pp. 38—39, 60.

DAHNK, E., »Musikausübung an den Höfen von Burgund und Orléans während des 15. Jahrhunderts,« *Archiv für Kulturgeschichte*, 1934, 25, pp. 184—215.

ECKHARDT, Otto, »Der Musikunterricht,« in *Die Mittelschule. Im Auftrag des Zentralinstituts für Erziehung und Unterricht*, Ernst Buhtz, Quelle & Meyer, Leipzig 1926.

ELSNER, Helmut, »Singgelegenheiten Zehn- bis Vierzehnjähriger. Ergebniße einer Befragung zu musikalischen Aktivitäten Jugendlicher,« in *Forschung in der Musikerziehung*, Musik und Bildung, Beiheft, 1972, 7—8, pp. 31—38.

ENRIKO, Josif, »Music Teaching as the Foundation of the Development of Musical Creativity,« *International Review of the Aesthetics and Sociology of Music*, 1971, II/2.

ERPF, H., *Neue Wege der Musikerziehung*, Schwab, Stuttgart 1954.

ESCHMANN, Wolfgang, »Musik — ein Medium der Persönlichkeitsbildung,« in *Rheinische Philharmonie*, Koblenz 1970, pp. 44—49.

ESSER, Ben, »Die Wiederbelebung der Volksmusik und die Lehrerbildung,« in *Mitteilungen der Pädagogischen Akademien in Preußen*, No. 1, Weidtmann, Berlin 1926.

FOUTS, Gordon E., »Music Instructions in the Education of American Youth: The Early Academies,« *Journal of Research in Music Education*, 1972, XX/4, pp. 469—476.

FRISIUS, Rudolf, und Ulrich GÜNTHER, »Politische und soziologische Bezüge im Musikunterricht, dargestellt an einem Ausschnitt aus den *Hymnen* von Karlheinz Stockhausen,« in *Musikunterricht an Gesamtschulen*, Klett, Stuttgart 1971, pp. 42—65, 143—180.

GHENEA, Cristian, »Rolul social-educativ al muzicii,« *Studii Muzicologie*, 1971, VII, pp. 249—293.

GOLDHAMMER, O., »Westgesang und Ostland-Lied. Die mißbrauchte Schulmusik in Westdeutschland,« in *Musik in der Schule*, 1960, 11/12, pp. 531—539.

GÜNTHER, S., »Die Bedeutung der Umwelt für die Musikerziehung,« *Die Musikpflege*, 1931, 1/11, pp. 521—536.

HAAKE, Claus, *Der Beitrag des Chorsingens zur ästhetischen Erziehung und Bildung der Arbeiterklasse in der Deutschen Demokratischen Republik,* Universität Halle, Halle 1971, pp. 320.

HILL, John D., *A Study of the Musical Achievement of Culturally Deprived Children and Culturally Advantaged Children at the Elementary School Level,* Ph. D. Thesis (Music), University of Kansas, Lawrence 1968.

HOFFER, Charles R., »Youth, Music Education and the New Sound Environment,« *New Patterns of Musical Behaviour,* Universal Edition, Vienna 1974, pp. 167—178.

HONIGSHEIM, Paul, »Übersicht über die bestehenden Volksbildungseinrichtungen und Strömungen,« in *Soziologie des Volksbildungswesens,* Schriften des Forschungsinstituts für Sozialwissenschaften in Köln, Vol. I, L. v. Wiese, Munich/Leipzig 1921.

HORNER, V., *Music Education; The Background of Research and Opinion,* Australian Council of Educational Research 1965.

INGEGNERI, Paul, *The Development of Music Reading Through Guided Listening Experiences in the Intermediate Grades,* University Microfilms, Ann Arbor 1970, pp. 353.

JAGER, Hugo de, »Musical Socialization and the Schools,« *Music Educators Journal,* 1967, LIII/6.

JENNE, Michael, »The Role of Tradition in Musical Education,« *The World of Music,* 1968, 10/2, pp. 8—16.

— »Soziologische Thesen zum Musikunterricht in der Schule,« *Musik und Bildung,* 1970, II/5, pp. 212—215.

JÖDE, Fritz, *Musikschulen für Jugend und Volk,* G. Kallmeyer, Wolfenbüttel 1924, pp. 64.

JOHNSON, James C., *The Introduction of the Study of Music into the Public Schools of America,* Kindergarten Literature Co., Chicago 1893.

KADUSHIN, Charles, »The Professional Self-Concept of Music Students,« *American Journal of Sociology,* 1969, 75/3, pp. 389—404.

KAPLAN, Max, *Foundations and Frontiers of Music Education,* New York 1966.

KARBUSICKÝ, Vladimir, »Die Musikerziehung zwischen Geschmack, Verhalten und Bedürfnis,« *Forschung in der Musikerziehung,* 1970, 3—4, pp. 56—63.

KARBUSICKÝ, Vladimir and J. KASAN, *Erforschung des gegenwärtigen Standes der Musikalität,* Prague 1964.

KESTENBERG, L., *Musikerziehung und Musikpflege,* Leipzig 1921.

KLAUSMEIER, F., »Der Einfluß sozialer Faktoren auf das musikalische Verhalten von Jugendlichen,« in W. Kraus, ed., *Musik und Musikerziehung in der Reifezeit.*

— »Das Musikinteresse der höheren Schüler in Köln und sein Bezug zur Konfession,« *Kölner Zeitschrift für Soziologie und Sozialpsychologie,* 1959, 11/3, pp. 460—495.

— »Radio-Hören und Musikpflege. Ein Beitrag zur geistigen Situation der höheren Schule,« *Kulturarbeit*, 1954, 6/1.

KOLNEDER, W., »Pädagogisch-soziologische Betrachtungen zur Neuen Musik,« in *Stilkriterien der Neuen Musik*, Berlin 1961.

KRAUS, Egon, ed., *Der Einfluß der technischen Mittler auf die Musikerziehung unserer Zeit*, Vorträge der Siebten Bundesschulmusikwoche, Hannover 1968, B. Schott's Söhne, Mainz 1968.

KRETZSCHMAR, Hermann, *Über den Stand der öffentlichen Musikpflege in Deutschland*, Sammlung musikalischer Vorträge, Paul G. Waldersee, ed., Leipzig 1879—1898.

LIST, George, »Ethnomusicology in Higher Education,« *Music Journal*, 1962, 20/8, pp. 20—26, 55.

MARROU, Henri, *Histoire de l'éducation dans l'Antiquité*, Seuil, Paris 1955.

MENZEL, Horst, *Jugend und Reizmusik*, Schriftenreihe zur Musikpädagogik, 2, Diesterweg, Frankfurt/M. 1969, pp. 78.

MICHEL, Paul, »Das Beethovenbild der deutschen Musikerziehung in Vergangenheit und Gegenwart,« *Musik in der Schule*, 1971, XXII/4, pp. 143—151.

— »Der Systemcharacter der sozialistischen Musikerziehung,« *Beiträge zur Musikwissenschaft*, 1969, XI/3—4, pp. 259—267.

— »Lage und Ausbildung des Musikers im 19. Jahrhundert,« *Musik in der Schule*, 1963, 14/3, pp. 95—105.

MÜLLER, C. J., »Körperpflege und Musik,« *Musik im Leben*, 1925, 1, pp. 97—100.

MUELLER, John Henry, »The Social Nature of Musical Taste,« *Journal of Research in Music Education*, 1956, 4/2, pp. 113—122.

* * *, *Music Education, Basic Concepts*, National Society for the Study of Education, Chicago 1958.

* * *, *Music Education for Tomorrow's Society*; Selected topics, A. Motycka, ed., GAMT Music Press, Jamestown (R. I.) 1976, pp. 83.

* * *, *Musikopleven og musiformidling: studier i musikkens psykologi, sociologi og paedagogik*, Akademisk forlag, Copenhagen 1975, pp. 236.

NETTL, Bruno, »Infant Musical Development and Primitive Music,« *Southwestern Journal of Antropology*, 1956, XII/1, pp. 87—91.

— »The Place of Ethnomusicology in American Education: Background for Discussion,« in *Papers of the Yugoslav-American Seminar on Music*, Malcolm H. Brown, ed., Indiana University, Bloomington 1970, pp. 321—330.

PAYNTER, John, »Music Education and the Emotional Needs of Young People. Towards a New Type of Research in Great Britain,« *New Patterns of Musical Behaviour*, Universal Edition, Vienna 1974, pp. 159—167.

PETSCHULL, Johannes, *Die soziale Lage der deutschen Musiklehrkräfte*, Ph. D. Thesis, Giessen 1924.

465

PIETZSCH, G., *Die Musik im Erziehungs- und Bildungsideal des ausgehenden Altertums und frühen Mittelalters*, Halle 1932.

RABIN, Marvin J., *History and Analysis of the Greater Boston Youth Symphony Orchestra from 1958 to 1964*, Music Education, University of Illinois, 1968, pp. 500.

RACKWITZ, Werner, »Beitrag der Musik und des Theaters zu sozialistischen Persönlichkeitsentwicklung,« *Musik in der Schule*, 1972, XXIII/1, pp. 1—8.

RAUHE, H., »Schlager, Beat, Folklore in Unterricht. Actuelle didaktische Ansatze zur Schulung des Hörens und Differenzierung des Wertempfindens,« in *Didaktik der Musik*, 1967.
— »Musikerziehung um Umbruch. Soziologische und kommunikations--psychologische Aspekte einer Reform der Musikdidaktik,« in *Mitteilung des Landesverbandes der Tonkünstler und Musiklehrer*, 1968, 4, pp. 2—7.

READ, Herbert, *Education through Art*, Fabre, London 1943.

REBLING, E., »Eine neue Situation. Probleme der Ausbildung von Berufsmusikern,« *Musik und Gesellschaft*, 1963, 13, pp. 649—654.

RECKLING, Wolfgang, »Zur Entwicklung des Musikschulen in der Deutschen Demokratischen Republik,« in *Sammelbände zur Musikgeschichte der Deutschen Demokratischen Republik*, Neue Musik, 2, Berlin 1971, pp. 272—293.

REINHOLD, H., »Musikerziehung zwischen Kultursoziologie und Musikwissenschaft,« *Musik im Unterricht*, 1957, 48/5, pp. 141—144.

ROEDER, Martin, »Über den Stand der öffentlichen Musikpflege in Italien,« in *Sammlung musikalischer Vorträge*, P. G. Waldersee. ed., Leipzig 1881.

ROMAN, Zoltan, »Higher Music Education in Canada«, *New Patterns of Musical Behaviour*, Universal Edition, Vienna 1974, pp. 178—183.

RÖSSNER, L., *Jugend im Erziehungsbereich des Tanzes*, Bern 1963.

RYSER, C. P., »The Student Dancer,« in *Arts in Society*, R. N. Wilson, ed., Englewood Cliffs 1964, pp. 95—121.

SAKUMA, Arline Fuju, *Education and Styles of Innovation: The Socialization of Musicians*, Ph. D. Thesis (Sociology), University of Washington, 1968.

SANDVOSS, Joachim, *A Study of the Musical Preferences, Interests, and Activities of Parents as Factors in their Attitude Toward the Musical Education of their Children*, Ed. D. Thesis (Music), University of British Columbia, 1969.

SCHOOF, Jack F., *A Study of Didactic Attitudes on the Fine Arts in America as Expressed in Popular Magazines During the Period 1786—1800*, Fine Arts, Ohio State University, 1967.

SCHUNEMANN, Georg, *Geschichte der deutschen Schulmusik*, Kistner & Siegel, Leipzig 1928.

SLUSS, J. H., *High School Senior Attitudes Toward Music*, Ph. D. Thesis, Colorado State College, Ann Arbor 1968, pp. 146.

SMALL, Chr., *Music, Society, Education*, J. Calder, London 1981.

SOKHOR, Arnold N., »Young People's Leisure Time and its Use for Musical-Aesthetic Education,« *New Patterns of Musical Behaviour*, Universal Edition, Vienna 1974, pp. 219—226.

SOWA, Georg., »Musik in der Schule und die Bildung von Soziabilitätstypen,« *Musik und Bildung*, 1972, IV/2, pp. 75—79.

SOWA, Georg, *Anfänge institutioneller Musikerziehung in Deutschland, 1800-1843*, Gustav Bosse Verlag, Regensburg 1973.

* * *, UNESCO, *Music in Education*, International Commission on the Role and Place of Music in the Education of Youth and Adults (Brussels, June 29 — July 9, 1953), Paris 1955.

VAN, G., »La pédagogie musicale à la fin du Moyen Age,« *Musica Disciplina*, 1948, 1—2, pp. 75—97.

MUSIC AND ARTS

ABRAHAMS, Roger D., »Public Drama and Common Values in Two Caribbean Islands,« *Trans-Action*, 1968, V/8, pp. 62—71.

ADORNO, Theodor Wiesengrund and Hanns EISLER, *Komposition für den Film*, Rogner und Bernhard, Munich 1969, pp. 215.

ALBRECHT, Milton C., James H. BARNETT and Mason GRIFF, eds., *The Sociology of Art and Literature*, Praeger Publishing Co., New York 1970.

ANTAL, Frederick, *Florentine Painting and Its Social Background in Fourteenth and Early Fifteenth Century*, Kegan Paul, London.

***, *Arts and People*, Cranford Wood, Inc., New York 1973.

BAB, Julius, *Das Theater im Lichte der Soziologie*, Kunst & Gesellschaft, vol. 1, pp. 247.

BAILBÉ, Joseph Marc, *Le Roman et la Musique en France sous la Monarchie de juillet* Minard- Lettres Modernes, Paris 1969, pp. 446.

BALET, Leo, *Die Verbürgerlichung der deutschen Kunst, Literatur und Musik im 18. Jahrhundert*, Heitz, Leipzig—Strasbourg—Zurich 1936.

BATTOCK, Gregory, ed., *The New American Cinema: A Critical Anthology*, Dutton, New York 1968.

BAUMOL, William J., and William G. BOWEN, *Performing Arts: The Economic Dilemma: A Study of Problems Common to Theatre, Opera, Music and Dance*, Twentieth Century Fund, New York 1966.

BELZ, Carl, »Relationships between the Popular and Fine Arts. Recent Developments,« *New Patterns of Musical Behaviour*, Universal Edition, Vienna 1974, pp. 84—91.

BENTLEY, Eric, *The Theatre of Commitment and Other Essays on Drama in Our Society*, Atheneum, New York 1967.

BIGSBY, C. W. E., *Confrontations and Commitment: A Study of Contemporary American Drama, 1959—66*, University of Missouri Press, Columbia 1968.

BOEHMER, Konrad, »Anmerkungen zu einem politischen Musiktheater,« *Oper*, 1969, pp. 63—67.

BOHNSTEDT, Werner, »Erwägungen zum Thema Film und Radio als Gegenstände soziologischer Erkenntnis,« in *Reine und angewandte Soziologie* (Festausgabe für Ferdinand Tönnies zu seinen 80. Geburtstage), Leipzig 1936.

BONTINCK, Irmgard, *Theater im österreichischen Fernsehen*, Ms, unpublished.

BURCKHARDT, Jacob, *Kultur und Kunst der Renaissance in Italien*, Bernina, Vienna 1936.

CASSOU, Jean, *Situation de l'art moderne*, Minuit, Paris 1950.

CORVISIER, André, *Arts et sociétés dans l'Europe du XVIIIᵉ siècle*, P. U. F., Paris 1978, pp. 248.

DAVIDSON, Colleen, »Winston Churchill and Charles Ives: The Progressive Experience in Literature and Song,« in *Student musicologists at Minnesota*, 1970/71, IV, pp. 154—180.

DENT, E. J., *Foundations of English Opera — A Study of Musical Drama in England during the Seventeenth Century*, The University Press, Cambridge 1928.

DILTHEY, Wilhelm, *Von deutscher Dichtung und Musik: Aus den Studien zur Geschichte des deutschen Geistes*. Leipzig 1933.

DUCROCQ, Jean, Suzy HALIMI and Maurice LEVY, *Roman et société en Angleterre au XVIIIᵉ siècle*, P. U. F., Paris 1978, pp. 256.

DUNCAN, Hugh Dalziel, *Language and Literature in Society*, Bedminister, New York 1961.

DURAND, Jacques, *Le cinéma et son public*, Sirey, Paris 1958.

EGBERT, Donald Drew, *Social Radicalism and the Arts: A Cultural History from the French Revolution to 1968*, Knopf, New York 1970.

EPSTEIN, Wilhelm, »Kino und Volksbildung,« *Volksbildungsarchiv*, September—October 1913, 5/3.

ERDMANN, Hans, and Giuseppe BECCE, *Allgemeines Handbuch der Filmmusik*, Schlesinger, Berlin 1927.

ERNST, Georg, and Bernhard MARSHALL, *Film und Rundfunk. 2. Internationaler kath. Filmkongreß. 1. Internationaler kath. Rundfunkkongreß*, Verlag Leohaus, Munich 1929, pp. 432.

EVANS, Robert Kenneth, *The Early Songs of Sergei Prokofiev and Their Relation to the Synthesis of the Arts in Russia, 1890—1922*, Ohio State University, 1971, pp. 302.

FINKELSTEIN, Sidney, *Art and Society*, International Publishers, New York 1947.

FISCHER, Pieter, *Music in Paintings of the Low Countries in the 16th and 17th Centuries*, Sweets and Zeitlinger, Amsterdam 1975, pp. 108.

FLEMING, William, *Arts and Ideas*, Holt, Rinehart and Winston, New York 1961.

FRANCASTEL, Pierre, »Introduction,« in Francois LESURE, *Music and Art in Society*, Pennsylvania University Press, Pittsburgh 1968, pp. I-VII.

FREHN, Paul, *Der Einfluß der englischen Literatur auf Deutschlands Musiker und Musik im 19. Jahrhundert*, G. H. Nolte, Düsseldorf 1938.

FULCHIGNONI, Enrico, »Musique et film,« *Revue d'Esthétique*, 1954, VII/4, pp. 401-415.

FÜLOP-MILLER, René, *The Motion Picture in America*, Dial Press, New York 1938.

FÜLOP-MILLER, René, and Joseph GREGOR, *The Russian Theatre: Its Character and History*, Lippincott, Philadelphia 1929.

HUACO, George A., *The Sociology of Film Art*, Basic Books, New York 1965.

LISSA, Zofia, *Estetyka muzyki filmowej*, Panstwowe Wydawnictwo Muzyczne, Kraków 1964, pp. 488. Germ. transl. *Ästhetik der Filmmusik*, Henschelverlag, Berlin 1965.

LOMAX, Alan, Irmgard BARTENIEFF and Forrestine PAULAY, »Choreometrics: A Method for the Study of Cross-Cultural Pattern in Film,« *Research Film*, 1969. 6/6, pp. 505—517.

LOWENTHAL, Leo, *Literature, Popular Culture and Society*, Prentice-Hall, Englewood Cliffs (N. J.) 1941.

— *Literature and the Image of Man: Sociological Studies of the European Drama and Novel, 1600—1900*, Beacon, Boston 1957.

MacCANN, Richard Dyer, ed., *Film and Society*, Scribner, New York 1964.

MARTI, Kurt, K. LÜTHI, K. von FISCHER, *Moderne Literatur, Malerei und Musik*, Flamberg, Zurich-Stuttgart 1963.

MARX, Karl and Friedrich ENGELS, *Über Kunst und Literatur — Eine Sammlung aus ihrer Schriften*, Berlin 1953.

— *Sur la littérature et l'art*, Ed. Sociales, Paris 1954.

MAYER, Jacob Peter, *British Cinemas and Their Audiences: Sociological Studies*, D. Dobson, London 1948.

MERRIAM, Alan P., »The Arts and Anthropology,« in *Horizons of Anthropology*, Sol Tax, ed., Aldine, Chicago 1964, pp. 224—236.

MEYER, Leonard B., *Music, the Arts, and Ideas*, University of Chicago Press, Chicago 1967.

MONACO, Paul, *Cinema and Society: France and Germany During the Twenties*, Elsevier, New York 1976.

MOORE, Thomas Gale, *The Economics of the American Theatre*, Duke University Press, Durham (N. C.) 1968.

PEACOCK, James L., *Rites of Modernization, Symbolic and Social Aspects of Indonesian Proletarian Drama*, University of Chicago Press, Chicago 1968.

* * *, *The Performing Arts, Problems and Prospects*, Rockefeller Panel Report on the Future of Theatre, Dance, Music in America, McGraw-Hill, New York 1965.

PETERS, Anne K., *Acting and Aspiring Actress in Hollywood: A Sociological Analysis*, Ph. D. Thesis, University of California, Los Angeles 1971.

469

PICKARD-CAMBRIDGE, Arthur Wallace, *The Theatre of Dionysus in Athens*, Clarendon Press, Oxford 1946, pp. 288.

POWDERMAKER, Hortense, *Hollywood, the Dream Factory: An Antropologist Looks at the Movie-Makers*, Little, Browne, Boston 1950.

RACKWITZ, Werner, »Beitrag der Musik und des Theaters zu sozialistischen Persönlichkeitsentwicklung,« *Musik in der Schule*, 1972, XXIII/1, pp. 1—8.

RANDALL, Richard S., *Censorship of the Movies*, University of Wisconsin Press, Madison 1968.

READ. Herbert, *Education through Art*, Faber. London 1943.

SACHS, Kurt. *The Commonwealth of Art Style in the Fine Arts, Music and Dance,* D. Dobson, London 1955.

SCHOOF, Jack F., *A Study of Didactic Attitudes on the Fine Arts in America as Expressed in Popular Magazines During the Period 1786—1800*, Fine Arts, Ohio State University, 1967.

SCHOOLFIELD, G. C., *The Figure of the Musician in German Literature*, Chapel Hill 1956.

SILBERMANN, Alphons, »Theater und Gesellschaft,« in *Atlantisbuch des Theaters*, Atlantis Verlag, Zurich 1966, pp. 387—406.

SPENCER, H., *Literary Style and Music*, New York 1952.

TOOZE, R., and B. PERHAM-KRONE, *Literature and Music as Resources for Social Studies*, Prentice-Hall, Englewood Cliffs (N. J.) 1955.

TREDER, Dorothea, *Die Musikinstrumente in den höfischen Epen der Blütezeit*, L. Bamberg, Greifswald 1933.

TU NGOC, »General Remarks on Vietnamese Music from 1930 to the Present and the Cross Influence between it and Literature,« *Tap chi van ho*, 1970, 5, pp. 208—237.

VALLAS, L., *Un siècle de musique et de théâtre à Lyon (1688—1789)*, P. Masson, Lyons 1932.

WAUGH, Jennie, *Das Theater als Spiegel der amerikanischen Demokratie*, Junker, Berlin 1936.

TRADITION AND INNOVATION

BARNETT, H. G., *Innovation: The Basis of Cultural Change*, McGraw-Hill, New York 1953.

BASCOM, W. R., and M. J. HERSKOVITS, *Continuity and Change in African Cultures*, University of Chicago Press, Chicago 1959.

BELZ, Carl I., »Popular Music and the Folk Tradition,« *Journal of American Folklore*, 1967, 80, pp. 130—142.

BRELET, Gisèle, *Esthétique et création musicale*, P. U. F., Paris 1947.

BROCKHAUS, Heinz Alfred, »Fortschritt und Avantgardismus,« in *Bericht über den Internationalen musikwissenschaftlichen Kongreß*, Leipzig 1966, pp. 25—33.

CAREY, James T., »Changing Courtship Patterns in the Popular Song,« *American Journal of Sociology*, 1969, 74/6, pp. 720—731.

CHAILLEY, Jacques, »Vue sur les lendemains d'hier,« *Polyphonie*, 1949, 3, pp. 63—68.

DALE, Ralph Alan, »The Future of Music: An Investigation into the Evolution of Forms,« *The Journal of Aesthetics and Art Criticism*, 1968, XXVI/4, pp. 477—488.

DANNEMANN, Erna, *Die spätgotische Musiktradition in Frankreich und Burgund*, Heitz, Strasbourg 1936.

DUNNING, Albert, »Die 'aktuelle' Musik im Zeitalter der Niederländer,« in *Bericht über den Internationalen musikwissenschaftlichen Kongreß*, Leipzig 1966, pp. 181—186.

FINKELSTEIN, Sidney, *Composer and Nation — The Folk Heritage of Music*, Lawrence and Wishart, London 1960; New York 1960.

FISCHER, Kurt von, »Das Neue in der europäischen Kunstmusik als soziokulturelles Problem,« *The International Review of the Aesthetics and Sociology of Music*, 1971, II/2, pp. 141—154.

— »Zum Problem des Neuen in der Musik,« *Musica*, 1971, XXV/3, pp. 239—242.

GERSCHKOWITSCH, S., »Die Kunst und der Fortschritt in der Massenkommunikationstechnik,« *Kunst und Literatur*, 1971, XIX/1, pp. 45—59.

GHIRCOIAŞIU, Romeo, »Traditii ale cîntecului patriotic,« *Studii de muzicologie*, 1971, VII, pp. 59—77.

HANNIKAINEN, Ilmari, *Sibelius and the Development of Finnish Music*, Hinrichsen Edition, London 1948.

HUBER, Klaus, »Die Musik in der Fremde der Gegenwart,« *Melos*, 1969, XXXVI/6, pp. 241—243.

JARUSTOVSKY, Boris M., »Die Musikkultur der Völker: Tradition und Gegenwart,« in *Kunst und Literatur*, 1972, XX/7, pp. 765—777.

JENNE, Michael, »The Role of Tradition in Musical Education,« *The World of Music*, 1968, 10/2, pp. 8—16.

KASDAN, Leonard, and J. H. APPLETON, »Tradition and Change: The Case of Music,« in *Comparative Studies in History and Society*, 1970, 12, pp. 50—58.

KISHIBE, Shigeo, »Means of Preservation and Diffusion of Traditional Music in Japan,« *Asian Music*, New York 1971, 2/1, pp. 8—13.

LISSA, Zofia, »Prolegomena to the Theory of Musical Tradition,« *The International Review of Music Aesthetics and Sociology*, 1970, I/1, pp. 35—54.

LIST, George, »Acculturation and Musical Tradition,« *Journal of the International Folk Music Council*, 1964, 16, pp. 18—21.

LÜTOLF, Max, »Zur Rolle der Antike in der musikalischen Tradition der französischen Epoque classique,« *Fischer Festschrift*, Katzbichler, Munich 1973, pp. 145—164.

MACEDA, José, »Means of Preservation and Diffusion of Traditional Music: The Phillippine Situation,« *Asian Music*, 1971, 2/1, pp. 14—23.

MACGILVRAY, Dan, »Topical Song and the American Radical Tradition,« in *Newport Folk Festival*, H. Glassie and R. Rinzler, eds., 1967, pp. 11, 36—37.

MELLERS, Wilfred Howard, *François Couperin and the French Classical Tradition*, D. Dobson, London 1950.

— *Music and Society: England and the European Tradition*, D. Dobson, London, 1946; 2nd ed. 1950.

SAKUMA, Arline Fuju, *Education and Styles of Innovation: The Socialization of Musicians*, Ph.D. Thesis (Sociology), University of Washington, 1968.

SEEGER, Charles, »The Cultivation of various European Traditions in the Americas,« in *The Report of the 8th Congress of the International Musicological Society*, Bärenreiter, Kassel-Basel 1961, pp. 364—375.

STEKERT, Ellen Jane, *Two Voices of Tradition: The Influence of Personality and Collecting Environment upon the Songs of Two Traditional Folk Singers*, Ph.D. Thesis (Folklore), University of Pennsylvania, 1965.

SUPIČIĆ, Ivo, »Note sur la tradition,« *Schweizerische Musikzeitung*, 1965, CV/1, pp. 22—27.

— »Umjetničko-historijska uvjetovanost u muzičkom stvaranju,« u *Rad JAZU*, No. 337, Zagreb 1965, pp. 221—239.

SZWEYKOWSKI, Zygmunt M., »Tradition and Popular Elements in Polish Music of the Baroque Era,« *The Musical Quarterly*, 1970, 56/1, pp. 99—115.

WERNER, Eric, *From Generation to Generation: Studies in Jewish Music Tradition*, American Conference of Cantors, New York 1968.

— »The Role of Tradition in the Music of the Synagogue,« *Judaism*, 1964, XIII/2, pp. 156—163.

WHITESIDE, Dale R., »Traditions and Directions in the Music of Vietnam,« *Daily Egyptian*, Southern Illinois University, Carbondale February 6, 1971, pp. 6—7, 9.

YAMAGUCHI, Osamu, *The Music of Palau: An Ethnomusicological Study of the Classical Tradition*, M.A. Thesis (Music), University of Hawaii, Honolulu 1967.

ACCULTURATION IN MUSIC. MUSICAL SUB-CULTURES

ALILUNAS, L. J., »Negro Music in American Culture. Sociological and Ethnomusical Interpretations,« *Journal of Human Relations*, 1962, 10/4, pp. 474—479.

AMES, Russel, »Protest and Irony in Negro Folksong,« *Science and Society*, 1950, XIV/3, pp. 193—213.

ANDERSON, Joannes Earl, *Maori Music with its Polynesian Background*, Thomas Avery and Sons, New Plymouth (New Zealand) 1934.

BABOW, I., »The Singing Societies of European Immigrants,« *Phylon*, 1954, XV/3.
— »Types of Immigrant Singing Societies,« *Sociology and Social Research*, 1955, XXXIX/4.

BEAUD, Paul, »Musical Sub-Cultures in France,« in Irmgard Bontinck, ed., *New Patterns of Musical Behaviour*, Universal Edition, Vienna 1974, pp. 212—218.

BORRIS, Siegfried, »Einfluß und Einbruch primitiver Musik in die Musik des Abendlandes,« *Sociologus*, 1952, 2/1, pp. 52—72.

BRAÏLOÏU, Constantin, *Vie musicale d'un village* (Recherches sur le répertoire de Dragus — Roumanie, 1929—1932), Institut Universitaire Roumain, Paris 1960.

CHU LIU-YI, »Folk Opera Flowers Among National Minorities,« *China Reconstructs*, 1962, 11/9, pp. 37—39.

CLARK, E. R., »Negro Folk Music in America,« *Journal of American Folklore*, 1951, LXIV/253, pp. 281—287.

COLLAER, Paul, ed., *Music of the Americas: An Illustrated Music Ethnology of the Eskimo and American Indian Peoples*, Curzon Press, London 1973, pp. 207.

CONKLIN, H. C., and W. C. STURTEVANT, »Seneca Indian Singing Tools at Coldspring Longhouse. Musical Instruments of the Modern Iroquois,« in *Proceedings of the American Philosophical Society*, 1953, XCIII/3, pp. 262—290.

COURLANDER, H., *Negro Folk Music*, New York 1963.

CRAY, E., »An Acculturative Continuum for Negro Folk Song in the United States,« *Ethnomusicology*, January 1961, 5/1, pp. 10—15.

DESCOTES, J., »La musique fonctionnelle,« *Polyphonie*, 1951, 7—8, pp. 71—92.

DE LERMA, Dominique-René, *Black Music in our Culture: Curricular Ideas on the Subjects, Materials and Problems*, Kent State University Press, Kent (Ohio) 1970.

DENISOFF, R. S., »Songs of Persuasion: A Sociological Analysis of Urban Propaganda Songs,« *Journal of American Folklore*, 1966, 79.

DENNISON, T., *The American Negro and His Amazing Music*, New York 1963.

DENSMORE, Frances, *The American Indians and Their Music*, The Womans Press, New York 1936.

GLASS, Paul, *Songs and Stories of Afro-Americans*, Grosset & Dunlap, New York 1971, pp. 61.

BIBLIOGRAPHY

HAMM, Charles, *The Acculturation of Musical Styles: Popular Music, U. S. A.*, in *Contemporary Music and Music Cultures*, Prentice-Hall, Englewood Cliffs (New Jersey) 1975, pp. 125—158.

HARRISON, Joan and Frank, »Spanish Elements in the Music of Two Maya Groups in Chiapas,« in *Selected Reports*, Los Angeles 1968, I/2, pp. 2-44.

HECKMANN, Don, »Black Music and White America,« in *Black America*, J. F. Szwed, ed., Basic Books, New York 1970, pp. 158—170.

HERZOG, George, »A Comparison of Pueblo and Pima Musical Styles,« *Journal of American Folklore*, Vol. 49, 1936.

— *Research in Primitive and Folk Music in the United States*, Executive Offices, American Council of Learned Societies, Washington (D. C.) 1936.

HOUSTON, James, *Songs of the Dream People*, Atheneum, New York 1972.

IRVINE, Judith T. and David J. SAPIR, »Musical Style and Social Change among the Kujamaat Diola,« *Ethnomusicology*, 1976, XX/1, pp. 67-86.

JOHNSON, Guy B., »The Negro Spiritual,« *American Anthropologist*, 1931, 33, pp. 170.

KATZ, Bernhard, *The Social Implications of Early Negro Music in the United States (1862—1939)*, Arno Press, New York 1969, pp. 250.

KITAHARA, Michio, »Acculturation, Survival, and Syncretism in Blackfoot, Flathead, and Dakota Music,« *Japanese Journal of Ethnology*, 1962, 26/3, pp. 45—48.

KURATH, Gertrude P., »Catholic Hymns of Michigan Indians,« *Anthropological Quarterly*, 1957, 30/2, pp. 31—44.

LACHMANN, Robert, *Jewish Cantillation and Song in the Isle of Djerba*, Archives of Oriental Music, Hebrew University, Jerusalem 1940.

LARSON, Le Roy, »Norwegian Folk Dance Music in Minnesota,« *Society of Ethnomusicology Newsletter*, 1970, IV, pp. 5—6.

LERMA, Dominique-René, »Black Music Now,« *Music Educators Journal*, 1970, LVII/3, pp. 25—29.

LIST, George, »Acculturation and Musical Tradition,« *Journal of the International Folk Music Council*, 1964, 16, pp. 18—21.

LUKAS, Victor Thomas, *The Traditionally Oriented Urban Folk Musician: Revitalistic Aspects of a Subculture*, M. A. Thesis, (Anthropology), University of Illinois, Urbana 1967.

McALLESTER, David P., *Enemy Way Music. A Study of Social and Esthetic Values as Seen in Navaho Music*, Peabody Museum, Cambridge (Mass.) 1954.

— »The Role of Music in Western Apache Culture,« in *Selected Papers of the Fifth International Congress of Anthropological and Ethnological Sciences, 1956*, University of Pennsylvania Press, Philadephia 1960, pp. 468—472.

McLEAN, Mervyn, »Song Loss and Social Context among the New Zealand Maori,« *Ethnomusicology*, 1965, 9/3, pp. 296—304.

McLEOD, N., *The Social Context of Music in a Polynesian Community*, M. A. Thesis (Anthropology), London School of Economics, London 1956—1957.

MERRIAM, Alan P., »The Use of Music in the Study of a Problem of Acculturation,« *American Anthropologist*, 1955, 57/1, pp. 28—34.

MERRIAM, Alan P., *Ethnomusicology of the Flathead Indians*, Viking Fund Publications in Anthropology, New York 1967, 44.

MERRIAM, Alan P., »Music and the Origin of the Flathead Indians — A Problem in Culture History,« in *Music in the Americas*, G. List and J. Orrego-Salas, eds., Indiana University Research Center in Anthropology, Folklore and Linguistics, Bloomington 1967, pp. 129—138.

MERRIAM, Alan P., and Waren L. D'AZEVEDO, »Washo Peyote Songs,« *American Anthropologist*, 1957, 59, pp. 615—641.

MULLEN, Patrick B., »A Negro Street Performer: Tradition and Innovation,« *Western Folklore*, 1970, 29/2, pp. 91—103.

NETTL, Bruno, »Change in Folk and Primitive Music. A Survey of Methods and Studies,« *Journal of American Musicological Society*, Summer 1955, 8, pp. 101—109.

— »The Hymns of the Amish: An Example of Marginal Survival,« *Journal of American Folklore*, 1957, 70, pp. 323—328.

NETTL, Bruno, »Speculations on Musical Style and Musical Content in Acculturation,« *Acta Musicologica*, 1963, 35/1, pp. 35—37.

NETTL, Bruno, *The Western Impact on World Music: Africa and the American Indians*, in *Contemporary Music and Music Cultures*, Prentice-Hall, Englewood Cliffs (New Jersey) 1975, pp. 101—124.

ODUM, Howard Washington, *Negro Workaday Songs*, Oxford University Press, H. Milford, London 1926.

RICKS, George Robinson, *Some Aspects of the Religious Music of the United States Negro: An Ethnomusicological Study with Special Emphasis on the Gospel Tradition*, Ph.D. Thesis (Anthropology), Northwestern University, 1960.

SLOTKIN, J. S., »Jazz and its Forerunners as an Example of Acculturation,« *American Sociological Review*, 1943, 8, pp. 570—575.

SMITH, Lucy Harth, »Negro Musicians and Their Music,« *The Journal of Negro History*, 1935, 20/430.

SPELLMAN, A. B., *Black Music: Four Lifes*, Schocken Books, New York 1970, pp. 241.

STEBBINS, Robert A., *The Jazz Community: The Sociology of a Musical Sub-Culture*, Ph.D. Thesis (Sociology), University of Minnesota, Minneapolis 1964.

SZWED, John F., »Negro Music: Urban Renewal,« in *Our Living Traditions: An Introduction to American Folklore*, T. P. Coffin, ed., Basic Books, New York 1968.

SZWED, John F., »Musical Adaptation among Afro-Americans,« *Journal of American Folklore*, 1969, 82/234, pp. 112—121.

475

THURMAN, Howard, *Deep River: Reflections on the Religious Insight of the Negro Spirituals*, 1955. Reprint: Kennikat Press, Port Washington (N. Y.) 1969.

TRAN VAN KHE, »Traditional Music and Culture Change: A Study in Acculturation,« *Cultures*, 1973, I/1, pp. 195—210.

TRAN VAN KHÊ, »L' acculturation dans les traditions musicales de l'Asie,« *International Review of the Aesthetics and Sociology of Music*, 1974, V/1, pp. 181—191.

URBANSKI, Janusz, »Sweet Beat and Other Forms of Youth Music in Poland,« *New Patterns of Musical Behaviour*, Universal Edition, Vienna 1974, pp. 80—84.

VITANYI, Iván, »The Musical and Social Influence of Beat Music in Hungary,« *New Patterns of Musical Behaviour*, Universal Edition, Vienna 1974, pp. 69—80.

WACHSMAN, K. P., »The Transplantation of Folk Music from One Social Environment to Another,« *Journal of the International Folk Music Council*, 1954, 6, pp. 41—45.

WALLASCHEK, Richard, *Primitive Music*, Longmans, London 1893.

WATERMAN, Richard A., »Music in Australian Aboriginal Culture. Some Sociological and Psychological Implications,« *Music Therapy*, 1956, 5, pp. 40—49.

WILLIS, Paul, »Youth Groups in Birmingham and Their Specific Relation to Pop Music«, *New Patterns of Musical Behaviour*, Universal Edition, Vienna 1974, pp. 108—114.

Index

Abraham, Gerald, 341
Academy of Marseille, 151
acculturation, 165 ff, 230
Adorno, Theodore W., 8, 41, 61,
    66, 74, 97, 99, 178, 351
aestheticism, 34, 35, 75
aesthetics,
    sociological, 37, 42, 71n
Affligemensis, Johannes, 335
Agricola, Alexander, 203
Ahle, Rudolph, 209
Aiguillon, Duke d', 152
air de cour, 109, 131
Albaret, Count d', 152
Alcman of Sardis, 107, 283
Alexander, the Great, 198, 215
alienation, 343
Allonnes, Olivier Revault d', 36n,
    62
amateurism, 57, 163
amateurs, 96, 120, 149, 150, 191
Amerval, Eloy d', 250
analysis, 63

formal, 62
historical, 62
'Ancients' versus 'Moderns', 334
Anet (violinist), 111
Anglois, Vaulthier l', 212
Anjou, Charles d', 211
anthropology, 31
Antistene, 198
aristocracy, 130 ff
Aristophanes, 207, 236
Aristotle, 118, 199, 282, 290
Arnold, Denis, 223
Arnoul, 116
art, performance of, 160
    sociology of, 21, 29, 33, 43n, 53,
        61, 76
    work of, 64, 77, 117, 199
artist, 50
asceticism, musical, 352
Ashurbanipal, 290
atonality, 344
Attaingnant, Pierre, 161, 246
Attali, Jacques, 159, 301, 302, 305

audience, 100, 122, 152, 154, 189
Augustus, 281
autonomization of, 175
Auvergne, Dauphin of, 286
Azevedo, L.H. Correa de, 321
Bücher, Karl, 7, 231, 232
Babow, Irving, 150
Bach, Johann Christian, 113
Bach, Johann Sebastian, 59, 107,
    111, 113, 152, 160, 172, 188,
    207, 209, 215, 243, 247, 265,
    268, 306, 315, 328, 330, 334,
    337, 349
Bagge, Baron de, 152
Baïf Academy, 109, 111
Balet, Leo, 17
Ballantine, Christopher, 18
Ballard, 113
ballet de cour, 109, 131
Banister, John, 107, 213, 244
Bardesan, 313
Barnett, James H., 56n
Baroque period, 17, 161, 256, 259,
    307, 308, 309, 337
courts of the, 144
Bartók, Béla, 91
Bastide, Roger, 53n
Beaud, Paul, 54, 61, 166, 181
Beaufils, Marcel, 17
beauty, models of, 340
Bedford, Duke of, 249
Beethoven, Ludwig van, 58, 113,
    116, 119, 133, 172, 188, 209,
    215, 250, 261, 263, 267, 326,
    330
behavior, collective, 177
Belvianes, Marcel, 8
Belz, Carl, 166, 186
Berardi, Angelo, 306
Berg, Alban, 344
Bergson, Henri, 180, 352

Berlioz, Hector, 110, 136, 215
Berthier, Nicole, 9, 151
Besseler, Heinrich, 94
Bianconi, Lorenzo, 214
Bible, the, message of, 310
Binchois, Gilles, 132, 133, 249
Blaug, Mark, 224
Blaukopf, Kurt, 8, 9, 19, 20, 66n,
    94, 96, 175, 184, 302n
Blume, Friedrich, 37n
Boësset, 145
Boïeldieu, François Adrien, 331
Bontinck, Irmgard, 179
Born, Bertrand de, 286
Bornoff, Jack, 191n
Borodin, Alexander, 214
Bossuet, 278
Bourbonne, Chartraire de, 249
Bourdieu, Pierre, 228
Bourgeois, Loys, 249
bourgeoisie, 129, 130, 131, 132,
    136, 136n, 145, 147, 148, 152,
    154
Bowles, Edmund A., 128
Brăiloïu, Constantin, 7, 24, 85
Brelet, Gisèle, 188, 231, 266, 298,
    326, 344, 350
Brenet, Michel, 153, 250
Brévan, Bruno, 18
Briceno, Luis de, 260
Bridgman, Nanie, 17
Britten, Benjamin, 96
Broecks, Jan, 99
Brook, Barry S., 18, 75, 82, 157,
    210, 244
Brossard, Sébastien de, 334, 337
Bruckner, Anton, 120, 315
Brunswick, Duke of, 242
Brutus, 199
Bukofzer, Manfred E., 17, 82, 135
Burckhardt, Jacob, 198

Burgundy, Duke of, 279

Burney, Charles, 334, 337

Buxtehude, Dietrich, 116

Bužga, Jaroslav, 138n

Byrd, William, 213

Caillois, Roger, 300

Calvisius, Sethus, 334, 336

Cambert, Robert, 137, 173

Campra, André, 106n, 112, 116, 278

Cape, Safford, 312

Caplow, Theodore, 7, 44

Capus, 249

Caracalla, Emperor, 216

Carapezza, P.E., 339

Carpenter, Patricia, 300

Carpitella, Diego, 244

Caurroy, Eustache Du, 204, 212

Cavalli, Pier Francesco, 242

Cazeneuve, Jean, 297

ceremony, 144

  definition of, 293, 294

Certon, Pierre, 204

Cesti, Antonio, 242

Chabanon, Michel, 178

Chailley, Jacques, 7, 15, 17, 58, 91, 106n, 244, 326

chanson, 246

chant, responsorial, 92

Charlemagne, 287

Charles the Bad, 212

Charles V, 136n, 144, 278

Charles VI, 277

Charles VII, 249

Charles VIII of France, 145

Charles IX, 109

Chartres, Duc de, 116

Chastillon de la Tour, Guillaume, 213

Chopin, Frédéric, 59, 113, 153, 214, 328

Choudens, Antoine Ch., 250

Cinesias, 120

Clark, Edgar R., 275

class, social, 125 ff, 196

Clemens non Papa, 278

Clercx, Suzanne, 15

Clovis, 279

Colbert, Jean Baptiste, 283

Colloredo, Archbishop, 208

Combarieu, Jules, 232, 233

communities, primitive, 90, 91

comparative method, 21

composer, 14, 60, 92, 105, 106, 159, 202 ff

  contemporary, 345

  publishing, 245, 246

  royalties, 248, 249

  traditional, 349

concert life, 158

concerts, 109, 148, 151, 154, 155, 297

  de table, 144

  free, 173

  public, 107, 109, 149, 154, 157, 164, 297

conditionality, 52

conditioning,

  political, 281, 282, 289

  socioartistic, 47, 321, 325, 327, 332, 360

  sociohistoric, 47, 81, 117, 126, 195, 223, 281, 321, 360

conditions, economic, 238, 240, 242

Constantine Copronymus, Emperor, 265

content, musical, 327, 328, 331

Conti, Prince de, 108, 116, 152

Copland, Aaron, 96

Corvinus, Matthew, 145

Couperin, François, 172, 326

court, music of, 95, 108
Courtenay, Peter, 285
Cousin, Victor, 147
Crane, William, 213
Cristine of Sweden, 308
criticism, 75, 101
    19th-century, 139
Crozat, salon of, 108
Cudjoe, S.D., 233
culture, musical, 156, 157
Dadelsen, Georg von, 138n
Dahlhaus, Carl, 31, 36n, 61, 63, 74
Danchet, 112
Darbel, Alain, 228
Debussy, Claude, 60, 215, 331,
    326
De Clercq, Jacqueline, 9, 155, 187
DeCoster, Michel, 9, 295, 296, 297
dehumanization, 343, 347
Delalande, Michel-Richard, 115,
    145
Deliège, Célestin, 76
Demant, Christopher, 291
Denis, Robert, 260
Derby, Count of, 285
Descotes, Jacques, 7
diffusion, 66
Diodurus of Sicily, 286
Dion of Trosa, 174
disfunctionalization, 179, 350
distinction, social, 209
divertissements, 145
Dufay, Guillaume, 315, 335
Dufrenne, Mikel, 37n
Dukas, Paul, 215
Dunning, Albert, 18
Dunstable, John, 249
Durkheim, Emile, 66
education, 117, 148

Edward III, 203
Ehrlich, Cyril, 164
Einstein, Alfred, 17
Elgar, Edward, 331
empirical method, 23
Engel, Hans, 8, 94
entertainment, 155
Epaminondas, 235
Ephraim, 313
Estreicher, Zygmunt, 233, 234
Ethnomusicology, 11, 27
ethnomusicology, 22, 24, 25 ff, 72,
    78
ethos, 118
Etzkorn, K. Peter, 81, 82n
evaluation, 75
explication, 74, 75
    musical 37, 38, 78
    sociological, 36ff, 41, 72ff
Fauré, Gabriel, 215, 326
Fenlon, Iain, 305
Ferdinand II, 144
Ferrara, Duke of, 203, 249
Ferté, Dutchess de la, 116
Finscher, Ludwig, 138n, 202, 203,
    335, 336
formalist docrine, 178, 346
Fouquet de Marseille, 131n
Francisque, Antoine, 260
Franck, César, 215
François I, 283
Frederick the Great, 115
free time, 183
freed time, 183
Freeman, Linton C., 275
Friedmann, Georges, 180, 183, 191
Fubini, Enrico, 155, 297, 337, 341
function, 143, 341
functions, social, 134, 61, 63, 95

Galant style, 130
Gerson-Kiwi, Edith, 196
Gesualdo, Carlo, 114, 172
Gilson, Etienne, 171, 230, 296
Girard, René, 301, 302, 311
Girod, Roger, 7
Gluck, Christoph Willibald, 107,
    110, 209, 289
Gombert, Nicolas, 278
Gonzaga, court of, 115
    Francesco, 144
Gossec, François, 152, 280
Gounod, Charles, 250, 331
Graun, Heinrich, 115
Grenonville (ambassador), 275
Grétry, André, 285
Grigny, Nicolas de, 326
Grimm, F. Melchior, 289
group, social, 47, 57, 60n, 65, 85 ff,
    99, 117, 125, 126, 130, 177,
    196
Gruber, Roman I., 16
Guédron, Pierre, 204, 212
Gualdo, Priorato Galeazzo, 308
Guignon, Jean-Pierre, 111
Guillaume IX Count of Poitiers,
    202
Guillemain, Louis-Gabriel, 249
Gurvitch, Georg, 24, 55n, 64, 125
Guyau, Jean-Marie, 29n, 56n
Hadrian, Emperor, 215
Halbwachs, Maurice, 58
Halle, Adam de la, 211
Händel, Georg Friederich, 107,
    114, 209, 268, 279
Handschin, Jacques, 30, 31, 105,
    263, 265n, 326
Hanslick, Eduard, 178, 179, 339,
    340, 341, 351

Hauser, Arnold, 17
Hawkins, John, 338
Haydn, Franz Joseph, 112, 120,
    158, 160, 203, 208, 326, 328
hearing, passive, 191
Hegel, Georg Friedrich, 179, 315
Heinemann, Rudolph, 97
Henri II Plantagenet, 286
Henry, Michel, 217
Henry V, 145
Henry VIII, 283
Herman, Mathias, 291
Hibberd, Lloyd, 15
Hickman, Hans, 127, 198, 211
Hilarius, 313
historian, 40
historicism, 34
history, 40
Hoebaer, Robert, 53n, 64n, 175
Honegger, Arthur, 96, 237, 268
Hood, Mantle, 27, 28
Horace, 207
Hornyak, Robert R., 57
Hosokawa, Shuhei, 296
humanization, 343, 344
ideology, 41
imitation, principle of, 300
induction, 70
inductive method, 23
Indy, Vincent d', 215, 331
innovation, 50
instruments, 256, 258, 259, 260,
    261, 262, 263, 266
  social roles of, 129n
integrality, 71
invention, 67, 323
Isherwood, Robert M., 306
Ismene, 198
Jachet of Mantua, 203

Jacquet, Jean, 260
Jager, Hugo de, 182
Janequin, Clément, 204, 291
Janson, Jean-Baptiste, 152
Jesus Christ, 286, 310
Johann Georg II, 204
Joseph II, 144
Josquin des Prez, 116, 172, 203, 249, 315
Kant, Immanuel, 184, 302n
Kaplan, Max, 7
Kastner, Jean-Georges, 292
Keiser, Reinhard, 112
Khoufou-'Ankh, 115, 198
Kinsky, Georg, 88
Kleinen, Günter, 186
Kneif, Tibor, 8, 61, 68, 293
Knepler, Georg, 18, 23
König, René, 7
Kuhnau, Johann, 285, 288
La Pouplinière, salon of, 108
La Trémolle, 285
labor, 231
    as a developmental factor, 232
    common, 237n
    division of, 224, 225, 227, 228
    manual, 229
Lacombe, 249
La Laurencie, Lionel de, 131
Lalo, Charles, 7, 29n, 53n, 60, 69n, 126, 225n, 232, 323
Lang, Paul H., 16, 82, 131
language, musical, 106
Laprade, Victor Richard de, 281
Lassus, Orlando de, 114, 172, 315
layer, social, 126
Lebègue, Nicolas, 281, 326
Legrenzi, Giovanni, 214
Legros, Joseph, 112
Leonius, 336
Leopold I, Emperor, 144, 176

Lesclop, Claude, 260
LeSueur, Jean-François, 286
Lesure, François, 18, 30, 68, 87, 92, 114
lifestyle, 145
Lisinski, Vatroslav, 280
Lissa, Zofia, 300, 326
listener, 92, 106
'listening' and 'hearing', 183
listening, active, 191
Liszt, Franz, 153, 154, 215, 267
Listenius, Nicolaus, 300, 335
literature, sociology of, 9, 61, 76
Lloyd, John, 213
Lobaczewska, Stefania, 18
Loret, 148
Louis XII, 116, 249, 278
Louis XIII, 147, 173
Louis XIV, 115, 145, 147, 172, 173, 217, 281, 283, 284, 305, 311
Louis XVI, 280
Lourié, Arthur, 354
Lowinsky, Edward E., 75, 147, 241, 354
Lully, Jean-Baptiste, 145, 209, 213, 283, 292
Lusignan, Pierre de, 277
Lycourgos, 282
Machabey, Armand, 326
Machaut, Guillaume de, 202, 212, 336
Macinus, Thomas, 292
Mahler, Gustav, 120
Mahling, Christoph-Hellmut, 214
Maillart, Pierre, 334
Mara, Gertrude Elisabeth, 111
Marais, Marin, 278
Marcel-Dubois, Claudie, 24
Marenzio, Luca, 114, 172
Mareuil, Arnaud de, 131n
Marix, Jeanne, 146

market, 162, 178
Marx, Karl, 49, 64, 225
mass culture, musical, 155 ff, 180
 ff
mass media, 94, 180 ff
Massenet, Jules, 215, 326
Mattheson, Johann, 337
Maudit, Jacques, 111, 204, 212
Mauss, Marcel, 257
Maximilian, Emperor, 145
Mazarin, Cardinal, 212, 242, 283,
 287, 288
McLuhan, Marshall, 187
Melani, Atto, 212
Melanippides, 120
Mellers, Wilfrid, 17
Mendel, Arthur, 75
Menger, Pierre-Michel, 9
Merriam, Alan P., 25, 26, 34, 92
Mersenne, Marin, 111
Merula, Tarquinio, 306
method, 35, 42, 43, 62, 63, 68 ff, 76
Mésangeau, René, 260
method, 35, 42, 43, 62, 63, 68 ff, 76
 comparative, 71, 72
 statistical, 73
 typological, 78
Metternich, Prince Klemens
 Wenzel, 286
Meyer, Ernst H., 18
Meyerbeer, Giacomo, 326
Meytus, Julius, 237
Michel, 249
Middle Ages, 17, 24, 49, 93, 128,
 130, 147, 148, 202, 203, 206,
 208, 216, 236, 283, 285, 309,
 335
 wandering musicians in, 176
middle class, 133 ff, 137, 146, 149,
 153, 165, 172, 177
Milan, Duke of, 249

minstrel, 146
minuet, 132
Moderne, Jacques, 161, 246
Mondonville, Jean-Joseph
 Cassanéa De, 111
Monteverdi, Claudio, 107, 214
Montigny, de, 249
Morales, Cristóbal de, 278
Moritz, 264
Mossolov, Alexander, 237
motivation, 116 ff
Mozart, Leopold, 209
Mozart, Wolfgang Amadeus, 107,
 113, 116, 120, 158, 203, 208,
 209, 214, 250, 263, 268, 273
 285
Mukerjee, Radhakamal, 53n
Müller, M.F., 62
music,
 aesthetic function of, 299
 aesthetics of, 28, 29ff, 47, 74
 art, 96, 121, 127n, 316
 as a profession, 156
 as instrument of power, 303,
  304, 305
 as instrument of social control,
  303
 as instrument of violence, 302,
  303, 304
 as status symbol, 307
 autonomy of, 12
 avant-garde, 347, 348, 349
 Burgundian, 133
 business of, 155, 162
 chamber, 108, 187
 church, 187, 92
 conception of, 11, 13
 contemporary, 97, 100, 110, 122
 copying, 158, 160
 court, 147, 304, 305, 306, 307,
  309

democratization of, 171 ff, 173
diffusion of, 95
'disfunctionalization' of, 174 ff
dissemination of, 160, 188, 189
engraving, 158, 160
entertainment, 97, 108
ethnic, 186, 26 ff
expressive, 346
field, 187
folk, 91, 225
French, 108
court, 147
function as a social symbol, 274
function of, 25, 26, 163, 280, 281, 297, 302, 352
galant, 337
Greek, 120
harmonic-homophonic, 322
in celebration, 299, 300
in ceremony, 295, 296
in ritual, 295, 296, 297, 298, 299, 300, 301, 302
instrumental, 262, 269
learned, 229
'light', 176
military, 290, 292
modern, 96
Oriental, 321, 322, 331
origins of, 232
political function, 280, 281
polyphonic, 322
popular, 127, 127n, 155, 166, 188
primitive, 91, 231, 256, 257
printing, 158, 160
program, 96, 172
progress in, 334
public, 96
publishing, 157, 159, 161, 164, 245, 246, 247, 248
religious, 239, 292

rock, 186
sacred, 309, 310, 312 ff
secular, 208, 309, 311 ff
serious, appreciation of, 176, 181
social function of, 99, 292, 299, 314, 359
social history of, 16 ff, 81, 138, 196, 224
sociology of, 5 ff
specificity of, 12
subculture, 100
theater, 187
tonal, 339
values of, 13
Western, 255, 311, 322 ff
youth, 166
musical culture, 309
musical life, 94, 95, 100, 111, 229
commercialization, 239, 251
eighteenth-century, 209
musical time, 298
musicians,
court, 307
guilds, 209
mobility of, 159
salaries, 240
social role of, 22
social status of, 25, 56, 57, 195, 197, 203, 205, 211, 214, 218
traveling, 209, 213
type of, 94, 95
musicology, 6, 12, 14, 15, 16, 19
Mussorgsky, Modest P., 214
Nattiez, Jean-Jacques, 62
necessity, 50, 52
Nietzsche, 339
nobility, 131, 134, 143n
Noske, Frits, 14n, 51, 335
notation, musical, 322
objectivism, 40

objectivity, 44
observation, method of, 74
Ockeghem, Johannes, 249
opera, 112, 134, 135, 136, 158
orchestra, Baroque, 261
originality, 330, 333
  objective, 328, 329
Orléans, Duke of, 289
painting, music and, 87
Palestrina, Giovanni Pierluigida, 328, 330, 336
Palisca, Claude V., 31
Parry, Charles H.H., 133
Partenio, 214
Patelin, Abbé, 249
patronage, 158, 204, 304, 309
Payen, Madame, 148
Pech, Karel, 182
Pepin the Short, 265
performance, 67, 94, 121, 128, 155, 160
  live, 58, 90, 92, 92m, 93, 161, 184, 216
Pericles, 281
Perotinus, 336
Perrichon, Jean, 217
Perrin, Pierre, 137, 173
Petrucci, Ottaviano, 161
Philidor, André Danican, 292
Philidor, Anne Danican, 107, 112, 145,
Philip the Good, 144, 204, 249, 277, 285
Philip-Charles of Öttingen, 144
Phillip of Macedonia, 198
Phillip the Bold, 212
philosophy, 38 ff, 47
  moral, 43
  social, 42
Phrynis, 120, 207
piano, 110, 148, 265, 266, 267, 268

Piccini, Niccolò, 110, 289
Pirro, André, 17, 134, 143, 276, 280
Plato, 118, 282
Platter, Thomas, 87
Pleyel, Ignace, 250
Plumb, J.H., 164
Plutarch, 198
Polymnestos of Colophon, 107
Pompadour, Mme de, 242
positivism, 43
Pötting, Franz Eusebius, 276
prestige, political, 276
Preussner, Eberhard, 17
Printz, Wolfgang Caspar, 334, 337
professionalism, 57
progress, 324, 338 ff
  theory of, 334n, 337
Prokofiev, Sergey, 237
Prudentius, 313
Ptolemy XI, 199
public, 10, 17, 65, 90 ff, 120, 121, 130, 133, 135, 137, 151, 154, 155, 157, 158, 160, 162, 163, 171, 173, 348, 354
Pythagorians, 121
Rösing, Helmut, 316
Radin, Max, 323
radio, 185, 186, 188 ff
Rameau, Jean-Philippe, 116, 152, 172, 278
Ravel, Maurice, 326
Raynor, Henry, 18
Rebans, Gervais, 260
recordings, 185, 187, 191
Reichardt, Johann Friedrich, 280
related disciplines, 24
Renaissance, 129, 147, 148, 161, 209, 241, 283, 307, 309
  courts of, 144
repetitiveness in musical

presentation, 159, 160, 161
reproduction, 343
Reys, Jacob, 260
rhythm, 232
Richard the Lionhearted, 286
Richelieu, Cardinal, 204, 286
Riedel, Friedrich W., 138n
Rijavec, Andrej, 325
Rimsky-Korsakov, Nicolay, 214, 331
Ringer, Alexander L., 167, 172
rite, Christian, 310, 316
    sacral, 316
ritual, definition of, 293, 294
Rococco style, 130
Rodolphe, Jean-Joseph, 152
Roger, Etienne, 247
Romantic era, 17
Romanticism, 59, 96, 130, 172, 177, 338, 339
Ropartz, Joseph Guy Marie, 331
Rore, Cypriano de, 203
Rossi, Luigi, 242, 288
Rousseau, Jean-Jacques, 235
Rumbelow, Alan S., 57
Sachs, Curt, 94, 234
Saint Ambrose, 313
Saint Augustine, 313, 334
Saint Bernard, 313
Saint Gregory, 287
Saint Louis, 285
Saint-Saëns, Camille, 215, 326
Sakadas of Argos, 107
Sallust, 199
Salmen, Walter, 18, 82, 176, 205
Sauval, Henri, 111
Sceaury, Paul Loubet de, 18
Scévole de Sainte-Marthe, 109
Schaeffner, André, 58, 59, 86, 90

Scheibe, Adolph, 334, 337
Shepherd, John, 274
Schering, Arnold, 82, 152
Schiller, Johann Christoph
    Friedrich, 286
Schmelzer, Johann Heinrich, 87
Schneider, Marius, 205
Schobert, Johann, 152
Schönberg, Arnold, 331, 334
Schubert, Franz, 188, 215, 286
Schumann, Robert, 58, 215
Schütz, Heinrich, 110, 114, 209, 292, 315
Schweitzer, Albert, 59
Seeger, Charles, 27, 28, 167, 323
Septimus Severus, 216
Sermisy, Claudin de, 204
Sforza, Cardinal Ascanio, 249
Sforza, Galeazzo-Maria, 144, 249
Shakespeare, William, 64
Shepherd, John, 274
Shostakovitch, Dmitri, 96
sign, 60
Silbermann, Alphons, 7, 8, 13, 74, 77, 88
Simmel, Georg, 7
Sochor, Arnold N., 98, 228
sociability, 153
social conditionings, 359
social demand, 58, 59, 114
social distinction, 143 ff, 165
social facts, 23, 66
social functions, musical, 13, 22, 146, 149, 154, 176, 150, 225 ff
social layers, 165
social life, 76, 88, 131
social *models*, 177
society, global, 47, 129, 130
sociological aesthetics, 29

sociologism, 33, 35, 75
sociology, nineteenth-century, 24
songs,
  trade, 234
  work, 234
Sorokin, Pitirim A., 40n
Souriau, Etienne, 36n, 65n, 68n
Spinoza, Baruch, 89
Spranger, Eduard, 315
Squarcialupi, Codex of, 335
Stamitz, Carl, 152
Strauss, Richard, 96, 153, 328
Stravinsky, Igor, 328, 344
structure, social, 62, 98
style, 129, 130, 132, 133, 134, 327
subcultures, musical, 165 ff
subjectivism, 40
Suetonius, 286
Sully, Duc de, 116
Susato, Tielman, 161, 246
Syagrius, 279
symbol, 60
symbols, social, 197
symphonie concertante, 138
Tacitus, 290
Taine, Hippolyte Adolph, 29n
Tallis, Thomas, 213
Tarde, Gabriel, 323
taste, musical, 117, 119, 121, 122, 134
Tavannes, Count of, 249
Tchaikowsky, Peter I., 331
technical environment, 180
technique, 345
Telepinu, King, 215
television, 182, 185, 186, 189, 190
  influence of, 183
Terpander of Lesbos, 107
Thaletas of Gortynia, 107

Theile, Johann, 112
Themistocles, 199
Theodoric the Great, 279
Thibault IV Count of Champagne, 202
Thoveron, Gabriel, 190, 191
Tinctoris, 335
Tiersot, Julien, 236
Timotheos, 120, 207
Titon du Tillet, 278
Todi, Luiza Rosa, 111
tradition, 67, 324 ff
traditionalism, 341
Tran Van Khê, 95
transposition, 60
trumpeter, 147
  fraternities, 146
Trumpeter ritterliche, 147
typology, 13, 21, 22, 98, 99
Tyrtheus, 107, 282
values, aesthetic, 36 ff
  human, 36
  sociological, 36
Verdi, Giuseppe, 274, 280, 289
Vidal, Pierre, 131n
Villa-Lobos, Heitor, 237
Vitoria, Tomas Lodovico da, 306
Vitry, Philippe de, 336
Vivaldi, Antonio, 214
Wagner, Richard, 60, 97, 107, 153, 209, 215, 326, 330. 331, 339
Walin, Stig, 209
Walsh, John, 247
Wangermée, Robert, 17, 129n, 175, 181, 191, 211, 246, 277n
Weber, Carl Maria von, 215
Weber, Max, 7, 22n, 267, 314, 322
Weber, William, 18, 161, 162
Wert, Jacques de, 115, 203

Wieprecht, Wilhelm Friedrich, 264
Wiora, Walter, 17, 18, 32, 82, 90,
    126, 129, 138n, 174, 300, 315,
    335
Wollheim, Richard, 53n
Woodfill, Walter L., 18
work, musical, 60n, 63, 64n, 69,
    91, 105, 110, 344, 345

Xenocrites of Locris, 107
Xenodamos of Cythera, 107
Yon, Ephrem Dominique, 315
Young, Percy M., 138
Zàccaro, Gianfranco, 18
Žak, Sabine, 18
Zimmerman, Franklin B., 138n